Measure liberty
by the safety of those
with unpopular ideas.

WMD MACHETE

by

Mark Plimsoll

An Adventurous and Romantic
Creative nonfiction Memoir
of a Global Citizen's Coming of Age

Copyright Information

*"Cultures with taboos against talk
about religion, politics, and procreation
create societies where people
become slaves to tradition. "*

Mark Plimsoll

As a literary experiment, WMD MACHETE uses a new type of English, in early twenty-first century called the language of "E," which eliminates the passive voice (and the wordiness of continuous emphasis that things exist, duh) to create an active, contemporary English that describes what did what, instead of "this existed doing that" as in He was walking (he existed in a state of walking), instead of "He walked" (we know he exists). This adds readability, immediacy, and precision to the memoir of the young author's struggle with two realities, one Anglo Saxon and the other Hispanic.

In this "coming of age" novel, we see hints of North America's future in twenty five years, when the Hispanic population becomes the majority, and so changes not only the demographics of the United States of America, but its culture. The author sweeps us along through a whirlwind of culture shock in this adventurous chronicle of a disgruntled industrial age young man's tribal and instinctual reluctance to accept a Third World view of the United States and its foreign policies. With Guatemala on the brink of war with Belice, before he can assimilate this alternative language, culture, and reality, along comes a new relationship and an earthquake that stops the war with the deaths of twenty two thousand people.

In sum, WMD Machete chronicles events that change one young American's blind patriotism into something else, and over the next thirty years, inspired him to write this "Huckleberry Finn" picaresque novel, perhaps the first Great Pan-American Novel for the Twenty-first Century.

Dedicated to Brett and Brandon, and all youth denied a future, and for those of any age who wonder how the other half lives.

WMD MACHETE
by
Mark Plimsoll

Table Of Contents

First Section: Gringotenango

CHAPTER 1: Meso-America

This begins with the first word, an Aztec creation myth that describes a cataclysmic obliteration of the earth and heavens, which made time stand still. Nothing changed until the Gods watched a blaze erupt from solid rock. One by one they jumped through it. The first God turned into the Sun, the second became the Moon, and the third, the Earth. As they whirled and danced, time became a God, and designed each day of our earthly existence.

Michigan, 1971

"So this is how the other half lives." I said. It looked like an aerodynamic, candy apple red, wood trim Catholic confessional with a sound system on four Firestone wheels. I bent down to open the sports car's passenger side. The new car scented air falls across my socks to escape into the swampy autumn night. I hunched inside, shut the door, then rolled down the window to let the pine scented breeze replace the fog of fresh lit cigarette smoke.

"This is how the better half lives." Her free hand clutched the steering wheel, a hand almost deformed by bulged veins that echoed the tangled nest of bracelets and dangled charms. Her rings clicked against the plastic steering wheel. I liked one in particular, a mood ring, like a tiny crystal ball. I wondered what the black color meant for our near future together. Her wavy mane of long peroxide blonde hair exaggerated the tilt of her head.

She untwisted her mouth from around her lipstick stained cigarette. "So what's your excuse this time?"

"Same excuse, damn brake lights out. Borrowed the money to get it fixed, but something came up."

"Oh yeah? Like what?"

"Like you. Who needs a car when you got friends? I need to talk to you, tonight. I don't have much time left."

"Who does?"

"Relax, let me show you a good time, and forget about my car for now. Look at you. You look great. New clothes, new car. What's the point of a sports car without a special friend to share it with? I'm saving you miles of loneliness. You should be thankful for my poverty."

"That's how the other half lives," she said. "They don't know any better. I do, and oh yes, I know you have money. You've got money saved for your trip, so you don't give a damn about your car."

"At the rate I save, it'll be years from now before I go. That's why I need you."

"I told you, I'm not going. Don't let that stop you, though. You go right ahead. Put on your backpack and go to Bolivia, or wherever the hell it is. God will not disown you."

She grabbed the knob between the bucket seats, popped the clutch and we bounced out of the driveway and onto the road in a spray of gravel. She could speed shift through the gears like most girls brush crumbs off their skirt. The motor's whine deepened for a moment as the car kicked forward and we both slammed back in the seats. The car shot straight as an arrow down the road, through thick oak woods and cattail marshes along the river.

I thought about the time, four years ago in eighth grade, I walked across the river ice to get to know her.

She snapped her fingers several times under my nose.

I reached under the seat to pull out a fifth of Wild Turkey whiskey and place it into her finger popping hand.

The dashboard light outlined her profile against the dark inkblot rush of forest that squirmed against the stardust sky. She drained the bottle, then rolled down her window to reach out and throw the bottle forward across the top of the car. The bottle arched into the headlight beams, kept up with us for a half second, and then crashed through the cattails and tall swamp grasses in the ditch.

"No guilt?" I said.

"Not me. I leave a trail of destruction wherever I go. I enjoy life on the sweat of others, and their misery doesn't concern me. That's my idea of order in the Universe."

She wiped her mouth with the back of her hand and smeared a small plume of lipstick from her lower lip to her cheek. She looked into the rearview mirror, said "Damn," and corrected it with a finger. She turned to me and smiled. "I love this car. Daddy can give me cars anytime he wants."

"You don't feel the slightest bit guilty? Didn't mom tell you to eat all your food, because children starve in Africa?"

"Of course she did. So what? It's not my responsibility, so no guilt."

"Come to Guatemala with me. It's exotic, like Asia, only two countries away. Think about it."

"I did think about it, for two seconds. I don't backpack, and you won't see me hitchhike anywhere. If I go, it's first class, baby. You can't afford first class."

"First class, no class. You miss the whole thing, the street, the people, the sounds and smells."

"You mean noise and stink, don't you? Sounds lovely."

"Let's take the bus together, you buy the hotel rooms, I'll buy the bus tickets. See the world as it is, not from some room that looks like a Holiday Inn no matter where you go."

"I told you. No bus, no hitchhike. That's how the other half lives. I'm in the first half. You go alone. Afraid to go all alone?"

"Not much. College kids travel alone all the time, from Europe and Japan. You see them downtown with their backpacks and maps. I've got a book on how to do it on five dollars a day."

"Yeah, right. Bumming cigarettes and hanging around Colleges, asking for a place to stay. You go, come back and tell me about it. Like I said, God won't disown you. Go around the world if you want. Nobody will let you die, not if they could help it, especially not a pretty young white boy, healthy, strong, intelligent. Someone will put you to work, if you don't get caught in some civil war or something."

"Disasters make heroes out of people."

"Not everyone, or it wouldn't be a disaster. That's God's plan. He's in all of us, we just don't feel him much. I know you don't believe, but God's inside you anyway. There's more beer under the seat. God sacrificed his son Jesus so that you should live. So God be with you, and send me a postcard when you get there."

"You won't even think about it?"

"No. Now where the hell is this bar? My fake ID doesn't look so hot. They better let us in, and this band better rock my socks off, or you're on my shit list till we graduate."

I reached down between my feet and pulled out two cold bottles of Schlitz beer and the church key, popped the caps off, and handed one to her.

"Here's to your socks off."

Teotihuacán and the Argentine

Teotihuacán, the ancient site, north of Mexico City and home of America's largest pyramid, means "City of the Gods" or "Where Men Became Gods". The Valley of Teotihuacán also served as home to the Cuicuilco Ticomán culture around the time of Christ, as evidenced by Carbon dating. They planned huge urban centers, constructed throughout the Tzacualli phase of Mexican history. By the Proto-Classic stage (AD 100-300), Teotihuacán served as the center for the New World's first true urban civilization. Through what archeologists call the Early Classic period (to AD 600), various cultures influenced Meso-America through conquest, governance, and cultural superimposition and synthesis.

The Teotihuacán hills contained obsidian deposits and records of workshops dated to 200 years BCE. The Pyramid of the Sun, 700 feet on a side, covers as much as Egypt's Cheops pyramid and contains over a million cubic yards of fill. Evidence suggests they faced it with cut stone, surfaced with plaster and maybe red paint. The pyramid took about a century to build. They embellished the courtyard of one small elegant pyramid with six tiers carved with feathered serpents that alternated with the god of rain, Tlaloc (an Aztec name), a squared off face with rectangles of stone for lips, eyebrows, ears and a characteristic T shape for eyes. A motif of seashells and waves surround them, to make a swirl of watery fertility, at one time covered with plaster and painted in brilliant tones of blue green, gold, and vermillion. Under the Pyramid of the Sun, archeologists discovered volcanic caves where ancients gouged out water channels in the rock floor. Ancient subterranean fire pits contained residues of burnt fish and shells from the lake.

The legend of the peripatetic God called Quetzalcoatl, or Kulkulkán to the Mayans, talks about a bearded white skinned God who departs but promises to return. This legend might date from Teotihuacán's earliest cultures, and over a millennium later, paved the way for the bearded Spaniard Hernan Cortéz to enlist the aide of subjugated tribes to topple their Aztec overlords.

At the huge pyramids of Teotihuacán, north of Mexico City, I attracted the interest of a bilingual Argentine man named Miguel, with shoulder length dark frazzled hair, facial features that showed his Italian and German bloodlines.

He needed someone to take pictures of him on vacation. We toured the site together, and when we mixed in with the Spanish speaking groups of tourists, he helped me understand the tour guides.

Miguel complained that all the showers in Mexico did not drain. "The placement of a drain at the lowest point in a shower somehow escapes the Mexican psyche.

"The Mexicans seem so proud of their calendar, that the Mayans invented zero before the Europeans, but after one week in Estados Unidos

Mexicanos, I see they invented nothing and have yet to discover toilet paper."

"Esta dos unimos what?"

"Estados Unidos Mexicanos. The United States of Mexico. That's the name of this country in Spanish."

Later in life, I learned that some Latin Americans consider people from Argentina as 'presumidos', which combines qualities like fatuous, presumptuous, pompous, vain, contemptuous of others, a too high self esteem, etc. and all this from a society that tortured and 'disappeared' almost half of a generation in the nineteen eighties, when their right wing government would push young 'dissident' couples out of open doors on airplanes over the open ocean and give their children away. In modern Argentina, the torturers and their victims now must face each other every day shopping at the grocery store or even over dinner, and practice the appropriate amnesia.

As we left the pyramids, Miguel took me to a spot where we could look back and see how the staircases ran parallel up the front face. They started as two staircases, yet up a level joined as one staircase, then split into two again.

He said, "You see that? It's crazy, the restoration is all wrong."

"What's wrong with it?"

"Wouldn't you think that a culture with talented astronomers, mathematicians, and a perfect calendar, capable of urban design and construction of pyramids, would place a greater value on symmetry? The Mexican archeologists' restoration left one staircase much smaller than the other." He noticed that the pyramid's restored areas, whose mortar bore intentional marks with peanut size pebbles, seemed "clearly inferior, and prove again Mexican ineptitude with even the simplest things."

Miguel offered to take me into Mexico City in his rental car. About a half hour later, a few miles away from the site, a police officer on a motorcycle pulled us over. Miguel turned to me and said, "Oh no. Here we go again. Don't say anything, let me handle it."

Miguel rifled through the glove compartment and extracted some papers as the policeman walked up to us, and then he pulled out his wallet to hand over his license with the car's papers.

The police officer, in his white helmet, sunglasses, and black patent leather uniform, asked Miguel to step out of the car.

When Miguel came back, he sat in the driver's seat and fumed with anger. "The bastard will sit there with my driver's license until I give him money. La mordida. You know about that? They pay these policemen shit, so they see me in a rental car and think I look American. All Americans have money, so they pull me over. What he didn't know is that I speak Spanish and much better than he does. I will shame him into letting us go."

The police officer bored of the wait and approached us. His white helmet gleamed in the stark sunlight of these cool Mexican highlands, and blinded me as he stuck his head through the window to start an intimate chat with Miguel.

Miguel pushed the door open, got out of the car, slammed the door shut and began to yell at the policeman in rapid staccato Spanish. His arms waved, fingers pointed at the cop, then he pounded his fist into his open palm. He walked up to the mute officer, and snatched his license out of the zombie officer's hand.

Miguel and the policeman looked at each other.

The cop looked at his feet, then turned and walked over to his motorcycle, got on, started it, and rode past us without a sidelong glance.

Miguel leaned down to stick his head through the driver's window and laugh.

"What?" I said. "How did you do that?"

"I told him he should be ashamed of himself. He stopped me because I look like American. He needs bribe to rich Americans, because they pay him bad, too little, so it's expected. He gives Mexico a bad name, and disgraces the police. But I speak his language, I understand, I am Latin American also. I work hard for years and years to save money for this vacation in Mexico. I don't make money like rich Gringo, I make money like the Mexicans do, little by little. I am not to let him rob me and destroy my vacation. He takes me to jail, OK, and I could die in a Mexican jail, but it will be his guilt."

We speeded south on a Mexican highway.

He clutched the wheel with both hands. "Stupid policeman. Make him a hummingbird, like that." He snaps his fingers.

"A hummingbird? What's that, an insult?"

"These little brown skinned, black haired, cannibal Aztecs believe their dead warriors follow the sun for four years, then returned to earth as hummingbirds."

Guatemalan Border

Twenty two years old and alone, I stood motionless and sweated, backpack between my feet, in line at the Guatemalan border. After almost two months of hitchhikes, buses, and trains through North America (which includes Estados Unidos Mexicanos), I could see Central America and Guatemala as a leafy horizon. One more river to cross, beyond this military outpost perched on the edge of ravines that held fingers of a great tropical lowland jungle.

I thought about how I got here, and why.

This dream come true took four years of sweat and loss of dignity as a dishwasher and busboy, car lot detailer, a maid, as a Carney in a bingo tent at Michigan Fairs, and nightmare jobs in factories where I became a robot. I sold my blood, time, and bodily energy. I signed up with the Teamsters Union to make donuts, ate too much bread, and convinced myself I saved money each time I slept in my car or in friend's basements. I steeled my resolve with on the job hatred of my situation, and flashback nightmares about my new car's breakdown in the deepest canyons in the center of New York City.

In High School, everything changed after I lost my virginity. After that, I wanted to ensure my access to beautiful females, and so I grew my hair long and learned to play rock guitar in a couple of bands, and frequented the library to research the best time to become a parent. Twenty two year olds procreated with the most success, the current literature said.

I spread my conceptual wings like the pages of National Geographic, and found most of the maps blank, so I decided to get out of my dysfunctional family nest and not look back. Not that they'd notice. Like any good WASP family, they expect complete independence by eighteen, and a distant estrangement soon after.

I graduated in nineteen seventy one, as the California "summer of love" in nineteen sixty eight reached Michigan. Late that September I took off on a hitchhike voyage around Lake Michigan and up to Minneapolis, north to Canada then west to Vancouver, down to Seattle, San Francisco to spend New Years with Quicksilver Messenger Service and meet Jerry Garcia, live in Berkeley with guys from New Jersey, visit Stanford, catch a ride with Navy sailors to Tijuana, Amtrak to New Orleans for Mardi Gras where LSD intensified the vision of Viet Nam vets who poured beer on the ground and cried for their dead comrades. Through it all, I lost the fear that I might go crazy, until I entered a traditional college.

College tried to brainwash me to become employable in a system I had no faith in. To avoid the draft for the Viet Nam war, I took couple semesters of college that included two Spanish classes. The courses felt designed as a sadistic rite of passage to destroy my curiosity and free will, reward conformity and obedience, to make me a good employee for business and industry.

The activities of my college age peers introduced me to a lifestyle of muscle cars, rock and roll, daily drug use, and women liberated by the birth control pill who expected sex from a man or insulted him as a homosexual.

I thought about a career in the military, and after I talked to a recruiter, the Marines called every other day. I also talked to friends with brothers in the military. One famous tough guy from the neighborhood came home with broken ribs, thanks to his drill Marine Sergeant, and a new, sensitive and caring personality, thanks to the anti-schizophrenic drugs.

The appeal of the Marines' promise, to beat boys down and build them up again as paid assassins for the state, escaped me.

"Join the army if you fail." The Bob Dylan lyric and WASP cliché paints the military as a last refuge for boys unable to cope, a place for those who want to remain adolescent forever and let others make important decisions about their life. These 'heroes' in their own eyes believe it necessary to brutalize others into submission.

I considered my next move both a small step for mankind and a giant leap off the edge. I crossed off my star crossed love affairs, limited my social life, and cut off all communication with those 'best friends' that take up too much time in idle chat, who bond with complaints about others. I avoided their emotional breakdowns and their need for a friend with a dry shoulder, or an open mind, to soil.

For four years, I stayed up nights to calculate my savings and the costs, until the day I turned my bank account into traveler's checks.

After an unreal and disciplined three days of courteous behavior toward my mother, to convince her I really wanted to hitchhike through the US and Mexico, she offered to drop me off on US 131 South, forty five minutes away.

She didn't believed I would go. I made no itinerary to give her, nor did we plan for regular contact.

"Let me know where you are occasionally," she said, with the expectation to see me at home that night for dinner.

Right away, a truck picked me up and took me south to Chicago. I then hitchhiked south to sleep alongside the roadside in wet Missouri. I rode with truck drivers, ex-cons, religious fanatics, and skinny long haired sex kittens in Volkswagens who let me off in the middle of the night to drive off in a cloud of perfumed frustration, probably because I appeared too naïve, I realized later.

Before my last ride stateside, I stood alone at an empty crossroad in the great barren desert grasslands near Van Horn, Texas. Dawn, a wet mist under a sky of twisted dirty cotton. My last ride overshot the mark westward, and I needed to backtrack a bit.

The hours passed slow, I sat on the ground or stood and shuffled my feet to warm my cold blood. I noticed black animals almost hidden in the sun bleached grasses. I parted the grass for a better view of huge black and silver grasshoppers, the size of my entire thumb. I picked one up. It seemed almost frozen, but as I raised it for a close examination, it hissed loud, seethed angry air through a row of open holes in the plates of its abdomen.

Hours later, I got picked up by a young man in a full produce truck, and we littered the road with bright green bell peppers on every curve all the way to the border town of Presidio.

In the next two months I would explore the Estados Unidos Mexicanos by train, bus, hitchhike, public transport in the back of pickups or donkey carts. Wrong turns, kidnappings, missed connections, sad goodbyes to unexplored virgin beaches and a not so sad goodbye to fellow Gringa adventurer. I survived on five dollars a day some days in spite of payoffs to policemen, through graceful utilization of predatory homosexuals' instant friendships, sleepless six hour bus station layovers, nighttime bus rides, and daily searches for cheap meals; fruits, beans and tortillas, sweet breads, peanuts, and plastic baggies full of fresh squeezed on the street orange juice to drink through a straw.

I discovered a hangover cure. Menudo, a watery tomato soup with chives and hominy, islands of mysterious greases, served with liberal doses of salt, limejuice, the clover-like leaves and soapy taste of cilantro, all to disguise the principle ingredient that absorbs the evils of a night's binge, rectangular strips of several types of cow stomach, all white as lard, some textured like tongue and some with a checkerboard of little raised flaps, like the pens of a miniature stockyard.

The odor reminded me of the muddy dairy farms of my youth. An acquired taste, hangover required.

I felt excited and alive, couldn't wait to cross this border to Guatemala and see the Highland Indians in the Land of Eternal Springtime, to see how they lived on a dollar a day. I hoped they might inspire me, and drag me out of this cocoon of disappointment in my fellow humans.

I suspected that my boyhood fields of Michigan served as dumps for industrial chemicals trucked in from Chicago, Detroit, or even Holier than thou Grand Rapids, by Mafia Teamsters to 'unintentionally' poison my deep woods springs, kill with cancer or otherwise ruin the lives of several friends who would never become a useful statistic of our contaminated rural neighborhood, because of America's mobile lifestyle. We kids played in big piles of white metallic residues and powders mysteriously dropped off in the deep woods, and never connected them to the asymmetric mutant ice blades in ice crystal rings around the forest springs we drank out of.

Michiganders my age coped with Winter's cabin fever with rock and roll, as they did every rainy day, whether in the muggy armpits of summer thunderstorms, or in the muddy molds of Spring and Fall. Trapped inside the house too often by prolonged periods of rain or snow, they sit inside with thick sweaters on, and socialize, their pasty white complexions colored by the clouds of cigarette smoke that lay in horizontal bands of thermocline layers. They stare incredulous at any cloudless sky, and feel privileged, as if before an act of God. Most Midwesterners venture out of their car exhaust gray, snow covered houses on the first sunny day with temperatures in the fifties. They put on shorts and wash the car with the ice water in the garden hose, shirtless, cigarette between chapped lips. Many grateful souls take all opportunities to lay out in the sun and burn the surfaces of various body parts to a painful tomato ripeness.

Weekends, the troglodyte warriors don black leather jackets, rev their muscle cars as a sonic prelude to the creation of long, two foot wide ribbons of burnt rubber on the road in front of their house, at the start of informal drag strips on the highways, or at the factory parking lot exit. They roar downtown to the rock and roll cellars early in the evening, before they 'charge cover,' an entrance fee to pay the band. There they glad hand and back slap, dangle cigarettes from their lips and develop hoarse whiskey laughs as they rub elbows with all the other anxious and sensually repressed spastic dancers that drink their confidence from beer mugs, and grow accustomed to the acidic tinge of vinegar from the unwashed plastic tubes of the bar's equipment. Beer, we hoped, helped us feel attraction or attractive in ragged blue jeans and flannel shirts. Alcohol makes people feel attractive, then irresistible with an intelligent wit, and if that proves false, more alcohol might make one forget the evening's disappointments or at least make it obvious you need help to get to bed.

Hopeless.

Like most young males, I felt ready for war, ready to pledge loyalty to a noble cause, but the recent ignoble end of the Viet Nam War filled my empty aches for service to tribe and humanity with cynicism and a healthy skepticism. I escaped certain brain death by the grace of a draft number of one hundred fifty, college attendance, and much credit it to the osmotic bravery and rationality of an anti-war movement fueled on respect for human rights.

Full of hungers and urges that I did not know how to indulge, I figured that if things did not go my way in Latin America, I could kill myself slow, with a real long, hard look around before I checked out.

Life as usual, for a twenty two year old boy-man.

Took me almost three months to get from Michigan to the Guatemalan border, all alone, especially alone in Texas and Estados Unidos Mexicanos, both foreign countries, I realized later. I looked again at the jungle horizon of Guatemala. A line of people passed through this military Gauntlet that separated me from the Land of Eternal Springtime. The line snaked toward a group of black booted Guatemalan military men who rifle through each and every poverty stricken person's possessions. Other soldiers stood behind them, angry expressions carved into their faces by manicured stupidity and a high testosterone brutishness. One chewed gum and his muscular jaws bulged in rhythm while a counterpoint pulsed above, in the brown black bristled skin over his temples. His index finger splayed too near the trigger of his machine gun with the safety mechanism up in the air, off, as he pointed the muzzle at us, or waved it around erratic, to move the line forward.

We few travelers from abroad punctuated the line of Westernized Latin Americans. Rural cowboy Mexicans fresh off the farm, fresh off retired yellow school buses as public transports, still marked with the name of some Ohio school district. The Mexican Indian's cowboy hats accentuated their stiff, half crippled movements with each little dip of its wings, like road kill turkey vultures, or rain troughs, worn on the head. From a historical perspective, it made about as much sense as Jews with Swastikas.

At first, I felt an affection towards the short stout indigenous women, over swaddled in scarves and thick layers of cotton dresses and blouses. They often glanced at me and made the sign of the cross, thumbnail to lower lip at the end. I asked about it with Mexicans who spoke English, and learned they do that to ward off the Evil Eye, from me. That pissed me off, and sometimes I threw them the Evil Eye on purpose. My vicarious osmotic lessons from Bela Lugosi and other Hollywood vampires taught me how to scatter a gaggle of indigenous matrons amid a flurry of air crosses.

Halfway through Mexico, since Oaxaca at least, I noticed a higher percentage of indigenous "autoctonos" Indians who wore their village clothes. The men wore normal Cowboy clothes except for knee length shorts of decorative horizontal red stripes, reminds me of pajamas, with sandals instead of cowboy boots. The women wore white blouses with embroidered decorative flowers, a blue jean denim skirt to the ankles, and very long straight black hair, sometimes thick as horsehair, braided over each ear. In general, they looked round faced with immense cheek bones, large and straight pointed nose, almond eyes, and full lips. At first I tried to sketch the differences of various Mexican and Mayan faces, but most of my sketches looked indistinct instead of Mexican; Navajo or Cherokee, Hawaiian, Pilipino or Tahitian, Papua New Guinea, Maori, I wouldn't know any better.

Two businessmen with briefcases stepped up for the inspection. One looked more urbane, the boss. He wore a very nice Cowboy shirt with a wide yoke across the shoulders, rhinestone buttons down the front and on both chest pockets, and new blue jeans. A big silver chain on one wrist competed with the gold wrist watch on the other.

The subservient man copied the other with cheap polyester that that clung and hung crooked, as if it melted a bit in the dryer.

They tried to play chummy with the soldiers, smiled a lot with teeth outlined in silver or gold.

Over the last month, I grew accustomed to the predominant black hair and tan skins around me, but not to my own exoticness in this context.

Schoolgirls often pointed and tittered, the other hand to the mouth. At first I resented all that attention, but something in their twinkle let me understand that the intrigue of the exotic goes both ways.

Ahead of me about ten people, a black haired Japanese lad stood with a glum expression, his skin a buttery yellow tan instead of the Mexican reddish brown. He wore a new US army jacket, like a long trench coat, olive green. I felt certain he bought it in the States. Maybe Californian. He looked back at me too often. Queer?

The soldiers interrogated him, and it didn't go well. I couldn't hear them, but seemed he spoke little Spanish. Even with the help of others as translators, they arrived at an impasse. He sighed in exasperation, leaned over with a shrug of finality, picked up his immense duffle bag rucksack and left the line to walk back toward Mexico.

He stopped in front of me to say "Hello. You American? Speak English?"

At first I felt suspicious. He breathed as if exhausted, nervous. "What's the problem?"

"You help me? Come, away from others. Please. I explain."

I looked at my place in line, about halfway. Could be another hour or more, and I would soon feel hungry. I looked toward the rear, saw twenty or so people behind me, and remembered that buses arrive a couple of times an hour to bring more people bound for Guatemala. No one else looked like they spoke enough English to help him.

I picked up my backpack and walked with him a discreet distance away.

"What's the problem?"

"They don't let me in. Uh, I uh, I don't show them money. Nuff money. I have money."

"How much money do you need?"

"No, no no. Money have. Money here." He pointed to himself, to his chest. "You help, I show. After."

I didn't understand. "What's wrong? Did they trick you? Steal your money?"

His eyes went northeast in a search through his vocabulary. "Trick? Trick? No steal. No. They want see money, nuff money. Or I no go in Guatemala. You have knife?"

"Sure, here's a knife." I pulled out my jackknife.

"Money here, in coat. I cut coat to get money."

So we walked further away, casual, then sat on a grassy slope to chat and enjoy the panorama of a long jungle mountain valley. It snaked away and disappeared into the distant milky humidity, a bluish hint of jungle mountains beyond.

"You from Japan, or Chinese?"

"Japanese. From Japan. I travel through United Stays, I like very much. Hamburgers in the Stays. You American?"

"Yes."

"Thought so. Sure. Like Americans. I have too much money, you know. Want to rob me."

"They robbed you?"

"No yet. Not show money, so people no steal, maybe ugly coat help." He laughed.

He took my knife and began to saw at the hem threads that held his coat together. He stopped to look around, talk, to hide his actions. He opened the hem, and then reached inside his coat lining to pull out loose bills, one at a time, to make a large wad.

After he sewed the jacket back up, we walked back to the line.

"Tank you," he smiled and nodded, like the echo of a bow. He breathed normal again. "Tank you."

Two hours later, we sat together on a bus and looked west over the long, humid sweep of the Pacific lowlands. The road wove through the mountainous western flanks of volcanoes, through rain forests of the Guatemalan highlands, as it led us to Guatemala City.

Many tourists visit Guatemala to see the folk art in the municipal market, an entire city block of a warehouse full of stalls located in the heart of the old downtown. From either the corner or mid-block entrances, corridors with cracked stucco walls led into a labyrinth that enclosed everything Guatemala produced in both hard goods and foodstuffs, plus tiny stalls with a window for services like locksmiths, knife sharpeners, and shoe repair.

Each stall's forty-watt light bulbs gave off a weak yellow light the colorful fabrics soaked up- the walls, ceiling, and floor space covered with clothing stacked, hung, and piled for perusal. Piled to the rafters of the huge building, even the stall's walls hung thick with embroidered típica clothing, bolts of fabrics with indigenous designs, display shelves for cheap Chinese electronics or plastic toys, storage shelves, etc. and served to separate each vender's stall from the adjacent ones. As the eyes become accustomed to the dim interior, one looks up to see steel rafters that support a metal roof, and holes that let in long spear shafts of sunlight through a smoky haze, along with a little more light that seeps in through unintentional skylights at the edges of the roof, streams of light which give the impression of an abandoned cathedral that spread its wings over this chaos of colorful activity.

The Mercado Central offered all the common everyday items and every handicraft, fabric item, pottery, food, metal utensil, etc. that any tourist or citizen of Guatemala needed. Everything that Guatemalans produced or used on a daily basis flows through this market, even the black market goods from other countries, stolen shipments from robbed trucks or ship containers the dockworkers "lost" in transit.

One entire end of the building contained exotic food stalls, lunch counters with two plank benches, where people sat to eat off ceramic dishes and dipped salsa from small three-legged volcanic stone bowls with dried scum-crusted rims of various colors. They chose their meats from skinned cow or pig heads, hog flanks that hung from hooks, or intestine-wrapped entrails. All around this restaurant stall section the fresh ingredients lay on display; tall piles of vegetables, glass cases of breads and cheeses, long counters with a slanted crushed ice bed for whole rosy bug-eyed fish, dusky perch-like tilapia, sea bass, chunks of white-skinned red shark meat, grey shrimp sorted into piles by size, whole mackerel and tuna, and piles of octopus, a black slime with lines of suckers.

Lines of stainless-steel industrial strength blenders stood ready beside shelves of mangos, bananas, oranges, sesame seeds, popped Amaranto, and vegetables to create nutritious milkshakes perfumed with strawberries, cinnamon, vanilla, and chocolate.

Many of the urban Indian workers wore their regional costumes to work, something Ladino Guatemalans cannot do without a plummet in their self-respect. Only the hip, who accepted the Sixties education of Peace, Love, and Rock and Roll drugs, or those artisans who find it helps sell their crafts, dare to dress típica. The modern Guatemalan Ladino woman's reluctance to appreciate and wear the beautiful and elaborate embroidery of the native blouses, which women all over the United States of North America pay exorbitant prices for, once imported into trendy urban boutiques, speaks to their institutionalized chauvinism for Westernized culture, and a socially mandated prejudice against the indigenous classes.

I needed a guitar to write music, and looked everywhere. The music stores carried some beautiful guitars so expensive I didn't want to travel with them. In the market, the cheap ten dollar guitars challenged me to tune them, then the frets would buzz, or the intonation so far out of whack that I could only tune it for one part of the neck at a time.

After a couple of days of search through all the music stores and several municipal markets, I found a cheap guitar with harmonics correct enough to play most of the neck. Something I could kick around with, and not worry.

Made me realize the important relationship between earnings and market. A market for people without much income won't carry quality products. A depressed economy cannot motivate producers toward an excellence none can afford.

Worst of all, people who don't know better find little to inspire their imaginations, and without wide experience, cannot judge quality.

Choice does not come cheap, and neither does expertise.

So far, my choice to come to Latin America widened my frame of reference enough to believe I stood a step away from the edge of civilization, yet I could still see the dark shadow of where I came from everywhere, that dark mound of polluted industrial caca we call the Rust Belt.

Gringotenango

About 400 after the birth of Christ, evidence suggests that Teotihuacán reached the height of its power and invaded Guatemala, about seven hundred fifty miles away. By persuasion or force, they influenced a city called Kaminaljuyúa to become a miniature replica of the Teotihuacán ceremonial city, near present-day Guatemala City.

Archeologists named this transplanted Teotihuacán culture "Esperanza" and point out that elite corps of Aztec engineers and architects ensured the faithful reproduction of Teotihuacán's minutia of detail, down to the slate slabs that support the lower moldings. The new copy used clay in place of the Teotihuacán site's volcanic stone, in spite of abundant availability in Guatemala.

Through the years, they built the platforms up like a giant layer cake; each period of construction left each previous effort buried under the new. Many layers encased the burial chamber of great leaders whose tombs hint at the extravagant wealth of the Esperanza elite, and their surpluses of food and human energy. For example, an enormous boulder in one tomb came from a mine on the Montagua River, two hundred miles distant, quite a feat for any culture without the advantage of wheels and roadway.

Behind the stairways that fronted each successive pyramid platform lay a God king's tomb. The leader's remains, surrounded by personal and devotional artifacts placed amid the ornate ritual burial furniture, comprise an archeological snapshot of his culture. The artifacts also suggest networks of trade, immigration, and other forms of interconnectedness throughout Meso-America at the time; a carved slate mirror like those of distant Central Veracruz, Mayan pottery from nearby Petén of Early Classic period (AD 100–600), Teotihuacán's Thin Orange pottery, Mayan-Teotihuacán ceramic artifacts, and a myriad of smaller Jade objects that reflect styles from across Meso-America. These, along with similar objects of other materials, may even reflect the mix of cultures and technologies within Kaminaljuyú society.

Downtown Guatemala City, late November, 1975.

After two restful mornings in my 'adequate' (too expensive) hotel, recommended by the previous night's Taxi driver, I looked for the cheapest hotel in all Guatemala City. My day-long search brought me into contact wit many young travelers. I entered many Colonial structures that reminded me of the palatial compound residences of Teotihuacán's noble families.

Teotihuacán houses flanked both sides of the Avenue of the Dead, each built around a square with sides about 200 meters long. A high wall blocked the view from the street, as in Colonial streets, where people see only stone and mortar walls with a few inconspicuous doors and windows on the lower floor. Inside upper class Teotihuacán houses, beautiful frescos commemorated events and rituals to honor their hierarchies of gods and their legends. Apartments interconnect around an open-air courtyard, like modern multi-family homes in Guatemala City. The Teotihuacán elite lived under flat ceilings, built with large cedar beams to support layers of brush and mortar, not only impervious to moisture, but also insulation from the intense heat of the sun, always high overhead in the tropics.

My new hotel came to me through suggestions from other travelers.

For $1.25 per night, I shared a Colonial house. Better said, I shared one of the house's huge rooms with four others. This Casa de Huespedes became a multicultural Mecca for the Five dollar a day travelers from all three human subspecies.

Pasty-white translucent young Caucasian backpackers from the US, Europe, and Canada mixed with beautiful tanned people of what geneticists call the Mongol "race," subspecies, or bloodline- those well-off indigenous Meso-Americans from Mayan Guatemala, Aztec Mexico and Incan South America plus the Asian Japanese or Koreans and South Pacific kids represented by Hawaiians, and representatives from the closer-to-our-roots and well-distributed dark skinned subspecies from Africa, all mixed with the Ladino kids, exotic blends of all three subspecies, who might have white skin, Mayan-Chinese eyes, and nappy brown-red hair in a smooth ball of tight, tiny curls.

We all struggled to understand each other's accent. The hotel offered three meals, vegetable soups, included in that $1.25 per person per day. Many fleet footed and fancy free mixtures of all three human subspecies streamed through the old colonial Guest House, although most represented affluent socialist brats whose parents paid for college.

The most curious and adventurous children from the more affluent environments travel the Third World to 'slum it' in a quest for knowledge of the world through easy living and cheap drugs. Many college graduates take a little time off to see the world, to dedicate oneself to the pleasures of youth, before 'settling down' to family and career.

American baby-boomers with trust funds enjoy economic security at low levels of expenditure, and thus helped invent a new lifestyle of-laid-back international idleness and recreational drug use, which people call "Trustafarian."

Our language barriers created an atmosphere of smiles, open trust, and a studied nonchalance about our possessions to avoid the insult of distrust. People shared stories and joints of marijuana (smoked in "secret") and traded books, advice, plans, and sometimes even their lovers.

To consider oneself a young sophisticate in late nineteen-seventy five meant acknowledgement of the recent end of the Viet Nam War, the Fall of Saigon as a testament to each nations right to "self-determination" against an Imperialism disguised by the Domino Theory opposition to Communism, even democratic communism. Many young people wanted to share in the new American Renaissance of creativity and multi-culturalism of Sixties music and guitar rock, Day-Glo art inspired by hallucinations, open sexuality inspired by The Pill and liberated females, the original New Age movement of Yoga, feminist natural health, and ubiquitous sister-and-brotherhood, a new ideology that included a love of Nature and rejected the Fifties values of 'full employment' (factory jobs for all, wives excepted) and unbridled consumerism.

Youth discovered old wisdom in Eastern religious thought in explorations of the world's non-Christian religions, all the more attractive when related to the alternative realities suggested by drug-induced consciousness. The classic Hippies' rejection of personal hygiene, possessions, and emotional intensity coupled with a Bacchanalian party style of nudity, free love or sex appealed to many young people, sexual deviants and predators, and people with sociopathic problems, often due to the Viet Nam war, who lived free from commune to commune. The mixture of the profane and profoundly disturbed, epitomized by Charles Manson, with those self-actualized pioneers of improvements in the human condition so stained the movement that many became reactionary after marriage and the responsibilities of parenthood, and backslid to become irresponsible uber-consumers or investors, with no curiosity about anything beyond their immediate social group, their tribe, or their own family's fragmentation.

Most of us gave lip service to a rejection of alcohol. We said it led to sluggishness, stupidity, and exaggerated violent tendencies among testosterone-overloaded men, though we admitted it lowered inhibitions and turned many females into potential sex partners. Many drinkers achieved milestones of personal sexual potential, even if they couldn't remember it later. From my slight experience with the use of drugs other than alcohol, I found that even though these drugs don't often make a person violent or fall down into a stupor, most could not compete with alcohol as an aphrodisiac, except one. Strong hallucinogens like LSD, mushrooms with psilocybin, or peyote cactus buttons and synthetic mescaline, changed the way one experienced reality and often came with side effects like paranoia, stomach cramps, nausea, and an urge to vomit, which temper amorous moods quite a bit.

Only Marijuana enhances sensuality and confuses the senses, which helps stimulate excitement while it elongates the passage of time, lucky for any precocious male who suffers premature termination of conjugal duties with a partner under the influence. Convinced that polite society needed more sex, we young people prescribed marijuana for efficiency and enjoyment when preceded by enough beer to ensure the availability of partners.

I wanted to learn Spanish in as short a time as possible through total immersion. I went out often to sight-see, do research on Guatemalan products to take back to the States, and find the best values on food or meals which often meant beg small family restaurants to prepare a simple meal of beans and corn tortillas, after I convinced them that I really preferred beans over meat with my false claim of vegetarianism. That meant frequent trips to the Central Plaza, the main square in the center of Guatemala City between the Palaces for the municipal and federal governments, the big Catholic church, and the cavernous Central Market.

Every day except Sunday in this Catholic country, people packed, pushed, and thronged inside the Central Market to barter and buy. At first, I hauled my backpack around and banged through the crowd or scraped my way down the dark labyrinthine corridors lined with merchandise in stacks of blankets and dresses wrapped in flimsy transparent plastic bags which easily tumbled to the dirty cement floor, a dappled color of fireplace hearth.

I walked head and shoulders taller among the masses of semi-urban Guatemalan Indian males, dressed as cowboys with a two-foot long machete holstered in a rawhide sling. Some of the shorter Mayan men carried machetes so long they looked like great swords, and drooped with a phallic and symbolic weight, as if loaded with the heavy responsibility of deadly force, the great leveler in man's war against Nature.

Here in the market, many Mayan women sat in the booths as sales staff, and wore a white or light colored típica blouse with baroque decorations, embroidered with large, hand-wrought flowers and leaves, over a blue denim skirt that hung snug across their hips and loosened as it fell down to their ankles. The hem, decorated with horizontal stripes of designs etched in thread, contrasted with the dark leather sandals that matched the leather like skin on the edge of their dusty feet, both cracked white around the edges.

Many Mayan women wore a long thin cloth, coiled into a thick serpentine circle, atop their head like the perimeter of a skullcap.

I bought some breads and cheese to take back to my room, and promised myself I would not bring my backpack along next time.

After a couple of days of restless sleep in the communal hotel, I heard too many complaints about "lost stuff" from the shared rooms, though none dared accuse anyone in particular. We all suspected each other. I again felt reluctant to abandon my stuff in the room, although I didn't possess anything of value except my traveler's checks, hidden deep in the substructure of my backpack. On another level, the poverty in Latin America exaggerated the value of my backpack's contents; the essentials for one person to eat, sleep, cook, and change clothes. Someone could walk off with the whole backpack easy enough, grab and run, no one around, no one to care enough to notice. No crime, no return of goods, no reward. Bad luck for me.

It felt bad to say goodbye to the fellow travelers, the sunlit flowers, the chilly mornings with coffee and bread, the stilted conversations against the melodic shrill din from the bird-filled cages, but the next morning before dawn, I said thank you and goodbye to the female staff who prepared the house's free breakfast, and made my way in a rectangular zigzag through the quiet city to the Terminal of Autobuses.

It loomed through the mist, dripped slick black and gray against the purpled light of dawn. As other people arrived, I watched them get out of taxis and pickup trucks, unload and walk inside with their baggage or heavy bundles. Some grunted under their loads with each step.

I stumbled toward them, avoided the deepest puddles on the broken asphalt, and felt dizzy, sick, shivers. Nothing to eat since yesterday afternoon. I could feel the full weight of my backpack. The points of my stored boots kick me in the small of my back with every step. Took my pack off, laid it on the sidewalk to open it and rearrange things, again, like so many times before. I squatted and felt the diesel-tinged cold whip up my khaki shorts with the polished steel of two-inch cockfight razors I saw lined up in clear plastic boxes on the sidewalk in Guadalajara. The wind outlined the sweaty imprint of my backpack with an icy wind, and I shivered.

At the entrance, the open double doors vomited a gust of dusty wind that tasted of fruity garbage and burlap, rotten meat. From inside, I saw people trickle in from various entrances to mill about in a short-stature, multi-colored crowd of Mayan and Ladino garb. Everyone' s hair looked as thick, straight, and black as a horse's mane.

I picked him out from a distance, tall, bearded, and long blonde hair. He walked up to me in the clothing of a Mayan Indian, bright red pajama pants and the intricate designs of a woven vest over an embroidered shirt of white cotton, now mellowed to a golden maple color. Pulseras, little colored woven bracelets, festooned both his wrists. From each bracelet dangled slender tails of tie-dyed threads like snagged strands of colored hair.

"Don't worry. You look worried," he said to me. "Say you're Canadian, and everyone will like you." A slight French accent. He poked his fingers into his beard as if in search, rubbed his temples, and then ran his fingers back to smooth the long, sun-bleached blond hair of his scalp-tight ponytail.

I felt irritated that anyone could so easily recognize me as American. I felt bad about that, as if I too served as a symbol for the Ugly American. Anyone from a country successful and rich provokes jealous criticism and blame from the have-nots. It made perfect sense to me at that moment, how others feel they always get the shaft, and the United States of North America gets the mine.

He asked me for a light.

I reached into my pocket to pull out some Mexican "Clasicos" matches, a little flat yellow box with a cover that depicted billows of smoke from a old steam engine train and an armless Greek nude female marble statue, and said keep the box.

He asked if I could spare an "extra" cigarette.

I gave him two unfiltered Mexican Delicados, ovals of tobacco wrapped in a sugar-soaked paper.

He lit one, and his eyes glanced about with furtive movements. "Welcome to the graveyard of American School buses, mate!" He forced a laughed. "Find your old high school bus, show me your name carved into the back of a seat, right where you put it a couple of years ago, and win a prize!"

"I'm not that young."

"Once in a lifetime, right now, and don't you ever forget it."

He walked away with short, rapid strides. With each step, his string-belted pajama pants sagged across one buttock and threatened to slip off. His faded red and green striped cotton pants of native Mayan fabrics dragged across a floor that carried a patina from years of inadequate maintenance, a gray sludge color, polka-dotted with dark smears of gum. He didn't look down at his filthy bare feet but strode fast, with a brisk swish as each callused foot stroked the floor. One hand held the cigarette up to his face. As he waded through the crowd, puffs of smoke marked his progress.

I went outside into the bus yard. Which bus should I take? I imagined how these American yellow school buses followed the heel-feathers of migratory birds, all headed south, to this Land of Eternal Springtime, with pothead hippies behind the wheel fueled by dreams of a quick buck in "import-export" through contacts with foreign military officers, school busses in exchange for protection and a load of marijuana, Mexican Heroin, or Colombian cocaine, probably stashed in bales of Mayan fabrics and hidden inside pottery.

From outside, the Terminal de Autobuses Extra-Urbanos looked like a great ad-hoc architectural disaster, a long semicircle of tin roofs held up by two-by-fours. The roofs protect the inner stalls of a large market full of fruits, vegetables, cloth, clothing, hardware, and house-wares.

I listened to people question the bus drivers, whenever they stopped their bellow of destinations- "Escuintla! Salamá! Chichicastenango!" as a substitute public address system to help passengers find the correct bus. A foreigner may not realize the joy given to these drivers when they convince a tourist, after much feigned scrutiny of maps and a long, feverish exercise in conversation without a common language, to get on this bus. The barkers say that their bus will take you direct and nonstop. Like all the buses, their bus takes you to your destination with a stop in every crossroad and village no matter what they promise.

To the drivers, it didn't much matter where you wanted to go. Some guidebooks suggest that the bus drivers consider all parts of Guatemala just as worthy of tourism as any other. Tickets paid in full mattered the most.

Children surrounded me, hands-out, their long eyelashes framed black irises like solid pupils, beggars, pure in motive and need. I saw gangs of them help other travelers with suitcases, three or four tiny pairs of hands on each, every one desperate for a tip. They spoke a few words of English, Italian, Spanish, Mayan, who knows- "One dollar, How oar you, Taco, I fine, food, I help, Ca-peesh, Where you go? Coca-cola," etc.

I tried to say No, with certainty, to all the children with happy eyes who begged me to pay them for the opportunity to carry my backpack. When that didn't work, they simply begged for money- with sadder, insulted, or even angry eyes.

After I passed enough of them, other children noticed and left me alone.

In Estados Unidos Mexicanos, I learned to accept help from children in secret, to avoid the concentric circles of frenzy that occurred once when I paid a child in public for a little help to get my backpack on the right bus. The child tugged my backpack to the bus, but couldn't get up the steps. I didn't know whether to feel good that I'd given him an opportunity for a little healthy paid exercise, or bad that I reinforced the corruption of a child who worked for money and neglected his own education in school, if offered or available. He appeared malnourished. When I paid him too much, the other children considered me Santa Claus and they mobbed me, a forest of calloused hands outstretched, dirty nails on the ends of long emaciated fingers, a brown picket fence through which I saw their wet eyes bright and shiny, their thick dusty hair cow licked by no pillow, the toothy desperation in their false smiles of hopeless joy.

Here, one Mayan child, determined to charm me, followed behind me. I heard his footsteps crunch across the gravel and it reminded me of a faithful, happy dog. I could not convince him to go away, so I decided to give him a tiny chore to do, and pay him too little, to get rid of him.

Without even the suggestion of pay, I let him help me find the correct bus. The man in the bus, with the child's help, convinced me to get on the bus with my backpack. I started to pull out my wallet but the man held out his hand to stop me. "You pay the driver. Not now, later. When the bus driver comes."

Afterwards, I slipped my tiny servant the phenomenal sum of an American quarter, and enjoyed his childish exuberance. He knew what it could buy. He fled to his friends all smiles, to show off or buy some candy, I supposed. I prayed he might use that same persistence to go to school for a career as an international diplomat, and give up sales.

As we waited for the bus driver, I watched how Guatemala's commerce forms a network of packets carried on the backs of Mayan men. They bussed in from their village's agricultural areas with immense loads of produce in net bags. I watched through the bus window to see how they walked under these loads as if against a hurricane wind, with a lean so far forward you think they might fall. They balanced huge loads on their back, over their hips, net bags three or four feet in diameter full of avocados, cabbages, oranges, corn, coconuts, whatever, and held them in place with the tension of a leather strap across the forehead. Like a backpack, but without adjustable padded shoulder straps, they kept the weight over their legs, atop their hips. As they rushed to take a place in line for any bus about to depart, their small-calloused feet stamped puffs of dust with each step, even on the Terminal's mildew-gray cement.

I recognized our fat bus driver by his black captain's hat. I felt the bus lean as he stepped inside and sat down in the seat. He joked with his companion, who stood in the doorway and bellowed out a list of communities.

With a startle, I realized I'd spent all my Quetzales, the Guatemalan bills given in exchange for Mexican pesos at the border, and needed to change my American dollars to the colorful paper notes that tourists often call monopoly money, decorated with the rain forest's iridescent Quetzal bird that gives the money its name- Quetzales.

I wanted to see one with its valuable three-foot long emerald tail feathers.

I walked to the front of the bus. I didn't know the rate of exchange, so I held out my American greenbacks to the driver. Both of the men came from the same mold, dark skinned, wavy greasy black hair, beer-fattened torsos in sleeveless T-shirts. The driver ignored me, and the other man swung out from the first step to hang from a vertical stainless-steel bar meant to help people board. He waved to the crowd and bellowed the route's destinations- "Quetzaltenango! Tontonicapán! San Antonio Palopo! Sololá!"

To get his attention, I stepped forward with my backpack in tow so he got the impression I wanted to get off the bus. He looked at me funny and told me the price again. I held up a mixed handful of United States bills and change, and said, "Quetzales."

He politely, with exaggerated purpose, pulled a wad of bills from his back pocket and extracted a Quetzal, and then a ten Quetzal bill, and said, "Un Quetzal. Un dolar. Cada una."

In Mexico, everyone thought it a good idea for tourists to carry dollars, because merchants like dollars, in case the Mexican Peso fluctuated downward. I didn't understand how they could assume the peso headed down. Why shouldn't the dollar nose-dive? However, day by day, the rate of exchange did change a little, both up and down. People feared the big devaluations. In Mexico, I learned to accept any rate of exchange near twelve and a half pesos to one dollar, a difficult computational task, even after I memorized a number of equivalencies for twelve and a half Mexican pesos to a dollar.

I repeated what he said, "¿Un dolar, un Quetzal?"

"Si. Un dolar, un Quetzal." With a smile and no haste, he gently took my money from my hand, counted it aloud, slow, and deliberate, bill by bill, as if he thought me an idiot. Then he took his Quetzales and started to count out my change, bill by bill, until he reached the same number.

He gave me the pile of Quetzales, then backed up and held out his hand. "Por el boleto. A Panajachél." and then reached into my handful of bills to extract the ticket price with care.

I put my backpack in the bus seat's overhead rack, used sign language to ask him to watch it for me. "No hay problema."

I went outside to buy some breakfast and a little food for the trip.

When I heard the bus purred to life with the stench of cloud of diesel fumes, I hurried back as more people boarded.

The bus crept like an overloaded yellow blood cell through the clogged main arteries of central Guatemala City, between old colonial walls of gray stone and cement, stained by the black breath of time and the scabby coats of once-vivid paint that now looked burnt as it curled, peeled, and fell to expose mortar, or stone or adobe bricks. Outside the heart of Guatemala City, the streets opened up with high-rise apartment and office buildings, interspersed with nondescript warehouses and open lots where the lush vegetation grew amid bare piles of iron car parts that stuck out of piles of rubble, dirt, and sand that glittered with broken glass.

Through the front windshield I saw a church, blood red, its spire like fire in the sunlight. I crossed the bus aisle to sit where I could see it clearly. Medieval and tall, an elegant fantasy mix of castle and church, the walls covered in smooth red tiles, no sign of life, its doors shut tight as if to protect a connection to another reality, protected against a world that could not match its beauty. The color-contrast to the Emerald City must house a weak and besieged witch with all the watery wisdom of the Anti-Oz.

Within an hour, we passed the city limits, and the Land Of Eternal Springtime unfurled its forests festooned with diamonds of dew that glittered in the bright morning sunlight. Pasturelands and cornfields rolled across the steep volcanic mountainsides where palm trees lined the ridges like the big-hair dos of skinny divas of country music, a slender stalked lineup of cheerleaders with pompoms.

When the bus speeds round a curve, everybody inside leans, as if in subconscious and unanimous opinion about the driver's ability to keep us within the Newtonian laws of physics. The driver tries to center the bus over the centerline on this narrow two-lane 'highway,' which often put us between steep cliffs and a drop-off. He took blind curves racecar style, in the wrong lane, and the old bus leaned enough that it brought the road cut of volcanic soils so close I could reach out and touch it, and break my arm. Then a curve the other way, near the canyon, and the wheels scatter loose asphalt over the edge of a drop-off into thin air, a snare drum roll punctuated by the whoosh of a few treetops.

Many times we rounded curves and almost killed something not far enough off the road- a mule, horse, herd of cows or goats, an Indian family and their dog, an old man who tried to steady a weather-grayed wooden cart behind two tired and startled horses.

The front of the bus resembles an altar, and whenever we survived a close call, the old ladies crossed themselves and held their thumb to their lips.

The windshield, framed in curtain trim of gaudy gold brocade, served as less a window than a diorama to frame versions of Jesus on the Cross with a clutter of white plastic Catholic saints, all lined up haphazard along the dashboard like fence posts. Hung from the rear-view mirror, a small cardboard Virgin of Guadalupe air-freshener swayed as if frantic, in contrast to the two decorations in the windshield corners- florescent green stickers with cartoon line drawings of buxom women, their expressions surprised, a small word balloon arrowed from their mouth as wavy lines radiated from their bulbous buttocks. I didn't understand symbolism, nor the Spanish, and my dictionary failed me.

Someone lined the entire windshield with a curtain trim of fuzzy balls, wine red, so that the driver's area reminded me of Mardi Gras, of a whore's cubical in New Orleans, where pedestrians on the street could see the rhythmic appearance of legs that stick out of two slits in a curtain, behind which a woman on a swing would make instant decisions to cross her legs, or show one leg, two legs on one side, spread legs, etc. Various rosary chains festooned the rear view mirror like clumps of seaweed on an anchor. In a flat area above the windshield, someone stuck a bunch of Christian crosses of wood and pewter alongside demonic red black and aluminum stickers for rock bands. On the back of the driver's seat, a reticulated plastic portrait of The Messiah stares at me with upturned eyes, and as I bounce up and down in my seat, Jesus' eyes open and close as if to say Oh my God, oh my God, oh God.

A couple of Mormon boys in the seats in front of me looked back and waved. I bet they knew more Spanish than I did.

Tried to write postcards. I carried a long cardboard strip of Guatemalan postcards that accordion together, not broken apart yet, all these landscape photographs printed in an ancient technology of large dots, like newsprint. It served as a travelogue of Guatemala; a market scene, the Indian's incense-filled Catholic church in Chichicastenango, the bottomless Lake Atitlán held up in the mountains by three volcanoes, some romantic seaside sunset with palms and a shack, Mayan pyramids of Tikál in the Petén region, jungle waterfalls with travertine-rimmed scalloped pools of pure cyan blue, pretty native girls in typical Mayan clothing, etc. Since I carried no camera, I valued them and wrote on them to friends, but never mailed them from Guatemala. I carried them all the way back home with me t_ o lose years later, long after I lost those friends.

The week since I crossed the Mexican border and bussed to Guatemala City seemed like a century. When I first saw the Pacific flank of volcanic mountain slopes, it seemed they ran westward to the Pacific floodplains instead of south. My internal compass would not listen to reason, no matter how long I stared at the map. The volcanoes' flanks slide down southward from Chimaltenango to the floodplains and pastures where droop-eared, hump-backed Brahma cattle lay in the shade of lone rocket-shaped-Ceiba trees. Farther south nearer the Pacific, sugar cane fields and beyond that, somewhere lost in the tropical haze, I thought I could see the low outline of mangrove swamps along the Pacific shoreline.

The highway climbed back into the sierra. Volcanoes loomed over the landscape from near and far, and on their flanks I noticed mini-volcanoes, blackhead pimples of rock, which stuck out of the volcanic uplift. The road fishtailed into the Sierra Occidental and wove its way through fresh-drenched rainforests of fog and steam as the land gives birth to clouds, instead of the sea.

Lago de Atitlán

The cacao bean, the source of cocoa and chocolate, served as money in Meso-America. Evidence suggests that people made counterfeit money, beans hollowed out and refilled, so suspicious people would bite the beans to verify their contents. Some archeologists think only the rich could afford to roast and grind up this bean money to make the chocolate drink.

After four years of fantasy, in a few hours I would see what originally captured my imagination- Lake Atitlán, my destination. Twenty-five square miles of 'bottomless' water trapped by a barrier of three 11,600-foot volcanoes.

The bus stopped at a wide, grassy crossroad clearing in the high rain forest called Los Encuentros. The air smelled fresh, wet, and muddy. Next stop, Lake Atitlán, so here many of us got off to eat some grilled meat tacos from the crude stalls that lined the parking area. Cooks attended large metal deep fryers that held about ten gallons of oil over coals hot enough to make the edges boil and fume. Pans held piled pyramids of breaded chicken or empanadas, pockets of dough filled with meat and vegetables.

I walked along the line of primitive stalls, each not much more than a counter under a canvas or plastic tarp awning, and felt queasy with the smell of rotten garbage and human excrement that wafted up from ravines hidden in the dark rain forest behind the stalls.

I asked for a bathroom, but they said No services, no building, and no water. I decided not to eat.

As the bus sped on, I caught my first brief glimpse of a far away glitter between tall pine trees. We tourists took cues from a cute Mayan Indian family, who turned to us with a smile to point at the window to warn us as we neared a break in the trees with another glorious view of the lake.

Terraced mini-fields scalloped the mountainsides, each defined by tiny canals perhaps used for hundreds or thousands of years to irrigate the rich volcanic soils. About the size of wide gutters, they divided and linked the fields in a network of water channeled from where the mountaintops hid their crowns behind the low ceiling of gray clouds. On some steep slopes, the quantity of tiny fields resembled fish scales. Different crops created mosaics of distinct colors and textures.

From the pine forests above Panajachél on the shore of Lake Atitlán, we could see across five miles of flat expanse of the lake to other tiny villages at the base of three volcanoes. A backdrop of blue sky cupped a milky humidity over the farthest horizon, the Pacific Ocean. This open-throated bowl of mountains, with three volcano teeth, cradles the lake as if it floats on air. The volcano peaks comb the moisture out of the West winds that funnel between them, winds which drive across the lake with so much force they decorate the water surface with distinct wave textures in gigantic serpentine paisleys of turbulence.

The road follows a gorge into Panajachél, then becomes the town's one street, a cobblestone trail lined with cement and stone architecture. Down side streets that turn into earth within a block or two, I see adobe or wood residences that disappear into the vegetation. Nearer the lake, thatched-roof 'luxury' hotels and touristy restaurants or trinket shops line the street.

Down this steep incline we bounced until the road continues for only a few blocks to disappear into the lake as a boat ramp. The brakes screech with the smell of burnt asbestos. Pedestrians rubberneck and watch our bus shudder to a halt.

Inside, everyone stands and tugs at their bundles stuffed in the overhead racks, then waits lined up in the aisle. An American tourist motions toward the lake through the windshield and says, "Busloads of people drown each year when their brakes fail."

I laughed a little. Didn't know if he joked, or tried to pass on valuable information.

He didn't laugh.

We lumber off the bus like stiff penguins to wait at the side for our luggage. After a couple of hours in the hot, sweaty interior, the cool mountain air, gusty and dry and pine-scented, invigorated me and made me impatient to explore.

The Mormon boys, in white shirts and ties, stood silent and deep in thought as the driver untied their bicycles from on top. They looked up and down the steep cobblestone streets with forlorn expressions.

Many people, mostly Indians, got off the bus at the stops along the way. About half of the passengers now looked Indian. I noticed two couples, retired Americans proud and loud, as they argued about the best ways to stretch their fixed incomes in Guatemala's 'dollar a day' economy. I wanted everybody out of my way. I wanted to get out and look at everything, and I noticed that nobody else felt my impatient urgency. Haste did not exist in Guatemala. People stay in the slow lane.

The Indian men from our bus walked down the gravel roads on sandaled feet or barefoot, bundles balanced on their heads or on their backs in net bags, the trump line headband across their forehead. The wide-hipped Indian women, swaddled in layers of clothing, towed a line of children, or carried them in a cloth sling or balanced on a hip, and sometimes also held live bedraggled chickens by their feet to dangle across their shoulders, head-down to cluck weak and wild-eyed.

Mayan Indian men in cowboy hats cruised the sidewalks. One carried a tall cage full of colorful songbirds that flitted about terrified. Another cage on the sidewalk housed a couple of parrots that squawked and complained as they chewed on the bars.

Lots of American tourists too, and for that, Panajachél earns the nickname Gringotenango, made from the word Gringo welded to Tenango which signifies "city" in Mayan.

A few old colonial buildings ran along the street, pastel shades of painted stucco walls punctuated by doors, windows, and rows of succulent plants that looked like green spiky tentacles of shy octopuses, heads buried in the planters. Thick shrubs and small trees adorned yards and made "living fence lines" that sprouted clusters of huge red flowers like wads of fluorescent tissue paper.

Another world. Some of the plants looked sinister, as if they might reach out and grab, once it got dark.

This town, near a major highway and with a spectacular view of sunset behind three volcanoes, showed its roots in both Mayan village life and international tourism. A mixture of sedate and dignified Guatemalan normalcy existed side by side with California chic, while even small hotels sported European influences and polyglot signage. Panajachél's renaissance created a happy boomtown that mixed ancient Mayan with old colonial, the Hippies' back to the primitive naturalism, and the sophisticated nature lover's appreciation of rare birds in gardens of endemic rarities.

The architecture and signage of one building impressed me with its modern sensibility. The use of wood and mud distinguished the House of Pies. In Spanish, pie means foot, so they also spelled it with Spanish phonetics as 'pay'.

I stopped to eat a wedge of fancy pie and gaze out into the street, transported back a hundred, two hundred years, among wispily-bearded men and their unshaven women, lost in the remnants of a complex indigenous culture that still expresses itself, although subordinate, from within Guatemala's European Catholicism.

I'd already heard about rental houses a couple of miles south of Panajachél, in a community called Santa Catarina Palopó. People there prepare meals for travelers, and rent houses for a song. I hoped they might want to defray the rent in exchange for lessons in English, or something similar.

I asked how to get to Santa Catarina, and people pointed me down a side road headed south. In about three blocks, the houses spaced out, the cobblestone road bent and turned into a dirt road. I walked a one-lane, tree-shaded country road between coffee plantations and soon realized that any of Panajachél's roads headed south that didn't dead-end merged into this one.

An expensive car drove by, a woman behind the wheel. In a heartbeat, I remembered why I hated Mexico's San Miguel de Allende and Acapulco. I'd seen her neurotic expression on too many a rich older woman there. I thought of them as the Art Moms, the divorced, well-off, loveless and perhaps unloved who lusted for fulfillment through creative expression. They wore too much make-up and expensive 'casual' clothing, as if they needed to out-Artsy each other, and a bored, slight pained and dull anxiety, as if they knew that life could not compensate them for all they went through- all the sacrifice and humiliation of matrimony and childrearing. They most likely refused to nurse their babies and used their husband's money to pay nannies to raise the next generation of ungrateful, unloved, and touched-starved children, the first baby-boomers. Now they fight against the ravages of time and lose any chance for a graceful fade because they live in fear of that final mortification, death without makeup, the loss of control over body functions and motor coordination, that results in soiled underwear and the flesh's final sag into whatever unnatural state all the ill-advised cosmetic surgery left it. These women already looked pissed off, as if they lived with a premonition that their premature death would happen any second, and on a bad hair day. Get out of my way, I have no time to acknowledge your existence.

A quiet Mayan Indian man sits bemused on his front step while his wife and daughters weave cloth on back-strap looms. He watches me clomp by. My backpack bounces like a monkey on my back. Did he ever see that spaceman, our spaceman, take his first small step for man, and the first giant step for mankind? Or was it a small, meaningless step for mankind, which those not male-chauvinistic acknowledge as humankind? Does he look at me and see a wallet filled with dollars, or a boy from a world he recognizes as poisonous, a boy who hopes to take his own first small steps for the species?

Did the Great Creator program all human with genes to desire a personal automobile? To get them ready, willing, and able to risk life and limb behind the wheel, to join the traffic-clogged veins and arteries of that bull-snort urban procession of trucks and automobiles in stop-and-go congestion with the growl, hum, squeal, and fume of incipient road rage? Programmed to believe the advertisements on TV, the First World of Lone Ranger images, everyone's desire for independence, alone in a sleek machine that bullets through the verdant billows of a mountain landscape, eyes glued to the ribbon of asphalt without notice of nature's grandeur, to imagine high-speed flirtations with other drivers, also insulated and relaxed at high speed, each in their illusion of escape, freedom, and perpetual youth?

Our ancestors paved the way to this multi-orgasmic grapple with the known universe. The synthetic television reality reduces humanity to a gold-standard yellow brick road that promises to lead to personal fulfillment alone in imaginary valleys of sweet fecund humidity or atop an oceanic overlook. The flowers of good fortune, like folded origami money, bloom in rainbow arcs over the soft green bosoms of ancient mountain slopes eroded round by the millennia. A foamy, wet river runs through it- and an asphalt ribbon runs alongside, the seam on Mother Nature's charcoal pantyhose. With my hands at two and four on the wheel of control, I put my foot down, in fearless defiance of all dangerous curves. The motor roars with an open mouth full of wind, a stainless steel luxury Extremis built on the lines of feline sex appeal, the metals mined at high altitudes in Bolivia by the grime-covered husbands of stout, infertile women who still wear black bowler hats because of a rumor from the turn of the century that it helps a woman conceive.

Someday, I should buy a car as a personal statement, an extension of my personality, like a perfect trophy wife with a perpetual purr, a high-maintenance utility that needs rhythmic injections and insertions of the credit card to keep the engine's throb and whine smooth, the exhaust hot, the vibration of wheels on the road a pleasant sensation. As soon as I get one of the two whores of Mordor, either rich or successful (whatever that means), whichever comes first, then I can make it all happen.

A bird swooped, eye-level, across and down the grass-tufted road in front of me, to chase insects that bolted at my approach.

The branches of cocoa trees on each side of this two-track lane meet overhead, and the sun dripped golden flashes that swam on the trail before me. The cool shade on the road shimmered alive, the dust glistened under my feet, a volcanic glassy dust that kicked up to settle like tiny diamond magnets.

The cocoa plantations alongside the road resembled a long unbroken park, a black-ink shade that stretched away under this grove of short but wide trees.

Other fruit trees mixed in. I saw the immature papayas, blond-green gourds the size of footballs, that hang as if weightless on trunks thin as the arms of starving children. These tall and slender papaya trees punctuated the undergrowth, their trunks textured by round black scars where previous giant compound leaves fell off. At the top, each large leaf radiated like an umbrella, each a giant green snowflake. The lower leaves almost hid the mature football-size fruits that suckled along the thin trunk.

When the forest plantation thinned out, I could see cacao trees up the valleys, the roasted fruits destined for chocolate factories in Europe, where they grind the seeds for three days to make a greasy micro-powder. Then they export that black cream back to the Americas as "Dutch Chocolate." Chocolate lovers appreciate its drug-like property, aficionados claim chocolate reproduces the feelings of love.

A young man sits under a chocolate tree and eats something out of a chocolate pod. When I stop to watch him, he offers me some, then signs Wait with his hand. He stands up, and stretches tall to reach up along the cacao tree trunk and cut down a pod. The fruit, the green ribbed cacao pod, clings to the trunk like a thirsty tick, an extra-terrestrial parasite. He shows me how to cut it open, and peal it back to turn it inside out. We use our fingers to scoop out a white custard matrix to eat, a sweet pudding.

I left him and marched to the rhythm of my own footfalls that raised little clouds of glittery reddish dust, like chocolate. I felt strong under my backpack, felt grateful for the sweet white cacao pod flesh, and felt the coolness of my sweat under the shoulder straps and across the small of my back. I hunched now and then to change the tension in the straps, with no particular reason, for something to do. When I passed small groups of people, women with children or a couple of men who carried machetes, we all mumbled Buenos Días or Adiós.

Midmorning, hot. What some might perceive as absolute silence, I heard as the roar of nature, the sound of wind without a breeze, the hum of insects the sun drove into the shade. I walked down the road through short fresh grasses, florescent green against the reddish chocolate-powder dirt. As far as I could see, ancient crop terraces scallop the mountain slopes. Built over millennia, these mountainsides, terra-formed by the Maya with stone tools, soak up the rains that shower abundance and sustenance over Guatemala, one of the very few countries on earth with no foreseeable shortage of freshwater.

Where the road neared the cliffs that overlooked the lake, the rich built unused houses that lay nestled behind walls topped with broken glass bottles set into cement to dissuade thieves. Thorny shrubs made fence lines that flowered, branched, and knit together, impenetrable. Like islands of irrigated green, tree canopies shaded small yards alongside twin strip gardens that flank the driveways.

Volkswagen Capitalists

The road curved down toward the lake and opened up onto a gravel wash. In the winter 'invierno', the May to August season of torrential downpours, water from all the mountainside ravines joined together here into a powerful flash flood. Big rains don't happen much in November, and only a small trickle of water wetted the riverbed.

Where it joined the lake, a half-dozen people dressed in their Sunday best watched an evangelical baptism.

I hear a motor putt-putted and echo on the road behind me, and glimpse through the trees a blue Volkswagen. I see the bug again, as it rounds a curve and splashes through pools that hide in deep tree shadow. The car's image shatters into shards of light when it launches into the full sunlight of the rock-lined ravine. It scatters the bones of white river rock, crunches through pools of gravel beds, splashes through drainage ditches of runoff streams, and wallows like a blue hippo through the dry riverbed of rounded stones.

I walk on into the shade of another coffee plantation.

They pass me, yell in a good-natured tone of voice, then skid to a stop in front of me, deep in the Cacao grove's shade. As I pass them, I hear one of the tourists in the car ask, in accented British English, "Where you going?"

"Santa Catarina."

"Want a cheap house, right?"

The three shadows in the car laughed. Looks like a young man with two girls. He leans out the window from the driver's seat.

"You'll love it there, beautiful. We live nearby. You smoke grass?"

"Sometimes. Depends."

"Like to buy some?"

"No way! What happens if I get caught with it?"

"You'll go to jail." All three laughed nervously. "And you don't want to go to jail in Guater-mahler."

"Like to buy a brownie?" One of the girls asked.

"With grass in it?"

"If it didn't have grass in it, think I would waste my time offering to sell it for a dollar fifty?" They laughed.

The girl stuck her slim pearl-white arm through the window and gave me a plastic-wrapped brownie.

I unwrapped it a little. It looked loaded with vegetable matter that swirled in tornadoes of psychedelic silage. "Is this good stuff or what?"

"Smell it. What do you think? Smoked lately?"

Warm chocolate aroma, with a hint of barn straw. "The last time I ate a marijuana brownie, months ago, I bet. I smoked a couple of weeks ago near San Blas with some Californians. We body-surfed the waves from a hurricane."

I bought a brownie for a dollar fifty, out of hunger more than anything else. I already felt like a stranger in another world, paranoid, my senses overwhelmed.

They took off. When the Volkswagen's sounds dissipated, the quiet hiss of silence, the wind or the rush of my own blood in my temples, surged back once again. I laughed, recognized my foolishness to believe I could escape my own drug-filled culture here.

My brownie proved to me the ubiquity of drugs, like dogs and cooking, part of the human condition.

Should I keep the brownie for later, with the risk that the police arrest me and start the endless negotiations for more money from my relatives in the USA, to pay everyone off- the police, judge, witnesses, court costs, jail costs, travel costs, lawyer fees, tips, and bribes and maybe never get out of jail?

For safety's sake, I ate it.

The road, bulldozed and blasted out of the mountainside, angled up steeply. I climbed off the road into the rocks to get a higher perspective, and sat on a rocky point far above the road to look out over the water.

On the far western shore, three volcanoes loomed over the lake. They bent the shapes of clouds that cruised in off the Pacific, about fifty miles farther west, far out of sight below the volcanoes' horizon.

The lake surface shimmered with a kaleidoscope of silver patterns where the wind tickled turbulence disorganized the surface of waves. Wafts of smoke and glints of sunlight on shiny metal or glass betrayed the locations of tiny villages along the shore. In the shadowy reflection of the volcano's skirts, the blue-black waters flickered with a mysterious stardust. The volcanoes' shadows slipped up the slopes from the inky lakeshore and tilted up through short forests.

Below, between the road and the cliff over the lake, the yards rich people's vacation homes sat empty behind high walls of brick and block or cement, with Mayan decorations sculpted into the corners and windows. I saw solid iron gates textured with ball peen hammer blows, doors of rebar and sheet metal, and windows with tiny panes, punctuated the walls. The houses sat smug and resilient, each empty except for the occasional caretaker in cowboy sombrero ,who trod the grounds slow, as if old, or stood idle in the shade, maybe with a hose pointed at a small garden. I saw a couple of workers dig with shovels, and another push dirt and stone around in a wheelbarrow.

Those rich enough to build such homes didn't need to live in them, or use them more than a couple of weekends a year, to achieve the desired effect.

I felt jealous already.

The Indian Village

Although Meso-American languages easily divide into 14 families, they also group into three super-families, called Uto-Aztecan, Macro-Mayan, and Oto-Manguean. The Uto-Aztecan contains the Nahua groups, and includes the Aztec empire's official language, Náhuatl.

Macro-Mayan consists of languages like Zoquean and Totonacan, though the largest group, Mayan, contains many mutually unintelligible dialects, some of which may still sound like language spoken over the past twenty centuries for the two millennia of Mayan cultures. A few of these languages may link into the Mayan literatures of mathematics, sciences, astronomy, medicine, and religious writings but almost every bit of that body of intellectual achievement disappeared forever, destroyed by Spanish clerics whose Catholicism demanded they burn those great libraries to save the Mayans' souls, while other Spaniards enslaved the Mayan people to farm, once those Spaniards gave up the dream of stockpiles of gold and instant wealth.

The mountain stuck out a shoulder here, into the lake, and road construction workers blasted whole sections of rock cliff out of the mountainside to expose the thick layers, mixtures of lava and accretions, dirt and volcanic deposits of dust and shattered black-glassy rocks, speckled and pocked full of tiny gas bubbles. I could see another half-mile of this curvy, up-

and-down road level off ahead to crossed a small alluvial plain. Slopes of green grasses formed an apron behind a tiny, one-road village along the shore, Santa Catarina Palopó, my destination.

In front of this lakeshore village, one long sturdy wooden dock, shaped like a cross with short arms, snuggled into the village's cove. In the village center's open square of reddish dust, a flower-shaped fountain sat in front of a white stucco church about thirty feet square.

I entered the village as the late afternoon sun slipped behind the volcanoes, and winds dropped down the mountainside with a pine scented chill. Dogs barked and ran out of nearby houses to join several that snapped at my heels as I walked. At one point, they surrounded me, held me motionless.

Children ran over to my rescue. They laughed, held the dogs back, and enjoyed all the barks and the wrinkled canine snouts, the pink gum-lined fangs. They ran their hands through the erect hair along the dogs' back, and laughed at the foamy fanged, saliva-spittled hatred that intensified as I stood there surrounded, unable to move.

These Mayan kids looked Japanese or Chinese, appeared much smaller and skinnier than their counterparts in the United States of North America. The boys wore bright red clothing, loose shirts and pants embroidered with intricate designs, and the girls wore blue denim skirts and red blouses with intricate multi-colored flowers embroidered across the collarbones. Some of the taller ones wore the circle of red cloth on their heads, a tight-wound cloth that bound their hair up into a ring, a round coil. I tried the little Spanish I knew, and they answered with smiles, hand gestures, and words that sounded Japanese with glottal stops like rocks dropped into a pond.

The children kicked at the dogs to keep them back. This went on for about ten minutes. I realized that they, like me, spoke Spanish as a second language. In effect, I'd arrived in Asia, China, or Nepal, for all the good my two semesters of College Spanish did me here.

All the howls and barks intrigued some older women who came over and addressed me in what my ears recognized, after much labor, as a baby-talk Spanish with a strange pronunciation.

With little suspicious smiles, they interrogated me- wanted to know where I came from, which at first I took to mean my nationality, or maybe from where I last spent the night. I didn't know if they wanted to hear Panajachél, or Guatemala City, or Mexico. I said Estados Unidos, or the United States of America, and they looked blank. I got better reactions with California, Alaska. They kept up the repetitions of Ooo Sah until I realized they meant USA in Spanish.

I claimed Uoosah, and they seemed relieved.

They tongue-clattered amongst themselves, then motioned to me to follow them as they chocked and shucked some curt words to the kids, which made the children drag the dogs by the neck skin back towards the houses at the village center.

A couple of men with Machetes walked over. After a very brief exchange with the women, they beckoned me to follow, they wanted to show me a few houses. The skies darkened so fast that I thought they might take me somewhere and do away with me to get my cash and all that great brand-new camping gear I used twice so far over these past months of travel.

I followed the young men past the church and the store, which sported the one electric light in town. Then we turned up the slope on narrow, boulder-strewn trails, footpaths that interlaced the small spaces around the simple houses and tiny bare dirt yards. The majority of houses seemed built of mud and sticks, the maintained ones sported a coat of whitewashed, and near the ground, the reddish chocolate earth tones crept up the walls to make a rusty stain for about two feet. Rain splash. At least Mayans placed windows to face the western horizon, to see the silhouetted grandeur of the three volcanoes against the sunsets.

Ten dollars a month, a fair price for two houses that shared a wall and a tiny yard. Each house a simple room with a door and window, and tucked around in back, a simple pit toilet with a modern seat and cane-walls for privacy and fresh air. I paid the man for a month, and they gave me a tiny frail Chinese padlock with two keys that looked stamped out of aluminum cans.

As night pulled its shade over the village, I stood in my new yard and smoked a cigarette. Around the lake, the lights of several towns emerged in a spray of twinkles, each village strung like fallen necklaces of fires to define the shoreline, and separate the inky lake from the black star blot of almost invisible volcanic slopes.

First Day

The cock's crow woke me at daybreak. I emptied my pack on the dry earth floor to do an inventory, paranoid about where to hide my money and the expensive items in my gear.

I needed food. My supply of oatmeal, cinnamon sticks, and my tin of whole powdered Mexican milk wouldn't last the day.

I hoisted my empty backpack and walked outside, turned to close the crude door of planks and sticks, and fastened it with that loose, tin-can Chinese padlock.

Bees buzzed around, turned into gun blue hummingbird helicopters that made tentative jabs at the morning glories and flowers that looked like furry rods made of glassy pink pinfeathers. The odors of wood fires mixed with the sweet perfumes of toasted corn tortillas, steamy cinnamon rice atole, coffee, and refried beans. In the still mountain air, the plants appeared to move, succulents with tendrils and arms that ended in extraterrestrial fingers, raked out to grab anything that passed.

Children watched me through leaf-toothed windows framed by the huge Aloe Vera plants, giant hands of green spine-rimmed demon-lizard tongues. These succulents often serve as fences, as between my yard and my western neighbor's yard below, about four feet lower down the slope.

In a village this size, everybody knew or saw everything. I wondered if anyone would steal my little five-dollar transistor radio from China, bought in a frantic last-minute Stateside search so that I could give it away in Guatemala at an opportune moment.

The clacks of parrots mixed with the fricatives of Cakchiquél, and I realized, at that moment, that my Spanish with an American accent added confusion to the linguistic mangle that these illiterate Mayan Indians accomplished with their Spanish.

On the way down, I explored some tangential paths, little more than drainage ditches carved into the volcanic slopes as part of house construction, rearrangements of the boulders and dirt to make the flat yard areas.

In a couple of places, the unmistakable stench of human waste slowed me down. With each step, I tried to place a foot atop a small clean rock or half-buried boulder that served as an island amid waterlogged paper detritus, squashed cans, parts of plastic bags and candy containers, and iridescent green fly-decorated piles where toilet paper melted like white frosting on chocolate cake.

A few people in the center of town walked slow, serene, and chatted in Cakchiquél. Lone men walked brisk in their pajama-like shorts, machetes at their sides. I headed for the little store, and passed a couple of houses where a man stood silent. Each one nodded and smiled relaxed, framed by the flowers that drape their gate.

At the store's window-counter, I waited behind a couple of short girls with waist-length hair, as they finished their purchase of a brown substance in a conical shape, reminded me of old ceramic electric line insulators once used on the crossbeams of utility poles, about where the Romans tacked up Jesus' wrists.

The girls noticed my curiosity. "Piloncillo" they said as they laughed at me and pointed at their strange cones.

An older woman with long gray hair smiled at the window-counter. "Azucar". Sugar. Beside her, a fat young girl smiled at me and played with a baby. On the back wall inside, plank shelves held boxes of cigarettes, tiny shot size bottles of hard liquor, bags of laundry detergent, and small household hardware items. A doorway led to their home's dark interior, and through the open back door, I saw another old white-haired woman hang laundry in the sunlit yard.

"¿Donde hay comidas?" Where can I buy food?

In clumsy Spanish came the reply. "Bueno, pués, en Panajachél, o Sololá."

"¿Restaurantes?"
"Panajachél, o Sololá."
"En Santa Catarina?"
"No. No hay."
So I started a long hike back to Panajachél.

Curt

Near the church in the village center, stuck right in the middle of where the main road widened into broad dusty village square, sat a well-kept adobe house surrounded by a white stucco wall less than a yard high. It struck me as out of place, built and maintained with a modern sensibility of uncluttered spaciousness. Two windows flanked the door, unlike the other houses. I assumed some American built it.

An Indian woman, in the bright red and blue colors worn by all the citizens of Santa Catarina Palopó, sat on her heels and wove with a back-strap loom. Straps held the loom tight around the small of her back, the other end fastened to the low wall. She worked the thread into a bright piece of red and blue cloth, all smiles and glances, happy as a bird.

I tried to talk to the woman, but she smiled and made a curious motion with one hand, as if to shoo a fly.

I realized that she meant to draw my attention to the house. The door opened, and a Greek God of a tanned Gringo man came out, over six feet tall, wavy blonde hair that fell over his forehead. He looked me over with his blue eyes, then smiled to put me at ease.

"Did you want to buy that?" he pointed at the woman's handiwork.

"No, trying out my Spanish."

"They don't speak much Spanish here. They know their numbers though."

"You live here?"

"Yeah."

"Lived here long?"

"About two years. Off and on." He put his foot on the low wall. Up close he looked young, but built like a soft, hairless version of Tarzan of the Apes, a jungle boy nursed on Big Macs and Strawberry shakes that stand up to a straw.

"I hear Panajachél's the place to get some food around here."

"You'll find more and better prices in Sololá. Market day on Fridays."

"What day is this?"

"I don't know. Not Friday. Not enough people on the street."

He looked up, screened his eyes to see the sun as it approached the volcanoes in the west. "You'd better go if you want to get back before dark. "

"Yeah, I know. I walked it yesterday."

"You'll get used to it. Say, stop by on your way back. I'll make you a cup of local coffee."

"Como te llamas?"

"Curt. Y tu?"

"Brandon. Nice to meet you. Catch you later."

The morning felt fresh, the sun probably rose in a clear sky but stayed tucked behind the tall mountains that cradled the village in its skirt. I followed the road out of the village as it climbed up their valley along the canyon's steep side. I hoped to find supplies in Panajachél. I didn't feel up to a trip to Solalá, to take the bus both ways. I wanted to relax and organize things in my two one-room houses.

Once in Panajachél, I stopped for a wedge of pie at the expatriate Californian's 'Casa De Pies' to refuel.

Not much in the store except candies, oranges, and soap.

I felt tired on the way back. The sunset painted swirls of clouds that scudded around the volcanoes' thirteen thousand foot peaks. Rusty oranges and vermilion splayed across a milky cerulean blue that mixed with the volcanoes' shadows. Long volcano shadows streaked high overhead upon the upper atmosphere. The colors reflected in the lake surface, crazy whirls of a million mirrors danced in the lake's turbulent winds. The darker textured areas of waves reflected light like pin heads, and traced the route of long powerful gusts.

The chill air prompted me to walk faster, so I made good time with my bags and pack full of sweet bread, bananas, oranges, and oatmeal.

Back in Santa Catarina Palopó, as I came alongside that anomaly of a Gringo-ized house in the middle of the wide road, I paused and considered whether to knock on the door or not. Didn't see the Indian woman, nor any dog around.

Curt's lights shone through the cracks around the boards that shuttered his doors and windows. Not many of the houses used glass for windows, too expensive and unnecessary, with the mild climate in this land of eternal springtime. Not many mosquitoes, maybe the dry mountain air and steep rocky hillsides eliminated the standing-water breeding grounds, while small predators in the lake waters ate mosquito larvae.

I knocked, and Curt opened the door, glad to see me. I walked around inside, tried to find a place to set down my bags of fresh raw groceries from Panajachél. The room's light hissed out from a kerosene lantern in the middle of a large wood table. Curt sat at the table in front of bowls of fruits so full they spilt over onto a pile of old English-language magazines. He leaned over and took away a couple of Mayan folkloric sculptures to give me a space.

As my eyes grew more accustom to the light and shadow, I saw a maelstrom of strange furniture and storage chests covered with Mayan textiles, net bags, carvings, wall hangings, paintings hung from the walls and tree-trunk beams.

Everything looked handmade; the table and chairs, carved wooden plates and oversize utensils to serve food, the back of the sofa's frame, carved from beautiful blonde pine wood tree trunks. On top sat a parrot, lifelike in the orange gaslight. The bird stared right at me, immobile, its great reddish eye surrounded by a round design of tiny white feathers as fine as hair. Even the iridescent blue-green metallic sheen of its feathers appeared real.

Then it raised one leg. It watched for some reaction from me, so still, without a feather ruffled, weightless, it put down the foot in slow motion. Then it walked toward me.

Curt said, "Don't pay any attention to her. Let her check you out, but don't get your fingers too close. She's the boss."

Whenever I scared it with a movement, it stopped to change its posture and threaten. It leaned back and hinted at a readiness to bite, mouth open, thick tongue a dark Brazil nut that moved like a snail.

"She bites hard. She got me a couple of times."

"Where did you get all of this stuff?" I asked. My eyes darted from one mysterious object to another.

"Mom and Dad collected all of it. Most of it's from Guatemala. Some from Mexico, South America, Central America, all over the Caribbean. Not as far as Columbia, though. They wanted to hike the Andes to Tierra del Fuego. Most of that stuff over there comes from Panama. Some tribe that lives on the San Blas islands."

"Where are your parents now?"

"In California, working."

"They left you here alone?"

"Sure, it's much cheaper for them to keep me here. They built the house for a couple of hundred dollars, and food costs almost nothing."

"I know! I bought a head of cabbage for three cents!"

"They robbed you!" Curt laughed. "I can walk back with you tomorrow and make sure they exchange it for the correct price." He reached over from where he sat and talked the parrot into a ride on his finger. The parrot stared at me.

"Would you like some wine? I've got some wine here somewhere."

He set the parrot down on the floor and it ambled around with one eye fixed upon me, as if it feared I might pounce on him.

When Curt got up from his chair, his huge bulk cast a tremendous shadow that eclipsed half the house. As wide as the doorway across his shoulders, his deliberate movements imparted a sense of dignity and grace as he poked among his parent's disordered possessions in search of the wine.

He acted comfortable with himself, so I asked "How old are you?"

"Sixteen. Just had a birthday."

"You go to school here?"

"Naw. There's no school to speak of. They want me to teach English, in Panajachél."

"Shouldn't you be in school?"

"I am in school, kind of. My folks think I learn more here than most kids in the suburbs do. They want me to experience what they call real life, from a primitive point of view, basic necessities and simple society, though things aren't as simple as they look. Mom says first, one needs to discover happiness within yourself, because where ever you go, there you are."

"Cool."

"Yeah, I think so. So I snorkel, climb the mountain, read books, learn Spanish, and go to Guatemala City once in a while, see a movie, buy something I want to read. Plenty of time to read.

Sometimes I sail, when they bring a boat. I love to sail." "What about school?" "I'll pass the GED test back in the States, easy enough. Mom's got a library of books for me behind that trunk over there. Ah-ha! Found the wine! Too bad it's not chilled. Where's the corkscrew now."

The green parrot walked up to the couch, up the fabric draped over the couch's back and then sidled along the wood toward me. It came right up to me. We watched each other with suspicion. Its pupils underwent a rapid change in size, the colored iris swirled like an oily kaleidoscope, and the zig-zag beak opened a bit, a bird snarl. It rubbed its tongue against the upper beak, like someone with peanut butter stuck to the roof of the mouth.

It crossed the cushions, climbed an end table, and then rappelled down Curt's chair with beak holds and foot-over-foot, to land with the softest of footsteps. It ambled across the floor to another sofa, grabbed a beak full of upholstery, and hauled itself up with a foot-over-foot until bent double, then stretched up for another beakhold. It used the technique to get over anything in its way; furniture, stacks of clothing, the legs and backs of chairs, loose woven cloth draped across big open chests which contained even more treasure from Latin America. the parrot made it all the way around the room to the other side of the table, where she stood now, a little sideways again, to come close and watch me with suspicion.

This close, she blazed with iridescent color, green with flashes of red and yellow, the beak a smooth carrot-orange seashell that started between those crazy eyes, pools of multi-colored gravel. Her rapid pupil-size changes bothered me. Happened too often, the pulsation in that rag of iris like an evil eye. Its eye feathers glittered under a red moonrise of eyebrow feathers which the bird could lift up agitated, or smooth down across its forehead. The colors graduated in a wave across its face, from blue-green on its skull to orange near the nose. The colors continued in a fade-out to black at the sharp point of its beak, opened a little in an alligator's smile, a guillotine-sharp finger remover.

"I can't find the corkscrew." Curt spoke with a little laugh.

"I've got a Swiss Army Knife."

"Why didn't you say so earlier."

I threw it to him. "Sorry."

"No, that's OK. I've got to learn to find my stuff someday. Neat stuff, still don't know what most of it is. Supposed to catalog it, spend hours at it. Took them decades to collect this junk, maybe more. I didn't get to go along on most of those trips, so now they hope to make it up to me by putting me to work."

"How do they expect you to know what this stuff is?"

"Mom took notes with descriptions."

He couldn't get the jackknife's corkscrew to go in straight.

"Got a little grass if you want to get high."

"No thanks. This place, the volcanoes, Indians that babble Japanese, it's enough of an alternate reality to deal with."

Curt laughed. "I don't smoke it much anymore. There's not that much to it. I'd rather go swim, then sit on the dock and watch the sunset. Get too paranoid on grass. Rather not think about thieves, the police, drowning, the military, war, rabies, kidnapped politician's daughters, murderers, and other stupid stuff like that."

"Rabies? Murders? Around here?"

"Rapes and murders, yeah. People talk, I don't know. Safer here than back in the States, don't you think? Here, everyone knows everybody. Everyone looks out for others. I can climb through those cornfields above town, and everybody knows about it within a day. I get high from the exercise. Life is good."

"Well, maybe what you don't know CAN hurt you."

He poured the wine and sat down. "Everybody says people disappear down here."

"Disappear?"

"Disappear." He pulled a baggy with a little grass in it out of the pocket of a shirt hung on his chair, and rolled a lumpy joint. He apologized for it as he lit it, a fat paper lightening bolt that dangled from his lips.

Curt took an enormous drag and handed it to me. He swelled up to his full height in the seat and took a couple of tiny sips of fresh air deep into his massive chest.

His bulk again darkened the room as he stood up. Curt smiled, and said, "Lots of good food in Guatemala," in that dope-smoker's airless quack. "Except meats. There's no refrigerator."

"In the market?"

"Neither the market nor here. There's a refrigerator in the store for sodas and beer. Sometimes he lets people store things there. They don't eat refrigerated food here."

We smoked. The room turned golden, the Kerosene lamp hissed a song.

"Is it my imagination, or does your parrot get closer and closer?"

The parrot, emboldened, walked across the table and inserted himself between us.

Curt laughed at him, and the parrot cut loose a guffaw so human I could believe an evil spirit inhabited its iridescent body. Those colorful eyes stared at me, one side of the head at a time, as it swayed from one foot to the other. It seemed intelligent beyond the sarcastic sound of its laugh, so unlike a hyena, or a mechanical clown. Curt could coax it to talk, sometimes, but I didn't recognized a word. Spanish.

I perceived emotions from this bird, an inter-species communication, in her proud attempts to appear fearless, or even dominant. She stood on one foot, motionless, to demonstrate her capabilities as quite beyond us.

Curt spoke, after a while. "They're real smart. When she gets mad, don't bug her. She's bitten me a couple of times, real good too."

"Bleed?"

"You bet. She warns you first. Then she'll bite to let you know she's really pissed, a careful bite, a pinprick of blood. Effortless. Just to show you how she can take your finger off."

The parrot fluffed itself and spread its wings as if to threaten.

"Down, Polly! Down!" I joked, and backed away from the table.

As Curt passed his hand near the bird, she made a half-hearted attempt to bite him.

Curt sucked on the last of the joint and said, "I like this part of the joint, the roach, before it's so short it burns the fingers. If it's good quality marijuana, you should feel pretty buzzed by then. I feel like, you know, time passes slower, so I notice colors and sounds, my heart rate speeds up. Sometimes I feel giddy, maybe it's the extra adrenaline, like when you stand on the edge of a cliff, you feel the edges of your own consciousness."

"You've thought about that awhile."

"I've got plenty of time here alone. I understand why people feel anxious and paranoid on pot. If you're not comfortable with yourself, then when you alter your mind, the changes confuse you, put you off balance. Me, I'm balanced. That's why my parents abandon me here. They know I won't get into trouble." He sucked at the little ember-glow between his fingers. "You want any more?"

"No, go for it."

"OK. To me the last part of a joint, held securely by this here roach clip or a hemostat thingy, the way it glows all out of focus under my nose, is one of the most beautiful sights in the world."

"Yeah, like it's the center of this golden treasure room."

"Like to hear some music?" Curt held up a Led Zeppelin tape. "My newest tape. Have you heard it?"

"They played it on the album oriented FM stations. You like it?"

"I listen to it all the time, not sick of it yet. I'm sick of all my old tapes."

Soon the dark fog of Zeppelin Jimmy Page's electric guitar riffed thunderous blues-derived music.

Curt said, "I wonder if Jimmy Page and Robert Plant ever imagined their music inside a Guatemalan bus."

We let the music influence the mood and chatted along, until the tape ended.

I asked Curt the time.

"About eight thirty."

"Must be later than that."

"It's December, remember. We don't get much late afternoon sun with those volcanoes in the west."

"What time do you go to bed?"

"Not till ten thirty or so. I read for a while. Study Spanish and listen to Mexican AM radio. It's a hassle to get Kerosene around here. I don't like to carry it, so I get someone to drive. I use sunlight as much as possible."

"Why don't you get electricity?"

"Why bother? I buy batteries for the tape player. Hate it when the batteries get weak and the music slows down."

"Put on the radio for a while. Let's hear what stations you get."

"Nothing comes in very good. Bad location, this valley." He spun the dial and the radio played nothing but static decorated with Mexican Polkas and the hoarse tobalcohol voices, accordions, tubas, and clarinets.

I thought about the month of rent paid, and what I would do here in an Indian village, surrounded by a darkness both physical and intellectual, a symbol of my own ignorance of their reality. That darkness threatened me, a vast unknown blank, a month, nothing planned, that extended through the Christmas season.

Outside, the faint barks of dogs reminded us of the village. Once in a while we heard the shuffle and scuff of gravel when someone passed in front of Curt's house.

Here we sat, hundreds of miles south of Estados Unidos Mexicanos, thousands of miles from my home, and just beyond these four walls, a village of Mayan Indians.

"So you've been here two years?"

"On and off."

"How has Santa Catarina treated you?"

"It's all right. It's no Mecca, but I'm not here all year long anyway. Panajachél has Discos, bars, restaurants, and plenty of different people each week. Plenty to do if you've got the cash. I don't go there much."

I leaned back and looked at all the colorful things that hang from the rafters. Weavings, paintings, maracas, fabrics, and knickknacks all vied for space and attention in the tangled room.

"So what kind of dangers do I face here?"

"Not much really, compared to California, for example. Some Indian children will steal small things, dogs will bite, but the most dangerous of all, the lake. The winds can pick up pretty fast, people drown all the time. Last week a dugout canoe capsized, two people swam to shore, but the rest died. Three people, I think."

"How many people can get into a dugout canoe?"

"A lot. It's the local taxi to go from one town to another. You either go all the way out to Sololá on an expensive bus, or cross the lake. No road goes all the way around the lakeshore. Too many steep slopes of soft volcanic material that collapses when it rains too much. Indians crowd into these canoes, don't know how to swim, and they die."

"Just the Indians?"

"Mostly. Most tourists know how to swim enough to make it back to shore. Indians drown."

We heard dogs bark up the street.

Then the dogs in the street in front of Curt's house barked and soon every dog for miles around joined in the uproar. We listened, then Curt opened the door. We heard the sound of an out-of-tune car headed towards the village.

The Writers Arrive

We went outside and saw headlight beams wash over the rock mountainside as the car crested the last rise. Then we saw the headlights curve and plunge down the arch of the bumpy road into the village.

At the bottom of the hill, we watch the distant car bounce hard and throw a shower of orange sparks from underneath. Then the sound arrives, and we hear the car's bottom grate atop the large boulders set firm in the roadbed. The driver didn't slow down, and the car charged onto the village's flat open ground to speed straight at us.

We both stepped back off he road and behind Curt's low rock fence.

The car pulled alongside us and slid to a stop.

"Well hello there!" a rough, deep, female voice intoned from within. "Glad to see other Gringos out here. Any houses for rent around here?"

In the faint light that bounced back from the headlights, her face looked like an old man's, with long thin graying hair that framed her sun-tortured, wrinkled skin. She looked like a white radish on dirty cotton, or oatmeal in a bowl of hair.

Their belongings filled the back seat and spilt into the driver's seat. Mired in the overflow on the passenger side, a tall quiet person with long hair stooped forward and looked at us.

I bent down to get a better look, and heard a deep masculine voice say "Hello" as he raised his hand in a faint wave.

Curt said, "The first house on the right might rent you a place up the hill from here. Come on. I'll take you."

Young Mayans scampered down the steep slopes from their homes. Quite a crowd assembled to follow the sedan, which chugged as if out of breath as we walked alongside in a warm cloud of dust and insects stirred up by the motor's fan.

After a brief talk, the landlord led us to the edge of the village and up through slopes of grass towards a house. We coaxed the frightened driver along with the help of her longhaired son, who sat beside her and urged her on through the sparse, tall grasses. "I hope to God there aren't any holes!" The brightness of the headlight beams blinded us. Tall grass hid both rocks and ditches.

She looked wasted. She squinted through the smoke of a cigarette that dangled from her lips. Lipstick gave her mouth some shape hours ago, but now the smear looked like a wound.

She drove on with her eyebrows up and fearful, and even as we watched her complain, she lit another cigarette and rubbed her face as if sweating.

Two Mayan Indian men with flashlights walked backwards in front to coax her on through the field. They motioned where to park, on a downward slope so steep that most drivers would reject it as a parking space. She lurched to a stop and cut the engine.

The big house, much taller than mine, enclosed twice as much floor space inside. More like a small barn, empty and dusty, with two dim electric bulbs that dangled on cobwebbed wires. The old Gringo woman and her emaciated son surveyed the house with bright eyes. They talked and gesticulated, got excited by the possibilities, and decided to take it. They exchanged money with the landlord on the spot, and he showed her how to use the padlock.

We pitched in and helped them unload the car as it pinged and popped to cool down. The crickets sang again.

Inside the house, we boys spread their belongings out on the hard earth floor. A couple of dogs barked close by, the car door slammed, an angry dog's growl, and a yelp of human pain. Then we heard her whiskey-and-cigarette sautéed feminine vocal cords voice the vilest curses in the English language.

The woman stumbled in with an armload of clothing, threw it down as she stood and gasped in the weak yellow light.

"He bit me!" she shrieked with her tobalcohol voice. She clasped her hands, then twisted herself to look down at the back of one calf.

I wondered if dogs in Guatemala received rabies shots, or if Guatemala hospitals stocked anti-rabies vaccine.

When she rolled up her pant leg, we could see the first reddish discoloration of what might turn into the dark purple and yellow of a palm-size bruise.

"At least he didn't break the skin." She said. She massaged her attractive calf. It looked forty years younger than her rugged face. "That poor dog," she continued, "I'm the ugliest thing it's ever seen!"

I said, "He saw you had nice legs."

"Why, thank you. Nice to hear flattery, for a change. Someone else thought so too, that's the reason I have a son." She got her son's attention. "Shotgun, say hi to this nice gentleman. My name's Ida."

"Brandon. Nice to meet you two. Looks like we'll be neighbors."

"Oh, much more than that. We're an oasis of English literature. If you ever need anything, come give us a holler."

As we unpacked, we filled each other in with the short version of the story of each life.

She considered herself a writer. "I don't come down here to Guatemala to become a writer, I come because I AM a writer!" Her portable library attested to her avant-garde tendencies, her intelligence, and role as a non-conformist. She parodied herself as the self-tortured expatriate alcoholic who wants to produce the Great American Novel. Their large library of books included old classics and some slim arty books of poetry and short stories, one with a cover that depicted happy toothpaste in love.

We shared wine, and discovered that everyone liked to smoke marijuana. No surprise, to look at her son, a super-emaciated six-footer with hair about a yard long, down to his bony waist.

We smoked some, and the let me borrow a couple of cigarettes to take the edge off my nicotine withdrawal nervousness.

Later I felt hungry, and said good-bye. I couldn't remember their names, or even if we'd introduced ourselves, but they already felt like family.

Curt stayed with them, to visit and help them settle into their new home. "I left the door open," he yelled through the doorway after me. "Don't forget your food."

First Walk Home

Meso-Americans often carved representations of inter-level Cosmic connectors as serpents, with portals as the yawned mouth of a fanged snake. From the front it resembles a short-armed cross, from the side a U shape, an open mouth. Classic Maya depicted the snake as a two-headed Celestial Monster that swallows the sunset, passes overhead, then defecates the sun below the Eastern horizon, similar to how the ancient Egyptians thought the sun traveled through the God Nut's body at night.

In the darkness, I scuffed my way through the tall grasses, on the lookout for ankle-twist potholes or trenches, and to scare away any snakes. I'd walked up this trail to my house one time only, in broad daylight, and didn't pay attention then. Now the marijuana suppressed those short-term memories. My peer's conservative voices from back home whispered in the back of my mind.

"Why do you think they call it dope?"

I stumbled through the grasses as if swimming through a thick blind darkness lit by the faint silver starlight. I hoped the moon might come up, but in this deep valley, hours and hours would pass before the moon flew high over the pine-covered mountain ridge behind the village of Santa Catarina Palopó.

As I reached level ground at the fountain in front of the church, the owners inside the store a block away turned off the light. In the new darkness in front of the store, I got my bearings and walked up the right trail, I hoped. Should take me through the deep rock trench between the fenced gardens of the tiny houses now dark and still.

I came to a fork in the rocky trail, one I neglected to notice before, with all my gawks at the extra-terrestrial plant forms that loomed over the trail. I went to the right, and found myself on a trail littered with loose boulders and garbage. A little further, and the reek of excrement, lots of it, both human and canine, forced me to reconsider.

Human shit smells a little different from dog shit. How did it get here? Did people come down here to squat in the mornings, or do they dump pails of the stuff over their fences, to let the rain wash it through the village and into the lake? I decided to back up. I kept my hands to myself and retreated.

I took the other fork, and thought I knew the general direction to my house. Dogs barked with an increase in viciousness as I approached to pass their master's house.

Many places along the trail became a soft cavern. Succulent trees overhead bowed under the weight of black explosions of leaves. The roots tangled into the trail's high dirt walls, and the branches intertwined into a live fence that sometimes met over my head. The vegetation, tropical and strange to me by day, looked like hairy monster heads now, spidery octopuses that leaned atop sinuous trunks and reached out motionless, as if in wait.

The little scimitar of a moon came out from behind the clouds, and I could see a little better in black and white. I stumbled up the other fork of the trail's eight-foot deep trench.

I rounded a blind corner and startled a guard dog, a spiky black shadow of snarls and rage-coughed barks, right above me. He looked down from a yard's embankment where I needed to pass. He lunged at me from above, fanged rage and foam, as if he dared me to walk under his yard. Coiled and tense, he bounced up and down with each throaty growl and bark, bounced weightless on toenails that clattered against rock, his iron-rigid legs in total readiness to leap down upon me and tear me apart.

I could see all of his teeth, and no matter which direction I stepped, he scurried to another break in the bushy fence to stick his nose out through the underbrush. He rammed his snout through, with lips pulled back so I could see fangs glistened with drool. As I walked slow, he darted ahead to another more advantageous point of attack. He lurched at me from above with admirable seriousness and dedication to his duty, overcome by fantasies of how he would sink his fangs into my soft neck tissues' tear away at stringy tendons and veins, and lap my blood when the spasms stopped.

No other route led to my little rented home. I stood still and hoped that might calm him. He became furious, as if sure I would hide to ambush him later.

I tried to soothe him with a soft coo sound, then puppy sounds, and he doubled his homicidal intensity.

In an effort to pretend to ignore him, I walked forward and ducked under the overhang of vegetation from his yard, with the expectation I would feel him pounce upon my back as I emerged on the other side. My neck hairs stood on end, tiny feelers that waited to perceive the wind of that attack. He didn't jump, and I didn't stop to turn around.

I walked right past my two houses the first time, but felt tipped off by a wordless sensation of unfamiliarity a little further up the trail.

The dog didn't calm down until much later, after I'd entered my house and prepared my bedroll, after I went around back to use the little stick hut of a bathroom, and after I walked a little up and down the trail in front of my house, to calm down and get used to how it looked in the darkness.

That dog knew I didn't belong here, didn't dress right, smell right, didn't know the right people, or wear the right clothes.

I soon found out that dogs and women share instincts.

CHAPTER 2: Indian Village

The Meso-American's sacrificial rituals and bloodletting teased these inter-level portals into brief existence, because of their Gods' eternal hunger for blood. The Shamans thought they could influence rain, crops, war victory, fertility, and freedom from plague and disease when an open portal materialized into brief existence. These portals connect the Heavens, the Earth, and the Underworld through which the King-god could travel and return, to become himself a portal of information from other levels of reality to his subjects, pawns, and slaves.

After a King-God died, the calendar era changed, his body became an old portal to entomb in another layer of the pyramid mountain temple. And so they built each layer upon the other layers, in imitation of their cosmology, each ruler within his level, above the tombs of his predecessors, analogous to the layers of Heavens, Earth, and Hells, analogous to the layers of history and society.

At sunrise, chickens, goats, mules, and a far-off automobile awoke to begin the day's racket to the aroma of wood fires, boiled milk and cinnamon, and toasted tortillas.

I got up every once in a while throughout the night to gaze, bleary-eyed, out my small west-faced window with a hope to catch the earliest sunlight paint the volcanoes. When it happened, the light struck the conical mountains from the top down, a weak red light on deep purple skies. It ripened to soft gold against the Pacific atmosphere's milky azure.

Cold air fell from the piney woods on the mountaintop and streamed through the village. It brought the scents of pines and the perfumes of flowered expanses on the forest floor, and hinted at the luxuriant damp soils of terraced vegetable plots, and steep cornfields that hugged the mountain above the village.

I waited for the air to warm up a bit, and then walked down to Curt's to pick up the food I left at his house last night. When I got back to my house, I realized I needed firewood, so turned around to scavenge what sticks and cornstalks I could find. The villagers left a precious little of such materials around. I found some long pieces of cornstalk, and a few bits of wood.

A little before ten o'clock, I ate my breakfast as the sunlight came over the mountain.

I wrote letters, but didn't know what to say, with too much to express, and a strange new world that begged my attention on the other side of my door. I admitted failure, put a swimsuit on under my pants, and went out.

The women grouped around the fountain chattered in Cakchiquél.

The Cakchiquél language sounds Japanese.

Blackbirds frolicked in the fountain as small Mayan women and tiny girls gathered around to fill clay water jugs. The birds perched on the fountain edges whenever the Indians left.

A little skinny girl, about six, sat on the fountain's edge and spat into the pool. She watch her spittle disappear as she stirred the water with her dirty fingers, then she splashed water onto her face and massaged her features with both hands. She dried her face and hands on her shirtfront.

Others came to dip water from the pool, while the more patient or hygienic waited their turn to collect the water that trickled direct from the small horizontal pipe that poked out from the fountain's central pillar.

I scooped out some water from the pool, pursed my lips together tight, washed my face and hands without soap, and tried to believe no one in Santa Catarina carried lethal contagions. Then I took the road that led away from Panajachél to explore the area on the other side of town.

As I climbed through Santa Catarina Palopó, I could look down into the back yards of Mayan homes and watch as they cooked, wove cloth, and tied together rolled bundles of woven reed mats to take to market.

Around the lakeshore, men waded into the shallows to cut reeds to weave into large floor mats, about seven foot square.

As the road topped its long rise out of the lakeshore valley, I came to the end of Santa Catarina's residential area. Before me, a rough road continued on its way around the lakeshore. I couldn't beyond the first curve.

Indians didn't own any cars.

Traffic kept some of the grasses in check. Of the cars and busses driven to Santa Catarina, looked like few went beyond to the next village.

I walked back through the village and went down to the shore where women wash clothes. They rubbed cakes of hard brown soap on fabrics laid out upon flat rocks, and then beat the clothing to loosen the dirt. They squatted in the shallows, their long denim skirts shone black with silver highlights. I noticed one stout older woman washed herself under her clothing. Her arm disappeared into the sleeve of her white blouse, the explosions of red floral embroidery danced around as she soaped her armpits, and around and between her breasts.

The village dock tiptoed high above the water, four feet or so, to avoid the large waves wind of powerful storms from the Pacific. The dock stood empty, decorated by a row of four herons. No boats moored, no cargo tied up, no people.

The Mayans used dugout canoes fashioned from single logs. Many lay beached near an unfinished dugout tree trunk, others worked as water taxis scattered across the lake's surface. Three or four cruised in the distance, dedicated to the long labor of transport from one shore to the other five miles away.

Boatmen maneuvered their dugouts with long poles as they cut reeds in the shallows. They piled up huge haystacks of reeds across the stern. Even when the canoes looked overloaded, the men showed no concern. They stood in the boat and poled in an act of nonchalant bravery noteworthy and impressive, when you consider that they couldn't swim to save their lives. Some boatmen waded to cut reeds. The cotton pajama shorts streamed with water when they pulled their loaded canoe to shore.

Throughout that month in the village, I saw few locals swim, only very young, naked children that played while mom kneeled in the calf-deep shallows to wash laundry on boulders.

The water taxi boatmen overloaded these dugouts to make money. The Mayans get in and let the oarsman paddle them across a lake famous for sudden winds, with only a couple of inches of wood above the water level. Mayans share the Catholic's blind fatalism, that this existence represents but one temporary and meaningless stage that takes us to a better one. They showed little concern for their own safety, nor for their children's.

Death did not warn or make people want to change things, but here reinforced a fascination with Death as a part of life.

I walked down to the shore. In the sunlit rocky shallows the water felt warm, but I debated with my lazy self whether to take a swim. I did need the exercise, so I sat down on a dugout canoe to think about it.

A half hour later, I found myself still in a deep rumination about whatever shallow thought came to the surface of my placid mind.

I took off my shoes and felt the water, to decide if I should start to undress for a swim, when I heard the sounds of a conversation, non-Indian.

Three foreigners, from Europe, came down to the dock with towels, and as they neared, I could hear them speak French. They ignored me, as if to demonstrate a cultural superiority, an attempt to ignore my existence and maintain the illusion of picturesque solitude. Pissed me off at first. But then I didn't call out to them either, for similar reasons.

The two young men accompanied a slim girl who wore a bright-multicolored woven beret, like Jamaicans wear, a traveler's long sleeve shirt, long loose khaki pants, and sandals. She wore her shoulder length black hair wild, uncombed. The way her loose clothing hung on her figure, it hinted at a fullness in all the right places.

I pulled up on my pant-legs to hoist the hems out of the water to walked through the shallows alongside the high dock.

As they walked towards the dock's end, they stripped down to their swimsuits and left a trail of clothing. She wore a black one-piece.

I walked back through the shallows to the beach and joined them up on the dock. They waved an answer to my hello in a way that made me feel I intruded. I wondered if they spoke English, or if they tried to ignore me because I represented male competition for their precious female companion.

I tried to break the ice.

"Where do you come from? France?"

The larger blond man spoke. "We come from Canada, she comes from France."

"You live in Santa Catarina?"

"About two weeks now."

"You like it here so far?"

"Too many tourists," the French girl said, in excellent English. "Stupid people, with cameras. Buses full of them come here on the weekends."

The other man spoke. "What part of the States do you come from?"

"Michigan."

"From the north, like us, neighbors, at least." He said, pleased to find another Northerner, even if not from the same country. "Well this water shouldn't feel too cold for us now, should it?"

"Nah." added the other, as he peered over the dock's edge at the dark deep water. "We're in the tropics, damn it!"

"Yeah, the tropics. We can take it."

I wondered if the water went deep, without any boulders hid beneath the dark surface that might split my skull. I stripped down to my bikini briefs. "Can you dive off of this dock head first?"

"Here?" The blond man looked out over the water. "Sure. Deep enough. Don't worry."

"Well here goes nothing." and I dove into the water to slash beneath the waves, not too far down below the silvery surface above. I coasted along under my own momentum and felt the cold water. As I slowed, tiny air bubbles loosened from between my fingers to stream by my face like jittery silver pearls.

I recognized my last words as a self-deprecation. I swam down into the blackness.

I think I saw the bottom about fifteen feet deep, and cold. I surfaced to see them stare at me from the dock. They wondered where I'd gone so long.

I can stay underwater a long time on my initial entry. Cardio-pulmonary response, a relic capability humans inherit from our water primate stage of evolution. That stage bequeathed us our sensitive fingers like raccoons, teary eyes like the pinniped seals, hairlessness like dolphins and whales, and our hair follicles angle in directions that would aid a primate that swam.

To get up on the dock again, I swam all the way back along the dock's pilings through the warmer foot-deep shallows.

As I stood up, I saw my unshaven reflection in the shadowed water under the dock. It shocked me into a new self-awareness. I didn't know what I looked like in this life without mirrors.

I pulled myself up onto the dock in time to see her jump off, her lithe torso stretched out over the waters in an arched dive.

Her dive brought to the surface of my consciousness all the hot blood of loneliness, and even though I didn't know her, it made me angry.

I didn't know why I felt so alone, but under the circumstances, a less analytical person might consider it love at first sight. I needed a better look at her but so far, I liked what I saw of her bravery, her spunk. From France, and she traveled alone. As Mark Twain wrote, "She had sand, a lot of sand."

I walked out to the dock's end and sat on its weathered edge. They swam together a little ways out, jabbered in French, which I did not understand.

The wind picked up, white caps decorated the lake with foamy waves as far as I could see. I sat on the sunlit dock and shivered.

"How's the water?" I yelled as my teeth chattered.

"Better than the air!" She yelled back.

I dove in straight at them, went deep, held my nose to push air into my ears and avoid the pain, and swam through the blackness, through the dusty shafts of dim sunlight that dance and flicker like long swords plunged through the silver surface above.

I saw them silhouetted above me. They tread water, awkward legs in a strange weightless dance. Ugly hairless apes, I thought, as I swam underneath them and beyond, out into the lake. In a steady rhythm, I pulled back the water with my hands, felt its resistance against my arms. With long strokes that propelled me to coast a ways through the slippery depths, I held my breath and swam like a frog. Water rushed by my ears, I heard fish calls, or perhaps the jaws of those that fed off rocks somewhere distant, the pop and click of electronic static or a distant motorboat.

I came up to a depth of about six feet and let too much air out before I broke the surface. Such clear water makes it hard to judge the distance to the surface. I lost buoyancy without that air, and worked to gain the surface and a breath.

Took in a mouthful of wave-tossed water with my first gasp, but didn't suck any into my lungs. I coughed under water to hide my incompetence. No fun, even if it doesn't kill you, nothing like a cough to empty the lungs and help you sink like a rock.

I lay flat, face down, and swam freestyle, the fastest stroke, though people call it the crawl. With a breath every third stroke or so, to swap sides, I worked my arms in great windmills to get warm. Didn't work. I headed farther out into the lake, then turned until I faced the dock again.

Switched to the sidestroke, which allows me to keep most of my face out of water and most of my body under, out of the cold air. I can look around with this stroke, and when one side of my body tires, roll over and swim on the other.

The muscular blond man swam up beside me.

"Enjoy your swim?"

"Oh yeah," I said, a little out of breath as we tread water. "Good exercise. Keeps you warm."

He laughed at me as we both sank low in the water to stay out of the wind, like two faces afloat. "What's your name?" and he spat some water.

"Brandon. What's your name?"

"I'm Dennis, Dennis from Toronto." He brought his hand out of the water to shake mine.

"Brandon from Michigan." I looked at the others way over by the dock. "And she" I nodded in her direction, "is with you?"

"Yes. Well no, not really. With us, yes. For now. For how long, don't know."

I heard the waves crash through the pilings, the larger waves slapped and battered down the entire length to the shore, like a child's finger against a picket fence. Slapped so hard the entire dock reverberated like a giant xylophone.

"God the air feels cold." The wind started to hurt my ears.

"We hope the wind dies down so we can get out on the lake."

I assumed he meant by dugout canoe, to somewhere. Perhaps to Santiago, the biggest lakeshore city, across the lake from Santa Catarina Palopó or Panajachél, where one could easily find a boatman.

We swam over to the others and tread water together next to the high dock.

Dennis introduced me to the woman, Yvonne. "She's a nurse, so with any health concerns, get with her. She's got a special needle for big butts."

She splashed him and turned to the other man. "And this is Gary."

"Hello." Gary said, his teeth clattering

Dennis explained, "He shivers all the time. Blood thinner than water."

"You know about the hot springs over there?" Dennis pointed north to where a cliff slanted into the water, a quarter of a mile swim away. On top, we could see the walls of one of those rich vacation homes.

"Might feel good, but I'd freeze by the time we swam back." Gary said.

Dennis went under. He came up soon in the same place, his swimsuit in his hand. He threw his shorts up toward the high dock, missed and they fell into the water again. He swam over to retrieve them and threw again. The swimsuit landed on the dock with a solid plop, motionless. Water dripped through the boards.

With a loud Wahoo! Dennis mooned us and let it float awhile before he pulled himself down in a moonset and sunk under the waves.

Yvonne smiled a crooked smile and rolled her eyes toward heaven for salvation.

I felt my hunger return, and that made me even more cold and tired. "I've got to go eat. I hope we see more of each other."

Gary said, "There's not much more of Dennis to see."

"Oh, you will," said Yvonne, "it's a small town."

"OK. We'll see you later."

I swam low in the water into the warmer shallows, to warm up a bit before I stood up to walk onto the dock and retrieve my clothing. When I got out to the dock's end, Dennis asked me to throw his trunks down, so I picked them up with a bit of show, as if I believed them contaminated or infected with something, and threw them way over his head out into the lake.

The Neighbor's Song

This morning I awoke with a familiar song in my ears again, a song sung by an Indian woman at her morning chores. She sang in an easy fluid voice so high and clear that it brightened up our mornings and shamed the birds into silence. The melody came from some tradition far from the scales I knew as a guitarist. It sprung from an ageless tradition of feelings, the effortless vibration of a born singer with a joyful voice. It came from the fountain of a pure, honest, and ancient tradition, from whence came all music until the Europeans discerned the mathematical relationships in the modern musical scales and crystallized frequencies with the piano, a blunt and dispassionate percussion instrument in comparison.

The melody moved without a scale I could grasp, it changed with enigmatic time intervals and perfect emotional pitch. The emotive voice played with the contradictions in the melody, the dilemma of a sad plaintive song that expressed the beauty of life, about how to live with grace through inevitable hardship.

I thought the song came from the house up the trail from my house, where a young Indian woman spread her washed clothes out to dry on the shrubbery.

I went outside to walk a little ways up the trail to listen, but when she heard my gate, she stopped singing. I walked up there anyway, and tried to talk to her, but she could not understand me and shrunk away. She refused to lift her face and look at me.

Her eyes could not see.

A pretty face, fine delicate features, prominent Mayan cheekbones, overshot teeth, and when she looked toward me, her whitish crossed eyes gave her a submissive and apologetic demeanor, at once comic and sheepish, as if in permanent expectation to suffer the ridicule of others.

In general, I found the Mayan Indians handsome and beautiful, in spite of the conditions in which they live. The girls stay infantile, skinny and short, well into their teens, and the full flower of youth fades fast among the mature. The rare elder must feel lucky indeed to join the few who pass maturity to reach an old age, graceful or not.

Friday morning, 7:30 too early, I wanted to make sure to catch the bus for Sololá. The bus passed through Santa Catarina Palopó at eight only once, and only on market days.

I got on the bus with all the Indians dressed in red. Some men brought rolled reed mats six feet tall, or things in tote bags that bulged too wide to fit between the seats. Some carried enameled pots that steamed when they lifted the lid, full of home cooked edibles to sell on the way and in the market.

Up above Panajachél, the main road follows the valley rim that cups the bottomless waters of Lake Atitlán. The bus passed through pine forests with trees outlined in dewy jewels. Sunlight, filtered between the tree trunks, created soft golden slashes of light that, as the bus sped through them, strobed the colorful scene inside.

Solalá Market Bat Jackets

The town of Sololá sits high on a rounded mountain slope, below steeper wooded mountains. With most of its houses hid out of sight on the hillsides below, it seemed the entire town consisted of the oversize market square.

All the indigenous men of Sololá wear the same style woolen jacket in pure white or a gray plaid, wide black collar, with a thin black ribbon that traced French curves and whorls, a formal sports coat crossed with an English marching band jacket. The embroidery's basic design consisted of doubled black lines that encircle the cuffs and outline up the sleeves. There the appliqué continues in a complex yoke to outline the shoulder blades and shoulders. Inside the space outlined by this yoke, the appliqué outlines a bat with wings spread to fill the space, an unmistakable Dracula outline with large, attentive ears.

I searched the Sololá market for a bat jacket, and although full of jackets that looked almost identical to what the village men wore, all sported an abstract curly-q rendered bat, instead of the stylized, recognizable bat. No market stall carried the bat decorated jackets that all the male residents of Sololá wore.

When I asked about this, I learned that local superstitions kept Sololá's bat jackets out of tourist's hands.

I almost bought a tourist model, white with black hand stitched embroidery, but I wanted a bat jacket.

Then I found a modern youth, a hippie Mayan college kid, who offered me a real bat jacket, told me the name of the bat in Maya, Zotz, and extracted from me a high price and the promise I wouldn't wear it in Guatemala. So I bought it and hid it in my tote bag.

When in Rome, do as they tell you.

I bought food pennies cheaper here in Sololá than in Panajachél, and a penny less could mean 30% less on items like cabbages, turnips, carrots, onions, rice, beans, etc.

Of course, I should count the bus fare too, but that I considered normal travel expense. I resolved to plan trips out of the area ,to Chichicastenango for example, with the return trip through Sololá on market day, Friday.

That never worked out.

Cross-eyed Singer's Shirt Sale

Mayan religious thought obsesses about mathematical and astronomical knowledge; they see Time as the root and ruler of their religious cosmology. Mayan priest-mathematician-astronomers conceived of an endless eternity of time, measured by a majestic succession of cycles, "bearers" or divine time periods, through which cosmic events and personages happen. Very few human cultures, such as the Zurvanites of Iran, worshiped time to such an extent. These cultures consider Time divine, and to the Mayans, each time period became a God.

The Mayans entertained a concept called cuxolalob, which signified a knowledge both rational and "supernatural," or perhaps a reflection of the role of each human brain's hemisphere, the left of linear logic and language, and the right of wholistic, nonverbal, artistic, intuitive, visual and musical, as if an aesthete counterpart to the logician. The Mayan's god of Time lives as an animate being, and its cuxolalob orders the universe, and predestines each of our days.

I woke up as someone knocked on the door.

At first I dreamt that Yvonne waited outside in the night. These past few nights since we met on the dock, I awoke several times resentful of my interrupted dream with her. The daylight streamed through the cracks in the door and shutters. I threw off my sleeping bag, jumped into my trousers, and opened the door. Blinded by the midday sun, it took me a while to recognize the cross-eyed near-blind Indian woman, the one who sings in the mornings.

"Espérame un minuto." I asked her to wait and shut the door to put on a shirt. Wasted motion, I realized, for she wanted to sell me a shirt she'd made that morning. She showed me a long sleeved shirt with two breast pockets, each with a button. Any day I wore this red shirt, I would fit right in with the traditional dress of Santa Catarina Palopó.

It fit me like a tent, but I liked it, and the manner in which it came into my life. I bought it for a couple of bucks and saved both of us the walk to the market.

Then she motioned for me to wait, ran back into her mud house, and came out with a lovely shoulder bag, just the thing I needed to avoid the overuse of my bulky backpack on market days. Red, like most fabrics woven in Santa Catarina, but with wide bands of black and white geometric skeleton or serpentine brickwork patterns. I used it as the final touch to my belongings, after I slung the guitar over the backpack, I looped its straps around my neck and shoulder to store pen and paper, cigarettes and matches, a stash of toilet paper, chapstick, maps, a book or magazine, water bottle, and nutritious peanuts and toasted tortillas to snack on.

I used that shirt often as a light jacket over the next two decades, till it fell apart, and each time I thought of her. I liked to show interested people how the black and white stripes portray geometric skeletal figures due to how the weavers stagger the black and white banded threads, which they produce through an ancient technique of tie-dye. They tie the cotton threads tight in numerous collars a measured distance apart, before they dip the thread bundles in the dye. Where bound, the threads remain white. The stripes on my shirt ran for thirty inches, from shoulder to tail, with alternate skeletal and geometric designs.

These Meso-American Hispanics, the Amerindian mestizos, Ladinos, or other mixes in Mexico and Guatemala, don't value their time. The marketplaces overflow with "artesanía" folk art that takes hours to produce, and sells for pocket change. People tell you how much something costs not based on how much time it takes to fabricate, but based on the raw materials. As if it makes them uncomfortable to charge for time, for the hours of production, perhaps because they believe they owe that time, at work or play, thanks to God, "Gracias a Dios."

How could they charge for something God gives all for free?

For a long time I puzzled over a common Latin American goodbye. When you say See you later or "Hasta Luego" until then, they answer "Si Dios quiere," which means If God wants it. At first, I thought they expressed the belief that things happen only with God's Will. That felt creepy and irresponsible to me, to believe that a fickle God threw monkey wrenches to make our plans go awry, to gum up the works, to put flies in ointments, and remove our free will, our ability to make things happen because of our priorities, because things matter.

I started to make sense of this phrase "If God wants it" as less a demonstration of irresponsible fatalism, and more as recognition that 'God Willing' expresses a sense of receivership of each moment, as a valuable and precious gift from God.

The Mayans consider time a God.

Rosa's Food Service
The morning after I bought the shirt, a pretty girl from next door visited. She looked twenty four but claimed she only "finished seventeen years," as they say in Spanish, a month ago.

These Mayan Indian girls either lied, didn't know what year their mothers birthed them, forgot how many years they lived so far, or their beautiful brown skin aged fast from the intense sunlight through the thin, clear mountain air.

I asked her about a domed earthen 'dog hut' in their yard. She explained, as best she could in her broken Spanish, that they call it a Tuj, a sauna for sweat baths. I didn't often see people bathe in the lake. She said I could use it someday, but I didn't get around to it, nor did they invite me.

I asked if anyone in Santa Catarina ran a restaurant or sold meals. No.

I tried my best Spanish on her, and that didn't work, so I tried my worst with hand signals, fingers to mouth. "Someone make food, feed me, morning (mañana, same word as tomorrow)? I pay." With that incentive to understand, she said "I make food everyday. One dollar."

"You bring food in morning, I pay one dollar. Ok?"

"Me, no." She blushed and dug her toe into the ground, hugged herself, bit her lip, and fought back giddiness. "My family bring food. My brother. You pay one dollar. Dollar fifty."

"One dollar."

"Ok."

Everybody around the world understands OK.

Soon, people gave me more evidence of how I, and probably most people, commit solipsism. We feel sure we think the only valid thoughts, and doubt the existence of anything we don't experience. I began to feel clues like weak radio transmissions from another galaxy, hints of the vast chasms between people's realities, even when we live side by side.

At first, I looked forward to each Mayan breakfast, but cooled to the idea in direct proportion to the meal's temperature. They brought it a little later and a little colder each day.

One cold bright morning, she brought her mother along with something in a soup bowl that resembled a big gray spider. It floated belly up, eight legs splayed, in a gray liquid that looked like used dishwater. I lifted it with a fork, and recognized it as a small boiled crab. It stunk like the bottom of a lake. In good humor, with the pleasant determination of an anthropologist among headhunters, I forced myself to acquiesce to their demands and agree to eat it in front of them.

With grim determination, I tried, my suspicions aroused by their complicity, their hands to mouth mirth and nonstop commentary in Cakchiquél.

My technique with thin stamped-metal bendy spoon amused them. I tried to cut the legs off and suck tiny slivers of meat out of the legs, as if the tiny creature merited the gastronomic technique of a giant Alaskan King Crab.

Maybe they didn't bother with the legs.

They demanded I eat the crab's middle, ordered me to, mom even got a little stern and testy, I thought. I resigned myself to an attempt to eat the rest, the whole crab, and so I picked it up out of the bowl and bent it, cracked the carapace open and squirted juices all over as they laughed at my squeamishness. Inside, ready for consumption, all dishwater gray, lay its guts, digestive tract, organs of elimination, gill plates, and two big gray wads of feathery tissue.

I couldn't force my tongue to taste the feathery stuff, but I managed to dissect and eat a few meaty parts.

Tasted like crunchy dishwater.

Another day, they again came together to offer me Atole. I love Atole, a liquid version of oatmeal made of rice, milk, sugar, and cinnamon. They called it Atole, but I didn't recognize it. Looked like more dishwater with potato chunks. They laughed when I took a tiny sip of it and declined the rest.

Practical jokes come with being human.

CHAPTER 3: Flocked Together

The Olmec society valued metals, and minerals they could carve; jade, serpentine, iron ore for mirrors, and cinnabar. Based in southern Mexico's Isthmus of Tehuantepec, the seminal Olmec empire ruled from 1500 BC to 900 BC, and influenced most subsequent Mexican and Central American cultures. In the west, archeologists found the largest Olmec mining site near Chalcatzingo in the Mexican state of Morelos, and decided it also served as a religious center because of its impressive location among three bare volcanic peaks that thrust up out of a flat valley. At the foot of the middle peak in a talus slope, huge boulders bear carved Olmec reliefs, similar to those at La Venta in Tabasco, about five hundred miles to the east. One depicts a well dressed Olmec woman of the upper classes. She sits in a cave's mouth under a cloud that pours down rain. It may represent a symbol of transmutation, of death or fertility, or a title stone for the 'pubic mound' of the central peak, situated between two volcanic peaks.

My landlord knocked on my gate one afternoon to explain that I owed them more rent money. I misunderstood, he assured me, ten dollars per month rent for each house. One I used as a kitchen and slept in, the other one as a living room, but when you live out of a backpack, food and sleep become the center of your universe. With no furniture, it didn't matter which of the bare earth floors I sat on. Only the kitchen window looked out over the lake, "Fine," I told him, "that one."

We both perceived the weakness of this solution.

The one gate to the yard gave access to the two house doors. No way to keep a person out of either house, if they wanted to get in. I doubted they could rent out such a tiny house while I inhabited its companion, and any new inhabitant of the other house would share the bathroom with me. I tried to reason with him.

Then he told me if I found a wife to live with, I could rent both for $15 dollars a month. "Go now, to Panajachél, and look for a wife."

That gave me an inkling of how these Indians think about these travelers' morality. If not representative of their own, it might represent what Mayans gossip about as they watch the shenanigans of young travelers.

Any lone male in the village threatened their womenfolk.

I needed to talk with Curt every couple of days or so, full of questions I hoped he might answer. I walked fast down the boulder strewn paths through the village to visit him.

I felt the absence of the old woman weaver at her usual post. Curt came to the doorway and said she "disappeared the last couple of days. Sometimes tourists buy the piece she works. They buy the loom with the back strap, fabric, wooden shuttle, balls of thread, everything, to make a wall decoration out of. Then she makes a new back strap loom from scratch."

Curt's mom liked to say that the Indians lived this way for the past several centuries, if not millennium. The females weave cloth and the males tend the gardens, the diet beans and corn, supplemented with any small game caught around the house, animals such as birds, fish, rodents, land crabs, maybe even insects to provide welcome variety and protein.

A tourist couple I met on a bus, East coast fruit and nut eating vegetarians, thought the indigenous Mexican and Mayan's diet near perfect, and responsible for their success as early City State civilizations. They claimed that a match of a grain with a legume like lentils, peas, or peanuts (all dicotyledons, distinguished by two seed leafs, unlike grasses that produce grains such as corn, wheat, rye, etc.) provide all of the twenty essential amino acids our bodies require to construct the proteins and enzymes necessary for good health.

They said the perfect proportion for Mexican diet would match "A half a cup of beans to six tortillas."

Most Americans don't live on peanut butter sandwiches, but it seemed like we did as kids.

Curt's parents wanted him to learn from the Mayans. I wondered if he tried the small game like rabbits, squirrels, monkeys, rodents, rats, land crabs, fish, minnows, frogs, tadpoles, worms, bugs, algae, gravel, whatever.

Hunger, the Grandmother of invention.

Kat

Most mornings I lost track of the days of the week, unless I noticed an increase in the number of cars that passed on the road through Santa Catarina Palopó, a reminder of market day in either Sololá or Panajachél. Most Panajachél market days, Curt didn't need to, or want to go with me.

Panajachél attracts many of the international tourists who visit Guatemala. I often met people from Mexico and Honduras, some from El Salvador, Costa Rica, sometimes even Colombians, Venezuelans, Brazilians or privileged families from Uruguay and even Paraguay. Guatemala swelled with tourists two weeks prior to Christmas.

The 'House of Pies' looked jammed at all hours this season. People from all over the world came and pursed their lips around the oversize plastic straws to suckle on exotic fruit shakes, between forkfuls of tropical pastry invention.

An oriental girl sat at a large table with two macho bikers, one a muscular mercenary type with short crew cut hair and a thick trimmed beard, the other a longhaired hippie adventurer with a pirate's hoop earring and matched necklace, a twisted loop of Navajo silver brocade encrusted with turquoise stones. He wore a red leather hat with feathers that angled from the wide brim, like a French Musketeer. A large knife dangled from his belt, not quite a machete, but lethal enough wielded by those muscular arms that now rested on the table like two sun burnt Anacondas. A sleeveless shirt, open at the neck, showed off a thick mat of chest hair and made him look Australian.

The oriental girl looked squeaky clean, athletic and healthy, tight jeans and a T-shirt that painted her curves. Her long shiny straight black hair undulated when she smiled and moved her body. She talked with a Californian's exaggerated animation, as if existence meant audition for stardom.

I looked around the room. At the other tables with empty chairs sat more "normal" people, though most people surprise you with a good yarn.

If I could sit at the Chinese girl's table with her pirates, I might learn something, like the good news she traveled alone. I walked up to them, took off my empty backpack to dangle it in front of my knees, and asked if I could join them. She looked up and said, "Sure." and moved her backpack off the forth chair.

After I'd ordered a piece of pie, I noticed the men called her Cat.

"With a K. It's short for Katherine."

They compared strategies in the art of barter, as they all claimed to deal in native handicrafts and folk art objects for export. A lull in the conversation gave me the opportunity to ask if they knew anyone who wanted to live in Santa Catarina.

"Where's that?"

"It's the next village on the lake, about three miles south of here."

"What's it like?" Kat asked.

"It's beautiful, of course. Indian village. You can rent tiny houses there. There's a dock on the lake, plenty of dugout canoes."

The two men got up to depart and shake Kat's hand. One bent down to shake hands, then pulled a little to impel Kat to receive a kiss on the cheek. Firm, insistent pull. I took notes.

I felt the Hippie glare at me, and thought his actions part of a subconscious attempt at psychological domination, as if to lower my self esteem or communicate that he thought me insignificant. Maybe I interrupted some illusion of a rapport with Kat.

She smiled at me a lot. To get away from them?

After the pirates took off on their thunderous motorcycles, I learned that Kat hailed from Los Angeles. She thought my landlord's strategy for rent extraction very canny and humorous, and laughed at the part where he demanded I go shop for a wife.

She asked me more about Santa Catarina Palopó and the Indians, if I felt threatened or perceived any danger there, and I coaxed her into the long walk back to the village to see for herself.

She let me convinced her, she said, because "I left my itinerary open today." She stood up, put on her backpack, threw enough money on the table for both of our pies and drinks, and headed toward the door. She looked back at me where I stood frozen, hand in my pocket, stuck in a finger trawl for the right coins to leave a tip.

"Are you going to Santa Catarina today, or not?"

Kathy Chi, or Kat as she preferred, wanted to talk about herself. A Chinese American college student well into work on an advanced degree, she considered herself an intelligent, bright eyed optimist with an open personality. The exercised an active imagination among the superstitious realms of Astrology and the Animist Syncretic Pantheism of China. She felt her life charmed and lucky.

She grew up accustomed to lots of people around, and found that people appreciated it when she told fortunes and gave out Zodiac personality profiles. When I pressed her on how much she believed in the influence of stars and planets on our life, she admitted she thought it great fun, but worthless. She made the stuff up, 'intuitively'.

She found her true passion in the arcane writings of Far East philosophies, Tao literature, and the pithy logic destruction of Japanese Zen one-liners. She loved poetry, and could make up Haiku for hours, she claimed.

She didn't appreciate my attempt to elicit a risqué chuckle when I asked if she knew the answer to the young man's Coming of age Zen Mantra, "The Sound of One Hand Clapping."

Dennis, Gary, and Yvonne passed us, headed into town, right at the entrance to the coffee plantations on the southern outskirts of Panajachél. None of us said much as we passed; our eyes met with a brief, soundless though polite salutation. I felt inhibited. I wanted a chance with Kat and preferred not to risk the slightest demonstration of interest in Yvonne.

I could see in the fleet expressions in Gary's face that Kat, a new, beautiful, and unknown face among us, set the boys minds aflame with conjecture. The presence of the two women kept both our groups pointed towards our respective destinations.

Kat and I talked most of the way back to Santa Catarina Palopó. That deprived her of the mystery of the cacao groves and the cliffs' rough volcanic majesty above, so I tried to shut up.

Silent people improve the quality of life.

When we overlooked Santa Catarina Palopó, I tried to impress upon her the crime of the empty, upper class homes along the shore did not house anyone most of the year, but she didn't hear me. She enthused about how beautiful the village looked snuggled in the mountainside's aprons, the one wooden dock mirrored in black on the great lake's silver surface, and the massive volcanoes so distant they appeared painted in flat gray against the midday sky.

After this long walk with her at my side, I thought the dock looked phallic, the lake wet, and the volcanoes, busty.

I could see Curt and Shotgun in Curt's front yard, each with a book.

As we passed them, they pretended not to notice. I looked back at them, and they waved like crazy people until Kat started to turn around. When I looked back again, and they both gave me the OK sign and leered, thumbs up.

I pointed out the trail to the house and she took the lead, her lithe build toughened on California's mountainsides. She hiked with a flow of effortless grace, paused once to look back at me and ham it up. She raised her sunglasses, took off her small blue jean cap to shake the sweat out of her bangs, then turned to bound away like a deer. Her hair fell as a shiny, black cascade across her backpack.

We passed through the vine covered gate into the yard of my two tiny houses of new adobe, and I felt good that the plants sported blossoms of fresh flowers. I felt the eternal springtime heat up my pants.

She said, "Great place for hobbits, even nasty ones."

From inside, she squealed when I opened the crude wooden shutters on the west window. The view appeared all the more spectacular with her China white features framed by Lago de Atitlán. The explosions of succulent plants grew like soft fingers of green crystals along the neighbor's red tile roof below.

"You look like you belong here." I said. "Mayans look a little Chinese. High cheekbones, almond shaped eyes."

"Almonds. My eyes are too small. I hate them sometimes."

"I don't believe you." But I did.

She said, "Don't you think the Mayans beautiful people, prettier than most Native Americans in the USA?"

"The Mayans have smaller bones, fragile, except for their cheekbones. They age so fast, don't you think?"

"Rough life." Kat said. "Did you ever hear the theory of two migrations of Asians into the Americas, from Siberia across the Bering Straits, and Navajo marauders arrived later, like Genghis Khan?"

"Arrived around the last ice age, ten thousand years ago."

"Brandon, want to hear my theory?"

I moved close to her, to share the view out the window as she spoke. I liked the shampoo perfume in her hair.

"Central Americans resembled Filipinos or Indonesians because of a meteorological anomaly."

"Meteorological anomaly?"

"A weather phenomenon. I discovered it on a map of ocean and wind currents. There's an oceanic 'counter current' that might have run from Indonesia right into Central America. It skirts north of the equator through the Doldrums, you know, where winds don't blow and sailors don't go, and maybe boats floated all the way, if they carried enough fresh water."

"You believe that?"

"I don't have to believe. I'm the fortune teller. I make others believe."

Thirty years later, scientists measured 600 year old skulls from southern Baja California's isolated Pericú culture, wiped out by the Spanish conquest, and recognized similarities to eleven thousand year old skulls from Brazil. Long, narrow braincases and short thin faces unlike most Mesoamericans shared similarities with skulls of Australian Aborigines, whom some anthropologist think settled Australia over forty thousand years ago, from Southern Asia.

Kat said, "In my anthropology class, I read that the northern Chinese share a common ancestral group with American Indians, that's why some have this fatty deposits over the eyes to keep the eyeball from freezing. You ever heard of the Laps, or the people of Lapland?"

"Take me to your Lapland."

"Brandon, I'm serious."

"The beautiful Laps of Lapland."

"They live above the Arctic circle, with reindeer."

"Santa Klaus. OK."

"They're white, Scandinavians, blonde hair and blue eyes, the works. The same fatty deposits formed over the Lap's upper eyelids, like Chinese eyes."

I scrutinized her features as she took in the view. First time I examined a Chinese person up close. I alternated between appreciation of her beauty, and alarm at her strangeness. Couldn't keep my eyes off her, I felt nervous, both fear and aggression. At times, I wanted to control her, possess her. "You're beautiful." I blurted.

"Thank you, that's sweet, but I'm not. I'm not ugly. Best case, I'm exotic. Fancy word for different."

Did I perceive her as beautiful, or feel an attraction to the unfamiliar, an instinct to widen my family's gene pool? How does one draw a line between attractive and attracted?

In Estados Unidos Mexicanos and most of Latin America, societies with over eighty percent Native American mixed with dark Mediterranean bloodlines, so now any blonde haired person looks exotic, like a glamorous movie star in the eyes of the darker populations. Some Hispanic American women try to dye their hair blond, and their beautiful, thick black Indian horsehair becomes a bloody piss orange haystack, which helps make true blondes even more glamorous to Latin men.

I didn't think of myself as blonde, but down here, my light brown hair, so common back home, makes me exotic, ten times more attractive in Latin America. Girls noticed me, and flirted. Part of it I believed cultural, but too much evidence came my way unasked for. Even from a distance, girls and women stared at me, and over the months, it convinced me that the rarity of my hair color attracted them.

"Why did you decide to live here?" Kat asked.

"I read about this area in an encyclopedia, and got curious, wanted to see for myself. Look at it, a lake surrounded with villages of Indians, each group in their village uniform, each person lives on a subsistence level in a paradise of picturesque scenery."

"And eternal springtime."

"Volcanoes. You don't see that in Michigan. And cheap! Pennies a day! The rent works out to thirty cents a day. I've bought time, time away from the States, away from gasoline engines, the rat race, and a lot of bad habits and addictive luxuries."

"You're a hippie."

"Maybe. What's a hippie? A revolutionary?"

"A drop out?" She laughed.

I stepped away from her. "Dropped out of a poisonous culture of illogical wars and inhuman factory work."

"Looking for some new values?"

"Looking for some old ones."

"Ah yes." She leaned out the window on her tiptoes, her face in the hot sun. "But you're rich down here."

"Rich? In what way?"

"The luxury to choose your own problems. And you can run back home if things go badly."

"What could go badly?"

"Illness. Or the war. You know there's a war brewing?"

"What war?"

"Don't you listen to the radio?"

"I do, but I don't understand it."

"Guatemala wants to go to war with Belize."

"So that's why they talk about Belize. Why?"

"The President of Guatemala, a former General, wants to take back Belize, the old British Honduras. Belize used to be a province, or state, of

Guatemala, but needed a better connection over the mountains. So Guatemala made a treaty with Great Britain. Guatemala allowed the Brits to lumber in Belize, in exchange for their promise to build a road to connect the two. England didn't build the road."

"So when does the war start?"

"Any day. Guatemala's sabers rattle every day on the news, another ultimatum to get a response out of Britain. It's ridiculous to think that a country full of black people that speak English need or want to unite with Guatemala. The General wants something else, cash maybe."

"Or the road built."

"Some say the Americans side with Britain, and might defend Belize, because the Guatemalan Quetzal always equals one dollar."

"I don't see the point, like we're supposed to feel guilty, right?" I leaned out the window with her, felt her body against mine.

"Brandon, guilt never does anyone any good. Why dwell on it? A little apologetic remorse next time you pay your ten dollars rent?" She laughed, and then pushed me with her hip because I stood there, mute and serious, lost in thought.

"Of course." I laughed. "Next time, I'll offer them a couple of problems to choose from."

"Five, maximum!" and she spit out the window and watched it arc over the bushes and into my neighbor's yard. She knew how to spit. Then she turned around, away from the window, and studied me. Her eyes darted from one of my eyes to the other.

Should I kiss her? Did I want to kiss her? I wished for more time to get to know her. I felt an attraction to her, didn't know why. I felt no sexual passion, but wanted to hold her, feel her body against mine, smell her, taste her. Maybe she likes women. She knew she charmed people, and followed specific travel plans, she told me on the walk here, as if to avoid complications. A college graduate with a career track. I followed no plan, except to explore, observe, and analyze the world with an open mind.

She looked at me, scrutinized me.

"Well, Kat? What do you see?".

"A sweet person." She said with a tender smile.

"Whatever that's worth."

"Oh, it's worth quite a bit. What do you know about life here?"

"Like what?"

"Like where do you go for medical help? Witch doctors? Do you know the infant mortality rate? Do any research about the local intestinal parasites, hepatitis, tuberculosis, the superstitious mistrust of strangers, the evil eye, the societal racism and class warfare, the people who disappear, the generations of enforced slavery?"

"No, I haven't done all my homework. I admit to some minor inconveniences, but then I might avoid death by car accident."

"In a bus, then. Thank your lucky stars you weren't on that bus with me last night. We about died. Several times."

"My experience also. But compare it to a cross town drive on a Los Angeles freeway."

Her litany of dangers sounded ludicrous to me, irritated me. "Where did you come up with all those dangers, US State department tourist alerts?"

"A friend of mine once lived in Guatemala City. He tried to talk me out of this trip. Said if I get a suntan, I look too much like a Guatemalan, and might get disappeared." She bumped me with her hip again. "He forgot to warn me about you."

"Are you worried about something?"

She whispered in a conspiratorial tone, "I'm convinced we live in a predatory universe." as she ran her hand up my spine like a spider.

"Like your import export friends?"

"Exporters." She corrected me, and dropped her hand from my back. "Machos, macho men. Kind of exciting!" and she forced a shudder and made a face. "Nice bodies, though."

I could kick myself for bringing them up. "I didn't notice their bodies, to tell you the truth. You distracted me."

"I like your body too." Kat felt my arms, and then hugged me, as if to reassure me. "And to think you're old enough to baby sit yourself."

"Hey, I'm well into my twenties." (Twenty two and a half.)

Through the window, we watched as boatmen hauled their reeds ashore. I stood behind her, my arms around her, as we leaned out the window.

"I don't know," she said. "It's nice here, but I want to get to Tikál." She took hold of my wrists and unwound my arms to back away from the window.

She walked towards the door, looked around, and stretched against the doorjamb. Her tight blue jean shorts beat a muscular rhythm into me, and I felt the blood drain into my weak knees.

I followed her out as light as a feather in a vacuum jar. My mood sunk into the mud, and in my head into a stunned silence that roared in my ears.

I wanted to talk her into a few weeks here, to get to know me. How could I convince her that something valuable might come of it? How could I convince myself?

She stood outside and scanned the mountains above, the village, the picture postcard afternoon, Indian village with Volcanoes.

"So romantic here." She said as I stopped next to her. She put her arm around my waist, and I pulled her closer.

She pressed against me, her soft twin pillows against my chest, and kissed me once, a brief peck as if to prove she controlled us, and then she rubbed her head against mine.

She smelled familiar, like snow, and I heard a one string banjo play a simple slow tune on a pentatonic scale.

"The Indians," she pushed me away, "don't display affection in public, do they?"

"So let's go back inside."

She laughed, and walked back to the doorway, reached inside to retrieve her backpack. "Walk me back to Panajachél?"

I hated the thought. "Sure. Let me get a few things."

The path downhill through the village, over rocks, around bluffs and banks overhung with succulent trees and rabid dogs, under tree roots from the fenced in yards of packed rocky earth, looked squalid and filthy.

I never noticed before how much I accept nature, and refuse to admit others don't.

Kat didn't appear to notice. She took photographs, and cooed at the color contrast of exotic green plants against the stucco walls near the ground, where the rusty stain of rain splash skirt ran around the adobe houses.

As we entered the main trailhead and passed the fountain where Indian women took water, she looked at me, mischief in her eyes, and danced a Southwest USA Native American pow wow stomp. Her feet kicked up clouds of dust. Her hand fluttered over her mouth to modulate the amplitude of her loud whoops, just like a Hollywood's wild Indians did.

I thought the Indian woman might drop their clay jars.

We both cracked up at the expression on their faces and then we ran like children all the way to Curt's house.

Curt stood outside with his parrot on his arm. "What's all the excitement?" he called out as we ran up.

We walked the last few paces to catch our breath, and then Kat did another war-danced around him, which scared the parrot so much she sunk her talons into Curt's arm.

Curt danced a strange crippled dance of his own, animated by pain as the enraged bird flapped and climbed by beak and talons up his shoulder.

We laughed until we cried, as Curt rushed the parrot into the house's safety to calm it down. From inside the doorway, the bird beat its wings and hissed at us.

I walked her back to Panajachél.

Back in my one room house, I kicked myself for a missed opportunity to invite her to eat. She held me spellbound, and nothing in my rural upbringing and lack of manners came to my rescue.

A few fresh, colorful mornings later, Shotgun and I chatted inside Curt's house and whenever people passed, watched them through his open doorway. Most waved, or said Buenos Días with a tip of the hat or a demure smile.

We planned to swim later, after the warmth of noon. To brave the lake's cold waters, we enjoyed a bottle of wine and warm companionship.

Shotgun told us about all the trouble his androgynous looks caused him over the last four years since he sprouted upward and grew his hair long. He said the Immigration Agents wanted to put him through a strip search at the Mexican Border to determine his gender.

Sounded like harassment to us. Didn't they notice his large Adam's apple, or lumpiness in his pants?

With his long delicate bones, fine features and beautiful light brown wavy hair that reached down his long back past his beltline, Shotgun did look sexually ambiguous in loose pants. He hated the way ignorant Guatemalans stared and talked about him, not even behind his back. He decided to change his ways, but not cut his hair.

He'd discovered that if he 'flipped someone the bird' with his middle finger extended, while he glared, that helped define him as a male, as did a good scratch to his balls. In Mexico, he "felt like taking a piss right in front of those bastards, right there along the roadside, like those fat Mexican men do."

Curt said "Guatemalans are too conservative, I wouldn't dare piss in front of anyone around here."

"It's like a different country."

We all laughed at that, and about Mexico, how crude and vulgar it seemed compared to polite Guatemala. We'd all seen Mexican men take a whiz along the road and wave at the bus with their free hand.

Maybe conservative Central America made all of North America appear vulgar and crude.

Shotgun grew up in Southern California, and that gave him a Chicano's slouchy walk. He also knew how to truck with giant strides and a lean backwards, which made him resemble a fashion industry runway model.

His long hair forced him into girlish gestures, with his hands or a quick bob of his face into the wind, to keep the hair out of his eyes.

"I guess I torture these macho Latinos. First, they think I'm this exotic super skinny sensual blonde chick, a wild promiscuous slut, the stereotypic Gringa they hope screws anyone anywhere all the time. Mexicans think Gringas are all sluts, to excuse their sexual harassment every time they see a real blonde. So Mexican men feel an attraction to me, when the me as female evaporates and I appear, they think I'm homosexual, and that's worse. They don't care if I'm a man. They try even harder! What's the deal, aren't there enough girls?"

Curt reminded Shotgun that his maleness might not protect him forever. Curt's parents warned him that in many Mediterranean societies, male prostitutes abounded, as they do in Estados Unidos Mexicanos especially along the highways at night. "Mediterranean cultures don't consider the man who penetrates as a homosexual, only the penetrated." Shotgun and I thought he joked with us.

"They consider the transvestite a deviant, and groups of men will beat one almost to death, especially if the queer says one of the men took him to bed."

"Yuck!"

So as preventative medicine, Curt and I demonstrated a more masculine way for Shotgun to walk. Curt found some extra towels and to the dock we walked, the three of us, chests full of air, shoulders back, heads high, hair out of our eyes, with determined gazes to see our farthest horizons.

Shotgun still looked like a member of Sweden's female volleyball team.

Not even a ponytail helped.

Shorts didn't help. His long athletic legs curved slow and smooth, with a wisp of almost invisible downy hair that glistened enough to attract attention.

Shirtless, he looked like a naked woman with a flat bust, a bulimic anorexic.

Once he expelled all the air in his lungs, he could put his hands on his hips and touch fingers in front and thumbs in back. His shoulders dislocated without pain. His double jointedness allowed him to tie himself into knots. He would sit cross legged on the ground, wrap his legs into a full lotus around his arms, and walk around on his hands. Probably could perform oral sex on himself.

Curt and I couldn't convince him to put on shows in Panajachél so that we could sell tickets.

We stood on the dock in the cool breeze, and dared each other to jump in. We moved around each other to avoid vulnerable positions that might get one of us thrown or pushed in by the other two. We circled each other barefoot on the hot gray planks, laughter and evasive feints of slap boxing.

This continued until Curt managed to grab us both by an arm at the same time, and picked us up as if tiny children. He threw us in like a couple of chunks of waterlogged driftwood. We fell five feet to the water's surface with a long scream. Curt laughed so hard he lost his own balance and toppled over on top of us.

Shotgun, tangled in his own hair, sucked in water and came up frantic. His hands raked the hair out of his face so he could gasp and choke and hack and sink like a jackknife. He clutched at us to push himself higher out of the water, and when calmed down, looked abject, betrayed and embarrassed, his face flushed, big eyes red and watering, like an Irish Setter.

The cold water inspired us to swim north hard, toward the hot springs Curt pointed out, at water level, at the foot of a rock cliff. Shotgun trailed us with his dog paddle. As a strong and young man, with a firm belief in his immortal indestructibility, he rejected our advice, our instant swimming lessons, and refused to copy our demonstrations of technique. Curt and I tried to tell him to keep low in the water, to submerge at least part of his head, so he wouldn't have to work so hard.

Though a short quarter mile swim, Shotgun convinced himself the hot spring lay much further from the dock. He called out to us, begged us to turn back. We ignored him, and built up his confidence with insults to his manhood. He stopped his vociferous complaints when Curt and I swam far enough away from him. Then he took all the advice he refused moments before and put his face in the water. He followed, a bit clumsy, but with a real fear of drowning, his self preservation won out over any ill advised effort to regain lost dignity.

Every fifty feet he would stop to say something, complain about the big waves, the cold, the hair in his eyes and mouth.

We swam away again, then back to him, tried to ignore his childishness while we laughed at him and enjoyed our parental duties. He did let us teach him how to swim on his back, which he enjoyed because it "keeps the hair out of my face."

"So would a haircut. Swim."

In the middle of the swim, far from both shores, we stayed near him to bolster his soggy ego.

As we neared the crack in the cliff, he swam fast. Curt and I stopped and tread water to watch his frantic grabs and bear hugs at the sharp volcanic rock. The average wave plucked him off. He looked too tired and too desperate to think straight.

We helped him tread water in comfort, in front of where the hot water issue from a wide v-shaped crack in the cliff. Beyond the crack, the eons of hot water scoured out a natural bowl, big enough for three or four people to squeeze inside.

Our skin prickled with needles of heat as we swam into the V-shaped caldron of hot water. We found seats more or less comfortable on the shattered rock, and kept enough skin out of the water to keep our bodies at a comfortable temperature. Sometimes even hotter water swelled up with a rush of bubbles.

"That swim wasn't that long. It looks worse than it is." Shotgun bragged. "I used to swim farther than that with the dog paddle."

Curt and I laughed. "Sure, but you forgot how tired you felt afterwards! A helluva lot more tired than you feel now."

"Shit!" Shotgun said. "I used to run cross country in school. Deceptive stamina, the papers said about me. Deceptive stamina, that's my middle name."

"Defective Stamen." Curt teased.

"Stamina." Shotgun corrected him.

"No Stamen, like the erect parts inside the center of a flower, you know the male part. Defective Stamen."

"You asshole!" and Shotgun splashed at us.

Curt leaned out the crack and stared back at the dock. "Hope no one steals our clothes."

Shotgun laughed and said, "Hey, no one gets into my pants."

"That's your tough luck." Curt grabbed him and in one powerful move, plucked him from his seat to push him through the crack into the cold lake waters.

Shotgun tread water, gasped and choked in the sudden cold, clutched and pulled at his face to rake the hair off as he flailed the water with the other arm to stay afloat. Then he calmed down, tread water, and glared at us.

His eyes darted across the sky, then he laughed.

He swam up to the entrance and splashed us with cold water, so Curt and I sank deeper into the hot waters.

Then he gave us a horrified expression. He yelled and lunged through the rock cleft into the hot spring as if he'd lost his manhood. We pulled him in, expected to find bloody skin over abraded bone, or a small crab to pluck from some sensitive part.

Shotgun shivered and tried to stand up out of the water. Wild eyed, he yelled, "What is it? Get it off me! Get it off!"

"Where? There's nothing there, where do you feel it?" we asked as we searched his body. He fell back into the hot water and then tried to rock scramble out of it.

We found nothing.

"Jesus!" Shotgun started to relax. "I banged myself a little, moving too fast." He rubbed one elbow.

"Next time, you ask nicely, and we pull you in." Curt teased. "Where did the nasty sea monster bite you?"

"You go out there, asshole! You'll see."

"What did it feel like?"

Shotgun raked his long hair out of his mouth. "Something swam around my legs."

"Is that all?"

"Most likely, your own hair."

"ASSHOLES!" Shotgun splashed us again.

"The Killer Assholes of Atitlán! Look out Shotgun! There's one by your hand!" Curt pointed at something next to Shotgun.

A crab sat under the surface, its eye stalks waved up at Shotgun.

"Yeaeccchhhkkk!" and he jumped to his feet on the slippery algae that covered some of the rocks.

"Hey, hey, sit down! You'll hurt yourself, or fall on us!"

"Get that bug eyed thing out of here!" He hung by his fingernails from the rock wall.

"We can't. He lives here. Maybe he'll cook himself, and we'll eat him for lunch. If he doesn't eat you first."

Shotgun sat down with averted eyes. He darted his glance out at the open lake. "There IS something out there."

"Sure. Fish, weeds, water, minnows, etc. Nothing to hurt you."

Shotgun glared at me, so I said, "Haven't you heard? You are the crown of creation."

"If you want something to worry about," Curt said, "worry about amoebas in your food and water. Or bacteria, or viruses. Even worms, there's plenty of worms to worry about. Intestinal worms, liver worms, lungworms, worms that crawl up through the bottom of your feet and come out under your tongue. How about those worms that get in your gut, then work their way out somehow, and you find them when they swim around under your skin. So then you cut a hole in your skin, attach a stick to the worm, and give it a little turn each day to try to pull it out and not break it. If you break it, it dies and then you die, real slow, from the infection as it rots inside you. Imagine a worm on a stick under your shirt for a month or so."

"Yeah, I've heard of that. My mom got infected by ringworm, but she said it's a fungus." Shotgun settled down comfortable again.

"Take her to the witch doctor," Curt said. "There's a Brujo, witchdoctor, in Santa Catarina Palopó that took me up to a cave, like a natural church, high up in the cliffs on the lake's north shore. Deep in the woods, a little cavern, candles and carvings, no one's supposed to go there, and it's real hard to find. He told me he could cure everything and everybody.

"Or he scares you to death in the process." Said Shotgun.

"Know what really scares me?" I asked.

They waited.

"A fish in the Amazon, smells warm piss and follows it, and swims right into your urethra. When it gets in there, a spiny fin on its back rises up and points backwards so you can't pull him out. It continues up your willy to lay eggs. Can you imagine any peaceful, loving male God that would design a spiny fish to swim up a man's dick?"

"Ick. I think I'll walk back to the dock."

"You ain't gonna make it, Shotgun. No way." Curt chided him with a smile. "I need a beer. Want to swim over to Panajachél and get some?"

"Sure." Shotgun said with sarcastic enthusiasm. "Go for it! Three miles! Like Tarzan to the rescue!" Shotgun stood unbalanced atop the rocks to yodel Tarzan's victory screech with spastic arms. Shotgun cupped his hands to pound his skinny chest like a gorilla. We all howled like Great Apes and filled the air with Australian kookaburra sounds from Hollywood's imaginary jungles.

A scatter of rocks fell into the water nearby.

We all froze into silent statues. The big lake 's quiet waves surged into our consciousness against the hot spring's hiss and bubble. I wondered if a rockslide threatened to entomb us.

Shotgun pointed high above us. I could see the distant silhouette of a wide brimmed hat. A man leaned out over the cliff's edge to look down at us. He motioned us away with his hand, polite but insistent.

We didn't move.

Then he yelled down in Spanish, "Váyanse." Scram.

"I guess he wants us to go."

"Tell him to come down here and make us!" Shotgun fumed. His hand shielded his eyes from the sun while he peered up and looked for trouble.

"Que están haciendo? Váyanse!" yelled the man.

"¡A disfrutar la naturaleza!" Curt yelled back.

"¡Basta! Por Favor, Váyanse de aquí!"

"Let's ignore him, maybe he'll go away."

Shotgun looked up and yelled back "Bastard!"

We laughed.

"Yeah look. There he goes now." We looked up and did not see the man. Then we saw a dark constellation of flecks against the clear deep blue sky, they grew larger as they fell, a handful of large, hard rocks splashed into the waters all around the hot spring.

"Shit," Shotgun jumped into the lake water first, then swam underwater to avoid the hail. Curt and I pressed our bodies against the cliff face and watched as more large rocks splashed about us.

In turn, we each dove through the cleft into the lake and caught up to the terrified Shotgun. We circled him and dove under, to threatened to pull him under. From underwater, we could see Shotgun's panicked movements, a dog paddle with an added kick against imaginary attackers.

He calmed down. We swam back to the dock so fast it didn't seem as far away.

To avoid the chill of the breeze on our wet skin, Shotgun and I swam through the shallows as long as we could. We walked ashore and ran out onto the dock. As we dressed, the light breeze hit us like an arctic blast.

Shotgun's teeth chattered. His blue lips trembled. I let myself shiver and chatter too, to ease his embarrassment. His extreme skinniness meant his skin surface comprised at least eighty percent of his total body mass. That cold water sucked all the heat out of his blood in seconds.

"You scarety cat." Curt poked fun at Shotgun.

"Yeah, yeah yeah. At least I'm not as bad as these Indians, or the Catholics, or the Catholic Indians, whatever they believe. Talk about scared. They build little shrines for their dead on every dangerous curve in the road. They even change the flowers and light candles in them every so often, for Chrissakes. If they took all that excess energy and put up guardrails along the road instead, people wouldn't die so often."

The Ride Back in Ida's car

Each death of a God-king necessitated another layer of temple construction, a tomb over the top of the old. They invented a calendar that measures time by unique dates encapsulated in periods of fifty two years, about an average life span. Each carved date referenced an entombed ruler, which suggests everything centered in the personage of these city-state Kings. The Mayans of each region felt ruled not by a mere human King, but by someone akin to the Pope, who represented a direct, inter-level connection to both the Underworld and the Heavens.

Days passed.

I tried to find a schedule for my life, a new ritual routine, but everyday changed. Too often I repeated the pilgrimage to Panajachél or Sololá for food and supplies, or necessities like toilet paper or cigarettes.

One day after a trip to the market, I discovered that my great bargain on oranges included worms. I didn't know little white worms could live inside an orange, that an insceet could get through the thick peel, loaded with volatile oils. I liked to show people how to make a tiny flamethrower with a lit match with an orange peel. Bend a quarter of an empty orange peel real fast, and the oils spit out will make a dramatic flare across a flame.

I fell in love with mangoes. The largest variety's peel came in green shades that turn to yellow or purple with a maple leaf red blush on the ends. Inside, the bright yellow orange flesh hid fibers strong as dental floss around a three inch long, flat, almond shaped seed.

One cold morning in the open air market, I stood among a small crowd of people who waited and watched a sturdy Indian lass, her hair in pigtails and her cheeks reddened by the chill air, serve atole. She smiled and showed her big lips and teeth, while she served Atole to a line of customers. The porridge steamed with heat and the sweet aroma of hot milk, rice, and cinnamon. She poured the viscous atole from bowl to bowl to cool it. With a bowl in each hand about three feet apart, she slung it from one bowl to the other to form a thick, steamy rope column that defied gravity. She poured on diagonal angles, without a drop splashed.

I bought food to carry back in my backpack. I hoped it would last for a number of days to avoid the long walk to Panajachél, but often what I wanted forced me to bus to Sololá. Even if I bought more food, the lack of a refrigerator turned life into a repetitive search for food.

I watched an older woman's strategy to select oranges. Squeeze each orange and juices bubble out any wormholes.

From hundreds of household in this area, some from much farther away than Panajachél and Santa Catarina Palopó, people and servants came to Sololá's grand market on Fridays.

I saw the writer mom and Shotgun. His emaciated hermaphrodite form caught a lot of stares in the Sololá market.

When they looked up and saw me, they waved me over to offer me a ride back to Santa Catarina.

On the way, she put on her educator's hat and lectured about Mayan civilization to enlighten her son and me.

I tried to imagine what the events she described looked like back then, with the population decked out in colorful woven fabrics, jewelry of wood, semiprecious stone, and iridescent feathers. The population gathered to watch their ruler, the God-king, and the priest class perform rituals to contact their Gods through rituals; ball games, blood offerings, public human sacrifice. All eyes focused on the King-god father symbol, his arms outstretched, as he stood on the uppermost levels of these manmade pyramid-mountains. Then he gave his subjects the State of the Union Address, the will of the Gods as communicated to him through the opened portals that connect separate realities.

With the city-state's King-god as the central visionary to orchestrate the bloody sacrificial theater, these Meso-American mass rituals probably looked like an outdoor rock concert, and served a similar tribal purpose. The extant paintings show Shamanistic dance and drums like today's Catholic obsession with death and blood, with Mayan peregrines who pulled thorn laden leather thongs through holes in their tongue or penis to offer their blood, both cultures similar in their resemblance to vampirism. Both ancient Mayans and modern Catholic Mayans carve bones, skulls, and ferocious half animal creatures to be their totems and Gods, terrible half Devils that speak with forked tongues like venomous snakes, their utterances foul with putrefaction like the snarl of big cats who pounce like thunder and lightning to snag the cautious critters that hear every drip fall from the canopies of the rain forests.

I couldn't remember her name, nor if we'd introduced ourselves the night of their arrival, too stoned, so I apologized and asked.

"Call me Ida. I've forgotten your name too."

Before I could answer, her son said, "Brandon, mum. I told you already."

"Why do you use Shotgun? Because you're built like one?"

"Funny man!" Shotgun laughed. "No it's because I'm a straight shooting fire breathing twelve gauge deadly and dangerous son of a, uh, pistol."

Ida gave him a light slap. "Hey hey, watch your mouth."

"Tell me straight, how did you come by a nickname like that?"

"Well Ida," he addressed his mom as a peer, "should we show him?"

"Go right ahead. That's what you're good at."

Shotgun ducked down and reached way under the front seat, then sat up and turned towards me in the back seat to display a rolled joint between his lips. "Have you ever tried a shotgun?" he asked, and pointed at the joint.

I didn't know what he meant.

"It's a nose hit. When I point this joint at you, inhale through your nose and I'll do the rest."

He lit the joint, took a big drag and then inverted the joint, coal first, and stuck it deep into his mouth. He motioned to me to come close to his face, and he exhaled and pushed out thick white smoke.

Ida turned toward us while she drove and said, "Tell us how you feel in a minute or two, when you get back to reality."

I inhaled as much as I could. The smoke felt cooler, the acrid sweet aroma and diffuse heat bit into my nose.

Ida shrieked, "Hide it!" as a Guatemalan Army personnel carrier, a flatbed truck with pipe fences that twenty men clung to, rounded a curve below us and chugged up the road toward Sololá. Shotgun stuck most all of the joint in his mouth and faked a smile as the army passed our haze filled car.

"Excuse my paranoia." Ida said. "We've got good reason to avoid problems with those assholes."

"Drug laws pretty rough here?" I squeaked out aloud, holding my breath.

"Who knows the laws? It's a big game of money and lawyers. That's what Mexicans call a free country; you can pay your way out of anything."

Shotgun took a couple of drags off the joint. "Ida," he squeaked, to not expel the smoke, "if they wanted to get us they could stop us and plant some dope on us."

"I do research" explained Ida, "on the fincas, the large ranches, the plantations. The trouble started the minute they noticed me asking questions, trouble at the national library in Guatemala City. Personal threats. The Guardia, Federales, came around the hotel to check up on us. Just friendly, they said, asking for our papers for the umpteenth time, even after they knew us on a first name basis."

"Why do they care?"

"Because the rich and powerful in Guatemala rule through a complicated system of what amounts to slavery. They don't want anybody with ideas from outside the country looking too close, someone who might call a spade a spade, if you'll excuse the expression."

"Such a small country, too." Said Shotgun. "Didn't take long to discover the major players. A couple of big families."

The landscape around us took on a new depth, beyond the mountainous vistas glimpsed through breaks in the pine forests along the road. A beautiful pastoral facade for the same technological nightmare I tried to escape, the social fabric of all of those factory rat people who worked hard for a decent life while they made others rich.

Ida, Shotgun, and I all felt the nightmare of inequality here in Guatemala; it hid beneath the benign green tapestry of ancient fields carved into the Mayan mountainsides for centuries, and still oozed the blood of human sacrifice at the roots.

We also felt stoned, and superior in our ability to recognize a country more primitive than our own, and then recognize the similarities. Ida said "You notice how the upper classes in Guatemala try to copy Americans in dress, cars, food, homes? That's how they measure success. Become like Americans."

"And we're down here running away from it." I said.

Ida laughed. "Running away to find a little more freedom. In an economy of a diminished scale, like Guatemala's, all of us expatriates and backpackers from the developed countries enjoy what the rich take for granted, the luxury to choose our own problems."

We agreed we loved the United States of North America and shared its common culture. We grew up in schools that talked of life, liberty, and the pursuit of happiness with equality for all, admired the Lone Ranger and rugged individualism, and learned to salivate at the endless stream of clever products advertised in a way that convinced us we couldn't live without this new improved product or service, and so we improve our life through purchases. We also agreed that beyond the public school system and consumerism, Americans often don't share a cultural heritage, but sometimes share a respect for diversity.

Ida told us that after the affluence and conformity of the fifties, the sixties' brought revolution and disillusionment. Many young people tried to define their own new and unique lifestyle, often with a stewardship of nature and a renewed interest in bodily health as a temple for the soul. Too many fell into recreational drug use, dysfunctional relationships based upon 'free love' promiscuity without respect for the complications of humanity's curse of violent jealousy, coupled with an inability to stay employed and the resultant damaged esteem and loss of interpersonal respect, caused many to run afoul of the law.

Shotgun said "We're the new Americans, a pure intelligence, idealism born of a comfortable childhood, peanut butter and jelly sandwiches and one a day vitamins, and the assembly line. Mom says for the first time in history, even lower class people can take advantage of cheap global travel. Look at us, we made it through two countries in under a thousand bucks for the two of us."

Ida said "Maybe too far away. The military shot at us a couple of times."

"We think it was the military."

Ida said "I didn't think we should stick around long enough to find out for sure who shot at us. In Guatemala, they say people 'disappear' as a euphemism for murder."

"Maybe it was thugs from the big coffee plantations."

"Why would anyone shoot at you?"

"I asked too many questions. I found out that Guatemalans associate a certain make and model of blue pickup truck with these disappearances. Someone's rotting body turns up along a rural road, and if you ask the neighbors, they often remember seeing a pickup. I talked to eyewitnesses, neighbors of a big coffee finca in the mountain, who saw them. There aren't very many cars, and too many bodies to count. They throw them into deep arroyos, and even if recovered, few make the evening news, unless they find three or so at once."

"Don't the police investigate?"

Shotgun laughed. "The police, like in Mexico, take bribes as part of their salary. They're paid hit men, and the only ones allowed to wear guns."

"Many people down here don't respect life." Ida said. "Especially not human life. Drunks lay as if dead along the road, and no one cares. Little children, malnourished into a scum mouthed permanent infancy, wander the streets and beg. They hang onto your pant leg and stretch out their rope thin arms palm up, with these dirty clawed fingers, you don't even want to get close enough to throw them a coin."

"That's just poverty, isn't it? There isn't enough money to help everyone."

"That's a laugh. Have you gone shopping for food yet? Costs pennies, and yet whole families live on the municipal garbage dumps."

"I don't see how you can assume Guatemalans don't respect human life."

"You will, after you get shot at a couple of times. Look, have you noticed how Guatemalans on foot, like Mexicans, fear automobiles? Like they expect the drivers to run them over at the first opportunity? As if cars didn't come with brakes. You spend a couple of months down here, you realize the truth to that. Any Latin American who can afford it gets a driver's license without driver's education, which creates a lethal and antagonistic relationship between the wheeled class and the 'peatones' or pedestrians. If you want to make a dangerous asshole out of someone, especially a young man, give him a gun without any training. Same thing with a car."

Over time, as travelers far from home, with little or no regular contact with those who might care if we disappeared, we learned to appreciate the everyday sadism of those who do not value human life, we felt less and less protected by our American citizenship.

We became mortal.

We learned to respect the oppressive reign of a foreign government.

Shotgun squinted like the eyeholes of a smashed sewing needle. "Hey, how old are you anyway?"

"Twenty. Maybe twenty two. Look younger, don't I?"

"Yeah. A little. How old do you think I look?"

Hard to tell, the long hair might make him look younger, or older, and his thin build might demonstrate an adolescent growth surge. He didn't attend school and traveled with his mother.

"Eighteen?"

"Sixteen."

"Same age as Curt then!"

"He's sixteen?!" they chorused in unison.

In the Writers' house

Artifacts suggest that earliest Mesoamerican cultures from the Preclassic (before 100 BC), such as the Olmec, first invented the idea of a connection between the three layers of reality as a cave or doorway. As a King-Shaman enters the portal, the "Feathered Serpent, or maybe sea monster, swallows him because he offers something sacred; leaves, tobacco, alcohol, human blood, sacrificial animals, etc. Afterwards the portal regurgitates the shaman. In Zapotec art, the serpent's open mouth contains a seated vision seeker who holds a leaf of the hallucinogenic Datura plant, still in use among America's indigenous cultures.

Inside Ida and Shotgun's one room house in the afternoon, most of the light came from the one electric light. Ida relaxed on a car seat, which they found abandoned in the tall grass nearby. She described how they dragged it into their house, after "rolling it over a couple of times to coax the scorpions and snakes out of it."

Her chain smoker's voice sounded even more garrulous after we smoked a joint. "After they shot at us a couple of times, at least we think they shot at us, we felt too paranoid to continue our work in the city, where everyone got to know us by sight, if not by name. We decided to make ourselves scarce, let things cool down a bit and hope they forget about us."

She smoked, and Shotgun continued for her. "That's why we drove in at night, over that lame excuse for a road. Useless to try and hide in Guatemala, everybody sees everything."

Ida said, "Even worse, they remember and talk about it to everyone. Imagine, people as strange as us, anyone could describe us in a heartbeat."

Ida's small hiccup laugh sounds like a nervous frog croak. "Here we relax, smoke a little, catch up on our reading."

We all helped them arrange their house. Curt stood on a chair to hang woven net bags destined to hold perishables up off the floor. Shotgun held up objects and asked Ida where she wanted them. Ida and I tried to unpack boxes of books, but started to read a couple of books we found.

I felt too stoned. Couldn't remember what I read long enough to understand the next line. I wanted to do something a little more active. "The sun will set soon. Anyone care to go for a little walk?"

Ida said, "No, I want the boys to help me unpack. I've got to get organized."

I left them indoors, to smoke grass, and redecorate.

Felt chilly outside already, still bright with the sun sliding down towards the volcanoes across a cloud scudded bowl of blue sky.

I started up some unknown trail. The houses spread farther and farther apart as I made my way up the slant between the terraces, little six foot by twenty foot plots of leveled ground connected by tiny irrigation ditches that distributed the constant runoff of water from springs somewhere above.

Scattered men worked the fields with hoes and small shovels to divert water from one section to another. They must do it all day long. I saw a couple of men irrigate by hand. They scooped a bowl into the water from the main channel and threw it into smaller troughs or on the field.

Quite a variety of vegetables grew under this intensive care. Anything grows in these volcanic soils at any time of the year. The crops appeared in all stages of development, sprouts, young plants, and the mature leafed out plants that overflowed their tiny rectangle fields.

Further up the mountainside, large cornfields took over. I walked on a slope along a trail that wove up through rows so steep each row towered four feet higher than the last. The cornstalks grew huge, maybe eight feet tall.

I stopped and peered between the yellow green bars of corn.

It changed my perspective on how Santa Catarina Palopó sat along the lake. From this vantage point, it looked less like bay on a lake and more like the flooded side of a mountain. The Indians built Santa Catarina Palopó without much flat land at all, except for a small alluvial plain that must flood in the rain.

The corn plants' tremendous height brought to mind the claim that corn originated in Guatemala. More native varieties of corn grow here than in any other country. These giant grass produce corn syrup sweetener, popcorn, grain corn of various colors, and silage which all together made it one of the world's most valuable foods for both humans and livestock.

Below me, Santa Catarina's whitewashed adobe one room houses spread out much farther and wider than I imagined, tucked amid the lush gardens and outcroppings of fallen volcanic rock. Indian women dotted the yards with bright red color as they sat and wove on their back strap looms.

I came to many forks and intersections in the trail.

How does a good hunter choose which trail to follow? He follows urges, not with a bunch of verbal rules and regulations, but with the goal in mind, a strategy sharpened by logic and broadened through holistic experience to make an arbitrary decision that results in a higher probability of payoff.

Could a modern hunter, raised on hunt magazines, bring home the bacon before a native hunter?

Better a rifle than a rock.

As the slope increased higher up, the terraced dirt piled higher, rows of corn like tight fence posts that grew almost on top of each other. Nearer the top, the trail twisted into switchbacks.

As I emerged from the corn, a few hundred yards below the visible rim of this circular mountain range that cups all this bottomless water of Lake Atitlán, a water column that goes all the way down through the earth to the China Sea, I guess, I looked up to see the wind gusts tug at the deep green branches of tall pine trees. A strong wind off the lake helped push me up, the warm air flowed up along the mountainside which now lay in direct sunlight. The turbulence traced patterns as it twirled through the corn, it made the corn stalks come alive, all those thousands of corn stalks danced like blonde haired stick figures, tall dolls caught up in a collective and violent hysteria.

The trail turned sandy, and steepened so that I used my hands to pull myself over the pine needle mat atop the rim of the valley.

I walked into a pine forest as clean as a park, the uneven ground thick with a soft bed of dry, brown pine needles a couple of inches thick in places. Although I didn't see any animals, something must graze these grounds so stripped of undergrowth. I followed the ridge to the right, south, away from Panajachél, and found an overlook, where I sat down to watch the volcanoes reflect in the rough lake far below.

Like glass shattered into colored dust, the lake surface swam with great swirls of turbulent wind channeled between the volcanoes. Purples from the volcanoes' silhouettes mixed with the deep blue of the sky's zenith. Golden clouds flew in from the rusty horizon below a milky blue green of ocean atmosphere in the distance.

"Hey there!" Someone called from my left. I turned and saw the French girl, Yvonne, seated a ways off on some tree roots.

I called out, "Hello!" and waved to her. My heart leaped at the thought that she watched me hike up.

"How long have you been up here?"

"I think I saw you at the bottom when I reached the cornfield." She sat there, as if waiting. "You come here before?"

"No. My first time. How about you?"

"One time before. Come here, better view, softer. Pine needles." She tapped the ground beside her.

She wore short shorts and a white shirt with tails tied above her navel, no bra, her tan skin flushed red and sweaty.

"Great sunset." I said. The wind blew her dark hair, combed it back out of her face. The sunset's soft glow set her flushed features aflame with healthy warm tones.

We watched the clouds gather and split apart around the volcano tops, like long drapes snagged on the three conical mountains that keep the waters of Lake Atitlán away from the Pacific Ocean.

"How long ago did you leave France?"

"Over a year ago. I don't remember. It's not important." She smiled. "Yesterday maybe. So far from home, and not so far. There I worked as a nurse, here I still see sick people."

"What sick people?"

"The village. Everyone looks tired and a little sick to me. Health problems. From the fountain, food, who knows? Lots of diarrhea. They're not very clean, don't you think? That's the nutty gritty of it."

"Uh, nitty gritty?" I shrugged.

"Nitty gritty, then." She laughed. She spoke with her mouth to the side, a wry one sided smile copied from some nineteen fifties European movie star.

"Nitty gritty." She shook her hair and laughed again.

I didn't know whether to look at her or the sunset. I stood up, nervous, and walked a few steps away to take it all in; her, the sunset sky, the pine forest, the village nestled below in Santa Catarina Palopó's valley the way I wanted to nestle in Yvonne's arms.

She sat and hugged her knees, stared at me as I stood before her. "What do you think right now?" She asked.

"I don't know." I lied. "I don't know which is more beautiful, you or the sunset."

"Oh! A romantic!" She teased me. "And a very good sunset. So how do I compare?"

"Very favorably. It's neck and neck, but the darker it gets the more you pull ahead."

"Thanks a lot. So I look good in the dark, when you can't see me."

"Touch has it's own beauty too."

My low self esteem surfaced full force when confronted by her European multilingual sophistication. My rural roots hauled me down into a dark, comfortable place of doglike subjugation, and I imagined she thought of me as little more than any other element of the scenery.

I wondered if she felt at risk alone with me so far from the village. "They say it's harder to go down than to get up."

"So you know how to go down, as well as get up? Clever boy."

I missed the double meaning. "Who knows? Maybe that's what keeps mountain climbers climbing. Supposed to be harder."

"Harder. How interesting." She stretched her legs, brushed off her tan thighs, straightened her shorts, and stood up. "I going down now."

"Mind if I tag along?"

"What?" She asked, and looked at me with concentrated concern. "The child's game?"

"Should I go down with you?"

"I might like that very much." She smiled. Again, I missed her double meaning, her joke flew over my head.

Her face brightened as she waited for a response from me, then she shrugged disappointed, and ducked under a branch to head off through the pines towards the trail. Her large knife case slapped on her hip.

I bit my finger and kicked myself with the heel of my boot as she turned back.

"Are you all right?"

"A bug, that's all. Almost bit me."

"Come along with me if you like. You can see me to my door like a gentleman. You'll feel better about it in the morning."

A couple of planets shone bright by the time we reached the start of the sloped cornfield. As the trail switch backed through the tall corn, we glimpsed two Indians ahead of us. We caught up to a barefoot boy who led an old, fat man with the use of a broomstick, without the broom. They both held it horizontal and the boy pulled the old man along. When they stopped to let us pass, we tried to talk to them but they didn't speak much Spanish.

The boy called the old man abuelo, grandfather, and spoke in the clicks and chowings of Cakchiquél for a moment. The old man turned to survey the horizon, then held out his hand for us to shake while he repeated "Mucho gusto."

We shook his hand in the limp Guatemalan fashion. Since they didn't understand our Spanish, we excused our selves, "Con permiso", and passed them to stride down the trail.

A minute later, Yvonne asked, "Did you notice that the Grandfather cannot see?"

"Blind? On this trail? You're joking."

"The grandfather feels the turns and dips in the trail through that broomstick. That's why they both held onto it."

We walked, or fell forward down the trail with each step, and talked. She refused to tell me her age. The past year she "explored North America" as she put it; Canada, the United States of America, and the United States of Mexico.

She met her boyfriend, the Canadian Dennis, through a friend in Toronto. She said they traveled with his friend Gary for the past three months, and she complained that they act like her bodyguards too often. "I like the USA, the open spaces, without people. Don't care for the culture, the lack of it, I mean."

We stopped, out of breath, to say goodbye at a fork where two trails led to our respective temporary homes. Before she turned to go, the moon peeked over the mountain and bathed us in its silvery light. She made me turn to notice, and I thought I saw a new light in her eyes, a new excitement that made me want to say something, but she turned and left, wrapped in her own arms and thoughts.

In my little house, I turned off my flashlight and the dark loneliness surged in so thick I could feel it muffle the life out of me. Made me want to jog back up the trail, find their house, and whistle low through the window to her.

I decided to walk down to the lake to sit and stare across at the few electric lights of Santiago on the far shore.

A symphony of sounds accompanied my thoughts of Yvonne; stars hummed and twinkled, except where the invisible black silhouettes of the three volcanoes blotted out their light. I heard the coo-coo of the gunmetal 'paloma' doves that folded their white tipped wings around them like a sweater, and cuddle together in the branches.

I tried to catalog the sounds; a chorus of croaks from slick green frogs that hunkered down in the shallows, the roar of lake scented gusts that combed through the trees, the wave slaps of whitecaps, the miniature surf swells that crash like long cymbals through the reeds that rattle against each other and whistle whip the air.

The wind calmed, and died.

I could hear my own absolute quiet, the eternal hum and sizzle within my own head, which in my youngest youth, I mistook for the furnace air that pushed through the ducts and registers in the house.

The lake's surface glittered with reflections of the bright dazzle of Milky Way, arched above the volcanoes. It made me feel even more insignificant.

Back in my dark hut, I couldn't get to sleep. Eyes shut or open, I could see her slim figure as it moved like a deer down the trail in front of me. We helped each other where heavy rains washed out the trail in steep patches of treacherous loose gravel.

The way she looked at me once, one look in particular, kept me awake with the memory of her eyes wide, pupils so black, soft lips bent into her trademark crooked French smile. I could almost feel the warmth of her hand in mind as I relived my life's most gallant moment, when she let me help her down the trail. Again, I imagined the weight of her body as she fell against me, and felt dizzy as we walked down a washed out trail, and I inhaled the perfume of her hair on the warm night wind.

I tried to analyze my predicament, my objectives, the reasons for what I did, and nothing made sense, but I felt good about it anyway. I hated the idea of life back home, sprawled in front of a television to rest for another day of meaningless labor.

How, where, and when do people find their place in this Universe? Why do most people need church once a week, and sex as often as possible? Right now, I would go to church everyday for sex once a week. Where do I search for happiness, or goodness, when I don't understand myself, how I fit, nor where I come from?

I tried to make the world fit together like a jigsaw puzzle, and the few pieces I knew about so far, the family farm, the factories, rich kids, dehumanized factory workers, academics at the University, Canada, Texas, Mexico, the Mayans of Guatemala, they all bashed against each other like pieces from different planets.

Maybe traditions offer a roadmap through time, a route from one holiday to the next; through birthdays, anniversaries, special days for mothers, fathers, Saints, labor, memorials, constitutions, declarations of independence, famous dead people or dead presidents, that pull us inexorably forward, shut eyed and platitudinous, weightless and thoughtless, like free balloons born on the fickle winds of time.

Maybe Christmas would reconnect me, or give me a clue.

CHAPTER 4: Holidays in Paradise

"What do you plan to do for Christmas, Curt?" Shotgun said, sprawled across one of Curt's chairs like a spider monkey. I looked up from my book and saw Curt feed his parrot cuts of fruit.

"I dunno. Buy the bird a present. Stay by myself, I guess."

"You're not Christian then?" I asked.

"I'm too young to know any better."

"He's the Lord of the Flies, man!" Shotgun shouted and threw a crumpled piece of paper at Curt.

"What's that supposed to mean?" Curt threw the paper wad back.

"It means," I said, "You feel like the head of our tribe of boys, older and wiser, but you're no better than a rotten pig's head on a stick. You missed some good books by not going to high school in the States."

"The Lord of the Flies led of a bunch of scared English kids marooned on a tropical island. Sort of a political science version of Robinson Crusoe." said Shotgun.

"How did they spend Christmas?" Curt wondered while he slipped the bird a piece of Papaya off the wide hunting knife.

"They barely got through Halloween!"

Shotgun and I laughed. Curt cooed at the big green bird and tried to touch its head. The bird let him, but got a little testy when Curt ruffled his neck feathers the wrong way.

The doorway framed the view. Dark out, but a full moon lit the scene across the lake where large clouds built up around the volcanoes from moist ocean winds. Santa Catarina Palopó lay in the mountain's shadow. Curt's house seemed like an American Space Capsule, the crew lost in the void of a sleepy Mayan Indian village.

"Anybody want to go to Panajachél?"

"There's a lot of tourists this time of year." Curt enthused.

"Shotgun, think your mom would go, drive us?

"Naw. She wants to read or write, all she ever does." He imitates Ida's voice. "That's why we came here."

I tossed the book aside. "Let's do it. I could use the walk. Anybody got money? I'll pay you back next time I cash a traveler's check."

Curt lent me some, and we left in the time it takes to turn off a light and padlock a door.

The chill inspired a couple of dashes down the long road we all knew so well.

As we neared the outskirts of Panajachél and left the haunted short forest of the Cacao groves, music flowed down the street from an open doorway. Light sprayed out of the house and lit a yard full of plants. We slowed down and the sounds sorted out. One man played electric guitar, a polka tune. He played bass line, chords and melody all twisted together.

As we walked in front of the house, we could see him seated on a couch inside, happy with his endless original song, oblivious to us, yet he smiled towards the open doorway as if to say 'I acknowledge your existence, even though I can't really see anyone out there in the darkness. Right now I'm kind of busy.'

Occasionally we heard sounds like distant machine gun fire.

Shotgun and I got involved in a conversation about Henry Miller or some such rot, we slowed down and Curt pulled ahead quite a ways in front of us. We saw Curt slow down and struggle to get his hand out of his pocket. As we approached him a few moments later, he threw something back at us. The orange fuse of a lit firecracker arched through the air.

Shotgun jumped at it, batted it back with his hand in midair, like a volleyball player. Sparks showered as it sped back at Curt, who ran down the road and let out a lunatic's laugh. The firecracker bounced across the road to ignite and vomit a thick spray of sparks, a dud. It hissed and spun around a couple of times before it died as a quiet little glow in the gravel.

"Got any more of those?" queried Shotgun.

"Sure!" Curt spun around and yelled back.

"Keep 'em!"

A half hour later, we walked down Panajachél's narrow streets towards the lakeshore. Curt stopped at the gate of a large modern house where, in one tall narrow window that flanked the door, a small electric sign imitated a neon glow with the feeble word ''. A substantial part of the walls of the house consisted of dark plate glass, and because outdoor lights shined on the plants, the reflections made it impossible to see more than silhouettes of people inside.

"What's the drinking age in Guatemala?"

"No one cares." Curt said as he walked to the door.

Inside, a yellow bamboo bar contrasted with a color scheme of deep burgundy color, except for some wood and leather chairs and the dance floor's obligatory Mirror Ball, like a giant cut glass beehive. The DJ played recordings of a Guatemalteco rock band that tried to copy the Rolling Stones, a group of white Englishmen who tried to sound like black bluesmen from Georgia. If I could find a little success as a white boy who played Guatemalan marimba music and a Georgia black copied me, full circle.

A steady flow of people, both dressed up and dressed down, percolated into the bar and it got crowded. People clotted around their favorite language. Everyone looked bathed, shaved, affluent, young and attractive, and my self esteem plummeted. I rubbed my face and felt my stubbly near beard, looked down at my rough clothes and caught my reflection in the mirror behind the bar to see a man of indistinct age, face blurred and buried under uncombed, overgrown hair.

I imagine the older tourists stay in their hotel's bar, fearful or "cautious", hands wrapped around warm cognacs while the local Juan Man Band played endless repetitions of Felíz Navidad, Guantanamera, La Bamba and Cucaracha, and Allá en el Rancho Grande.

These young women stunned me with their beauty, their makeup, and provocative eveningwear. These Catholic American women knew how to dress with style, in diametric opposition to the frumpy Hippie culture recently popular in the States, or the Midwest's casual disarray in layers of serviceable clothing.

As we downed a couple of beers, our eyes grew accustomed to the low light level and the beer gave us confidence. I saw the unreachable attractiveness of the women diminish. Minute by minute, they appeared less intelligent, more artificial, gaudy in their polyester clothing, cheap.

Some people travel in disguise. They live out their own fantasies. They may try to look rich, mysterious, or act haughty and omnipotent, to lower other people's self esteem. When Americans mingle among the less well off, they call it 'slumming.' Other Americans like to act as if they own the place, or could buy it.

If this Guatemalteco staff could see these same American vacationers in their home environment, they would find normal stiffs who think they receive inadequate pay for too much hard work for too many hours a day per week after week, to earn their one or two vacation weeks a year. As Ida described Guatemala's forms of indentured cultivators, many of these tourists also slave to service their debt, trapped in jobs they can't afford to quit.

I spotted the young man who owned this bar, or rented this house for this purpose, as the man the over groomed homosexual waiters sucked up to, the disk jockey with reddish tinted hair piled up into a moussed pompadour. Better living through chemistry. I disliked him in a blink, perhaps for the overabundance of jewelry, rings, bracelets, earrings, and even a gold tooth. Third World elegance.

Looked like Guatemala's upper class, children of all ages received carte blanche to enjoy their holiday in Panajachél. A short drive from their enclaves in Guatemala City, they find an opportunity to mix with Europeans, North Americans, and Asians like the Japanese who traveled halfway around the world to stay at one of the two little seven floor hotels that overlook Lake Atitlán.

We all land here, tourists to a sensual Mecca, a temperate microclimate island in the tropics, and slum it together, expatriates and ruling class, to change languages from competent to incomprehensible, from a Cuba influenced underworld hip Spanish to an English invented by American rock fans on marijuana and psychedelics. How easy for the Third World citizens to impress their date with this cheap excursion, the Mayan Indians as picturesque as the geography, the open air hotel rooms cool enough year round to ameliorate the sweaty overheated rewards of successful seductions. The modern Gringotenango lakeshore resort serves as a place where tourists get dizzy on alcohol in a safe capsule of modern lights and perfumed flesh, oblivious that a cocoon of two Old World traditional cultures, both primitive and homicidal surround them.

Sometimes I wanted to lie down in my rented hut and moan away, full of shame for my unshaven face, lack of appropriate clothing, inability to talk Spanish, and my working class roots. Here in this , I relived all the snubs and social rejection of high school, whenever I noticed a girl's smile or glance and felt lit sarcastic. Later in life, I realized that a girl's smile might represent flirtations, but in those days, I usually misread and ignored these open invitations like a perfect fool.

In the Indian village, they saw me as an outsider, a source of income, harmless, a curiosity to people with little curiosity.

At best, I felt above it all. I meditated, and became one with my low self esteem. I owned it, and it opened the door to a strange sense of union with the dirt of the earth.

I ordered another round for us, stood there lost in my circular thoughts. Too loud to talk, too crowded to walk. A constant flow of people passed us as they circulated through the bar, a change of scenery that delayed boredom moment to moment.

I watched Shotgun fixate on women. Every once in a while he would glance at me and make his eyebrows and scalp go up and down in a message that a pretty girl approached me from behind. When one arrived from Curt's direction, he pulled his hair and pointed with it to pass along the alert.

A girl stopped in front of Curt, looked up at him and smiled, then pointed her finger and jabbed it into his meaty chest. She yelled, "I know you, don't I?"

"As long as you want to." Curt said with a confident smile. They shouted into each other's ear and shook hands, and then vanished together into the crowd.

I circulated, and as I moved among them, these over dressed women transformed before my eyes. What looked like, from a distance, an exotic Mayan beauty, turned into a crude Chinese brush and ink drawing on pasty base cream. I imagined these women applied blood red grease on lips chapped from other lips. They smiled with red dove chevrons over coffee yellowed teeth. The elegant women of the unexercised class evaporated into emaciated vampires with laughs husky as ancient crypt hinges. Their crab carapace sternums sprouted bony appendages from the shoulders sheathed in a thin skin streaked with spider legs of black hair.

To add to the confusion, healthy buxom women, athletic or soft, like any woman with piles of luxuriant hair that stood in stiff salute to 'better living through chemistry', offered a modern challenge to testosterone driven males. Where does technology end and the woman begin?

Small wonder men love the beach, where bikinis shrink in direct proportion to distance from home, and the truth comes out.

Shotgun and I talked to a young Guatemalteco man dressed in imported Italian clothes, as he pointed out several times. He could get us dope, he claimed, if we fronted him the money now. Then later we could pick it up at another address in Panajachél.

Great plan, give a stranger your money and make it easy for them to rob you. To make it safe, he offered to leave his passport with one of us.

"Not necessary. We trust you." Shotgun decided.

"Take it. You need it so he can identify you. Just don't get so stoned you forget to give it to him so I can get it back."

We eyed the girls while the dude went on his errand with Shotgun's money. Shotgun wanted the grass to give as a Christmas present to his mother Ida, "even though it's her money."

People away from home get tempted to do things prohibited at home. They jump into intimacy, try a different personality for the weekend, rent a sports car, gamble, buy sex, waste themselves on booze and drugs, wake up and either not know what happened, or not want to remember.

Travelers whose ships pass in the night like to cross gangplanks because every new acquaintance becomes the promise of a perfect confidante who we won't see again, and will not contact anyone we know back home. So we allow our nightmares and fairy tales to mix and dovetail, as Demons of Self Destruction lay in wait to ambush our Angels of Optimism. Over the course of a bus ride, one hears a life history unfurl with more than you want to know detail as a pump for our own confessions.

As for instant love on the road, amorous intoxications become luxurious and anesthetized, safe in the knowledge that a relationship will not last past the next bus ride.

I noticed Yvonne, my heart jumped. She came in with Dennis and Gary from Toronto and found a group of French speakers at a table to my left. Yvonne turned to face me, without acknowledging my existence. It made me so nervous I went outside for a walk.

I lit my cigarette and leaned against the gate out by the main road. I turned to face the entrance to the ' and tried not to look hopeful.

Nobody followed me out. I fantasized someone might want to, but then sunk with the thought that I appeared poor, dressed for a muddy funeral in Patagonia.

A bar employee came out of the and muttered in broken English about the beer mug in my hand. He hurried over to me, overexcited, saying something about robo, robbery.

"You think I'm stealing the beer mug?"

"No no no. You no unnersten' me. Police take you money, no beer in street."

I opened the door to the and passed Yvonne on her way out. She said Hi as she passed, without much of a glance in my direction. I kicked myself for not handing the waiter the half full beer.

Then Dennis and Gary followed her out. They ignored me as I held the door.

I found Curt with a couple of girls at a table, so I wedged my way in with a vacant chair scooted from a nearby table full of dirty looks because I acted too fast for them to comment.

We all pretended to enjoy ourselves. With the music too loud, I suffered their yells into my ears, shook my head negative until I gave up and laughed 'yes' as if I could understand, like the rest of the participants in this charade of camaraderie.

Shotgun bounded up about fifteen minutes later, and motioned to me with frantic points to his bare wrist as if he wore a watch.

"Hey man, come on! I looked all over for you! We got to get going!"

"Yeah, yeah yeah. I'm coming."

I made a move to get up and Curt put his heavy hand on my shoulder and leaned close, his face contorted in a mixture of mock anger, astonishment, and a plea to stay.

I tried to move away from the table and couldn't. Curt held me in place with a giant hand that trembled with anger. He leaned to my ear and yelled through a forced smile, "You lost your mind? I need you here. Her friend wants to meet you. Don't abandon me now."

Curt thought that no real red blooded American man would go and him alone with these two beautiful girls. It did not compute. "I like these girls," he said to me in Spanish (these girls please me), then switched to English. "Stick around, help me get to know them. Give me a break. Hey, I'm sixteen, I could use some advice."

"Advice?" I said. "Run. Don't pay for their drinks. No me llaman la attención. No me caen bien." Translate that to "They don't call my attention" or I did not like them much, and "neither of them falls well to me" which means I don't like them. Spanish throws the responsibility elsewhere, things let themselves fall through your fingers, nobody drops them.

Shotgun put both hands on my shoulders with a little massage and leaned down next to my ear. He looked from one girl to the other, raised one hand then the other to get their attention, and said in a loud voice, while he rubbed his hands together like a waiter, "Goodnight you luscious babes. Wait right here and when we return, I promise to get you stoned out of your frickin' minds, so you'll let us go where no man has gone before!"

He knew they would not understand even if they could hear through the music. They smiled at him, laughed, and shook their heads Si, si. He smiled back and blew them a kiss Adios as we worked our way through the crowd to the door.

I felt good about my decision to follow Shotgun. I knew how these teenage hormonal rushes, which for the moment kidnapped the man's man Curt we knew and loved, cause a dangerous stupidity and a deafness to reason in most male adolescents. They reduce a man to a whispered whimper, a pussy whipped antisocial mama's boy, a servant or taxi driver for some cock tease girl. Not that we all don't enjoy it, until the fog on the rear view mirror clears up, and we see no one in the back seat. A man shrinks to listen to a woman's interminable whimsical chatter, and nothing but complete and constant approval preserves her affection. Otherwise, the boy drives aimless through the night until she disappears. He drives on, feels rejected, jilted, cheated on, despised, used, and manipulated.

An older man once told me that every boy must come of age, and turn off that rainy street to nowhere with a mean woman, get on the expressway alone, and find that place near the state line where boys with emotional damaged go to buy a ticket to become a man, the adult bookstore.

What did I, the fatherless one, know about women?

Perhaps God plans it so every man could meet a girl worth the dedication of a man's life, all his energy, time, love and money. Maybe once a lifetime, with one compatible girl.

When?

Maybe Curt should follow his instincts, which scientists surmise exist on a cellular level, imprinted on the male genetic code, a strategy of procreative success through survival of the fastest and swiftest, which equals fitness, play the field, juggle various seductions at the same time, infiltrate other couple's relationships to mate poach, cheat if coupled, accept all opportunities for one night stands, and impregnate all of them whenever possible, and move on to the next batch.

Curt's youth prevented him from a useful appreciation of the situation. When these cinnamon skinned, almond eyed, affluent party girls looked at him, they saw an exotic blue eyed blond Surfer God from California. Perfect.

If he could convince them of his wealth, irresistible.

The Seed of Sin

Shotgun and I hurried down Panajachél's dark streets to the other address to pick up the marijuana. We asked directions, and after much confusion from people on the street who do not need or use addresses, we arrived at a modest hut made of long poles set vertical, like a rectangle fence, topped with a palm frond roof, a 'palapa'. Inside a kerosene lamp burned.

"Buenas Noche."

An old shirtless Guatemalteco, barefoot and dressed in worn dress pants, came to the flimsy bamboo door and let us in.

"Como estás, conoces este gente?" and Shotgun showed him the passport.

The old man put the passport in his back pocket. "Si, si. Como no. Me dijo que les entregara esto, muchachos." and he lifted an ornate saucer over a porceline tea cup to pull out a baggy full of dope. Shotgun examined it and complained about all the seeds, looked like fifty percent seeds.

Shotgun blasted off. "What! He told us he could get sinsemilla!"

"Sinsemilla, sinsemilla. Todos quieren sinsemilla. Sinsemilla no hay. Si quieren, quitan Uds. las semillas, entonces." The old man wrapped his arms around himself and adopted an attitude at once serious, concerned, yet not without a touch of threat. His country.

"What did he say? Shotgun asked me.

"If we want sinsemilla, we take the seeds out."

"Ask him how much this bag cost."

"Quince" the man said without prompting. "Fifteen dollars."

"Shotgun, that's not a bad price in the USA."

"Shit! He knew I wanted sinsemilla, Ask him if we can try it out."

I asked him.

Not in his little house of sticks, he said. Then he waved his hands to signify far away, please.

"Shotgun, he wants us to smoke it somewhere else."

"I gathered that." Shotgun stared down at the baggy full of seeds he paid good money for. Bad mood.

"Shotgun, you look like you're in a bad mood."

"Shit."

"One thing you gotta remember. You've got the power to change your mood right there in your hands.

"What do you mean?"

"That there's a mood altering drug."

"Well, ok. Let's go. Hope mom's happy about it! We'll clean the seeds out of it before we give it to her. Sinsemilla." He laughed at the deception.

He raised the fist that enclosed the little baggy and shook it as if angry. "Time to alter my mood."

We walked along a dark road into the Cacao plantation, and rolled a joint to smoke on the way back to the . Near the lake, we noticed our legs felt strange on the sloped pavement and cobblestones.

Shotgun said, "I forgot to tell you, I looked all over for you earlier, in that . I ran into that Frenchy Yvonne you're so stuck on."

"Stuck on?"

"Like a broken record."

"I thought you never remembered who she was!"

"You never catch on to the joke, that's all. Yeah, well she told me you went outside, then back inside. She's prettier than I remember, up close. You over her, or what?"

"Hey, nothing to get over."

"Talk to her. I talked to her easy enough."

"I didn't. Didn't see her, I guess. Couldn't walk up to her while she hangs around with those two guys. What if one gets jealous or something? If she was my girl, and walked up a mountain all alone one afternoon and came down with some guy, I'd watch out for her No place to hide on that trail. Did she say anything else? Mention any names?"

"Yes she did." Shotgun held his silence like a squirt gun full of laughter pointed at my vulnerability. I could feel him about to explode with mirth at my mfort.

"Yes she did what? Tell me, you asshole! Dink!"

"Look at this! Dink, he calls me, I'm only the messenger, don't kill me! Let's see if I remember clearly, hmmm. I believe she said you were too nice."

"Too nice."

"Yes, I'm sure that's exactly what she said."

"You know she doesn't speak English well." I lied. "She mispronounces, or said something in French you didn't understand."

"You're the one who should practice your Frenching, not me."

"What did she say?"

"What?"

"Tell me. You're pissing me off."

"Oh. Well that's different. I said hi to her as she passed on the way to the bathroom. You should try that some time, hang out by the bathroom. All girls use the bathroom at least twice an hour."

"OK, great idea. Next time. You talked to her?"

"She talked to me." Shotgun waited for a reaction. And waited. Then he continued, "Came right up to me, stopped, and said Don't you live in Santa Catarina? So I said yes, and I said you know my friend Brandon."

"Good work."

"She said He's a friend of yours, right? I said yes, and she said he's too nice, isn't he? So I said, not like me at all, and she laughed, reached up and held my chin to give me a little kiss. On the cheek. Don't get bent out of shape. Then she went into the bathroom. When she came out, she hurried by with a little wave. That's all."

As we walked, I thought about that for a long time, until I believed every word. Shotgun looked serious when he pronounced those words, as if in transmission of a coded message.

We bought some fireworks from a street vendor. The very moment we arrived at the door to the , Yvonne came out, followed by Dennis and Gary. They acted much friendlier, drunker, and stopped to shake hands and chat.

They wanted to know what we paid for the fireworks, so they could tell a good deal as it got nearer Christmas. "Better get them soon, the way these Indians love to shoot off fireworks every night." Dennis complained.

We could not find Curt inside the . The two girls he sat with earlier said he took off, after he encouraged them to stop by his place in Santa Catarina.

Shotgun and I went downtown and found him at the House of Pies a little before they closed at one. He'd finished his late night snack, but we all ordered a different flavor of pie and cut them into three pieces to sample the Californian chef's exotic concoctions.

Thus fueled for the long walk home, we took off and entertained ourselves as rowdy boys do. We ran and pushed, insulted each other and slap boxed. At one point, Curt grabbed both Shotgun and I, one in each hand, lifted us both suspended by our belts like suitcases, walked to the roadside, and threw us into the bushes.

At the cliffs over the lake, about two o'clock in the morning, Curt showed us the tied bundles of fireworks he bought. Where the road ran close to a high cliff over the lake, we lit them and threw them over the edge. The big lake swallowed the sounds like a sprinkle of rain on a hot tin roof.

Christmas Party

In one carved stela, the Mayans depicted the Milky Way as a feathered serpent from whose belly hung symbols for both lunar and solar eclipses. From those symbols and its open jaws issue the floodwaters that destroy creation. Below, an Old Woman Goddess of Death and Destruction flexes long talons on both her fingers and her toes as she empties a bowl of floodwaters. At the bottom, a Muan bird of evil omen perches on the head of a black War and Death God, whose spears and staff point downward.

As result of the sporadic meetings between various households of expatriates who lived in Santa Catarina Palopó, a plan emerged to hold a potluck Christmas celebration. For the celebration, the Canadians offered to lend their house, high up the slope above the village, as the most comfortable and scenic. There we could do whatever expatriate travelers might want to do, without so much preoccupation about the ultra conservative Mayan villagers.

The view from the house took in both the village and lake. The three of them felt at ease about entertaining a bunch of strangers because they planned to vacate the premises before the first of the year.

Curt and I made a big salad for the potluck. We filled it with avocados, cabbage, lettuce, onions and cut three varieties of raw squash into cubes. Shotgun and his mom decided not to go, and opted in favor of a nice Christmas evening at home amid the normalcy of all their other evenings. From now to then, Ida said, she might need to ground Shotgun for some deviation from her rules. After all, most boys of sixteen still peek out from under mom's wing. Curt said Ida told him once that she didn't appreciate the example of a sixteen year old who lived on his own, and that she hoped Curt would try real hard to remember that Shotgun looked up to him as a role model.

They way I saw it, Shotgun and Curt could do the same things, and whatever Shotgun did made him look like a goofy, skinny kid while Curt did the same thing and looked like a big mature responsible guy in a silly mood, and if anyone didn't approve, either Curt's hairless squeaky clean wholesomeness or his gargantuan proportions convinced them to shut up about it.

We arrive early and noticed that the Canadians' landlord stood nearby with his family, as if to demonstrate humility and servility, at least to those of us who arrived first. They lived nearby, and came dressed in their usual pajama style village uniform. His three elementary age boys, all very polite and well behaved, watched us for about ten minutes, with scared monkey half smiles, from in between their father's trouser legs. Once accustomed to our presence, they ran around the corner of the house.

Dennis said they knew about the party. Maybe they want to protect their property.

Then the father reached into his paper bag of fireworks and showed them to Dennis, who declined to buy them. No, no, not for sale. Through sign language, he promised to give us all a fireworks display, Mayan style.

We waited for others to arrive, and chatted as best we could with him. He questioned us to make sure all the guests arrived to see his show. "Todos?"

As the lasts guests brought in their bowls of food, Dennis warned us all to line up against the house because "the landlord's pyrotechnic display begins in five minutes."

We looked at him, confused expressions on our face.

"I'm serious, folks. If you value your health, put your back against the house." He'd seen this show before, several times in the last couple of days.

As we gathered next to the house, the Indian man reached into his brown paper bag and pulled out a wad of firecrackers. Then he bummed a cigarette from Dennis and used its coal to light a common fuse to a handful of firecrackers. He held onto it almost too long, then threw the bunch so it started to explode right over our heads.

In a flash, all the Gringos hugged the wall under the house's tin roof overhang. The first few air born explosions sent lit firecrackers in all directions, on the house roof, in the grass and dirt in front of us, and down the grassy, tinder dry slope.

The children ran under the explosions as if through rain, and relished the excitement when firecrackers landed on them. Terrified, they brushed them off with explosive mirth, or tried to bat them out of the air with their little bare hands. Firecrackers exploded by their ears, and they reacted to the ring of tinnitus as if mosquitoes attacked their ear.

The man hurled bundle after bundle of firecrackers up into the air to explode in machine gun bursts of staccato that echoed off the canyon walls above the village. Cascades of sparks and explosions rained down around the Indian man and kids. They giggled at our fearful expressions, and mocked us. They acted incredulous, as if they could not believed we never saw fireworks before. Our terrified behavior convinced them, as we cowered under the eaves, backs pressed against the wall, of our unfamiliarity with these smallest caliber firecrackers.

His children ran in circles around small grass fires until their father stamped them out.

We hugged the wall and talked about how we expected someone to get hurt, burned, or worse, a grassfire, as the landlord's giddy laughter, inspired by the antics of his children, made him more and more careless in his display of bravery.

He spun himself around with his eyes covered to throw firecrackers with blind abandon. We cringed into each other's arms and painted our bodies against the wall.

The show stopped. The father relaxed, smoked his cigarette. No one hurt, but I thought ears might ring for days, maybe till death. The children reached into the brown paper bag again and again, in a stupid and hopeful search, controlled by magic thinking, they expected more firecrackers to appear at any moment.

As the family left, the father's hands rose to tip his sombrero rim toward us. We saluted back in kind, as best we could without cowboy hats. The family smiled and beamed as we shuffled about and pretended to feel excited about the fireworks. They showed us a good time, and strutted proud as if they proved their superiority.

We breathed a collective sigh of relief as they disappeared.

A half hour later, we twelve sat down to eat. The sun dropped from a glorious red sky toward the ocean, and hid somewhere below our volcanic horizon to send shafts of golden light between the volcanoes which streaked the clouds high over our heads. The light tinged to orange, then painted the bottom of the clouds with crimson fire. From our high vantage point, the lake reflected clouds and sky, as the winds churned the surface colors into a mosaic of visual echoes.

I met real Germans for the first time. The party attracted three of them, each traveled alone.

One man tried to ruin the sunset.

A German loner, dressed in mixed elements of colorful traditional garments from around the world, embarked on a relentless effort to convince us of Afghanistan's supremacy as the most beautiful place in the world. Whatever he said sounded like "My life, which I share with you all now, should interest and fascinate you not because I lived it, but because of the way I will tell you in your own language with my vonderbar German accent. And the way I tell you, succinct and artful as I only I know how to tell you, if you listen carefully, you come to the inescapable conclusion that your life doesn't amount to squat compared to mine."

I doubt if we demonstrated the appropriate level of gratitude to appease his sense of personal worth. I snuck away from the crowd to write a few notes in a cute little pink booklet I used to keep a journal. This night I hoped to fill a substantial section about these young world travelers in Paradise.

As we all helped build a small campfire outside, a scorpion broke cover from the woodpile. We surrounded it and tapped it with our shoes until it weakened enough for someone to pick it up with a pincer made from a broken stick. A rare and wonderful display of collective primate curiosity motivated us to work as a team and defeat the danger to the clan. I don't believe many of us acted out of fear, or any discernible group goal beyond a vague notion, an instinctual appreciation, that one scorpion on a stick beats thousands in your shoes.

The well traveled German, whom we wished to transport to Afghanistan as soon as possible, ended up with the long end of the scorpion's stick. I tried to get closer, for a brief examination of the scorpion, a bug which I'd never seen before. I begged him not to throw it away but to pass it over and let me get a good look at it, but he ignores me as I follow him, and walks to the yard's edge to throw my scorpion down the canyon into the brush. Big hero, my savior, what an ass.

I wanted to pretend to stumble, give him a little bump and push him over too. Maybe I should continue to 'stumble' and manage to roll a couple of large rocks after him for good measure.

Some of the travelers started a vacuous conversation about the absolute superlative nature of the current sunset, with a sly sarcasm of a shared joke as we tried to drown out the endless stories about Afghanistan. And so we invented an antidote to this dictatorial Nazi of Tourism.

When he received our subliminal message, he stalked off a little ways to poke at the ground with his stick. We watched the sunset in blessed silence, and passed a couple of joints around with caution, in case the landlord's family lurked nearby.

After a smoke, I stole off a ways in the tall grasses and sat down, hidden, to write my observations in my little book in the last echoes of daylight. A breeze of chill mountain air convinced me to head inside.

The Canadians instructed us to carry our paper plates and plastic utensils to "the fireplace", a place in the corner where a fire pit kept the food hot.

As we ate, another new face, a 35 year old German man, recounted his adventures around the globe. He explained this passage through Guatemala represented the midpoint of his latest sojourn, a tour of The Americas from Patagonia north along the continental divides.

He planned to drive his 'Panamanian' Motorcycle into the United States of North America, then through Canada to Alaska, then return to Germany. There, he works in his Artist's Studio, and selects photos of people and places from his trip to draw and paint at his liesure. He then takes his drawings and paintings and plies the lecture circuits around Germany.

Imagine his popularity in the Europe's Society Clubs, an egocentric artist who spouts Goethe and Bob Dylan with a cold, precise Germanic superiority. Wagnerian furies whine and wail in the background of his mental slideshows, as he draws pictures with words, and drags the hidden Third World's harpies out into the light to reveal them as forces of ignorance, an illiterate Good and Evil. He claims these societies deserve the governments they get. "They shoot themselves in the foot when things get good, and investors run away."

He kept sketches rolled up in a couple of cardboard tubes, and he brought a tube full to the party to show us some of the fruits of his labor. Not bad. He also takes thousands of photos to fill in the details while back home in his German studio.

After dinner, a curious me catches him alone, outside, at the campfire. I ask him if he's married.

He looks me over, as if to reach a decision about whether I'm gay, then shrugs it off and says "A girl came with me on half of this trip through South America."

"German girl?"

"I met her in Germany, Dutch woman, and we left there together, but her family comes from Austria. Raised in Hungary."

"Where did she go?"

"She got tired of the traveling, and wanted to go home for a while. These modern women, you can't find a good one, and if you do, you can't get her to agree to stay home anymore." He picked up a stick and poked the red hot, ash covered coals. He laughed. "I've learned that women keep two sticks in the fire. Maybe more."

"Why didn't you go back to Germany with her?"

"Not an option. I plan these trips too carefully, everything in order. The distance traveled and the time it takes to complete makes my journeys extraordinary. I cut my own throat if I make little trips. No one cares about things everybody can do."

"How long have you been on the road?"

"About ten months and thirteen days. And I worry this trip will be too short if it takes two years out of my life."

He also attempted to monopolize the conversation, like the German jerk that loved Afghanistan and threw my scorpion over the cliff. So alike, I suspected congenital factors.

"Are there a lot of people like you and the other German traveler in Germany? You two seem like twins."

"In Germany, we get long vacations. Each worker gets about four weeks of vacation a year, and many Germans save their weeks from year to year to travel for a month or more. Few as successful as I, of course."

"What makes you a success?"

"Most Germans fear excellence and pride. They became timid and apologetic, you know. We Germans must get over this ridiculous guilt about the Jews. Genocides happen throughout human history, nothing special or unusual about ours. Germans didn't invent genocide, and genocides still go on, everyday in some part of the world. The biggest genocides happened in North America, Africa, and China. Germans do not deserve such vilification alone, you know. The whole world should appreciate how thoroughly we industrialized the process. Nobody committed genocide as efficiently as we Germans."

Inside, the jerk that likes Afghanistan so much started a demonstration of the fine points of New Guinea tribal dancing. He acted as if he heard our most private inner voice, How can I learn? Where should I go?

He made a total ass out of himself, all of us knew it, and many comments suggested as much. He ignored them and continued his duty to provide us with cultural enlightenment. We tried to enjoy it for the theater of an overweight German who thought he danced like an aboriginal native. By the time he caught on that no one would join him in his impromptu folk dance anytime soon, he could find no graceful way out, and his embarrassment mutated into anger at us.

He mumbled and stammered, shocked by the depth of our ignorance and mean spirit at Christmas, then blamed us, people like us he said, for all evil in the known universe, and then stomped out the door and into the night.

Through the doorway, I caught a glimpse of him as he strode fast down the grassy slope in the light of a half moon. Thought I could see a thundercloud around his head, music with lightning bolt Beethoven chords that jabbed and blotted at his halo.

What sweet torture, to suffer such under appreciation. Happens to the best of us all the time, I imagine. Pearls before swine and all that.

I turned back to our party, and tried not to fixate on Yvonne. I tried to avoid her, not look her way, and not betray my base interested in her. Neither of us talked much to the others. Once I thought she looked too long at me.

I talked with a young couple from Oregon, and maneuvered myself so that I could glance past them to keep my eyes on Yvonne.

The woman from Oregon caught on, and turned to see who captured my interest so.

"The French girl?" She said. "Well you're not alone in that." and she elbowed her companion.

Another couple, a woman and a man, came late, and darkened the doorway with such hesitancy that it created a moment of breathless, paranoid drama.

Later, when the man started a conversation with two young, chubby female backpackers from an Iowa college, it gave me an opportunity to followed my interest in his partner, an American girl who looked familiar.

Over the past month, we met a couple of times in the Sololá market, chatted a total of maybe fifteen minutes, but here we greeted each other like Hispanic cousins, with a hug, a cheek kiss, and three pats on the back.

She laughed, looked around, saw her boyfriend's back as he talked to another couple, and then she pulled and pushed me towards the door to sneak me outside. To avoid problems, she said.

We stood on the grassy slopes under a sky that swirled with the Milky Way and got to know each other.

She explained how she lived with her current boyfriend in small motor home, but she first entered Mexico a few months ago with another rich man in a much larger motor home. She tried to convince me it took her by surprise, to ver that her surrogate daddy thought he deserved an affectionate return on his investment of hospitality expenses, the three months of transportation, food, gifts, and occasional shared hotel rooms to cut costs. I laughed at her, asked her if the hotel rooms came with champagne and room service, and she said yes. She sounded proud that she strung him along all the way down Baja California to ferry over to Mazatlán, then through central Mexico, right up until Mexico City, where she managed, with tact and artful histrionics, to weasel from him a fair sum of money to 'travel back home with' in her state of emotional crises.

What state did she hail from?

Alaska, she told him. Needed airfare. So she saved her honor and acquired a little money to burn. She soon headed south though, and conquered her current boyfriend in the Yucatán. They planned to continue south to Venezuela, where he hoped to work with geophysical teams that prospect for oil reserves.

We went back into the house at different times, like lovers who hide an affair, though we never kissed. We might as well have. I perceived openness to a kiss, telepathic communication a few times that created clumsy moments when she tugged on my shirt, or lost herself with dilated pupils as she bit her lip. Maybe she ovulated at that moment. Could've stolen a kiss if I wanted to. Yeah, I wondered what I would do if she acted a little more innocent, or at least honorable, so I wouldn't get my guard up and think her either mercenary or a mere manipulator of men for the fun of it, to feel power.

I, as a proud, young, callow cad, knew that either a higher percentage of bare skin or more prominent frontal protuberances would easily sway me. The blouse's topmost button stayed latched. She could have offered that small token in a gesture of openness.

Dennis fed the fire and it danced high like orange and yellow crepe paper, and roared back at the chill night air that streamed invisible through the open doorway.

Gary suggested he eat some fire, and Dennis laughed it off.

But Gary persisted, and forced Dennis to tell us all about his work in the circuses that travel across Canada and the northern United States of North America. In one of his more recent duties, he worked as a helper for a sword swallower magician.

"Do the nail trick, Dennis! Show them the nail trick!" Gary and Yvonne egged him on.

"Ok, ok. Somebody find me a nail. Not too big, not too small." Then as people presented nails for his inspection, he rejected most as too small. "I can't believe you can't find a nail in here big enough."

"Big enough for what?" Many asked, intrigued. "What's he do with it?"

Gary said, "Watch this." And pointed to Dennis, who stood in the center of the room.

Dennis produced a huge nail from his coat pocket and smiled deviously. "I just happen to have this with me. I've saved this nail all year long, for this very night." he kissed it and looked at us, then chortled a demonic laugh.

The nail measured about four inches long, shiny, clean, and straight.

Dennis showed the nail from all angles, beat it on a rock to prove it a solid metallic object, and said, "What do you say I push this up my nose?"

We laughed

Then he took hold of the flathead end and aimed the pointed end straight and level at the center of his face and pushed it, then retreated, pushed again toward his nose and retreated, to build up suspense.

We all booed and hissed.

Then he demanded quiet, and faced the fire, held his chin up so that his under lit face contrasted against his own shadow on the adobe wall. Then he pushed the horizontal nail into his face, perpendicular, into one nostril, buried it to the nail's head.

He spun around so that we could all see the trick's lack of a trick.

The trick hit home with the realization that no trick existed. He turned to look right at each of us, and then showed us his profile. About an half inch of the nail stuck out of his head from his nostril.

Hysterical with laughter, we asked him to pull it out slow and let us examine it. He did, falsely demure, as he wiped the nail off with his shirt and handed it over.

The chubby backpacker girls scrambled for it first, convinced of some mechanical trick, and squealed "Oh my God!" as they handed each other an ordinary large nail.

"This trick depends on a little known fact about the nose. The nasal passages that lead to the sinuses and throat go pretty much straight into the head, not upwards, as we tend to believe from the shape of the nose. Watch closely now."

He turned to show us his profile and pushed the nail into his left nostril, buried again. He turned to looked at us, and we laughed again.

"Let me try!" Some reached out for the spike.

"I'm not responsible for any nosebleeds, remember. Use smaller nails at first. Make sure they don't end in a sharp point. Wipe them clean, and push them in careful, careful, maybe with a little spin. Lubricant up there helps, so don't blow your nose. I'm serious. Look for an open passage, don't force it. If you feel the point stop against tissue, try the other nostril."

"Oh, come on!"

"Serious. The nostrils open and close, each one opens for about six hours at a time. It will tickle and feel funny at first, you might even sneeze."

Sure enough, those of us that tried it found an air passage straight back into the head, not angled upward.

A half hour later, the good food, wine, and rare air at this elevation took its toll, we yawned at each other, and the fires died down as no one moved to get more firewood.

As soon as someone decided to depart, everyone concurred and stood up to go. We said Merry Christmas to each other at the door, and separated toward our temporary homes on trails lit by the relative permanence of the Milky Way and other far flung galaxies of deep space.

Celestial Snake Monster

The human mind seeks patterns in everything, in history, in personal behavior and ritual, in the habits of animals and the growth of plants, in the random swirls of stars across the sky it invents the Constellations. What looks like stars to us, mere points of light, upon magnification contain entire galaxies larger than ours.

The Mayans saw our Milky Way galaxy as a serpent, arched across the heavens, that swallows the souls of the recent dead, of the cursed, of the recent sacrifices, and the soul of any Shaman who dares to enter a portal to the sky. Used as a decorative motif on many buildings and artifacts, this Celestial Snake Monster, as carved by the Mayan artisans of the Classic period, appears as serpentine vertebrae with two heads, one to swallow the sun at sunset, and one to disgorge it at sunrise.

From what I wrote down at dusk, almost illegible, people's reactions to the sunset made me think about cosmology.

"The eye loves sunsets like the tongue loves candy. Sunsets feed our need for beauty and rest, a survival mechanism like the tongue's taste for sugar. People see the sunset as a goodbye to the daylight, to conscious life, and it becomes a symbol of life's temporary passage. Evolution might favor creatures that take pleasure from the color changes of sunrise and sunset. Crepuscular changes of habitat, diurnal and nocturnal, mesh in the sunsets and sunrises, when those two groups of predators and prey intermingle to inhabit the earth for twelve hours."

I also remembered to write a couple of reminders. "Need toilet paper and dental floss, oranges and peanuts. Should I buy a bicycle?"

My notes continue. "When the daylight softens, the pupil opens up, and the world appears with a shorter depth of field. Focus on something near and the background blurs. As the sunlight on clouds passes from white to yellow, orange, and then red, the sun appears to expand due to the thick lens of atmosphere near the horizon, red light rays bend the most, as the sun sinks into the horizon to become a pinprick of hot reddish orange for an instant, then disappears.

"The earth's gravity affects the red rays of the visible spectrum because they're less energetic, so they bend and curve through the gravitational field, like a lens, around the earth. We look at a red sun on the horizon, but in reality it already lies beyond the line of sight, set and sunk, below the horizon. The red light rays give us an instant replay of the immediate past.

"After the sun sets, the eye's iris yawns open like a person in love, like an owl's eye, all black pupil with a slim ring of color, the doorway to the mind. The ground gives up that day's solar radiation as heat, infrared vibrations of photons, as the stored energy from the rainbow frequencies of sunlight becomes the chaos of heat in low level radiation, and random molecular motion.

"A cold wind blows over these Guatemalan highlands. Invisible planets fade into bright spots in the purpled firmament, soon surrounded by the shards of a cold, crystal matrix of stars. Billions of stars salt the night sky. Those bright stars outside the Milky Way represent galaxies larger than our Milky Way, filled with trillions of stars and views of other galaxies, each of which spins through clouds and gasses of the vacuum, each with its supernovas and black holes. We, as the eyes of the universe, see how it arranges itself in layers and levels of organization. The earth seems smaller than the smallest piece of dust, itself an infinite number of potential subatomic particles and positions."

With overcast skies, the three volcanoes wear little cloud hats that swirl and change, grow long tails that stretch the width of the lake and beyond, far over our heads. Sometimes the clouds reflect red light underneath, as if from a lava lake inside the volcano.

Some tourists climb the volcanoes with Indian guides to see their craters. Dangerous. Not only because of the steep trail through unstable ground, or the chance of volcanic activity, but stories circulate about how criminals rob, beat, or rape tourists along the way. Some say plenty of tourists disappear and nobody ever hears about it.

One night I watched the sunset behind the volcanoes and it struck me how people say, in hushed tones, that Guatemalans disappear all the time, and nobody cares. Disappearances happen all over the world, all the time. We all share the sin of that criminal negligence when we do not protect each other's human rights. Maybe we also share the duty to protect each creature's right to exist and enjoy the pleasures of life, even domesticated animals raised for food, and beasts of burden.

Maybe it doesn't make logical sense, but I felt it as I watched that volcanic sunset, and recognized the Mayan village as an ark of humanity in case of flood. I never forgot.

One night, that same night perhaps, in this Christmas season, I woke to the sound of many voices, an insistent choral, loud, and chanted in time to buzzy rhythm instruments, like tambourines made out of rattlesnake tails.

I lay in my sleeping bag on the chocolate powder sandy dirt of the floor inside my little adobe shoebox of a house, and fixed my stare into a vortex of colored blackness. The sound grew louder, came closer, a torrent of echoes of voices and a battalion of footsteps that crunch across loose rock crunch. The sounds grew stronger, and came up from the village center on the trail to my house.

Then it sounded like a big crowd of people entered my yard.

I jumped out of the sleeping bag naked, put on my trousers and shirt, pushed my bare feet into my unlaced boots, and ran to the window.

I whipped it open in time to see, by the moonlight as they passed in front of the house, a long parade of morose Indians in a ponderous march up the trail. The procession extended as far as I could see, not far in neither direction due to the switchbacks. West towards the village, the trail dropped out of sight. Eastward, it wound up the mountain slope and bent around the house of the blind woman who sang when she hung her washed clothing on the bushes to dry.

Nobody glanced left or right. The whole village must turn out for these midnight events. Then came seven or eight Indian men, heads bent as if to watch each footfall on the rocky trail, who bore a heavy litter made of two beams of pine log that supported a platform. In the middle of the platform sat a wedding cake in a circle of candles which allowed me to see it rested upon another miniature construction, a long church, or a baby's casket.

The candle flames played tricks with the light, cast grotesque, spidery crab shadows of the exotic plants to dance across the whitewashed walls of houses.

The procession made its way up through the trail's rock steps and boulders, turned the corner, and out of sight. Over the next twenty minutes, the chant grew distant, quieter, and mixed with its own echo, as the footfalls diminished, became soft as moonlight, and then disappeared.

The cold beans and cold tortillas brought to me each morning by the boney slim Indian girl, Rosa, the daughter of my landlord, often churned my innards in an intestinal pillage that ravaged my guts. The food sped through my system with an immediacy that challenged me to light a cigarette as I hurried to the outhouse, the little flimsy structure tacked onto the rear of the house. I sat there, under some bush with balled explosions of leaves like thick grass, with the crude plank door open, to enjoy a view of the volcanoes and a bit of the lake over the neighbor's roofs.

I treated all my drinking water from the village's fountain with 'purifying' chemicals, either military issue white pills or iodine tablets, both bought from an Army Navy surplus store in Michigan.

I decided to stop Rosa's breakfast deliveries.

The problem cleared up in a few days, and later, I found a medicine in the pharmacy in Panajachél, which I took a slug of before I ate, which I imagined annihilated the little bacteria that tried to make a meal out of my intestines and my food, and poison me with their toxins in the process.

I decided that everyone in Latin America must suffer in secret the traveler's diarrhea called Moctezuma's Revenge, the malady that afflicts even the affluent in four star hotels. I heard that the immune system overreacts to new benign bacteria where ever you go. Without systems of sanitation and waste water removal, bacteria causes health problems for everybody. No wonder so many people seemed underweight and unhealthy and didn't live long, with all the filth, poor hygiene, lack of health care and quarantines, lack of sewage systems, and drainages that overflow into the streets with each heavy rain.

At twenty two, I didn't appreciate that many common bacteria, spread by poor hygiene and unpurified water, cause diarrhea and disease that kills millions of babies each year.

The best goal in life becomes the rarest of undeserved gifts, and escapes the notice of the majority of us with deceptive simplicity. We should all enjoy the great luck to survive to a very old age, with lots of friends and great, great grandchildren.

Each day swept by with glorious weather that changed every hour, a visual feast, and I accomplished nothing. I felt supercharged, like an explorer on another planet. Too much to see, to learn, to read about. I still couldn't speak enough Spanish, and could see my competency recede into the distant future with each new realization of the difficulties.

At first, I spent time with Shotgun, most often on days when he ran out of grass and we put our swimsuits on under our khaki shorts and visited Curt's house to read books. Shotgun learned to swim to save his life, but it took too long to convince him to take that first jump into the cold waters. The boy's skinny frame needed insulation. The cold reached his bones right under his shirt. His teeth chattered a little before mine did, but Curt didn't get cold.

Inside Curt's house, I sat where I could look out the doorway. Whenever anyone passed, I looked out and hoped to see Yvonne, alone.

One afternoon I did see her, and I thought it a miracle, even though everyone in town must walk by Curt's place since it's right there in the middle of the only road, in front of both church and fountain, near the store, with a view of the dock.

I saw someone swim in the lake, and realized how I tried to convince myself that those three left Santa Catarina right after Christmas. She swam into the shallows, then stood up in thigh deep waters to shake a spray of droplets out of her hair. She walked towards shore along the dock's pillars, where her bikini spread like black paint as it merged with each vertical shadow.

I put my book aside and walked out the door without a word. Behind me, I could hear Shotgun ask Curt "Where's he going?" and I imagined Curt's wide shouldered shrug. Then I heard a loud "Oh, no!" and I turned around a couple of times to see them both drag their chairs to the doorway to claim the best view.

When I looked back again, they fought over possession of Curt's binoculars.

She walked out to the end of the dock and lay down. The gusty breezes blew through her wet black hair and moved the thick cotton cords that tied her bikini top across her shoulder blades.

My footsteps resonated in the dock's dry gray wood. She sat up with one hand to her forehead and shielded her eyes from the sun as she stared at my approach.

After we said hello, I feigned a casualness I didn't feel and started to strip down to my swimsuit.

I asked her "Feel like another dip?"

"I'm not warm yet. This wind, it makes the sunlight cold if you are wet, and I'm almost dry. Enjoy your swim." She laid back down, chin on her hands.

"If you feel cold, you should move around. Come swim with me. You get used to it if you swim, because once you get in, it feels..."

"Cold."

"Very cold." I laughed. "But you feel cold here too."

She closed her eyes, and I noticed how the sunlight caressed her long curves and drew a black shadow outline around her.

I sat on the dock's edge to dangle my legs. "I need the exercise. If I swim hard, I stay warm." The morning sun shone white, so bright it hurt, and the humidity paled the three volcanoes. "I thought you left already."

"I did. We left together, but I came back. I wanted to stay here longer. They didn't want to listen to me, because I'm only a woman."

"I don't want to leave either."

"I wanted to say goodbye to this place in my own way."

"What way?"

"I can't explain very well, but I must find a way to say goodbye to Santa Catarina so we will remember each other forever."

She sat up and looked around. Her body flexed with electric intensity when her muscles tightened against the chill air. She lay down on her back, closed her eyes, and arched her back. She stretched out her arms and made fists, then stretched each of her muscular legs. She swiveled each foot in little circles and a hint of washboard musculature appeared on her flat stomach. She inhaled deeply, then laid the backs of her hands over her eyes and relaxed, lithe and supple, a bronze cipher against the gray weathered boards.

A few moments later, she reached out and grabbed her purse, rummaged through it, and pulled out a bottle of tanning lotion and threw it to me. It skidded to a halt against my thigh.

I stared at it a couple of seconds, then said to her, "No thanks, I don't use that stuff. Too greasy."

She sat up, put her elbows on the towel. "You don't understand. It's not for you. Put it on me."

"OK. Where do I start? Front or back?"

With a half smile, she rolled onto her stomach and said, "Do a good job on my back, we'll talk about the front later. OK?"

I sat on my heels, poured a dollop of white grease that smelled like coconut into one palm, rubbed my hands together, and massaged her back. I looked towards the village, and saw Curt and Shotgun, in doorway of the house, engaged in a violent tug of war over the binoculars.

I didn't want Yvonne to see them. "Could you turn a little more towards the lake?"

She moaned and rocked under my hands. "Why? So I won't notice your childish friends?"

Curt and Shotgun could see my face and she couldn't, so I rolled my eyes and head, and otherwise made orgiastic gestures of ecstasy, and they about fell over each other with laughter.

"Is Dennis your boyfriend?"

"I don't know. Why do you ask?" she said.

"Self preservation, I guess. He's not violent, is he?"

"Don't worry. He doesn't own me. Nobody owns anybody."

"I used to think like that, before Guatemala."

"If he gets upset, his problem. We'll split up soon anyway."

"Why? Back to France?"

"Not right away. I travel with Dennis and Gary, but things change, sometimes not fast enough."

"You love him?"

She grunted.

I poured out some more of the white, slimy, partially hydrogenated oil and wondered, should I start with the thighs or the calves? How close should I come to her round buttocks?

I massaged one leg, my hand cupped underneath the front to massage front and back simultaneously. "Where do you go next?"

"To San Jose on the Pacific Coast. You know the place?"

"Never heard of it."

"It's on the map. You do have a map, don't you?" She turned over to sit and look into my eyes. "Want to swim?"

"You've got sunscreen on only half your body. You'll tan like a circus clown."

She pulled my hand into both of hers and looked back towards the village. "Your friends with the binoculars."

She stood up, pulled me up, and took a wide step sideways and began to do some stretches, bent over or half turned into graceful birdlike positions, her back arched into an impossible swayback. Her arms moved like rubber over her head, movements of classical Hindu dance or Gypsy Flamenco, her head thrown back. She stopped to look at me, then looked toward the village where Shotgun and Curt still tugged at the binoculars. "Twelve years of dance classes. Oh look, Here they come. Like clockwork."

Dennis and Gary, towels in their hands, walked the trail that led down from their house.

She looked at me with her half smile, "How do you feel? Here comes my lover and his faithful dog."

"You can handle them, right?"

She scrutinized me. "We'll see. Maybe I finish the break up here, on this lovely dock in Santa Catarina. Good way to say goodbye, no?" She glanced at their progress through the village. "He tries so hard not to understand. Let's swim."

She walked to the dock's edge, her hands on her hips, and stared down into the water a couple of seconds. Gusts of wind made her waver in place to the sounds of birds and the clunk of a sodden wooden paddle against the side of a dugout canoe, the sizzle and slap of waves that brushed along the near shore.

Yvonne took three quick steps backward then ran forward and jumped into a high, smooth arch and like an arrow, shot beneath the waves to disappear without much splash. She stayed under a long time, surfaced quite a ways out, and continued to swim away, out into the lake.

I ran to the edge of the dock and without a stop, dove in and swam underwater as long as I could. I surfaced and swam freestyle until I caught up with her.

We floated on our backs, our faces islands in the water, at rest upon the heave of swells. I felt her brush against me. Then she grabbed my arm and we sat up to tread water together.

We watched Dennis and Gary back on the dock, as they undressed down to their swimsuits.

She spoke soft, in short gasps, conspiratorial.

"You swim fast. Caught up to me, easily."

"Breath control. A child could do it, with eighteen years practice."

She laughed. "Come to San Jose. Look for me there."

"Why? To share your interpersonal disaster, or what?"

"I'll be alone by then. I don't like to play games."

"How long will you stay there?"

"I don't know. I don't plan anything right now." She held on to my arm underwater, as a secret token of affection. "I want to see more of you, that's all."

"There's precious little of me you haven't seen. This must be the smallest Speedo in Guatemala."

"I go tonight, or tomorrow, now that I've done what I wanted to do."

"What?"

"Say goodbye to Santa Catarina." She smiled and then laughed at me. "Let's go back to the dock before I get rescued by those two!"

Dennis and Gary dove from the dock as we swam in together.

We swam up to them. She said hi, then ignored them and led me on a long breaststroke through the weedy shallows, then a walk to the shore. I helped Yvonne up onto the tall dock. After she dried off with her towel, she threw it to me and said, "So your teeth stop chattering."

"Enjoy your swim?" a male voice came out of nowhere.

We looked around and saw Dennis and Gary tread water underneath the dock.

Yvonne said, "Very much, thank you."

She reached out and held on to me for balance while she slipped on her sandals.

I called down to them. "I thought you all left Atitlán days ago."

"We went sightseeing. We go for good tomorrow." Gary announced.

"You can rent our house, if you're interested." Dennis added.

"Yes, the best location in Santa Catarina. I may look into that." I lied, and put on my clothes.

Yvonne ignored all of us, lay down, and rubbed oil onto the leg I'd neglected.

The silence felt awkward, so I said "Well, I've got to go."

No one said anything.

As I left, I wished them a good trip, and Yvonne looked up at me with the vacant gaze of her black sunglasses to say, "Bon Voyage" and blew me a kiss.

I noticed the absence of Curt and Shotgun in the doorway.

Later I thought about what Yvonne said. She didn't say goodbye, but Bon Voyage, Have a Nice Trip, as if in challenge, a dare, a final enticement to take her up on her invitation.

If I followed her, I might fall on my face.

Have a nice trip.

Machete Attack

Shotgun and mom Ida discussed with Curt about why Indians in the village crossed themselves, like good Catholics, when Shotgun looked at them. They repeated for my benefit what happened a few nights ago, when Shotgun and his mother walked alone on the road from Panajachél.

Three Indian men, dressed in the style of Santa Catarina Palopó walked toward Panajachél along the road. As they came alongside Shotgun and his mom, the men pulled machetes, faces contorted with snarls of hate, and said things unintelligible to the Gringos.

One broadsided Shotgun's ass with a machete, gave him a good slap. When Ida and Shotgun ran away, the men chased them down the road, with no laughter.

I asked Curt if he ever heard of similar problems in the village, and he said no. His parents employed villagers to construct and maintain their house, and the villagers offered to look out for Curt when his parents left. He said the Mayans thought Curt brought luck to the village, as if oversize adolescent white boys possessed mystic spiritual powers.

"Never had any problems here." Curt said. "I feel like the white giant, the King of the Valley, and I'm only sixteen years old. No problem. Back in

California, I got problems. Assholes want to beat me up all the time, because I'm so big."

Shotgun and mom Ida thought they better vacate Santa Catarina sooner than later. "We've been through this before," Ida said. "I bet the men discuss Shotgun's sexuality, and it only confuses them more."

"Confuses Shotgun, too." Curt said.

Ida continued, "Maybe someone paid them to scare us. The wrong people already know where we live. I feel like we're being watched where ever we go."

I said, "I may forfeit of my last few days of rent to head off for San Jose."

"Why? This has nothing to do with you."

"It's not that," I shrugged. "I would love to help in any way I can, but something's come up. I should depart tomorrow."

Shotgun chimed in. "Something's come up, in a bikini perhaps? It's amazing how a handful of suntan lotion will change your plans, and your friends, no?"

They tried to convince me to stay. "You can't leave on New Years Eve. We have to toast the new, out with the old, and all that."

After I described part of my conversation with Yvonne, they accepted the hopelessness of their argument.

As I walked home, I smelled the wood fire smoke and listened to the peaceful tranquility of a village without cars, where the wind whispered through tall grasses and rustled thick leaves and dried palm fronds, insects buzzed past the ear every once in a while, and from a distance, the inquisitive yelps of young dogs.

He who hesitates may not always lose, but a lost opportunity haunts forever. When the fickle finger of opportunity prods a vertebrae or two, the luckiest recognize it and anyone with any backbone should jump up to confront their fate.

Everyone truly alive wants to walk up to the edge of a precipice to look down and fantasize their fall.

It angers me when people won't look. They run from nature, their own human nature, the same nature that supports and surrounds us with unappreciated beauty and glory. Too many people feel terror alone in nature, like young children who fantasize bogeymen at night. In the deep woods, they can't feel the cathedral of nature, the shafts of light where insects hover like angels. In the desolate arid expanses, they think a poisonous viper waits in every shadow, and in the rare silence of night, they fear their own imagination.

People who fear travel, who fear the unknown, can never know themselves. We all begin life happy as puppies, then we mature as things kick that stuff out of us. Traditions help people control each other, let us ignore fundamental truths; about our origins, sex, the segregation of us into classes, the greed that motivates versions histories and wars between nations. Instead, society instructs people to self censor themselves into parodies of the neighborhood cliché. They do not know when to laugh unless others laugh first, and that destroys their curiosity and makes education impossible. After that, they rely on superstitions, magic thoughts, and the judgmental, gossipy brainwash of their neighbors.

With so little time left for me in Santa Catarina, it inspired me to take advantage of the day and walk south, to the next Indian village along the lake. The path's two tracks proved that cars went this way, but the long grasses spoke volumes about how few did.

When I came into the village of Santo Tomás, I noticed the poverty much more than in Santa Catarina. The houses needed repair, the plants around the houses needed water, and someone needed to remove the bloated, rotten carcass of a dog, swollen like a hairy sausage, that lay on the beach of wet sand.

I noticed a small hand painted sign that said Restaurant, and turned down a foot trail that led toward the lake. A European man mixed cement to apply to a strange structure built over a twenty foot cliff. He would build his dream hotel here, with a little diving board cemented onto the rock above a deep round caldron, the remains of a lava tube carved into the lakeshore. He came from Poland, and married a Guatemalan woman with family in this village.

He offered me a meal of beans and tortillas, because by Thursdays, he ran out of supplies until Sololá's market day on Friday. As I ate, the village children surrounded me. They looked dirty and disheveled, their clothing torn and worn. Most of the girls carried a handful of pulseras of woven cotton, and demanded that I try them on, and buy some. The man tried to run them off, shoo them away, but they laughed and spit at him.

I took out my camera to take a picture, and they said Capiche? Capiche? with a hand held out for money. I tried to take a picture of them, but they would hide their faces and put up a finger and yell No, no. They want the money first.

When they realized I would not buy either pulseras nor photographic rights, they insulted me, and told me "Usted es malo, muy malo." They thought me a bad person.

I couldn't get away from that village soon enough. After I ate, I bought some water from the Polish man and walked back toward Santa Catarina.

The sound of machine gun fire assaulted my peaceful reverie as I walked along the deserted gravel road high above the lake. I rounded a bend, and saw an army man run along the road toward me, his rifle held across his chest. When it seemed he would run past, I put up my hand to stop him.

He stopped and wiped at the sweat that ran down the sides of his dark indigenous features. He jutted his chin up as if to say "What?"

"Hay problemas? Todo está bien? Que onda?" I tried to think of a way to ask whether I should turn around and run, or present my wrists for handcuffs, or my temple for a bullet.

He looked confused, then sensed my insecurity and said "Todo está bien." He waved me forward, then ran off down the road behind me.

Ahead, a few more bursts of machine gun fire scared a flock of birds out of the underbrush. I rounded the curve and looked up into the scrub brush and cactus on the mountainsides, and saw camouflaged soldiers on a steep slope. They crouched amid the prickly pears and scrub, and moved furtive and crouched from one treacherous foothold to another.

I ignored them, and they ignored me. I rounded a curve and felt relieved to get out of the line of fire. As I walked on, I heard a spray of machine gun bullets every ten minutes or so.

Later, I asked Curt about the soldiers.

"Where did you see soldiers?"

"Before I got to Santo Tomás."

"You went there?"

"Not much to see. Bunch of mean kids."

"Should have asked me first, I could have saved you the effort. They're communists."

"What do you mean?"

"The village elected communists. My mom says they're jealous of the success of Santa Catarina, because here they make money from tourists who drive here for cheaper prices on fabrics and clothing. Then there's the people like you who rent houses, adds a lot of money to Santa Catarina's economy. Santo Tomás lies too far away for the majority of backpackers. Why bother to rent there, when Santa Catarina is prettier and close to Panajachél, and the dock isn't rotten. Some say the United States pays the Guatemalan army to put on those displays of military force, to convince the people to throw out the communists."

So what if a community decided to try communism? Doesn't democracy entitle all people to enjoy respect for their self determination, no matter what their political theory?

The Party on the bus I missed

I couldn't sleep. I packed, ruminated, unpacked, changed my mind, and packed again through most of that night and by early the next morning, I felt exhausted and excited about my departure. I knew by heart the list of my meager belongings. Mess kit, dry foods, sleeping bag, a wad of mosquito netting, hiking boots, my two changes of long clothing, shorts and almost bikini professional swimmer's European model swimsuit, ten dollar Chinese transistor radio, flashlight, an blank page soft cover journal with a pen and ink sketch of a Catholic church on the cover, a matching tiny pink vest pocket size booklet of blank pages for quick notes to the journal, maps and a couple of relatively heavy paperback books picked up at that guesthouse in Guatemala City. Still unopened. Too much to do during daylight to find time to read, and then all forgotten whenever Ida arrived with her collection of recommended books.

I felt the presence of the Quetzals and Traveler's Checks in the green money belt under my waistband. Each still equaled one American greenback dollar, and that gave me comfort. Easy math to convert currency.

I stuck my right hand in my pocket and felt the presence of my useless car keys. The other pocket carried a truncated toothbrush, some chap stick, and loose change for small emergencies, like the two peso entrance fee into bus station toilets, paid to somebody who sits at the door and gives you about eighteen squares of folded toilet paper as a receipt. I buttoned my back trouser pocket over my wallet, and made sure to zip the most accessible pockets of my backpack. I checked again that my precious toilet paper rode on top, then the map, then a book and the small flashlight I used to read at night on the bus.

I hurried through Santa Catarina Palopó too early to say goodbye to Curt. I didn't want to miss the bus, so I walked fast. My backpack's bounce became an accompaniment to the soft, muffled rhythm of my footfalls in the dusty gravel.

This early in the morning, I heard Panajachél's businesses literally open up, metallic screeches as owners hoisted up the metal barriers, similar to manual garage doors in the United States, which protect their glass display windows at night.

I felt relieved to see the yellow school bus, curbed at the bus stop on the cobblestone street, gurgle diesel. Everything seemed in place, all ready, turned around and pointed uphill, pointed out of town.

I felt thirsty, so I put my backpack on the ground at my feet, then gave a street vendor a Quetzal and watched as he squeezed three halves of oranges into a huge a paper cup. I heard the bus motor rev, and felt my blood drain into my knees as I watched it pulled away from the curb without me.

I left the orange juice on the little cart's counter and ran after the bus with backpack in hand. I almost caught up with it, but then my backpack zipper opened. Stuff fell onto the steep cobblestone road behind me, to scatter and roll away downhill.

I felt the beautiful opportunity for a romantic tryst in San Jose fade away as I watched the bus go by, the rear windows so close and unattainable. Then I noticed someone wave from inside the bus.

Kat laughed at me from behind the dusty glass. She held up a bottle of wine and toasted my predicament, and the bus faded away into the diesel fumed distance.

She might party with Yvonne. I felt certain. Girls talk, compare notes, laugh and squeal at each other's revelations. I cringed at the thought they would ver they both knew me. They would laugh and carry on, and make fun of the barely curious glances of Guatemalan Indians, unsurprised by the strange antics of tourists.

What a life, two beautiful women, a bottle of wine, a four hour bus ride, an unknown destination, and no agenda, and I'm left in the middle of Gringotenango to chase an unraveled roll of scented, floral print toilet paper I stole months ago from a hotel in Mexico City.

I walked back downhill to drink the orange juice I paid for, and muse on life's injustices.

Second Section: The Ninth Hell

Observant clients of Mexican prostitutes report how some press on a man's coccyx, the last, inflexible section of fused vertebrae we call the tailbone, because they believe those bones contain, and hasten, a man's sexual potency. The Maya call that bone "fire" as metaphor for the cosmic portal that links the three (sometimes four) major divisions of the universe: the Underworld, the Earth, and the Heavens.

CHAPTER 5: Puerto San Jose
New Years Diversion in Antigua

Some cultural artifacts from the Classic Maya (100 - 900 AD) reveal their multileveled cosmology divided into three regions; the Heavens, the Earth, and the Underworld. Mayans linked the three together with images of a World Tree (the Ceiba tree) or "Tree of Life" or even "Crocodile Tree," which researchers think they named "Six Snake", a creature with deep roots that puncture the Underworld, and high leafy treetop branches to comb the Heavens of the Milky Way. Caves appear as metaphoric apertures between levels of their cosmology, as do doorways, springs, fire hearths, all analogous to the body of animals and people; the mouth, anus, and vaginal openings, each loaded with its own symbolic significance. A deer hoof in Mesoamerica can represent the female genitals. Thus they built a familiar body cosmos, built upon what they knew of geology, climate, animals, body functions, fire, and transmutations of clouds to rain, food through animals into excrement, rain through the ground into springs, wood through fire into smoke, and life through the portals to death, the levels of the Heavens and the Underworld.

After a couple of hours on the next bus, I arrived by night to walk around the old capital city, Antigua Guatemala, with beer in hand. This New Year's Eve I felt the traditional pressures to go through the motions of procreation, and no hope in sight.

We dateless men sat in the ornate bar of an old colonial hotel and watched with frustrated amusement as couples, the upper class Guatemalans in formal attire, walked by. They ignored us, or glanced over us with what I perceived as an obvious and irritated disdain. After all, we travelers visit to watch the locals. Their way of life becomes our spectacle, our TV show, an evening's entertainment, as they filed through on their way into the grand Ballroom for their elegant upper crust New Year's Ball.

I thought we looked like a varied and intelligent group, a couple of Americans, some blokes from some England or Australia, an Italian couple lost in each other. Not one of these party goers said good evening or Happy New Year to us. They seemed mean spirited to a one, immersed in a studied attitude that injured us as we saw their delight in obvious insults aimed our way.

A Brit leaned over to whisper to me, "These Guatemalans. I wouldn't give the time of day for the lot of 'em. Got a jolly big problem with their own self esteem, you ask me, I say."

A thunder from outside reverberated within these thick Colonial walls, and bits of plaster fell from behind the baskets of hung plants, where the stucco chipped off to reveal those picturesque inaccessible corners of exposed stone wall, as if to excite painters and photographers.

More warlike explosions of pyrotechnics filtered in from outside. A symbolic massacre of the year gone by. The odor of gun smoke wafted in when the door opened, along with the occasional obscene squeals of Chinese fireworks that bounced off the colonial buildings to spin in the street with orange rooster tails of sparks.

I paid up and headed outside to catch the show.

A Guatemalan man struck up a conversation with me on the street. Short and prematurely balding, he held a drink in his hand and pointed a pinky finger at me to ask "Are you an American?" in an accent which sounded close to American English. He pointed to my backpack, and explained to me in the vestiges of a once fluent English that all the cheap single rooms in town got booked for New Year's Eve months ago. Therefore, we should solve our mutual dilemma with a shared double room, which, he explained, worked out even more economical when you consider the other amenities of free breakfast, good security, room service, clean sheets and towels, along with the high class luxurious accommodations.

This scrubbed squeaky clean, coifed, and over-cultured young man of the Guatemalan upper class, once inside the quarters, lent me a hand mirror in which I saw my bearded visage framed by the long locks of hairy disarray. In shock, I stared back at myself as an unwanted, unwashed, longhaired tormentor who with sudden recognition, crept into my consciousness and began to set up house. Without a mirror, I rarely saw myself over the last two months, only when I happened to glance at my reflection in a window.

He gave me a small hand mirror, and left, with the plan that if he returned to find me here, he would show me around Antigua.

I shaved off my beard and moustache. It took a while, but he didn't return.

I went down to the hotel lobby, and met an American sailor who told me about his Seaman's papers. Unbeknownst to me, I could get my own papers processed back home in Michigan, because many seagoing ships call on various ports around the state. About the same age as I, we both enjoyed his brag of his travels around the world, how he works on ships to cross the seas, then disembarks in some exotic locale with a healthy paycheck to spend on his overland explorations, until the next job at sea.

"Sounds like heaven, but what kind of work do you do?"

He spoke with a Buffalo New York accent. "Hard work. Manual, dirty, sweaty, sometimes dangerous. Forget about a job you might enjoy. Everybody thinks they can enjoy work, get paid for fun stuff, but the fun stuff everybody wants to do. People do the fun stuff for free, so nobody pays for it."

"Somebody must enjoy their work."

"Who cares about the work? While the ship sails, day, night, hour, every second, she pulls you to some new place, or a place you knew once, now either half forgotten or changed enough to look new. Everywhere, anyplace, takes more than a lifetime to get to know."

"What about marriage, a home, children?"

"A dream, maybe someday. I'm young and happy all by myself right now. Women wait in every port for a sailor, sometimes two or three at a time.

They like the idea of a boyfriend who neglects to visit but sends money. Financial security. I scramble for each job when I run out of money, like the next guy. No different."

We toasted each other. He bought another round of beer, and we settled back into that quiet stupor that dons a sullen expression. We watched the rich Guatemalans pass and ignore us. The tuxedo clad doormen admitted them into the inner sanctum of the opulent ballroom, an allegorical heaven that happens a couple of times a year, beyond those massive carved doors and down a long corridor where the music of a small orchestra wafted out each time the big ballroom doors opened.

The sounds of war outside reached a hysterical pitch, a murderous rapture of human exuberance, an orgy of controlled destruction to laugh in the face of death. The barman said Happy New Year, Happy New Year. The bartender put on Auld Lang Syne.

Nobody but the American sailor and I knew a bit of the words, and we didn't feel like singing.

The sailor left with the lame and insincere excuse that he felt tired. Off to carouse the streets, I imagined. I went up to the room.

The young Guatemalan, with whom I shared this room, showed up a little later with a similar complaint about his attempt to enjoy himself, or as they say in Spanish, divert himself.

We walked out outside together, and into Antigua's main square. From the street vendors' kiosk kitchen trailers on two wheels, we sampled spiced tortillas, (rolled up and fried in lard), corn on the cob, picaya (a vegetable that looks like chicken feet), fruits with red pepper, nuts and candies.

About three in the morning, we walked alone amid the old city's ruins, as the wind swept the streets of the New Year's eve litter, all the multicolored shredded paper and lumps of burned fireworks which the wind pushed into the gutters and against the walls and corners.

The city still celebrated. We heard, saw, and smelt the Firecrackers explode in all quarters of the city. The light from the high explosions illuminated this ruin of a once great colonial capital in flashes. We saw skeletal ghosts of stone, the remains of high crumbled walls, ornate fountains that no longer flowed, broken arches and aqueducts, and dark streets lined with solid block walls.

A lake destroyed this city, once the heart and capital of Guatemala. A lake that fell down the side of a volcano. In seventeen seventy three, Antigua served as the Capital of Guatemala, a colonial city with magnificent architecture and Roman aqueducts. When the Santa Marta earthquake caused the side of the tall volcano's crater of ash and rock to disintegrate, the lake emptied down the side of the volcano and into the city of Antigua. Imagine a dam on the top of a mountain in sudden collapse, the entire lake fell through town, an immense wave of white water and boulders that ripped apart the thick walls of stone architecture. After that, the Spanish Royalty ordered the city abandoned, and its treasures moved to the new site of Guatemala City.

Within the national borders lie twenty seven volcanoes, all potentially active. The one that towers above this city, majestic and full of earth's potency and permanence by day, imparted an extraordinary palate of colors as a backdrop. Then on one innocent day like any other, an earthquake broke the side of the cone, and the high lake fell in a torrent of mud and rock to slam the town with millions of tons of accelerated fury. Imagine a wall of earth and water as it rushes down from the top of a twelve thousand foot volcano to slam through town. Some of what survived still survives today in its ruined state, a monument to the disaster, to the feeble works of man and the omnipotent cataclysms of nature.

Through the fireworks' flashes we walked as if in a harmless dream of war, all noise and smoke. The strobe light explosions painted black shadows that streaked from the base relief of ruins, arches, and fortress thick walls. We walked a circuitous mile, dodged the drunken traffic that whipped the paper shards into whirlwinds, and returned to our shared room.

Roommate's Attack

Since at least the Late Post Classic, the Aztec's hereditary guild of armed merchants traveled far and wide across lower North America and the northern Central America, to find luxury goods for Aztec noble families. Known and feared as the Pochteca, they demanded the lands through which they passed swear allegiance to the Aztec empire. If not, they provoked incidents that gave an excuse for the Aztec army to intervene. Thus, by trade or conquest, they helped the upper classes accumulate wealth and territory.

He didn't talk to me much throughout our sojourn from bar to bar, punctuated by cheap deep fried snacks or grilled meats bought from street vendors. A tour of Guatemalan culture, he called it. I felt his constant regard for my face, but blamed it on our language differences.

Once in our room, he said that while we walked around Antigua, I carried my eyebrows high up on my forehead, "like this" he demonstrated, his face in wonder, "like a child" he laughed.

So what, I thought. I felt drunk, and wanted to sleep. I told him goodnight.

As I started to undress in my bedroom of our spacious hotel room which consisted of three sections cordoned off by wide archways with white curtains. He comes into my alcove with the flimsiest excuses, to ask if I need a razor, when he knew I shaved earlier, he returns again and again. Then he wonders did I want another cigarette from the pack he bought me? Did I think it a good idea to rent the room for another night so we could rest and avoid the New Year's rush home, etc.

The alcohol didn't make me so stupid I couldn't see his motive, he wants to see me naked. So I unfurled my sleeping bag atop the bed and zipped myself inside to finish undressing and avoid the huge four poster colonial double bed's pristine white sheets. I said thank you for everything, I'm too tired to think right now and I'm going to sleep, goodnight.

He would leave. For a while. But he returns; now he wants to talk. Asks the dumbest questions of a one dimensional nature. Did I like the tacos, did I have a girlfriend, did I feel grateful that he took me on that walk, to drink all those drinks he bought me, and didn't I appreciate and enjoy the tour of downtown Antigua?

I said yes, thank you, I'm going to sleep, goodnight, and he would leave. For a while.

In frustration, he returned to my room in his underpants and laughed as he tried to unzip my sleeping bag.

I'd tell him to get back to his own bed, in American English and in my own version of Spanish, but he complained it wasn't fair. He couldn't sleep.

I said that's not my problem, I'm going to sleep, goodnight, and he would leave. For a while.

Next time he returned with a determined attitude of insolence and self righteousness, reached out to unzip the sleeping bag and insinuates his hand inside the zipper and toward my genitals.

I push his arm away, and say "No."

Again he tries.

"Stop it."

Again, and I scowled, grit my teeth, and asked him "At what moment in the evening did you decide I wasn't a human being anymore? When did that happen?"

He sat on the chair beside the bed, put hands on his knees, and sunk down between his shoulders, his body in a slight sway from side to side. He stared at me and his expression became more and more pained.

I wondered what he might try next.

He left.

Minutes passed.

I counted my breaths. I put pen to my tiny journal by the streetlight that shined through the window, and wrote "I ruined his plans and now I feel guilty, even though he tricked me into this situation. Every horny man needs sex, a drive for pleasure, an instinct for indiscriminate fertilization, a necessity with about as much importance as a pleasurable piss. Women ver that and resent it always. The male human's catholic promiscuity, even when called serial monogamy, reveals an ambition for multiple partners. The universal fantasy of male sexuality becomes pornography, a depiction outside the human context, where people become objects to pleasurably excite or mistreat, with their cries of anguished pain or pleasurable extremis, often difficult to know which. Good sex sometimes resembles rape. The human animal's mixture of sex and aggression may speak to the patriarchal society's fundamental morality of invasion, conquest, and possession, a military way to say violation, rape, and sexual slavery. Young men commit almost all crime because they are genetically programmed for war. There's too many men on the planet, so as a resource, their value comes from their expendability. Every time one man whacks off, his ejaculate could fertilize billions of eggs. So this idea of love must come from women. No matter how small the village, a lot of people find their mate. Love happens between people regardless of age, sex, orientation, size of the village, or social norms. This bastard doesn't care about me at all. He cares about his physical needs right now. I would feel better about him if he made me believe that he held my happiness as a higher priority than his own. I should remember that the next time I'm hot for some girl."

With the journal tucked away, I lay there with eyes open and tried to sleep.

I could feel his presence even when not there. I imagined he sat there in a funk, stared at me through the walls, and considered various ways he could attempt to overpower me. Perhaps he kicked himself about the missed opportunities to drug me earlier in the evening, or steer us toward a gay hangout. Perhaps he toyed with other options with other people, should his first plan fail. A visit to a gay bar might allow him to get help, call some friends over to overpower me. He might consider a change in tactics, to lay low tonight, and then tomorrow morning invite me on a tour of the countryside in a rented car, to apologize and start the seduction anew.

Right now, I hoped he felt convinced of my humanity. I lay awake and stared at the ceiling, watched the blobs of color ebb and flow through my field of vision for an hour or so, until I felt so relaxed, sure he slept, that I dozed off and passed out.

His actions inspired a Eureka moment. Thanks to that homosexual male, I appreciate what my own testosterone inspired horny male behavior looks like, and feels like, from the recipient's point of view. I decided to treat all future potential sexual conquests as people first, and maybe my wildest fantasies might one day materialize, that a woman might use me as her sex toy.

As they say in Spanish, her 'consolador,' her consolation, a human dildo.

Instead of a much needed long hot shower followed by what I'd promised to do, call down and request room service deliver our free breakfast on silver trays so we could eat together in luxurious surroundings, I got up earlier than my roommate and caught a city bus for a serpentine, two hour ride through the darkness of the new year.

While trapped on Route Seven, which went everywhere except the bus station, I saw most of the quake destroyed old capital city before it took me to the station. There I caught the first bus to Guatemala City and escaped before dawn from Antigua Guatemala.

To keep the New Year tradition of retrospective introspection, I analyzed my life so far, and fought the utter boredom of that task to keep myself awake, to no good purpose.

I dreaded the thought of tomorrow's trip to San Jose. What did I know about Yvonne? She spun webs, and then enticed me to enter, but why? To help her ease out of a relationship?

And why, violent boyfriend?

I wondered if this bliind worm between my legs controlled my brain, if I allowed sexual tension to enhance my feelings for a French girl whom I spoke to, alone, maybe an hour and a half, total.

Those two nights I lay awake into the wee hours of the morning. All my unresolved circular questions and tangential thoughts robbed me of sleep. The third night, I got out of bed and packed the backpack, left my keys on the pegboard behind the front desk, and woke up the boy on the cot to unlock the door and let me out for a long walk through the quiet, predawn streets towards the bus terminal.

Plenty of time to think about things on the bus. San Jose lay a hundred and five miles from the capital, yet it would take half the day, with all the stops in every village along the way.

I saw no reason, other than Yvonne, to go to this Port town, which the guidebooks mention as forgettable with consistency. Travelers describe it as small and dirty, an open air brothel of cheap whores for sailors, with a large commercial cargo vessel grounded on the beach.

Imagine, Yvonne and I under a quarter moon that floats through a purple sky. We would lay horizontal on the beach, locked in a kiss on the wet shiny slant of sand, while Pacific waves crashed and pushed frothy sheets of wavelets between our dovetailed legs. Little crabs skitter, and seagulls hover and cry out with raucous calls of insult and irritation.

I could taste the salt from here to eternity.

The bus wound through the mountains that ring the Valley of the Cows to the sounds of static mixed with a cassette of Credence Clearwater Revival's Greatest Hits. I sat in the back of the bus to sleep, but the owners of this old yellow school bus wired the stereo system to rear speakers with ripped paper cones, which spat out Born on the Bayou and Bad Moon On The Rise.

I fell asleep to a fuzzy version of "I like the way you walk, I like the way you talk, oh, Suzy Q."

Woke up on the long flatlands of the Pacific shelf and saw groups of Brahma bulls nested under the rocket fuselage of lone Ceiba trees. They chewed their cud and stared through little clouds of gnats that hovered like smudges.

Something in my pants tried to break through my zipper, while Credence Clearwater Revival sang "There's a bad moon on the rise" which sounds like there's a bathroom on the right.

I tried to write a general, nonspecific postcard, but couldn't think of anything except "Arrived San Jose late afternoon. Wish you were here."

San Jose looks like three streets that turn into sand and run straight into the sea between a spread out, ramshackle community in competition with about five species of palm tree. The center of town grew around the intersection of the docks, railroad tracks and those three beach destined streets decorated with a few restaurants and shops whose merchants offered wares from within the hot shade of crude canvas tents.

A high percentage of women sauntered the long street to the beach. Most in short shorts and halter tops, with a loose long sleeve shirt. Overweight women, whose eyes sought any and every man who passed.

The transfer of cargo from truck or train to ship, or ship to truck or train brought a constant flow of tourists and sailors on brief shore leave to run this female gauntlet in a search for cheap thrills.

I asked around for a good place to eat, and many people asked me if I liked Chinese food, as if quite a novelty. In a small one room wooden building with the top half of the walls of window screen, I sat at a crude, unfinished wooden table with salt and pepper shakers from China and ordered from an inexpensive menu of unrecognizable names, bilingual in Spanish and Cantonese. The skinny half Chinese Guatemalan brought me a delicate porcelain bowl that contained a white soup ninety percent noodles, too salty, enhanced with monosodium glutamate, flecks of green and orange scraped vegetables, and three wrinkled green peas that evaded my spoon.

My backpack bounced against my back as I walked down the road through tiny sand drifts to find a hotel near the beach. I hoped to see Yvonne before she saw me, to assess her status with her companions, if not alone.

I took off the pack to change boots for tennis shoes and rearranged things to minimize the discomfort against my back for the next jog of my hot walk. Sweat ran off my nose, down my temples, and matted the hair about my ears.

The pack still rubbed uncomfortable against my sweaty back in this salt muggy tropical heat, and again I thought I could rearrange the contents and lessen the impact of boot soles against my lumbar spine.

I tried. I failed.

The paint on the hotels' wood planks peeled in the salt spray and sun. They looked almost identical, two stories high, each story's upper half made of window screen, the upper floor rooms accessed by a second floor walkway around the building.

A couple of blocks from the sea, I saw a small hotel with a more recent chalky pea green paint that peeled off salt blasted gray wood walls, so I took a tiny room on the second floor. The screened windows let in the sea breeze, and I thought it might stay cool, but soon realized the bare wood slanted ceiling did not deflect the energy of full sunlight on the roof, but radiated its heat downward. The exterior paint's green tones continued on the inside of the planks as the walls of the room, and contrasted with the gray weathered two by fours and boards of the roof underside, and the gray echoes of a small, unpainted table and chair.

The tropical sun straight overhead, and the oppressive, merciless humidity, pushed me out the door on a walk to the sea. The winds kept the wide street swept clean of sand, and the gaudy pure colors of crude hand painted signs announced the entrance of each bar. Sweaty fat whores hung in the doorways like hams, and called out to me in a quiet guttural language I pretended not to understand with a smile and a nod.

Port town. In front of the pharmacy liquor store, a sign stuck in a barrel announced champagne on sale, a dollar fifty for three bottles wrapped in a plastic net bag. Three brands unknown to me, perhaps stolen by a customs official and turned over to a family business to dispose of. One bottle claimed to contain port wine, and I bought some for the coincidence, to experience the port on port.

I wanted to borrow the store clerk's corkscrew, but he insisted till he opened the bottle for me. It tasted like industrial alcohol mixed with carbonated grape drink. I sat in the nearby shade and finished the first bottle out of thirst. It bestowed upon me an inventive courage and a sense of humor which helped me squirm my way out of the whores' clutches in a friendly, graceful way for the rest of my strolls up and down the main street to the beach.

I took a side street to avoid the crowds and check out the residential area. Two rows of beachfront houses blocked access to the beach. I could hear each wave's crash, as I walked on cement sidewalks decorated with miniature sand drifts, and the large fleshy leaves of what some call broadleaf evergreens. Nothing like evergreens, one could call them thick leaf deciduous in a constant molt that never loses all their leaves.

The sea lay more south than west of any point in this centerless town. Only the one main road that flanks the railroad to the pier gives public access to the beach.

I went back up the beach, curious to check out the tall, industrial strength, modern metal pier glimpsed from my second floor room.

As I round the corner of the last house, I could see down the beach to the black pillars encrusted with water level rings of mollusks and barnacles, and up into the palm trees, a sky painted with reddish black mud.

I felt my eyes go out of focus, and looked down at the expanse of black sand, sun baked to chocolate powder. I could see waves smash in white explosions against the reddish black mass with a metallic thunder and hollow reverberation. Gradual recognition flooded my field of vision, as I perceived the background of palms filled by a rectangle of rusty metal.

An oceanic ship, beached parallel to shore, eclipsed a third of the sky toward the west. It materialized out of the atmosphere as I walked forward, and took on an inappropriate immensity as the backdrop to tiny humans on the beach under toy sized palm trees.

I tried to imagine the storm that brought this ship ashore, some immense wave that broke the ship's moorings. It floated in sideways, and ran aground so that the rear half now sat mired in dry sand, with the prow's first twenty meters surrounded by a shallow pool. The ship's nose pointed enough out to sea to protect a little kiddy pool of shallow water that mothers let their children play in. The pool's water level changed with each wave that smashed against the other side of the bow.

The ocean waves' powerful blows pummeled the steel plates, and it sounded like the whole vessel shook with each reverberation. Children screamed and laughed as they waded ankle deep in a pool that filled to chest deep with a suddenness that made them bolt in panic through the explosions of spray to their parents. The greatest sprays made fan shaped explosions of rainbows and diamonds, a white peacock tail as big as a house that fell in slow motion over the silhouettes of thrilled toddlers.

Saturday morning, I assumed people would fill the beach. I saw scattered individuals and family groups spread around in pools of shade, but none looked like the Canadians.

I decided not to swim and walked back to my hotel room, to drink some wine and read a little. I hummed something that sounded good to my sodden eardrums from the inside, something related to the harmonic frequencies of trains and traffic, to the slow beat of the ocean's constant throb and the cymbal crash of wave spray.

Back in my screened room, I recalled my request for a beach view. Instead, I saw a view of the main road that opens up onto the beach two blocks away. I could see a line of sunlit palm tops, like bright green mop heads, against the chocolate metal of the ship that obscured the Western sky.

I unpacked and relaxed with a bottle of cheap wine and a book in the comfort of a bare wooden room with a bed and a desk and chair, screened doors and windows equipped with wood shutters for protection against tempests. By the late afternoon, I reached that stage of drunken oneness where a lucid transcendence, or a latent translucence, paints the world in whitewashed pastel tones. Everything stammered and shimmered, and my thoughts turned base and transparent, like gossamer butterfly wings hung wet on the spider webs of a ramshackle architecture.

I slipped on my bikini swimsuit, got out my white long sleeve long tailed shirt I use as sunscreen, locked the room with the cheap, colorful, flimsy Chinese padlock the hotelkeeper gave me, and plodded barefoot toward the sea.

No need for shoes or sandals in a beach community. No health department rules here to demand shirts and shoes. With sidewalks so hot, I ran from one pool of shade to the next.

The beach, with its monolith shipwreck, recalled the end of the world, post industrial; the huge metal blot on the bright blue sky a reminder of the plague of industrialization and the repression of workaholic conformism. After several of these jaunts through the gauntlet of whores, I felt no inhibition here, even with consideration to the conservative Guatemalan culture. On the last sidewalk near the beach, I took off my shirt in the shade of a palm and piled sand on it as a safeguard against the powerful gusts of sea breeze which blew things inland, into trash piles caught under the cockroach infested underbrush at the edge of the sand.

I wanted to get into the ship's shadow. I walked out onto the black sand, and felt knife blades of heat cut into the soles of my feet. I ran back into the shade, cooled my heels, and tried to sprint out to the ship, but again the heat and pain overwhelmed me about half way. The third attempt got me less than halfway before I turned around. I tried again, and proved I could not reach the sea without burnt feet.

I gave up, and sat down in the shade to analyze the situation.

More and more people arrived. Small young families for the most part, they reached the beach sand and sought the palm's pools of shade to settle into and take off their shoes. They feared this Nestles chocolate powder of black volcanic grains mixed with glassy quarts and pearl white bits of shells. The salt and pepper mixture absorbed so much solar radiation that when families tried to walk across it barefoot, the sand burned their feet and forced them to run, with a wide stride dance and scream, to the nearest shadow, their children reduced to tears until rescued by parents.

As I watched each family stake out a palm shadow far from the water, I realized that the ship's tilt prevented its shadow from a wide advance across the beach until late afternoon.

With my white shirt in hand, I found an alternate route to the ship, a walk in the long shadow of a tall palm tree. Then I crossed to some tables shaded by bamboo a short sprint from the ship's thin strip of shadow along the port side.

I buried my shirt against the ship and walked into the pool by the shop's bow.

I swam out from behind the protective metal wall of the bow and into the explosions of spray, and felt the turbulence of the frothy, broken waves pull me under. I tried to swim out beyond where they broke, but when I dove down to hug the sandy bottom and let the wave break over me, the turbulence plucked me like a rag into gravel filled depressions where the turbulence bent, folded, and bounced me off the bottom over and again. Out here beyond the bow, the waves bounced off the ship to meet the new ones, and where they met they doubled in intensity. I tried to escape with a quick dive to grab handfuls of sandy bottom. Futile; with a murderous, mindless simplicity, the turbulence plucked me off the bottom and rubbed me across the corrugated sand like a washboard. Then it churned me around in a sea foam washing machine thick with sandy water to stone wash me into a fatigued version of my former self.

I rolled around powerless, underwater, with no idea which direction up, or when it would allow me to surface without a great wave slap in the face at the exact moment I must inhale, or pass out.

The worst waves come in sets, and things calmed down enough for me to surface with a suit full of sand and fight a strong sideways current that slipped seaward along the ship's flank. I swam hard through the murderous collisions of waves and wave bounce, both on top and underwater, to get a foothold near the bow. I bent underwater to pressure my feet into the sand, and scrambled up the steep sand to a calmer haven around the bow.

I sat in the shallows of the bow's pool and examined the situation. I wanted to find a discrete way, or place, to empty the handfuls of sand out of my suit and not attract notice or the police.

Behind me, a young girl in black slacks and a red and white striped skin tight tube top strode through the sand straight at me. She wore black shoes with high elevator soles and thick high heels.

She squatted over her heels on the hard wet sand near me and said hello, even acted relieved to hear my fragment of Spanish. I felt a alarm at her lack of girlishness, no giggles, no flirtation. She breathed as if tired.

She wanted to know if I wanted a girlfriend. She wondered how long I might stay in port, and if I arrived on a ship, or by bus. She wanted to know which hotel I stayed in, and then she wanted me to take her to my room.

She slipped into her Pidgin English to make sure I understood, "You make love with me in room?"

"You think I could fall in love with you so fast?"

She shrugged. "Love? I do not know. Fuckee suckee. In your room. We go now?"

I swam out into the pool and watched her as I slipped my suit down to my knees underwater, and tried to shake the black sand out of it.

She watched me and began to smile. "What you do?" and made a man's masturbatory motions with one hand and laughed.

I got most of the sand out of the suit and its one little pocket, pulled it up, and walked out of the pool.

"Ay, que hombre, cochino. Malvado. You bad boy. You pay me now. For looking."

I try to explain, "Mucho areno en mi traje. Ya no. Lo saco," in horrible Spanish.

She sat down in the shade of the ship again.

Like one of the undead, a vampire slut so pale by daylight, this pretty girl next door drowned herself long ago in hopeless ambitions for a better life out of the dysfunction of her broken family, where she experienced incest and inherited a boisterous, vulgar, culture of false happiness that did not value education or understand personal discipline. The hand to mouth fatalistic existence spends today's resources as a response to future shortages, and thus bankrupts the future. Now she works the oldest profession, mines the most base of the human condition, and acts insulted when a man injures her artificial self image and degenerate cosmology, which tells her that by virtue of her youthful beauty and slimness, all real men want her at first sight.

"You homosexual? You gay? We go to room now?"

I looked at her, angry, insulted.

She smiles, happy to get this reaction from me. She might convince some men to pay for the opportunity to prove their manhood, and prove her wrong. She might even enjoy a small victory herself, as she lets their fake caresses fondle, and watches their excitation build in maudlin anticipation yet ebb in confrontation with the reality of this polluted empty shell of a girl. So she feels competent and successful when men debase themselves on top of her, and if all goes well, it means as much as a drunken pee, a pleasurable physiological relief for a man. So she insults and provokes men to demonstrate of their manhood, to plough and pound her in an act that more resembles rape than sexual union, which proves her assumptions about men.

We moved into the shadow of the ship. Sweat beaded and ran down on our faces and reflected the bluish sky. I suspected we both felt hung over. I asked her if she wanted a real boyfriend.

"No. Too much trouble."

She sat glum, and I said nothing. After about five minutes, she got up and moved on without a word. I watched her walk across the sand on her tall platform shoes, a slim feminine girl, hips still prepubescent and narrow but on the way to that sallow cellulite that slim limbs never exercised gather in dimpled shadows. Her shoulders already sloped into the shrug of a profound apathy that refuses to struggle against gravity.

I walked to the pool at the ship's bow and rinsed out my sweaty, sandy shirt. When I put it on, it felt cool and I revived. To leave the shore, I sprinted from one palm tree shadow to another, and took note that as noon approached, the shadows moved farther apart.

I walked and drip-dried back to my hot room. The day felt too hot again when my shirt dried.

Alone, bored and tired, pissed I didn't feel drunk. I wanted to nap but dreaded the lost hours, and the headache pulsations of my exaggerated heartbeat, startled by the myna bird screeches from the neighbor's yard.

Hung on the back of the chair, the net bag that once held all three bottles of cheap champagne wine now cradled two torpedo shaped testicles. They gave me a pirate novel inspired, Hemingwayesque urge to get drunk and act dull, natural, and macho, like his Post Traumatic Stressed cast of war crippled atheists and existentialists. I recognized the urge as bankrupt as Latin America's need to feel part of the "First World" through blind consumption of brand name cigarettes, alcohol, automobiles, and icons of femininity disseminated through glamorous images in movies and magazines, skinny women who jumped to life off the pages of some male New York homosexual fashion designer.

Without a corkscrew, it took me five minutes forever to get through the cork with the smaller blade of my Swiss Army Knife. With the first poke through, a miniature geyser of champagne erupted in a tiny stream of mist which I pointed out through the screen towards the confused faces of a young family that passed on the street below.

I downed the bottle. Hemingway made me do it.

I stumbled out the door, grabbed a handful of the two by four wood rail, and felt its green paint shards peel away from the soft wood rot and weakness. I turned around, locked up, walked careful down steep wooden stairs into the solar radiation of mid afternoon, and clumped toward the commercial district, determined to buy a pair of sandals to liberate my feet from these industrial strength boots' steel toed solar ovens, or my tennis shoes that now duck quacked through loose soles under the toes.

I tried to walk normal and felt one leg shorter than the other, off balance, so I slunk along the shady side of the streets, to spot Yvonne before she spotted me.

Sancudos and Whores

The human mind searches for patterns to organize information, and if a pattern doesn't exist, the mind will impose one. The Meso-Americans and other indigenous cultures demonstrate this fractal logic; like complex images rendered from a single mathematical formula, computer savvy artist-scientists can produce entire landscapes from one formula. Dendritic patterns like a leaf's veins mimic other things that branch, like trees, or rivers system, and so a leafy tree can resemble clouds which resemble mountains, etc. All these images a computer can render from one formula for a leaf's veins, perhaps analogous to the way the infant's brain learns, through new connections between layers of neurons that build upon the previous latticework of defined patterns.

The Meso-Americans saw the Universe as a multilevel reality analogous to the body, with mouth, intestines, and anus, a digestive tract that connects cosmic domains of blood hungry Gods and the Earth, as a giant turtle or crocodile. Their worship of a city-state God King between star heavens and an underworld of mysterious death and corruption becomes a cosmic snake whose lair's entrances serve as power points to portals and doorways, mountaintops, underground rivers, springs, and caves, all interconnected passages of transmutation. Clouds give birth to rain which falls from the heavens and drains into the mouths of the underworld, which gives birth to springs, rivers, plants, and volcanoes. Sometimes angry gods throw fire from inside the rain, to scorch the earth and sacrifice man, animal, and forest in wildfires that produce a smoke which feeds the sky's darkest clouds.

After another Chinese meal of noodles peppered and decorated with miniscule cubes of nameless batter fried vegetables, I walked to the beach again, to watch the sunset from the stern of the ship. Afterwards, I returned to my room and watched twilight turn to nightfall.

I turned on the light. Invisible little critters, so small they flew right through the screen, bit my exposed skin and sucked my blood. I turned the light off and used my mosquito net as a blanket, tried to sleep in the heat and suffered attacks until about 10:00 PM.

Then, in spite of the heat, I put on pants and long sleeved shirt to explore San Jose by night.

The whores called out with more spirit and animation at night. Their clothing disappointed me. They changed from the day's beachwear of short shorts, skimpy shirts, and bikini tops, to their night look of long gowns with synthetic fur on sleeves, collars, and boas. Mosquito repellent. I suppose they hoped for an all purpose, virginal urban elegance adequate for dance or dinner, denatured and deflowerable. From their ears and around their necks dangled glassy flashes of color that competed more than complemented the patches of sky blue meant to add concavity over their shallow Indian eyes, with pools of rust smeared onto their coco skin cheeks. Slim crayon drawn arches above their shaved off eyebrows and petroleum based mascara that smudged like glue under their plastic eyelashes changed them from exotic Meso-American females to clownish imitations of glamour magazine models.

The whores, often grouped in threes, watched me approach along the sidewalk, and as I passed, they grinned to show teeth yellowed, blackened, missing, or golden which I took as evidence to judge the length of time and relative success in their chosen profession

They said, "Fuckie suckie" with eye contact, the shaved eyebrows raised a little but the crayon lines stayed put. I wondered why they bothered. Any interested man easily identified the sex workers. Might as well get a "yes" tattoo on their foreheads to save all that vulgarity for a more appropriate moment.

Then the eternal circus with various perennial acts. To survive, I tried to act like a sailor ashore after too many long months at sea with the boys. One whore flutters a hand to her neckline and jerks the blouse down to expose soft cleavage, folds of fat squeezed into position by the intricacies of corsets and torture bras. Another whore kicks a shapely leg out through a long slit in her mosquito net gauze skirt. A third waits in a pose that seethes with a proud and certain sexuality, with confidence in her good natured flirt because she knows what attracts the boys, because she's a man.

Once in a while one stepped in front of me and exposed a nipple which stared at me like its owner, who waited for my response. If I acted immune to their offers of nocturnal accompaniment, the whores dropped the act. They wondered aloud if I wanted a homosexual, then confessed their frustration in tones of exaggerated exasperation to complain "No hay barco." No ship in port. The town came alive, they assured me, when a Navy ship docked in the port.

"Every girl you get cheap now. You come with me. All night, cheap. Cheap cheap cheap."

With a ship or two in port, I imagine this town fills with sailors in minutes. Prices would inflate in relation to alcohol consumed or to the desperation of the sailors' swollen sausage balloons of flesh, filled with a Milky Way of spermatozoids that elbowed for release from their prison, twin kiwi fruit that dangle between the sailor's legs and clang together like cowbells and call out to these scantily clad shepherds. When opportunity knocks in San Jose, it looks like all knockers available. Most Free Market

Capitalist people would approve of profit at another's expense, if only to win at the Game of Consumerism, when the perceived value of each purchase beats both the price and the amount sweated to earn what it cost. Those who come out ahead in the exchange of money or services rendered, win at the game of Consumerism, and believe it all part of a "normal" pursuit of happiness.

Young men cause the majority of casual vandalism and violent crimes. They suffer sexual frustration and express it through violence, inspired by macho competition, and the low self esteem of jilted people with an unformed, adolescent morality that allows homicidal jealousies. Some young men go so far as to defeat the incest taboo, or reenact their own background of "normal" abuse with their sex partner or own children.

Sailors and soldiers get naughty because they plan to leave port in a matter of hours or days, and so broaden their experience as both victimizers and victims. Careless, overconfident sailors learn an expensive lesson in why not to stumble around alone, drunk. They move in groups of at least two, make themselves known and then scarce. The whores recognize them as economic opportunities, migratory fish that come with a supply of money from a more opulent universe, and as targets for all sorts of crime to liberate that money and redistribute it to whores, street thugs, bar owners, police, and even other sailors.

Many of the 'putas' looked young and fresh at first sight, but a glaze settles over their false smiles, the squinted eyes hide a bloodshot blush, the skin dry and flaky from last night's indulgence, with a residue of chronic alcoholic dehydration intensified by the climate and their long, sweaty labors under some sailor's sexual frustration with alcohol induced impotence. The whores and sailors share a boisterous vulgarity that shouts of the 'wild life,' from their cover of darkness, into the houses where normal families rest in their sleepy world. The whores simplify life to a vampyric hunt for cash deposits from men with foreskin wallets full of greenbacks, while the sailors regard women as urinals for semen.

All is fair in the sailor's escapes from tedium at sea and the influence of long periods of captivity and boredom fertilized by liberal doses of alcohol. Sensitive young stupid sailors become insensitive old stupid sailors, if they survive. They lose all types of virginity, the years jade them to what they once found exciting, now all too familiar. They sing to drunkenness and search out the famed nightspots of uninhibited depravity where they join the self deluded "relatively rich" in a misguided campaign to reduce poverty and enjoy life among the common and brash, vociferous, open, brusque, vulgar, boisterous, and fun loving, but hopeless culture of whores, with its propensity to cause emotional, family, and social chaos.

Once in a while I communicated on a human level with one whore or more, and saw them mutate from whore to human being. We hacked it out between two languages, their limited English and my limited Spanish. Most told the same sad and probably untrue story to tug at my heart strings. Good girls gone bad, the man she loved ran off with another woman and left her pregnant to fend for herself and her other children (fathered by other men, she forgets to mention). Then she gets kicked out of her home, out of her father's home, or the next place her newest boyfriend provides, etc. So she left her baby with mom in Guatemala City, or with her sister or some informal, unrelated 'cousin' in another 'home' town, and escaped to help support them with the easy money earned in port towns.

One twenty dollar trick earns almost a month's wages at a real job.

The literate write home to mom and paint a picture of honorable employment in a restaurant, and enclose a little cash so grandma can raise another child in the same circumstances that produced this whore.

I met whores that came from neighborhoods where they say all, which I take to mean a high percentage of, young girls work as whores, and become mothers as a side effect.

Anthony Newfort, Adventurer

Much later in the cool of midnight, I sat in an all night restaurant and sipped a tall glass of Horchata, the sweet rice drink made with milk and vanilla.

A bedraggled blond man stumbled in for a midnight snack, "To avoid a hangover." he says to me, and flops into a red plastic chair nearby.

I motioned him over. He opened his large leather shoulder bag and produced a business card that proclaimed 'Anthony Newfort, Adventurer'.

At the prompt of my open hands in a slight sign of curiosity, he explained that he, a professional chef, worked in first class hotels all over the world to finance his life as adventurer, 'a photojournalist for a liberated mankind,' with the man emphasized.

In San Jose, he worked on a photo documentary of whores.

His professional contacts with the whores enabled him to develop a friendship with some of them, and unexpected fringe benefits came his way. "You should get a camera. I carry one all the time, don't put film in it."

"Never loaded?"

"I use several cameras, but the one I use most, No! Never takes a picture. But they think I'm in love with them, makes them feel beautiful, because I pretend to take so many pictures of them." He rummages in his shoulder bag and shows me a number of impromptu Polaroid photos of whores. "You should carry an unloaded camera, it pays for itself in fringe benefits."

"Fringe benefits?"

"Once you get their confidence, they take off their clothes, they flirt, pose, lay on the ground, get on all fours, dance around, free fellatio, everything else at bargain prices. Those fringe benefits."

"Think you'll ever get married?"

"Marriage costs too much, and it's just a long term form of prostitution. I like the variety. Rather buy into a membership brothel, a nudie Playboy club you know, based on the supermarket model, or cafeteria style. Good for the girls, too. Everybody knows the real professional girls, the smart ones, guard their health. And the class of clients and the whores, that keeps everybody on a level of professionalism where they know the boundaries. Don't call me at home or at the office, don't threaten to talk to my wife, I won't get jealous of your boyfriend."

"What's so great about variety? Don't you see anything you'd like to keep around the house?"

"A wife might demand her own pleasure, and sometimes I'm too busy to take the time. Sometimes a man's only got five minutes to get 'is rocks off, then I'm out the door."

"You use women."

"A girlfriend once said that if men needed to seduce a toilet every time they took a piss, they would head for the bathroom with chocolates, jewelry and flowers, recite little poems and say I love all day long, never forget anniversaries and special occasions. That's the kind of rot girls go for, and call it Love."

"What is love?"

"What do you think?"

Anthony's food arrived. He said "Love is a beautiful sensation that lasts about fifteen minutes, then you roll over and fall asleep."

"Don't you miss the romance, the true love, all the wanting and jealousy? The intensity of anticipation?"

He wolfed down his Chinese noodles and talked with his mouth full. "Frustration you mean. Much more efficient to go to prostitutes. I think the French invented Romantic Love about two hundred years ago. Don't believe in it. Look at western civilization, written about since Homer, three or four thousand years before Christ. Men get together to pillage, rape, and capture women to take home to their harem. Yet some anthropologists say matrilineal societies, where women boss the men around, engaged in far more promiscuous sex. Women walk around half nude, everybody promiscuous, and led happier, less neurotic lives because every man got some on occasion, without any extra responsibilities, without any shame, guilt, or declarations of love or exclusivity. No jealousy, nobody killing each other for some imaginary indiscretion. When women rule, men don't know which babies they fathered, and everybody lives in peace and harmony."

"So who's the father to the baby? Who provides the food and shelter, protection?"

"The whole village. Actually, the mother's brothers, the uncles, take the role of father."

"Where is this happy society?"

"Deep in the jungle, I imagine. Soon as they get discovered by the Western world, they learn to feel shame, start wearing clothes, want mirrors and compete with each other, get jealous, and soon they're just like us. Happened in Hawaii, Trobriand islands, South Pacific. Don't know much about it, really, I'm not that kind of anthropologist."

"What if you met a woman who really turns you on, knows how to please you and wants to really rock your socks off?"

Anthony said, "Variety is the spice of life. And the word Spice is the plural of Spouse."

"You don't think there's one special woman, girl, you'd want to spend a lifetime with, to give birth to your babies?"

"Maybe I'll find her in Tahiti. Plan to go there. Tahitian mothers give their daughters sex education, teach them to do this dick squeeze, make their pussies tight. Perfect, no? Must feel like you grab yourself when you're inside her, with tits and buttocks all within reach. Girls learn from mom how to do exercises, get a good squeeze down there."

"You believe that stuff?"

"It's true. Women learned this stuff a couple of hundred years ago, before the Catholic Church convinced the heathens of their original sin, inborn depravity, and separated Man from Nature. Imagine how different the world might be if the situation reversed, if the Tahitians sent missionaries to Europe to colonize and enlighten the Anglo saxons and Iberians. Instead of sports on TV, men would watch porno soap operas, while the women bar-b-que in the back yard with the kids, and the young pretty girls would dance around topless in grass skirts, to flirt and pick out their next lucky man from all the happy boys who loll around and wait their turn."

"Their turn?"

"To disappear into the bushes with a girl. Maybe with a couple of guys and her."

"Couple of guys and her?"

"You're not into that? Oh well. Nobody's perfect."

"So when do you start your photo documentary?"

"Got here a couple of days ago. You should come with me, check it out for yourself."

"When?"

"I'm through for the night tonight. Tomorrow I'll show you around San Jose. Meet you right out front here, on the main drag, sometime after I wake up. Sometime afternoon, sound good?"

Back in my room, I sat up and smoked a cigarette, deep in thought with pen in hand to scratch notes for an hour or so. The sea breeze whispered through the palm fronds and window screens. Those mysterious bite and run 'Sancudos' went to bed two hours ago, now only the mosquitoes rammed the screen from the outside. I could hear their miniature airplane motors drop a tone with each impact. Those vampiritas that extracted blood out of me earlier, now hunkered down somewhere to digest it, or chased each other around in the darkness to copulate and lay eggs.

Sometime midmorning, I fell back asleep because I woke up pissed, pen in hand, my journal on the floor beneath the bed, and I dove headfirst for it. Not a good way to discover the intensity of a hangover. I breakfasted, or broke fast, on the grape flavored champagne. Another hot afternoon, and the cheap champagne's insignia leered at me from the trash basket as if it knew about the thick, blueberry funk that pounded into my head and stabbed when I moved my eyes.

My groggy feet waded through the beach sand that drifted throughout the town. The sewer and ashtray stench flowed out of the bars with the music and made me nauseous.

I avoided the whores near the beach and headed for the restaurants near the tracks.

In my condition, I dreaded the chance I might run into Yvonne in San Jose, so I wandered down side streets and found a little café with two tired faded sofas and a coffee table loaded with magazines in various languages.

I wrote letters and waited for Anthony Adventurer to pass by.

He saw me first, and came in with his arm around a Ladina whore. He stood in the doorway to call attention to himself. He turned to look out at the sandy street, put one hand up to shield his eyes from the sun, and intoned for my benefit, with his Britannic lip set stiff under his upturned nose. "It makes a grown man cry to think how most people live a life of quiet drudgery to save money for travel when they retire, and by the time they retire, they're too old and set in their ways to enjoy it."

She smiled up at him, her eyes beads of hematite.

They sat down at my table so close together they almost shared the same chair.

He leaned forward as if to conspire. "I've figured it out this morning. This entire town's a brothel. Everybody needs the extra cash. When they get to know me, fathers offer me their daughters, wives compete to give me Spanish lessons. When you get their confidence, every school girl wants an English tutor."

"How is your Spanish?"

"I talk to everyone. Cheaper than Spanish lessons," he assured me. "I speak the three big languages of Europe, English, French, and German, and after a few more weeks in Guatemala, I'll speak Spanish."

We slinked off down the sunlit streets to a small cement house on the main drag, near the train tracks. He conversed with people at the door, and they motioned us inside. A small living room, couches, a television, and in the back wall a beaded curtains covered a doorway that led to a hallway.

Anthony amused them as he spouted all the off color Spanish words I could never find in my dictionary. His stilted staccato flowed almost unintelligible, but the Guatemalans laughed and covered their mouths in a feigned shock.

He asks for the girl Alejandra, the whore he wants to photograph.

The young man says she sleeps. "I don't think she got lucky last night. She might get up soon."

We sit down to wait.

Anthony says "I am hell bent to discover the extremes of my own sexual energy, now, while young, while I have the energy."

"Shouldn't you find a special someone to do it with? A like minded female explorer?"

"Any girl like that wouldn't stay with me long." Then he gives me a lecture on infidelity.

"Know why a faithful man falls to a prostitute? I figured it out. Imagine a sailor misses his girl, and feels jealous, that's natural, in any long distance relationship. He wonders if she's fooling around. So he gets drunk, and his mates, his supposed friends, play around with his feelings. They try to convince him that some drunken bloke ruts atop his girl this very instant, and she enjoys the shit out of it, too. He tries to brush them off, but he thinks about what they said, can't stop thinking about it, about how they described this imaginary big sweaty beefy guy, and how she bites his shoulder and sucks his fingers to beg for more. She doesn't give her boyfriend a thought, that's what they'll say, and eventually he believes it. He lives in a world full of men who brag about things they never did, and hears the stories about respectable women who never talk about their secret life. He feels guilty about not writing his girl, but doesn't want to write too often and appear soft, like all he does is write to prove his faithfulness. So it eats at him, like a sore throat you notice every time you breath. He becomes susceptible to his buddies' next argument, that he needs to protect himself, in case it's true she's found another. He should get a girl for the meantime you know, at least buy a prostitute, as an insurance policy, you get me? Against the off chance that his girlfriend gets regular bonings by some other bloke. Then he can fall back on his little beforehand revenge, maintain his stability in the face of bad news, you get what I mean."

"You think so? But when he gets home to his girl, wouldn't the truly faithful man's guilt show somehow, and cause her to doubt? Women's intuition, like radar, you know? She might catch him, or feel it, when he lies. Wouldn't that cost him plenty, both to reassure her, and to somehow redeem himself for his unfaithfulness?"

"Jesus you're naïve. How many faithful people do you think you know? You trust people, that's your problem."

"What about disease? I don't care how many condoms you put on, there's a chance that you catch a disease. Imagine a guy that brings that home to his girl."

"I put my whores through an entire medical exam before we get down to it. They do the same to me, to all men, the smart ones. Done right, it's part of the fun and laughter."

I watch the whore on his arm, who doesn't speak English, as the beatific smile sags into a grimace of tired low self esteem. She throws her arm around his shoulders as he wipes his mouth with the napkin. "Fuckee suckee? We go now?"

He peels her arm off, and pats her thigh.

She decides to go.

Anthony kisses her goodbye and shows her to the door "as becomes a gentleman," he says.

We sit back on the two sofas along the wall for a while, smoke cigarettes and drink Horchata.

We stepped out into a too bright world, over exposed and washed out in the tropical sun, and put on our sunglasses before we kicked up the powdery sand on some back roads.

Anthony confesses his obsession for an albino Negro girl.

We knocked at a house where Anthony knows several working girls live. A young fat boy guides us through a doorway draped with light fabric curtains. He motions us to sit on a too low couch that looked like horses sat on it.

Anthony calls out "Blanca..." several times in a high sing song voice, and from beyond another doorway with a gauzy curtain that swayed and billowed in unfelt surges of air, a woman's voice gives Anthony permission to enter.

He goes through alone, but I can sort of see through the curtain. After a brief discussion full of laugher and hugs, Anthony pulled back the curtain and beckoned for me to approach. I stood up and looked through the curtain's aperture to see the albino black woman, a soft and veined whiteness waddled in a kaleidoscope nest of Mayan blankets on a sofa sized bed.

"She's a beauty, isn't she? You don't see this every day."

Anthony beamed from her to me, as I feigned enthusiasm.

Blanca's face mixed features from Negro, Mayan, and Spanish bloodline; almond shaped eyes with steel blue irises, big cheekbones and lips, High forehead crowned by a sponge of kinky yellowish white hair tied into a pony tail pom pom. Her eyebrows merged in a thin line of white fuzz over the bridge of her nose. I resisted the temptation to look where the blanket folds revealed a narrow glimpse of her white cleavage, like an after image, a film negative that falls out of an old book. Both swollen expanses peak out as she lets the blankets fall. Their translucent whiteness contrast against the colorful woven Mayan blanket, like two immense pearls on colored sand, big as ostrich eggs in a nest of rainbows, two half gallon scoops of melted vanilla ice cream in baggies with two swollen strawberries to poke out near the bottom.

Anthony's hands scrambled into his small shoulder bag and rummaged around with urgency. He pulled out two cameras like a ball of black spaghetti. He carried on a constant conversation with Blanca, talked to her, cooed to her, took her hand and repeated beautiful, I love you, and she relaxed and smiled more and more, and teased him back. He pulled at the blanket to uncover more of her, inch by inch, as he snapped away with that empty camera, and adjusted f-stops on the loaded one.

The translucent skin sacks of her mammary glands hung by a network of tiny stretch marks. They both pointed down, like two half gallon plastic bags full of milk, and lay in comfort against the soft rounded mound of her white belly. The landscape of Blanca's skin flowed in unbroken tints of whiteness, down from her shoulders with just a hint of clavicle, down to the bluish shadows between her soft bulges in two long, graceful arcs of fish belly white skin to the shadowed regions of her rounded belly folds. There, faint silvery stretch marks from several pregnancies traced little wiggly rivers across her landscape's rolls.

As Blanca's nudity increased, so did the speed of Anthony's dedication to his craft. With frantic motions, he snapped photos with both cameras until he stopped to rewind film, opened the camera, changed canisters of film, and store the exposed roll in his camera bag. All the time he chattered to her nonsense about marriage, what their children would look like, how all England would treat her like a queen. He paced around Blanca like a happy fox with a cornered mouse. He talked to her, kissed her forehead, arranged and pulled at the blankets till they both laughed and fought over his insistence to expose everything. He flirted with her, sat beside her to hug her and coax her into position for another photo. He proclaimed her beauty to all present, and effused thanks as if to signify time for another pose, all in his atrocious Spanish made worse with a British accent, his face flushed red and streaked with rivulets of nervous sweat.

Like a voyeur I stood there and felt guilty pleasures, though she did not excite me. I wanted to leave Anthony to his avocation. To say goodbye, I told Anthony we could meet later on the beach.

He smiled at his blue veined model, and loaded more film for another twenty four shots, while he pretended to take photos with the empty camera. "Ok, I'll catch you later. I'm going to slow down now anyway, and see if I can get some. The really raunchy stuff sells for big bucks sometimes, but I need a bit more privacy for that show. She's fantastic, I'm really crazy about this girl."

I could see it worked. He coaxed the albino negra into her most vain, flirtatious, and sublime femininity. She hugged herself and ran her hands over her body to accentuate her round outlines. She used her massive softness like a weapon, and pointed portions of its bluntness at Anthony, who moaned like a soldier wounded in action.

I parted the cloth curtain over the doorway, and retraced my steps through the tiny house with a polite smile and an Adios to anyone who looked my way.

Outside, I winced in pain as the sun on the salt white cement street knocked me blind.

I walked and thought about Anthony Newfort's claim that variety, the spice of life, comes from the plural of spouse.

I hung out near the beach, but wandered farther into the residential areas. My anxiety about Yvonne prompted me to keep a lookout yet stay hidden.

This town, this beach, didn't appeal to me, lined with shacks that rented as houses. And all the whores! Might send a romance inclined French girl back to luxurious Antigua, to relax in that shattered Colonial splendor.

Met up with Anthony around sunset, so we walked up and down the beach on the wet black slope of sand packed hard by the waves. I felt comfortable with him, and I asked his permission to take a few notes in my little pink journal.

"Not at all," he said. "By all means, write. You write, I take photos. Same thing."

As we approached the beached ship's stern, it caught the sun's reddish light and looked like a building.

Anthony said "One of my first nights in San Jose, I watched the boat from my room, by moonlight. You ever notice a metal ladder hangs down from the deck, bout midway?" He points and tilts his head, uses his arm as a rifle.

"Yeah."

"That night under the full moon, I watched two men walk up to the boat. One boosts the other up to the ladder, then stands guard after the other guy climbs up. The guy on the boat comes back to the guardrail about ten minutes later, and waves down to his buddy. Then he holds up a small box, which he drops over the side so his buddy can catch it. Then he climbs down the ladder and they both walk away."

"So?"

"The next day, I noticed a guard there, all night, at the bottom of the ladder. Never noticed a guard there before. Maybe there was one, I don't know. Maybe they didn't post a guard until someone stole the box. Or maybe the thieves paid the guard to disappear for an hour or so."

"Did you tell anyone what you saw?"

"Why? Stick my neck out? Something valuable, in a box big enough to see in the moonlight, that no one thought to take from the ship before?

Look there, see that guy next to the boat? Tell me that's not a guard. You might notice if one stood there before, wouldn't you?"

"You're right. There wasn't one there a few nights ago."

An armed guard stood under the chain ladder that cascaded down the black cliff of the ship's port side.

From then on I noticed that at any time of night or day, a guard with a rifle squatted in the shade of a nearby palm, or stood in the shadow of the hull.

That afternoon, I walked down to the beach with new, indestructible sandals made out of old automobile tires to run across the sands of hell and into the boat's cool shadow. The cool air gave me the impression the immense wall of iron saved up the night's coolness.

The soldier guard rejected my efforts at a conversation. At first he smiled a little, then acted like he didn't understand me, but about the fourth misunderstood question, he made hostile motions with his jutted jaw and unslung rifle. He expected me to move along, so I did.

As I left, I asked him if he wanted a hamburger or water or anything, and he lowered the rifle at me.

Maybe he thought I would poison him to gain access to the boat. Maybe he suspected I might spy, or steal, or maybe he felt attracted to me, or someone who might threaten his masculinity, a penetrator.

That night I dreamt of Lake Atitlán. I could see the three volcanoes from Puerto San Jose, see across the flat Pacific lowlands of sugar cane, the foothills and fields of corn. I saw rangeland where Brahmin cattle lay droop eared in the shade around the rocket shaped trunks of Ceiba trees. Volcanoes blotted out the sky like the side of that ship. I dreamed I climbed upon a spider web of trails and ropes. At the top of this volcano size ship stood Yvonne. She tried to hand a jeweled box down to me, but laughed and withdrew it, then disappeared. I reached out from my tenuous perch on the wind blown rope ladder, everything out of reach.

I woke up in a sweat. A whore's dark laugh blows down the street below me, a newspaper, the flutter of wings.

Tomorrow I should leave San Jose. From what I'd seen of this port town, I thought Gary might convince the jilted Dennis that San Jose could provide exactly what the doctor ordered, as Anthony explained to me, something men do for each other, as buddies.

The sweaty armpit of San Jose educated me in the fecund perfumes of the tropics, the seaside putrefaction, the semen odor of one tree's flowers, the sour fruity smell of fleshy fruits that drop rotten and untouched by bird or rodent, and the hot wafts of air around the whores, who used cheap perfume to cover their personal mix of oterh people's sweat without success. These perfumes became palpable, a cloud to tint clothing, a dust in one's hair, a taste on the tongue, a grime on the skin. They became my evidence that organisms procreate without inhibition in the tropics, and my time in this groin of Guatemala, debased me.

Another image of Yvonne came to mind.

I saw her get off the bus, take one look at Puerto San Jose, and get back on the bus.

Nicaraguan Mosquito Princess

I left Puerto San Jose early the next morning. I stared out the bus window as it entered Guatemala City on the lookout for attractive women that I could undress in my mind's eye, until I saw the Red Tile Church.

Anachronistic, it seemed created by another universe, a touchdown of an extraterrestrial force from the past, a castle from Mars constructed to attract and inspire, to urge us to lift our eyes upward. The building shined with a passionate red flame, a symbol of a union of the sacred and the profane, the dilemma we face in how to use our God given energy while mired in the mud of necessity. My own ignorance of how anyone could create such a stern beauty in a world so drenched in carnal corruption, a world of hunger and insecurity, bereft of opportunities for personal satisfaction, deficient in knowledge, without the simplest intellectual resources such as books in libraries, made me want to get off the bus and pound on those massive closed doors until somebody answered for this situation.

Everything seemed the same at Hotel San Jose in Guatemala City, and I felt something akin to nostalgia for the restaurant's decorations of dried frogs locked in stomach to stomach copulation, and that dilapidated pelican hung in mid dive over that dim, narrow, pipe crossed corridor.

I didn't expect to meet a Nicaraguan Princess.

The doorway to Her room opened right behind the front desk, and across Her doorway hung a curtain of beads, through which she buzzed in constant motion, both to keep up with Her energetic yet polite six year old daughter, too mature for her years. One of those efficient and useful kids that think adults waste too much time.

The Queen communicated as much in her haughty tone of voice and excellent manners.

The Princess dressed in Haitian robes of African influenced fabrics, great wads of necklaces sparkled against Her dark skin and looped down across Her upper chest. Her black skin looked like a charred wood, Her features carved from the darkest tones where the sunlight hit the middle of her forehead, cheekbones, shoulders. Other places, She shone with a deep reddish mahogany, except the palms of her hands, white but more yellow than mine with fold lines traced in black. Her black painted fingernails looked thick and strong as bear claws.

Her interactions with the hotel manager and Her own daughter exposed Her poise, civility, and high expectations of others.

The Hotel Manager said the Queen made it a point to talk at length with everyone, and my turn came.

She spoke British English with a faint Caribe African accent, both musical and staccato.

"I know this will be hard for you to understand or believe, but I'm the last princess of the Mosquito Indians, a tribe of people in the hills of northern Nicaragua."

I categorized her as educated, intelligent and beautiful, with both physical and moral strength, but I knew that even a self described tribal Princess, like anyone who lived long term in this flea bag hotel, would absorb a little of the ambiance like a stain. By infection, she must feel like a complete failure at Her own confidence game, with Hotel San Jose as her address.

With refined and regal gesticulations She related stories of persecution and injustice suffered by her people, a community of Indians who intermarried with black runaway slaves brought over from Africa to the Caribbean by the Spanish to cut sugar cane.

The Princess' tiny daughter sat beside Her on the bed and toyed with a box of jewelry. Baroque fabrics, tapestries and hung robes and other examples of thick Royal clothing crammed their hotel room.

"I'm here in Guatemala to get some support for my people. They trust me. We are all alone in this struggle, but they've sent me on ahead, because I'm educated, and I speak with the voice of my people. I am their last hope, and I am committed to help them. I need money to do that." The Princess asked me to help her decide which piece of jewelry to hawk on the streets or surrender in a pawnshop, to support Her correspondence with political leaders around the globe.

"I am the only one left to speak for my tribe and for many of Nicaragua's oppressed minorities. They depend on me to fight for their rights, of ownership and self determination, their right to decide their own future democratic rights, as a free people, as world citizens."

Which sounded like "Ah um dah only wuhn lef' to speke fo' my tribe and fo' many ahf Nicaragua's oh-ppressed maeeno'eetees. Dey depen' ohn me to fight for dey rights, ahf ownahsheep ahnd self-deetahminayshone, dey right to decide dey owen footah deymocratic rights, ahz ah free peepo, ahz wah-old seaty-zens."

She claimed to be on guard against assassination attempts and campaigns to smear Her reputation. Her enemies will try to kidnap Her daughter, and send The Princess false news from home to detour The Princess from Her mission.

She said people around the world express interest in her cause, people in Germany, Australia, Denmark and Sweden. She communicates with the Royal family of Sweden, and "some Congressman in the Unite Estates send me lettuce of encouragement."

I tried to look impressed.

"You could help me, help my people, ee-measurably if you would only buy some of my Jewelry, or even just to donate some little money. The money goes to a good cause, a very noble cause. Right now we have no money to eat with. I must buy food for my daughter, and I will still need money to continue the struggle in my people's name."

I gave The Princess some money, just in case she spoke the truth, and in case there is a God, and wished Her good luck.

I didn't tell The Princess what I thought. Unless they strike oil in Mosquitoland, she'll never get what she needs from the rich and powerful. What's in it for them? Why bother rock someone else's empty boat? It's a big ocean out there, and everybody gets their own waves to deal with.

Worst of all, I thought that the best luck would bring her the worst of luck. What if her tribal lands did sit atop oil reserves or gold deposits? Powerful people would hasten their extermination and they would lose the very autonomy they wished to maintain. Better that no one cares, that they somehow survive the slow crush of expansion from other ethnicities, the Latinos, or the Mayans who run further into the forests to escape the chainsaws and guns of ranchers.

Years later, I got a better idea of the abject poverty that people suffer due to the social strata of power, which tends to marginalize any non-Western, non-Consumer cultures while it caters to international businesses in search of cheap labor. They equate constant growth as progress, measured by the expansion of industrialization into underdeveloped societies full of cheap, ignorant labor ruled by despots.

Fifteen years passed before I again heard about the Indians on the Mosquito Coast of Nicaragua and Honduras.

Fifteen years too late, I believed her.

At twenty two years of age, in a fleabag hotel in Guatemala, I met one of the last Princesses of Nicaragua's Mosquito Indians, but didn't believe her, because I didn't look for the most parsimonious explanation, the simplest and most probable reality.

Who else but a Caribbean Queen could rise up out of unendurable hand to mouth poverty and global racism against those with the dark skin of African descent to become an educated, English speaking, multicultural beggar in a run down Guatemala City Hotel?

It took a dead pelican, comic dried frogs, and the bankrupt Black Queen of a Mosquito Coast tribe of interbred Mayans and escaped African slaves to show the son of a long dead American doctor, who wanted to see how the other half lives, how his own background blinds him to the truth.

The Chess Master

The next couple of days I counted funds and estimated how long I could postpone my return. To make plans, travelers spend hours over maps with fellow travelers. I ate lots of beans and corn tortillas only because I doubted I could live on banana splits from the Mayan Ice Cream Queen.

One Sunday, I took a bus to the park on the north edge of town, and walked along a sidewalk where thirty or so people played chess on a row of tables set up in the shade of elegant trees.

At the end of this long line of chess games in progress along the sidewalk, I noticed an obese redheaded man in front of a chessboard adorned with gold tiger statues on the corners. His baleful eyes bugged out over protruded lower lids, pulled down by the weight of his red flecked jowls lined with red ink squiggles of varicose arteries, lids that yawned open to reveal blood red raw meat inside. His thick lips appeared loose and flaccid, wet and pendulous, and they trembled like corned beef in a pout as he breathed through his mouth and appeared agitated whenever he contemplated his next move. He took his opponent's piece with the dart of a fat ham of hand, a grunt, and a sort body of hop that reverberated across his body's thick layers of flab.

So what if he played Chess better than anyone else in all Latin America? I decided he represented a warning that intellectual fanatics risked a long fall into obsessive behavior, a substitute for normal physical pleasures, like exercise and sex. I doubted a person could exist very long in the real world once removed from the physicality of life through obesity. He gave up normal good health and must not realize how he denies himself the natural pleasures of any simple creature that belongs in nature. He divorced himself from his own body when he transmuted himself from mere mortal to become obese Chess Master in a black verses white universe on a checkerboard. A knight trapped in his own crusade, a Grand Inquisitor of chess skill, his physical presence imposed not only a gigantic intimidation and symbol of superiority, but also a death sentence to his chances of quality of life, of spouse, children, health and long life.

He enjoyed too much food, in stark contrast to the majority of people in Guatemala. Like others who lust after the status symbols of convenience and consumption, those who refuse to go to the corner store unless they can drive their ostentatious car, he created himself in their image, an obese "First World" urban denizen. No matter that when they get out of their car or into a shower, they resemble fiddler crabs torn loose from their shells, a dead meat gray shapeless mass dragged around by brute force.

Historical forces from the Northern Europeans' Catholic Church, perhaps inspired as much by a fear of winter as a worship of its sterility, emphasized the authority of the church as they convinced people to distance themselves from nature and deny themselves as a verbal consciousness, with animal needs, and the same God given abilities to enjoy life. Animals don't commit suicide. Obese people do, in the slowest and least cosmetic manner.

Maybe he suffered a disease, a glandular irregularity, a genetic defect in a couple of appetite suppressor genes, or he lives with his mother who cooks immense quantities of gourmet foods spiced with salt peter to destroy any urges to procreate.

The obese and infirm must not think about the poor hospital worker who turns them over for their sponge bath throughout their final weeks, nor about the undertaker, the coffin maker, nor the grave excavators. They must not feel any guilt about the shear quantity of recyclable nutrients they carry with them to the grave in this world full of starvation and neurotic women who idolize the sickly skinniness of fashion models.

Industrialization and consumerism furthered the Church's destructive dogma of a chasm between humans and nature. They exist as dysfunctional cultures, of production and consumption, without a relationship with the biosphere. People who live by industrialization, and those who profit through the blind acquisitiveness of other people, often must ignore their lifestyle's non-sustainability, and push all living things closer to the edge of extinction.

I remember how everyone laughed along with the award winning and famous television advertisement where an elegant mature woman in the prime of her life, dressed in white gowns like a Greek Goddess, points her long alabaster finger like a lightning rod and says, "You shouldn't mess with mother nature."

After I recognized the Chess Master as a stereotypic example of what happens to people divorced from their own physicality and oblivious to the charms of Mother Nature, I decided to dedicate the rest of this trip to a long crawl up her skirt.

CHAPTER 6 New Yearning

Throughout history, archeological evidence reveals that many cultures considered the sacrum bone, the lower spine's widened area of fused vertebrae that curves onto the pelvis, as the source of male fertility. Many cultures created artifacts out of the sacrum bone with exaggerations to its face-like aspects. Some cultures consider it the focal point of each life's resurrection, through which the individual rebirths. Both Plato and Leonardo da Vinci thought a man's ejaculate flowed from the vertebrae, from the spinal "marrow" in the central nerve cord column to the urethra and out through the penis, because of the similar appearance of spinal fluids and semen.

In the Classic Period (100 - 900 AD), Mayan artists noticed that the sacrum looks like a "skull" with eyeholes where the vertebral column's branches of nerves emerge. Mayan artists sculpted the image of a skull at the base of a crack in the scaly shell of the Earth Tortoise or Crocodile, from where emerges the Corn God, Ah Mun, the ruler of the vegetable world, a youthful deity who wears a headdress adorned with one erect ear of corn, the penis shaped fruit loaded with hundreds of seeds for future fertility. Mayans depict him in fights with the Death God, Ah Puch, a skeleton man who rules the Ninth Hell, whose glyph becomes the sixth day sign called Cimi. When the Corn God Ah Mun wins over Ah Puch and death, it causes a rebirth, a resurrection of the dead, rejuvenation, increased longevity, and perhaps, immortality.

On buses, I often kept my shoulder bag on my lap, so I could allow my hand to grab a handful of my rock solid, bus-vibration inspired, super pressurized early morning hard-on.

I thought about where I came from, two thousand miles from Michigan. That distance represents, with speeds that at best averaged fifty miles per hour, a potential for more than forty hours of velocitized tumescent excitation. It seemed like half the time on buses, I either enjoyed my hard-on, or went to lengths to avoid one.

In a heroic effort to avoid sexual frustration, I might start a conversation with an old, ugly Mexican cowboy. Alternatively, I might flirt with a Nun who thought she used to speak English, or prod a dull secondary student out of his catatonic fixation beyond the bus window to hear all about his plans to become a rancher. I found my biggest challenges in conversations with idiots where I hid my yawns and pumped hard to dredge up a little fool's gold.

On a bus, my fear of a public wet dream causes insomnia. I let myself sleep after those around me slept, or appeared to. Everybody looked like they slept all the time, almost no one read anything, not books, newspapers, nor magazines but a few males concentrated on the tiny Mexican book size illustrated novels that featured panel drawings of low rent Zorros who rescue nude female blondes with breasts bigger than his head, and an ass like his horse's.

So I traveled drowsy, which increased the turgidity and made my condition chronic. I bought a light blanket for a little privacy and warmth on all night bus rides to avoid the expense of a hotel, and often awoke to resent the blue denim tightness, over my fly, the bronze zipper a sharp toothed rasp against my tender mushroom. I check for the wetness of its tears of loneliness, and held it to give comfort and shelter from a world that refused to understand. The poor thing would stretch out full length spasm with insistence.

I learned to awaken in fear, with a fresh boyhood recurrent nightmare of 'copious quantities' of tapioca to further yellow my cotton underpants and stiffen a newly darker blue area of denim over my crotch. In my fearful hysteria, I awoke from a dream where semen slithers its way through the forests of mons pubis, drips along both sides of my inner thighs, slides down the leather sack that contains my two furry satellites, and puddles in a subterranean region along my continental divide. Those moments brought me as near to religion as I dared approach, and I thanked God that not once did it ever become a reality.

But in those climactic moments of bus dreams with one of the seven high school girls whose intimacy I craved, I awoke convinced that those around me conspired to hide the joke. Did anyone else notice the sweet smell of success? What does that slight smile on the face of that man across the aisle mean? The over long glance of the sweetest, most innocent young girl becomes accusatory.

Did I make any strange noises in my sleep, as a dog might make, when you scratch its chest?

In total, I estimated almost twenty hours on this trip, to date, of turgid discomfort on busses. Thank God not too many hours in a row.

Women who cry foul and bemoan the injustice of both menstrual cramps and the frivolous sexuality of men should try an hour or two of testicular blue-balls, just for comparison. Menstrual cramps win for long term inevitable torture, but women should know the consequences when they keep a man in unreleased sexual excitation for hours. A girl who teases the cobra might think about how she would act if avoidance of menstrual cramps depended on an orgasm.

I remember rides on the School bus on dark, six AM subzero mornings, the snow illuminated by starlight. Next stop, one of white-blond Frisch twins, or Amy Dykema with her firm milky jugs that stretch her sweater a little more each day. Then we pick up Cathy, who hates any references to bovines or her hips. At the end of a long driveway that leads to a ramshackle house built out of what construction sites throw away, we pick up my favorite, the mulatto with frizzy hair Crystal, who claims "Russian Jewish extraction." She gives me a half smile, then turns to sit down next to me in a slow motion that exaggerates her exaggerated hindquarters and gives me a surge in blood pressure my young heart does not yet understand.

Then they might ask me questions like "Why you hold all those books on your lap? Put them on the floor. Let me borrow one. Why won't you I let me see your book?" Ha ha ha. Maybe they did, or didn't appreciate the fact that regardless of whether or not a girl sat next to pubescent boys like me, a woody grew like an instant beech tree, a boner swelled rock hard and bent against the pile of five books on his lap until he thought they balanced there like Chinese acrobats on Sunday night's black and white television ritual called The Ed Sullivan Show. If these savvy girls wanted to take credit for my missile silo, why should anyone spoil their fantasy?

Upon arrival at school, I descend the bus steps with my books held in front of my groin. One of the girls pulls at a friend's elbow and turns around to ask me, "Feel pretty up this morning?"

Freshmen high school girls adopt a new way to smile that suggests to me their mothers told them more about boys than we knew about ourselves.

Some guys might know a few things, through their dads, uncles, older brothers, cousins, neighbors, counselors, etc. but not fatherless me.

I figured out what little I knew from the encyclopedia. Those guys that knew how to date seemed like hoodlums, the rough boys that shaved early and never studied enough to get good at it and learn to enjoy it.

When I first started to hang out with serious cock tease high school girls, I got blue balls a couple of times, and vowed to avoid it through a daily purge of my procreative juices. I enjoyed this time to myself, and looked forward to it each night. I tried to drag each session out to twenty minutes or so, with the conscious intention to train myself so that I could pleasure a woman to her satisfaction before my own climax.

Throughout the whole trip down the North American continent to Central America, I found it impossible to follow this nocturnal ritual as often as necessary.

My predicament reminded me of that shared dorm room in college, where I first recognized my imprisonment in Maslow's Hierarchy of Needs.

Once a person receives food, clothing, and shelter, they bungle through the jungle to find someone with whom to procreate, an act that occurs with greater probability and frequency in safety and comfort. Then a person wants to belong, then needs to decide on some goal, something to do with all this comfort and free time on their hands. The highest level of human existence Maslow termed self actualization, where people achieve success doing what they love to do. He studied Lincoln, Thomas Jefferson, philosophers, artists, and other exemplary humans with the hope to uncover a principle or psychology of excellence. He realized that most people never achieve self actualization because they cannot satisfy the needs that build a foundation for self actualization. Each level of need leads one to strive for a the next, even more difficult, level.

This life long long process of lifestyle design, discipline, and satisfaction of needs may lead to 'peak experiences' that others miss, or can't feel, in a sunrise, the way birds fly in silhouette in front of lofty clouds, the sounds of music or a magic moment of a well interpreted song, a mountain landscape with waterfall, or the front lawn. Something that feels like a spiritual awakening. These experiences can provoke profound changes in the individual, who recalls such moments as important, unforgettable, and noteworthy.

Maslow thought this helped explain how what he termed 'self actualized individuals' accept themselves and others. Self actualization leads to an independence from the culture and society in which they live. This aloofness may cause social discord, but and also brings them few, but very close, personal friendships. Self actualized people can devote their life energy in a conscious search for solutions to important (to them) problems, which may lead to improvements in the human condition for the greatest common good, as Confucius postulated as the root of ethics and morality five hundred years before Christ.

Poor Einstein, to see what military minds did with his elegant theoretical work on the nature of reality. He wondered what in the universe remained constant, if time and space could fluctuate, and discovered their relativity to the speed of light.

In the meantime I remain stuck on a lower level of need and walk around with exaggerated interest in females, their self decoration and laughter, every dart of their eyes toward me, and every jiggle as they walked away. I inhaled their perfume as they walked passed, and admired the contours of hips, lips, and tits. The high hemlines of miniskirts called attention to what they revealed, and I responded to every one. The tease of a plunged neckline kept me on my toes as I stood alongside them on packed busses to sway together on every curve, to relish discreet snuggles against their softness. A woman's athleticism attracted me as a challenge to subdue, as their baby fat passivity inspired me to try and awaken the lioness of passion that lay imprisoned in their bubbly, vacuous voluptuousness.

Once ensnared by beauty, the obsession manipulated my activities, my route and thoughts. Where they walked, my eyes followed and I strove to intercept, to get close and assure myself that any brief meteoric recognition of appreciable beauty represented a work of art, a rare beauty, an manifestation of the divine. Of course, this love at first sight, as in great art, often results from a happy coincidence of light, form, image, and execution, and most of my pursuits led to disappointment, but once in a while a woman stupefied me, and I felt outclassed and unworthy, and ran away.

I felt that hunger, did not feel safe to pursue satisfaction, did not belong, did not feel comfortable, and although I knew what I wanted to do, to write music and collect experiences to write about later in life if I survived, this distraction by female beauty tortured many wakeful hours, and often invaded my dreams.

On those days of youthful health, my unexpurgated lust changed me, encapsulated me. I looked out through my own eyes as if from inside a prison cell, entombed in a hell of frustration, on one of the lowest rungs of the ladder of Maslow's hierarchy of needs.

Hotel San Jose's Electric Shower

In the Valley of Guatemala, near present Guatemala City's western edge, over 200 earth and clay mounds dated to the Late Formative (300 BC–AD 100) period may represent the doorway between two cultures, that of the lowland Maya and the Izapan's culture, influenced by the Olmecs from Mexico's isthmus of Tehuantepec. Inside one mound, a log tomb preserved the treasures of a deceased nobleman, buried with an accompaniment of many other bodies, perhaps sacrificed slaves, subjects, prisoners of war, or citizens (volunteered or forced) into the burial event. Archeologists excavated around three hundred and fifty objects, some perhaps three and a half thousand years old, which included various types of worked Jade; beadwork jewelry, necklaces, mosaic masks, ear spools, and figurines. They also uncovered beautiful multicolored pottery containers, chlorite schist bowls, and worked volcanic rock.

138

The inclusion of curious mushroom shaped stones may point to ritual use of the hallucinogenic drug psilocybin, found in a common mushroom which resembles other mushrooms with sometimes lethal toxins. A ritual that featured ingestion of mushrooms might alow the most skilled Shamans the choice of who to entertain, and who to kill.

Just after dawn, we entered a modern Latino community somewhere on the outskirts of Guatemala City. The bus driver pulled us into what looked like an abandoned gas station, and turned off the motor. The bus stopped with a giant hiss of escaped gases from the pneumatic brakes. Then the quiet muffled the sounds of travelers exhausted by boredom who roused enough to glance out the window and slump back under their jackets or blankets that shielded them from the highland's chilly air.

A sweater clad group of five long haired Indian women with big, dirty, misshapen cloth bags came out from behind the building. They gathered around the bus driver as he opened the motor compartment and poked around for space to stow their cargo.

I dozed off, then awoke to the slam of the metal panel motor cover. The driver took money from the women, and they entered the bus to fill the center aisle with bags and stout bodies.

The sky lightened into an airbrushed dawn streaked with red rays. I hoped that the sun would come out before we passed the Red Tile Church. I saw it from a long way off, as we crossed the top of a slight hilltop that gave us a glimpse of the entire Valley of Guatemala City.

Fifteen minutes later, as the bus approached it, the sun broke through the morning clouds and the shiny tiles looked like wine with flickers of golden electric lightning across the surface. As the bus passed, it looked almost transparent with reflections of the glorious sky, almost fluid with rivulets of sunlight.

No one but I noticed. The others on the bus, asleep or awake, didn't turn their head, while I felt as if electricity passed from the church into me. As we drove away, I took out my journal and tried to describe it.

I awoke when the bus slowed to a crawl to negotiate a couple of tight corners through stair step size potholes. It pulled up diagonal against the bus terminal, a long airplane hanger turned into a cement stable. Through the glass, I could see five dark bus line offices with broken equipment and ad-hoc restaurant menu signs of destinations. Fifteen minute stop, many stood in the aisle to get off the bus, and I wedged among them with my shoulder bag low in front of my zipper.

I stood and followed the schoolgirls as they got off.

The bus terminal's floor, a chaos from multicolored polka-dots of chewing gum stains, made me dizzy.

The girls pushed and pulled each other to glance back at me to giggle and hide within the group as they walked toward the bathrooms, their faces mottled with flush and acne, a demonstration of raw teenage ridicule that fails at both discretion and wit.

I decide to explore Guatemala City on foot, from the Terminal de Autobuses Extra-urbanos to the central Central Plaza, and look for a cheap hotel.

The Terminal de Ferrocarriles (Railroad) reminded me of images of Asia, swarthy exotic people in the daily drama of a pedestrian infrastructure that brought the foodstuffs to the urban masses, the farmers and dockworkers, pushcarts, wheelbarrows, and trump-line backpacks. Their shadowy hulks moved about the docks, unions of masses of muscle with boxes and formless bags from palettes they pushed around on carts like oversized roller skates.

Not far from the terminal, the large window display of a coffee shop grabbed my attention with plastic imitation pastries, cakes, toys, dolls, two dead frogs in a miniature bed embraced in the missionary position.

I backed up, yes two frogs in frontal coitus, three lizards stuffed into poses of See no Evil Hear no Evil Speak no Evil, and a dead bird that hung upside down from his knees with a beak in a cartoon smile, four baby alligators with guitars and a trap set bent and lined up like rock'n rollers, "Los Rocodrillos."

I peered inside to see the rest of the restaurant, and realized the coffee shop belonged to a hotel.

I found a door nearby under a drab, crooked sign, painted many years ago. Vague letters whispered "Hotel San Jose".

A sleepy young man first pretended he couldn't understand my Spanish, and then tried to point me toward the tourist section of town, but I convinced him that I needed a cheap room. He led the way past the restaurant's doorway and into a darkness of labyrinthine medieval corridors, as black and gray as old photographs. My backpack bumped and scraped on pipes along the narrow passage. Bare wires, spider webs, and live spiders decorated the walls. A couple of times as we walked, he flailed about with one arm to pull unseen strings that turned on bare light bulbs that dangled from wires or fixtures once attached to the cement ceiling.

He motioned me to lower my head to pass under the splayed wings of a stuffed pelican. It swayed in the faint breeze fanned by our passage as we walked on, the fingerlike projections of its macabre shadow clawed the air.

I examined the pelican. A zigzag corpse bent into a caricature of a Pelican's dive, in nature not graceful, a dirty white W with a long neck and splayed feathers, the translucent jaw pouch spread out like an old worn sock. I couldn't imagine why the taxidermist went to all that trouble to create such a misshapen ugliness.

On the seashores, 'los Pelícanos' like to sit on the docks with a regal air, and at sunrise or sunset, I saw them fly in squadrons of three to six. They follow the wave crests and peel off to dive, like demented swastikas against the ocean sky, to grab any fish exposed in the translucent green wall produced as each wave enters the shallows.

He showed me to a tiny windowless room, lit by one bare electric bulb, which possessed one modern convenience, he assured me with great pride.

At first, I suspected he played with me, that he spoke false and sarcastic.

He drew back a mineralized black plastic shower curtain to reveal the inside of a black metal box, the shower stall. Thick chips of black paint peeled off on all three sides. His hand urged me to look closer.

I noticed one typical garden faucet water valve knob on one pipe, and asked him if they had hot water.

He smiled, two gold teeth glinted, and he pointed to the showerhead. He explained, in a halted Spanish that waited every four words for a sign of comprehension from me, that this little cylinder mounted into the water pipe at the showerhead heats the water with electricity. He twisted a dial on this machine to impress me with its temperature control.

I noticed the electric cord drooped down from the showerhead, wrapped around the water pipe twice, then hung in a graceful half circle out the shower doorway to the wall outlet.

Perfect. A shower stall/electrocution chamber. My electrocution would dim the hotel's lights and alert management to change a fuse and call the coroner.

I dipped my shoulder to liberate myself from the backpack and dangled it on my feet, asked him the price, then said OK to signify that I found the room acceptable. He motioned for me to leave my pack on the bed with a "no hay problema" echoed by both of us several times. Thus trapped, I followed him out to pay for the night.

I found my way back down the corridors to my new room, undressed, and examined my nakedness in the small mirror over an unpainted writing desk, then stepped into the shower.

The showerhead's water pipe passed through what resembled a small coffee can. The dial on the side marked off a semicircle with gradations from Frio to Caliente. I turned the round metal lawn faucet handle mounted at belly button level on that one little pipe, and the water came out frigid cold, a fifty degree spray that reduced me to shivers in seconds. I wondered where such cold water came from, in a hot tropical country full of volcanoes.

I pulled the wet chord attached to the tin can on the showerhead, and expected to feel one hundred and ten volts of wall current push electrons through my arm, across my chest, groin, and legs, and out my feet to escape to ground with the shallow hurricane of black water that slipped down the drain. I waited for the water temperature to change, and then stepped out of the shower to escape the icy water and manipulate the device from beyond the curtain. I turned the dial all the way to Caliente, and expected to hear the hiss of steam as the water passed over hot electric coils. The temperature warmed. A little.

I waited for about ten seconds, the amount of time it took my teeth to chatter like ice cubes in fine crystal, ten seconds that took hours to pass. My arm felt the shower of water like a blizzard of ice needles. I turned down the flow of water. As the flow turned into tiny threadlike trickle, the water heated up.

I stepped back into the shower. That trickle of hot water thawed my frozen body, a ribbon at a time. I wondered about the technology that prevented the electricity from a quick run down this dribble of water, through my heart and spastic body, until I died there on the floor, a white Gringo pretzel in extremis.

The Guatemalan soap smelled like the chemical rose scented Air freshener odor they spray on plastic flowers for funerals, but it smelled a lot better than I did then, my last swim in Lake Atitlán now a memory from days gone by.

With the luxury of a shower stall in my room, I first thought I could do myself when I pleased, and would often. Not so. As a friend once claimed, as if to talk me out of onanism, that in one twenty four hours he did it twenty seven times. My efforts at a personal best convinced me that quality trumps quantity.

I got used to this black shower stall, and in a strange way, came to love its cosmic darkness, which began to symbolize the lack of a woman, a wife, in my life.

The recent invention of the Birth Control Pill in the sixties created a sexual revolution of Free Love coincidental with the Hippies who rejected what they saw as a System of workaholic consumerism whose profits fueled the Viet Nam War. When hippies rejected traditions and unhooked from the workaholic world, they rediscovered what it meant to live unwashed and unashamed of their humanity. Many people experimented with a new situation where women took control over their own reproduction. Women could copulate as freely as men, with little fear of pregnancy. Not that men ever feared pregnancy.

For the first time in human history, the average daughter now had a good reason to live independent of her family. And if some young female experimenter lived with a cute roommate, liberal doses of alcohol and other recreational drugs tipped the scale of probability toward bisexual threesomes, which became a principal seed image for fantasies that branched and convoluted like the rivulets of warmish water over my chilled skin, when I did myself in that sprinkled blackness.

I slow danced and walked tiny circles under a hot trickle, all lathered up, to charm the cobra for ten or twenty minutes. The first time I loved myself in the shower, it hurt, my serpent's clotted venom came out like a knitting needle made of sandpaper. The floodgates must open more often or the river silts shut. I knew that if I didn't blow for a week or so, it got painful to climax, like the urethra narrows or the jelly thickens, feels like something rips open with the expulsion of those first dollops of hot caulk. I lost no time to take advantage of my black shower with a long bout of muscular tension under that hot rivulet, and the first paroxysms took my breath. I shuddered and shook, stifled the urge to howl, my toes curled under, and I lost my balance to fall against the back paint chipped wall with the thunderous boom of the thin sheet metal stall. My blunt cobra spat a galaxy in slow motion, squirted dayglo phosphorescent aluminum flake donut glaze through that little tinkle of water to slap the wall in Milky Way arcs across the pitted black paint. It streamed from me in spasmic pulse after pulse and formed, in mid flight, paired dumbbell drips that spun and hit the wet wall to start long, sluggish slide toward the drain. Looked like the black wall melted. It flowed slow towards the floor to form jellied amphibian spermatophores that I swept down the black open throat of the drain with a foot that trembled on a rubber ankle.

I recovered, stepped out of the shower and into a room full of chilly Eternal Springtime air. I felt clean and energized. With some warm clothes on, I raided my stash of money, located passport, pen and paper, loaded up my handbag, and stepped through the door to explore the city.

I locked the door, and from the next room, a troll of a stocky Guatemalan stepped out. He rubbed his eyes and glared at me as if to blame me for interrupted sleep. One thirty in the afternoon.

"Buenos Días," I said.

"Buenas tardes."

Good morning, good afternoon you mean. He gave me the impression my noise woke him up, or that he strained to listen to every whispered pant, or maybe he intuited every move I made in the shower, because he did, too.

I gave him the shoulder and marched down the dim corridor. The sunlight struggled to enter through layers of dust and cobwebs over tiny vent windows high up on the walls, beyond the water and drainage pipes, which ran everywhere.

Dead end. I missed a turn somewhere. I made note of the dead Pelican, a feathered chevron mounted as if in a dive. Years ago, some short Guatemalan hung him high over his head, level with my face.

I passed the front desk and came to the dim restaurant's open door. Shafts of bright sunlight streamed across the room's empty tables and chairs. The shafts entered through the curtained front window, above the display cases where I knew dead frogs dressed like the Beatles played silent music for frogs that copulated on a copper wire brass bed.

I entered the restaurant.

A round fat man, with greasy prematurely gray hair around a shiny bald spot, sat up as if electrocuted from behind his newspaper. He motioned me to sit anywhere, and stood up to grab a menu and shoot me a big smile with a mouthful of teeth outlined in gold.

"Mañana." I told him, and backed away to explore the city.

The Iglesia de la Merced, a Cathedral built of huge stone blocks carved in Neoclassic style and hoisted by a power greater than man, rose out of an apron of rust red tiles. It hinted at supernatural forces greater than those the Mayan Indians believed in. After the Santa Marta earthquake of 1773 destroyed Antigua, the old capital city, the Spanish crown ordered the city abandoned, and its polychrome iconic art treasures moved here. Catholic cathedrals seemed designed to frighten and inspire the credulous, those who feel small and weak, into a faith in large things with a baroque labyrinth of purposeless illogic at the core. The building's stone glowed with a copper orange tint, and the wide flat apron, fashioned from darker red blocks, reminded me of the blood of sacrificial victims. So far, I did not notice any rock this color in Guatemala's road cuts, but the twenty seven volcanoes must produce a great variety of rock. For this cathedral, they chose a color so uncommon it looked unearthly, perhaps to represent divine origins, to leave the Indians with an indelible sense of wonder even as they fill the churches with bluish smoke of their Copal incense, as they did atop their pyramid temples before Spaniard invaders dismantled them to build the cathedrals that now house Catholic icons meant to inspire the faithful to accept blood and body of Christ on their tongues for the redemption of mankind.

Not much improvement on the same tired theme of the Mayans, an attitude adjustment through horrific reminders of mortality. Serves the same function as horror films, to make one jump into another's protective arms.

Newspapers in Guatemala often carry a cover photo of bloody carnage, a gangland homicide victim, auto accidents, gruesome and graphic injuries, photos of corpses with amputations, or amputations without corpses.

In a nation of illiterates, blood sells papers when the headlines can't.

My hiking boots clomped across that dried blood apron to the Cathedral's entrance. I tried not to let it intimidate me. I pulled open a small door cut into the massive wood of the huge arched doors, thought about rebirth, and walked through the antechambers and down the center aisle. From a row of high stained glass windows, dim shafts of light slashed diagonal through a slight fog of humidity.

My eyes adjusted and I saw paintings of Stations of the Cross on the walls, cubby hole niches with saints and angels, the black box altar draped with a huge crochet doily, the divine podium with its little cobra, a brass hooded reading light. As a backdrop, pillars with giant brocades of carvings flowed up like twin towers of golden seaweed, full of little angels that frolicked and hid amid the golden vines like chubby white flowers. In the center of the wall behind the altar and podium, a huge statue of wounded Jesus in manikin color, pinned up like a butterfly, mascara eyes rolled upward to bury halfway under the eyelids.

Stillness.

Tiny noises, the titters of mice, pigeon coos outside against a high window, a batwing rustle from the alcove roof, the creak of new shoes.

I sat inside a confessional I couldn't think of a thing to confess, a void in my social learning due to an upbring oblivious of Medieval notions like sin and redemption.

Another, more voluntary, ignorance allowed me to walk into places where others feared to tread. I found glass coffins that contained white shrouded bearded saints with the same injuries as Jesus on their wooden hands. Alongside the pews, round pillars sprouted that looked like ashtrays, in the shape of tree mushrooms, that held little ponds of water. A cushion covered two by four on the floor in front of the pews assuaged the knees of a few old women who prayed with heads wrapped in long black scarves.

Catholicism and the old Mayan or Aztec cosmologies both abound in victims and bloody sacrifice. A magical progression from Jaguar boy, victors as sacrificial victims, virgin sacrifice, virgin birth, then God's infanticide of his own only child.

Man, the crown of creation, a self proclaimed mirror image of God, the most developed, evolved, diverse, and complicated organism extant in this corner of our small known universe, a creature inclined to demonstrate an endless capacity for physical, spiritual, intellectual, moral, and heartfelt self abasement through abuse of others.

The meek and merciful shall inherit resentment and inevitable bondage to the bloody hands of one they saved.

Maybe I would feel different after a thirty mile crawl over cobblestones with planks tied to my hands and knees, then through city streets of greasy diesel dust and pigeon shit, to the back room of this church to pin my prayer request atop hundreds of others'.

I left the church, made a big circle and a few discoveries. A few blocks east or west of the three main one way business streets, each city block walled in its own small community of houses, each with independent windows and entrances. The individual dwellings, very few three stories high, shared the street side walls with the neighbors, but at different heights and colors. The doors and windows of various styles, decorated with wooden shutters, wrought iron grills, stone frame window boxes, tiny balconies, etc punctuated these walls and gave distinct character to each household.

I wondered what the houses looked like on the inside.

Ermita del Carmen

Next day, I dressed without a sound in the predawn darkness.

Inside the hotel, I followed stairways upwards and emerged onto the roof, a flat area with clotheslines, a couple of crude cement water tanks built upon short pillars, and a row of cement sinks.

From my high vantage point, I noticed a little lighted knoll crowned with a church on the northeast horizon, near central Guatemala City, the oldest section.

Back in my room, I found it marked on the map as Cerro del Carmen, a church surrounded by a park. I escaped out the door without breakfast as the maid unlocked the front door, headed for the market to purchase the day's supplies.

The dark, dampness and dew enhanced the city's textures. Rock stained black, shiny polished granites, baked brick and tile, pockmarked volcanic stone, and sidewalks squares repaired with various tones of reddish cement made of volcanic sands.

I walked through invisible clouds of breakfast aromas, hot corn oil, fried eggs, toasted tortillas, vanilla, wood fire smoke punctuated by short bursts of stink from black water drainage, rotten fruit, piss, and excrement which I assumed came from stray dogs, until I accepted the dearth of dogs and the prevalence of rural Indians. A few cars puttered by to break the morning song of wings and wind as parakeets streamed overhead.

On many streets, a stout matron or malnourished maid in apron threw water to sweep their sidewalk and the road in front. Some flung big bowls of water to arc a spray halfway across the road, or used the fan of water from a hose like a broom to sweep out the tiled corridor that led into their house.

Deep in the predawn urban canyon of the oldest part of Guatemala City, I overshot my goal, the little church on the hill, and doubled back to approached the "Cerro del Carmen" from the northeast side. Bare dirt footpaths wound through natural meadows under a small forest, punctuated with groomed patches of flowers. The trails connected picnic areas, open spaces with metal grills that overflowed with gray wood ash.

On the hilltop, alongside an ancient, small, whitewashed church with a rounded roof on the cliff side end, huge pine trees stood guard and whispered with each breeze.

The Church's black stained dome adorned the west end, pointed toward the city. On the other end, toward the sunrise, ornate pillars, one on either side of the heavy wooden doors, framed the entrance. A driveway looped in front of the church and then spiraled off down the hill. A little round tower, like a two story cement lighthouse, stood in the center of the circular drive. A sign proclaimed the church "Ermita del Carmen", which translates to Carmen's hermitage.

I walked around the church on bare footpaths lined with gardens of exotic plants in flower. Even the trees adorned themselves, some with great red roses like upended flamenco skirts, some with pious white carnations, another kind responded to the slightest gust with a perfumed rain of yellow petals the size of bumblebee wings.

As dawn broke and the sun came up, the birdsong swelled to a din that chorused and swirled in my dizzy head. I peered up through the branches to spot the birds that made that roar of sound, saw nothing. The sounds turned into a chorus of female voices in song. It came from inside the church.

I walked over and peaked through the dark entrance, and saw the interior draped with a great pyramid of pure white gauze streamers of cloth, each about a foot and a half wide, that peaked at the dome's center and came down to the pews' outer ends. Sunlight streaked in through high windows and lit up the white walls. Tied to the giant white gauze ribbons, hundreds of balloons floated like pearls in slow motion. Nuns in white winged hats filled the first rows of pews.

I retreated to a nearby cement bench under the pines to listen to them sing.

A perfect peace, a rare respite of order and beauty in a chaotic universe, born of human faith built upon the backs of a people conquered and enslaved four hundred and fifty years ago.

Little did I know, that one predawn morning one month from now I would try to sleep on this narrow stone bench in terror alongside a woman with whom I'd already spent an almost sleepless night.

Low clouds rolled in and clumped together to darken the day. From this high vantage point, I saw them dance to the slow airy melodies of the nun's songs.

Guatemala City almost filled this long valley as a horizontal galaxy of yellow streetlights framed by distant mountains. Below, an adobe brick factory made a reddish ochre checkerboard, patches of domino shaped rectangles lined up on the long edge to dry. On the distant southern horizon, I saw the powder blue outlines of tall, modern hotels near the airport.

The architecture of each city block reminded me of a centipede rolled into a square, each bug's segment a separate house, each house itself a donut shape of red tile roof, with a central open space. Sometimes I could see into that courtyard's upper floors to see compartmentalized balconies festooned with huge potted plants and trees in flower, cages where parrots or turkeys squawked, and rows of clotheslines with scarecrow shirts. The houses shared both outer and inner walls with their neighbors, but each house enclosed its own courtyard.

Around each courtyard, the roofs of round red tiles slanted inward. Tiles shaped like a halved thigh length section of pipe lay in two layers, rows of one lay open upward, and the top layer opens downward to straddle the seams between troughs. They drained rainwater inward into the courtyard. I liked the idea that each home enjoyed absolute privacy in its own courtyard jungle, with rainfall diverted into roof runoff and collected in fifty gallon oil drums to provide extra water and help control courtyard floods.

I sketched a tree in front of the church, because of a hole in the tree trunk's middle, through which I could see part of the church. The side of the church from this angle looked like a rectangle between six square support pillars, with the dome over the farther western end.

I sat in the grass and tried another sketch of a species of tree that grew branches as regular as a ladder, and each branch a series of smaller branches that ended in round explosion of needle filled branches like balls of long green fingers.

Maybe a Norfolk Pine.

The nuns stopped singing. The valley's urban cacophony surged up with a motorized rush of wind and hisses, beeps and honks, and the thunderous rumble of big metal plates as empty trucks stamped across potholes.

A misty rain fell, and I sketched as long as I could.

Guatemalteco Intellectual

The Popol Vuh, one of a very few books that remain from the Maya, comes from the Highland Guatemalan cultures and talks about their cosmology and creation myths, like the Bible. They believed in multiple creations, each destroyed by floods, of three previous worlds. The Popol Vuh chronicles the adventures of first humans, the Hero twins, who fool the Gods and represent cosmic principles themselves, similar to the Chinese Yin yang symbols, with the Sun a representation of the Heavens and Life, and the Jaguar to represent the Underworld, and Death. Dwarves inhabited a first creation filled with darkness, yet built buildings. Everything became ruins when the first sun dawned and turned the dwarves to stone previous to a flood that destroyed the world. In the second creation, the Dzolob "offenders" inhabited the world, again destroyed by flood. The Maya inhabited the third creation, but they too succumbed to flood. This time, the fourth creation, the Maya believe humanity a mixture of all the types of people that came before.

A well dressed young man came over and stood beside where I sat. He watched me draw a while, and then said, "Good job" in Spanish. He motioned with his hand, wanted to sit beside me and watch.

He squatted on the heels of his shiny black shoes, his charcoal gray dress pants stretched tight over muscular thighs.

We conversed in 'Special English' and sign language, as most people of different languages and cultures can, when pushed. Each half understands the other and nods assent anyway, and each side of the conversation stalls while some mysterious back burner sorts out new word symbols into messages and responses of equal intelligibility. A smile and repetitious "yes" can buy a little time for things to clear up a few sentences later.

"You know this church?" he said in Spanish.

"No, not much."

"Spanish conquistadors built this, first church, here in Guatemala, first in all of Latin America. Ermita del Carmen."

I looked up the words in the dictionary, to show him I could. Ermita means Hermitage, a place for monks and nuns.

"I go to college. You go to college?"

I felt warned, his tone accusatory and the two of us, alone, me a stranger here, and far from the busy street's police officers. Did he plan on a robbery, to snatch my wallet, hit me over the head? I figured him a little smaller than me. He noticed my hesitation.

He looked around and said, "Nobody see, nobody care. ¿Cigaro?"

"Sure."

He stood up for easier access to a front trouser pocket and took out a pack of cigarettes with three left.

I stood up too, and we lit up. Then we walked behind the ancient Church, where the rock edged walkway ran along a cliff that looked out over Guatemala City.

"This valley" he waved his arm to take in the flat expanse of this wide valley high altitude flatland between distant mountain ranges, "called Valley of Cows. Now look, mostly all houses. Cortez came here, with Bernal Díaz de Castillo. You know him?"

"No. Cortez, si."

"Bueno, this place very old. When Spanish come here, they see Guatemalans like animals, like sheep for God. Spanish show Jesus to Mayans."

I tried to help him out. "So Jesus could save them."

"Like America save Guatemala?" he gave me a suspicious look, as if critical of my American education. "In this place they see the Quetzal bird, so beautiful."

He fished in a trouser pocket to pull out a Guatemalan dollar, similar to Estados Unidos Mexicanos' money, so colorful the most crass tourists from the United States of North America refer to it as Monopoly money, or 'play money' for board games.

He showed me the drawing of the long tailed green Quetzal on it, then handed me the bill. Then he put his left hand out.

I got out my billfold, wary that he might try to snatch it from me, and took out an American dollar to hand him.

He stretched the American dollar out, and showed me Washington's picture. "Who this?"

"Washington. Father of the country."

"President, no?"

"The first president. Yes."

He held up the Quetzal, pointed to the bird, then the head of an Indian chief. "You know who he is?"

"No."

"You think he president?"

"No, I doubt it."

"You know how much Quetzal worth?"

"One Quetzal, one dollar."

He said "¿Por que? Why?" and stood with a frozen smile as he waited for my answer.

I said, "What do you mean?"

"You come here through Mexico, right? All right. You change money into Mexican pesos, twelve to one. Fine. In Guatemala, you change money one to one, one Quetzal for one dollar, all the time, every year, year after year. Strange, no?"

"No. Maybe the Guatemalan treasury measures the Quetzal against the dollar."

"Look at how beautiful the Quetzal is."

"Very beautiful."

"You know, they say it printed in the United States. If so, why does the United States not make pretty money?"

"Because they call dollars greenbacks?"

"Like military, you see. Military green. Green go. You know Gringo' green go? Why they no change color of American money?"

"Why?"

"That is so strange, is it not? Always same color? Make it easier to copy?"

"Why would they want that to happen?"

We looked at each other, as if we each recognized a long row to hoe. He must convince me the United States of North America would gain from easily counterfeited money, and I must convince him of my country's noble incorruptibility.

He finally said, "Insurance policy. Easy for people to print when they need to buy things."

"Why would my government want to make it easy for counterfeiters?"

"Guatemala grows bananas. You know what the United States produces?"

"Apples, oranges, vegetables, lots of stuff."

"You buy vegetables here, what you think of the prices?"

"Incredible, so cheap."

"The United States does not produce vegetables for the rest of the world. They make guns."

"So you think counterfeiters buy guns from the United States?"

He said, "What year you born?"

"Nineteen fifty three."

"OK. One year after you born, the United States government take away the Guatemalan President."

"Where to?"

"What that mean, where to?"

"Where did they take him, where did he go?"

"They take him out, away, put in another president. American Army come into Guatemala, planes bomb boats, and United States take our President away from us."

"Was he a dictator or something?"

"We voted to elect him president. Democracy. Like that."

"You think the United States would do something like that? Why? For what? We don't make war in Central America."

"You know, in nineteen fifty three, one American company sells all the bananas in Guatemala."

"What do you mean all? In the market?"

He lay back exasperated and thought of another way to put it. "Look, Guatemala sells bananas to United States. One United States company sells bananas from all Guatemala. Understand?"

"Yes."

He said, "Today, almost twenty five years later, one company sells bananas. Guatemala's bananas."

"Yeah, so what's the point?"

"Do you know about our Presidential election?"

"No, nothing."

"We, the people of Guatemala voted, but the man we vote for, he not President. The loser, he is President."

"When did that happen?"

"Last year."

"The man who won the election is not president?"

He shrugged his shoulders. "No. He is not president. The man who won is not president, because the United States don't like the man. Same thing happened in nineteen fifty three, but this time, without Army. More quieter."

"Are you sure about that?"

"Of course! Everybody say so."

"Who counts the votes?"

"No matter who counts votes, no matter who votes. Depends on who United States wants for President of Guatemala. To serve American business."

"You think American business depends on bananas?"

He looked at me blank. "I don't understand you."

"You think the United states steals your elections to control bananas?"

He looked unsure. "Yes, yes I think so. Maybe I unnerstan you mean what is."

"If you believe what you say, tell the newspapers."

"Everybody knows already the problem."

"Tell someone. Even if everybody else admits it's wrong and still doesn't care enough to change anything, you should still try. Democracy comes with responsibility."

"My friend, every year hundreds of Guatemalans killed, disappeared, and no one knows who, or why. Maybe I know newspaper will print my letter, without name. How I deliver that letter? You carry letter for me? You take my letter into newspaper office? No one will print such a letter, so those letters don't exist. Instead, I will disappear. Maybe you too."

I visualized a time five hundred years ago, when European people first walked up here to see their new church, the first permanent infiltration of Western culture and religion in the Land of Eternal Springtime. The Mayan world forever changed, infiltrated by people with ideas from another continent, driven by greed for gold, unable to maintain their religious perception of a common humanity or "soul, nor share a perception of equal moral worth, which excluded all possibility for democratic, or at least cooperative, participatory government across ethnic and cultural lines.

They did coexist, and intermarry. The Spanish did not kill the indigenous inhabitants off, like the English and Northern Europeans accomplished in the United States of North America in what humanity must remember one of humanity's true genocides, not an ethnocide or culture war, like most wars, but the state mandated eradication of humans as representatives of a genotype, the so-called "Mongol" race of Native Americans.

He asked to see my paper map of Guatemala, and showed me how to get to a park with a large three dimensional map of the entire country of Guatemala. "The road stop here, barranca, you know? Yes, a cliff. All streets in this park stop."

He looked around, asked me the time, then said he must return to his family, so we parted.

For once, a Guatemalan or Mexican did not invite me to their house, or at least force me to write down their name, phone number, and address.

Seemed like he rushed off in fear.

I looked around and noticed a police officer headed our way.

If he believes what he said, he may also believe he saved my life, and his, at that moment.

I wondered about the political reality of all this, and if true what he said, if it ever got back to the citizens of the United States of North America, would anyone care? Everyone in the states knows most Americans live blissful, innocent, affluent and noble lives relative to most people on Earth. Bananas cost so little in Michigan. At ten cents a pound, the store might take three or four cents which left six pennies a pound to pay for the grocery store distribution, transportation out of Guatemala, and shipment within Guatemala. That wouldn't leave much for the banana pickers who carried those green, back breaker size bunches to get crated and shipped.

Moms tell us to eat up because people starve in Africa, and never stops to think that if we didn't feed so much corn to cows and pigs in immense feedlots, that same amount of corn might feed ten times more people that the meat could.

I walked to the main thoroughfare and took a northbound bus. We passed through a more spacious and modern part of the city, and then entered a park under the boughs of huge trees. The bus circled around a fenced off area, and within which I saw a large cement area, like a playground filled with spires of termite mounds, elongated, tall slender cement volcanoes about three feet high.

A sign explained the map exaggerated the vertical scale for clarity, and above the map one could climb a platform that stretched out over the map to offer a more expansive view of the entire country. Little triangular flags labeled the place names of towns, Mayan Archeological sites, mountains, rivers, and other points of interest.

A spot of blue, labeled Lago de Atitlán, sprawled up the side of a volcano.

The young man's words haunted me. Often when I repeated back to him what I understood from him, he said yes, correct, but I still couldn't believe that he wanted me to understand that the United States overthrew his country's president back in nineteen fifty four, in my first year of life, over some bananas.

If true, he could not communicate to me enough details to convince me that no situation existed to mitigate a blatant violation of sovereignty and democratic principles. Some National Security fear, or even a threat of Communist expansion. Maybe I didn't pay attention in High School.

The Ladinos and Indians enjoyed common citizenship but not equal in the way they dressed, spoke, earned money, nor owned property, though they liked to claim mixed blood. How would anyone find common ground among all these Guatemalans? The Mayan Indian Villages, themselves without a common language, could somehow link arms with the industrial workers, and the riveters would hold banners with the farm workers who waved their pitted dull machetes alongside the mestizos who complained of lost birthrights yet must unite with, or fight against, their own extended bloodline, the Spaniards who believe their pure European bloodlines give them a conqueror's right to the realm and all its subjects.

I stood and stared at the map of Guatemala in 3-D and it began to drizzle. The fourth dimension, which many refer to as Time, reared up on the horizon like a band of haze, a cloud formation more and more substantial the longer one lived. I stared into the march of history and saw my own reflection, as an American, with European blood, a white person, a male, who enjoyed the fruits of past generations of genocide and social injustice.

It all made me hungry, and I thought of McDonald's, or the Dairy Queen downtown.

What a confused Guatemalteco. Blame the United States for everything, because everything works in the United States of North America. We invent, the rest copy us.

European culture, maybe all temperate cultures that work together to survive cruel winters, rely on a work ethic that expects everyone to work hard, and shame on you if anyone sees you loaf.

In Mexico and Guatemala, you loaf every chance you get, to cope with the heat.

Then again, if the United States of North America went away, things might get worse, or "go south" as the cliché goes.

Then who would buy all those bananas?

Mayan Ice cream Queen

"The Mayan girl ran off the trail and into the forest, then stopped in her tracks. Big water droplets fall from the high leafy canopy. She pants. Her young bosom heaves under the bright colors of a woven blouse, wet and clingy. Her thick black hair flows down in inky tracks, pasted to the sides of her face and down across her shoulders where it makes almost legible arabesques of tapered calligraphic strokes. She gazes up into the forest, acts as if she sees something, as if it calls to her. She walks slow, step by step, to the base of an immense tree with buttress roots

like rocket fins. Up in the center of this Tree of Life, a skull grins down at her. She stares, and when she holds out her hand, the skull spits into her palm. She closes her fist and her eyes as the skull speaks. You will give birth to twins, and they will become the Hero Gods who teach the entire Pantheon of Mayan Gods the meaning of fear."

Based on the Popol Vuh, one of very few Mayan books that survived the Spanish conquest.

Should I go back to Santa Catarina? Would Yvonne wait for me in Puerto San Jose, tanned on a towel alongside the Pacific Ocean?

The next few days I spent in a semi-sarcastic mood, resentful of how much time I thought about Yvonne as I roamed the streets of Guatemala City. I busied myself on a search for the best cookies in the bakeshops. I wandered into luxurious gold leaf cathedrals, tried to make beggars sing or dance for my money, perused bookstores for that perfect small cheap illustrated Spanish Dictionary until I found one.

Three full color sections of twenty pages each, and cute black and white illustrations on every newsprint page, both mixed into the text and alongside in the margins.

I tried to exude aloof confidence, an Elvis meets James Bond cool, as I searched for the cutest girl in the city.

Then I saw her. She worked in an ice cream shop.

I developed an appetite for a banana split in the last fifteen minutes before they closed every night. I agonized as the hour approached, got super rational about my motives in an attempt to avoid the run across town through twelve blocks of dark, gritty back streets for an ice cream. I felt no hunger, and I would arrive all nervous and sweaty from the exertion to see a girl I couldn't talk to. I stand in front of her and wrestle with my own fear of women and try to keep my eyes from continuous fingertip roams across her face and the soft bulges in her white uniform. I try to act casual, even when I see the other patrons smile at me, and I blush.

My lack of functional Spanish prevents us from a conversation, I think, but deep down I know it doesn't matter. We both smile, blush, and pretend I don't drink her with my eyes. She fails to hide her enjoyment of my nervousness and her own pleasure in the silent acknowledgement of my infatuation, adoration, tribulations, and glandular fixation. Sometimes when she bends toward me to scoop some ice cream, she seems to point her open collar my way so I can look down her shirt. Or she pulls up her white skirt a little too far to climb a small stepladder and reach another stack of paper cups.

We both know why and how often I make this pilgrimage.

I felt myself blush hot in front of the people who ate ice cream alongside me. They knew. They noticed the target of each of my furtive glances, as they lick the rivulets and drips that run down their own cones. I knew they could feel the heat of my inept passion, even though I couldn't understand the comments that made them laugh and look at me in unison. This happened several times, without fear that I might catch the joke.

I could tell, the way her expression became sheepish when she glanced at me, that she apologized for their words.

She made my love feel both pure and shameful. Her innocent grace and lower class servitude contrasted with my cautious callousness and youthful intrepidness, the traveler's intoxication fed on a brew of false and feigned cultural superiority broken in places by open eyed curiosity. I enjoyed the illicit and taboo, the unknown danger, and risked these late night excursions in a foreign city because I wanted to talk to her in the language of sweat and tension, twine my fingers like the buttressed roots of a great tree sunk deep into the hot fruit scented tropical mud. Continents of culture and class separated us.

I wanted to cover her flawless body, tanned without tan lines, with my pinkish body of translucent skin, pure white where the sun never shines, and swim upstream into her happiness. I wanted our caramel children to smile because the world welcomes them without regard to their color, nor their parent's color(s) of skin, hair, and eyes.

I embarrassed myself night after night. I insulted my education, culture, and family with this surrender to the vulgar call of my glands, which I heard recast in the noble tones of a fight against discrimination and intolerance.

Perhaps I fooled myself, but she looked happy to see me, discreetly, and I perceived a special smile reserved for me. I wanted to believe it, that she waited all day to see me, and thought about us. I felt I'd fallen in love with her, the way she moved and smiled while she filled ice cream cones, scoop after scoop, and took money.

Yet I played it so cool, not brave enough to talk to her, or find the courage to stay and even try. Each night I left and hated my cowardice.

What if something happen between us? I dreaded it, because I knew that no matter what my feelings, my political status must force me back to the States and get my head straight, pregnancy or not, which I felt both improbable and certain, impossible and inescapable.

One day, after I bought another ice cream a few minutes before they closed, a young man came in and they flirted together with so much animation I felt she did it to hurt me. As they laughed together, I slunk out through the open wall. Instead of my usual flight back to the Pensión to avoid my urges to stay and stare at her all night, I stopped at the nearest corner.

The clients left. I couldn't tell if the young man left.

I saw the lights go out when the shop closed. She came out with someone who either came unseen to pick her up, or worked with her. A taxi drove up, and they both got in and left.

I hated the idea they might see me, notice me all alone on a dark street corner in the off hours of commercial Guatemala City, under a misty drizzle, with sweet and sticky ice cream on fingers and lips, no reason to stand there except to see her.

For the first time, I realized my silent attention over time might set off alarms, make her fear me, and put me in danger from her Gringo hater Guatemalan boyfriend.

On the way back to the Hotel San Jose, I hopped from bar to bar in search of a couple of beers to take the edge off my excitement, to tranquilize my urges to run around all night in this strange and exotic city, an explorer lost on another planet full of dangerous situations and unknown rules.

I wandered new streets and got lost several times on the way to my hotel, and reminded myself again that the night boy locks the door around eleven. I knock, increase the volume, until I wake up the young lad who sleeps on an army cot on the other side. He opens for me and again warns me, as he does every time without fail, not to stay out at night, too many dangers, do not tempt all the bad people in the city to rob the ignorant Gringo. Stupid, stupid Gringo, nothing to do after the shops close except bars, so you get drunk and walk through a city full of drunks, putas, and thieves.

"Stupid, stupid Gringo." he clicks the door behind us. "One of these nights, the police will come and ask me to identify your body full of blood and bullets. Don't talk to girls. Girls, I know what you look for. You only find bad girls, putas, on the street. You show your money, they take you to a room and a man hits you over the head. If you wake up, you lucky to be alive."

Inside the hotel, three blind turns deep into the black bowels of the pipe lined hallways, I'd flail around for the string to turn on that one pale forty watt bulb, which puts it into a fast swing, a pendulum on its own electric cord. I hurried down the corridor under the dead dirty yellow pelican.

My heart leaped as its Devil fingered winged shadow lunged at me.

CHAPTER 7: Hawaii, Guatemala

A couple of Gringos, a slim bearded man and his bratty seven year old daughter, stayed for a few days in the Hotel San Jose, while they accumulated supplies for a secret mission.

Over three days of short conversations within chance encounters, he and I developed a certain mutual respect at a distance. We both liked to read books and felt confident of our opinions with each other, but not so inflexible we denied ourselves an education. I badgered them both, with slight ridicule, about their secret mission.

He surprised me one morning, as we both waited to pay for our rooms.

He told me they would leave as soon as they received a package from the States. With a resigned reluctance I didn't understand, he almost begged for my friendship. He needed someone he could trust. "In case anything should happen," he said, "I want you to know where we're going, and why. You say you'll be in Guatemala for a while, if you ever hear that something happened to a Gringo and his seven year old daughter, go to the consulate and tell them what you know."

"Ok. What should I say?"

"First, you need to know that my wife's looking for us, and she's rich enough to hire detectives and pay them to travel anywhere in the world. It's a long story. We need some time apart right now. My wife will say that I kidnapped my own daughter, even though she doesn't believe it herself. In the long run, this will save our marriage. All you need to know is that I want us to get back together again."

"What if some bad ass detectives get to me first?"

"Don't tell them anything. Her father's a Mafioso, and that's more than you need to know. In case you didn't notice, every time we've talked, no one else was around. No one in this hotel knows we've had a conversation, and I want to keep it that way, for your sake too."

He told me they headed for a remote village, on the Pacific coast. "Latin America's not like the United States. You can pick your century when you travel. I like the eighteenth century. No cars, telephones, no electricity. Someplace where people walk or ride horse."

"Have you been there?"

"Can't wait to get back. You should see it. Stick houses for ten dollars a month. No gringos."

"Tell me where, and if you want, I'll show up and they'll have two gringos to get confused about. Like a cover, you know."

"Ok, but you have to promise you won't tell anyone. I mean no one, it stays between you an me. If you come, that's fine. If anyone else comes, I'll know you told someone."

"It can't be that remote."

"Come and find out. Alone."

"Tell me how to get there."

"Take a bus to Chiquimulilla. It's almost to El Salvador. From there, ask around, and find the bus that goes to Hawaii."

"Hawaii?"

"Don't tell anyone." He looked past me.

I looked around, and noticed someone enter the hotel and walked toward us. When I turned back to him, I saw him walk away down the hall into the hotel.

I felt excited that I might see a part of Guatemala far off the tourist trail, on the Pacific Ocean, with clean air, mangroves and coconuts, mild ocean tempered climate, and a stick house for ten dollars a month.

I imagined there exists, within Mexico and Guatemala, entire communities that still exist within nature, within a social context where the arts flourish, people enjoy plenty of free time to play with children and talk to each other, in the absence of personal automobiles, television, and no reliance on energy from oil. They don't mind the odors of a hot, sweaty humanity, nor the frequent and unavoidable skin to skin contact in packed busses or the informal vans and pickup trucks of ad hoc mass transit through these humid tropical climates.

For the first weeks in Latin America, I felt a paranoid suspicion that all others lurked about to rob and pickpocket, until, to my surprise a couple of months later, I felt comfortable and at ease, even relieved by their presence, as we rubbed and jostled together on a crowded bus. I found it easier to put my trust in the basic goodness of others, when I realized that they would try to protect me in direct proportion to their expectation that I would try to protect them.

The more cash money I carried in my billfold, the more paranoid I felt. At first, that limited the things I allowed myself to do, pressured by my relative wealth to thoughts of a rental car, to insulate and isolate myself, as the rich need to protect their loved ones from a desperate humanity. The filthy rich need a car with bodyguards.

In Latin America, I felt ashamed to see how easily they trusted each other, and trusted us itinerant poverty stricken travelers, trust enough to invite us to share life with them for a meal, a night, a vacation. Yet it also took me too long to realize that people often lied when they introduced me to cousins or brothers and sisters of no blood relationship. These impromptu family memberships occurred because they shared Godfathers, or neighborhoods in childhood, or through the friendships of both sets of parents, co-parenting, and through the existence of Godparents and extended family connections through grandparents. Anyone could become your brother, or cousin. Any good friend can become a member of your family.

What might the poorest Guatemalans think of the poorest Americans in the US, that 'dirt poor' minority that the failed middle class falls into, with their color TV sets in several state subsidized rooms of a decrepit apartment complex? America's poor downtrodden masses bathe in the glow of television, beer in hand, while kids crawl the carpet and play with cigarette butts, an unpredictable car or two parked on the bare dirt lawn drive off to collect their government welfare check and food stamps at least once a month. If they find a job it threatens their welfare, so they stay unemployed, unmarried, and procreate to boost their income.

Their cats and dogs eat better than people in the underdeveloped world.

Even a dog in the United States of North America sleeps inside with people, or in a dog house, or in a garage filled with more things, the majority unused, than most people in the underdeveloped world could own in a lifetime.

I needed to get away from Guatemala City, where my limited activities included a daily grapple with Spanish and my illustrated dictionary, a march between my quarters and the post office with the hope to glimpse Yvonne, and my nocturnal missions to the Ice Cream Shoppe, driven by my obsession for the forbidden fruit, the Mayan princesita. This appetite promised only milky obesity, a Catholic sexual frustration, and ridicule from the girls she worked with, to I might become accustomed to, in exchange for the opportunity to worship her beauty.

Young girls read men like headlines.

The descriptions of an undiscovered paradise from this mysterious California gringo cinched it.

I decided not to pay for another night, but to leave that afternoon and beat them to Hawaii.

In Guatemala City's main bus terminal's back gravel bus lot, if you ask the bus drivers who wait for fares when the bus leaves, they say in ten minutes. Then, if you happen to board an almost empty bus, everyone waits for more people to fill the bus up, hour after hour.

The fat driver of this bus tried to catch forty winks under his shiny black captain's cap. The rolled up shirtsleeves of his white shirt revealed a heavy gold watch and numerous silver bracelets.

I sat alone for thirty minutes, before I realized that my few companions with the same destination abandoned this bus, and now waited on another bus nearby, almost full. I changed buses, and soon we lurched off, elephantine, through potholes in the gravel lot and down the narrow backstreets of town.

Alongside the driver, our colorful conductor, a huge black man in black dress pants and patent leather shoes, rubbed his immense abdomen and pulled at the hem of his clean T-shirt. He leaned out the door and grinned against the wind. His voice boomed out the exotic Indian names of our destination towns to the pedestrians on the sidewalk.

"Escuintla! Chiquimulilla! Guanagazapa!"

He repeated various announcements each time we pulled into one of the unmarked, informal bus stops scattered throughout the residential areas of the city.

This primitive system informs even illiterates about the destinations for each bus. Then the slight framed, pajama clad Mayans tighten their grim faces into grimaced smiles of exertion as they hoist huge loads onto their backs and haul them over to the bus.

The conductor climbs atop the bus, and the driver and other men helped push each awkward rope net bag up the bus's side. From on top, the conductor reaches down to pull the loads up, where he takes rope and string and knits everything into a misshapen mountain of cargo on the roof.

The bus headed southeast for a couple of hours, and the bidirectional flow of people through the bus door tended to trickle outward with each stop in little communities or crossroads along the way.

Towards late afternoon, I sat alone, the last and only passenger on the bus.

Only the driver and conductor remained.

Out the window, the flat tropical lowlands unfurled in lush green of tall grass pastures dotted with Brahma droop eared cattle knee deep in muck. Fence lines defined by rows of trees led to hummocks, forested islands. The cows lay in groups in the shade of lone ceiba trees to chew their cud under little clouds of insects flew in tight masses, that hovered in place and caught the sunlight like spheres of dust.

Because I knew little about Hawaii except its name, I began to fear that the Gringo lied to me, and inspired me to go on a wild goose chase. The silent driver dropped the black conductor off, which left he and I alone on the bus.

I waited for a word, a sign from him. I walked to the front to make sure he knew I existed, that he hadn't forgotten me.

I retook my seat toward the rear of the bus, but after a time I walked up front to ask again about Hawaii.

Silence. Then his big hand raised up slow, to motion for me not to worry.

His impatience with my distrust seemed all too obvious. I pestered him too often en route, to make sure he still remembered where I wanted to go, paranoid I might lose a bus connection in one of the small towns where we hesitated to pick up passengers.

If I so much as stirred in my seat, he would raise one hand, as if to bat a fly. I thought it a joke we shared, at least I hoped so.

We drove on through the vast and flat Pacific lowlands, punctuated by tiny settlements of shacks of unpainted gray planks set in bare yards of brick red mud with chickens, pigs, and great bushes in flower. Ceiba trees, the national tree of Guatemala, stood graceful like lone sentinels, arms wide open as if in prayer. The long vertical trunk often swollen in the center, and the buttress roots, eight or nine feet tall, resemble rocket fins, complemented the smooth aluminum colored bark to make the trunks look like rocket drawings from the fifties, .

The road became a one track lane through tall grasses and swamps. Whenever we passed through a grove of trees, it got so dark I thought the sun set. The afternoon waned, and still we rode on, a nightmare ambulance ride to an insane asylum.

We stopped, or rather ran out of road, in front of a very small but sturdy cement tienda all alone on the edge of a swampy pasture. He turned the motor off, and I heard birdsong and the composite buzz of millions of insects. As the bus motor cooled down, it pinged and gurgled.

Along the edge of this overgrown pasture, the government, or someone, excavated a large irrigation canal from here to the mangrove forest about a half mile away. From where the road stopped and the canal began, right in front of this shack with a store window, two track paths came out of the tall trees and intersected in front of the store.

The driver's shoes swished through the wet grasses over to the store, then he moved around the back and out of sight.

Silence.

Motionless in the canal, about seven log canoes, in various stages of repair, floated in the black mirror waters, moored to a little boardwalk.

IN the shadows, I saw one loaded dugout contained cases of beer wrapped in rope net, and burlap bags bundled together, so overloaded I didn't recognize it as a dugout at first, then I thought someone forgot to unloaded it hours ago, and it sunk a little minute by minute from a leak that no one noticed. I expected it to head for the canal bottom any second.

My bus driver returned from around the corner of the store with another man. They chatted and laughed, traded all the latest news and gossip, I imagined. Then the driver got into the bus, started it up, and drove off without a word to me.

After the bus left, the man closed up the shop and locked it.

I stood beside my backpack in the tall grass, watched the man work without a word to me. He didn't even acknowledge my presence. Wondered if he wanted to leave me there.

Then he motioned for me to hand him my backpack. He carried it to the canal and put it in the overloaded canoe.

Then he untied the rope that moored one end of the canoe and walked along the shore to pull it broadside to the little two plank dock. He took a casual step into the rear of the dugout and motioned for me to follow. He held on to the dock's slim planks to steady things. The black water, within two inches of the canoe's top, clung like thick oil as if to wrench itself over the side. As sure as the late afternoon's humid sunlight softened the edges of the distant mangroves, I knew my weight would sink this canoe.

He noticed my concern, laughed, and urged me to get in, even pointed at his watch to hurry me.

I got in, slow motion, with many a breathless pause as I moved to sit down. I put my hands out on the bulky cargo to distribute the weight off my feet. I felt my blood drain away as I saw, in my minds eye, the black waters surge into the boat. I knew how to swim well enough, but I didn't know if I could rescue my backpack and save myself from the whirlpool caused by cases of beer falling off a dugout canoe.

I let myself let go in a slow collapse to sink soft atop the bags of potatoes and grains. Motionless, I listened to the small waves I'd caused as they lapped against the canal shores and bounced back to the boat.

I looked around, decided to breathe, and noticed a place I could sit, on the stacked cases of beer, and pointed them out to the boatman.

He smiled at me, motioned for me to sit on them, then turned to yank on the starter cord for a small Evinrude outboard motor, two and a half horsepower, so tiny it escaped notice behind the load.

The engine coughed and sputtered clouds of bluish white smoke that drifted out over the quiet mirror lagoon in graceful contrast with the blotchy green ink of dark jungle. He motioned for me to untie the last line so we could glide straight down the wide ditch's perfect reflection of sky between the high treetops.

South, full speed ahead, for what seemed like a mile or so, and once inside the mangrove forest we entered a wide channel that ran east and west, parallel to where I imagined the Pacific Beach lay. He took curves like a racer, straightened as much as possible with a wider curve where vegetation allowed.

The canal averaged thirty feet wide, but vast islands of hyacinth floated together and often choked it down to much narrower passages. The black waters mirrored perfect images of the undersides of water hyacinth leaves and the mangrove treetop silhouettes. The mangroves drop strange straight branches, like spears or plumb lines, from somewhere up in the leafy branches. A pointed knob adorns the end, and it seemed like it would plunge down like a spear someday, and once anchored in the mud, a new mangrove tree would sprouted. My theory, don't really know. It reminded me of old German World War I hand grenades on the end of spears.

Great herds of skate bugs danced across the surface tension, and in the larger open areas, I heard the waves of our wake splash into the tangle of mangrove roots. A great checkerboard of rhomboidal waves criss crossed behind the canoe.

Maybe this silent boatman knew he took me to my death.

Everyday the rest of your life dawns on you as the rest of your life, that endless final vacation, with a mythic, silent figure at the helm of a boat that takes you down a black river towards the winedark sea of forgetfulness.

Four-eyed Fish

Some animal, fish or frogs I thought, jumped away at the dugout's approach. Sounded like each animal made three or four fast leaps out of the water, accomplished by splashy flops, like skipped stones. The animals fled from both sides of the boat.

I asked the driver about them. He slowed the canoe down, said, "Quadrojos" and pointed to his eyes, then to the water ahead of us.

Four-eyes, he said.

I could see two froggy eyes stuck out of the water ahead of us that moved across the surface in a zigzag swim. When we drew near, the eyes shot out of the water and splashed away. I saw two more ahead, then two more eyes further on. Once I learned to recognize them, I saw hundreds at play along the canal.

"A fish? Pez?"

"Yes, fish."

Then I remembered, from some distant wildlife TV program or a book, a bug eyed fish that kept the water's surface at eye level, and each eye enclosed two pupils, one for above water and the other for underwater. I assumed such odd things rare, but they populated this canal more densely than frogs populate the summer ponds of Michigan.

Some stretches of the canal tunneled through mangroves whose canopies knotted and twisted high above us, raised on rectangular tangles of roots and slender trunks like spider legs.

The beige wounds of fresh sawn limbs stuck out against the dark backdrop and attested to the constant efforts of men to control the tropical exuberance of nature and keep the channel clear.

Islands, created by thousands of Water Hyacinth in bloom, floated along the edges and down the canals to threaten our passage. Their flowers glowed, ghost white around a dark center, and stared from the leafy carpets of their flat islands. The boatman leaned a little to correct the canoe's tilt as we sped around them. By instinct he avoided the cul de sacs that almost formed in front of us in the slow currents.

We did not get trapped, all credit to him.

The sun set fire to ponderous cumulus clouds that billowed off the Pacific and backlit the dark masses of mangrove trees overhead. We cut through the coffee color waters, and passed banks of tall cane grasses topped with feathery blond flowers, where hundreds egrets roosted like bone white ghosts of flappers from the Twenties, can-can girls, all bent into the letter S, all the unpronounced S's that Habanera Cubans, and other Latin Americans with an urban Caribbean accent, drop by the thousands.

As the sky's colors faded into twilight, we beached on a steep bank of dark sand held in place by a stand of coconut trees, one of the few breaks in the mangrove wall. Children, then a few young men, ran toward us from stick houses lit by lanterns and candles on the flat dunes. Seven or eight grown men ran like children and jumped down the steep slope of sand to the canal. They unloaded the beer and baggage from the dugout, handed smaller things to the children, then two young men at a time hauled the burlap bags up to a little store with an electric light.

Through the underbrush, I could see candles shine from within houses, made of vertical sticks, tucked under a grove of tall coconut palms.

I could hear the distant ocean, the hints of thunderous crashes that reverberated up and down some long beach on the other side of theses huts.

The boatman led me to a thin old man who wore a stained, old fashioned tank top T-shirt that sagged around his little basketball pot gut. The boatman explained that Don Martinez, founded this settlement many years ago, to make me understand that he served as host and chief, and my principal problem solver.

He asked me if I needed a house to rent. He seemed like a sweet old duffer with wet eyes. We would talk more later, he assured me, after he attended to other business. He called out to one of the young boys to show me the habitations.

One electric bulb radiated a little yellow light as a noisy gas generator growled behind the store. Hawaii defined itself in the darkness, a haphazard community of one room houses built of thin sapling sticks, by the lights from candles or lanterns. the light revealed people reclined in hammocks, or seated around tiny tables.

The boy showed me a row of dark houses, and I picked one about three doors down from the store where Don Martinez lived. Far enough away for a modicum of privacy, and near enough to dissuade thieves.

I noticed that these stick houses, when illuminated from inside, become transparent with a person's movement. Anyone who walks by can see right through the wall, as if the sticks turn invisible. The motion causes the scene to flicker like a slow movie animation.

One day I thought of a way to correct this problem. Make the sticks run horizontal instead of vertical, and force any Peeping Toms to jump or bob up and down to see through walls.

I wanted to see the ocean before it got any darker out.

After I stashed my backpack in the house of sticks, I took off my shoes and ran through the sand. Darkness engulfed me away from the store's electric bulb and the noise of the generator. My vision turned black and white, and I saw a thick lightness that obscured the horizon, like a bit of milky sky that changed shape and undulated above the dark sand beach.

I ran past a little wood slat fence sunk into the sand at the boundary of the settlement, and on across open sand towards a grove of tall coconut palms. I sensed something strange underfoot, and stopped to find myself in a huge sand field covered with four foot wide pale spiders. They looked like colossal spider crabs, some almost two yards across with twenty inch long legs sprawled in radiating pools, as if dismembered and gutted, their center gone, blonde beasts blown apart by shotgun blasts on the dark sand.

My heart beat fast with adrenaline. I froze. Arranged in geometric rows up and down the beach, spaced apart with precision, hundreds or thousands of them, pale in the starlight on the black sand, covered the ground between the palm tree trunks.

I stepped close to one four foot crablike blotch, my eye on the hole in the center, where the twenty or so legs joined together. I leaned down in the black and white darkness, and recognized a huge fan palm frond with a scoop of sand in the middle. Someone laid each one out with a handful of sand to hold them against the wind. Laid out to dry atop the black volcanic sand, exposed to the intense tropical sun.

After I calmed down, I faced the onshore breeze and took a look around. The pale undulations of the horizon turned into wave froth and ocean spray, from ten foot high waves.

I left the palm frond field and continued towards the sea. At the top edge of a steep slope of black sand, I stopped and looked down at the crash of surf and felt the wind drive salt spray into my face. Each wave piled up into a mountain of water that curled forward into a brief tube then collapsed against the beach in a thunderous collision that exploded with violent billows of atomized sea water.

While I sat on the sand, stars appeared in the purpled sky, the earth tipped, and I felt it lunge. Each wave crashed like hungry outstretched arms to fling clouds of mist into the breeze. The wind brought salty perfumes of seaweeds and fish, flowers and putrefaction. Whenever the winds calmed for a few seconds, I heard sounds from behind me, where giant mop heads of palm trees swooned a song of sighs and the dry fronds of their drooped skirts rustled and whispered against each other.

I sat there, and felt like I belonged, while I watched a million tiny stars form a Milky Way so bright it lit up the sand and sea.

When I returned to the settlement, the old Spaniard Don Martinez introduced me to his wife, Doña Martinez. She looked alert and healthy, an old Indian woman with hair tied into a thick salt and pepper pony tail that accentuates her Mayan nobility through a nose dominated profile. She looked accustomed to hard labor, a stout body with a little pot gut. She wore an apron a bit longer than her below the knee skirt, and the way she wiped her hands made her switchback veins stick out like those that wriggled across her teakwood calves. She looked at me with a calm, inner elegance, an aloof silent pride that demanded respect as it commanded your cautious attention.

I recognized her as the village witchdoctor, the sage, the feared and respected.

Don Martinez asked if I felt hungry, as he pulled a plastic chair away from a table on the sand. He motioned for me to sit. Without a word between them, Doña Martinez made hand motions for me to wait, and then strode off to the kitchen area, an impenetrable darkness behind the store's tiny counter window. Don Martinez offered me a verbal menu, with careful pronunciation, of rice, beans, carne de res (beef), pig meat (he corrected himself to say "ahorita no hay"), or chicken, which I ordered without a word to the price.

Doña Martinez came right back out to set my place with plastic plate and tall plastic glass, some thin metal silverware, and then made sure to center the salt and pepper shakers. She gave me the first of a few rare smiles. When she did smile, you felt everything in the universe relax in place.

Halfway through my meal, Don Martinez came out with two candles and lit them at my table.

Then he went behind his building, turned off the generator, and plunged us into the eighteenth century, and the silence engulfed us, broken by soft sounds in the underbrush, plants rustled by wind, or small, cautious animals.

Midnight Intruder

Near Tapachula on the Pacific coastal plain, the Izapan civilization created a large ceremonial center of over 80 earth and clay pyramidal mounds covered with river boulders. Reliefs carved into stelae depict their mythology with scenes of warfare, the Sacred World Tree, ceremonies, decapitations, meetings of elders, and deities reminiscent of the Olmec's. East of Izapa, on the Pacific slopes of Guatemala, the archeological site of Abaj Takalik reveals sculpture in three styles: Olmec-like, Izapan's, and Classic Maya. One stela carries the date AD 126, earlier than monuments from the Maya lowlands. In front of each stela, the Izapan artisans

placed round altars the form of toads, an amphibian that lives in burrows, which
could symbolize both transformation and ownership of portals to the underworld.
The skin glands in many toad species contain toxins as a defense against predation,
and some contain a potent hallucinogenic drug. Shamans could use this drug from
the back of Zac, the toad, to disorient themselves or others, and convince others of
their power over the portals to the levels of reality.

On a narrow wood bunk in my little room of sticks, I fell asleep lulled by the sounds of the surf, and dreamed the planet breathes through those long curls of waves. I stayed warm enough under the billowy mass of my mosquito net as a sheet.

Long after midnight, someone's footsteps awakened me. I stared into blackness to adjust my eyes, then peered between the vertical saplings of the wall to look outside, at the sandy starlit spaces between the palm trees and the scattered stick shacks.

A rooster crowed. I made out the silhouette of a man, black against the gray of star filled sky, who stood within the sticks of my shack's walls, immobile in the corner.

I watched him, he watched me.

I asked, in a low voice, so as not to alarm anyone else, "Who are you? Who's there?"

I heard a footstep, but the man did not move.

A distant rooster crowed. A series of large waves crashed against the beach.

I threw off the mosquito netting, swiveled my body off the tall wood frame cot, stood up nude, inhaled to make myself look as big as possible with lungs full, and got on my tip toes to look taller.

Then I walked toward the corner.

The man dissolved into my own long shirt hung on a hanger.

I fixed my eyes on the black corner below, as my field of vision danced with the sparkles of darkness. The ocean quieted, but the wind rustled the palms that towered above the settlement. I jumped with each nearby bright rattle and scrape of palm fronds.

A separate clot of darkness, about the size of a small football, caught my attention. Something huddled down into the black powdery sands and pressed against the base of the wall of sticks.

A rooster crowed, I startled. Then it moved.

A toad, the size of my opened hand, tried to head butt a way through the sticks to get out. I made a tentative grab at him, and he hopped across my little room to the other wall. He bounced his head along that wall of sticks with a weak jumps that eluded my hand.

When he reached the corner, I controlled his movement, and he tired. I gained enough courage to hold him down and get my fingers into his warty armpits.

Seven inches round, he must eat birds and Chihuahuas. He measured over ten inches long when stretched out as if in mid jump on his short fat legs. In proper toady behavior, he tried to piss on me.

I carried him to the doorway so that his piss fell along the wall, opened the little gate of sticks that pretended to serve as a door, and gave him a gentle toss to hear the soft squishy thud of his body as it hit the sand.

I awoke to a rooster's crow about 3:00 AM, and a chill convince me to unpack my sleeping bag.

The bushes rustled a couple of hundred yards away. Maybe raccoons, coatimundi, ocelot, nutria, or armadillo, but most likely, toad.

First Morning on the Beach

I awoke often that dark cold morning, with each cock crow and gust of wind. When the sky lightened enough to see, the sounds of morning in the human village, the dogs' bark and babies' cry, I put on some pants and my Solalá bat jacket to walk the beach. I could hear dogs bark rabid as people walked past their master's house, and the sounds of cooks who scraped metal spoons on cast iron or aluminum pans. Fires crackled with spilt oil, hens cackled and scraped the dirt near cocks that strutted and stretch their necks to crow again as they crowed throughout last night. I glimpsed, through the vegetation, candles and small fires flicker from inside the houses of sticks.

Young men came out of the scattered huts to gather the dried palm fronds into great piles on the beach. Most of the spread fans measured about six foot long, and so sturdy the men walked all over them. They folded the dried ones along the rib veins so that each one made a tight, yellow, accordion bundle, like a Japanese fan. Then they tied them together.

Other men arrived with bundles of fresh green fronds to spread out and dry in the harsh sunlight to come.

Back in my little room of sticks, I put on shorts and a sweatshirt for a barefoot jog along the beach. I ran where the steepest and dampest sand solidified into a seawall, and the chill sand lent wings to my feet.

The waves looked smaller today. In the distance, the sea spray obscured the beach, as it did behind me. I felt caught in a magic landscape of sunrise and planets that shined over both horizons of land and sea.

I ran along the shore and watched the waves soak the sands to a deep coffee black. Little animals buried in the beach sand extended two little arms to catch food as the water slipped back down the slope, and created a stationary wake as the water slid around and over them. They looked like tiny boats that sped up the beach's slope with enough speed to remain stationary against the slip.

From the top of the sand shoreline, I could see over the beach to the mangrove swamp, and above the treetops, far away on the horizon, I spotted three distant volcanoes, two to the northeast and one to the northwest, a faint darker pale blue against the palest of milky blue horizons.

The shore faced south, and as the sun came up near the junction of land and sea, its colors refracted through the salt spray into oily rainbows on the wet black sand. The dry dark sand appeared damp, until the sky lightened enough to cast light on the powdered chocolate dryness.

On cue, as if by magic, pelicans passed at the precise moment sunlight hit the wave tops. They flew in a diagonal line, wings half bent without a flap, in groups of three or more. They followed the long waves that piled up into a transparent green mountain ridge. Sometimes the waves suspended schools of fish high above sea level, trapped in a triangular aquarium. Then the pelicans might dive into the waves and come up to sit on the surface, water streaming out of their mouths, as the ballooned skin under its chin emptied.

Succulent plants sprawled across the black sands from the highest heaps of sand. When the first rays of sun highlighted this vegetation, swallows appeared to skim up the bugs roused from their night's sleep.

I jogged a mile or so down the beach. A large cross stood vigil over the sand, rough hewn planks made from two large straight mangrove roots. It leaned a bit, held up by boulders placed to reinforce the weak foothold in the sand.

I doubted this mound of boulders contained a body. Maybe like the shrines along the highway, it commemorated a boat and loved ones lost to the sea. Perhaps a frightened plea to calm the storms and hurricanes, a physical demonstration of Christian faith, a silent sentinel ever watchful for the lost to return home, and a reminder of the salt-wind monster that coughs up both sustenance and destruction in furious infantile tantrums that last for days, oblivious to human misery and fear, without a care for human love nor death.

I ran on though the haze of salt spray, and every once in a while, surprised one of the immense white hogs that rooted through the fresh debris left by the high tide.

In this first hour of daylight, people began to walk down the beach alone or in small groups on their morning errands, faint distant ghosts in the beach haze. We materialized to each other as we drew nearer, and I could make out their clothing and packages, or bundles and pots balanced on their heads.

They looked at me with wonder and suspicion as I jogged up to them. When I got close and if our eyes met, I panted "Buenos" and continued on.

I saw a tall woman ahead in the mists. She carried a vase shaped object upon her head that echoed the undulations of her outline. Her long, lightweight skirt blew about her legs with each step.

I felt tired, and broke stride to walk and catch my breath.

From forty feet away, contrasted against the beach spray and sunrise, she materialized out of her own silhouette to reveal a beautiful young woman inside that curvaceous outline. At twenty feet, I felt self conscious to realize she could see every detail of my face and eyes in full sunlight, as I adored her, the way her arms up akimbo to the load upon her head accentuated her full breasts, and the way the damp fabric adhered to her dark skin.

As we passed each other, I felt speechless, and felt that her direct gaze and smile, with a faint nod of her head, acknowledged my adoration.

I walked back to my room of sticks to make a small fire in one corner and boil some oatmeal in powdered milk. After breakfast, I bought a cigarette from Don Martinez and headed for the palm frond outhouse in back of his store. Inside, two holes in the planks served as seats, and a few sheets of newsprint as toilet paper. I sat there and smoked, let a couple drop, and heard an immediate commotion as something big crashed through the underbrush toward me. It slobbered and grunted with each heavy footfall, ran up to the back of the outhouse, rammed into it, and commenced to growl and grunt so that I thought a Brahma bull might tip the outhouse over with me inside . I jumped off the seat and peered through the hole, and in the shadowy light, saw the profile of a monstrous sow's face in full tusky smile, tipped sideways to force its head under the boards to eat my excrement.

To cool off, I tried to swim all alone in the mighty Pacific, but after too many close calls, bounced off the bottom near the turbulent shore, and too paranoid farther out, alone, where I thought about sharks, muscle cramps, and imperceptible rip currents, I decided to try the canal.

Children played in the shallows near the little sand beach near the boat dock. I first checked, by feel, the area near the bank and under a fallen stand of mangroves that men pruned back in their constant battle to keep the canal clear for transportation. All along the coastal length of the brackish, tea filled canal, the scars of sap-weepy cuttings stand out yellow orange against the mangrove's lush green leaves.

I swam through the coffee waters by feel, cautious, with hands in front of my face, and found no submerged stumps or branches. I climbed up the mangrove roots into the trees, and dared a swan dive off a high mangrove branch into the black canal waters. After that, some of the older children overcame their shyness and swam with me, and a couple of older boys followed suit and climbed up to the branch to jump in feet first.

I swam cross the canal and climbed up roots into the mangrove branches. The iron hard smooth wood of the mangrove trees allowed travel from tree to tree. Some of the pencil thin branches could hold my weight, and the roots interwove to create tangles up to ten feet high, like the muscular arms and legs of ten limbed Martian wrestlers.

A young Guatemalan man named Arturo wanted to make friends with me. He took me to fish with him in his dugout a couple of times. We each cut a small stick about a yard long for a fishing pole, and attached line and hook. Then he poled the canoe along the canal and looked for bays that might lead to one of hundreds of hidden watercourses that thread their way through the mangrove swamp. We fished the dark pools in deep shadow, sheltered under thick, low mangrove branch overhangs, and we fished large open fields of water hyacinth with a shrimp net.

As he poled the dugout along, he found plenty of opportunity to teach me the word for duck, in the sense of "Look out, a limb low enough to hit your head!" Agáchase!

We caught lots of small fish, perhaps perch and bluegill, the largest the size of a big hand.

His skilled eyes could see the hidden mouths of small channels. We pulled on branches and ducked under walls of leaves to enter tiny watercourses between the "knees" of rectangular roots. A couple of turns later, and I felt cut off from the world, lost in a claustrophobic tunnel of vegetation, accompanied by the deep woods buzz of insects and the call of startled birds, the plop and splash of unseen things that jumped into the water nearby.

The mangroves closed over our heads like a cavern. We fished, and when too long without a nibble, moved on. We couldn't see ahead far enough ahead to know if the small channel led to the open water of a hidden lagoon, or a dead end mangrove root cul de sac whose submerged knees threatened to capsize us as we tried to turn the dugout around, sometimes from precarious perches on the mud slick, iron strong but finger thin spider-legs of mangrove roots.

Whenever we entered a wide open area, usually a shallow swamp with hyacinth islands in flower, it felt like the sun came out. I heard the birds sing, and watched the bees zigzag and gather thick fuzzy golden boots of pollen, while dragonflies hovered motionless and then darted fast as an arrow, weightless helicopters that disobeyed the laws of physics.

Arturo pulled his shrimp net out of the puddle of water on the dugout's floor, then walked to the bow. He motioned me to silence, set his arm into motion with a couple of rhythmic underhand swings, then cast the net far out over the waters like a Frisbee. The lead weights on the circumference forced the net open in flight to make a big gauzy circle. When it hit the water, the weights pulled the net down fast, and trapped everything underneath. He pulled the cord attached to the center of the net and it drew the weights inward, to close and ensnare anything too big to escape through the mesh. He hauled droopy doughnut shaped net bag to the side of the dugout, and dumped the catch into the bottom of our dugout canoe. Snails, fish, water bugs that looked like brown tea leaves, and various sizes of shrimp all tried to flop, flip, scramble or climb out of the dugout's pool between our sandaled feet.

He let me pole the canoe on occasion, as he stood perched on the prow to watch for any increase in surface ripples that betrayed the presence of shrimp or schools of fish. He laughed at my technique in tricky maneuvers around islands of water hyacinth or along the tunnels of mangroves, where I tended to use the pole above water to push off mangrove roots. I almost tipped us over a number of times, but he kept his balance like a surfer.

Over the week, he tried to teach me Spanish, even though he said he couldn't read. Arturo's wife Yadira cooked us a wonderful meal once, loaded with vegetables like quisquil, a small, bright green, translucent squash with soft spines and a puckered smile at one end, about the size of a woman's fist.

They never married, neither civil nor blessed in the eyes of the Church, in spite of their avowed Catholicism, love for each other, and three children. A common practice in rural areas, he assured me. Never enough money for marriage.

I helped Arturo and Yadira harvest Ajonjolí, sesame seeds, one day. The crop grew in very small manicured patches out on the sands. We cut the plants and stacked the stalks upright to dry. With plants cut days before and now dry, we shook the seed out onto a canvas tarp to pick chaff out before we poured it into burlap bags the children held open.

Back at their stick house home after this harvest, Yadira treated us all with conserva, a delicious cookie made of sesame seed and spiced honey.

After his wife leaves us to wash the dishes, we smoke cigarettes and wait for the oldest child to run all the way back from Don Martinez's store with two cold beers. Arturo talks in a hushed conspiratorial tone. He wants a watch like the ones he saw the sailors wear in the port town of San Jose. "My ambition", he said, "my big dream of all my life." He thinks it may take him a few years to save up the money.

I could imagine in this barter economy, or with wages at a dollar a day to support his family, he might never save the price of a two hundred dollar watch. And for what? When does he need a watch? No appointments, no schedules. If the sun shines, you work. When night falls, you sleep.

Imagine the day when he ruins his two hundred dollar watch with a few drops of shrimpy water, will he see the superiority of my fourteen dollar "waterproof to fifty meters" black plastic wristwatch and recognize his foolhardiness? I hoped he might think twice and make his family a higher priority, or become a competitive consumer, an educated shopper, determined to get the most bang for the buck. Then he might see the real difference in value between a cheap fourteen dollar waterproof plastic tool, and the metal and glass glitzy brand name badge of status that will not only disillusion him, but probably ruin his relationship with his wife.

Meals with the Nursing Woman

As a symbol for a doorway, as portal or connection between the three major divisions of the cosmos, the Double Merlon design might date from before Olmec times (1500 BC) and shows up in stone sculpture around 200 BC. It occurs in examples of Maya, Mixtec, and Aztec art, both contemporary and ancient. Some see a meaningful connection between the Double Merlon and a cross section schematic of sunken patios, or walled ball courts, from the Middle Formative Period ruins.

Today, the remote Lacandon tribe still use Double Merlons as symbols for a house's doorway, though their doorways do not resemble Double Merlons. On the Lacandon's "god pot" censer (a clay vessel to burn incense), the Double Merlon forms part of the rim's lips, and frames the head of a deity as it thrusts up, as if birthed, between the two protuberances.

I asked around for a restaurant, to see if anyone sold meals of vegetables, beans and tortillas. No one took me serious until I claimed vegetarianism by doctor's orders. I wanted to find cheap, simple food, because Don Martinez specialized in rooster meat, cooked with skill and variety by his Mayan witchdoctor wife, as tough as the turkey, but even if I believed meals of rooster would put a dent in the nocturnal noise levels, I couldn't afford it.

One household a half mile down the beach sells meals, sometimes, they tell me.

Late afternoon, I hiked along the beach dunes, through the salty mist of spent waves that blurs the beach, to find the house. They say look for the closest house to the sea, the only one with its own well.

I found it, recognized the well cover like a wagon wheel of planks atop a three foot tall tube of rough logs to keep the sand out.

A little three plank table sits in front of their house of sticks. Their home consists of three buildings for various functions. A couple of kids run out happy to yell and jump around me like their two wag tailed puppies to announce my presence.

A slim, statuesque barefoot woman in a gray sleeveless dress walks out of the kitchen shack. With each step, her mid-calf dress wraps itself to the curves of the forward thigh to flutter behind in the strong sea breeze. As she walks, she wipes her hands with a faded, striped dishtowel, knits her brows and thins her lips which I interpreted as a warning.

She greets me. I smile, but she remains aloof and down to business. We try to communicate. After she sorts out my Spanish pronunciation, she understands I want to eat, and motions me to sit, without a smile.

"What would you like to drink? Coca-cola, Manzanita, Cervesa?"

"¿Horchata?" I ask her.

"Si, hay horchata." She looks at me with a sidelong glance. I wonder if she feels suspicion or frustration that I would drink what she prepares for her family, instead of what she could sell for profit.

She returns with a tall glass and a pitcher of the vanilla cinnamon flavored rice drink to set on the table

I see a man approach down the beach, a faint silhouette against the misty sunset. The kids run to him. Her husband walks over to greet me like an old friend, with familiarity and a big smile. As our hands meet in the traditional, light touch, pale nothingness of a Guatemalan handshake, I recognize the man as my boatman on the Stygian waterway, the man who piloted the dugout that brought me to Hawaii through the hyacinth choked canals.

Hard to recognize him now, in a T-shirt, shorts, and sandals. He helps her set the table for three, then excuses himself "Con permiso" and goes into the kitchen to help cook.

She comes out with a blanketed bundle in one arm, a baby a few months old, its skin a coffee and cream color topped with wisps of chocolate hair. She sits across from me.

As her husband serves the food, she opens her shirt and takes out the most beautiful mammary gland, a soft swollen roundness with a perfect tan and, an unexpected shock to me, no tan lines. Her unblemished expanse of skin made my eyes feel out of focus. Shaken, I tried not to reveal how much I wanted to milk her with my eyes, and so controlled my glances to appear uncontrolled, as if her full breast interested me not more than the two pups and their cow bone, the vulture that circled above the beach, or the sun on the tight curly nap of her husband's hair as he carries more wood into the shack.

She cradled the caramel colored baby in her arms, and it begins to nurse. He suckles with faint slurp noises as his little arms spread out to hug mommy's softness. The little fingers wiggle in vain attempts to grasp the smooth surface, a vast and soft plain to his larval digits.

I thought I could feel my face blush when she looked at me, direct, stern, prolonged, as if to gauge my reaction, to drown any of my impure improper natural thoughts with her own social superiority in this situation. Her personal dignity as mother disarms the male psyche, her strength rooted in motherhood, itself a testament to her personal experience with the one track, linear motivations men think they can hide behind walls transparent to female intuition.

I manage a wane and, I hope, dignified smile of reassurance. I don't know how I should react. My upper lip sweats more than most people's anyway, and in this humid, seaside heat that begins each day at nine thirty or so and continues to emanate from the sun soaked sand for hours after sunset, I invent ways to make it a joke to wipe my lip so often, feign nervousness when I feel nervous, or blame it on hot chiles in the salsa, "Me enchilaste."

She doesn't smile back.

Her husband sits down to eat with us. I feet an instantaneous heartburn, my stomach refuses to digest.

With grace and dexterity, she breast feeds her baby with one hand and eats her meal with the other, even rips tortillas into sections to use as a spoon with one hand.

I concentrate on my own meal. Later I look up, and realized that without my notice she managed to drape a white cotton diaper from shoulder down over baby, to block my view, or as a shield against the sunlight.

I stopped by there at my convenience to eat, sometimes twice a day, but more and more often, after the long walk down the beach, she might say they ate everything, no food remained to prepare.

As the days passed, I felt accepted into the community at large, and at least tolerated by their family. They acknowledged my membership into something bigger than family, into a primordial village larger and more real than any nationality, ethnicity, or culture. I belonged to the family of man, and we all shared in this, the Human Condition. We all live motivated by complex social needs and a search for basic necessities, frustrated by scarcities and unmet desires, and the commonality of our hungers unites us.

Not even my diligent platonic attitude towards her muscular, lithe, brown, active and healthy female body, could purge my brain of impure thoughts about the softest parts of her. My vague membership in their family failed to activate any instinctual incest taboo. Without intention, I probably paid a little too much attention to her, and worse, in the presence of her husband. I became too familiar around both the adults and their kids, and I bet that scuttled our relationship.

Even without another restaurant for miles, except Don Martinez's, they weaned me away from them through bad treatment.

They conspired to run out of food too often. She lost patience with me, refused to decipher my half Spanish, and it felt like her husband ignored me yet lurked around without reason.

Other times, she and her husband refused to prepare me a meal because of a scarcity of food for their family, they said. It confused me. I couldn't imagine what they did with the all the money I paid them for meals. In a dollar a day economy, they either didn't charge enough, didn't operate with a profit motive, or would rather not suffer my presence in their life because they saw me as an uncommunicative stranger, a young male, a person with incomprehensible grammar, from a distant land of ill repute.

To those accustomed to days of hunger, voluntary fasts become a normal part of life.

Took me years to appreciate the most obvious reason my relationship with the family evaporated.

As a male, her husband could read my mind.

The Fishing Co-op's TV

Hawaii distinguished itself as one of the first communities in Guatemala to form a Fishing Co-operative, and as a reward for collective endeavor, and to share the communal profits, the community voted to buy a television set. They built a simple canvas room on a cement slab in the open space in front of Don Martinez's store, to double as a main square for the collective's meeting hall. By day, they sometimes opened up the thin sides of canvas and to reveal the cement foundation and pillars that supported the tin roof, which protected people from the brutal overhead sun.

In the center of the cement floor, they built a wooden altar and placed the Television on it. People came and revered it for a couple of hours a week on specified evenings, or whenever Don Martinez decided to run the gasoline generator. Both children and adults sat cross legged on the cement, or outside on the sand, to watch some stupid soap opera made in Estados Unidos Mexicanos with actors that all looked Caucasian.

More people lived around Hawaii than I imagined. Hidden away from our community center, some houses made of cement and brick with ceramic roof tiles stood empty most of the year, and served as cottages for city dwellers. The local inhabitants, all poor people, lived in houses of sticks, roofed with lightweight "shingles" of folded fan palm fronds thatched into "palapas"

I heard of another expatriate American in Hawaii. A big girl, everyone said. She lived here for the past six months as part of an independent Latin American study under the auspices of a college professor in the Capital.

The televised images introduce the beach dwellers to advanced technologies like "electro-domestics," electrical kitchen utilities, and cars. The images also make the beach dwellers feel insecure about their own lifestyle, which helps lure them to the cities, the promised land of luxuries and universal economic success. TV gives them faith that with a job, they will earn enough money to buy status, health, glamour, happiness, and endless youth.

Too bad that so far, no financial incentive exists to reverse the polarity and bring images to the developed world of 'underdeveloped' nobility and their humanity balanced with nature, in contrast with First World's neurotic urban landscapes of work ethic nature haters in an unsustainable culture that values efficiency, competitiveness, and acquisitive ambition and ignores contamination and damage to the environment.

Here, I watched TV with these technological virgins, and saw with dismay how television's amplified colorfulness, light speed image transitions, and complex soundtracks charm the guileless and uninitiated. The images beckon and smile with an alien seductive beauty, then become recognizable and something to identify with, even though the visual medium demands excessive animation, congruent to the Mexican's extreme histrionics but in contrast to the reserved Guatemalan's. The images instruct them in how to behave, and give them a false impression of a 'correct' way to live, with the acceptance of violence and gratuitous sexualized imagery. Young people's moral frameworks tend to deconstruct in the photons. The seductive images wet the innocent's appetite for the "developed" world's products, as seductive cartoon consumer goods dance to become indispensable necessities in their eyes. Only the literate can appreciate planned obsolescence, the engineered tendency for things to break a short time after the warranty expires. With Latinos that do migrate to the first World, of the small percentage that avoid the trap of inner cities, rural enclaves, or urban slums and enjoy a First World lifestyle, most (almost all the women) will live underemployed and underpaid, beyond their means, perpetually in debt. They don't realize those ambitions will lead them away from their traditional roots and divorce them further from nature, to isolate them within an urban reality that controls their activities all day long, five or six days a week, to dig themselves into a job they can't afford to quit because they buried themselves in debt.

Subliminal messages infect like a virus. When indigenous people first receive television signals, they see no images that reflect their surroundings, nor people that look like them, except on the news, in reports about protests against the government, or live broadcasts about crime, poverty, tourism, or tragedy. From this they conclude that television's reality, of glamorous soap operas and Hollywood movies, must represent the superior reality, more real than theirs, a reality that beams from somewhere else, a higher reality, a nobler universe, somewhere beyond their reach.

In this, Television resembles religion.

They lose faith in their own uncertain environment, and perceive a better, expansive, ordered, and unlimited horizon of potential in these urban images.

Television and movies, in general, exaggerate the developed world's luxury and glamour, and suggest that the majority of people live like that. People get the idea that the 'real' world exists somewhere as seen on TV, and that they will find the good life in cities full of expensive cars on smooth, well lit roadways, huge electrified homes awhirl with gadgets and toys with kitchens where hot and cold water falls out of chrome tubes. They want to live a life of blue or yellow fluorescent mouthwash, and dream one day they will invite all their friends and family to perfect social functions thrown by a tall, svelte, high class, usually fake blonde, hostess for hire.

Those with unfilled social needs imagine that civilized people sit around with friends in discos, perhaps a part of their own house, as a partially nude girl with too much eye makeup serves cut glass crystal glasses of icy slushes that glow in rainbow colors under little paper umbrellas. Everyone smokes cigars or cigarettes, and the smoke drifts into a blue and red strobe light haze in a room that throbs with dancers.

The family oriented see TV dreams of a heaven where each small nuclear family lives in a perfect, multi floor mansion, and no visible means of support.

TV convinces people they should live a life of riotous consumption with unlimited discretionary funds, no visible means of support, pockets full of mad money for fashion, cars, jewelry, alcohol, and then pay for psychologists, "shrinks" that promise to solve all manner of personal problems related to anxieties with unknown causes.

Like religion, television beams from somewhere beyond, to welcome them into a realm of social standards they must accept on faith, in direct proportion to their loss of faith in their natural environment.

To afford the brain poison of broadcast television, they work long days on a rigid schedule each week, and get a small vacation of one or two weeks per year, if lucky enough to receive benefits or consideration, to enjoy themselves.

Vacation, a chance to experience nature, if they value the opportunity, to again return to the simple pleasures of a place like Hawaii, where trees burst into flower to perfume fresh ocean breezes that waft through sea side cottages of sticks. They could lay in shady hammocks strung from two trees to escape the afternoon sun, and let their mind invent relaxed daydreams that dance to the sounds of children and chickens and dogs. Or they might lay in their spouse's arms at night, lulled by the cool night's endless surf music.

Without TV.

One twilight after sunset, I walked the beach and saw, far to the west over the Pacific ocean, the silent approach of lightning strobed cumulous clouds. I watched it approach and grow larger for about an hour, until I heard the first dull gong tones of thunder, the hints of an immense, tempestuous fury from inside the swollen cloud towers.

That night, as I lay on my cot and listened to the torrential downpour's roar in my flashlight's beam, I saw sheets of water scurry across the sand to coalesce in wide rivulets. One came through the sticks of my hut's walls, through my fire pit, and out the other side on its way to the mangrove canal.

Ponchien loves Strawberry

One afternoon, the slim bearded man and his bratty daughter arrived by canoe at the dock. As if by magic, the village's young boys came to help them unload enough supplies to last a couple of months without contact with the outside world.

The Gringo greeted Don Martinez like an old friend and soon rented a large shack of sticks about thirty feet across the sand from mine. The men and children that unloaded the canoe balanced huge lumpy canvas bags on their heads for the short trek across the soft sands to his new home.

I greeted them and they invited me to come back in a few hours, after they unpacked a few essentials, to share a meal with fresh ingredients.

He and his daughter cooked up a fantastic meal, under the circumstances, based on pancakes with fresh vegetables.

The seven year old pantomimed the mature attitude of a perfect woman of the house. She completed each task with a haughty competence that exaggerated itself into a sarcastic mock with each needless instruction from her father. Her eyes rolled toward heaven as she dropped her hands to whine "I know, dad."

He continued to flip flapjacks, his face swallowed by thin scruffy facial hair that allowed his eyes to peek out and smile at her for an instant.

I bet he grew his beard out to help hide from his wife, although still a rare gringo in Guatemala. The beard also helped him hide any displeasure with his daughter, I thought.

We ate a salad of fresh ingredients from the City, with fresh local fish from the sea or mangrove canals, and a drink made of powdered milk, cinnamon, and chocolate boiled in water pre-boiled for ten minutes to sterilize it first.

He told me about his quiet and civilized divorce, his painful separation from his wife who he will forever consider as the one true love of his life.

This perfect woman, the mother of Brianda, doesn't know where her ex-husband and daughter went to.

"You mean you kidnapped her?"

"Legal terms, I don't think like that. I'm not a lawyer, nor do I respect them. I did what I saw in the best interests of my daughter, like any responsible father."

"You think she's better off here, in remote Central America, cut off from all contact with civilization?"

"Better than at home with a mother that's too distracted by her own personal activities to pay attention to her daughter. Brianda's at that age where she needs somebody to be there for her. I need time and isolation to write the novel I couldn't finish with her mom around. Brianda's better off with me. I'm dedicating all my professional time to finish this novel, so one hundred percent of my personal time I dedicate to Brianda."

"How long have you been writing?"

"I was born a writer. It's something you know inside, a gift. It's not easy to balance the life of a true artist with the demands of work, marriage and childcare. If the baby coughs, someone must attend to it, even though in the long run, we must consider art much more important. Art delivers the knowledge that will beautify the future."

After dinner, we lay back to smoke cigarettes in a couple of comfortable camp chairs he'd bought back in California and shipped to Guatemala City.

"My name is Doug, Doug Tralfagar. You can call me Doug, but I want you to remember my last name, Tralfagar, and when I'm famous in a few years, you can say you knew me when. I won't look the same. I plan to cut off the beard by then."

"What makes you so sure you'll get famous?"

"Everyone waits for the Great American Novel. This is it. My book details the Hippie generation through the eyes of two lovers, exactly the way it happened, taken from my true life experiences."

"What's the name of the book?"

"Ponchien loves Strawberry."

Brianda's ears perked up. "It's about my mom and dad. Ponchien Loves Strawberry, and their going to get back together and live happy ever after. Right dad?"

Of course she believed her parents loved each other and must get together. Inevitable.

"Part of the reason why we decided to come to a place so remote springs from my wife's well financed efforts to find us and take Brianda away from me, by force if necessary. And it would be necessary to take her by force. I love my daughter."

"Why do two people, so perfect for each other, separate?"

"That's the thing about true love. Like that movie what's its name, that said something about love, when you love someone, they don't need to hear you say you're sorry. When two people intertwine their lives, it's inevitable that one develops faster than the other, then vice versa, at various times. They leapfrog along, first one ahead, then the other. I'm supposed to apologize to her for where my life took me? I tell her she can do what she wants. Up to the point where our lives start to unravel. That's when I put my foot down."

"What drove you two apart?"

"My wife drove the three of us apart. I admit that on one level, her actions may be necessary steps in her personal development. Unfortunately, and she took those steps with another man, and violated our union, our vows, our trust. How could I ever trust her again? Morally I knew I should do nothing about it. I didn't own her. She has the right to live her own life, and I understood that. But when I saw that my acceptance of her past actions gave her permission to proceed, that I allowed her to chose a course that hurt our family and threatened our daughter's emotional wellbeing, I took Brianda out of that situation. So we came here, and found Hawaii."

"You went back to the States to get supplies and these great camp chairs. Did you see your wife?"

"No, no no no. We hid. Mutual friends assured me that contact with her would be tantamount to walking into a mother bear's den. My wife will pass through this stage of her life, Brianda will mature, I'll find a publisher, and the book will come out. Then I'll have my own money and not depend on her family's resources. She'll learn to respect me and come to her senses. We'll become a family again, all three of us, or continue with this miserable separation. In the meantime, Brianda's with me."

"Isn't that kidnapping, even if she is your own daughter?"

"Everything in life depends on your point of view. To a criminal on the run, all cops look like pigs, and to the police mentality that follows orders without question, peaceful hippies and young idealistic college students that don't support the president need their heads bashed in. Therefore, they shoot and kill a couple of adolescent kids for the good of society. Anyone would admit that's wrong, except for those who worship authority because it gives them authority, a police mentality. So I've taken my daughter into protective custody. Who better to look out for a child than her biological father?"

Brianda snuggled up to offer kinesthetic support to Big Hairy Daddy's argument.

As time went on, the thought that I should tip off her mother resurfaced every so often. Not out of any moral indignation, but because the brat rubbed me the wrong way from the beginning, snot nosed, know it all, lapdog daddy's girl that turned the both of them into smug isolationists. They loved each other, and it gave me the creeps to see them watch the moon reflect in each other's eyes, with Brianda curled in his lap with her arms draped weak around his neck. She stared into the hairless parts of his face.

Within a few days, Doug put me on the spot. He asked me how I felt about his course of action with his daughter.

I figured the heat probably affected him as did me. It made us both too horny, with no opportunity for release, and that frustration made us cranky. So I said, "Divorce hurts kids a lot. My father died when I was a bit younger than her, and I thought that duty forced me to mature in an instant, to take his place. But then girls mature earlier anyway. Brianda should feel safer here than in a public school, don't you think?"

Sure, I lied, for the sake of green salad and store bought bread. I felt sickened at myself, to say something so hypocritical about it, but he caught me hungry.

Doug smiled, I think, somewhere under his beard. "That's the way I see it. Good to hear it from you. We need you on our side."

I could see it, all right. "We're the Gringos out here, we better stick together."

I tried to love them and cherish them as my fellow compatriots, even though I suspected Doug a communist. Since grade school, we learned that Communists aimed nuclear weapons at us, and took orders from Satan. In atomic attack drills, we kids ran into the school hallway to line up against the wall and hug our knees. In college, I learned the next step. Kiss your ass goodbye.

Any political discourse threw Doug into a frenzy of paranoia. He perceived most governments as puppets of the United States and part of The Conspiracy. Anytime I could imagine the other point of view or the middle of the road, he said "You're another one of those treasonous vipers ready to call the States and tell my wife and Interpol where I am."

He held his political convictions too close to his chest in a poker hand of secret, heartfelt, superior and certain knowledge of The Conspiracy bolstered by arcane anecdotes, the source of his bluff. He loved to end discussions with "You don't understand," or the terminal "You wouldn't understand."

I owed Doug a little loyalty for the tip about this paradise, although I figured he appreciated another Gringo's presence as a little insurance, another element of confusion to those on his trail. So I decided he let me in on his secret Shangri-La with planned premeditation. Now that I knew him, when I reviewed our first week of short encounters, I could see how he tested me and sized me up as young, sincere, harmless, and respectful, and therefore controllable or useful to him.

At first I helped out with the daily cleanup, as arranged, but like most twenty two year olds, I didn't feel it important to figure out where he liked to store all the stuff. I figured the process of home organization entailed constant rearrangement as improvements came to mind.

Doug felt I should follow his ad-hoc placements with precision and total recall, so he could "get to work and write" which meant lay back, with a pen in one hand and a cigarette in the other, to close his eyes and think behind his huge sunglasses. He seldom appreciated how difficult I found it to keep up with changes in their methods and organization.

For the first few days, after each meal we often kicked back and smoked a few cigarettes, mostly Doug's, and took turns on beer runs to Don Martinez's window counter convenience store. After we threw back a couple of beers, or when I felt bad about some mess or mistake I made, I ran to Don Martinez's to buy a couple more. My guilt level stayed high after the fright I gave his daughter the first time I hid in a small space under the canvas flaps of the table's cover that served as their cabinets. I jumped out like a rabid dog as she walked up in the twilight.

I thought Brianda cried real tears that time, as she jumped into daddy's arms. Later, I thought otherwise, as I recognized her control over those spigots for tear ducts.

Brat.

After we drank into the darkest twilight, he often decided to leave the dishes till morning, "to save on batteries."

I rarely shared breakfast with them. Instead, I jogged down the beach on many of those cool, pre-dawn mornings. Doug complained he did dishes "way too often" and let us know the task lay way below his station.

I wanted to test him, but his buffoonery, or photographic retention (impossible to know which) in his devotion to arcane scientific detail won out. And, as an open eyed Californian, he saw and analyzed the weird, wonderful, and fresh firsthand, while the rest of America played catch-up with a slow and overly critical acceptance a couple of years after California introduced it.

I grew up way down that road, in rural Michigan, about two years distant from California. Our 1968 summer of love happened in 1971, the year I graduated, the year girls who rejected my offers to take them out on dates all through high school became liberated women who would see me around midnight at some illegal beer party in the boondocks and offer to share our fledgling hormonal impulses in the tall grasses out back.

Right-handed Sex

"Doug, what do you know about those four-eyed fish?"

"A little. Latin name, Anableps anableps, ranges in the mangrove and brackish swamps throughout southern Mexicano, Central America, and northern South America. Gets over a foot long, most about six to ten inches. Each eye's pupil divides into two horizontal sausage shapes. The fish cruises right at the surface level, the upper half sees above the water while the lower half sees underwater. The two eyes' upper halves stick out of the water. There's an oval shaped lens in each eye that directs light at distinct angles of refraction to compensate for the differences between air and water. But that's not the weirdest thing about them."

"No? What is?"

"Their sex life."

I waited, sucked a drag out of one of his cigarettes, and put my head back to exhale a veil in front of a glorious Milky Way sky behind ink black palm silhouettes that rattled a tremulous hula above us.

Doug continued. "Four-eyed fish must mate either right handed or left handed. So right handed males find left handed females, I suppose."

"They masturbate each other?"

Doug ignored my joke. I thought he joked.

He was serious. "Each fish's sex organ works either from the right or the left. The male's sex organ comes out to the right or to the left, and each female's vagina opens to the right or to the left, so that a 'right handed' male must find a 'left handed' female."

I didn't know whether to believe him, or resent him for his humorless disdain. He knew I couldn't find a useful reference library south of UCLA.

Decades later in college, I read that the four-eyed fish's sexuality orients right or left, and I remembered Doug, and wondered if he reunited with his wife, or his right or left handed.

Doug's superiority, so obvious to himself and due to his own diligent and disciplined efforts, gave him the right and duty to belittle everyone else. One day I realized, after many observations of his interchanges with various locals that stopped by to sell him something, why Doug resisted any improvement in his Spanish. He needed to humiliate others. He refused to adapt to local expectations of behavior, and wouldn't adopt a learner's attitude, but maintained personal distance through an attitude of cultural superiority. Bad plan.

I grew to hate Brianda because she mirrored his attitude. Because of her love for him, she learned his contempt for others. She treated me as a threat and intrusion into her relationship with him as his golden haired lapdog.

Get a life, I told myself, when I'd lay awake after dark at about ten or so, and shake myself back to reality after my muffled laughter about another fantasy of revenge against the stuck up little twit. I daydreamed about how to twist sticks and wads of long black hair found on the beach into horrid spiders to leave on top of her favorite box of cereal, but abandoned the plan because she'd know whom it came from.

I moved her things from place to place, but her pointed questions dissuaded me from that tactic.

As if by a mandate from a higher consciousness, I slipped into a secret mission to find any chinks of fear in the brat's armor. Then I could worry them into open wounds that festered into doorways for her worst nightmares.

Through an instinct born of righteous indignation, I learned to terrorize her, without any conscious decision.

Suppose I see her and Daddy Doug stroll toward me through the coconut groves long before they see me. I might squeeze myself into a palm shadow next to their trail and jump out with a bark that giggled, because I foresee how her body will shudder as she leaps into daddy's arms to hang like a pendant from his stiff neck, while his stare says "I am not amused."

One twilight, I tiptoed and scurried across the sand that separated our shacks to slip under the canvas that covered the storage benches they used as a kitchen. Brianda reaches to pull up the canvas and I launched out on all fours with a gruff dog-snarl to scare that smug half-smile of childish self confidence off her face. She falls flat backward, flails sand, crabs her way to hug her seated daddy's knees and beg him to pick her up, while she chatters adult-rated insults at me, like spider monkeys scurrie into trees to throw poo from a safe place.

Doug mentioned other people as acquaintances, never as friends. The way Doug talked in English about others persuaded me not to get any closer. He liked to admit that none of his acquaintances merited his friendship, but "I give my friendship almost as freely as others earn my enmity." Direct quote from the writer. He spoke about no one but his wife with the slightest affection, for Brianda's benefit, I suspect.

I decided to put more distance between myself and these two Californians, who lived secret lives in Paradise to escape the wrath of misguided Mom, the Mafia's daughter, the unfaithful wife, the better off without them.

I needed to protect my own reputation in Hawaii. Not only did I see Doug as the quintessential Ugly American who refuses to learn their language and social niceties, he uses a false sense of cultural superiority as a threadbare security blanket to cradle himself in.

From anecdotal examples of his wife's family money, I got the idea that the authorities might arrive any day with a warrant to arrest the kidnapper. And they might, by force of bribe, take me back with them to testify.

A few days into my spontaneous campaign to terrorize the pompous brat, Doug walked over and told me in his laconic monotone "it makes sense for us to not share meals anymore, since we don't think you pull your weight with the cleanup."

He whispered, "Brianda decided she didn't like you."

I felt a little hurt, and then cheered up as I thought about how my social failure would forever free me from Doug's tone when he talked down to me. I learned a lot from him, and he from me, but the manner he used when he forced me to learned from him injured my self esteem, week enough in a land where I couldn't communicate.

I can appreciate the invaluable gift of a knowledgeable friend, but if their attitude communicates they believe you wrong and stupid all the time, unrelieved by laughter or reciprocal listening, only the strong survive. It tired me, and I gave up.

A few days after he booted me, he waved me over with a sincere smile. He said "things have disappeared, and I wondered if you'd seen anyone around." He always said he hoped I might keep an eye out towards his place, whenever they left camp for any length of time.

"Sure," I said, as I relished the fact that he crawled to me to accept his society again. People walk through here all the time, to and from the store, beach, canal, TV. You've got so much, they've got so little."

"I expect them to treat me with the consideration I give to them." His voice sounded muffled.

"You're voice sounds different. Toothache?"

"Not quite. Remember that festival a couple of days ago? Well, some drunk came over and tried to talk to me. I didn't want him near my daughter, and I tried to shoo him away, but he followed Brianda and I. Tried to approach us several times. Looked to me like he wanted to pick a fight with me, no matter what. I tried to avoid him, nothing worked, so I gave him a clear nonverbal message, a little shove. Pissed him off. Maybe we both drank too much that day. He got too close again, and I took a swing at the guy. Mistake. I missed, he nailed me, didn't see it coming. He cold cocked me right there in the sand in front of my daughter. Brianda freaked out and attacked like a little banshee. She screamed and cried, and that got everybody's attention. People ran over to help, and the guy ran off."

"Did they catch him?"

"For what? Everyone knows him, but they blame me. Don Martinez says they want him to kick me out of Hawaii. Every time he sees me now, his face looks like he's gonna cry."

"Why's that?"

"Why do I think they want me out, or why does he look like he might cry?"

"Both."

"They think I caused the trouble. Don Martinez's face gets flushed and wet because he feels responsible, ashamed he let me come live here. Remember, he founded this community. I've damaged his reputation, and the idea that tourists would help these people out. He wants these villagers to believe in progress and education. Us Gringos represent the future. He told me we should know better than to resort to violence. So I let him down. Who gives a shit. Looks to me like a bunch of criminals."

"Who does?"

"These people. Looks like plenty use Hawaii as a hide out."

"What do you mean?"

"Why do people come here to live? They don't catch enough fish to live on, as far as I can see. Bet most of these families came from criminal stock, like Australians. Criminals wanted by the cops, or drug dealers on the run from violent assholes that want to balance accounts, want revenge, or worse."

Projection of his own situation? I wondered.

After that confession of bigotry, I felt vindicated in my campaign to put distance between us, but our similarities, our shared nationalism and culture, put me square in his camp in the eyes of this community, whether I liked it or not. They see me as his friend, his paisano, his compatriot.

No sign of my one friend here, Arturo, since the day I stopped by his house and found his wife, Yadira, alone. She told me without a glance, "Arturo's not here today. He left to work in a nearby town" as she continued to cut vegetables for the soup.

I found her attractive. I wanted to hang around and talk awhile, because she often revealed intelligence and curiosity, within the limits of her husband's macho domination, and I wondered if her personality would change with him not around.

I took a seat at the table, and offered to help her. Her Ladino Mayan mix of features gave her full, sharp sculpted lips and a slight flare to her nostrils, an exotic lift to the outer corners of her mango shaped eyes. Her soft, full and healthy body intrigued me, almost visible behind the simple light cotton dresses most of the women in Hawaii wear.

She refused my help, and said, "No, no. Women's work," and then said something I did not understand, and could not get her to repeat.

She acted nervous, and she did not offer me any water or food, which felt strange. Most Guatemalans offer you their last piece of bread.

She refused to talk to me, wouldn't answer, shrugged her shoulders. After a few minutes of silence filled by clanking dishes and the wind from my twiddled thumbs, I felt uncomfortable, so I made a big production about the time, looked at my cheap plastic watch, showed it to her and told her to dissuade Arturo in his selfish ambition to own an expensive Rolex.

I got up to leave.

"Bye." she said, without a glance.

Later it dawned on me that she knew the other villagers, all of them, even though they live apart and out of sight of each other, everyone notices everything. A man who visits someone else's wife raises eyebrows and enters the fourth dimension, time, as something to talk about for weeks, months, years, decades.

Too much peace and quiet, nothing to read, no continuous adult education. What else to think about?

To the local men, Doug and I represented their worst nightmare, two single male Gringos, with the resources to steal their women and take them to some Developed Nation in the First World. Worse, and more probable, we might deflower or defile these local girls and women, moms and grandmothers, leave them with child and disgrace in their public's eye, while we flee beyond their reach or influence.

Cowboy Movie

The Olmecas of Veracruz state in Mexico knew how to make concave mirrors of iron ore one thousand years before Christ. They pierced them to wear as a pendant around the neck. The optical qualities of these concave surfaces could potentially cast bright sunlit images onto flat white surfaces from within in a relatively dark enclosure. Outside on a clear midday, these mirrors might ignite tinder at the focal point of reflected sunlight, like a magnifying glass. Any Olmecas in possession of these mirrors, whether kings, queens, witches or priests, could demonstrate these supernatural powers to influence others. The mirrors themselves might serve as emblems of a certain class of citizen, prophets, priest, rulers, or shaman witchdoctor healers, all Godlike humans with the power to reflect reality to an intimate group, or create fire, or inspire fear in an entire community so that they will dance, perform incantations, and sing songs to reach a state of trance and recognize the world as a reflection, an image superimposed upon time.

One morning a grizzled old man, sturdy from decades of hard work, came to Hawaii and set up a tent on the beach alongside my house of sticks.

He convinced, or bought, Don Martinez's permission to use electricity from the generator, and then hung out at the store all day to spread his promise of a cowboy film that evening. He sold some tickets, and to some of the more aggressive young boys, he gave groups of tickets for them to earn a commission. He encouraged everyone to spread the word, one night only.

He and Don Martinez both carried the coils of orange extension chord out of the store. They walked together across the cocoa sand to the Fishing Co-op structure. Don Martinez opened up one canvas side and pulled back a panel of corrugated tin to reveal the Television set on its altar. Don Martinez smiled at his companion, plugged it in, turned it on, turned up the volume, and stepped back.

The full color image of a beautiful white girl with too much makeup appeared. She cried and gesticulated a frantic distress through the glitter of static. Mexican soap opera, although she looked Italian. Estados Unidos Mexicanos leads Latin America in Television soap opera production, which they call "novellas" because they often begin as works of literature that begin and end, in contrast to the multi-season decades long lifespan of soaps on American television. As in most soap operas, histrionic actors agonize over the plot's various sexual affairs (in Spanish, they call them "love adventures") in the pursuit of new infidelities and confidences, until they uncover each generation's untold secrets about who fathered whom.

Don Martinez crossed his arms over his proud, inflated chest.

The other man took a step back, crossed his arms, exhaled, crestfallen, hunched forward, as if confronted by the end of his career.

Don Martinez turned off the TV and unplugged the extension cord to hand to the tough old man.

He dragged the orange electric extension cord across the sand toward the beach, past my stick shack, to where his big bundles of canvas lay, which he then untied and spread out.

Within a couple of hours, he set up a miniature circus tent, about twenty five feet square.

All afternoon, the squat tent's greasy gray black canvas panels flapped in the sea breeze. It reminded me of a great bat, the camelhair tent of a slaver's harem of Nubian virgins, a portable adult theater, a slaughterhouse of innocence.

I felt worse about it the longer I looked at it, so I peaked inside.

Smelled like motor oil. After my eyes grew accustomed to the dim light that seeped under the canvas, I saw the screen and projector wrapped in roped cloth and plastic against the back wall, two soldiers, one with a bazooka, both fossilized and still, who hid in shadows. The wisps of sand slithered under the canvas and blew into little dunes around their feet.

At dusk, the inhabitants of Hawaii came with their children to crowd inside the greased canvas enclosure. The canvas did keep out the daylight that lingered over the ocean. After the village boys, fathers, and grandfathers settled into their seats, I entered and moved around to the back.

They sat cross legged in the sand and muttered as the man turned on the noisy projector and started the movie, a grainy, scratchy old black and white Hollywood western, dubbed into Spanish and distorted through loud amplification and inadequate speakers.

I peeked out, from under the canvas, to watch the sunset purple twilight, and glanced back inside to watch their reaction as the movie started.

In one of the shots near the very beginning, a band of five distant horsemen charged at the screen, as if to run right over the audience. From the far distance, the horses came at full gallop, seven spastic ink splotches in front of a dust cloud.

The camera shot from ground level, about the height of our eyes as we sat there on the sand. The horses thundered from out of the distance, picked up speed, and kept right on toward us, as if to burst out of the screen, immense healthy black and white horses with foamy bits, wild eyes, and metal shod hooves that stomped explosions of dust.

As the horses fill the screen to ride right through us, children scream and claw their way out of the arms of the men to flee the tent. More than half of the audience panics and scrambles on hands and knees to the edge of the tent, where they wriggle like crabs under the tight canvas to escape.

The horses did not come out of the screen to trample those of us who remained. I saw people lift the canvas from outside to peek in, then crawl back under the canvas to reclaim their seats in the sand. They giggled, felt around with their hands for lost hats, smoothed their shirts, and shook sand out of their cuffs. Grandfathers with gap-toothed smiles hugged their nervous grandchildren who sobbed and giggled at the same time.

I thought of the time I tried to interest a Mayan Indian boy in magazine photos of airplanes and automobiles. He showed no interest.

I wonder now if he couldn't see them, could not understand.

CHAPTER 8: Venomous Squamates

One morning, I sketched a number of things from imagination into my sketchbook journal. One pen and ink turned out very well, a muscular three dimensional snake dragon, a prehistoric reptile from sword and sorcery fantasy science fiction. I regarded it as the extrapolation of a boy's dinosauric quest for power through big ugliness, the sex starved adolescent man's wish fulfillment for dominance and sexual conquest, which parallel's a girl's expression of phallic worship through the desire to surrender to the giant strength and vertical mobility of a gentle unicorn.

With a ball point ink pen, I created a long S curved viperous dragon, covered with scales. It turned back to looked out of the page with a sardonic smile full of long teeth that dripped with venom.

Because of the time spent on the sketch, I jogged a little later than usual. The smells of cooking fires reminded me of Fall in Michigan, the odor of burnt leaves, dry grasses bleached blonde by the August sun to grow mold in the days of rain. The trees displayed exuberant colors of yellow, orange, and red as the leaves gave up the ghost of chlorophyll. January, and I longed for Halloween, the hay rides through the country side on a wagon pulled by a tractor driven by the meanest man in the neighborhood. How civilized it seemed, to trick or treat with the threat to commit acts of humorous vandalism like streaks on windows of soap (or wax if we felt mean), or brown paper bags set on fire on doorsteps with dog poop inside to relish the moment the owner opened the door and stamped out the fire, or the joy of a secret arsenal of rotten eggs to settle old scores with stinky anonymity.

Here in the tropics, I felt everything green after the New Year insulted the appropriate advance of four seasons, and everyday when the cool yet muggy mornings turned into a tropical heat that sucked one's energy and de-accelerated the rhythm of life, the work ethic seemed like an impossible ideal, a myth from another continent.

I jogged alone every morning, and considered everyone else my moral inferior, until the sounds of children or laughter accentuated my solitude and unhappy bachelorhood.

One late morning, I stumbled over the rise of a small dune to look down upon a large naked white girl. A Gringa, tucked into one of the deeper dune valleys, sunbathed in the cool morning air, with most of her ample surface area exposed. Skin so white, my eyes felt snow blind for a second. She rolled around like an albino elephant seal to cover herself with the towel she lay upon.

I stopped mid stride and watched her huff and try to cover her expanses of nudity with the insufficient beach towel. Her long blond hair, parted down the middle like a butt made of straw, hung in two thick braids that ended in pigtail knots the size of shaving brushes. They whipped across her face as she threw nasty looks at me, and lurched after more of the sheet.

About six feet of her larval whiteness writhed and kicked up the sand in that small dune hollow, a fish in a sugar bowl. She seemed put together with rude slabs of white grease blubber, designed by Norse gods with intentions of hard labor without a squeak of complaint, a rough hewn gem in need of long term tumbles for polish and refinement. I doubted the existence of any self described woman tamer who could whittle down this prodigious relic of Viking femininity. Her frantic motions to hide her voluptuousness made her plump white bread rolls of fatty tissue heave around like cow's udders full of catfish.

She looked like whale ready to process.

I tried to act nonchalant, but after I greeted her, she reacted to my boyish charm with angry contempt, unimpressed and antagonistic. My attempts to break the ice with talk about the weather met with frosty glares that threw daggers of icicles meant to gash my insouciance.

I said "People told me about you, they said hey, there's another Gringo in the area. I'm surprised we haven't met before. I don't quite remember, but they did tell me your name."

"Connie."

"Nice to meet you. Name's Brandon."

She didn't even smile. "So now you've met me. Enjoy your stay." She turned her back to me.

I jogged on.

Whenever we passed the next few weeks, I saw no sign of a thaw. She acted like everybody should consider her the only real resident Gringo, Anglo Saxon or Nordic Laplander, whatever, because she lived in Hawaii the past six months, longer than any other current expatriate resident. I imagine the mere presence of other Anglos broke her delusion of explorer on the National Geographic frontier, and all the attendant self aggrandizement that the discoverer feels with fantasies of a first contact from the true civilized world. Imagine the sense of purpose of a young Peace Corps woman on her first assignment, all alone, as a giant white being with yellow hair, among diminutive brown skinned Ladinos with black hair. She wants to believe that most of the residents never before saw a white person, let alone a monolithic unpigmented and translucent one. Her path leads to perpetual legend, a live myth, a part of their cosmology to last for eons because she will change their world forever.

Whenever we found ourselves close to each other, she sent me nonverbal reminders to amplify the distance between us. After each of these few encounters with her aggressive stare or cold shoulder, I walked down the beach to sit and let the waves massage my bruised ego and bring me back to paradise.

Years later in retrospect, I felt I knew her better, and decided her rejection of me serves as evidence that she, perhaps on a nightly basis, wrestled with Lesbianism and often lost.

Sea Snake

One day, as I sat deep in thought about a story of a manta ray that washed ashore and how I wished I could see something like that, I heard shrill screams of giddy children, both gleeful and terrorized.

Down the beach, some children chased each other with the top of a long shrub of denuded branches. Near the top in the thin twigs, a long slender snake draped limp.

The children screamed and laughed, and ran from the child who carried the bare shrub, who laughed with insane pleasure, power mad. With each attempt to throw the snake at the other children, those closest screamed and laughed with a shivery note of terror. Each time a child dropped the branch, another closed in to grab it to enjoy lethal power over others.

I ran down towards them, and noticed the pallid whiteness of Connie's face rise up like the moon to peek over the top of a sand dune. She pulled on a parachute size T-shirt and almost fell as she bounded over the top of the dune, her towel tangled around her feet. I could smell the coconut oil as she passed.

I ran after her.

The children's shouts mixed fear and glee, "It kills, it kills you!" as they chased each other.

The skinny snake's limp curves seemed lifeless within the branches, as the child in possession twisted the branch to keep the snake off the sand, to thrust it at other children.

They stopped their game as she approached. I grabbed the branch and broke off a section, about three foot long and straight. The snake fell onto the sand, motionless, emerald green in sunshine.

She yelled at me to leave it alone, and I ignored her.

It sported a lateral stripe along the sides, and its long triangular head ended in a very flat rectangular box of a nose instead of a curved or pointed snout like most snakes. Its little tongue flickered between its twin rows of lip scales like a tiny spark of life.

The tail flattened and widened, vertical, like a rudder. A sea snake.

The children yelled "Veneno," and huge Connie translated it for me with pedantic professionalism, as if to prove her superiority in Spanish. "They say it's a poisonous snake, it will kill you. Don't mess with it. Just let it go."

I used the small branch to pin it down behind the head, then picked it up by the neck and forced its mouth open with a twig. I didn't see any fangs, but the vibrant green plastic toy head shape, coupled with the kids continual yell about how it kills, gave it an aura of danger and poison, an inscrutable denizen of the sea, foreign and exotic.

Perhaps it got sick at sea and washed ashore.

I squatted down to the cocoa sand and felt the reradiated heat of the sun. I felt sweat run from my temples to chin as I let the exhausted animal go and jumped back as if it might spring to life with some deep reserve of lethal energy. The children batted it around until it died, or finished dying.

For most of the day, I noticed a huge cloud build up over the ocean, and by sunset it matured into a massive thunderhead. The dark bottom smeared downward as rain fell and lightning played about and through the anvil cloud. Many people, attracted to the beach to watch it, talked about the danger of floods and waves in little Hawaii, built upon dunes about two or three meters, six to nine feet, above the sea.

The sun set right over the beach and it took a long time before the last rays of red light disappeared from the cumulus cloud's wispy cirrus crown. The atmosphere over the sea glowed a creamy yellow behind the cloud's dark shadow.

The moon came up inland, over the palms and mangroves, announced by a golden glow over a far volcano.

The cloud's color in twilight shadow ran through a rainbow, from rust red to green to deep blue. In the East, the earth's orange rimmed shadow moved up and trailed the almost full moon into a red streaked purple sky.

An hour or so later, the rains came, and everyone scurried into their huts to hang in their cocoon hammocks to stay dry, while rivulets invaded their huts.

My shack's wooden bunk allowed me to dry my bare feet with my 'other' shirt as I sat and thought about my plan to write songs. No one down here appreciated rock guitar, they expect you to sing and I hate my voice. I felt self conscious anyway, but after I saw how Mexicans sing together in buses or as audiences, American music culture seemed weak and commercial.

In Hawaii, I couldn't play guitar very late into the night because I didn't like to write by candlelight, and I felt inhibited because we all slept in a silent humidity that carried sounds over great distances, far beyond what reason would call earshot. All the villages sounds became ghosts of lives separated by spatial and temporal distances, the most distant sounds a message that relayed what happened moments ago.

Depression hit me, and I wrote it down, a la e. e. cummings.

nobody alone as me. i own alone. no one to talk, no language shared, everyone misunderstands whenever i open my mouth. we smile like perfect idiots and chase our misinterpretations like a dog's own tail, like at home with family, or in high school, college, wherever I go.

nothing to do in Hawaii on rainy nights except myself, in the luxury of privacy, thanks to the noisy darkness and the beaded curtains of rain. when the downpour ends and the sky clears, the black and gray beach scene outlined in mercurial moonlight taunts me. i hear the worst thing imaginable, the gasps and moans of violent pleasure, an echo of the pulses of surf, the endless loops of Earth's shoreline, a copulation of land and sea that stitches this planet like a baseball.

Next day I took advantage of packed wet sand and walked East, all the way to the mangrove channel's outlet to the sea. A few fat men cooked chicken tacos for fishermen, who prepared to go out to sea in little rowboats. The fishermen piled weighted and buoyed fish line nets in the bow, waist high haystacks of transparent noodles.

Got back to Hawaii a little after dark. I slipped the bit of wire that 'locked' my decrepit sapling door to the frame of the one room stick house, and noticed some activity at Don Martinez's tienda.

One matron sized woman who drew her face in black lines of makeup, stood and shook out her long black hair, her weight on one leg, chest out, as if in a pose for a beer commercial. Behind her, two older white men, one bearded, addressed Don Martinez through his shop's window counter.

All carried leather purses like camera bags, and wore sandals and knee length khaki shorts, straight brim straw hats, and loose, tropical print short sleeved shirts with front pockets. They belonged in Miami, or the Keys.

Don Martinez wiped his hands on a cloth as he walked out from behind the counter to motion them to a table. Then he sat with them to talk. Doña Martinez came out with four cold, wet beer bottles to give one to each. She waved away their money, because the Don would not allow his guests to pay.

I never saw Don Martinez drink a beer before, nor give them out free, so I grabbed my dictionary and walked over.

Pot bellied Don Martinez basked in their praise as proud founder and chief resident of this outpost of civilization. He smiled wide enough to show the spaces behind his eyeteeth where molars once gleamed.

From deep in the store's darkness, I imagined the immobile Doña Martinez's hatred, her fixed glare twin sparks that burn under her haystack of gray hair as she watched her husband kowtow to these invaders.

Don Martinez made sure we introduced ourselves to each other, then got up and motioned me to sit at the head of the table, in his chair, to drink his untouched beer. I protested, but he took my arm and maneuvered me into it so he could slink off to some unnamed task. After his trademark subservient bows, hands pressed together in a Chinese supplication, he scurried off, his bare feet whispered through the sand, to join his wife and become silhouettes in the eternal darkness of their mysterious home behind the store.

The three came from Guatemala City, from the American University. They told Don Martinez they wanted to rough it and rent a few days in one of the house of sticks, to check up on Connie's independent study.

They spoke English, and invited me to their home whenever I got back to Guatemala City. They wanted to know why I came to Guatemala.

"To learn Spanish."

Teacher Berta then asked me something in Spanish, and by some grace of her careful and educated diction, I understood. I must have answered well, too.

Then she asked me, in very good English, how I learned my Spanish vocabulary.

"The dictionary."

"A bilingual dictionary?"

"No, I searched all the bookstores in Guatemala and found this thick illustrated one. Has little pen and ink drawings in the margins, and two sections of full color pages. Unfortunately, I didn't notice a bunch of blank pages in the D's."

Her eyes widened in appreciation of my genius.

I rummaged through my shoulder bag, pulled the dictionary out, and handed it to her.

The beardless man started to ask me the usual stupid questions, if I knew this swear word, or this gross anatomical term, but she shushed him.

"You read it page by page?"

"Oh no. I use it to try and understand the newspapers that come through here."

She looked relieved. I realized too late I had blown my claim to genius.

"How long have you been traveling?"

"What month is this? Four months ago, then. Almost two in Guatemala."

"You don't have any problem with the culture?"

"Like what?"

"Culture shock."

"Oh no. Culture shock. No. Culture? What culture? Stone age around here. They only talk about food and sex, and I never see them bathe often enough."

The bearded teacher spoke up. "Only Americans want to bathe everyday. I bet when you first got here, you saw this as paradise, now you see everything dirty and primitive."

"Culture shock?"

They laughed.

I said, "No, no no no." and failed to convince myself.

Flaco says "Now he sees Guatemalan people as lazy, ignorant, diseased or dying, dangerously stupid, and intellectually dead. Maybe even murderous, with hatreds he cannot begin to understand. You feel it sometimes, the way they look at you, or ignore you on purpose. Am I right?"

"Sort of. Partly."

"Come on, kid. You hit it on the head, Norman. Culture shock. They really do not talk about you, at least not when you think they do. But murderous? Yes, that is the truth. Life is cheap, and yours is worthless."

"I like Guatemala. It's beautiful, the Mayans make wonderful fabrics."

Flaco said, "Maybe you don't have culture shock. Yet. Maybe you left a girl back home, and you miss her. You feel homesick, you dream about it, want to find other Americans so you can discuss all the things you hate about where you are."

They all laughed.

"Now hold on, give him a break." Norm said, "Culture shock causes real and serious problems, and starts after five or six months away form home.

The skinny Flaco chimed in. "Yeah, people feel homesick, then get sarcastic about the world around them. Soon they hate everything different in the culture around them. They reject it as obviously inferior to the miserable lifestyle of their family, the way they live back home, which they ran away from."

Norm said, "Life sucks, no matter where you run."

Berta said "No matter where you go, there you are."

I thought a few seconds in the silence that followed, then said, "I don't feel my attitude changed much since I left the States. "

Berta said, "I know what he means. Even though I'm American, when I live in America, it feels like I'm all alone in my car all the time. I work too hard everyday, I make too much money, and never find time to enjoy it. Life without nature, without a social life, few people care about beauty and art in their life. Buy, buy, and buy again. Search through newspapers for ads and coupons for something else to buy. It's hard to see your own culture from the inside, invisible as water or glass, a window you can only look out of. When you go outside, then you can look back through that window and see a different frame around it, and begin to compare things."

Flaco touched my bicep with the back of his fingers. "Back to you. Do you feel your attention span shorten lately? Find yourself in constant repetition of mindless routines to fill your day? Did you lose interested in social relationships?"

I shrugged. "I guess so. I don't speak Spanish very well yet."

"Travelers talk with people from their own culture to verify their observations, to reassure themselves they know the truth from the civilized world where they enjoy the best of everything. Of course, it's not true. It can never be true, not for anyone. So be careful, because the stress of culture shock can make you sick. Physically sick."

"I don't feel any different. I wasn't very happy in the United States, either."

"Bravo! We'll all drink to that then!"

We leaned back in our chairs, took swigs from the beers, and looked around at the stick houses scattered under tall coconut palms. The southern sky above the western half of the beach still glowed with the rose and melon colors of late sunset. In the light hot breeze, we heard the surf's music mix with the hot rustle of palm fronds overhead, and bird calls, regular like the metallic squawks of a factory's conveyer belt, came from deep within the mangroves to the north. The thick leafy walls of mangroves muffled the sudden splashes of water from small animals, frogs, diving birds, four-eyed fish.

"Ah, it's so beautiful here."

"Amen."

A large insect flew in a zigzag across the table, as if to illustrate the viscosity of the humid, salty air.

"Si, pues. Pero ya no, ya nada no se puede continuar sin fin."

They explained it to me. Filter out the Spanish double negative verb form and reflective irresponsibility that gives objects free will, it translates to "Yes, sure. But now no, now nothing cannot continue itself without end."

"Everything ends, eventually."

Drunk Guatemalan Reporters

The National Museum of Ethnology in Leiden, Netherlands contains a jade plaque known as the Leiden Plate, inscribed with the earliest developed Maya calendar date found. The reverse side contains a Long Count date of 320, and in spite of its provenance, found along the Caribbean Coast among the ruins of a more recent civilization, its style resembles much older artisan styles from Tikál, snuggled deep in the rainforests of Guatemala's northern state called the Petén. The front shows a wealthy Mayan lord who holds his foot on the neck of a captive.

While we talked, we heard a motorboat in the distance on the canal. The roar grew louder, came alongside, and then cut as the boat beached at Hawaii's dock. We heard loud voices, laughter.

Flaco said, "Oh oh, drunks."

"Berta, so sorry about your paradise weekend."

In the dim light of Don Martinez's store, we saw the top section of a big speedboat with three tall white men in their thirties, and a couple of much younger women. Instead of the usual polite and inhibited Guatemalan behavior, one of these men ran around the girls in a pantomime of nimble quick, in either a bikini swimsuit, or his underpants, neither appropriate in conservative Guatemala.

Another helped the second of three girls ashore.

The third man hindered and tried to intercept the ones who helped push and pull the girls up the slope of soft sand.

Looked to me that the buxom blonde got the most attention, in spite of her thick, stiff wild orange haystack of hair. Reminded me of a synthetic plastic Halloween wig to scare children.

These six urban and somewhat overweight Guatemalans stumbled and lumbered across the sand up to the tienda.

They pounded the counter, made impossible demands, and otherwise treated Don Martinez like a servant.

Two of the toady Guatemalan men came over. The one covered in black hair wore a sleeveless T-shirt and underpants. They shook hands, and presented business cards to the teachers.

The business cards claimed they worked as part of the President's press corps, as state journalists. One of the men said, in good English, "I take photographs for the government. Where are you from?"

"United States." Then the teachers explained that they worked in Guatemala City, and oversaw a local Peace Corps project.

The big bear looked at me and said, "What chew name?"

"Brandon."

"What chew name, Juan mor-eh time-eh, pleez?"

I used the Spanish pronunciation. "Brahn-doan."

"Condon? Good. We need condones here tonight." He laughed alone.

Berta whispered to me that he'd made a joke with my name, turned it into condoms.

Then this ape-toad, in a black T-shirt and underpants, scowled at us and said something cross in Spanish about the United States.

The bearded teacher smiled, and retorted like machine gun fire in Spanish. Then Flaco said something that made both teachers laugh.

The hairy guy stood immobile and stared off into the blackness of mangrove swamp beyond our conical pool of sixty watts of light. He looked at the empty beer bottle in his hand, and motioned that he wanted to buy the teachers and me another round of beer.

They refused, which I thought strange.

Several people warned me that to refuse when someone offers to buy you a drink might insult and lead to a serious situation like an invitation to fight. The teachers refused, with steadfast smiles that lacked humor. The big monkey's brow corrugated, and his black eyes squinted into linear masses of tangled spider legs.

He spun around and yelled for Don Martinez, who waited motionless in the store window counter.

As the hairy guy and his friend looked at Don Martinez and tried to order beer for everybody, the teachers signaled "No" behind their backs.

Don Martinez bowed quick and hurried out with a paper pad I'd never seen him use before. He distracted the men with his short list of available food and took their order.

The big guy stood there and swayed, then threw his beer bottle into the bushes.

Flaco said something in Spanish to the guy.

Norm seconded it.

Berta registered her disgust, crossed her arms, and refused to look at the drunk.

That began a low volume, but surly, argument in Spanish. For a moment, it looked like the hairy guy wanted to beat up Norm, but his buddy grabbed him by the arm and dragged him back to their party.

I needed one of the teachers to fill me in.

Norm said, "We asked him politely not to break glass around here, where so many barefoot children play."

"What did he say?"

"He said the same lame brained thing I've heard a million times down here. It gives you an idea of the racism and inhumanity that goes by the name of class in Latin America."

Norm, Flaco, and Berta said in mock, almost in unison, "People without shoes should watch where they walk."

The third fat guy in his undershirt came over to ask what happened. The hairy guy tried to stop him, but with a quart beer bottle in each hand, he couldn't wave his friend away. Then both pushed each other around, yelled and sometimes pointed toward us. At moments, I thought the big hairy guy wanted to beat these skinny teachers into a patch of fruit stained sand, little tufts of hair and tiny wrist watch parts on top.

"Look at them," Norm said, after they lumbered off a ways. Photographers, I bet."

Flaco said, "Probably shot more guns than photos."

Two guys came over to us, and spoke in Spanish, (I asked what they argued about afterwards). "You guys have a problem with us buying you a couple of beers?"

Norm looked up at them, met their motionless glare with his for a few seconds, then said in a calm voice, "I have a problem with people like you, who should know better, who dominate and repress the working classes, especially the Indians."

The fat man said, "What are you, some kind of leftist commie?"

The ape-man said, in a tone of voice that sounded like gargling, "Everywhere in the world, one class dominates the rest. We all got a boss, don't we? Everybody gets pushed around by somebody else. You're from the United States? United States? Ha. The United States keeps its foot on the neck of the Guatemalan Government, so why should you care if we keep our foot on the Indian's neck?"

"Because it's wrong." Berta said.

He scowled down at her.

She smiled, her upturned face confident and almost rapturous in the protection of her gender.

He squeezed the brown glass neck of his full beer bottle. "You know the difference between right and wrong? Wrong is dead. Only the lucky wake up to wonder about right and wrong. People with wrong ideas lose their friends, their jobs, even their families. But some people like you, never learn, and those kinds of people..." He threw his bottle like a hand grenade. It spewed beer and flew into the darkness over the almond bushes to thud onto the sand. "... disappear."

No one said anything. The two men sneered at us, made motions as if to wipe and shake sand off their hands, and went back to their party.

I noticed one word used often, aplastar, and asked the teachers what it meant.

"Flatten, smash, put down." Both teachers made a movement with their leg as if to crush out cigarette butt.

"Like that thug said," the woman said. "everybody feels a foot on their neck. They both work for the government, so they're a little more educated. They say the government dominates the Indians, like the United States dominates Guatemala."

"Does the United States dominate Guatemala?"

"Don't you think it odd that the Quetzal equals one dollar, exactly, all the time?"

"A young man at the Ermita del Carmen talked about that. He said the United States wouldn't let Guatemala's elected president become president."

"Which election?" The teachers laughed.

Norm said, "Here's a little clue. A man came up to me last week, someone involved in a Catholic relief organization, and wanted to know if he could send documents back to his Catholic superiors in the United States. He wanted to mix his Catholic church mail into the mail I send back to the Peace Corps offices in Washington."

"Why was that?"

"He felt that the Guatemalan government looked through all his mail, so he didn't feel free to express his concerns about what goes on here."

"What did you tell him?"

"I told him to forget it. The Peace Corps communications get searched through, too. But not for the reasons he thinks."

"Yeah, the Catholic relief worker thinks the Guatemalan government wants to control information that heads out of Guatemala. The Peace Corps, which should operate through diplomatic channels beyond the reach of the governments, must let the Guatemalan government search Peace Corps mail. Know why?"

"Because the United States wants to help the Guatemalan government find the people responsible for all the disappearances?"

"No. Because they ARE the people responsible for the disappearances."

"Who? Which?" I asked.

The three teachers looked at me and waited. I knew they waited for me to figure it out, but I didn't have a clue.

Norm said, "In what year were you born?"

"Nineteen fifty three."

"The next year, in nineteen fifty four, the US Government overthrew Guatemala's president, Jácobo Arbenz Guzmán."

"You believe that?"

"Oh yes. It's well known, outside the U.S."

"How can you believe that? How is it possible that the U.S. can throw out another country's president without anybody noticing?"

"Like they did the year before. The CIA starts a campaign to brand the president as a Communist, as they did to the Iranian president the year you were born, and no one complains."

"Were they communists?"

"Not really. They weren't anti communists either. That's the beauty of a truly democratic society, tolerance for different opinions. Look, if the United States truly spreads Democracy, they would let other nations elect Socialists, Communists, Mormons, Anarchists, or Feminists, whatever. Guatemala elected President Arbenz Guzmán in a free, democratic election. He had the mandate of the citizens, but that didn't stop the U.S. from overthrowing the government of another sovereign nation. You know why?"

I shrugged.

Flaco said, "Because a tiny country like Guatemala bought back some unused banana lands that belonged to an American corporation."

"So you think big business controls the U.S. government?"

"Big business is the U.S. government, especially when the head of that corporation is the US Secretary of State's brother."

"Who?"

"The Dulles brothers."

"Even if that were true as a coincidence, you think it's so easy to remove the President of another country?"

"Yes. Even now. The U.S. manipulated last year's presidential election here in Guatemala. In 1975, Efrain Rios Montt, a Pentecostal Protestant, won the popular election but never took office."

"Why not?"

Berta said, "Let's go back to Arbenz. The poor people of Guatemala needed more land to homestead. Large landholders, even the President's family, got their land cut up and parceled out. United Fruit Company, a giant corporation, owned thousands of square miles of Guatemalan lands, even though they produced no bananas. When the Guatemalan government took back some of that unused United Fruit Company land, they repaid the company at the tax assessed value. Fair enough, right?"

"That doesn't explain how a company could force the U.S. government to topple Presidents."

"Because then CIA director Allen Dulles once sat on United Fruit's board of directors, and his brother still did. The company probably demanded a US Intervention to protect its interests. American businessmen, or the American government, they both control each other, so they felt President Arbenz threatened American business interests and therefore, National security."

"Couldn't be that easy. Why didn't any Americans do anything to stop it?"

"They hired people to manipulate public opinion. In the McCarthy era, if you seemed tolerant of communist ideas, you could be arrested, tried, and convicted of Un-American activities. They exaggerated what was going on in a way that would paint Guatemala's president as a communist."

Flaco said, "Remember the Domino theory? Before Vietnam, the government wanted people everywhere to believe that communist countries infect their neighbors. Thus if Guatemala falls to the communists, it would drag down Belize, Honduras, El Salvador, and even Mexico. Then we have Commies on our own doorstep, as they put it."

"You're joking."

"I wish he was."

Norm spoke up. "You think it might be a joke because maybe you know a little about Guatemala. You think, Cute little country. Nothing to fear. Yet the U.S. government spent over seven million dollars to train anti-Arbenz dissidents in Honduras to help in the overthrow. Even so, the invasion didn't go well, until the U.S. Air Force came and dropped some bombs on some boats. The whole thing was a mess. The Guatemalans tried to buy used weapons and arms from Europe, so the US bombed a boat in San Jose, and killed some Guatemalan troops as well."

Berta continued "After the invasion and overthrow, the new militarized government of Guatemala confronted a population that distrusted it. Everyone feared a long civil war, so they outlawed unions and erased the few gains toward democratic progress and social justice of the previous administration. And that's where we are today."

Nearby on the sand, the party people shouted and laughed. As the sky darkened, they demanded that Don Martinez keep his store open and run the generator for the one light bulb.

"What do you mean, where we are now?"

Berta nodded toward the revelers. "They think they can control things with terror and death squads, professional torture techniques learned from U.S. military schools like West Point, or from U.S. military advisors, and now we have thousands arrested or killed, disappeared, over the last twenty years."

They danced with each other in the pool of sixty watt light under the bulb as if a mirror ball over disco dance floor. They carried their drinks in hand, gave each other body rubs, and stole kisses as the music repeated from their two eight track cassette tapes, one of Led Zeppelin, and the other a mix of current Bubble Gum popular music, like "I Believe In Miracles" by Hot Chocolate with the lyric 'Where you from? You sexy thang.'

They stopped their group grope dance to sprawl, legs open, on the plastic chairs to pant out of breath. Two of the men looked over at us with eyebrows scowled into a V shape.

Reminded me of gun sights.

I still didn't get it. "How could the United States get rid of another country's president?"

"Very easy. The CIA did it first the year before, when they toppled the president of Iran. CIA operatives paid people for some street theater to make it look like a popular communist revolt in the streets, then with a little U.S. military support, the president runs away. All this in spite of Time Magazine, which named Iran's Premier Mosaddeq their Man of The Year for nationalizing oil away from the British."

"Didn't anyone notice what happened?"

"Maybe they did. So what? Who cares? Even within the country, useless, because the CIA knows how to manipulate local newspapers. It always looks like a problem with Communist rebels. Then the United States rides to the rescue."

I couldn't believe that no one would complain, no one would notice. "What about evidence? Photos? Eye witness accounts?"

"Newspapers circulate photos of murdered Guatemalans and even label those photos to depict dead Communist rebels, or civilians killed by these Rebels, or say that Communist rebels killed Guatemalans. Newspapers identified Communist insurgents killed by the Guatemalan Army even before Communist insurgents existed in Guatemala. The photos might show people the CIA murdered, or maybe those the Guatemalan Army tortured into false confessions for more names of innocent people to disappear."

"If this is true, why doesn't Guatemala press charges against the United States?"

"For what? Now they really do have Communist rebels and a civil war. It kills thousands of people a year. US policy created a permanent guerrilla movement, really quite a bit like the American Revolution against the English."

"Against who?"

Berta ignored me. "Unfortunately, it's often in the United State's interests to prevent democracy. Democracy has the potential to change government with each election. Not good for business. Easier to manage long term dictatorships."

"You want me to believe that the United States can march in and take out another country's elected government? Why doesn't everyone know about it?"

Berta stood up and said, "Excuse me, but I want to watch the sunset on the beach, then I will retire to my little stick house and read. You men can stay here and continue to solve the world's problems."

She reached into her purse and pulled out a business card. She bent down with a pen to write something on it, then handed it to me. "When you leave here, all roads lead to Guatemala City to go anywhere else. Here's our name and number. Call us, and let us know how things turn out. You look intelligent, so I tell you, don't waste your time here. Stay away from the local girls, or the boys will kill you. A month or two, don't stay too long. You'll get sick."

"I'll get sick?"

"Contamination. You'll ruin your kidneys, or liver."

I looked at the other two men. "Contaminated?"

They nodded gravely. "Most all of the fertilizers, herbicides, and pesticides used on this side of the mountains drain down to this mangrove canal along the coast. And they use well water, shallow wells."

Berta continued, "Don't stay here too long. Please, call us, promise me, we'd love to talk to you again, find out how it all turned out, when you go back to civilization. Nice meeting you."

As she walked away, the music stopped, and the drunken revelers nearby paused mid step in their stagger dance. The women coughed their laughter to a halt, and the men's laser eyes aimed at Berta.

As Berta walked across the sand, the wide woven scarf around her hips exaggerated the serpentine hip motion of soft steps through the loose sand.

The teachers took a swig of beer and clunked the bottles on the table to break the spell.

I grew up in the country, and can lay in the tall grass to watch the clouds in their slow surge and pull across the sky, as if suspended in a gelatinous mass. I recognized the red winged blackbird's trill, even in Guatemala. I remember my seven year old self, that first Spring in the Michigan countryside. I put on rubber boots and learned to cut me a long stick to hike through the fields, woods, and swamps in the foggy wet mornings. I saw the ice cold waters teem with thousands of hatched crayfish, each the size of a pill bug. I grew up alone in nature, and expect insects to crawl across my skin. They do it for a living. I got used to it, and didn't mind much if one fed off me every once in a while.

Some people freak out. When a bug lands on them, they want to spray the adjacent hundred hectares with poison.

City kids don't walk down wooded paths in their childhood to find mountainous piles of glittery white powders from fifty gallon drums strewn about the undergrowth.

We kids ran through the stuff, and didn't think about it until years later, when memories of strange ice formations around springs linked to high incidence of leukemia among our friends, a statistic that the establishment refuses to measure, because we Anglos tend to move out of our neighborhoods.

It made more sense, when people I trusted told me, with great mirth, that the Mafia controlled Chicago's hazardous waste removal contracts, and witnesses saw hazardous waste removal trucks stop at midnight, in the middle of the street in the inner cities, to pour the stuff into the drainage systems that lead to the rivers and waters of the Mississippi system down to the Gulf of Mexico.

Imagine the pollution that drains into this Pacific coast mangrove forest from the industrialized agriculture and the lack of sewer systems in the Guatemalan highlands.

I didn't know what to think. Maybe these two American academics worked as CIA operatives, or Communists, and wanted to test me. Or they wanted to put me up to something, give them information about what happens in Hawaii after they leave. Maybe they need a scapegoat. Guatemalan President's photographer catches young man from USA in net of drugs and arms, corrupted Peace Corps, in a remote seaside brothel. That kind of news item might make a mother leave her child to rot in a Latin American prison.

I changed the subject. "You guys know what happens with all those the fan palm fronds on the beach."

"They tie them into bundles and transport them by canoe and truck to a town in the mountains. There they make baskets and those straw cowboy hats you see rural people wear throughout Latin America."

"Sombreros cost only a dollar, after all that work."

"Imagine how little the frond cost, or how little each individual worker in Hawaii earns for his part."

The sunset wind died down, and the mosquitoes came out to buzz our ears and bite our legs under the table. We passed around a can of insect repellant.

"What do you know about this war with Belice?"

"Guatemala considers Belice a lost territory, a county or a state, that the British stole from them, because the British never built a road to connect with Guatemala."

"That's true. Guatemala's leaders want people to avoid the domestic situation. They use this war for a smokescreen to hide what really goes on inside Guatemala. Belice, a beautiful country that speaks English and has a tiny upper class Tourist industry for Scuba divers, would give Guatemala it's own little Jamaica to attract American tourists."

Flaco says "You can think of Guatemala and Belice like retarded sisters, with Britain and the USA as two bullies that use them for sex."

"Not this again," Norm groaned.

"This again. Listen, bullies let their girls squabble for the fun of it, for the show. Nothing changes their relationships, afterwards everything's about the same. Actually a little mud wrestling between them, a tiny civilized war, and both Britain and the United States sell more arms to both Belice and Guatemala. For men in power, they like it when men get killed off, makes more women available. From an international perspective, both nations become even more indebted to international banks and other governments, and the sale of arms helps each super power's economy, while the arms dealers and other middlemen get rich."

Norm laughed, rubbed his face with one open palm. "As citizens of a superpower, what's not to love about a little war? We always come out ahead, and there's hundreds of them on any given day, all around the world."

Nearby, the party slowed down. The Bear began a psychological torture of poor old Don Martinez, who cowed and bowed in uncharacteristic humiliated servitude. The noble man I'd met as the proud founder of Hawaii winced each time his hairy tormenter barked at him to get more beer, snacks, move tables and chairs around. Then they ordered Don Martinez to put them back. Don Martinez wrung his hands and begged his captor for permission to go and help his wife prepare their food, to bring the ordered round of beer, to escape.

Maybe the Bear's female companion rejected him, she seemed embarrassed. She stood in a model's slouch against the wall of the store, refused to get pulled into the mass grope dance, and watched the Bear take it out on Don Martinez. When the Bear sprawled into a chair and seemed to sop into a stupor, Don Martinez escaped behind the store window and into the inner sanctum of the kitchen.

His party girl, dressed in a black two piece bikini under a man's unbuttoned white shirt with some black garment tied around as a belt, slinked over to our table.

Her hair and suit still dripped with water from when her companions threw her into the canal a half hour ago. Without a word, she took Berta's wooden chair next to me and sat down heavily

The chair started to fall over. The chairs tended to sink into the sand; we each fought a constant battle to keep them level.

We caught her before she breaded herself like a Kentucky chicken with Hawaii's beach sand.

"Thank you," she said in good English. She held out her hand to me. "My name is Angela."

"My name is Brandon, and this is Flaco and Norm."

She listened to our conversation for a few minutes, then interrupted to question me with non-sequiters about how I arrived and from where. Her black hair, cut short a little below her ears, swung forward like an old Roman gladiator's helmet that dripped with dew. Her English, as bad as my Spanish, amused us to both to discover how often we misunderstood.

She wanted to know why someone from "Uoo sah", the illiterate pronunciation of USA, came to this remote edge of Guatemala.

The American teachers chattered in Spanish with each other. Our table ignored the bawdy loud jokes that the toad men in underpants yelled out for all, as Don Martinez piled supplies onto the store's windowsill for them to carry to the speedboat moored in the mangrove canal.

The speedboat started, and then it sped off.

Alarmed that they left this girl behind, I asked her where they went.

She said, "Don't worry. They come back after they put things in the house where we sleep tonight." She pointed over to the nearby table, where two of the men sat cozy with the other two women.

"The house belongs to his uncle. Rancho Grande."

Quiet reigned for an hour or so, until the boat returned.

When they heard the motor approach, the two men in underpants stood up nervously, their hands on shoulder holsters I failed to notice before. They peered around foliage as if in a spy movie, to identify the boat as it landed and make sure things looked OK.

Those two drunks stood at the edge of the only electric light source in all Hawaii, and acted like they thought no one would see them.

The boatmen cut the motor and it glided up to the dock.

Silence.

The light dimmed and sputtered as the generator behind the store coughed and changed speed. Dirty gas.

One of the hidden men called out. "What the hell took you so long?"

"What the hell makes you two so stupid you pull a gun on me? Put 'em away. If I wanted to 'chingarles', you'd both be dead by now."

Angela wanted to know what kind of parties they throw in Michigan.

I tried to describe those high school or factory rat parties where a house full of strangers use and abuse all available drugs and listen to rock and roll so loud you can't hear, so people yell into each other's ear, and still not understand.

She squealed and said it sounded like great fun, until I pointed out that people didn't dance much in the United States.

"I can't believe you, people don't dance." she said, her eyes black as wet coal, steady as tugboats. "All people love to dance. It's something in the blood. Like making love. You, like a man, you always want to make love, don't you? So it is with women, we want to dance, to laugh, to make love."

"Not the Christian Reformed. They teach their daughters to turn the lights off, open their legs, and cross their arms. To enjoy sex means to sin, and they must get to Heaven. I don't see why it matters, they also believe that everyone's already selected and written in a big list of names, so you can't join Jesus with good works, even if they canonize you, unless your name appear on that list."

"You pull my hair? In Latin America, we dance. You see Cubans dance? Like sex, the way they move."

"I've seen Mexican's dance." I thought about a bar in Chihuahua, one of the few that allowed women to enter, at least one class of professional women, the sex workers. Those Mexicans didn't dance sensual. I saw Mexican Indians dressed like Cowboys, and they danced stiff and awkward, often pot bellied men with toady no-necked women held in a headlock. But I couldn't say that.

"You see Salsa dancers? Cubans? Sexy, no?"

"Angela, where I grew up, nobody's Catholic. The people came from Holland, Christian Reformers, Methodists, Calvinists, all Protestants."

"Protestantes?"

"Yes. Almost everyone. Europeans first came to America to escape the Catholic Church. Protestants don't like public affection. No sex. No hugs, no kissing, not even on the cheek."

"We always kiss on the cheeks, even with people you don't know so well. And with people you know, well, you can hug and kiss right there, where ever you are."

"I saw Mexican men hug, slap each other's backs, and caress each other's shoulders. But not in the United States. In Mexico and sometimes in Guatemala."

"How do people salute each other then?" She often bent forward when she asked these questions, as if to tempt me with her cleavage, an inspiration, a soft promise.

"They shake hands."

"They never dance? Don't Americans like sex? Sex is a dance."

"We dance rock and roll, not really like Latin dance. If you have a wedding or something, you have to request a dance permit from the government."

She thought I put her on, that I joked with her, "You pull my hair," she thought I pulled her leg, as we say in English.

I offered to buy her a beer, but she refused and pointed her chin toward the other members of her party. "They buy my beer, when I want one."

"Are they friends of yours?"

"Not really. I hate them. I want to be your friend." She touched my thigh in secret, then withdrew her hand.

"What are you doing all the way out here with them?"

"They pay me to come with them. I don't like them."

Then I understood why her face sagged at rest after each animated flirtation. A professional woman. She wanted to swap clients. She wished to abandon her current clients, escape them, and hang out with me, as a young American male, who might represent a lot of easy money to her, if she could hook me. Hooker. "Why do you go with them if you don't like them?"

She ran her finger up and down my backbone, once, then put her hand on her lap.

She said something like "I need more money than most people in Guatemala. I want to live in Miami. No stores in Guatemala City carry fashion from Europe. I go to Miami once, with clients. They bring me to stores, wonderful, buy things to me. I feel wonderful, like bird of paradise, beautiful and happy. I laugh so much there. You know Miami?"

"No. New Orleans."

I tried to ignore that a woman in a wet black bikini sat on a wooden chair that sunk slow and tipsy into the sand. She untied the thin black sweater from around her waist to drape across her shoulders and shield her against the chill and mosquitoes.

She pouted at me, pointed with her lips, and said "You don't like me, do you?"

Her companions in their underclothes, male and female, laughed and began to dance to American static filled Credence Clearwater Revival pop music played through a tiny AM radio.

"I like you better than them."

She smiled, put her hand on my thigh for a moment. As we talked and drank, I never ran out of beer. Without my notice, the teachers bought me a beer, then another.

Then the Guatemalans, perhaps with hopes of an enjoyable spectacle a little later, came over to say hello and buy our table a round of beer, which Don Martinez brought over without a smile.

The teachers smiled and toasted our benefactors with a gracefulness that did not arouse my suspicions until much later.

The Warning

The Classic Central Veracruz sculpture and art fixates upon the ball game, the ball courts, and associated paraphernalia. At El Tajín, Late Classic period (600 - 900 AD) artisans made elaborate reliefs on the walls of the ball courts that give us the details on how the players used their equipment. These sculptures of players wore stone yokes, called Yugos, heavy belts to protect their hips from the impacts of the hard rubber ball as they jostled it up and down the court. The yugos portray the marine toad, replete with thick poison sacks behind its eyes, and with a human head in its mouth.

Everybody stuck to their own conversations for a while, but as soon as she left to find the outhouse, one of the teachers moved into her chair to whisper to me. In a conspiratorial tone, in English, with a low, theatrical, ominous voice and a decoy smile, he said "Do you know what's going on?"

"No." I said.

"She likes you. She wants to be with you." He said, as he pulled me to my feet, clapped me on the back and walked me off into the darkness away from the group of drunks that danced to a crazy song on the radio. The cassette player played the spastic voice that sang the lyric "I Believe in Miracles, Where You From? You Sexy Thang" for the fifteenth time.

"Yes, it appears that she likes you." Norm said, a beer in one hand, a cigarette in the other. The sad little electric light flickered as the generator chugged and coughed on a sip of dirty diesel oil. "And that's your bad luck."

"What do you mean?"

The teacher put his arm around my shoulders and we walked behind a hut. "You're a good looking, healthy young man. You want to stay that way, to bed. Don't say goodbye, goodnight, see you later or anything. Leave, and don't think about her, or that she might follow you to your hut. She might. We will cover for you, and say you don't feel well, that you can't handle your liquor, and everyone will understand."

"Why? What's the problem?"

"These people are gangsters. Government gangsters. Could kill both you and the girl in a second. You disappear, like it never happened, like you never existed. No one will find you, no one will know, no one will dare say a word and you will disappear like cigarette smoke. Look at them."

The three men and two women under the little electric light danced in a huddled mass, stumbled over each other's feet, laughed and drank beer or poured it into each other's mouths, all engaged in a mock hump orgy of drunken togetherness.

"These people, their society, represent power in Guatemala. Probably have machine guns in the boat. They showed us their business cards right away. They do publicity for the government. They are connected to the right families, the rich and powerful, or maybe drug smugglers, the same thing. You might get the girl, not much of a prize for the risk, or you might get killed. Is she worth it, a one night stand, which you will have to pay for one way or another, perhaps with your life? Either way, it's fun and games for them. They live for chaos and violence. You have no choice. Either way, you must disappear. You disappear on purpose to live another day, or they help you disappear forever."

For a millisecond, I didn't believe him. "You're kidding."

"You think they like you? Did they say something that gave you the idea this is the start of a beautiful friendship?"

I felt the finger of an infected whore run up and down my vertebrae.

A Predatory Universe, as Kat said. The crushed and the crusher, the recipe for disaster almost complete. Jame's Bond's recipe for a Martini, "shaken, not stirred" means a little afraid but not emotionally touched. Start with liberal amounts of alcohol, add a dose of jealousy and the quiet rage of rejection, and the agitation of a depressed, bored prostitute that hates herself and so cannot care about others.

I stood in the middle, as a handy symbol of America's domination and tacit presumption of superiority. Each American abroad faces an alternative reality that clashes with the familiar symbols of status among consumers, and in self defense, we become the ugly tourist who deprecates other cultures as inferior, dirty, backward, and corrupt. That First World tourist attitude a low self esteem until it festers into a passionate hatred and a desire to get home as fast as possible.

My world could explode at the end of alcohol fueled short fuses, sparked by the promise of tiny meaningless acts of violence, where intimidations culminate in blows or a small splatter of gunfire, the echoes swallowed and muffled like hyacinth choked wave eddies in the canal's mangrove currents. My body sinks into inky nothingness below a trail of bubbles. Villagers cower in their huts of sticks, and pray the angels of death pass them by. The instant end of a twenty two year old American lad's short life, a boy who escaped the Viet Nam War with two years of college, with a total life experience to add up to maybe thirty beer hangovers in six years in which he broke at least three hearts and suffered five or six rejections of his caddish inability to commit to marriage. He could still remember almost every single time he made love to a woman, each of their faces and bodies, with the beginnings of a little amnesia about their complete names.

Poof. Smoke and mirrors.

The citizens of Hawaii, if they dared to would only say anything, would shrug and say "He left."

Yeah, left the planet, left the known universe.

As disappeared as any Guatemalan neighbor who feuds with a well connected neighbor, and never hears about the visit their enemy made to the authorities, to ensure a little lie left in the right ear would eliminated that entire family's residence on earth. Dead leftists make the best leftists.

I remembered the words of Burly Schroeder, neighbor, farmer, insurance salesman and owner of the most beautiful real estate in the area. Great expanses of tall sand dune hills covered with hay fields and oak forests punctuated with sugar maples. Hidden out of sight from the road, a small lake filled one forested valley. From the sandy beaches we heard loons call and watched Fall's colorful majesty reflect off the water's unruffled mirror to herald the coming Winter's skating rink of smooth ice. When I told Burley my plans to travel to Guatemala, he looked at me and said, "God be with you. I hope you find what you're looking for."

I could wait a while longer for my union with the Great Beyond. This disappearance idea would come too soon no matter when, no need to rush things.

With too many beers in my gut, I slunk off through the village, stayed within the straight avenues of palm tree shadow cast by the store's little yellow light bulb. I didn't know for sure where she might go to pee, and I feared I might bump into her in the semidarkness. If we did by chance meet, I visualized various ways to usher her away to the noisy seashore for a quickie.

What if she likes to make a lot of noise?

I zigzagged through the huts and across the wide beach to the steep hard black sand where the Pacific waves roared ashore, then ran down the beach bent over to stay out of sight as I circled around to my shack.

Three shacks away and out of sight, I could almost see where Don Martinez's generator lit up his party patio, and almost pinpoint from where the sounds of drunken laughter bubbled and echoed. Too close. Once inside my shack, I took care to pull shut, without a sound, my gate-like door, open wood slats tied together with rusted wire. I crawled onto my bedroll in the darkness and fumbled about for my sleeping bag's zipper, while their laughter and party squeals grew louder.

I thought about the teachers, how they cared enough about me to give me warning. On the other side of the equation, if anything happened to me, it must also happen to them, as potential witnesses and fellow despised Americans. They protected me out of self defense. They rescued all of us, and maintained order from a near freefall into the irrational, reptilian, and homicidal chaos of mass murder.

That girl. All alone now, to face those she humiliated. If she tried to find me that night, she didn't succeed.

I knew that if she found me, this ache for her would carry us away, down the beach a ways, where our lips and bodies could meet like waves on the wet black sand, to crash in an explosion of spume and spray.

They might find us there exhausted, the funnels of their flashlight beams outlined by the humidity of our breath, our bodies clasped together wet, covered with black sand, seaweed, and blood as our bullet riddled bodies slip beneath the waves.

Sunrise Moonset Jogs

The Mayans depict their rain gods, called Chacs, as anthropomorphic creatures with protruding noses, fangs, and large round eyes. These friendly gods aligned themselves with the common farmers and workers to pour their favor down in the form of rain, fallen from the gourds they carried. When these Chacs flung their black obsidian stone axes, carved into intricate multi-blade shapes with curly-q decorations, their lightning scattered fire through the heavens, and thunder broke the sky gourds open to spill rain. Mayans believe that frogs accompany these Gods, and that the songs of frogs herald rainy weather.

The frogs croaked, a hard rain fell. Thunder and lightning, everyone ran to their shelters. I heard Don Martinez's stop the gasoline generator, light went out, and the drunken laughter faded into the distance. I half dreamt, fantasized, asleep and then awake. I heard the boat motor roar to life, then speed off down the canal where the mangroves muffled it like a gloved hand.

A gang of frogs called together in chorus from a lagoon not far away.

After the rain, a silence swept over Hawaii's stick houses. It covered us all, a thick blanket, dark and humid, impassive. The palm tops sighed, insects whirred close by my ears, and the deep relaxed silence of nature allowed the fizzy music of life to fill my ears.

I snuggled in my down sleeping bag, and fell asleep.

Something woke me up.

Again, the silhouette of a man stood within the slat gate door to my hut.

"Who are you?" I said in Spanish. "What do you want?"

The roar of silence.

He didn't move. I got out of bed sleepily, felt drunk and dreamy, and approached the doorway where he stood. My heart pumped and I felt flushed with thick ears and a stuffy nose. I tried to control the way I breathed, to not make noise.

Again I stared at the silhouette of my own jacket, which hung unneeded there on a hanger since my arrival.

Something made a noise behind me. I turned, saw nothing. Then I heard two footfalls in the small drift of leaves inside my hut. Adrenaline kicked in and I felt cold blood run wet up my legs. My hairs stood on end upon my goose bumped flesh.

I saw the toad, took two steps across the room and picked him up with my fingers below the fat poison sacks on each side of his bullnecked head. I held him out away from my body so he could pee all he wanted without a drop on me, carried him to the door, and threw him out of my hut.

This time, he felt relaxed in my hand, and I regarded him as an old friend.

That next morning, and on five or so nights after each full moon, the moonset so lightened the sky that I awoke with the chill of the wee small hours on clammy skin, and thought the sun would rise in a few minutes.

Once I jumped into my shorts to jog across the palm fronds laid out days ago, now bleached by the sun to an almost white tan. I ran along the sandy shore, directly east into the faint red glow of sunrise where the beach met the sea.

Behind me, the full moon set where the beach met the sea. January sixteenth, nineteen seventy six.

I felt relieved and alive. I survived last night. Now I owned the beach, the sea, the sky, the sun, the moon, and three tiny volcanoes glimpsed on the horizon above the mangrove forest.

What a shame. After a quarter of a century of life in Michigan, I now discovered the incredible beauty and majesty of light and magic that occurred in the heavens every 28 days, a moonset sunrise. Too many clouds in Michigan to notice the obvious juxtaposition.

On each full moon, the earth sits between the sun and moon. The moon orbits the earth like a disco mirror ball, to reflect the sun, and so always points at the sun's position on the daylight side of the planet, with a full moon that faces the sun on the other side of the earth, or a crescent smile to a sun on the horizon. The new moon cruises the daytime skies with the sun, to cross its face for a solar eclipse, and a full moon darkens when the earth's shadow causes a lunar eclipse.

I realized how the simple observation of the north south migration of these moonrise sunsets and moonset sunrises would lead to the astronomical measures of equinoxes and solstices, the ratio of length of day to night in temperate latitudes, and the rain to dry seasons in the tropics, where the sun stayed more or less overhead through all twelve months. The sunset/sunrise and moonset/moonrise moved north in Fall, and south each Spring.

To the west behind me, the moon set into the salt spray that obscured the distant junction of land and sea. It turned gold against a red purple horizon, and the colors reflected on the ocean and wet shore, they shattered into ripples as each wave slipped back, an inky mercury, a watery mirror of the sky that slid down the black sand's incline.

The sun rose up over the junction of land and sea, and painted a cold yellow on each wave's bluish plume of spray, swept back by the offshore breeze, like the manes of white horses in full gallop.

I ran on exhilarated, across the trailheads which man and animal wore through the scant vegetation, a low carpet of succulents and beach plants. Sometimes the paths led into little forests that sheltered houses of sticks where people cooked breakfast over tiny fires.

My toes gripped the hard packed wet sand, my tracks animal, a sign without the heel of my foot. My eyes and body felt a keenness of sensation, healthy and alert, and felt the earth as a companion.

I survived last night's whores and murderous bastards from civilization to see this day.

My eyes combed the washed up tangle of jettisoned flotsam. Acrobatic swallows swooped close about me, as we cruised the thin strip of beach between vegetation and froth topped waves, the surges of water that curled, crashed, and ran in a flood up the steep black slope, then slipped back into the sea with a fizzy sound.

A strange shape caught my eye.

CHAPTER 9: The Oldest Totem
Proto pompous

Archeologists think a proto-Mayan culture known as Chicanel, from the Late Formative (300 BC - AD 100) period, created pottery dishes with wide doubled-over grooved rims, bowls with composite silhouette, and "ice bucket" vessels. In spite of the ubiquitous appearance of "Venus" figurines (depictions of female torsos with exaggerated hips found in excavations of many human cultures around the world), Chicanel ceramic figurines of either sex remain unknown. To some, this lack of evidence suggests that instead of stone or fired clay, they sculpted in wood, the dominant substance of their culture, which would not survive very long in moist and tropical environments.

Something like a handle, a thick lever, a shaped white piece of driftwood caught my eye. About seven inches long, its resemblance to man's primal digit, the capital I, the root of all evil, the lone shoot, the spike of life, the nocturnal nail and fountain pen of my wet dreams, the organ of insertion that serves my genome's prime directive of propagation, the proud and selfless declaration of my fulsome maleness, and the singular reason for all that useless truck men put up with from girls, put my jog into a rapid backpedal.

I picked it up.

Carved from a piece of light pithy wood, white with a tinge of yellow, it filled my hand like the real thing, and I claim some familiarity. I felt fascinated, but looked around to ensure my privacy.

Maybe a practical joker, like us Michigan kids who threw tethered guns or axes along the road on a steep hill to tempt cars to stop. Then as the car backed up, we'd reel in the lure and disappear into the underbrush, to watch our victim search in vain.

I didn't see anyone. I turned it over in my hands.

No knife marks. It looked and felt like a realistic portrayal of a very aroused tumescent member in my hand. A real woody. I only knew my own, a little larger than this sculpture, which reassured me. I speculated that a man or boy sculpted it, though I didn't see why a man would, nor how I knew. I doubt that a woman made it because throughout history, women didn't sculpt much, don't know why.

Maybe men love to touch like women love to feel.

The artist took great care, the subtle curves and contours of the corona too perfect, from a live model, or a live part of the artist. In my hand, I could feel how the sculptor hinted at the three columns of spongy tissue that hardens a man's procreative injector with hot blood in those almost painful moments of full turgidity.

I stood up full, my back to the ocean breeze, and admired it in the light of a new day. The shadows around me filled with blue from the luminescent sky. Three pelicans flew in a formation that followed the parallel crests of wave break.

A dildo? Did Catholic women use wooden dildos? The pithy wood would make it hard to lubricate. Most probable, a talented and excitable artistic boy with more than time on his hands on this vacant stretch of beach.

Maybe it washed ashore, an offering, a ritual object. Maybe this small relic functioned as part of an ancient Mayan fertility rite, set to sea with other gifts in a miniature dugout canoe. Would someone carve this with such care and realism to leave it in a pile of driftwood on the beach?

As an icon, the phallus may predate the most ancient of clay Venus figurines, those Buddha-like female torsos on wide hips and thighs with bloated mammary glands over pregnant stomachs, which represent humanity's oldest sculptures.

Too bad wood does not fossilized easily. We lost tons of prehistoric art done in wood.

I could see the volcano on the horizon. A long cloud trailed from the summit. Perhaps the Maya thought of these streamers of vapor as the earth's joy juice to fertilize the sky, a point blank smoking gun wielded by tectonic movements, the cinematic long drag on a cigarette after the commission of acts both violent and creative.

Many mornings, the phallic towers of volcanic plumes tickled the underbellies of pubic clouds that rise from where the moist rain forests pant steam. The clouds cling and blow like wet skirts around the flanks of these sierras, exhausted vampiric hookers grateful for the dawn though its spells their death. A portal between the worlds of Earth and Sky, a seed that sprouts flowers of tremendous cumulous clouds. They build up slow in hours of humid foreplay, and spread out to paint the zenith with a cottony blanket of row upon row of soft, round mammary swirls. The imaginative and sensitive artist and shaman classes, in a culture committed to Magic Thinking, might convince the authoritative and legislative classes of the necessity of passionate sculptures, human sacrifices, and prolonged orgies to placate a huge swollen volcanic mountain that threatens to destroy their world with the typical male anger of frustrated sexual tension.

Throw it a couple dozen virgins.

I held in my hand a ubiquitous, cross cultural, cross millennia joke about the male gender's one track mind. The longer I thought about who might carve this, and why, I convinced myself that a bright young Guatemalan boy about sixteen years old sculpted it in a powerful rush of hormones. His sexual confusion, a new attraction to women and the homosexuality of his auto-eroticism forced him to literally come to grips with his own prime mover. So he wrestles with an aspect of his life he didn't understand, indulges himself in it, and creates this objectification of self love, carved and sanded smooth to perfection. An over excitable young male artist's own member would model with pleasure, erect and immobile as a rock, to pose for those long moments of self examination for the hour or so it took to carve.

I didn't dwell overlong on how he celebrated his masterwork's completion.

I thought long about how to get it home with me, but didn't relish the idea of a confrontation about it at a border crossing. After all, customs might consider it an art object, or the morality police might consider it something worse, and I might involuntarily join the ranks of a criminal element that languished in prison.

I threw it back upon the pile of driftwood.

Days later too late, I thought to mail it home, with the hope that a U.S. Customs Agent examination of international packages would consider it folk art and pass it on.

Village Games

One interpretation of a carved bass-relief sequence in the North Temple at Chichen Itza describes a ritual passage of an initiate. A superior being awakens to guide him on a journey to speak to jaguars and control a lance (mastery of 'will power'), then with his left hand over his solar plexus and his right on his penis, he becomes 'tuned to the vibration' of one of these meter-long stylized stone phallus, as the Tree of Life emerges from him. Farther along the path, he holds a dismembered penis in one hand and his nose with the other, and vomits 'negativity' from his headdress onto a disembodied head (peyote ingestion and indigestion?), and continues on the path to join a feathered serpent-god in the clouds, and become reborn through the jaws of a serpent. Along this path, the head symbol deteriorates 'along with his ego,' and the figure of an eagle replaces it.

While crazy theories often come from the overworked brain of imaginative "scientists," they also speak to the ubiquity of ideas such as these penis cults, still extant in India as a recognized religion. One should hope that 'universal archetypes' like human instincts to fear snakes and spiders, floods and heights, also tend to propel us from the male-dominated tribal hatreds, penile rapaciousness, homicidal jealousy and acquisitive war, towards a rebirth into 'superior beings', leaders that accept others and respect each person's right to free exploration of ideas and cultural lifestyle, which in sum promotes human progress in peace, art, and love.

The next weekend an inter-village Fiesta held in a settlement called Madre Viejo (Old Mother), located to the west up the canal, would unite Hawaii with other invisible settlements in a series of track and field events and a big dance.

All that week the village girls, whose caramel colored skin contrasted with their red shorts and white, sleeveless, numbered T-shirts, practiced basketball on the cement court in the middle of Hawaii, alongside the Television hut. Everyday a couple hours before sunset, two slender graceful girls swept away the wind blown sand so the teams' worn sneakers wouldn't slip.

One day they told me a long, sad tale about how the bus took off with their basketball inside. The next day, I noticed they practiced with a soccer ball's black and white polygons.

I planned to go to the fiesta with them, and afterwards continue on westward to leave Hawaii, to backpack down the beach to the town of Monterrico and catch the bus back to Guatemala City.

That next Saturday afternoon, all Hawaii crowded into a couple of flat bottomed boats about three times longer and five times wider than a dugout canoe. A little canvas canopy kept the sun off those seated in the middle, but ten of us in the bow and the driver, with his hand on the outboard motor's handle in the stern, would crisp in the sunlight that flickered through the mangrove treetops.

We wound our way through the clear water between labyrinthine fields of hyacinth islands. Our boatman found a clear channel, by instinct or habit, even where the flat islands of fleshy leaves threatened to block the way, when stretches between the islands grew narrow as we approached. Mangrove branches interwove over our heads to create a cavern of leaves and the mangrove's pendulous spear seeds. The white flowers that dotted the islands glowed florescent in that cool shade, like the white hoods of nuns.

Felt like an hour and a half later, when we stopped at a small dock.

Atop the sand dune slope that dropped into the mangrove intercoastal canal, a pickup truck waited for us. We climbed up the sandy slope and over the tailgate of the pickup; the women's basketball team, the men's soccer team, family members, other athletes, citizens of Hawaii, and I. We clung to a pipe fence stuck vertically out of the sides to surround the truck bed.

The pickup glided and fishtailed down a smooth sand road that curved around underbrush and tropical hardwoods. The tree branches overarched and protected us from the brutal sun, but every once in a while, people called out "Agáchase!" warnings to duck and avoid decapitations or loss of cranial integrity from low branches.

In a half hour or so, we arrived at Madre Viejo Aldea, a place where two rural roads met to make a T. Villagers put the final touches to the erection of a temporary tent, half the size of a small circus tent, with a single post in the middle. Musical equipment, electric guitars, keyboards, a trap set of drums, and a line of timbales and conga drums stood on a raised stage in front of the single wall of canvas that would block the sea breeze.

Next to the large tent for the dance, a smaller peaked tent hid the electric generator. Through the open side of this small tent, I could see about six benches and an altar with icons and votive candles that burned with flames invisible against the strong ambient sunlight. Every once in a while, one or two of the older people went in, crossed themselves, knelt or sat in the sand to pray a little, and came out to rejoin the party.

Stocky women steadied tall slender girls who climbed upon chairs to fasten colored crepe paper along strings of electric lights that followed the underside of ridgepoles and rafters in decorative dips and scallops.

We from Hawaii walked together in representation of our village as we entered their village. I saw no houses off in the undergrowth. Some people from our group scattered to buy six packs of beer at a tienda and carry it to the basketball court.

Weeks ago, the girls on our team decided on blue uniforms. They gathered bluish shorts and painted their tennis shoes, all crowned by a loose tank top sleeveless white T-shirts with their Hispanic surnames across the back yoke and red numbers, front and back, applied with appliqué or red paint.

The two teams of lanky girls played basketball in earnest competition. Some of the darker girls wore their thick, kinky hair in a huge ponytail pompom. They looked more powerful, and stood head and shoulders taller than the cinnamon skinned Guatemalans with Mayan Indian bloodlines. Their black ancestors, Africans sold into slavery to escape from plantations or freed by pirates, added to the genetic diversity in Guatemala over the last four centuries. Few girls on this coast looked like the shorter inhabitants of Lake Atitlán, who probably remain close to one hundred percent Mayan in their genotype.

At half times and time outs, the referees threw a bunch of lit firecrackers over the heads of the players. Firecrackers exploded and scattered starbursts of secondary explosions to hit several girls who crouched and ran with arms up and hands atop their heads to protected their hair or ears. Firecrackers bounced off their shirts, bare shoulders, and hair. One fell on a tall girl with kinky hair and strange little bumps on her skin, hit her shoulder and exploded, burned the skin, and created a small weepy wound. She acted like it meant nothing, didn't hurt, and after the break she continued to play marked by that wide chevron of wet red tissue.

After the men's soccer game, which I didn't watch because I knew nothing about soccer (and any red blooded American male who must choose between men's soccer and women's basketball must watch the girls), everybody went back to the tent area where vendors put the final painted touches on numerous stalls or stands to sell fried foods, drinks, candies, and candles for the devote Catholics.

We ate around sunset, accompanied by sounds of birds and other awakened nocturnal wildlife from deep within the mangroves. As if in answer, the amplifiers spit out sporadic keyboard and bass tones, as the band tuned up and did sound checks.

"Uno, dos, one, two, three, cuatro." The musician at the microphone winked at me, the Gringo.

Crown the Queen

One radical interpretation, of a carved bass-relief sequence in the North Temple at Chichen Itzá, judges it a description of an initiate's ritual of passage. A superior being awakens to guide the initiate on a journey where he speaks to jaguars and holds a lance, symbolic of his mastery of 'will power.' Then, with his left hand over his solar plexus and his right on his penis, he becomes 'tuned to the vibration' of one of these meter-long stylized stone phalluses, as the Tree of Life emerges from him. Farther along the path, he holds a dismembered penis in one hand and his nose with the other, and vomits 'negativity' from his headdress onto a disembodied head (a sign of peyote ingestion and indigestion?), and continues on the path to join a feathered serpent-god in the clouds, to rebirth through the jaws of a serpent. Along this path, the persistent head symbol deteriorates 'along with his ego,' until the figure of an eagle replaces it.

While crazy theories often come from the overworked brain of imaginative "scientists," they also speak to the ubiquity of ideas such as these penis cults, still extant in India as a recognized religion. It makes sense that many of these 'universal archetypes,' like the instincts to fear snakes and spiders, floods and heights, tend to keep us from harm. They also may rouse less desirable and inappropriate responses, such as tribal hatreds, penile rapaciousness, homicidal jealousy, and acquisitive war. The ubiquity of myths that deal with rebirth into 'superior beings,' may evince a genetic foundation for the attractiveness of things like self-help books and religion. Diversity promotes the continuation of any species, and in humans thus creates the evolutionary need for inspirational humanistic leaders of friendship and diplomacy, leaders who can consider alternative viewpoints, accept others ideas, and respect each person's right to exist as an individual, with individual dreams, desires, talents, ideas, and personal development, which in sum, will promotes human progress and the survival of all.

After most people finished their meal, a man took the mike and made some announcements. He wore a white short sleeve shirt, untucked, square cut, with two columns of three pockets each down the front. People applauded after what sounded like interminable lists of names of people to thank.

The mayors gave speeches, and called new people onstage. They thanked each other with a profusion of repeated complements, gave and accepted awards, ribbons, and plaques for the competitions in track, soccer, and basketball. The other competitions and races took place in some area far from this central tent. Throughout the day, I heard no cheers to draw my attention.

More people arrived. I asked someone what happens next.

"Van a coronar la Reina de la Aldea."

I thumbed through my Spanish-English dictionary in the dim electric light. They would crown the Queen of the Village, the girl who received the most votes.

Over the past month or less, people voted for the Queens with money; when they bought things at the local tiendas, they found the candidates' coffee cans on the counter. Each candidate's team decorated their coffee cans with the candidate's Xeroxed photo, wrapped and scotch-taped around the can, with individualized decorations of colored paper, ribbon, and aluminum foil.

The spotlight came on as the girls paraded out in white evening gowns, which increased the volume of the murmurs and public commentary from groups of men nearby. I saw the men leer, a lot of chin rubs and elbows in each other's ribs. Men migrate away from the women at social functions, and en masse they felt free to express themselves as machos. The faces of women on the other side of the tent flashed critical and sarcastic, heads nodded negative, until one of their relatives came onstage as a contesant, then sections of their crowd erupted in cheers and upraised arms.

The younger men hooted and roughhoused, pushed each other around and shuffled a quick slap box, as they admired this feminine beauty. They jumped upon each other's shoulders for the momentary advantage of height. Five or six climbed up a nearby tree and hung there, wrapped around the almost vertical branches like monkeys, with a clear view to twelve of the most beautiful young women in the area.

Every one with black hair, straight or wavy or kinky, due to the predominance of Mayan, Spanish, and African ancestors. Back in Michigan, I suspect none of these girls would feel enough self esteem or peer pressure to enter any beauty contests, but my last three months in Latin America gave me a new perspective on beauty. I could imagine the Midwestern criticisms because these girls don't fit the standard Dutch model of beauty with blond hair and alabaster skin. Their lips too fleshy instead of thin, and painted a deep bright shameless red. Their skin, exposed to the sun, took on a color darker than possible for Midwestern tans, and their obsidian black eyes would frighten those who expect a brown eye and a defined pupil.

Their youth gave even the skinniest girl a soft, healthy voluptuousness. A little extra baby fat, obvious through their white evening gowns, gave supple smoothness to their bodies. I could imagine a similar scene in Arabia, and anyone of these young virgins would fetch top dollar with slavers.

Only one seemed comfortable in her own skin; the others acted shy, raised a hand to screen their eyes from the light, slouched to minimize their new womanly curves, didn't know what to do with their hands.

One well-endowed girl tried to hide her frontal protuberances, so recent they decorated her chest without surrender to gravity. The evening gown design swaddled her thin waist in extra fabric to tone down the exaggerated curves of bust and ample hips. At first, I saw her as freakish, and could not imagine a Michigan girl would dare to enter that exuberant body in a beauty contest. I could not keep my eyes off her, and fantasized how she might look without clothes, in various horizontal dances. My mind changed, as I responded in involuntary ways to these fantasies, and she won me over. She convinced me of the error of skinny women who succumb to the dictates of predominantly homosexual men in the New York fashion industry, who put clothing on women so skinny they look anemic, malnourished, ill, and sexy only to pederasts.

What man wants to hug a ribcage of bones?

She became a Goddess from India, freed from six hundred years captured in stone on temples devoted to carnal love and beauty. They knew about beauty way back then in India.

My favorite to win the crown, an angelic beauty, by and large free of overt sexuality, seemed pure Mayan. With her mango shaped eyes set apart and forward on a round flat face, she looked hand-drawn. Asian eyebrows on a doll's forehead, prominent cheekbones that tapered to full lips in a faint smile, and very long straight black hair that fell beyond her waist, created a vision so out of place, it amplified the subtle curves under her white sequined gown.

When the spotlight panned back and forth across the row of contestants, the skin-tight white evening gowns shimmered like water, glittered like rainbows, and threw electric sparks. Giant rhinestones, like iridescent scales of fish, outlined their motions and flowed in filigree patterns and French curves to catch the colored lights from the long lines of bulbs strung along the spokes of the circus tent frame. Sparks danced with every excited breath that heaved those firm, adolescent bosoms.

After too much talk and jokes I couldn't understand, the master of ceremonies announced the names of the three finalists. The other girls streamed off stage, my favorite included, to leave three excited girls, two slender, and a girl whose body outshined her personality.

More people climbed up on the unstable tables and stood on chairs in the sand. Young men climbed the tent poles, and pulled themselves up the trunks of trees, whenever one dropped, exhausted from the effort to get a clear view over this sea of black-haired heads.

As the announcer read the name of the third runner-up, the attendants came out with a robe and a crown, while the two contestants that remained trembled and hugged each other.

When the second runner-up heard her name, the winner's eyes overflowed with tears of joy. Her hands flew and fluttered like pigeon wings to her face, to cover her open-mouthed cry of astonishment, her features a twisted mixture of pain and joy.

The announcer read her name, Xelerina Kabah Salamanca or something that mixed Spanish and Mayan, and she hugged the MC, the two runner-ups, the attendants, the announcer, and said then said long thank yous to her parents, people who voted, neighbors, God and church, the Government, the people Guatemala, and even visitors from other countries as she looked over the crowd to where I stood.

I blushed.

Everyone clapped.

Perhaps they judged her right as the most beautiful young girl. Slim and elegant, her features outlined in fine wavy black hair, a fine strong nose, soft rounded jaw, and demure recessive chin. She painted her lips with a cherry red and stayed within their fleshy limits to look swollen with fruity youth. Her eyes and natural black lashes now dripped with tears and streaked her rouged cheeks with a grey mascara sludge.

She delivered a practiced speech, something about how she hoped that her coronation signified the arrival of culture in the Aldeas, these rural neighborhoods throughout the forgotten Guatemalan hinterlands. She proclaimed that from now on, thanks to these Fiestas and the good will between communities, Guatemala's citizens would reap the advantages of knowledge and culture not only in Guatemala City, but also in the agricultural regions, the beaches and plains, the highland mountains and cloud forests, and into the jungles and deserts. And most important, these advances come promised to all Guatemalans, for Indian and Latino as equals, no matter what their color, background, their family name, or their income.

With the most sincere and intent expression, and a magnetization of her eyebrows toward her nose, she asked for applause in support for all the good people that put so much work into this definitive moment, a moment that would change the future for the better for all humanity and the universe at large, etc. etc.

At the very end, she thanked God and the pope, and everyone applauded.

Up to that moment, I could believe the world needs more beauty contests.

Guillermo

Throughout the Classic and Post-classic periods, the most important ceremonial and scientific center of the Northern Mayan civilization, which spread over the modern Mexican states of Yucatán, Quintana Roo, and Campeche, lay in the northern part of the Yucatán peninsula, at a site now called Chichen Itzá. Some archeologists theorize that the Toltecs from central Mexico conquered the region in the tenth century, and some think the reverse happened, that Chichen Itzá conquered the Toltec Tula cultures.

Within temples of Chichen Itzá, shapes protrude from the middle of walls, shapes like the heads of penises. In Chichen Itzá's small structure known as the Temple of Venus, the first discovered Chac Mool came to light, along with a large collection of "cylinders" that resemble stone fence posts with one end rounded and smoothed. Today they lie piled and stacked in one area under some trees like firewood, with no interpretive information posted. At least one researcher suggests they represent ceremonial phalluses, used in rites of passage into the elite class's adulthood, or a priesthood, of the privileged.

The Classic Mayans carved the Chac Mools as a reclined male figure with 'big ears' that resemble headphones, most often with knees bent, a flat plate held over the stomach, face turned to the side. Chac Mools may represent the "Divine Fire" or the transmutation of low frequency sexual energy into higher energies, as in many cultures' theories of physiology, such as Kundalini Yoga. A recently discovered Chac Mool reclines on one hip, one hand behind the small of the back near the fused sacral-coccygeal vertebrae, the other hand over the solar plexus and sculpted penis (since broken off by modern prudes). A carved cross over his face resembles tape to seal his mouth and nose, but allows him to see and hear, and "keep silent."

I bought a beer, and walked over to the side of the pickup where three young Ladino men from Hawaii talked and laughed. They shared cigarettes, and offered me one.

As we smoked, one Latino man took an interest in me. He looked Arabian, with kinky hair, shadowed jaw from his shaved beard that left his skin bluish, a hawkish nose, and intense angry black eyes under long black lashes.

He said "I call myself Guillermo," the way Spanish says My name is such and such. He asked me the usual banal questions that travelers suffer, but too often put his hand out to touch me on the arm, hand, or shoulder. Then he said something which I didn't understand, but made everyone laugh. This he used as an excuse to put his arm around my neck and reassure me. He pulled my face close to his for a quick backslap of encouragement, as his forehead touches mine.

The other two watched all this with an amused attitude I couldn't fathom. Then they made some comments I didn't understand, but spoken with a seriousness that outlined a clear difference of opinion with Guillermo, who I felt forced his friendship upon me.

Then they left me alone with this guy.

He glared into my eyes. I felt uncomfortable and asked him "What's up?"

"Nothing. Let me buy you a beer."

"No, Guillermo. I'll buy my own, don't worry."

"I'm not worried, please, my pleasure. Wait right here, and I will go buy you a beer.

He ran off before I could say no, ran to the little stall nearby and opened one of the ice chests full of cans of beer. He bought one, opened it, grabbed a paper cup, and ran back across the sand. As he came, he poured the beer from the can into the tall paper cup.

I held out some money to pay him, but Guillermo wouldn't take it. He acted insulted, and convinced me to put my money away. "Friends buy each other beer.'

"You can buy the next ones for both of us."

Whatever.

I wanted to put some distance between Guillermo and I, but didn't know how to break away and not commit some social misstep.

I saw a couple across the sand. They walked hand in hand towards the beach into the late afternoon sun, their silhouette and the tops of the dunes shimmered with heat, painted by sunlight to look like a photo in silver and black. Best of all, I did not lie. "Excuse me, I want to take a photo." I left him there with my beer, alone and a little confused, at the side of the pick up truck. Maybe I could avoid him for the rest of the day even though I owed him a beer.

An example of the problem of primitive reciprocity in human society, and its utility to cement relationships, welcome or not.

As loudspeakers filled the air with Cumbia music, people chose partners to dance with.

One man, beyond the outer perimeter of the tent's dance floor, hung onto a ribbon that radiated from the tent's center pole. He moved in a slow circle while a woman on the ribbon's forward side asked each couple to pay before she allowed them to slip under the ribbon. They worked their way around the dance floor, and ensured that dancers paid as long as the dance continued, song after song.

I watched from within a group of young men with beer, and like many, nursed each beer for as long as we could in the heat, to look cool and not spend money too fast. Many of these Latino Guatemalans offered to buy me a beer, which I learned early in Hawaii to reject. I couldn't allow it. One beer represents too great a proportion of their meager incomes. At one beer per day, they could drink away their entire income.

Somewhere in Guatemala, people must earn the average dollar a day, but that affluent neighborhood eluded me so far.

This Guatemalan generosity made me feel ashamed and guilty about my relative wealth and ability to earn in the United States, so I held onto my half-full beer to fence off their constant offers. I also feigned a problem with my stomach, a common enough occurrence among the local population, and expected among foreigners, which enabled me to block their offers to buy me a meal.

As the band announced the last dance, an older woman came off the dance floor and dragged me into the fray. We danced, my new friends hooted and encouraged me, then mocked my clumsy attempts to dance the Cumbia. I decided to use my vast repertoire of spastic free form rock and roll moves, but the song ended, to everyone's relief, and I fled.

Hunger prodded me to look for something to eat, but the food vendors packed up long ago, when they ran out of food.

The musicians started the disassembly of their equipment, and people accepted that as the signal of the event's termination.

Our contingent from Hawaii gathered belongings and family members into the pickup trucks. I stood near the mangroves, out of the way, and watched the procession of people pass by to return to their respective villages.

Guillermo saw me, and came over to give me a big unwelcome hug. He gave off an odor that suggested he found more than a couple of beers to chug down in the interim.

He wanted to buy me a beer.

I said no.

Then he thought I should buy him one.

This late in the day, not one vendor's stall remained.

With a great noise, a rush of wind and sandy salty dust, the circus tent collapsed into a pool of canvas and rope. Several men folded it with effort and urgency, then wound it with ropes into a giant sausage shape that took several men to lift into a truck.

Guillermo pulled me toward the mangroves, down a little path between the short bushes that petered out into an open space between branches. Although reluctant, I went with him, curious about what he wanted to show me, but the path led nowhere except out of sight of the rest of them.

I turned around to walk out.

Guillermo tugged at the back of my shirt.

I shook him off and jumped away. Once outside the bushes, I saw the others gathered around the pickup, and walked fast toward them.

Guillermo caught up to me and threw his arm over my shoulders, laughed, and took up a loose kneed and casual gait, as if to pretend that we walked around like that all afternoon.

At the pickup truck, our other two young friends approached, a half smile both of their faces.

Guillermo tried to convince me to go for another walk with him. "Come on, we've got time."

I asked the other young men "Do you think the pickup will leave soon?" I thought they might take it as a clue, and help me avoid Guillermo's advances, but they acted insecure about something, did not want to meddle. Later I realized that my question could also signify that I wanted time to hang out with Guillermo.

They looked at him, then at me, then back to Guillermo to examine both our faces. Guillermo's face sincere, his eyes implored with the intensity of a puppy. I do not know what my face said, but deep down, I wanted to remain distant friends. Very distant. Continents apart.

Someone said "The pickup won't leave for a while. No te preocupes (don't worry yourself), it won't leave without you."

Guillermo grabbed my upper arm and pulled, "Come on, let's go for a walk. Vamos a dar un paseo." We go to give a pass, literally. He dragged me off a few paces, then I stopped.

He turned to me with a look of frustration that cemented his facial features under furrowed brows. Then he grabbed his cock through his pants. He came close, nose to nose, and mumbled something I did not understand.

I turned and started to walk back to the pickup, and he grabbed my arm and wheeled me around. His face communicated an emotion between anger and astonishment, as he put his arms out in a soundless shrug, as if to question, "What gives?"

"Let's go back to the pickup truck."

"We've got time! Why do you want to go back?"

"I want to go back to Hawaii."

He acted like my words struck him as the dumbest thing ever. He reached for my arm with one hand, and grabbed his crotch with the other. I twisted out of his grasp, then turned to walk back.

He ran in front of me and pushed my chest to stop me, dared me to take another step. At least, I thought he meant that.

I told him to calm down, calm down. He let his arms fall to his side, let out a breath of air, and turned his bowed head to the side as if in thought. I stepped around him and headed for the pickup and the others, and felt that all eyes looked at him and me.

He caught up to me and walked beside me, but did not put his arm around me.

At the pickup truck, the two young men talked and giggled at us a little, but Guillermo's glance calmed them down. Guillermo made one more surreptitious intent with his eyes. He pointed with his eyes at the bushes, then he looked toward me with immobile head. The numerous eye rolls toward the bush made him look like he suffered a seizure. I stood and leaned against the pickup, felt secure around my old friends from Hawaii, and watched him try to entice me into the woods. He gradually escalated his private messages to me with unsubtle motions of his hand over his groin.

Some people laughed, low and careful. I didn't look to see at what.

Guillermo became self aware again, the spell broke, he stopped his little show, and walked away with a jaunt meant to cover his dejected frustration.

I planned say good bye here to my Hawaiian friends and walk to Monterrico, and now I must avoid this pissed off Guillermo. My friends from Hawaii tried to talk me out of my long walk, which would take all night. Most waved their hands to coax me into the pickup, and many said I should return with them to Hawaii in the barge.

My two friends thought the beach at night too dangerous to walk alone to Monterrico. Many people from several communities saw me, talked about me, and now knew my plans. That might tempt someone to wait for me in the darkness to rob, or worse.

People from five different communities knew about me. Perhaps I looked too long at somebody else's girl, so I choose caution as the better part of valor. I could try to leave another night without so much fanfare.

We boarded the pickup truck, fewer of us than before. I asked where the other people went, and heard the explanation that many stayed behind with friends.

Silence in the pickup. A few girls looked at me and smiled. A man made a comment and everyone giggled a little. I looked at him and put out my hand as if to shake hands, the way they implore someone to explain.

"Poor Brandon," he said to everyone in the back of the pickup. "Confundido."

Invisible low branches swished by in the darkness overhead, and forced everyone into a paranoid semi crouch. Even if seen in the truck's headlights, they came in so close and fast you couldn't duck fast enough.

"Brandon está confundido." The young man repeated to make others giggle.

We rode on without conversation, and many dropped their heads and slept.

Seemed like an hour to get to the canal dock where we left our barge canoe, then another half hour to load.

Perhaps around midnight, we started back. Most of the young men slept together on the floor and benches, while the women and girls sat up to give them room, or laps for their heads. We cruised though the cavernous darkness of the mangrove draped canal, with the accompaniment of the small outboard motor's raspberry noise.

I could not sleep. Fireflies drew white line arcs through the branches over our heads. I could hear the series of plops when four-eyed fish bolted at the boat's advance. A small ribbon of sky between the mangrove treetops allowed the Milky Way's light to illuminate the clear channels around the mats and islands of water hyacinths. The water hyacinths bloomed at night, thousands of flowers, white eyes that stared in horizontal populations across the massive black islands that made missing jigsaw puzzle pieces of the smooth gray mirror of reflected stars.

Brandon está confundido. Confused.

Turtle Egg Hunters

The cosmic portals transform fire, water, earth, and smoke. The constellation of Orion shines down as the fireplace of the Heavens. Its three Hearthstones of Mantle, Fire pit, and Hearth contain the fire itself, the smoky Nebula of pillared clouds, a womb of star formation around the middle "star," a galaxy we see within the constellation Orion. As the house's fireplace serves as a portal where the material world of wood disappears from Earth as light and smoke, so we might believe the sky must contain a fireplace, a return portal where the Heavens materialize earth from light. As the Heavens and earth both suffer the ravages of fire and smoke, so they must suffer an oceanic wave of death and destruction, as earthquakes turn solid ground to jelly, as rain falls from the sky to liquefy earth into deadly rivers of mud. Earth, air, water, and fire, the coagulation of blood that ran from a heart ripped out of a sacrifice who breathes the last breath, as Jesus expires on the cross in back of every Catholic Mass. Each person's perception of the spirit world awakens with the acknowledgment of the disintegration of life's reality. The Heavens reach down to touch the earth and create water and fire. Clouds form above volcanoes and mountains, forests, or bodies of water. The open portals of caves and volcanoes allow the Underworld to belch rock, smoke, steam, and air. And the Gods gave humans an ephemeral existence on the tiniest layer of all, a thin green coat of life that exists between air and earth, between heaven and the underworld, a layer we call the biosphere.

A few nights after the inter village competitions, I decided to walk the length of the beach all the way to Monterrico.

I liked the idea of a walk through the coldest part of the night, to walk the seven miles alone, across the empty, lawless stretches of remote unpopulated beach between small rural villages. I should and reach Monterrico in time to catch the seven AM bus, and so avoid the cost of a hotel room.

Someone shook me awake from a soundless sleep. I looked into Don Martinez's concerned face, and wondered how he arose with so much energy, and probably without an alarm clock, while it took me some time to remember my own plans.

I pushed my sleeping bag into my backpack and shouldered it, gave him the key to the useless lock. We walked under the palms toward the ocean, and stood together on the black sand beach, on the edge of his creation, his Hawaii, to say goodbye. The clear night sky looked gray with so many stars. Easy to see the constellation of Orion, which Don Martinez pointed out several times to over emphasize it. "Keep Orion on your left side and you won't get lost."

I don't know why he thought it so important. Turn left, fall into the Pacific Ocean. Veer right and fall into the mangrove canal.

Don Martinez tried to talk me out of it. "Too dangerous. Ladrones. Robbers." He held his hand out to mimic a gun.

"I have little for them to steal."

"People here muy pobre. (Very poor.) Hay gente mala. (There exist some bad people.) Que hacen cosas malas para divertirse. (They do bad things for fun.) Debes tener cuidado. (Take care.)"

When I said, "See you next year," his face looked frightened for a millisecond before he managed a smile. He put both hands out, palms down, to tell me to slow down, and said, "Maybe in a couple of years." Then he clasped his hands together, tilted his head back as if to gaze down at me with the angelic smile of someone enamored with a sunrise.

I thought he might want me to get a wife and a good income before I came back, to change my status as rogue male and improve my potential benefit to the community. Took me years to realize his instructions to keep the constellation Orion on my right until it set would also ensure that I did not return to Hawaii.

I headed for the beach's firmer sand, and strode along the dark Pacific by starlight. My backpack bounced in a rhythmic song with each step, and a strap rasped against a bass string of the guitar lashed on top

This past evening, I witnessed the Burning of the Devil, a holiday ritual observed throughout rural Latin America, they said. People in the village, almost every household, lit bonfires and by their light I got a much better idea of how the colony of Hawaii covered a very large area.

Piles of coals still glowed red and smoked when the wind blew along the beach. I imagined how all these bonfires raged earlier this evening, the flames high while men ignited strings of firecrackers to drive the Devil out of their village, family, forests, and self, and send him back to that Christian or Mayan hell where he belongs.

After I walked a ways, I felt nostalgic for the place. It took so little effort to pack my bags and walk out of that short lived world of daily routines. Never again would I walk around with a hunger for another glimpse of that young girl's fullness silhouetted against the beach spray and sunrise, her arms up akimbo to the load upon her head, her shy smile that acknowledged my adoration.

People ahead of me on the beach betrayed their presence with brief flashes of their weak yellow flashlight beams. They disappeared as I approached without a flashlight.

Bandits?

I presented an easy mark. For this attempt to reach Monterrico, I told no one of my plans except the Don and Doña Martinez.

If I saw more than one person approach with a flashlight, I assumed they couldn't see me with their flashlight on, and I hid myself. I watched for places to hide, and kept visual note of piles of vegetation that might hide me and my pack if I needed to flee.

They might also hide an assailant.

I hid once when I saw a flashlight come straight toward me. A man approached, all his attention focused downward as he scanned the sand. After he passed, I walked on and discovered the reason for these insomniac wanderers.

Turtle eggs.

Where any huge sea turtle comes to shore, it leaves a peculiar trail that looks like a tank tread. The trail leads back and forth from the ocean to the ravaged nest, now excavated and clean of eggs. The hunters dig through the sand to gather up the leathery white eggs, considered a delicacy, although illegal. In Guatemala's economy, turtle eggs offer an opportunity for a poacher to make quite a bit of easy money. One bag of twenty eggs sold to tourists for a dollar or more per egg equals a month's income from hard work on ranches or farms.

I remembered the taste of a doomed turtle egg eaten on a little beach near the town of Huixtla, near the Mexican border of Guatemala. Salt and lemon juice did not cover the raw chalk flavor.

I kept track of the Belt of Orion's stars, and thought about how it contains the Great Nebula, and near Alnitak, the easternmost star, the Horsehead Nebula. So many stars become entire galaxies through a telescope, and the empty space between, full of intergalactic clouds with more galaxies beyond.

A telescopic scan of one tiny area half the size of the moon could catalog tens of thousands of galaxies, each with billions of stars. Makes me feel less than insignificant.

Orion moved toward the horizon up ahead, where the beach stretched out before me, straight as an arrow, along a dark and nebulous line of waves roared in long booms against the sand, the snores of something gigantic in a fitful sleep. At its quietest, I could hear the rustle of wind blown sand and the hiss of wave water that slips back to sea, a brief quiet before the next set of waves assault the beach in tremendous explosions.

The spray falls and swirls around me like a million stars.

I walk through the middle of the universe. The clear night sky shines with light from billions of years ago, a vast window into the yesterdays of the universe, under which I walked into a new tomorrow.

Monterrico

Before dawn, I glimpsed a distant Monterrico glitter with low streetlights under palms trees. I felt exhausted under a backpack that seemed full of rocks. On the farthest outskirts of town, long low mansions of the rich occupy sections of beach. People in Hawaii said I would see the President's weekend residence, and how the rich try to cordon off sections of the beach with broken wooden fences for their own private and personal use. Go right through them, they said.

When I entered Monterrico, I saw one other person awake in these wee small hours. I asked him how to find the main road, and where to catch the bus.

We stood on the main road, and he also waited for the bus.

The bus arrives at eight and leaves at eight thirty, so there remained two hours to sleep. I didn't want to sit on the hard cement. The young man told me I could rent a room cheap for a couple of hours from a hotel across the street. I got a room on the second floor of this new cement hotel, with metal and glass windows that cranked open for the day's coolest breezes, and on that breeze I heard a beautiful Mexican song.

Somebody loved that song, and played it over and over in the near distance, at a clear and vibrant volume that accompanied the quiet birdsong of these early morning hours. Like a piece of theater, the song contained a couple of dramatic halts that emphasized the singer's art. A man's voice ran from a whisper to an operatic yell, a plaintive whine to a confident shout and laughter. His rendition captivated at least two people, me and whoever played the song, if not the whole city of Monterrico.

I stood at the window as the eastern sky began to lighten, fell in love with the song, and wondered if I would ever find it.

Years later, I discovered the song, a classic sung by an icon in Mexican music, and part of his movie released that year by the same name. Vicente Fernandez's "La Ley Del Monte" describes a star-crossed romance with the basic plot of the movie "Little Shop of Horrors" inside a two and a half minute song.

I didn't sleep at all, and about the time the man in that distant cantina ran out of Quetzals, I shouldered my backpack and hurried down the stairs and out onto the street to wait with a couple of other people at this mysterious, unmarked bus stop.

Outside, a young businessman in white shirt and tie without a sports coat stood beside a woman in a light cotton skirt that billowed slow in the delicate sea breeze. The broadleaf evergreen trees along this sidewalk grew as tall as a four story house, and their muscular branches stretched over us, adorned with umbrella rib arrangements of leaves big as footprints. I picked up some fallen leaves and they felt thick as waxed canvas, with two distinct surfaces, shiny dark green on top, and silvery dusty underneath.

About every ten minutes, a pair of headlights brought us to attention and hopefulness as a prelude to disappointment.

The night sky purpled beyond the leaves.

The bus clattered into view twenty minutes late. I saw, through the windshield, the fat driver in a white shirt and tie. The brakes squealed, a cloud of dust and diesel fumes enveloped us, and he jerked the crank that opened the door with violent bang. He rubbed sleep out of his eyes with the other hand.

We entered the empty bus. After a few blocks and a few more stops to pick up people, we pulled out of Monterrico. The cement road turned into a sandy lane lined with tall trees that cut between the pastures and forests of the Pacific lowlands. I enjoyed the rush of cool air through my open window, and watched the golden tones of sunrise saturate the sky.

The volcano's shadows streaked the sky's zenith in purple, way up above the rush of branches, and merged into the darkness over the Pacific Ocean.

On long rural stretches of dirt road, the bus stopped at every crossroad to pick up a couple of people, school children, or old people with big heavy bags destined for the market. After an hour and about twelve miles out of town, the bus seemed filled with people and their bags.

Then the bus quit. We coasted to a dusty stop under the trees.

The driver couldn't get it started, so he flagged down a young man on a small motorcycle, who turned around and gave the driver a ride back to town.

We waited through the morning hours, and felt the sun bake away the cool of night.

He came back on a different motorcycle with a man in a T-shirt, who gave the bus a thorough examination. He crawled out from underneath to cross himself and pronounce it dead. People laughed, took their things off the bus, and looked for soft patches of ground to sit in the shade.

The two took off on the motorcycle toward town.

About two hours later, after I'd gone through a rainbow of reactions from irritation, frustration, desperation, anger, and into heat exhaustion, the Guatemalans seemed as complacent as cows.

A big pickup truck pulled alongside us and stopped. The bus driver stepped out with a heroic grin, and shooed us into the open back of this pickup.

We climbed into the back, hoisted the loads in, and got everyone in on top of the load. we jammed against the pipe reinforced sides as the pickup bounced down the sandy country lane. I thought it miraculous that all of us, plus the big bags of cargo, the corn, peanuts, cloth, nuts, etc. all managed to cram into the back.

The driver stopped to pick up more passengers and cargo at a couple more stops. We pressed against each other, bounced, got hurt, cried and laughed together, until we reached a major paved highway intersection, and half the people got off.

As we continued down our sandy road we took advantage of more space to make ourselves comfortable. We sat down, and the Guatemalans plundered their cargo for food to eat. Women offered fresh cooked pastries and tortas (sandwiches made of football shaped rolls), men pilfered their crates of vegetables and one took out a fireplace log, maybe to sell at the next stop.

We jostled along, ducked the low branches, and gazed at endless Pacific lowland fields where droop eared, lyre-horned Brahman cattle lay in the shade of ceiba trees and chewed their cud.

Ceiba Trees

In Mesoamerica, the Ceiba (also known as Kapok tree) represents the Meso-American's Sacred World Tree, much as the Bible's Tree of the Knowledge of Good and Evil tainted the Garden of Eden. With fruit that corrupted Adam and impregnated Eve with evil, it took innocence as a state of grace at the same time it cursed all women forever with menstrual pain and dangerous childbirths. The archetypal story may also express how women invented agriculture. As if due to a programmed genetic response, the males, no longer of primal important as hunters, learn to dominate and enslave females when societies develop agriculture.

Some psychologists believe that archetypal mythic stories exist deep in the shared brain, perhaps in the genetics, of all human beings and thus exist, recognizable, in Mayan cosmology. One feels tempted to say that Adam and Eve fell under an influence from within the branches of the Mayan World Tree, the same one that harbored the skull that spat into the palm of the virgin mother of the Twin Brother Gods. These Trees of Life, Trees of the Knowledge of Good and Evil, both end human innocence with their symbolic death snakes as conduits between a shadowy Underworld of secret information and an imperfect Eden of earthly innocence.

As the site of Christ's crucifixion, the four Gospels of the New Testament mention a skull shaped hill near Jerusalem called Golgotha or Calvary, said to contain Adam's tomb. The Bible says a virgin gave birth to Jesus as the son of a human and God, and Jesus becomes a "sacrificed lamb" who returns from the underworld of the dead "reborn" for mankind's benefit. The Calvary cross resembles the Latin cross, which resembles a European version of the Mayan's World Tree, most often mounted at the apex of three pyramidal steps.

Like layers religious thought, a Meso-American pyramid often contains the tomb of a God King in each layer. As the Meso-Americans believed in Coatzecoatl, a white skinned bearded God who would return to them from the East and pass through the coral reef's breach at Quintana Roo's Tulum, so the Christians await the return of Jesus, the Son of God. Quetzalcoatl, or Coatzecoatl, or Kulkulkán, did return to Cuahtemala (Guatemala) personified by Hernan Cortéz, the white skinned bearded Spaniard who helped Mexicans win their civil war against the Aztecs and paved the way for European cultural dominance and the eradication of most Meso-American cultures.

We sped along the white dirt track, thankful for the brief shade huge rocket trunk Ceiba trees cast over us from their high, smooth, muscular branches. One of the world's most beautiful trees, the roots and trunk combine to make a rocket shape. A slight bulge in the middle of the long branchless trunk narrows toward the bottom where the buttress roots look like rocket fins from science fiction movies of the fifties.

The pickup paralleled the beach without a glimpse of it, and fishtailed down the sandy track. Each bounce caused us to lurch from one jerked handhold on the pipes to another.

Sometimes one rider asked others nearby to signal the driver to stop. They relayed the message with quiet discretion in spite of the wind and engine's roar, the wild whoosh and flap of boughs of vegetation. Those nearest the cab pounded on the roof to get the driver's attention. He stuck his head out the window as he drove, and people would yell the name of some crossroad or invisible community, or maybe a family name. Then he knew where to let people off.

At each stop, they ask others to hoist their bags over the pipe fence, and then waved goodbye. The driver idled until he heard the shrill voices of the slim, athletic, gap toothed older women yell "D'lante! D'lante!" a contraction of adelante, forward.

The road turned to flank a wide, jungle clad river that moved in a slow slide toward the Pacific. Islands drifted in the current; clots of hyacinth, fallen trees and tangles of branches and cane, and chunks of riverbank bush and weeds brushed the edges of extensive aquatic fields of lily pads, areas of green flagstones with magnolia blossoms on stalks a foot above the water.

Our road dead ends on the edge of a twelve foot yellow dirt cliff above the river. Long flat barges cross from one side to the other below us. We park alongside other buses

The driver helped the women get down off the pickup's tailgate while below in the river, a man poled an immense barge toward us.

On the other side of the river, a bus waited beside an ice cream stand. Looked like Paradise from this side of the river, or at least a more civilized world, if not the industrialized one. In the humidity above the far horizon, the hotels of luxurious Iztapa made rectangular smudges, a tourist Mecca developed on the Pacific, seventy miles by boat from the headwaters of the Rio María Linda at Lago de Amatitlán.

I felt excited about the possibilities of the Big City, and looked forward to when my Mayan Princess would hand me an ice cream cone with that sly, shy smile.

For the first time in months, I thought about her. I felt hot, sweatier that the midmorning humidity.

Next time I saw her, I promised myself to ask her to go out with me, though I might stammer, blush, drop my cone or my pants or hers, or sprout an inflamed zit on the end of my nose. Worst case, she ridicules me while her boyfriend beats me up. Best possible case, she rejects me, the simple path to 'over and out'.

What if neither happens, and instead she smiles, agrees to meet me one Sunday afternoon in the Central Plaza, where she explains how much she wants to learn English and live in the USA?

CHAPTER 10: The Pensión

When the bus entered Guatemala City, I felt excited by the prospects in an urban environment, the freedom, the choices, anonymity, the shared neurosis of carnal beings in an artificial world where an educated privileged class profits from everyone else's basic needs.

After the experience of life in Hawaii's garden of Eden, I better understood rural flight, even my own out of the Michigan hills, reverted to wild with plans for a future suburb.

The Red Tile Church burned into my mind's eye like a miniature Emerald City. My eyes darted from left to right windows, to catch a glimpse before we passed it. I wanted to see it from the other side, from this new direction as the bus sped towards the center of town, and so I clawed at the old yellow school bus's window to work it up before the church came into view. The city seemed four times larger than when I left a few weeks ago.

When the Red Tile Church materialized alongside the bus, I almost missed it. It seemed drab and rain stained in the midday sun, without the shards of reflected light from the polished red tiles. The big wooden doors on immense iron hinges remained shut tight and dark like the charred remains of paper confessions, the door into an abandoned mausoleum. I imagined the Anti-Oz on an upper floor inside, an old long haired Spaniard in a cape who writes with a long feather quill dipped into homemade ink, as the dust swirls through shafts of light that angle down from the round, iron crossed acoustic windows in the belfry. Inside, I imagined cats slink about the scaffold stairways, and dust dried spiders hang stretched on their last webs.

This time, my third visit to Guatemala City, I decided to stay longer, and so walked around and talked to everyone and anybody until I heard of a cheap place to stay. Got lost on the way, but found a little guesthouse, a Pensión, not far off the beaten track, where I could rent a bed for a couple of weeks.

I shared a small room with a skinny student from El Salvador who hoped to graduate from some college in Guatemala City. The other guests who lived in the house included a young Spanish couple and their three children, an old man, the grandmother, and a greasy thug that looked like a thick necked, hyperactive Guatemalan of Italian Spanish Mayan Sicilian Arabic extraction.

The housemother, and I assumed her two daughters, cooked and served meals a day, swept and cleaned, did laundry, and boiled up large tubs of water for the baths, when asked.

Many healthy young men want to exist in a perpetual physical horniness dangerous to their psychological balance. They become addicts to the excitation of both love and war, two states of manipulation of the future almost identical physiologically, only the dipstick's angle of dangle measures the difference between an amorous young man and a homicidal one.

So the most reasonable and sane of those young men seek sexual relief, perhaps as an antidote to the lust for warfare, which might merely express that part of the human brain analogous to a male bird's need to display for females.

In the cheapest hotels, I'd go down the hall to the communal men's bathroom, on the off hours, to find solitude, and get all lathered up to excite myself, but too often I thought some guy might walk in, or I think about all the other guys that stood in that exact spot to kick out the jams as a substitute for a natural one plus one.

The aftermath took the most effort, with pubic hair clotted white with a mineralized residual mix akin to Elmer's glue and wheat paste that answers cheap soap with more coagulations and tangles. I imagined those little sperms so happy to jump out, all excited and ready for the big race to the egg, billions of little cannonballs shot out into the light like so many lottery tickets. Then they see the paint chips and mineral deposits on the shower walls. After a sight like that, I bet their little tails wrap around anything to avoid the spiral journey down the drain.

I much prefer it alone in my room ,where I can take my time, on average about twenty minutes, which I calculate might endear me to a girl friend, if I ever get one. I pant and stroke with my Kleenex or toilet paper ready, and as I approach the point of no return where tingles run up my spine and I feel pressure at the base of my totem, I don't know whether to slow down and prolong the pleasure, or jump over that cliff edge of breathless sensation, faint and religious, thankful for life and this corporeal realm.

But in this family oriented guest house, at that climactic moment a super paranoia takes hold, some useless evolutionary precaution, and I imagine I hear someone in the next room cough, as if they could feel the vibrations emanate from my room.

Then I face the problem of the disposal of soaked paper towel, or stolen restaurant napkins, if I remembered to grab a couple. In emergencies, I use toilet paper and throw it under the bed until morning, but sometimes it glues itself to the floor. Sometimes the paper leaves tiny wads, like hard white heat treated plastic pills, that decorate my short hairs for days.

To avoid any odor of my body's basalt, I hit upon the idea to hide the stained napkins inside a paper cup and crush it, fold it over. To get these cups, I order an expensive drink from a modern fast food restaurant. The act took on so much added meaning I would blush when handed the drink, it became foreplay. On the way home, I tried to slow down and take my time with the drink, and not rush things. For variety, I would order drinks from other vendors, and sometimes they pour the pop out of the valuable glass bottle and into a plastic baggie with a straw. They wrap it with a twist tie or rubber band, and hand it over with a smile. I've used the transparent baggies for the same purpose, but I thought they looked odd until I realized they would seal away any odors from the crushed Styrofoam cups with their genetic treasure inside. That helped me believe that no one, not even the maid, would smell anything, unless they went out of their way, something which I did not doubt either.

At times I resented the whole situation and urgent recurrent need, even if the epitome of pleasurable.

So far, Latin American men acted much more open about sex than this Midwesterner with Victorian age grandparents felt comfortable with. Instead of a tacit taboo topic untouched upon in polite society, Mexican men expressed something about carnal relations whenever they breathed. They smirked about various vegetables, and invented innumerable and unavoidable puns that detailed parts of genitalia and secondary sexual characteristics. Their need to pepper earnest conversations with references to the sons of raped women, goats, and cuckolds seemed as ubiquitous and necessary as food to the Mexican psyche. I wondered if the Mexican male sees sex as a sin to commit as often as possible in defiance of the majority of decent Catholic girls, or did they want to leave a good impression with the guys?

If I ever wanted a hot bath, I needed to ask the women to heat up water and wait for it a half hour or more. I made up some excuse for my flushed and sweaty appearance, a jog, exercise, a fever, etc. but I never mastered the lie.

If I jacked off in the afternoon, it meant I would take a bath in frigid water, because others used up the hot bathing water in the early morning, and they used the hot water kettles in the afternoons to wash the laundry.

If I took a cold bath at night, I might wake others up.

In general, I prefer to masturbate late at night, when everyone else remains so quiet you can hear a fly's footsteps.

In the early evening, if I succeed in a quick, soundless strangulation of the rooster and a stealthy erasure of the evidence, a glaze of sweat covered me.

I became paranoid of any absolute quiet in a house with so many people. After my participation in a few dinner time conversations (in a Special Spanish for my benefit) about how various people in the house suffer insomnia, hear everything, and get up to walk around at night, I became one of the insomniacs.

By day, people walk past the flimsy, acoustically irrelevant door all the time. If anyone realized I remained in my room for over an hour, they thought I killed myself. Their combined curiosity, or a vague social concern for my wellbeing, forced any one of them, the house mother or daughters, cleaning lady, the maids, or another houseguest, to stop by on some pretext to inquire about my welfare. The girls invent tasks. They want to clean the room, wondered if I feel hunger, need a bath, or might I help them please with an English word, anything, to convince me to open the door.

One day, I tried to exercise in my room, get all sweaty and hide my pleasurable activities behind the sounds of pushups and squat thrusts. The rhythms differed too much, and right in the middle of my wild eyed uncoordinated spastic paroxysms and preoccupation with jelly control, I heard the pitter patter of at least two pair of feet in counterpoint to repressed laughter. The sounds came from the other side of my thin door and faded off. I could see in my mind's eye, through the door and into the courtyard beyond, how they hid and smirked amid the foliage and the hung laundry's rows of ghosts.

For a while I tried cold showers, but then I wanted to warm up, and again felt tempted by the most pleasant way I knew to generate heat.

Our Neighborhood Bar

An upright stone object, which some suggest functioned as a ball court score marker, adorns the sculptures of the Mayan ballplayer's U-shaped belts. These markers appear in two forms: Axes (Hachas in Spanish) with thin stone heads, and palm trees (palmas), carved in low relief enmeshed with other life forms. The paddle shaped stone Palmas often carry decorations that illustrate sacrifice and death, which some archeologists call the Veracruz style ball game. Post game ceremonies featured sacrifice of a team, either the disgraced losers, or perhaps the heroic winners who felt they earned the right to die with free passage to ascend to a realm of reward. Artifacts and decorations give us a picture of ceremonies atop the pyramids, where attendants hold victims down as the priests' cut and rip the live hearts from their bodies to hold aloft and show the populace how strong it beats. The heart counts Time and flows red with the blood that nourishes the Gods. This heartbeat, that once marked each second of a person's life, now beats independent of the body. It breathes and slows down to that final gasp, a symbol of the passage into death, of the sun into night, of time as God, of our mortality as inevitable, a time-tested way to shock people and influence their future behavior. The similarities to European clergy's bloody icons and tortured Christs who bleeds upon wooden crosses, probably preconditioned the Meso-Americans to accept the Catholic Church and Christianity.

One day, I entered a nondescript neighborhood bar and discovered, once accustomed to the lack of light, a scene both medieval and modern. The architecture hinted of big timbers underneath with wood panels, chairs of thick rawhide fastened to sturdy wood legs with bronze clapping, heavy framed paintings, chandeliers made of elk and deer antlers, and polished steel or silver artifacts from Spain. The place glowed with candlelight and bourbon bottles, yellow ale in heavy, rose tinted glass beer mugs, and a fat barman in a bowtie who reads the papers in silence.

Located on a street that diverted behind a small hill on the east side of Guatemala City, I thought no one except the immediate neighbors ever found their way there. I lost my way several times when I tried find it, and so became familiar with that part of the city.

One evening, I walked in and saw Dennis from Toronto. He sat alone at the end of the bar, with a beer and a cigarette.

I walked over to say hello, and flashbacked to myself six years old, when I darted across the street on a three wheel bicycle and felt the vague presence of a car that screeched to a halt to my right. I could not stop myself then either.

I tapped him on the elbow.

In a practiced bar reflex, he turned on his barstool then leans back to recognize me and shake my hand.

He looked surprised. "Brandon, isn't it? How did you find me, Sport?"

"I discovered this bar. How did you find it?"

"Got a bed not too far from here, a hotel and food for a buck and a quarter, three meals, you heard about it?"

"Yeah, I used to stay there myself." I pulled up a chair. "Anyone to safeguard your belongings?"

"No. Pay to use the hotel's safe for important stuff. They can steal my toilet paper, most valuable thing in my backpack. Haven't seen you in, what? Three or four weeks?"

"About that. I went down to the Pacific for a while. Where did you go?"

"The Pacific. San Jose. We didn't spend much time there," he spoke, picked his teeth, and stared straight ahead at the mirror behind the bar bottles. "Didn't like it much."

"I know what you mean. Whores, cheap rot gut, and horny sailors. Vacation paradise, for a certain type of person. After San Jose, I lived in a village on the Pacific, in the boondocks, Peace Corp and a fishing cooperative."

"You went to San Jose?"

"Only two days ago. Then I went to Hawaii, Guatemala."

"Sounds romantic. You and the coconuts. Alone?" Dennis took a drink.

"Always. Keeps me light on my feet."

He sat silent, played with his cigarettes. "Have a beer?"

I nodded, and he attracted the bartender's attention the way we learned to in Guatemala, with a light shshsh sound, then made a circle with a down pointed finger to order another round of beers.

We smoked our cigarettes and slugged down our beer. The slight rasp of an unbalanced ceiling fan drew attention to the dim quietness of the mahogany room. When the silence felt awkward, I said, "Ever seen anybody else in here?"

"What do you mean?"

"Not a very popular bar. No one's ever here. I figure they launder money."

"Why? Because it has nice furniture, and stuffed animals?"

"No one's ever here. I bet they pretend it has a big clientele, and deposit drug money in its bank accounts as bar profits."

"Well I'm here, Sport. You surprise me, Brandon. The last person I expected."

"Likewise, I'm sure."

He stared at me, so I made a circular motion with my finger pointed down, and he did not brush it off, so I ordered another round. "Your friends?"

"I don't know. Gary split for Canada."

"And Yvonne?"

He took a sip real quiet, as if to give me a chance to realize my breathing stopped for a moment. "Split too. Still in Guatemala, I think. Why do you asked?" and he smiled and turned to stare, eyes fish dead, which I took as a false display of cluelessness.

"You and Yvonne split up then?"

"Split up, although it feels like down to me." He turned and looked back into the mirror behind the bar. "Happy to hear that?" He smiled at my reflection.

I also looked into the mirror at his reflection, half hidden behind the liquor bottles, to gauge how much he thought me his rival, and how much he fantasized a sweet revenge as he turned into a mean drunk.

"One more beautiful unattached girl. As a man, who could complain about that? Maybe I'll bump into her." I thought he might blame me for Yvonne's faded attraction for him, though I couldn't explain how, more than the fact that I would hate anyone who climbed through an almost vertical cornfield with my girlfriend a few days before we broke up.

The entire village noticed us come down the mountain together. Ida and Shotgun asked me about it, said people made comments to them.

Ida said people all over the world get the same idea when a boy and a girl come out of the bushes.

I felt his stare, and realized he caught me too deep in thought. No crime, but he looked at me hard and said, "Let's cut through the bullshit. You come clean with me and I'll give you a road map to your own future, deal?"

"Deal. Traveler's code of honor. We won't see each other again, so here's to honesty."

We lifted our beer mugs and clinked them together.

"Right!" Dennis said, downed the rest of his beer, wiped the foam off his lip with the back of his hand, and threw his arm up high to motioned for another round. "You seem like a pretty regular guy."

"You can leave out the pretty."

"When Yvonne first saw you, she pointed you out, said there's a handsome boy, a real pretty boy." He relaxed a little, slurred some words. Did he pretend to feel drunk?

"Her words? Pretty?"

"Not exactly. We both speak French, and as I remember it, she said puerre."

"What does that mean?"

"A fickle man, so boyishly handsome he learns to live off of women." He received his beer, and played with the foam that spilt over the top. "Maybe she meant you look like a nice guy, sweet maybe. She loves to spoil innocence. Tell me the truth, Brandon. What happened when you two climbed up above Santa Catarina together?"

I felt giddy inside. "You mean Yvonne and I? On the trail through the corn?"

He turned on the stool to face me and give me an insolent stare.

"We didn't go up together. We met on top of the ridge."

"How many times?"

"We met once. I mean by chance, not even once! We barely spoke, nothing romantic. We watched the sunset up there, and then helped each other down the trail as it got dark."

"Nothing romantic? Watched the sunset? Idiot." He spat out the words. "How do you think she felt about it?"

"OK. Maybe the romance of the situation got lost on me. Someone else could picture a guy, a girl, the tropics, sleepy Indian village, terraced cornfield hillsides, pine forest overlook, a dramatic sunset behind three volcanoes, twenty five square miles of water to reflect it, maybe some might think that a little romantic."

"You're breaking my heart."

"We didn't even talk. Didn't get each other's life story or anything. She didn't interest me much."

"You almost convinced me for a second." Dennis squinted at me and waited.

I continued, "OK, she's sexy, easy on the eyes. We were like any two people, didn't matter what gender. So what I'm a guy, she's a female, big deal. We didn't kiss goodbye, say see you later, or any of that crap."

Dennis stared far off into the wall mirror behind the liquor bottles, someplace beyond our reflections.

"You're how old?"

"Twenty two."

"You look younger. Maybe you don't know the score, yet. Men always think about sex, and it doesn't take women long to understand that."

"I agree, but that doesn't make all men gigolos."

"You've had girlfriends, right?"

"Sure."

"Then you know how people get tired of each other, most of the time, after the first month or two, three on the outside, when they begin to really know each other."

"Did Yvonne and you have a fight about me?"

"Yvonne said she wanted space, to leave her alone. Next thing I know, I look up and she's a comin' down the mountain with a man. You say that was chance?"

"As pure as the driven snow."

"I saw you go up after her."

"I never saw her until I got to the top. I swear."

"She didn't invite you up there?"

"How could she? No phone in my place. Your place got a phone? You seen a phone in the village?"

"She could pass by your house on the way up, or writes a note, sends an Indian kid to give it to you."

"If she knew where I lived, which I doubt."

"eHow many Gringos do you think live in Santa Catarina Palopó? Of course she could find you."

"At least you know my side of it now. Ask her yourself if you don't believe me. Wouldn't she tell you?"

"I waited to see if she'd tell me on her own, Sport. She didn't."

"She didn't tell you what?"

"Nothing."

"Then she told you the truth. Nothing to tell. Nothing."

"Suppose there was, would she tell me? To get me all upset over nothing? The thing is, Brandon, we didn't talk much at all after that." Dennis stared into the lands beyond the mirror, and waited.

"So you thought she and I, that something happened?"

"How would you feel? I waited, and she gives me the cold shoulder. That makes me angry. She acted sneaky, refused to talk to me. I couldn't sit by and watch her start something with another man right under my nose. She declared her independence, came and went as she pleased, and kept me in the dark to drive me crazy. I tried to act unconcerned and ignore her. Maybe that's what made it happen."

"Made what happen?"

"She fell in love with you, and decided to break up with me."

"Oh yeah, right." I felt surprised and flattered, got so hot under the collar, I tried not to blush. I thought I might drop my beer to divert his attention. Instead, I acted angry. "I don't even know the girl, and you say she fell in love with me?"

"Tell me first, what on earth," Dennis plucked a plastic straw, out of a glass full, stirred his beer and offhand said "brought you to San Jose on the mighty Pacific, Sport? Out of all the places in Guatemala, all the tourist places in the highlands and all the Mayan ruins in the jungle, what convinced you to see that sweaty armpit of a port town?"

He stirred his beer, smiled, and glanced at me in the mirror, to watch my expression change as I delivered my next answer.

I wondered if he knew she invited me to San Jose. "Tourists go to the ruins, to Chichicastenango or the Petén. I think I'm a traveler, like you and Yvonne and the others in Santa Catarina Palopó. We go where the tourists don't. San Jose looks good on the map. There's only three main roads in Guatemala, and it's the main Pacific Port. In spite of what people say about San Jose, I went because I like to swim."

"Swim? So why are you back in the city?"

"We all bump into each other in Guatemala City, don't we? Everybody comes here to get their mail."

"True enough. Every road brings you back to Guatemala City." He closed his eyes and swayed a little as he waited for me to continue.

I decided to call his bluff. "That day we went swimming in Lake Atitlán, Yvonne did ask me to come to San Jose, but I didn't. Not right away." I lied, "No one saw me there. "I thought she might try to use me to help pry her away from you."

"Bravo!" He toasted me. "The truth comes out! Any tidbits you've failed to mention?"

"Like what?" Did he think I would volunteer for some revenge fantasy he nursed on for over a month?

"Oh, like displays of affection, sweet nothings in the ear?"

"We brushed against each other while we tread water. How's that?"

"Touched what?"

"Toenails, I think. Maybe forearms. Does that count?"

"It counts, Sport. It counts. Like when she leans against you to say goodbye, follows you out of bars, hangs around Santa Catarina Palopó to talk to you before she can even think about leaving, little things like that. I notice. I keep track."

"Sounds like you wrote the book. Pure fiction."

A couple came in like one person, hugged together so close they pushed through the bar's Old West swinging doors to twitter across the floor and bounce their way into a shared booth seat in the darkest corner. They proceeded to fill the air with incongruous flutters of sexy laughter within that somber hunter's bar, full of furry desiccated trophies frozen in long toothed sneers of bravado.

"Did you leave the day of our swim?" I tried to derail his train of thought.

"Yes. Yvonne seemed so tired of our arrangements there, yet she stalled about leaving, found any excuse for not leaving, until she spoke to you." He drained his glass, ordered another round.

I watched the bubbles in my beer, felt superior to him. His jealousy helped keep me in Yvonne's consciousness. His jealousy forced her to think of me. I should thank him, but couldn't categorize it as a favor. Not yet.

This conversation ended there, for me. I knew where Dennis stood, what he believed, and my vague idea about how they parted fleshed out a bit. They both used me as an emotional wedge to divorce themselves. Maybe Dennis wants us to get drunk enough to unleash his testosteronized aggression, the icy cold wrath of a scorned Canadian's three weeks of sexual frustration. I imagine he might tie me to a dog sled's runners and take me round the Arctic Circle, all of it. At fifty pounds heavier than I, and a circus athlete, no contest.

I tried not to feel too concerned about it. I would rather use diplomacy to get out of interpersonal skirmishes. Profuse apologies as a low energy alternative, a momentary metamorphosis of my confident attitude into one of ingratiation, coupled with an unwillingness to resort to blows even if I catch a jab or two on the face. That might buy me enough respect or time to defuse, or extricate myself from, the situation.

Then again, Dennis hated me for the entire past month, and might take revenge against me for that. A man on the edge of drunk often dives into danger.

"What did you guys do in San Jose?"

"Gary loved it. We left Yvonne in the hotel and went out on the town, and Gary latched on to a very pretty whore, got to know her and her whole family in no time. Her boyfriend and her child weren't too crazy about him hanging around, but he paid their way. Yvonne spent her days at the beach, doing her lizard thing, as usual. She stretched out in the shadow of that ship and tanned in the shade."

"My God, ship's huge, isn't it?"

"And right up on the beach! We couldn't believe it. Gary ran up to it and yelled 'Momma! Take me home to Canada!' and we all cracked up." He laughed, "A good time, I guess. We made up some songs. Bars and whores and does and don'ts and little mamsy pansies, a kid'll eat panties too, wouldn't you? Or how about this one? Port town, sailors for tail or cunt. Rooms to rent, Quetzal a month."

"How did you and Yvonne part? On good terms?"

"The best," he said. "Gary and I got back to our room one night and she'd gone."

"Didn't she leave a note or anything?"

"Oh yeah. Don't worry about me, catch you later, thanks for everything, no hard feelings, enjoy your trip, empty fuckin' rot like that. We didn't talk much at that point anyway." He drifted off into some memory. A few more people came in, took tables behind us.

I finished my beer.

"Let me buy you another." Dennis pleaded, and could not accept my negations as an appropriate response. "It's the least I can do, after all you've done for me." He slapped my knee and ordered two more.

"What did I do for you?"

"You freed me from tyranny. You deserve a medal, a national decree, and a hero's welcome. So go on, play innocent, no idea why. Time to listen to the multitudes sing your praises! A toast to the beauty from France, and her Prince from... Where you from, again?"

"Michigan."

We clanged our glasses together.

"To Brandon's Michigan!"

"And back again! Dennis, you still miss her, don't you?" He sunk into a stupor.

"Sure," and he starts to mangle words as he sings lines of pop songs. "Don't you always scenic go, that you don't go on what you got till it's gone?" He downs a swig, wipes his lips and looks around the bar. "What are little girls made of? Candy and spice and everything nice, till they grow up to make bastards of us all."

"Spice is the plural of spouse."

"That's right. All women, like Jesus, become fishers of men. They hook each one, and keep as many as possible hanging on the line. And she's a French girl, for chrissakes! They think of sex like handshakes. You're lucky if they bathe in between partners." He giggled.

"What is it about the French?"

"Sex is their national pastime. She wants to make her life a feminist's soap opera."

We each threw down enough thick, medieval Guatemalan coin to cover the drinks.

The lovebirds get up to leave. We turned to nod goodbye as they twitter to each other in their own little world. Arm in arm, that alternative reality left the bar.

We ordered another round, and played a game of pool.

Then Dennis said, "You haven't ever lefter you the best part."

"Lefter you the best part?"

"Let me parter you the best. No. Let me TELL you the best part." He cleared his throat, and thought it funny, coughed to get over his giddiness.

He leaned back in his elegant barstool carved from Petén hardwoods, and looked at me too long.

Made me nervous. "What?"

He fought back laughter as I grew more uncomfortable.

"Look." He leans his face close to mine, sits there and pants, breath stunk of kerosene, his blue eye steady gaze with lids in a slow droop. "You seem truthful with me, you tell me the truth, at least I think you do, and I respect you for it. I respect you. Let me level with you, Sport. For a long time now, I blamed you for how Yvonne and I split up. I planned to kick your ass bloody, promised myself I'd do it next time I saw you." He paused to let that sink in.

It of sunk somewhere, but I felt too soggy to feel threatened anymore.

He put his hand on my shoulder and said. "I don' wanna anymore. I miss her, sure, weeks now, and she's doing OK. Good luck. Tha's all I wanna say now."

He looked at me. Looked back at his drink, and did a slow dive for it.

After he took a swallow he said, "Got something to say."

"Me? No. You?"

"You bet I got something to say." He leaned close, conspiratorial, as if someone might overhear, as if they could understand English well enough, even if they did overhear us. "After that night, you know when you watched the sunset together, things changed. Everything. Well not exactly that way, almost. It accelerated the process, that's what it did."

"What process?"

"We bitched at each other, first in fun, but Gary hung around like a child, tedious. No privacy, you know. Imagine. Anyhow, after she met you up there, it felt over. I mean nothing. Like brothers and sisters, only guilty and resentful. A man gets angry, without sex. Starts fights over silly things, argue."

"I know what you mean. Like married people."

"Wait. There's more." He held his hand up to stop me from talking. "Much more. She dreamed about you, Sport." He studied my face to get my reaction.

"How do you know?" I asked incredulous.

"She told me. She talked in her sleep." He giggled. "Out loud, plain as you and me right now. I lay awake, I could tell she dreamt with someone, someone else."

"She mentioned my name?"

"No. But I've got magic to ferret out the truth. Remember when I put the nail into my nose? Tricks, my good man. I've learned centuries of magician's lore in the circus. I learned hypnotism."

I felt instant skepticism as I looked at him and tried not to let it show.

"You don't believe me. Hypnotism. Suggestion. It's not what you think, it's what you are."

I took a cigarette from his pack and lit it, as I said "Magic sparks from the fingertips, shiny watches swung before the eyes, that sort of thing?"

"You're already hypnotized by what others suggest you should be. Advertising. Real hypnotism started out as Mesmerism, and they sold it as animal magnetism. Psychologists call it suggestion, no matter. Remember subliminal messages at the movies?"

"You mean sex?"

"No, well yeah kind of. That gets in there too. People discovered that messages flashed onto the screen too fast to read influenced the number of people who bought popcorn and hot dogs. Declared illegal, too powerful, devious, unfair. Takes away the right of choice."

"So?"

"You've taken drugs, right? Sometimes reality ain't real, and it ain't what our parents thought."

"What's this got to do with Yvonne? You turned her into a Zombie?"

"Wish I could. Make a hell of a lot of money in San Jose."

"So she talked in her sleep, right?"

"In her dream. He rolled up his sleeve like a magician. "You won't believe this. Get this." He pressed close again, his hands open to make a window frame. "She's sleeping in one morning, right? I hear her mumble, and see her eyes closed but her eyeballs underneath moving like she's watching something move."

"Dreaming."

"Yeah. So I make some light sounds in the room, and she doesn't wake. I cozy up, say, 'Hi, Yvonne. What's up?' but in French, of course." Dennis paused.

"And?"

"She acted surprised to see me. She dreamt, I could see it on her face. Then she asked what I wanted. I didn't feel positive sure she still dreamt, but I went for it anyway. I asked who she talked to. She said, "None of your business." So I said 'Yvonne?' And she said 'What now?' I said, in a very reasonable voice, very smooth, 'I've got a letter here' 'Give it to me' she says. 'It's not for you. It's for that person you're with. She said 'give it to him then.' So I knew she talked to a man. I said, I can't give it to him until you tell me his name. 'He can tell you himself' she says to me. So I gambled. I told her he can't tell me because he doesn't speak French."

"Like that, she blurts out my name. Brandon?"

Dennis snaps his fingers. "Maybe she didn't say Brandon exactly, or I didn't hear it clear as a bell, you know, but she said something in French. I heard what I wanted to hear."

"Maybe she faked it, and used my name because it bugged you the most."

"There's more, Sport. She and I talked about her dreams later, when we got on more like brother and sister, advice and stuff, you know. She incorporated that imaginary letter into her dream. The letter in the dream contained a poem I sent to her once, a real good one, one of my best love poems, one she lost on the trip. I think she got mad at me early on, and threw it away before I got a chance to copy it. Spiteful Bitch. She dreamed you sent that letter to her, which I took as a clear sign she replaced me with you, at least in her dreams."

"And you helped."

He laughed at the irony. "She falls in love with you because of a poem I wrote her!"

"I swear, Dennis, she doesn't even know me."

"Settle down, don't get your panties in a bunch. It's chemistry, or fate. Her obsession with you got worse each time she saw you. At the disco, the Christmas party, swimming."

I thought about it for a while, looked for answers in the froth of my beer, and asked, "When did you see her last?"

"Couple of weeks ago. I bet she's looking for you, Sport."

"Sure?"

"She gets what she wants from the men she chooses. Never let her think she lost control. Try to convince her that she seduces you, not the other way around. If nothing happens between you two, it's because you're too stupid and innocent. That makes you irresistible to her. Look, no matter how small the village, every person finds someone to love. She isn't attracted to short brown men in pajama shorts and sandals, so here in Guatemala, she finds scant few eligible bachelors. She's in full flower, an exotic French orchid hid somewhere in this jungle, and you're the pollinator wasp ,the honeybee. Just follow your nose and reap your reward, my man."

The barman delivered two more. I figured Dennis ordered them with a glance.

"This beer's warm" Dennis said to no one. Then he motioned to the bartender, "Ice cubes."

I asked him why the ice cubes, and he told me he liked to chew on them when he got drunk. Reminded him of his childhood in Canada. When the ice cubes came, I took a couple and plopped them into my beer.

"Bottoms up."

We drank.

Dennis licked beer foam off his fingers, dried his hands on a napkin, lit a cigarette, and spoke with a German accent. "Vee men must shtick togedder, and forget dees ridiculous guilt about our misogyny."

"Do you think it helps to talk about this stuff?"

"Hey Sport, I'll tell you one thing, in your shoes right now, I'd try to find her and pray to God I don't. You won't regret it at first, but later you'd like to kill yourself. Or her."

"Doesn't it seem suspicious to you? This dream and all, she faked the whole thing. It suits her purpose, to get away from you, know what I mean?"

We drank in silence for a while, and then his words rattled in my ears like the ice cubes in my beer.

"She thinks of herself as an expert in male behavior. She loves to tell stories of her adventures as a seductress, a manipulator of men, an alchemist of infatuations. You will be transformed, if you hook up with her. No one stays young and stupid unless it kills them first. Enjoy your education."

Drunken Bawl

We left the bar arm in arm, and felt each other's young muscles tense in competition. We separated and faced off against the chill of Guatemala's high central valley, to walk the empty streets alone under the stars of a predatory universe.

We walked an arms length apart all the way back to the center of town, then across Guatemala's empty Central Plaza, the vacant theater for each day's pageant. He taught me a couple of Canadian drinking songs to sing as we marched through the park.

Our song woke up the dogs and a couple of alcoholics dressed in the disintegration of cotton denim and hand woven Mayan fabrics. They sat up out from under flattened cardboard boxes to look at us cross eyed, then leaned away from each other to cough and spit once before they lay back down.

An old schizophrenic woman, a mountain of shawls, saw us come her way, became frightened, and shuffled across the street. She stopped at the sidewalk's next pile of filth and garbage, and plundered about with her foot.

We shared the last cigarette, tensed against the chill, and dared the thugs and hoods to come out and try us.

Then Dennis took a swing at me.

I felt the wind, or heard the rustle of his jacket, as Dennis leaned away from me to draw his arm back for a punch aimed at my chin. He missed.

I pushed him away. "What's that for?"

"You think that's it about you and Yvonne? She left me with your name on her lips. You're fucking ridiculous! All your posturing, the purity of poverty, I recognized you right off, another American middle class socialist brat with enough money to exist as a starving artist in paradise, another Gauguin among the Natives. A trust fund, that's how you do it. A shit head who slums around to benefit from other people's poverty. Got news for you, they don't need your fake charity or your money. You Americans, with your demonic encoder rings from a cereal box, geniuses in your own minds, pathetic pretenders who lust for economic success because you equate wealth with personal accomplishment, personal worth, and general happiness. Jesus wants you to be fucking rich, says you. I should kick your ass for you, do the world a big favor. Fucking Americans."

"This is about Yvonne, right? So leave me out of it. What's she to you? You met her on the road, easy come, easy go. You wanna marry her or what?"

He swung again, and we both lost balance and clutched each other in a drunken dance.

"Hey Sport, you know the difference between a man in a fight and a man making love? If you don't, you're dumber than I thought. Not much difference at all. Almost identical, fucking scientists like that Kinsey pervert say."

"Everybody's been talking about that. An erection. A man in a fight doesn't have an erection. Otherwise they're identical. So what?"

"You better hope I get an erection, or I'm gonna kick your ass!" He came at me again.

I stepped aside to watch him stumble off for fifteen feet, then he stopped himself.

"Dennis, you know the night watchman at your hotel? That young boy who sleeps by the door to let people in at night?"

"Yeah."

"You think he's cute, don't you? Kinda small, slim butt, soft feminine eyes?"

Dennis stood unsteady and panted, out of breath, to glare at me. "You might say he's cute. Did you think he was cute?"

"Asshole."

We sat on the Church of Merced's apron of red stone slabs. We both made vague comments about its beauty, as we bobbed and faded in and out.

I became the insignificant center of the universe, an insect, so small in front of the cathedral, its front a face with arched, stain glass window eyes turned heavenward, the door a mouth frozen in a giant yawn.

I wanted to get rid of Dennis, and reminded him about a gang of Guatemalan street boys that beat a young male transvestite close to death one recent night.

Before I could mention it, the world spun round, the sky fell upon me, I couldn't breathe, my elbow slipped off my knee, and I threw up.

Parque Zoologico

Archeologists refer to deposits of distinct pottery styles as horizons, because they help link concurrent cultures to the same time. Techniques of pottery manufacture and style, the decorations, shapes, and colors, spread through travel and trade with a cultural intermix on the edges of regions. Horizon markers for the Early Formative (1500 - 900 BC) include the tecomate, or globular neckless jar, and Olmec excised pottery, especially with decorations where red pigment color zones lie among incised lines, or with the sophisticated use of "rocker stamps", a technique where potters impressed the wet clay with the edge of a stick or shell.

After the Olmeca's influence waned around 900 BC, other "Mamom"
cultures coalesced into what became the Middle Formative (900 - 300 BC) cultures
of the Mayan lowlands. Archeologists refer to this timeframe as the Xe horizon, and
its female figurines often help to date archeological finds.

Ceramic horizon markers for the Middle Formative (900 - 300 BC) exist
over much of Meso-America, through the diffusion of a very hard white pottery
decorated with incised lines, and by solid pottery figurines that stare with large eyes
formed by a punch. The mysterious people who replaced, perhaps overthrew, the
Olmeca at San Lorenzo (900 BC) made similar pottery and figurines.

These "Mamom" cultures shared some styles with the later Highland Mayan
cultures with monochromatic pottery in red, orange, black, and white, and their
figurines, with punched and appliqué decorations, most often depict females.

Someone knocked, several times, the next morning and sent my
hangover into a painful throb. She knocked every five minutes, until I invited
her to open the door. She asked if I felt all right.

I pointed to my head and made hand motions as if I held a beer mug.
She laughed. No one bothered me for a while.

Much later, I made my way downstairs to the kitchen. The 'house
mother' boiled a huge pot of vegetable chicken soup atop the cast iron gas
range. They offered me a bowlful, and cooled it with a spoonful of green
leaves of cilantro, cut up fine and mixed with chopped onions, chased by the
acidic juice of a lime half. They knew I knew how to do it, but they wanted to
dote on me. They forced me to drink plenty.

Then that Italian muscle-head came in and teased the maid in
Spanish. He made up some story about the maid and I in my room together,
with the most obscene of Guatemalan hand gestures, his thumb inserted
rhythmically between the same hand's forefingers.

The maid reddened, looked like she might cry, and then ran out of
the kitchen. The housemother scolded the jerk, but he laughed too hard to
hear her, and walked away.

I went back to the room, to rummage through my pack for any
aspirin, and read.

Later that day, I took a bus to the Parque Zoologico, got there an
hour or so before it closed. Time enough to see the few animals they cared
for. The tapirs nuzzled each other like happy pigs. As usual, the big cats,
ocelots and jaguars remained out of sight in the day.

The reptile exhibit interested me. Throughout my boyhood, I caught
snakes with impunity in Michigan because I thought only one little pigmy
rattlesnake lived there. I got bit twenty seven times by non-venomous
snakes, fifteen of which by the same mean, scarred up black watersnake.

At one point in the reptile house, I felt faint and so dizzy I weaved a
bit and reached out to steady myself. Maybe the hangover, dehydration, or a
lack of calcium or something. Happened right as I stumbled up to an empty
exhibit.

In front of a glass display case with a pool of water, a small book lay
pinned open. I recognized the book as American, in English, one of a popular
Pocket Field Guide series. These slim full color books detail a species on

each page with an illustration of the animal or several related species, and a tiny line drawn map of continents shaded with the range of each animal.

The book showed a long, green, flat tailed Sea Snake, a representation of the snake caught on the beach in Hawaii, the one the kids threw at each other until I picked it up and forced its mouth open and thought that without fangs, it represented no danger.

Someone at the zoo used a transparent yellow marker to highlight the text where it explained that one bite meant death, the venom injected by means of small fangs set in the rear of the mouth.

At that moment more than any other, my youthful immortality ended. I recognized youth's fearlessness as an instinct to ignorant bravado, a genetic program that gives young men the power to become brave, loyal soldiers who risk their lives to protect their tribe, and thus swell to heroic proportions.

CHAPTER 11: The Petén

Since the nineteenth century, archeologists and explorers uncovered Mayan ruins in southern North America, from central and south Mexico into the vast regions of the Yucatán's three Mexican States of Chetumál, Yucatán, Quintana Roo. The region of Mayan influence extends down into Northern Central America, in Guatemala's Petén, and along the Pacific Coast from the southernmost Mexican state of Chiapas south into Honduras and El Salvador. Even more Mayan ruins may lay undiscovered throughout the region's forests and swampy jungles, hidden under the vegetation.

More than 50 known sites deserve consideration as major. Most lie in the Central Subregion, with the greatest concentration in northern Petén, where the Mayan civilization's roots run deepest. The Petén region covers the Northern third of Guatemala as a southern continuation of Mexico's Yucatán peninsula, a mostly flat Karst topography of limestone built of sediments deposited undersea millions of years ago. Tikál, the largest and best known Classic site of the Central Subregion, lies amid this Karst topography of limestone where the vegetation depletes the scant accumulations of soil nutrients. Yet a population of tens of thousands lived there for at least a half a millennium to leave a record in stone of the Golden Age of Mayan civilization.

To see how the other half lived, I lived on the cheap and discovered a rainbow of ways the other half lived, like a mountain climber on the summit sees more mountains beyond, or a scientist discovers that answers to questions lead to better questions. I wanted to see other parts of Guatemala and the world, not only contemporary, but in the past, to get a handle on these conquered cultures lumped under the term Meso-American. I wanted to see Tikál, but when I added that to my itinerary, a cash shortage loomed ahead like a giant stop sign.

I wanted to stay longer than planned. After all the work to get this far, I wanted to extend my journeys beyond Tikál, into Belize and Honduras, maybe to Brazil.

Brazil fascinated me as a country with sixteen or so terms for various 'racial' mixtures. I mistook that as an indication of a tolerant and classless society, instead of evidence of one of the most segmented and discriminatory society on the planet.

I walked to Guatel, the Guatemalan phone company, to use the public phones lined up on the sidewalk in front. From inside one of those powder blue half-egg plastic cowlings, I called home to ask mom to transfer the rest of my funds to Bank of America's international unit so they could send it down to the Guatemalan branch. Next day I called her again. She said everything OK, it would take a few days for the funds to clear the banks and arrive in Central America.

My guitar and extra stuff could stay in the Pensión while I traveled with the little cash left in my money belt. I suspected that more money lay hid in the structure of my backpack.

The money from Michigan should arrive by the time I get back from Tikál.

I decided not to fly, but to take the long bus ride through the Petén to Tikál. The bus ride meant twenty four hours cooped up in an old US school bus, instead of a couple of expensive hours on a plane. It cost over a hundred dollars to fly, and at five dollars a day, that one flight would cut a month out of the time my money allotted me.

I would rather see the country than fly over it, I reasoned.

The bus left the station around sunset. This school bus came with the original kid sized seats, two on the left, three on the right with a narrow, almost central, aisle. When three adults tried to sit in the right side seats, myself and two stout Mayan women, I got pushed over until I sat on the aisle, literally, with about five inches of my right buttock on the seat and the rest of me suspended in midair.

On my left, a huge, fat, Hispanic 'Negra' black woman straddled the center aisle from her seat. We supported each other through body pressure, like bricks in an arch, and saved each other from the embarrassment of a fall to the floor with each bump. We wedged in so tight, on rough stretches of road we grunted together and inhaled to help pressure our way back firm onto the seat.

I wondered if the word purchase, when used to mean a firm hold to keep from slipping, evolved from such a bus ride. I purchased a five inch purchase on that seat with my ticket, and couldn't wait till someone got off the bus to improve the situation.

As public transportation fueled by the profit motive, buses also serve as local service. The drivers pick up anyone who waits alongside the road, no matter how full the bus, to let them stand and ride until they reached the correct crossroad or trailhead in the middle of nowhere.

The pressure never let up. Most of us would sit on this bus for the long haul. All through the night our heads bobbed upon our chests, and the luckiest, exhausted into sleep, lolled their heads back and snored. A chilly damp air came in through the windows and made us grateful for the press of hot flesh on either side.

Almost sleepless, I felt exhausted when I saw the sunrise come up in rosy streaks behind the boughs of giant trees and the palms along the high ridges, ink blot silhouettes like fashion models with big hair. As the sky lightened, I could see how precarious our route. We often careened down a one lane gravel road, a delicate ribbon scraped into the face of a jungle mountain cliff side above a drop off into a gorgeous canyons full of the tops of trees in flower, perhaps hundreds of feet tall, or mere bushes that resembled stands of gigantic broccoli, difficult to distinguish which.

The first time the bus stopped to drop off some Indians, I stood up to wiggle and insinuate my way forward from the bus to beg the baggage handler to let me ride up top with him.

To convince him, I hid my sheer terror and desperation of another twelve hours sandwiched between the sweaty shoulder of the Negress and the cotton cushioned shoulders of the two stone faced Mayan ladies, my butt suspended over the open aisle, and tried to convince him through open adulation of the jungle, the sky, Guatemala.

Still he refused to permit it.

I asked him where he rode.

He pointed up top.

Then I pleaded to his humanity, complained about the ache in my back, the open space under me, the pressure of the fat ladies, and it would make more room inside the bus. "Soy joven, no voy a caer." I'm young, I won't fall off the top of the bus. I pictured myself sprawled out like a big cat stuck like Velcro to the flank of a big yellow elephant.

He smiled, and agreed. We shook hands. He showed me how to climb up on top.

For the next five hours or so, I stretched out and massaged my overworked left leg in a great happy sprawl across the lumpy rope-net baggage on top of the bus. The baggage handler and I smiled at each other, no fools. He smiled a lot at first, but got serious to put a hand out and warn me of the approach of trees with low branches, or curves with steep canyons where the bus lurched and bumped over boulders impossible to bulldoze flat.

I tried to write impressions in my tiny pink journal, kept in my shirt's vest pocket. Flowers, fluorescent reds and yellows, covered some trees like snow, as if sunlight kissed the upper layers of leaves into blossoms to delight us. I tried to imagine what the jungle looked like from inside. Singular tall palms marched in line along the high mountain ridges and reminded me of Old Western movies with Indians in full war bonnets.

I wrote and wrote the best I could, to get it all down, between the lurches and bucks atop the shifty cargo. On one violent surprise bump, I flew into the air and came down near the edge of the bus and started to slip off. The baggage handler grabbed my belt, and I panicked, both hands clutched handfuls of rope and baggage. I heaved myself back to center and noticed my journal slip from between my fingers to flutter across the baggage. I dove for it, but it bounced around my fingers and caught in the wind.

The baggage man pulled me back by the belt, as I watched my little pink journal flutter in the wind of our passage to butterfly over the edge of the bus, and spiral down into the leafy chaos of the jungle canyon.

I watched it fall through space, a pocket-size rosy orange stapled paper artifact that tumbled into the flowery mounds of vegetation, a record of three months of travel in handwritten English few could read, almost nobody here could understand, that no living person would ever see again.

The baggage handler looked at me and smiled, shrugged, and gave me the upside down smile. Fatalism. I felt sick. All those notes to myself over the past months, the observations, poems, song lyrics, ideas, snippets of conversations, names and addresses.

I thought of a few tidbits reread recently in idle moments, and how I felt proud of the words when well put, or lucky that I kept such a record of ideas and interests for future pursuits. I also lost pages written in my special script, designed for pitch dark on bumpy buses, a large scrawl which I often failed to decipher.

The bus stopped to let us eat about midday.

The space inside the bus opened up towards afternoon, when more Indians left than got on. Then the driver and baggage handler ushered me inside the bus, and refused to let me ride up top.

In the muggy heat of afternoon, many of us sat and slept.

Right at sunset, the rumor spread through the bus that we approached the jungle rimmed lake, Lago Petén Itzá, where the map shows an island city called Flores. We stopped alongside a square building at the edge of the lake and saw the lights of Flores' houses reflect across the calm lake surface in long wriggles of thin white ribbon.

All forty of us got off the bus, most Ladinos, eight or so tourists travelers like me, and a few Indians who shouldered huge bags and bundles to strike out toward a small bus terminal market nearby. Others got into dugout canoes to cross the lake to Flores, or other communities that glittered with diamond fires along the distant northern lakeshore.

As darkness fell, the electric lights of Flores painted a fantasy city on a small, low island of rock. I could either walk all the way across a low, one-lane automobile bridge to the island city, or let a boatman in a dugout canoe paddle me over the calm lake's mirror surface.

The bus drivers loaded the bus with the bags and bundles of people headed back to Guatemala City.

The boatmen refused to take any travelers to the island. They said, "No hotels in Flores."

The nearest hotels lay many miles away in the jungle, on the way to Tikál. The taxi drivers circled us like sharks and offered us outrageous fares, at almost the cost of a hotel room. It illustrates the problem of greed and corruption in captured market economies, and contrasts with the gentle humanism of Latin America in general, with the Mayan Indians who sell you their loom for twenty bucks even though it takes days to rebuild one.

The richer tourists took that long taxi ride into the jungle to find the hotels and hunter's lodges nearer Tikál.

Impossible on a five dollar a day budget, and all of us 'budget travelers' felt trapped. We gathered in polyglot knots to relay the same information over and over, that the workmen and the three guards opined unanimous, "All Public transportation stops for the night, and starts tomorrow at seven o'clock."

The guards invite people inside the shelter of the storeroom, to lay down amid the baggage and bundles, and sleep all night for five dollars per person.

A swindle, but manageable, and the thought of what the mosquito filled, snake infested, rain soaked jungle swamp would do to us by morning encouraged all to reach into their wallet.

So a reluctant stream of travelers, about twenty in all, entered the storeroom, a large windowless cement rectangle with a tin roof unattached at the top of the walls to let mosquitoes in. I came in late, and staked out a somewhat level group of bags to lay down atop, careful not to crush whatever they contained.

After a while, I heard the screams of some of the others, and recognized German accents, then the Spanish word for rats, rata, intoned with several European and American accents.

The gaps between the bundles, net bags, and cardboard boxes created a haphazard maze, a miniature city, with thoroughfares on the cement floor of the storeroom and higher passageways over the tops of boxes and between the plastic or rope net bags that bulged and leaned into each other for stability. I could hear the scrapes and nibbles as the rats scurried about or stopped to chew.

I dropped off into a light sleep, face down, but woke several times with a rat right underneath me. Each time I struck out blind, angry, fearful, and disgusted, but quiet to not wake the others.

The lapels of my Sololá jacket hung down into the crevice between a box and a bag of wooden artifacts. One time, I woke up to find a rat eye to eye with me. It clung to the front lapel of my jacket.

We both panicked. It exited through the neck of my jacket as I wore it, and I jumped up about four feet into the air from a prone position. I felt the rat's warm fur brush my cheek and ear, and heard its claws rasp on my collar for a foothold.

Didn't sleep very well after that.

Rainforest

Meso-Americans quarried limestone to build with, and often came upon intrusions of hard glassy igneous rocks to make arrowheads, spear points, or knives to work wood and stone. They used obsidian, black volcanic glass, to create elaborate decorative items, even eighteen inch long 'knives' shaped like bizarre alphabet letters with complex edge decorations similar to their serpent head architectural embellishments. Mayans also manufactured a cement-like mortar and plaster out of burnt limestone or shells, but never invented a true arch, which limited the size of rooms inside their stone temples.

Over the millennia, acid rich ground waters from the decomposition of leaves ate away at cracks in the layered limestone rock to form underground river systems and 'cenotes', or sinkhole water wells. The Mayans believe in an interconnected Underworld of underground rivers from which cenotes surface like hungry mouths, doorways for the soul's entrance into the underworld.

People roused themselves in the first glow of dawn. Many of us wanted to get out of the storeroom before sunrise, and as soon as the guard unlocked the door, several of us bolted outside to smoke a cigarette. The shore of a smoky Lago Petén Itzá melted into the jungle fog, but you could approximate it by the line of orange lights in the mist, where people prepared breakfast over open fires.

I waited alongside the storeroom with the others to take the first public bus headed to Tikál.

The bus sped along on a good paved road through the jungle. A couple of times I could see a couple of shacks where wood smoke wove through the trees. The bus passed bare grey dirt clearings where ladino men stood and looked at us with their machetes in hand, while small dogs and dirty faced children played nearby. Short legged, barrel bodied Mayan women with round heads and owlish faces walked along the black earth trails that intersected the road. Most balanced large bowls on their heads filled with water, or masa for tortillas, or maybe hot food to take into the tourist zone to sell.

As the bus sped along, I toyed with the idea of a walk through the expanses of jungle with sparse habitants, straight north into Mexico's Yucatán Peninsula. Tales of little known ruins, uncharted unknown territories, primitive tribes of Indians, and isolated encampments of criminal Chicle gatherers piqued my interest. The possibility of an encounter with venomous Fer De Lance snakes, a huge rattle-less diamond backed rattlesnake, aggressive and known to chase people, influenced my decision.

I wondered about how to walk, or somehow traverse, the hundreds of miles of empty green on my map labeled Petén. Few people lived there, maybe with good reason.

Why live so far from civilization? A need to hide or escape? Maybe these chicle gatherers got their bad reputation the hard way, they earned it. In the jungle, people probably exist as hunter-gatherers who fish, find vegetables, hunt, locate honey, lumber, or otherwise mine some resource to sell, in constant movement for your family's sustenance. Or maybe they work for contract and gather chicle, or guard and harvest cultivated jungle fields of marijuana.

I bet the men who lived in such conditions outnumbered woman by a long shot, and might consider me the next best thing.

The bus passed a few crude wooden bungalows with hand painted hotel signs. At last we drove into a large clearing made for a parking area, where uniformed transportation workers herded us into little shuttles to drive us into the Parque Nacionál.

We drove with the windshield wipers' slap as a rhythmic counterpoint to eight track tapes of Cumbia music. The flat gray of the windshield looked like the view from a plane that flies through a cloud, except for hints of treetops where the fog lessened.

Our bus arrived at the park entrance with the cars of the day's first tourists, and we all unloaded into a soggy forest.

I noticed a few groundskeepers walked around with rakes. The forest reminded me of Michigan's oak forests grazed by cows, the underbrush cleared away, a slight green fur of grass. Cool and shady, but very wet under the tall and too slender vine-clad forest trees. I could see my exhalation. Water condensed on any flat surface, and droplets grew fat and fall from the leaves as water grenades.

It drizzled on and off all morning without stop under the trees, which continued to drip long after the drizzle stopped. The music of drips, chirps, twig snaps, and buzzes merged into a gentle murmur.

This soggy quiet shattered into mad vortexes of leafy tornadoes as a troop of monkeys screamed, leaped, and chattered above, in the canopy. They seemed to call out to other similar hubbubs in the leaf-muffled cathedrals, and awakened other creatures to start a cascade of sounds from big mouth birds and raspy insects that each argued for sonic domination.

Few bugs flew around, so I looked for more in the undergrowth and found plenty. Many sported bright colors and hornlike protuberances. Spiders with horned or spiked projections, bodies resembled spiky crab carapaces, stalked the floor, hid under broken branches, leaves and bark. Others spun invisible orb webs in a spiral to the middle, where they sat and floated like spiky plastic.

Guatemalans and Mexicans alike describe each and every spider as "Veneno, venenoso" venomous, one bite, dead, etc. I lost faith in their knowledge, but I don't go out of my way to touch spiders as a rule, period. I feet much confident with snakes.

I used to feel more confident with snakes, before Hawaii.

Tikál

Of the six temple pyramids that loom over Tikál, the Temple of the Sun stands 230 feet high as the tallest structure ever built by the Meso-Americans. Lintels of sapodilla wood, once decorated with colorful reliefs of Maya lords on thrones amid luxurious surroundings, still span some doorways. Excavations of Late Classic tombs extracted collections of bone tubes sketched with beautiful detailed depictions of Mayan rulers and gods.

Research at this largest of Mayan ceremonial sites suggests that the Chicanel people (Late Formative 300 BC - AD 100), built the earliest structures that underlie the Tikál Acropolis. Both at Tikál and Uaxactún, architects used white stuccoed platforms and stairways flanked by polychromed masks. Corbel vault roofs, stone A-frames, gave an arch-like ceiling to long, narrow rooms.

In the extreme northern part of Petén that borders Mexico's Yucatán and Quintana Roo states, discoveries of other large sites (Calakmul and El Mirador) with cultural conformity suggest that a huge Chicanel population existed under central political rule.

The areas around Tikál, when analyzed through satellite and air-borne radar and enhanced with false-color photography, show an ancient canal system for irrigation, and ten huge reservoirs to store up potable water for Tikál. As it became the grandest Mayan city of all, Tikál grew to over 3,000 structures, and small mounds accreted a new layer with each new ruler or regime to become these temple pyramids, all within six square miles. Archeologists estimate the population at 10,000 - 11,000 people, with as many as 100,000 within the agricultural area that served Tikál.

The Spanish relate that the Maya buried their dead beneath the floors of their homes, which they then abandoned, so the evidence for the great number of homes around Tikál may not reflect the number of live inhabitants at any one time.

I climbed the biggest pyramid, two hundred thirty feet of tiny steps, aided by a low chain suspended knee high on iron poles driven into the rock along the pyramid's central staircase. The steps, steep and wet and too shallow for the whole foot, did not invite people to pause, pass each other, nor rest. Some people did stop to make a slow, careful turn to enjoy the view while they caught their breath. More elder, rather than teenager, attempted the climb.

When this first group of tourists got halfway up the pyramid, blue sky peeked out between the low cloud fluffs of shattered jungle fog.

It took a while for us to pull ourselves up to the platform on top. On top, I stood above the height of the jungle that surrounded Tikál, and I felt the sense of authority and mastery over all I surveyed, and imagined how it might feel to take part in a ritual so high above thousands of people. As the sun evaporated away the last of the low clouds and jungle mist, the day warmed up enough to force people to remove their sweaters and wear them looped around their necks. Below, the teenagers and parents felt the heat of the sun and humidity and unfolded their arms to tie sweater or jacket around their waist.

The temple illustrates the methods of Mayan architecture, platforms built on a cemented rubble core, once covered with thick layers of plaster. Rooms at Tikál illustrate how Mayan architects used the corbel vault principle, where they achieved over-arched structures by laying brick walls tilted inward, until they meet at the top to press against each other for strength and stability.

When the sun came out, so did the groundskeepers with rakes across their shoulders. Between the pyramids and other complexes, the flat mown expanses of 'courtyard' areas shined and glinted like wet emeralds in between the black fungus stained limestone temples. They stuck up like the snouts of whales through the leafy chaos of the jungle canopy, with some trees in full bloom with big clusters of yellow and red blossoms.

I wondered how the Maya maneuvered the blocks of stone up steep slopes against the pull of gravity. Thousands of workers could build a long inclined plane to construct each side. The Maya left no evidence they used wheels except on toys.

On top, the Mayans constructed a shallow room that resembles a full size version of the tiny Catholic shrines along the road where a traffic accident took the life of a loved one, except that here, no one put plastic flowers inside, or lit candles every six hours.

From the ground, the pyramid's shape also enforced a false perspective, as if the top signified a point near an infinite distance, which exaggerates the size of people on top.

When civilizations gain enough leisure time through successful agriculture, rulers need monuments as proof of their powers. The surplus of food and person hours liberates people to explore and discover, invent lifestyles and culture, stratify society, divide labor, and invent clubs for its masons, doctors, teachers, architects, artisans, courtesans, etc. to pass on their esoteric knowledge. At some point in the evolution of many societies, the necessary megalomania of a born leader convinces their populations to build temples and monuments to honor theirself. Thus the ruling class begins to appear to the multitudes as the Gods themselves, with supreme powers to cause death, enhance life, and cure people who get well on their own.

The last doctor who treats a patient that would get well no matter what, gets all the credit. The cured tend to credit the last treatment instead of their own immune system.

Tourists on the way up complicated the first group's descent along that one chain lifeline. The wet steps, nearest the chain very polished and rounded by millions of tourists sneakers, seemed more hazardous to those in descent.

I figured out why. If one falls while headed up, one stops. Fall on a descent, you accelerate. Much worse.

Imagine fifteen hundred years ago, how the successive generations of Mayans watched, awestruck, as these monuments grew, king after king, layer after layer. Imagine the sensations of subjects and strangers alike when they come to Tikál for the first time and see the massive proportions of these manmade mountains and the intricacy of the sophisticated embellishments in these ceremonial centers.

I walked across the spacious fields of short, lush, well manicured, and very wet grass between the pyramids.

A huge population of people once lived and worked in the nearby area, even if Tikál served as site for ceremony instead of what we now think of as a functional city. Hard to imagine that life under today's conditions. Where did they grow all the crops necessary to sustain Tikál's laborers and priesthoods?

The pyramids today peak out over the jungle treetops. Did men build such temples on purpose among such tall trees, or did open fields once surround Tikál? Where did the rock come from, and how did they move the blocks of stone without wheeled wagons?

Detectives in Time, we search through the rubble of human garbage for the story of prehistory, and discover the route our ancestors traveled to invent today. Curiosity forces us to reconstruct forgotten histories and unearth abandoned cities to decipher the stories of failed societies, often victims of marauders or culture wars that end in purposeful eradication of the weaker.

The most important things to look for in excavations, to dust off and bring to light again, may not exist in the architectural ruins or the extant remains of monuments to military leaders, but in the libraries, churches, and on the walls of homes, evidence that may reflect the human psyche, the graphic clues that lead us to conjecture about their dance and song, matrimony and child-rearing, all the social learning we call tradition.

I listened to the tour guides explain the ball courts, where the players competed in a football-basketball game with a ball of solid rubber, the chicle sap collected from the local trees. They bounced this solid rubber ball off their hips and aimed at stone hoops, vertical instead of horizontal, placed high on the walls of the ball court.

I can't imagine anyone's hip could smack a big solid ball of heavy rubber that high up the wall to pass through the feathered serpent decorated stone hoop.

The other tourists listened with their mouths slack and open. The tour groups sorted themselves by language around each translator/tour guide to receive questionable knowledge in their native language, without question.

Many of these international travelers wore trendy jungle hiker's boots, khakis or bright colored shorts, jungle 'playera' T-shirts or 'beach shirts' printed in Hawaii with colors to drive butterflies crazy, andsometimes with a long sleeve sweater as a light jacket.

Sweat didn't cool us. The high humidity clung to us, turned sweet and sticky, and attracted many tiny bugs to fly about and land to annoy us.

I felt soaked to the bone, dirty and sweaty from two days of travel, chilled to exhaustion as I took the shuttle back towards camp.

The National Park offered a campground with bare spots on the ground protected by a waterproof thatched roof. Park personnel said we shouldn't try to sleep on the ground. If you did not carry a mosquito net and hammock to stretch between the roof's poles, some local merchants rented them.

I walked around the forest as the drizzle misted everything again; all the tree trunks black with water, all the leaves and branches bejeweled with tiny prismatic rainbows, the ground and air dissolved into a gray unity in the distance. Seemed every branch, leaf, and blade served as a nest, or as thoroughfares for a myriad of ticks, gnats, mites, and the leaf cutter ant processions. Each ant marched in line with a leaf sections like miniature green sails. The line undulated along the forest floor and led them back to their underground den.

I knew this jungle would never let me dry.

The dampness got under my skin; each mosquito bite promised infection with fungi, bacteria, parasitic worm, or some bug that burrows into a hair follicle and makes a trap door of a patch of skin to protect the den for its litter.

I decided to take the shuttle bus back and visit the island city of Flores, or "Flowers," which other travelers said sat on the small rock island in the middle of lake Petén Itzá like Alcatraz prison. Not worth it, nothing to see, they said.

As the bus sped along the narrow jungle road, I glimpsed bungalows on stilts, thatched roof domes, walkways with peacocks and parrots, and signage with evidence of sportsman culture, mounted wild boar heads and carved wood jaguars frozen in mid-snarl. Many signs used the word Trofeo. The apex of modern civilization, the corporate warrior flies down to Guatemala to pay big bucks to hunt where they guarantee a trophy to bring home and brag about for decades.

The bus drivers and local people pretend no hotels exist on Flores. They must work together to spare the tiny island community from the onslaught of tourism, and probably receive a commission on the people they herd toward the bamboo and rattan woven logs of bungalow hotels.

Netherworld Boatman

The Petén's rain forests contain the oldest dated Maya stelae, although earlier prototypes exist in the Pacific coastal plains, and in highland Guatemala.

A the Late Formative (300 BC - AD 100) proto-Mayan outpost of the Chicanel culture built enormous temple pyramids in the Yucatán peninsula. The Cave of Loltún contains a figure of a leader that resembles the Izapan style, carved in relief beside mysterious hieroglyphs and a notation in the 260 day count, which casts doubt on Mayan authorship of the calendar.

At sunset, the bus dropped us off at a little cluster of buildings on the mainland end of the small causeway that led to Flores. I wanted to avoid another night in the rat-infested storeroom. A crawl into the slug-slimed bushes to battle mosquitoes, to risk a confrontation with ocelots or coatimundi, seemed better in comparison.

In the still humidity, Flores reflected on the lake's black mirror. The few large lights reflected in straight white lines, wavered every few minutes by tiny sets of waves from distant canoes.

One boatman waited to take passengers to Flores.

I asked him about hotels on Flores, he said not a one, but when I pushed him with questions about what Guatemalans do when they visit Flores, he said that some families on the island operated posadas, or casas de huespedes, informal guest houses. I bartered with him about the price to paddle me to Flores for a few minutes, but he would not come down. He smiled and pointed around at the other empty canoes pulled up onshore, their owners nowhere around, as if I could wait for them to return, or try to steal a canoe.

I got his point. He waited here alone, without competition. He smiled.

I paid him what he wanted, and crossed by dugout canoe, accompanied by the beautiful mirror image of Flores that burned upside down on the still surface of the jungle lake.

Mist hung in the dark air, even after a hot sunny afternoon like today's. The haziness along the distant lakeshore blurred and exaggerated the few lights of lanterns and fires, where jungle clad inlets and bays nestled tiny outposts of humanity, a few houses at a time.

The boatman said they call Flores the oldest inhabited city in Guatemala, maybe in all the Americas, never abandoned for thousands of years.

He paddled me to an ancient dock of fungi-blackened rock, urged me to step ashore, and turned to paddle back to the lakeshore.

I walked off to find the posada, which he said lay a short walk up a slight hill on the main road. Black stains of ancient water traces ran over the dark gray stone of colonial architecture. It looked medieval without streetlights. Easy to imagine that behind those walls, dragons and witches sniffed at my approach.

No one on the streets. I didn't see any sign of a guesthouse. No one to ask, so I walked to the highest point in town, an open cement square with basketball hoops on each end. Then I walked back to retrace my steps.

The guesthouse hung out the tiniest sign.

A small elder woman with big sunken black eyes came to the door and allowed me entrance. Her left hand gathered an orange shawl under her chin. In slow motion, she led me up a stone staircase along the wall, open on the side, then into a short hallway. She opened the door to a small stone room, pushed a plastic toggle button the color of a yellow tooth to turn on a weak light. She gave me the key, and hulked back into the gloom.

The Witch's Sobrina

The Mayans believe that the god Itzamná, Lord of the Heavens, rules over the Mayan pantheon. Although considered benevolent most of the time, he bears resemblance to aspects of both Kinich Ahau, the sun god, and Ix Chel, the moon goddess, who often takes the role of an evil old woman.

I dropped my backpack to the floor, sat on the bed, and felt weak. The stones gave off an odor of wet dust. Guatemalans ate dinner hours ago. I forgot to eat in the excitement of Tikál, then captive on the bus. I hungered for vegetarian food, beans and tortillas, so I headed downstairs.

The slow motion woman told me I would find everything closed, but maybe a small place on the corner might reopen if I knocked.

I hurried out, and up the age-blackened stone blocks and cobblestones of the sidewalk and wondered if they once belonged in the walls of a Mayan temple.

At the corner, I looked around but did not see anything. I believed my new landlady, the directions too simple to not understand. Up two blocks, on the corner.

I took the one option available, and walked down into a narrow dank stairway and knocked on the world's skinniest door, wedged between rough-hewn stone jambs, a medieval monstrosity made of thick heavy wood planks bound with iron bands.

An tiny woman, pasty white warty skin with a straggle of white hair on her forehead, stepped out dressed in a colorful poncho, a black woolen hood over her head. When she saw me, her eyes widened to reflect the few streetlights. Musty fumes of old, hot oil bellowed out from inside.

"Closed," she said. "Cerrado."

"I'm dead from hunger." I put my hand over my stomach. Nothing to eat in over twenty four hours, and exhausted from the midday climb on the pyramids. I begged with sincerity. "Please, beans and tortillas, I pay you well."

She hesitated, then smiled a three tooth smile and pulled me inside by my sleeve. She steered me firm, as one would a child, and deposited me at one of two tables.

Then she pulled at her hood and slipped off the colorful poncho from under the hooded cape. She combed back her thin greasy strands of yellow white hair with bony fingers and stood before me for an instant, dressed in a white peasant dress with the open woolen cape and hood, a thin female Merlin the magician.

More a forgotten cellar than a restaurant, the uneven, dried mud floor and bare stone walls worked against each other at odd angles; compressed, claustrophobic and distorted, bowed by the huge beams that held up the street level constructions above. A dark buildup of sooty grime covered everything, a veneer of ages of hot corn oil smoke which swallowed all the yellow light from one sixty watt bulb that dangled in the middle of the misshapen room.

She fed the stove's ashy coals some sticks of wood, then placed a large flat sheet of iron over it. In a few moments, the forked tongues of flame licked at the skillet as she ladled refried beans onto it, and then surrounded it with tortillas.

She busied about in the gloom, so near the lantern that her giant shadow flitted across the walls like batwings that changed the shape of the room in throbs and gushes.

I sat exhausted on a hard wooden chair that threatened to tip over, and tried to write but the ink turned to smoke and stung my eyes with the scent of burnt tortillas and the scorched skin of hot peppers, and a steam of spices emitted from the refried beans.

She poured me a blood red glass of an acidic Kool-aid which she called Jamaica, and then pantomimed how she made it earlier that day.

She pulled out a paper bag of dried flower tops, shriveled black but with a strong red tint like licorice, and explained through sign language how to put a mass of the flower tops into water to soak for a few hours. Then she pours the liquid through a sieve to filter out the plant residue.

She put a rose colored plastic teapot full of sugar on my table, stuck out one bony finger at it, then to my glass. She cooked and cleaned and swooped about as if to dodge her own shadow. The room spun as she circled my table to set silverware, a plate, a primitive spoon stamped out of sheet metal, and three three legged molcahete bowls, carved out of bubbly black volcanic rock, which contained the remainder of the day's hot sauces, one green, one red, and one with a clear liquid over flakes of leaves or something, like empty of whatever it contained.

I understood her Spanish better than I did most Guatemalan's because she knew how to get her point across with cackles and coughs. Her waxen hand flipped tortillas over the yellow flames that wiggled against the carbonized gloom of the stove.

She looked at me too often and ate me up, a toothless sea siren trapped on land, an ancient spirit with an egg-eyed silver glitter that saw the future through the crystal ball of the cataracts that floated behind the bloodshot crescents of whiteness in the cathedral of darkness inside her hood. She swept it back with a rigid bent arm, robotic from a lifetime of repetition, a handful of fingers with swollen joints as a shield against the bright sunlight of her lost youth. The robe, charcoal by the flames of stove and candlelight, contrasted against the diaphanous material of a white peasant dress that clung to her sagged, though agile, body.

Her voice sounded strong and controlled in contrast to her frail femininity, and so appeared disembodied out of nowhere to my ears, an aural hallucination in that brittle, stone enclosed space. "Where you from? You go to the pyramids? You like Guatemala? You stay here long? You come back to Guatemala? You all alone?"

She acted like she understood my Spanish, but perhaps she said yes to everything just as I did, and went on.

She spoke to me in baby talk. "You like Guatemalan muchachas?"

"Oh si, si, beautiful, beautiful. I never see Mayan girls before."

She seemed disappointed for a moment, then shrugged it off. "Mayan girls pretty, no, no. You look handsome. I find you a Guatemalan girl."

"I don't know how to speak Spanish."

"Talk?" She cackled. "You get married, get Guatemalan wife. Good wife. She teach you talk. Better no talk."

"I've got to get back to the United States. How could I take wife there?"

"Bus. If she a good wife, she go where you go, she make you happy, she do good things." She gave me the Guatemalan sign for copulation, thumb between first and second finger, "and you don't go nowhere. Stay in Guatemala." She laughed.

I ate. She pointed to the molcahete bowl that contained clear liquid with a few vegetable remains on the bottom. She pointed at it and made motions with her fingers at her mouth as if too hot, yet as if she wanted me to try it, to put it on my food. "Pruébala. Chile Piquín. Prueba."

I looked closer and saw tiny bulbs on a tiny piece of stem, like miniature green cherries or olives.

"Chile Piquín." She says, and motions again for me to try it.

I put one tiny little chile on my tortilla loaded with avocado and beans. Her eyes widen and she smiles, yes, yes.

So I chew away at this little hand grenade from hell, mash it around my mouth and swallow before I feel the first faint sparks of what felt like a nuclear core meltdown.

My eyes watered, my nose ran, I begged for ice. "Hielo, heilo."

No ice. She offered more tepid Jamaica flower water.

I over chewed tortilla and beans to wash it out of my mouth. Nothing stopped the bonfire that spread through mouth, to nose and down throat. My ears smoked, and I could feel a sensation of coldness, like a wet death, spread from my solar plexus across my midsection. I became radioactive and glowed red, sweated through pores in lips, temples, ears, neck, and on down as the stuff passed through. It seared my guts with hot coals, blood red and furrowed, steam-filled blisters, third degree burns.

She asked if I had a novia, a girlfriend. Then she said, "You wait here, I come back with girl for you."

"No, wait..." I slobbered.

"My sobrina. Very pretty. And young."

"Sobrina, No, wait, don't go."

"OK." She sat and watched me eat, chuckled as she waited for me to finish and pay.

I used up a mound of napkins to dry the sweat, snot, and tears off my face. I hurried and ate to not keep her long.

She noticed and motion for me to slow down. "You in the hotel? Si? When you finish, we go and meet my sobrina."

"No, please. I need to sleep." I slobbered.

"You need to go to bed. Not the same thing."

I did not know then that sobrina means niece. I thought she might sell me her granddaughter as prostitute for the night. After a Spanish lesson in the correct names of relatives in a family, I understood sobrina, and then began to wonder if she wanted to set me up for a matrimony instead.

After the meal, I paid her, and ran out the door to my guesthouse where I fell into bed fully dressed, and slept for twelve hours.

Next day, I got up and out in the early afternoon. I walked around and saw most of the island. Buildings crowd atop this small stone outcrop island. Few people walked about, except the uniformed Catholic School children that play basketball on the cement court in the village center, the highest ground.

In the light of day, the stone houses appeared medieval yet suggested a quiet affluence, perhaps home for centuries of the area's Mayan and ladino ruling class.

I wanted to stay longer, to meet the witch's sobrina. I might find an educated, upper class, stylish, bilingual Mayan doll, but her parents would recognize me as an ex-hippie who can't speak Spanish, can't pay a dowry, doesn't work, and doesn't go to college.

Perhaps a fundamental choice offered itself to me there at that time, a crossroad of destinies and alternative realities. Maybe I thwarted a secure future of exotic romance, hard work, and familial happiness, but I did not go out of my way to look her up.

From the look of her aunt, I could imagine her sobrina, my future wife, as a wildfire of sensual passion. Our nuptial union would conjugate like irregular verbs in a nighttime ceremony of jungle drums. I could imagine the whole village carried pine bough torches around a nine foot tall bonfire. Tethered, leather loin-clothed, sacrificial virgins danced tied to posts with weak strands of fresh grass rope. The virgins' flirtatious smiles inflame the village males, who try to provoke these conservative provincial Mayan Indian Maidens into further indiscretions, until they reveal their eagerness to lay spread eagled between trees and donate their virgin blood for the benefit of my wife's new family, and me.

Third Section: Yvonne

CHAPTER 12: Way Out Of This

As the bus hurtled through the black night, Yvonne dreamt.

Her eyes moved, the scene behind her eyelids responded. She watched herself from a balcony that overlooked the inside of a blood bank, as she walked on the floor below, in a tight red sweater that her mother knitted in France, years before, when it happened.

She watched herself go from one teller's line to another and then turn away after she again recognized this teller as one of her mother's old boyfriends.

People in white coats pushed racks of sample trays on wheels through the crowded lines, racks of tissue samples that squirmed in test tubes labeled like beer bottles.

The workers drove the racks through the rounded, steel reinforced bank vault doorways that dripped like the mouths of caverns.

Yvonne the watcher-dreamer followed them down smooth reflective white tile corridors, past wooden doors, then cage doors where she avoided the hands of naked skinny idiots that grasped and drooled at her from between the bars. They pulled at her clothes and jostled her, and propelled her along.

She woke up with a startle. The bus hit some potholes as it entered the first high suburbs of Guatemala City, spread out over the valley below. Square blocks of cubic brick houses marched up the wide gentle slopes of the Valley of the Cows. She remembered she needed to go to the bank, and then remembered she owed Dennis something.

Ridiculous, she scratched her uncombed hair, matted by the bus ride, and tried to think to herself in Spanish.

Her face screwed up, eyebrows unsymmetrical. Stared out the window, noticed herself and her mouth screwed over to one side of her face as she bit on the inside of her cheek. She drew her knees up and locked them against the school bus seat in front of her. No one in three countries bothered to write on it. Boring.

She tried hard not to think of Dennis, so of course she did. As the day progressed, the hot bus floated in time, a meaningless procession that whooshed, vibrated, and bumped along from one stop to another. It stopped at every crossroad. The villages strung together on a zigzag timeline from prehistory to a rustic modernism wrought in poured cement. The smallest villages, and the rural outskirts of large communities, resembled the prehistoric Indian village of palm frond thatch roofs over rectangular stick or adobe homes. Giant hand-painted advertisements covered any bare cement walls, the largest areas of factory or agricultural storage building walls, and walls in the town centers. The signs shouted about spark plugs and Firestone tires with cartoon characters alongside announcements of popular music concerts, dances, soccer matches, etc. Some of these events happened over two years ago, some promised to occur in a month and a half. Painted signage for fast-food restaurants and political campaigns featured crazy wild eyed yellow cartoon chickens who shouted in the bright purples of three dimensional serif fonts.

A spider web of electrical cables overhang Guatemala City's boulevards. Colorful plastic signs, raised as high as mosque towers, glowed and tempted throughout the night in a non-verbal baby language that the rural Guatemalans and all recent arrivals to the capitol, soon learn about; the Dairy Queens, MacDonald's, Kentucky Fried Chickens, and Pizza Huts.

She felt hollow inside; it grew until she felt her chest might collapse in upon itself, an iron taste in her mouth, as if she ran cross-country with a machete between her teeth. Tears welled up in her eyes as she thought of Dennis, the last in a long line of failed relationships, her latest victim. She saw herself, knelt beside the road of her life, her gaze locked into distant memories that illuminated her, a soft eyed animal in a car's headlights.

Don't act like a fool, she told herself. She blew her nose and wiped her face with her bandanna, and laughed at herself for her brief wallow in self pity as she tucked it into her pocket.

It reassured her to cry real tears, to feel anything with a child's honesty, to believe that she still felt anything other than the hypocrisy of a shallow saccharine sweetness that she used to make others happy. Maybe others found their maturation did not mean mutation into a grim mass of cynical manipulation. The happy idiots.

She thought of her recent past as a black junkyard of sensations, all those magical things once familiar to her childlike curiosity, when repeated too often became the adult's mindless addiction. She relished her childish reactions to the new and spontaneous of life, her unambiguous tears or laughter, her delight in new people, music and clothes, even the sad pleasures in the self absorption of a shallow nostalgia and insincere remorse.

She tried to regain a confidence she once felt in her ability to remove herself from situations, to cease to exist, to divorce herself from her own body, her life, her pain, to survive the torture that others inflict for their own pleasure.

Her first loves became confused with the pleasure of mischievous guilt. They pulled her out of depressions and made her feel like a child again, one who giggles at the prospect of certain punishment, yet inches closer to the precipice, dares to cross another line, and push someone beyond their limit, one more interruption for each 'not another word.'

Tears proved to Yvonne that a little flame of innocence still burned, a little girl inside shared the cage of her ribs with the cold stone of her heart as a pillow. Bright eyed and full of a blind trust that expected the mercy of others, that little girl could still believe in God, Santa Claus, and a White Knight to take her away into a universe of happiness and hope, happy ever after. Whenever she felt denied, the little girl ranted and railed, and only love or sex seemed to placate her tantrums. As years went by, Yvonne secured proof that the little innocent survived, and could dig herself out of the sticky tar pits of whatever Yvonne suffered on each of these escapes, these instant solo trips farther and farther from home.

A mother's arms, her father's lap, a hug from a friend, a bed shared with a girlfriend, the passion in Dennis's warm body, they once gave her comfort, she thought, and it pained her again to see herself wind up so selfish and alone, and uncomfortable. These self exiles from her familiar world of France, carried her to this New World which she grew to know and perceive as unformed, a larval fetus, artless with no history, tainted by an infantile violent culture, with little reason to exist.

Work to Live: Time is Tomorrow, in Mexico, where people work to live, and time catches up to you bankrupt. There's never enough money for necessities, but always enough time to do something unnecessary.

North of the Mexican border, she got to know many people who Live to Work. She learned the American work ethic, that Time is money, and people use the gains of their employment to acquire things and plan for a distant future of free time that may never come, or come too late, when decades of unhealthy habits take their toll. People hoped to retire with the resources to go where they want in their "golden years," yet most compromise and do whatever their ill health permits, like move to a warmer climate.

In American slang, to Make Time means sex, to Make Love, which Yvonne respected as a vital part of life, irrefutable, and one of the things she resolved never to do without, a rule to live by since the tragic death of her first high school boyfriend.

The frustrations of her miserable 'free-spirit' mother, who lived more than half a century in intense hated of her role as a wife and mother, gave Yvonne the example of what happens when one negates or sublimates that hedonistic urge to couple and procreate. The woman who gave Yvonne life, lived as a prisoner in perpetual servitude to her role as wife and mother, unpaid servant to both husband and children.

They both blamed the divorce on Yvonne, whose physical body matured with a suddenness that took the wind out of her mother's illusions of her own youth and attractiveness.

Mom recognized daughter's immaculate involvement. Yvonne's full lips, baby fat curves, and youthful innocence inspired, in even the purest and noblest of healthy men, a primal urge to procreate, or at least go through the motions for pleasure. A dangerous instinct which God's law attempted to sublimate through the incest taboo, which increases the excitement level for men who become stepfathers, and those who fear the power of mature women. Those men who obsess over the non-skinny version of childlike femininity, the soft roundness and full blossom on cheek and lips, bosom and buttock, became her fan club. The love and solace she sought from her father, the protective man who knew how to sooth her whimpers and stroke her sad confused little head, became mixed with their painful midnight secrets which she wouldn't understand for another decade.

Yvonne's mother could not forgive anyone, especially not God, for what happened.

Her mother told Yvonne, like a mantra, to not shoulder that responsibility. Chance forces things upon people without regard to merit, reward, nor punishment. "It only matters how you react to things. Over reaction is the worst you can do. Take things slow, don't blame anyone, not yourself nor the devil nor God, because in this world, things happen without reason, and it's nobody's fault. Try to forget, and concentrate on the beautiful things in life."

Yvonne knew mother offered that advice too often, and its repetition helped prove mother's guilt in Yvonne's eyes. Only fools build dams where water cannot flow.

Yvonne, now an ocean away on another continent, alone without travel companions nor a man to cling to for love and protection, wondered if she could find a group of Latin American girls to learn Spanish from, girls that wanted to talk English or French, girls fascinated by the romance of Paris or New York, or who dream of life in the United States. Maybe a friendly family might take her in as a stray, to appease their humanitarian urges, or because they need a nanny who would work for room and board and a little income she might save for a ticket home.

Yvonne herself, in perfect freedom, with money in the pocket and a little in the bank, wanted to feel young, beautiful, and fully alive, wanted to feel on top of her world, a beautiful place of whims and happiness, perfumed by the scent of flowery adventure blown to her from a distant hothouse on an exhausted wind.

She wanted to know her capacities, her limits. She compared herself to other people, in other situations, other stories. Could she survive exotic locales to commit incredible indiscretions, even crimes, and become infamous for intrigue and political influence, or noteworthy for one heroic act, or lionized for a lifelong devotion to a campaign for others' benefit? She asked herself over and again, and answered each time with a Why not, until she recognized herself as someone who peered at the highest forms of love and humanistic altruism as if at lofty mountain peaks while her legs mired in the muck of how little she could love herself. Moment by moment, controlled what she allowed herself to experience, and denied her the self knowledge, the macro-cognizance, where self help begins, the "auto-superation" in Spanish, the 'self going beyond' where one climbs upward through tugs on one's own bootstraps.

She thought "Maybe I could lift an automobile in an emergency, an instant reaction to the sight of my own baby trapped underneath it. If one could love others as a mother loves her baby, those instincts might impart a super-human strength to rescue others."

"Or I could live with a band of smugglers on the Mexican / USA border. I have no friends or family to worry about." She thought, "Why should they help me get rich, when they could turn me in, any time they need a sacrificial lamb to throw to the police?"

She wants to taste the full palate of life's bounty, to travel and love, before youth left her behind. As a younger adult, she imagined her future as a happy and accommodated wife in a life driven by career, marriage, home, and children. Before she settled for that, her ego painted another goal, to milk her youth for all the freedom and advantage she could, because at any moment, all her plans might add up to nothing, thwarted by marriage, pregnancy, accident, ill health, or death.

Therefore, she rejected the necessity of motherhood, ignored the importance of her biological clock, and believed only in physical health. She accepted the psychological conflict of independence in opposition to her God-given feminine obligation to continue the species, to pass on her genes and ensure her offspring's health for the first eighteen years of life, at best with a husband.

The bus tires slapped against the cracks in the ribbon of pavement that wound through these mountains. The scents of a sun drenched jungle after the rain, and the steam of pools where fallen tree flowers floated, created a fugue with the intermittent aromas of villages, the stews and soups, ripe fruits, toasted corn tortillas, and raw sewage that runs down the mountainsides to create the perfume of Central America.

The bus window admitted the stench of hot tropical carrion that rotted somewhere in the undergrowth. It made her grimace, and clung to her loose white shirt like a stained reputation. She felt herself shrink and wither within, reminded again of the young unmarried woman who fears a transition into wooden spinsterhood and a lonely future of repentance.

Let Dennis and Gary play hide and seek with venereal disease in a port town full of sailors and whores.

No one ever kills themselves over love. If they do, they confuse love with self interest and depend on others for their self esteem.

"Poor Yvonne," she thought to herself, "she feels sick and depressed when alone. This thing grows in my brain, and wants more and more affection all the time, it needed more and more with Dennis, more than Dennis provided, or ever could, more than he told me he wanted to give. I should be queen. I should demand pure devotion and abject adoration. Men are stupid, and cannot understand a mother's unconditional love, which is the minimum a woman should expect from a man; love without a hint of criticism, no advice as its disguise, no matter how well meant."

The rush of the bus droned on.

"I should do something, find something, go back to school, even though I don't want to, to prove I can, to commit myself to something, and stick with it. I made a mistake when I left. I'm too young to pick a career at this stage of my life.

"I can't commit myself to anything but an insane asylum."

Yvonne woke up in the bus and shook off the dream, her fingers meshed into the hair above her thick eyebrows. She calmed her breathing and tried not to look at the passengers.

The Mayan Indian lad next to her stared straight ahead, as if he could see through all the heads that bobbed in the front seats, through the scratched plastic barrier behind the driver and through the driver's head to enjoy the wide screen scenery framed by the drapery trim decorated windshield ,a line of fuzzy burgundy balls that swung in unison as the bus heaved from side to side.

She dreamt they diagnosed her with a cancer of the imagination, that her growth and change would go on and on without stop, until she knew everything and experienced everything, and no longer felt any appetites. She became the end in itself, a female Buddha in permanent enlightenment, her brain a sieve of razors that no longer functioned as a filter to separate the good from the chaff, but cut everything up into tiny, digestible and useless pieces, an entropy of random noise, a turgid, formless warmth instead of a pointed intellectual microscope. She would examine her goals with the cold blue light of spiritual logic.

Long ago, she noticed that everyone cherished the idea they suffered an unusual amount of childhood pain. Every child becomes its own executioner, the adult who must dismember it and cast aside the useless parts. Each milestone of development, each fundamental memory, becomes warped by the weight of subsequent reckless discoveries laid on top, the sedimentation of internal secrets and external burdens. Impossible for a noble child to survive the fall, not with all the King's whores nor all the Queen's men. Not with a mother's blind love of the neighbor's husband, not even to spite her stepfather's public hypocritical affectionate hug, or worse, his embrace of mother while his eyes bore into hers and made her remember how his tongue licked her belly to seal their little secret.

No matter how he lost her as a daughter, she never accepted him as a father. He failed to fulfill the child's need for a savior and hero, so he convinced the girl of his ability to dominate.

And so she first became aware of macro knowledge, when she could see the small change in the size or shape of an idea. Concepts became clay, lumps that once learned call attention to itself, the way a new word learned appears as if by magic in magazines, newspapers, signage, books, and conversations. The once noble unicorn becomes a peripatetic erection, the motif of the male's instinctual mandate to inseminate and move on. The concepts grow, and cause subtle changes in the weight of opinions or beliefs. She noticed many new ideas discolored her child's view of a beautiful reality. She recognized that as one reason people take precautions before they talk about the most important ideas, ideas about politics, money, religion, and sex.

For many years, she sought the truth of things which others fear to address, or acknowledge.

In one of her explorations, she became blonde to explore the quality and quantity of a blondes' enjoyment of life, until that bastard of a negro African college student killed it all for her with one insult.

"Only women believe blondes have more fun. Men want blondes, and say blondes have more fun, because men have more fun with blondes. Men who know women think blondes, both real or not, want to become perfect lovers, at once flirtatious, sensual, capricious, silly, and symbolic of cleanliness. Bondes want to believe in themselves as sex goddesses of bloodless purity and golden holiness. That makes it even more fun for a man to humiliate a blonde, to debase her and abandon her, for her own education."

When she thought of school days, it pained her to think that she could not keep friends. In high school, she could not keep boyfriends. She didn't like them after she got to know them, or they bored her and brought things into her life she didn't want to deal with, or they demanded more time than she could give, time she wanted for herself.

She wanted to improve herself, to learn how to give of herself, but felt she wasted time with others.

Her friends felt she rejected them, so they rejected her.

Now, with all the time in the world, she couldn't think of any surrogate friend or adopted family nearby for her give to.

She alienated her friends and family on purpose. She didn't need intimates after she learned that friends don't understand her feelings and thoughts, which flow quicksilver fast and bifurcate like lightning along the black bottoms of cloudy ideas.

All little girls love daddy, until they get old enough to want a horse, a unicorn, that winged promise to fly her away from a house full of poltergeists born of impossible lusts. The happy home turns into a hopeless mausoleum devoid of movement. Domestic moments no longer charm, the quality time of doll houses becomes robotic, and eyes that once met like warm lips in a slow swirl of sunlit spring flowers changes to suspicion, recriminations, dirty looks, lies, and veiled threats.

Yvonne rode each virile unicorn as long as she could. She held on tight for each ride, and took the reins to make him change direction with her whims, or at least shut up and land to let her move on.

Yvonne slumped against the bus window, stared right through both her own reflection and the Guatemalan cityscape that spun past. She felt the wild winds of her reproductive chemistry howl with urgent loneliness, another ovulation with the full moon that called out to the werewolves of her dreams. Her young body stretched against the plastic seat, felt its contact hot and sweaty, and breathed the diesel perfumed city air that rushed through her open window. It combed the hair back along her temples, sleek black ringlets streaked across her ears, a mop of ink that shivered like cold crows and exaggerated her tan, aquiline features.

Sometimes when she felt depressed, in a deep dive through an ocean of self pity, the recognition of her powerlessness to control her sex kitten emotions awoke the cat within her, an attention starved feline that hungered to prowl and in frustration, extended the sharp claws of self flagellation.

The bus passed buildings and under as rushed down the boulevards toward the city's center. The lights of signage played across her face and brightened her reflection in the glass. Hidden under her white Bat jacket from Sololá, worn backwards like a blanket with the embroidered sleeves thrown over her shoulders, she cupped a breast with one hand.

She glanced at her Indian companion on the seat next to her. He stared straight ahead, hands on his knees. His beaked nose and dirty straw cowboy hat bobbed with the bus motion nonstop for hours. He showed no interest when she offered him a magazine in Spanish. What did he think about, she wondered. I must attract him. All healthy young men share the same instincts. Homosexual? How does an illiterate mind think? How do all these Mayan dialects work as symbols of thought? Do they care about anything beyond the agrarian world of village society?

Maybe he thinks he comes from an upper class Mayan family.

Yvonne laughed, to think a Mayan Indian might use a bank.

How many times did he get the chances to sit next to a beautiful French girl who expects the unwanted attention of men? Imagine, a girl from another continent, a citizen of one of the seven industrialized nations. She speaks three languages, her culture birthed the world's premier language of diplomacy and the highest social graces, not to mention a tradition of culinary arts envied the world over.

Where does he hide the masculine curiosity that kindles the spirit of exploration, that inspires war and rapacious conquest, that fuels the desire to learn and invent the achievements that benefit man and society the world over?

She felt tired and bored, and thought it hopeless to start another conversation with an Indian in Guatemala, and listen to their strange Spanish syllabic strings of welded words roll like rosary beads off an illiterate palate. A mind that lacks words, without a visual symbolic component to communication, lacks the path to understanding, continued education, and acquired knowledge of all things important in the developed world. Little wonder the back of bus seats sport no words, and little graffiti decorates the urban walls or sidelined railroad cars.

Yvonne thought Guatemalans don't read books.

She turned her head away and swallowed hard, tried to stop the tears that welled up from that black pit of tar inside her which she struggled to ignore so many years.

Ah, but this stone face young man here beside me, she fumed, inhuman. Happier than I, complacent as a cow, who without fear lunches at the unsanitary food stalls at important crossroads in the highlands.

These Catholic Mayan Indians worship in a church that preaches in the dead language of Latin, and forces them to memorize prayers by heart, to chew God's name in rote repetition in Spanish, a second language they speak only for commercial reasons, and never learn to write.

She remembered the beauty of the sunset at the Gringo's Christmas party in Santa Catarina Palopó, the reflection in Lake Atitlán, the star filled night, the view of fireworks from across the lake launched throughout the night, flowers of short lived flares that tapered off into darkness and much later, the hollow bang reached their ears.

She covered her face with her hands as if to sleep, and cried. Her shoulders shrugged with each sob. She squirmed in the bus seat to hide it.

Depression makes us see our slightest personal failures as permanent and terminal defeats, due to the a poisonous influence of an external world that dealt us one too many blows in too short a space of time. Depression forces one to suck in deep the hurt and nurture it there, long term, to make it part of us. To recognize futility and mortality makes us strong, and allows us to put to rest the past. When done, we perceive reality anew, as it exists, neither good nor bad outside our perception and reaction to it. As a coping mechanism of survival, developed by millennia of human evolution, depression teaches the brain to accept the blows of callous events, to bury them in the mind and seal them off, and then learn to reconstruct the reality of life with new neurons and synapses.

Yvonne thought she might meet someone, she planned to meet someone, to help her bounce back. She knew how to turn her cold self inside out, to expose the warm ember of her soul to the light of day but only in the presence of someone who offers the hope of their own spiritual heat for her to suck dry. She becomes the vulnerable for someone who needs to feel like a hero, a prince, a rescuer. She imagined herself as the emotional vampire, the wounded cannibal lioness hidden inside the skin of a beautiful gazelle, motivated by that lost waif who looks out from between her ribs in fear and distrust.

Tomorrow the hunt starts for her next enabler.

Yvonne meets Dr. Mendez

Fire transmutes the material world into the spirit, an analogy of how life leaves the body in death, and the body disappears into dirt. Archeologists interpret one Pre-Classic (1500 to 100 BC) clay figure as an old man, a fire god, who carries an incense burner on his back.

Late afternoon, the bus pulled around the gritty back streets near the bus terminal to unload passengers. She waited for her bag at the side of the bus, while staff opened the side hatches.

She felt a finger of fear run up her spine.

Alone, in a big city at last, where rural Guatemala mixes with the outer edge of civilized modern reality. To her, it looked like chaos, filthy and primitive, class stratified and bigoted, dangerous. Around her, she watched the incessant stream of agricultural products, a view of the food supply that first class travelers, who dine in the finest restaurants and make international comparisons of recipes and service, spices and prices, seldom see.

She thought her Spanish, awful a few months ago, got worse in Santa Catarina Palopó with the Indians and the Canadians' influence. They got along fine on grunts, smiles, and finger points.

She shouldered her pack and walked out of the bus terminal, past the dock workers and delivery men who waited with wheelbarrows to manhandle crates of produce from the train platform warehouses to trucks, pickups, and buses. The smells assailed her refined French nose as she stepped across puddles, juices from rotten meat and spilt vegetables, that ran in black rivulets to the gutters, a sun heated vile soup.

Some of the men eyed her.

At least, she comforted herself, most Guatemalans represented a race of either stocky small men with delicate hands, rounded shoulders, short necks, and small features on moonsize faces, or anglular hawklike men with sailboat noses, small eyes and little facial hair. Since she entered Guatemala, she felt relieved about the size of the men, and the probable inconsequential dimensions of any pushy member that might force an entrance. Small comfort in extreme situations. She thought she might hold her own against most of them in an attempted rape, maybe even two at a time without the influence of alcohol to stretch things out. She wanted to kill her fantasy attackers, but considered cooperation, and rehearsed how she might bluff her way into a sexual friendship, and escape. She felt so confident she might either charm them into a comfortable hotel with a greater chance for her escape, or exhaust her attackers before they did anything to physically change her life forever, and once they fell comfortable asleep, rip their hearts out with a fireplace poker. Or she might convince them to pay her.

She walked proud and confident, her impetuous gaze set in the general direction of the town's center. 'Why didn't I pay more attention to the guidebook on hotels near the terminal' she thought, distracted by the sights and smells amid the chorus of loud bangs and scrapes as workers loaded and unloaded crates and great ballooned nets full of fruits and vegetables.

Later in the day, her eyes squint against the caused by the bright sunlight. Each street side wall sported a complex veneer of breaks and repairs, paint peals, nicks and scratches that uncovered layers of advertisements painted over each other onto the cement; images of spark plugs, loaves of bread, babies, political banners, and Coca-cola. She sought out the small word Hotel or Casa de Huespedes painted vertical, alongside a nondescript door, hidden in a jumble of plants and paint chips.

Guest House. Should she inquire? She walked on.

Her pack became a Brahma Bull on her shoulders. The city's bustle and activity felt foreign to her. She became a cipher and felt invisible, eccentric, a time traveler, or astronaut on another planet.

One man took notice of her and whistled. That brought her down to earth with a crash, her illusion of separateness killed by a squeal of tires, two men who yell at each other, with a couple of common Mexican oaths of anger and Yvonne understands a new dimension of macho, each man a chignon, a violator of your mother, worth nothing.

Too many cars.

Nearer the city center, the air felt cool and perfumed; wood smoke from street vendors mixed with diesel fumes from the busses that pass like empty Catholic shrines, oblivious to the waves of impatient commuters at the bus stops.

She came to a busy crossroad and turned the corner to see, way up the street, the Golden Arches. They reminded her of the ends of two sanctified hamburger buns, purified to yellow light, up ended ready for human consumption. They beamed like twin golden halos that crown a nutritious lie, a delicious double breasted seduction, into the dark tropical sky.

She deserved a break today, at Mac Doughnas, or Ma Doe Nahs, as they pronounce it in Latin America. She decided to take a roundabout route to acquaint herself with the area and search out a place to stay. Far easier to tell people she lived near McDonald's than to use street addresses that no one else used.

On side streets, she encountered families of poor indigenous people, old Mayan women with two generations of children, camped out on the steps or entryways of dark colonial buildings. They collected cardboard to improve their shelter, and at night slept in shop doorways or on the sidewalks with newspapers over their bodies and heads. Some wore tattered shawls and filthy serapes to ward off the night air's high altitude chill. Their black marble corneas and pupils, set in light brown and bloodshot, followed those who passed on the sidewalk. They greeted each person with hand outstretched as eyes implored, and an unintelligible moan of a whisper oozes from between their crusted lips.

Near MacDonald's, she came upon a Dairy Queen ice cream shop, a piece of the United State's fast food consumerism she resented. French fries, how dare they blame that on the French? She shrugged, pulled open the door and her nostrils felt the acridness of perfumed chemical disinfectants as blasts from the air conditioning blew the curls of her hair off her face. She entered this spaceship from an extraterrestrial world, everything shiny and clean and unnatural, an anonymous corporate environment of chrome, red brick, and white plastic framed within a plate glass cage.

She walked into the First World, another reality, a very well guarded reality. Behind the door, in her peripheral field of vision, her illusion of First World security shattered with the intrusive presence of an armed military man in green camouflaged fatigues with an enormous machine gun cradled in his arms. The incongruity of military in Franchise America wore off, as she considered it from the aspect of intrusions of the First World into the Third, the haves near the have nots.

The size of the rifle's curved magazine, a swollen fistful of lethal phallic projectiles, made her feel weightless, vulnerable, and paranoid in Latin America, where kidnappers consider victims expendable until proven wealthy.

An affluent Mayan family in line at the corner talked with their clicks and clucks, sweeps and squeaks. In spite of the photographic illustrations, they remained confused by the bilingual, in English or Spanish, menu and lists of drinks, malts, ice creams, flavors, and toppings until the counter staff resorted to Mayan.

She took a table near the wall where she could eat her banana split and view the street through the plate glass walls. She kept an eye to the guard, and wondered why an ice cream shop needed an armed guard.

This franchise, a symbol of First World Consumerism and product homogeneity, attracted the affluent Guatemalan kids and tourists alike.

At one table, about seven Japanese people carried on a polite conversation. Two groups of Japanese travelers compared cameras in an animated show and tell. They laughed as a group, dressed and moved alike, clones of inscrutable conformity, she thought.

Maybe the government put guards here to take notes and listen, to discouraged journalists and revolutionaries from discreet encounters in public places where they might feel safe from an ambush by secret Military assassins in pickup trucks. The guard might operate a little camera, make lists of who comes and goes, their license plate numbers, their friends, and whoever they contact.

A young Guatemalteco approached her, held out a five Quetzal note in his hand, a paper rainbow of color.

"I think you dropped this." He said to her in English.

She got into her bag and looked in her coin purse, "No, I don't think so."

"Oh! That's good for me then, isn't it?" he said in American English with a slight Spanish accent. "Where are you from?"

"The south of France."

"Oh really! You speak very good English."

"Thank you." She replied without a glance. "So do you."

"Oh no, you flatter me. Do you mind if I join you?"

She looked him up and down, unconcerned that she might appear rude. Harmless, about 18, a soft pudginess like many upper middle class youth who deny themselves the physical pleasure of exercise with the luxury of indolence. She thought he overdressed on a budget, like a minimum wage bank teller. "Sure, sit down." She removed her purse made of Indian cloth from the table and set it beside her pack on the seat.

"How long you live in Guatemala?"

"About a month, down by lake Atitlán."

"Oh, very beautiful there. Panajachél. Did you like the Indians?"

"All right, a little too primitive. When I lived in Santa Catarina, I wanted a hot bath."

"Santa Catarina, yes, I know it. You didn't get sick there?"

"Once or twice, not too bad. Why?"

"My father's a doctor. He complains about the Indians, the way they cook and don't bathe, they throw garbage around. They wash clothes and everything in the lake."

"Something wrong with the lake? Bad water?"

"Everybody do laundry there, and kids go to the bathroom in the streets. It all washes down. They get diarrhea and skin disease, eye disease, who knows what else."

She shrugged, eyed him with mock suspicion, as if she thought him an over protected alarmist. She studied him while he waited for her to respond. So she asked him "How did you learn English?"

"I go to the American school here. My mother is American and she wanted me to go to school there. So, I go. Nice school, nice teachers. Very good, I like it." He noticed Yvonne about to finish her ice cream. "I like to talk in English, harder than Spanish. At least, for me."

"Oh yeah?"

"Oh yes! It is very confusing. Spanish, very easy. You try to learn Spanish? You understand?"

"If you speak slow. Must study more, I don't study enough."

"I could help you if you want. Here, let me give to you my telephone number." He took out his wallet, removed a business card, and wrote on the back of it. "You need a hotel also?"

"Yes." She looked at his business card. It advertised a glass repair shop. On the back, she read his name, Jaime, and a telephone number. She tucked it into her purse. "Do you know the city well?"

"My mother used to stay at a hotel near here. Not too expensive, comfortable, classy but not pricey, she says. You want to see?"

"Yes. I need a good hotel, and a friend. Thank you."

Yvonne walked beside Jaime as he talked. His soft pudgy body and big sad puppy dog eyes suggested to Yvonne a sexlessness so profound she doubted he missed it. Well good, she thought. Simplifies things, like a brother.

He took her to the Spring Hotel, not far from the Dairy Queen, in the center of the colonial architecture of Old Guatemala City. He knew the boy who tended the little portable bar that served as a front desk, and as she paid for a room, he backed away and said goodnight.

Her room, large with ceilings twelve feet high, contained a large double bed, a desk with a mirror to write upon catch up on her postcards, and a bathroom with private shower and tub, sink inside, not out in the bedroom as in too many rooms. Her own room made her feel secure, like an adult, an independent woman.

She examined the shower, and an electric wire that ran up the pipe to the little element mounted on the water pipe at the showerhead. She took a long warm shower under a slight spray of hot water. She stepped out frantic with shivers. She dried her hair with the towel, examined herself in the mirror, and alternated her bare feet on the icy tile floor. Wrapped in a dry towel, she jumped into bed to drown herself in the thick, cold coverings.

When she felt warm enough, she leaned over the side of the bed to rummage around in her backpack and retrieve a couple of books. She read by the light of a lamp near the headboard, until she dropped off to sleep.

She woke late the next morning, dressed in her kahkis and walked outside to sit in the hotel's open air courtyard near a cage with a big green parrot. She asked for the free standard two egg breakfast that comes with beans, tortillas. She smelled the aromas of the wood fire ,the coffee with cinnamon, her eyes enchanted by the three ceramic bowls of red and green hot sauces, and a bowl of diced onions, tomatoes, and cilantro that waited on the of the cement table top that, designed in a mosaic swirl of multicolored square tiles.

Then out to the diesel-pungent streets full of Ladinos in white shirts and business pants, and colorful Mayans. She stopped at a giant Bank of America to change some money into Quetzals. When she got back to her room before the two o'clock checkout, the hotel clerk gave her a message.

From Jaime, "Call me."

She called.

Jaime invited her to come dine with his family that night, and would pick her up at her hotel. She paid for another day and wondered what top do for another day in the city. She rode the buses aimless, and walked around downtown to window shop, half-hearted.

Jaime picked her up at six, punctual as promised, in a clean, shiny silver late model luxury car as big as a boat. They drove down the city's busiest roads, headed south into the new developments nearer the airport. Jaime described the haunts of the middle and upper classes, the movie theaters, and the bars of each of the new hotels, not so much as a brag about some debauched lifestyle, but as if he hoped to impress her with how much he knew about it.

Here and there, Northern European style peak roofed homes sprawled between the traditional colonial architecture, a triangular skyline punctuation, with gardens that broke the street-long stonewall of colonial architecture. The southernmost parts of the city filled with tracts of suburban residences that flowed over the hillsides, dendritic patterns of winding surface roads, capillaries to cellular single family dwellings modeled after the ranch style suburban architecture of the United States, except done in cement.

In the low light before sunset, Yvonne noticed a glitter and sparkle atop the high cement block walls that surrounded many suburban communities.

"Look how pretty!"

Jaime said, "What you look at?"

"The sunlight on top of that wall."

Jaime said, "Broken glass. To catch thiefs. They break bottles and put the broken glass into wet cement. People do not jump up the walls."

"Couldn't a thief smash them off, or use a blanket to cover the glass?"

"Sometimes. Not much. People got dogs, too. Rich Guatemalans scared, too many poor people."

Yvonne laughed to think of Guatemala's poor indigenous Mayans as criminal. Their small stature, passive lifestyle, serious devotion to gardens and weaving, and ancient religious ritual mixed with Catholicism didn't lead her to high crime rates. "I think the rich people more dangerous to the poor ones."

"I agree, some very bad. They steal, and kill people, and nobody care. It take away their hope when police, the military, and the politicians do bad things all together, and protect each other."

Yvonne watched a police car go by with lights flashing. "People say the police and army kill Indians, and other people disappear."

"If somebody say that, maybe it's true. The Mayans live in another Guatemala. Not the same Guatemala I live in, but our maid still lives there, sometimes."

"Guatemalan Indians don't live in Guatemala?"

"They live in a state of self defense. Since thousands of years ago. Too many languages in Guatemala, because the groups stay away from each other for centuries."

Jaime drove off the main road and onto a suburban side street that led into a gated community. He waved at the guard who stood with a rifle in the window of a little cement building the size of a big closet. Yvonne noticed the street's cul de sac after six one story houses, each with its own two car driveway. Landscaped yards and tall wrought iron fences with ornate gates surround some houses. Jaime pulled the car into driveway and stopped at the closed wrought iron gate. He got out and opened it with a key. They drove through, then Jaime stopped again to step out and walk back to shut the gate.

Jaime drove up into one of the first driveways and parked the car. They got out and walked to the front door. He knocked. An indigenous girl, a servant, answered the door and let them in.

Jaime presented Yvonne to his father, Dr. Mendez, a middle age man with a bald head and a very large wide nose that pointed down and made a triangle with the thick frames of his heavy black glasses, which slipped down whenever the Doctor spoke. Amiable, he spoke often and with a bemused smile, delighted to show off his considerable vocabulary in an imperfect English with wry enthusiasm.

Dr. Mendez went to school in the United States, where he met and married an American, a citizen of the United States of North America. They separated after a few years, and then remained married though separated for long periods in two separate and unequal countries.

As a repeated joke whenever his children complained, Dr. Mendez explained he liked to say something like "Life is a one way road, a struggle down one path to one inevitable end, like digestion. We born, we survive our family, to find a mate, make children, and accept responsibility for their food, clothing, and any complaints for the next eighteen years. We husbands find a job and work, and keep on working, in spite of the stupidity and envy, the meanness and hatreds, the nepotism and injustice. We become depressed and disillusioned, and sometimes don't treat our family good. And the best anyone can hope for, to survive. To wake up each morning to suffer, to work, to see the corruption, all this illness and injustice, until we become uselessness. Maybe the luckiest get Alzheimer's disease, God's way to let us slip back into the shadow of our previous life, a slow backpedal through young adulthood, youth, and childhood, back into diapers and then death. Now what was it you thought so important?"

Manuel

As if to enclose a ceremonial area, the Olmecas built a "fence" made entirely of upright shafts of basalt, black rock crystals thick as thighs, beyond the main plaza at La Venta in the state of Tabasco, Mexico. North of this, Archeologists found a mound that contained several tombs, where the Olmecas also built a fence of basalt columns around at least one of the tombs. Inside, accompanied by magnificent ornaments of jade, archeologists found the bundled remains of two children entombed over three thousand years ago.

Manuel, Jaime's younger brother, skinny as a rail, hatchet faced and hawk nosed, and much more excitable than his studious brother, spoke English as well as most who attended the American school in Guatemala City. In the family, they regard their intelligent youngest child as naturally obnoxious. Yvonne fascinated him, and this sexual attraction brought out instincts that turned him into a sixteen year old smart ass nuisance.

Dr. Mendez's thorough though rusty knowledge of American English enabled him to catch his most of his son's oblique Freudian slips and off-color remarks. He reacted with a long, slow peer at his son from over the top of his glasses, slid down his nose for effect. When that did not work, he raised one finger and intoned something that Yvonne would hear many times throughout their hours together, "Manuel, un aviso. Solo uno." One warning, only one.

Manuel inherited his father's nose, and all hoped someday he might grow into it.

By the time Yvonne finished dinner, she tired of the intricate conversation in slow English and fast Spanish. To make matters worse, Dr. Mendez tried to translate a number of jokes in Spanish for her.

Jokes do not translate well, for reasons as much cultural as to the constraints of vocabulary, timing, flow, and surprise. She learned some Spanish from all this, but little she would remember to use. She tired of her forced laughter after they labored to explain an unfunny joke to her from Spanish to English, which none of them knew well enough to handle these subtleties.

Before sunset, they decided to take Yvonne home. All three went along for the drive. They toured a part of the city far from the main roads, through blocks of neglected adobe dwellings that crumbled onto the sidewalks, empty lots and auto parts, abandoned dreams and a hard reality.

They cruised through a rough part of town.

Ahead on the corner, a figure hunched under a streetlight in the cold. As their car passed, he watched them, his vacant eyes stared through them at nothing, head shook a tangled thicket of stiff black hair, his hands tucked deep into his tattered coat pockets to anchor somewhere in his solar plexus or groin area.

"Half-man, half-ape." Dr. Mendez said as an aside, and pointed back with his thumb.

After a round about, circuitous route into the city center, they dropped Yvonne off at the Spring Hotel. Jaime asked how long she would stay in the city. "We will go to a farm next weekend, and want to ask you to come along."

Tired, she did not feel excited about anything at the moment, but without a plan, she said, "I would like to go, yes, very much."

In her huge room in the Spring Hotel, she felt small under the thirteen foot ceilings, the smooth expanses of ancient stucco over masonry, the ornate carved wood moldings and cornices sculpted by hand perhaps two hundred years ago.

She read at the desk for a while, then moved to the bed and propped herself against the headboard, with an oversize pillow on either side. She fell asleep with the light on, the book fallen across her lap.

The white pillows looked like the wings of an angel.

All that week the Mendez family called and invited her over to eat, or take her to some point of interest, to help Yvonne feel like part of their family. She grew closest to the teenager Manuel, and sometimes enjoyed the bony play of his energetic clumsy youthfulness. His older brother's pretentiousness, his nods toward the suave urbanities of an imagined intellectual bohemian lifestyle, made her laugh. She called him silly, which endeared her to Manuel. Jaime's Guatemalan friends, artist wannabees and international tourists that shared coffee and conversation about what the newspapers carried on the front pages that day, seemed elitist, pretentious, and conformist to Yvonne. Only those with Hippie pretensions dared to wear any of the exquisite Guatemalan fabrics ,which Jaime sneered at as too "tipica" (indigenous) and low class.

When Saturday arrived, the whole family piled into Dr. Mendez's car and drove out of the crowded city streets on narrow asphalt roads with few cars. They followed the high ridges through rain forests and coffee plantations, the steep mountainsides sculpted with the rows of tiny terraced fields that produced vegetables in the rich volcanic soils, a continual and traditional method used for hundreds, maybe thousands of years of Mayan farmers.

The car climbed up the verdant hillsides into the forests, then followed a ridge that led to a narrow but flat mountaintop coffee plantation farm. She explored the perimeter, peered over the edge of canyons around the house and yard, and saw the steep mountainside drop down away from her as deep ravines filled with terraced corn rows that defied gravity and erosion. Here also, as in Santa Catarina Palopó, they plant corn on slopes too steep for cows.

They took a walk through along the ridge to enjoy the pastoral scenery of steep valleys of corn, orchards, and distant pastures of pure green dotted with black and white cattle. They bent over on hands and knees to climb from one row up to the next.

Back in the yard with other members of both families, they played croquette, traded language pointers in Spanish and English, enjoyed the cool air at this altitude. She won at croquette, and over-ate a delicious meal prepared by a staff of three or four servants. She asked for seconds of dessert, an egg flan bathed in a brown sauce made of cooked cinnamon and raw sugar .

The sunset bathed the landscape in a way that brought out the complex horizons and layers of mountains and volcanoes that marched off into the hazy distance. In the twilight, they drove her back to the Spring Hotel, and she fought to remain awake and take part in conversation.

Next Saturday they planned to drive her 300 miles to the jungles of Lake Isabél, and as the day approached, Yvonne prayed that a forecast of rain would not dissuade Dr. Mendez.

When she asked about the weather forecast at dinner Friday night, they acted surprised that Yvonne held the weather in such esteem. With a fatalistic flourish, Dr. Mendez remarked, "Neither sleet nor storm nor dead of night will keep me from my appointed rounds. I swear, rain or shine, like an American postman, we go to Lake Isabél. Only one place I worry about. A mud puddle. That is all."

"A mud puddle?"

"You will see."

Next morning, they drove south out of the city and turned north east. The highway took them out of the forested mountains and through a dry cactus desert, a badlands of erosion where eons of volcanism layered the parched bare earth in tones of sulfuric yellows, bootblack and browns, rusty reds and deep purple mauves. To the accompaniment of classical music on cassette, Yvonne watched the terrain and climate change as they drove upward into cooler mountain forests, then down into the dry desert hills, then into lush tropical plains with irrigated plantations of citrus fruits, sugar cane, and bananas.

The sky hung low and dark. After hours of participation in a long conga line leapfrog of cars that passed each other without reason, the road ran out of pavement. Everyone slowed down yet still proceeded at a dangerous velocity through ruts filled with rainwater and wet caliche, a slippery mixture like wet chalk, made of limestone ground into a fine white dust.

At times the road, two lanes wide, consisted of three bumpy ruts, with great white mud bog holes that threatened to trap each car that "made a run for it" and sped through, the motors revved while the wheels threw a rooster tail of mud to arch behind.

Then the road opened up into a cleared area in the jungle, and the traffic piled up into double lines of cars. A couple of trucks sat stuck, wheels painted thick with the white mud ooze. Drivers pulled their cars off the road on both sides to wait and see if anyone got through.

Some men tried to walk ahead, balanced on the thick wet edges of mud tire tracks that filled with white trickles of liquid mud. A few men talked with the truck drivers and tried to figure a way out of the mess. People sat in cars and talked to those nearby, who got more information from those who walked by.

"Let's get out and see what's up." Dr. Mendez said.

The four opened the car doors and stepped out to walk on the tall ridges of mud. Their shoes caked up thick soles and bumpers of chalky clay.

Dr. Mendez seemed to enjoy this little problem. He watched and smiled as one by one, cars from both directions tried to make it through the mud and around the trucks. Most made it, due to the simple folkways of Guatemala, where young men and gallant elders joined in a concert of cooperative assistance. Altruistic strangers nearby ran to the aid of automobiles bogged down in the mud, to push it along until the wheels regained traction. Larger automobiles created more difficulty for any driver that tried to negotiate the S curve around the two trucks. Many moved forward with too much speed and a dangerous amount of inertia for the helpers who constrained the course of the automobile around the S curve to avoid the two stuck trucks. These old boat-size cars from the sixties tended to slip sideways and stick in the dirty cream colored muck at the sides of the main ruts. When that happened, more men strode out to the car and pushed, as twin rooster-tails of mud flew for yards from under the fenders. They pushed the rear of the car sideways back onto the main route to improve the car's traction in the shallower mud.

Yvonne and her escorts got back into the car. Dr. Mendez waited, his head out the window, for an all clear signal from one of the truck drivers who acted as traffic controller, while Jaime opined that nothing but a wrecker could resolve this situation. He sounded fearful and blamed his father. "In spite of you being a doctor, your medical school, your Hippocratic oath, you risk our lives because you are terco."

"Terco? What's that?"

"He doesn't know when to change heez mind for nobody."

"Stubborn?"

"Yes, that's it." Manuel slaps the back of his father's seat. "He's Stoe-born!"

Jaime tries to correct him. "Stew-burn."

Manuel: "Not stew-burn, stow-born!"

"Stoeborn."

"Stewburn."

Yvonne said, "You're both stubborn."

As if in answer, Dr. Mendez smiled and gunned the engine. They spun out of the line of cars, and fishtailed down the road. Through their feet, they could feel the car's bottom scrape and bang against the highest clots of mud and gravel, as the car straddled the ridges made by big truck tires.

Yvonne grabbed the seat in front of her and held on tight, the car bucked and lurched in and out of deep ruts as it spun and slipped around the two mired trucks, threw a high rooster tail of white clay, and spun across the bog and up a rise onto firmer ground.

On the other side, people who waited their turn to come through waved congratulations and applauded as the Dr. Mendez drove by with a big smile, both hands still clasped tight on the wheel, his glasses way down his nose.

Up the road they sped, chunks of white clay flew off the tires and banged into the wheel wells.

"I need a beer," said Dr. Mendez.

They pulled onto the grasses in front of a small gray wood plank shack that served as a storefront house at the side of the road. They walked a red dust trail between small 'palapas,' palm frond thatch roofs like umbrellas that shaded small rounded plank tables with a circular bench made of halved saplings. Dogs lay underneath in the shade. Their tails wagged listless in the heat as flies bothered about.

Dr. Mendez and the boys bought beer while the owner told them this time of year, it sprinkled on and off for a couple of days, then would clear and cool off.

They drove on, the car a capsule of civilization on a white limestone scar through the lowland rain forest.

As they neared Lake Izabél, the sky's gray blanket broke into patches of blue.

CHAPTER 13: Lake Izabél

They drove across the bridge over the Rio Dulce, which drains the Lake Isabel's water toward the Atlantic coast and the Bahia de Honduras. They slowed down to look upstream and down, to see its flanks of impenetrable jungle, and then drove on through the verdant wilderness. A slow rain began to fall in droplets so large each one splashed its own ring on the windshield.

Jaime yelled "Look at that!" and pointed north out his window towards the lake.

Dr. Mendez raised a finger to warn. Jaime moved his hand in front of Yvonne's face to point down at a huge stone building built on a peninsula.

"Castillo de San Felipe de Lara," said Dr. Mendez. "Built in sixteen fifty two by the Spanish to keep pirates out of Lago de Izabél."

"Could we see it?"

"My uncle lives next to it. You can to walk it." He paused, as his sons broke in with their estimates of how long the walk took, "In about fifteen minutes."

Soon after they crossed the bridge, they turned down a small track northward which led to a village of tiny wooden shacks suspended on blocks or pillars about two feet off the ground, little wooden dwellings all colored like ash, light gray with a skirt of black stain, or fungus, that marked the reaches of rain splash. They drove through the tiny village over the intense green of wet grass, each tire in its own footpath.

Men appeared from between the wood shacks, mostly Negroes tanned a deep black, with very little Indian descent apparent. They wore long church pants, and white short sleeve shirts, black dress shoes or sometimes barefoot. Some carried a small stick to swing haphazard in front of their feet, as if to disturb the bush and flush out any poisonous snakes. The black women wore bright colored full length skirts, silk screened tropical prints, or solid pastel sack dresses. Many carried loads upon their heads, gigantic glass or pottery jars, wooden boxes, or cardboard packages tied with thin twine.

Children played in the dust of bare paths, in the green grasses at the side of the trails, between the shacks, in and out of broken down abandoned automobiles. They played hide and seek along the foot paths between the shacks, and pushed each other across little bridges made of lengths of broken board that span canals fed by fetid trickles of black sewage water from each house.

On the other side of the village, large pineapple fields stretched across the hillside to the wall of jungle. Dr. Mendez turned down a lane that led back into the woods, and then down a mown slope until the track gave out in an immense yard that sprawled under an orchard of great trees, with tall Royal Palms like sentinels on the lakeshore.

The old one story American ranch style house needed paint, but the red trim and shutters, still bright, set it off from the three green walls of jungle and the mown yard that ran to the lakeshore. A screened porch enclosed the side that faced the lake. The tall trees dotted the lawn in geometric equidistance, their branches intertwined above to give shade to most of the lawn.

Parrots and tropical songbirds flew about and squawked in agitation when the Mendez family got out of the car and walked toward the house.

Dr. Mendez and Manuel unloaded the car as Jaime and Yvonne waited on the steps for the inhabitants of the house to acknowledge their arrival.

Jaime explained that Dr. Mendez's uncle, now an old man, once hailed from the States, and used to think of himself as an American, but rejects that identity now. He no longer liked to speak English, seems to enjoyed his life alone, and refuses to discuss politics. For decades, he and his wife operated this hacienda as a home, farm, and commercial dock on the lakeshore. They raised animals, tended pineapple fields, and sold gasoline.

When the uncle appeared, dressed in a sleeveless T-shirt, dress pants and sandals, he seemed half asleep, unable to acknowledge anyone's presence, as if unsure if he dreamt.

"My uncle is a famous man here," bragged Dr. Mendez. "He sells gasoline to boaters. For many years, he was the only man on the lake with gas pumps on the dock, and the only man who could repair their motors."

The uncle looked around in silence, as if to ignore talk about himself, or ignore his company, or wait to see if he wakes up from a dream.

He made a small gesture with his arm to something Dr. Mendez asked, which meant he offered the screened in porch for us to 'camp out' inside, away from most of the mosquitoes. They carried the suitcases and supplies across the lawn to the entrance of the porch as the dark sky threatened rain. From the house, the boles of the tree trunks framed the featureless grey expanse of the lake.

Dr. Mendez came out of the house and gave a flashlight each to Jaime, Manuel and Yvonne. "You'll want to see the castle before it gets dark. Use these to explore inside."

The boys and Yvonne picked their way across a pineapple field, down paths between the shacks of another small shantytown, then into a wet, overgrown path along the lakeshore.

Yvonne remembered the view of the Castle from the bridge, how it sat squat and silent, a black stained gray against the darker gray waters, a mass of stone built on a rock peninsula stuck out into the lake at the exact mouth of the lake, as if part of a rock formation, a natural dam, that that created the lake eons ago.

Manuel's skinny frame tried to dodge the branches that hung into the trail. "A tour boat goes up the river. We used to go by boat, but they don't tour the Castillo any more."

"Manuel, you are afraid of this road. The boat costs too much." Jaime chided his big nosed younger brother.

After a pause, Yvonne said "Are you afraid, Manuel?"

"No, it's wet, dripping, and I hate all these spiders. Sometimes the army comes, men with guns."

"Manuel, you are the one crazy. Afraid." said Jaime.

The vegetation, which encroached upon the almost unused road until it narrowed down into a tiny trail, dripped on them, a wet cavern of green. Long grasses splashed against their legs and intensified the muffled scurry of animals close by in the underbrush. The long grasses soaked Yvonne's pants up to the crotch.

Yvonne glimpsed their destination, the chocolate and gray blob of the Castle's wet stone walls, as a background beyond small openings through the vine clotted trees.

The trail ended in an open mown area at the foot of the castle wall. They skirted around the castle and reached the lake where they stepped from one slippery rock to another. The lake waters funneled into the river's current at this spot. Objects float by and pick up speed near the castle.

"Do you want to swim?" Yvonne asked.

Yvonne looked at the Castle, the dark cloudy sky, the waters that moved past this narrows, out of the lake and toward the mouth of the jungle lined tunnel called the Rio Dulce.

Manuel pointed downstream at the river. "They filmed a Tarzan movie in there, in a wide lagoon called El Golfete, down the Rio Dulce to the Bahia de Amatique in the Golfo de Honduras."

"Is that the same as the Golf of Mexico?"

"Yes."

Yvonne said "Lets swim, then afterward, go into the castle before dark. It will be dark in the castle day or night, right? That's why we brought flashlights. Do you want to swim first?"

"Yeah!" Manuel said, excited about the vision of Yvonne in her swimsuit. "Let's go back over there, in front of the castle. Come on." The obnoxious imperious tone in Manuel's voice often provoked people, and motivated them to ignore his suggestions.

Jaime said "I don't think we should. Looks dangerous."

Yvonne scoffed, and worked her way across the boulders along the castle's walls until she came to a place about twenty feet below the ramparts where the canons once repulse the pirate ships.

"Yvonne, did you wear your suit?" said Manuel.

"No." She sat down and untied her shoes. "We can swim in our underclothing, can't we?"

Manuel grinned and took off his clothes. Jaime squatted and felt the water, stood up and announced "It's too cold."

"Not too cold." Yvonne answered with finality. "I love to swim. Wash off all this sweat after all that time in the car. Water feels cold at first, you get used to it."

"I'm comfortable." he said, and then sat down on a rock. He watched Yvonne and Manuel strip down to their white underclothes, careful not to lose their balance on the narrow, wet rocks. He looked at Yvonne, noticed the translucent whiteness of her tan lines. For the first time, he noticed a white person's tan, and how her skin's whiteness peeked out from under her bra and panties. The whiteness amplified her fleshiness, made her look even more full and soft.

She felt hypnotized by the false contrary motions of the lake surface, wind waves that moved against the current, the distant uncertain areas of whitecaps, and the tiny patterns of glitter that lined the shore. Random waves lapped and splashed against the flagstone boulders at their feet.

She undressed down to her bra and panties, wrapped her clothes around her wet shoes, and threw them to a flat area at the foot of the castle wall. She walked across the boulders like flagstones, to stand on a wide, flat boulder and stretch upwards with her hands over her head to pull her body out full, like hot taffy, the abdomen so flat and narrow it accentuated the firm roundness of her lean breasts and the smooth musculature of her buttocks and thighs.

Jaime remained dressed and watched Yvonne with eyes widened and pointed like canons. He clutched both hands below his fat belly and shuddered a moment.

Manuel stood shirtless, a statue with shoes and shirt in hand, as he stared at Yvonne in slack jawed adulation for some moments. He took off his pants and his legs trembled as he stepped from boulder to boulder in search of a dry spot for his clothing.

Manuel followed Yvonne from one smooth water worn rock to the next to reach the last big boulder which jutted into the lake. Her wild and wind driven mass of hair played about her shoulders. Manuel stumbled, because he could not keep his eyes off her.

She pretended not to notice. She stood outlined against the wet tropical sky, the jungle across the lake softened by the haze of humidity. She hated to swim in her brassiere and panties, white barriers between the skin and the environment, a synthetic reminder of how repressed society tries to contain the pleasures of life, the happy beast within, the false sin of hedonism, the surrender to nature, which she thought religions should worship and not fear. She wanted to return to the fold, fall into the pleasant scheme of things which sustains all creatures in all times ever since the creation.

The human male's domination of science refuses to admit that hedonism and sexual selection by females serve as the principle motors of human evolution.

Yvonne wanted to unite with the glorious Earth and live as an expression of elemental nature, an adult creature in search of the intense personal pleasure that dovetails with simple social emotions, creates family relationships, and cements people together for long term societal plans. A relationship of interpersonal pleasure with one person, with homicidal jealousy, keeps the promiscuous destructive side of wild passion under control.

Yvonne crouched and sprung out headfirst into the water in a flat, shallow dive, She skimmed across the surface and out into the lake in two strokes. Then she disappeared underwater.

This alarmed Jaime. He yelled to Manuel not to do it, not to crack his head open on a submerged rock with a dive like that. She did not surface right away, and the two boys stood there and uttered swearwords in two languages until she did.

Manuel laughed and pointed when she surfaced, and hopped to the water's edge to follow her example. He hurled himself into the water like a deer, seemed like more than his four limbs splashed and flailed as he tried to keep his head out of the water. He strained to keep his head too high, and dogpaddled with a happy grimace. He tried to catch up to her with youth's energy. He did not notice or appreciate how easily she swam, low in the water, with a rhythmic sidestroke in a big circle, to wait for him to catch up.

She floated on her back as he approached. Manuel paddled around her like a faithful dog, and gazed long at her tan body under the surface. The round protrusions of her sheer white bra broke the surface like islands, and changed shape with her motions, and the pressures of soft waves.

"You are so beautiful," he said in a low and nervous voice.

She floated there, her face above water, her ears under water, oblivious to what he said.

A giggle of relief swept him, replaced by a shudder of fear. "Yvonne! Yvonne!" he cried out as he touched her underwater and stared back towards shore.

She righted herself and tread water. "What's wrong?"

They heard Jaime yell from the shore, from upstream, where the dark outline of the castle seemed to shrink in the distance.

Manuel and Yvonne drifted downstream with the current, towards the mouth of the Rio Dulce. The nearest shore looked too full of vegetation impossible to climb through to get out of the water. As the water escaped down the Rio Dulce, the current grew stronger and threatened to wash them away to the Caribbean.

Manuel panicked, and swam wild, his arms flailed in a splashy dog paddle. His eyes darted from the shore to Jaime, to the river's mouth, to the castle, and back to Yvonne as he examined his options and looked for salvation. He thought he should act like a hero and stay with Yvonne, who swam like a fish and didn't seem alarmed in the least, or he might bolt for the nearest shore and lose face as he scrambled and clutched at thick grasses and barbed vegetation that rained ants and insects, in a ridiculous effort to save himself and lose himself in the impenetrable tangled mass of plants.

"Swim with me, Manuel. Calm down, and don't fight the current. Follow me." She felt no danger as she swam against the lazy current to stay in place, but Manuel's panic concerned her. She turned and led him at right angles to the current toward the shore nearest them, and looked back to make sure he followed without panic. When she reached the waters protected by the peninsula of the castle, with less current, she led him upstream, but not so near shore they might bang their legs against rocks or waterlogged branches. She talked to Manuel while they swam.

They both mocked Jaime, who jumped up and down with wild pulls of his hair and frustrated thigh slaps with his little fists balled up tight. He shouted commands, and hit himself in the palm, frustrated that they ignored him, angry in recognition of his impotence, his inability to help in any way to resolve this imaginary crises which only he perceived.

When they swam upstream even with the castle, they fought against the current to round the peninsula of boulders and enter the almost still waters of Lake Isabel. Jaime walked back and forth, then jumped from boulder to boulder back to the castle wall, near where they left their clothes. He stood cocky and triumphant, as if his cowardice paid off, that because he avoided all dangers, he remained to save their lives with his calls of alarm. Jaime reached down to take Manuel's clothes in hand, as if he expected them to get out of the water right away.

To Jaime's exasperated horror, they swam up near him and then out into the lake again. They stayed out a distance from shore, where Jaime could not hear them, and Yvonne taught Manuel how to swim on his back and maintain his position against the slight current.

"Did you hear me out there?" Manuel whispered to Yvonne.

"Hear you what?"

Manuel felt bold, a man. "Hear me when I say to you, You are beautiful?" He said with a strong whisper, a cold gasp, out of breath and over excited.

Yvonne swam up against him and let her body brush his. She said, "No, I did not hear you. That is so sweet of you. Thank you. A woman likes to hear such things from a man, sometimes. Depends on which man."

Manuel gushed adulation as he smiled, and did not realize she teased him.

Jaime interrupted with a shout from shore, his hands in his pockets, a picture of misery, the outsider, the coward who found danger where none existed. He begged for attention, squatted on the rocks, walked and hugged himself in the shade of the castle wall. He yelled, "Come in, it's cold. Let's go back. I want to see the castle."

They swam to shore and walked out of the water unsteady, from submerged boulder to boulder, and then shook the water out of their hair and wiped themselves off. They used their shirts as towels. Jaime puffed himself up as he watched them shiver into their clothes. "Lucky I saw you in the current. I yelled at you to come back."

Yvonne did not look up. "Ni modo." Useless. "The current is not strong."

Manuel used his shirt as a towel. "I think it feels strong. Sometimes too strong." he said in an attempt to maintain his status as hero in a brush with death.

"Good place to learn to swim, because here You swim to remain in place, so the river will not carry you away." She looked at Jaime. "You don't swim, do you?"

"Oh yes. As a boy. I float on my back also. But I am not a boy anymore."

"Oh!" laughed Yvonne, "Too old to swim. You should swim with us. I think you are lazy."

Manuel laughed at Jaime without a glance toward him. He bested his older brother this time, and now with deliberate effort, Manuel acted older, sure of himself. He finished toweling himself off with his wet shirt, then used it as a whip to flick at his older brother's fat butt. It connected with a loud snap.

Jaime yelped, looked at his brother in anger, and started to rub his butt, but stopped when he saw Yvonne smile although she ignored them.

Manuel laughed again.

After all, Manuel swam almost naked with the almost naked French girl his brother brought home, and his brother didn't.

Inside the Castle

They passed through the main castle entrance and walked across a courtyard of stone blocks set so tight that grasses sprouted in very few places. The small size of doorways reminded Yvonne of the stature of the Spanish Conquistadors, short men who could survive the cramped spaces in wooden ships for the months of meager rations to cross the Atlantic.

Various size two story structures of cut stone blocks loomed up on the four corners of the fort. In the center, a wide staircase led underground between two long, low stone barracks.

"Imagínate," said Jaime, "the Spaniards built this fort and put canons up there, with gunpowder and metal balls. They shot metal and stones at pirate ships that tried to hide in the lake. The pirates attack the villages for food. They take people and make them slaves, too."

They stood at the ramparts and looked out into the lake, the distant view alive with dark banners of rain that swirled and danced down from thunderclouds. A light drizzle fell as they walked the castle grounds.

They explored the courtyard's rooms and passageways, then took a wide central stairway that led down into darkness like a ramp. At the bottom, they entered a large room with little alcoves, like a Catholic church's spaces for tiny altars, along both walls. The three flashlights played across the dark wet stone.

"What are these arches?" Yvonne motioned towards the row of alcoves.

"I think," Jaime's voice echoed in the dark, "they chained prisoners there, to bend them down, not let them stand ever. To torture them."

"Disgusting." Yvonne said, and shined her flashlight's pool of yellow light across the gray ceiling. "What is this?"

A round, dark mass hung from the center off the ceiling then began to wiggle and move.

"Abejera!" Jaime shouted. Beehive.

"Abejas, no, está moviendo!" Manuel negates his brother, says it moves.

"Si, pues!"

They shined all three lights on it, and tiny glimmers of red reflected back, tiny pinhead coals. Then the mass writhed like a sack, expanded, melted, and pieces flaked off, to drip and break apart with a strange explosive violence.

"Murcielagos! Bats!" Jaime bounded towards the door in a low crouch, his flashlight held up by his ear to help fend off the bats of his imagination. He scrambled out and up the steps as a couple of bats shot out alongside him. Leather winged shadows fluttered past his ear, winged shrews with fang toothed mouths that clicked and squeaked. The slaps of their frantic footsteps mixed with the squeaks and chatter to echo and amplify as they bounced off the cold, wet stones.

As Jaime's voice faded into the courtyard above, Manuel backed up stiff, crouched against the wall, his flashlight beam darts and flies about as he fends off unseen attackers, or aims the light to follow a bat's erratic flight.

Yvonne crouched down, stayed bent at the knees, her head up, her flashlight aimed steady on the group of bats still attached to the stone ceiling.

"Let's go! Let's get out of here!" said Manuel, as he slid his back along the wall towards the stone steps that lead out to the daylight. A few more bats broke off. Manuel abandoned the doorway and fled up the stairs, abandoned Yvonne to face the bats alone. Yvonne switched off her light after his exit.

Better, almost pitch dark, she thought to herself, as the scuffle and pandemonium of Manuel's terrified voice and actions turned into the buzz of silence decorated with the chirps of bats.

She faced the blackness of the farthest reaches of the long room, and let her eyes grow accustomed. Then she looked around at the prisoner's alcoves, and imagined scenes from previous centuries, since sixteen fifty two. Then she turned and walked towards the bright rectangle of light, the wide staircase that led up into a cloudy day.

Manuel's silhouette appeared at the top, head first, then more as he came to stand at the top of the stairway. He called out frightened, with a quiet and tremulous "Yvonne? Yvonne?"

Jaime called too, from a little farther away within the courtyard, in the whispered voice people use when they do not want others to hear. "Come on! Manuel, Yvonne. Someone comes!"

Yvonne turned on her flashlight and walked out of the blackness, up the stairs like a vampires, her hips undulated with each step. The flashlight beam, at first a diamond of yellow light in the gloom, dimmed and paled in the increased sunlight.

Manuel shined his flashlight toward Yvonne and screamed, "Look out!"

A bat flew past Yvonne and out the doorway, missed both of them by inches, fluttered and swooped towards Jaime who fell back on the stone steps. His feet slipped from underneath him, and as the bat shot straight up into the sky, he slid down a couple of steps on his rump and yelled "Ow, Ow, ow" with each bump.

Manuel rushed to help his brother. They crouched and peered upward at the dark shapes that streaked erratic over their heads.

Yvonne didn't react. She knew a lot about vampires. She once studied them, remembered how their tiny clawed thumbs stick out from the top middle of their membrane wings of veined leather that stretches between long toothpick finger bones. Their piggish blind faces reminded her of Foo Dogs, those ceramic canine guardians from China. Worst of all, she remembered a horror film that featured a vampire bat's froglike motions as it crawls toward the sleeping victim, unaware even as the bat begins to feed with open jaws and twitchy lips, teeth so sharp they incise the flesh without notice, the long tongue curled to corral and lap up the blood.

On the steps, Manuel helped Jaime to his feet.

Yvonne laughed. "You two should make movies. Comedies."

Jaime stood motionless, his hand to his ear, and looked at the others. He said "Listen! Someone calls us, from outside the castle. Come on! Hurry!"

They ran across the castle courtyard, down the wide steps, and through the gate.

Outside the castle gate, as if posed at the jungle's edge, Dr. Mendez and a tall black man waited with flashlights on, the ends shone with a faint yellow under the overcast afternoon sky.

Dr. Mendez smiled and said, "Come to eat, before the policía get here."

"Did someone call the policía, poppa?"

They talked in Spanish, and then Manuel turned to Yvonne. "They closed the castle to tourists, and so if they catch us, they can fine us five hundred dollars for each."

As they left the Castillo de San Felipe de Lara's grounds, they turned off the trail and stayed on the road, and in a few minutes passed a sign as big as a barn door that detailed the new prohibitions. Manuel chattered at his father, who, at a fork in the path, gave the negro a pack of cigarettes for the favor; he warned Dr. Mendez about these new regulations of trespass to the castle, and thus avoided any trouble with the local authorities who would love to fine a doctor from the city for each person caught within the castle.

When the man left, they walked back through the darkened jungle on another trail, and Dr. Mendez made light of his pack of Benson & Hedges cigarettes, which he said carried his "family's coat of arms. "Vini, vidi, vici. I came, I saw, I conquered."

They returned on another little used path that passed between two green walls of vegetation whose newest branches leaned far out over the path for light. They ducked, or stepped around, the droplet-laden branches to avoid a free shower of water and bugs, but the tall grasses soaked their pants again.

Yvonne walked slow and dropped behind out of sight. She stopped to let them get further ahead, then cocked her head to listen to the jungle wilderness that flanked the wet path.

Yvonne thought about vampires, about older men who seek young women to procreate, about harems and polygyny. The Indians' mystic bat jackets in Sololá, the vampire movies of Hollywood, maybe the bat represented the universal archetype in for male sexuality in the human psyche. Bats both revolt and inspire. Maybe the human genome contain a genetic, programmed fear of bats, an archetypal memory of a long ancestry as cave dwellers in uneasy association, an instinctual connection between bats and disease, to recognize evil in these sightless, weightless mammals.

Imagine the horror among cave dwellers who share their residence with a population of vampires. Would their witch doctors connect the presence of vampire bats and rabies? A person, then the family, falls victim to a curse of madness, and one by one everyone in the tribe succumbs, mouths full of froth, dumb blank stares of rage, stupidity, and violence, and then a slow, feverish death, as sick bats rain down from colonies on the cave ceiling. The social order breaks down, the aged chiefs of the tribe decide to appeal to their Gods. They shuffle through the darkness to awaken a twelve year old girl, and cover her mouth with a hand. They wrap her in her own deerskins and take her outside, into a moonlit meadow deep in thick jungle, where a group of men fornicate with her, as an offering to their Gods, a sacrifice, or a gift to another, stronger clan.

A terrified mother awakens at night, throws off her own skins to sit up and see her dream come true, by the light of a nearby fire's dying coals, where strange men in ritual orgy take their pleasure atop her daughter. Then her vision clears and she sees the bat's tongue siphon blood from her own child's face, the same Bat-god embroidered across the back shoulder yoke of the white Sololá jackets, which none but the men of Sololá can wear.

The bat lives in the portals that connect the underworld to the world of green, the sunlit world of women and children who play in the wet gardens under rainbows. The bat lives in the black interstitial, unconscious spaces between the blue pearls of days. The bat crawls across the bedcovers, a hairy inkblot of nightmare, to suck life out, and leave infection behind.

Men.

Dinner on Lake Izabél

After a late afternoon cafeteria style dinner eaten off three folding tables lined up across the lawn, a black man lights a gas lantern as the sun sets, then collects the paper plates and metal forks. The men sit and drink beer on well maintained wooden lawn furniture, kept clean and painted white by the black servants. Mosquito repellent, shaped into coils like electric stove elements, burn with a red glow under each chair and from strategic locations under the tables, or upwind near the base of trees.

Throughout the dinner, they conversed in Spanish, because the old American did not like to speak English anymore. After the old man left, they spoke English also, for Yvonne's benefit. The other household members and guests, a couple of older women, an aged Honduran gentleman, and two Guatemalan men, also spoke some second language English. Yvonne and Dr. Mendez brightened up. So much English piqued the two boys' interest, which kept them quiet and polite.

Dr. Mendez and one of his relatives, uncle 'Tio' Beto, a man about forty, took a walk around the giant lawn with Yvonne and described a friend who learned English over the years through cheap, pulp fiction cowboy and Indian tales of the American Southwest that friends sent him.

Dr. Mendez drained the last dregs from his long neck beer bottle. "Con permiso. I must go to the house."

"I'll go with you," said Tio Beto.

As they walked towards the screen door, he raised his beer bottle high as if in salute, and then threw it high into the air to arch into the noisy jungle at the lawn's edge.

They stopped to listen, motionless as a statue, eyebrows up with expectation, to hear it crash land. When the bottle broke deep in the bushes with a chuk! and a wind chime tinkle, the doctor said "Hope it doesn't rain tomorrow."

"I hope you get your wish." said Tio Beto, as he tossed his bottle after Dr. Mendez's. They all listened, cheered a little when they heard the glass smash and chatter against itself.

"Why did you do that?" called out Yvonne.

"To get our wish, of course."

"But what about the broken glass?"

"What about it?"

"Someone could get cut."

Dr. Mendez said, "Let me tell you a Guatemalan proverb: Those without shoes must watch their step." Then he walked away to enter the house. The uncle, Tio Beto, took his seat with the others.

Jaime watched Yvonne's face. "My father, he strange man. A doctor say this, imagine, no?"

"Si, eso es." Yvonne answered with her crooked smile, stood up, diplomatic yet with a touch of French disdain and intellectual superiority, and walked toward the lakeshore.

Manuel got up to follow her. "Sometime I think he like to hurt people."

"That might be a reason people become doctors, also."

"But not a good reason. He writes big, writes big lines, a big pen, one with flat on the bottom..."

"Like this?" and Yvonne made a wedge shape between her two hands.

"Si, like that. He writes this big. You know what that mean? A person signs too big, it says vanidad, how you say when they think they better than everyone else?"

"Pompous vanity? Sound like your father?"

"Egomaniaco?" he said.

Yvonne laughed at the boy's big words to describe his father.

He laid his hand on her arm. "For sure and true. He hates people when laugh at him. You watch, he very nice now, but wait and you see him get crazy, wait and see." Manuel looked at Yvonne sideways, a goofy smile stretched to bare both rows of teeth, a parrot beak on his hatchet face. He froze like that, stared from the corners of his eyes, held the grin, and bobbed his head a little, up-down, in affirmation of his own words.

For the rest of the evening, Yvonne noticed that Manuel kept close to her, and now stared at her without reservation or furtiveness. His incessant interjections irritated both Yvonne and his father, who sent Manuel away so the adults could talk freely.

"About what?" he complained.

"About you if we want to. Now go."

The conversation turned to a shared synopsis of the American's long history on Lake Isabel, a pioneer from another world, who brought the technology of outboard engines for the boats. "He sold gas from the dock here, and only he knew how to repair their engines. He became the wealthiest man around. But the people so poor, the criminals stole the pumps from the docks, and kept robbing him. He worry much about his wife's safety. The criminals get caught, the bring the pumps back, because such a small number of people scattered around the big lake. The best people in thses communities don't like the criminals, and they tell the police who did it."

The men agreed that the stress of such a problematic existence in paradise sent his wife back to the states. Year after year, the old man's stubborn will proved insufficient to make a big success out of any one of his ventures, and she refused to come back. His ambition turned into resignation.

When Manuel caught Yvonne's eye from across the great lawn, he gave a little wave and wink of conspiracy.

It embarrassed her.

She enjoyed it too much.

That night about twelve of them, the men, boys, Yvonne, and two children, slept on cots packed within the porch. The screen walls offered an effective if flimsy protection from the threat implied by an incessant hum of insects beyond the walls, and from the jungle's screeches and hoots, or the long quiets interrupted by the stealthy sounds of a heavy body that crunches through the undergrowth. A lack of cots put the boys on blankets on the hard floor, a slab of cement that wore six or seven chipped layers of enamel paint in various tones of blues, oranges, yellows, and the latest, a tile red.

Each bed received a single sheet that couldn't keep anybody warm against the damp chill, but helped keep off the mosquitoes.

On lines stretched tight across the yard between the giant trees, the swimmers' wet clothing hung with the laundry. The clothing swung and flapped like ghosts when gusts of wind moaned through the trees.

Restless, she could not sleep, and when she did, her dreams woke her up.

She needed to go to the bathroom.

She rubbed her cold hands on the sleeves of the thin white cotton robe they gave her, and then sat up. She tried to make out all the haphazard figures on cots, or bent into question marks wrapped in blankets on the cement. She stepped off her cot and picked her way deeper into the porch, toward the house. The door handle froze, locked. She did not know the layout of the house's interior anyway, and as she peered through the door's glass, she realized that once inside she would not know which way to turn first. Might stumble into a bedroom and get shot before she found the bathroom. She knew they slept with guns nearby, as she recalled the stories of robberies.

She didn't want to wake anyone. She decided to go outside. Might find an outhouse somewhere, or she might squat behind a tree, but the thought of all those mosquitoes dissuaded her. She picked her way between the dozen bodies once more, all the way back through the sleepers crowded into the long porch, toward the screen door. She startled when someone coughed, or snored loud, or failed to breath in a bout of apnea.

She opened the screen door and stepped out into the lush yard. As she walked, the wind picked up and blew her light robe into wings. She brushed the hair out of her eyes as she neared the brush at the lawn's edge from where she heard the complex whine of thousands of species of insects.

A mosquito buzzed around her ear. She shook her mane of hair in a couple of whiplashes, and walked into the cleared area in front of the lake, where the breeze kept the mosquitoes away.

Behind a tree to shield her from line of sight from the house, she gathered the robe and knelt to urinate. She wiped herself with her hand, and washed her hands on the dewy grass.

The lake spread out before her, lights twinkled along the far shoreline and defined the visible expanse. She stood faced into the wind like the masthead on a great ship of earth, her black hair combed by the wind and her alabaster temples shined in the moonlight, her nipples tightened and pointed through the sheer fabric. She locked her knees and leaned into the west wind.

She felt powerful, filled with youth and energy, and she wanted open herself up to the universe. She spread her arms and legs and let the wind caress her.

The energy of earth and water possessed her. The wind made the fabric heave, cling, and tremble over and around her limbs. She smiled a little, her nostrils dilated as she took great breaths of the sweet night air, perfumed by the pale bluish flowers that dotted the bushes, flowers closed by day, now in night blooms to attract moths and nectar bats.

She turned her head toward a light, a flash, across her peripheral vision. She turned and stared toward the house.

Someone walked toward her.

She thought she could see a cigarette glow follow the route of someone who strode down the lawn's slope toward the lake.

Maybe a firefly.

She gathered her robe about her, clutched it close to her, and again felt the night's chill.

She did not recognize him until he stood right in front of her and offered her a cigarette.

Maybe she recognized him as the owner's son, Polo or something, she thought, but he did not dine with them earlier. She'd never seen him before. She took the cigarette, took a drag, and let the smoke out slowly as she looked away and handed the cigarette back to him. She remembered him as handsome, and wondered how she could remember.

He flipped his cigarette into the grass and reached out with both hands to grab the lapels of her robe near her collarbones. He pulled the robe down across her shoulders as she remained with her head turned to the side. The silky fabric slid down across her chest and bared her white breasts to compete with the moonlight. He continued to pull it down, until his arms encircled her hips, and the fabric imprisoned her arms behind her back.

He coaxed her to lie down on the grass where they both moved as if underwater. He kissed her, and she wrapped her legs around him.

She awoke in darkness on her cot. She wondered, did she dream that walk, dream she leaned over Manuel, asleep on the cement? Did her nightshirt fall open to reveal the full moon of her stomach above her pubis, a shaved arrowhead of blackest night? The shirt opened like lips to swallow him, and her nipples stared back, she felt sure of that. Did Doctor Mendez come in? Did she ask for the bathroom? Dr. Mendez replied, "Go out in the bushes." he said, "Don't wake anyone. Do you want me to go out with you?"

Oh yes, please, ¿Por favor? Did she really ask him to? Did she share the warmth of the bald doctor's body on the wet grasses while she dreamed of another, or did she meet the absent nephew, or his disowned son who may not be his son? Did she still sleep?

She remembered the wet fields, the grass between her toes, the cool of the wind. She looked down to see pieces of wet grass stuck to the top of her feet and she felt weak, flushed, recognized a sensation, a familiar post-extremis sleepiness, and tried not to explain what she could not.

With the dawn's light, they got up early and dragged themselves about, disheveled and bleary, in the chill wet air. They all agreed the cold took them by surprise. Yvonne heard their voices, remembered where she was, and awoke completely with a start. Her hands slipped down the sides of her body to her hips. She sighed, relieved, to find her panties on. She decided to look for clues in the behavior of others.

She dressed under cover of the robe.

No one said anything; no stares pregnant with desire, anger, or rejection. She heard no double talk, and no one seemed to communicate anything she could not understand, nor say anything meant for her ears only.

Puerto Barrios

Zacatenco and Ticomán cultures produced many examples of terra-cotta dolls, found in tombs of the agricultural Pre-Classic periods of (1500 to 100 BC), and some statue-like figures of women that might represent fertility goddesses, or "Patron Saints" for good harvests. Double-headed figurines from Tlatilco provoke controversy about whether they represent a feminine version of the legendary birth of the twins (From the Mayan book The Popol Vuh) that would shake up the pantheon of Mayan Gods, or another supernatural creature to symbolize the concept of duality, like the Chinese Yin yang, or a representation of feminine duplicity perhaps used in rituals by the lovelorn to change someone's mind, to make a woman make up her mind, or make a man see something that does not exist.

After eggs and bacon, Manuel asked Yvonne to help him convince his father to take a detour on the way back to visit Puerto Barrios, on the Gulf of Honduras. Dr. Mendez did not like Puerto Barrios, and that inspired Jaime to help change his mind. After fifteen minutes of pleas from the three of them to change his mind, he acquiesced, as he said, for the sake of a pleasant journey home.

They drove about seventy miles down a flat jungle road, back across the Rio Dulce, on a road that more or less followed the river downstream to Guatemala's Atlantic Ocean port town, Puerto Barrios.

Hot, humid, and rotting, wood buildings decayed into the rusted junk along the road, and strange fecund odors filled the air. Large, well muscled black men hauled things around on their backs or in carts and wagons. Old wood hotels sagged and listed with the jaded fatigue of the spent whores, the skinny black women with flat breasts who leaned through doorways and broken shutters to lock eyes with any males that passed.

A cacophony of salty fishy smells filled the open air dockside market. Huge obese black women sat on short stools in front of tubs of fish, experts that behead and gut fish six days a week. They discard the entrails on immense piles of offal, and throw the cleaned carcasses into galvanized tubs of bloody water.

Yvonne got used to the smell, and remembered how the ocean's incessant cough tosses up unimaginable and repulsive flotsam to rot on the beach, too much for any human energy to alleviate. Why should an industrious utilization of the ocean's bounty smell any different? The odors faded into a humid tropical backdrop, and she turned her attention to the people and noticed their quiet dignity, the smiles, polite salutations, the open gaze. While the fat women cleaned fish, their light cotton dresses, looped low across ample bosoms and pulled up over their thighs to tuck around their middle back, exposed and outlined smooth round folds of dark flesh, the top surfaces charred black by the sun. Each looked up and smiled as they scooped offal out of bug eyed fish carcasses to throw on a pile of guts already two feet high beside them. Then they threw the gutted fish into galvanized tubs to join the other black carcasses in the bloody water. The fat women seemed happy and unembarrassed, neither by their occupation nor their display of corpulence, comfortable within the scheme of things.

The men looked muscular and healthy to her, a contrast to the pudginess of Dr. Mendez and Jaime, or Manuel's skeletal skinniness.

"Look at the filth." said Dr. Mendez, "Imagine all the exotic bacteria around this community. Disease, stench, dead babies, diarrhea sick infants, infections, endless, hopeless."

Here, everything existed in a state of decomposition; ad-hoc ready made flimsy and temporary buildings that looked as old as those almost rotted away, or blown away, by hurricane and high seas, or the floods of wind driven wave surge. Everything recycled in impermanence, the shattered pieces tangled together again to make new structures. On the edge of the inhabited areas, the maimed limbs of bush and branches swallowed immense piles of driftwood and trash. Trash lay strewn about everywhere, as if people expected nature to take care of it, by vulture, wind, wave, or jungle. Other places, people wage a constant battle against nature, but here humans co-exist with nature, and expect the jungle and sea, as agents of decomposition in this wet hothouse of life, to erase or swallow the trash of human activity.

Few tourists walked the streets, but Yvonne watched two female tourists for a while and then told Manuel she thought they came from France.

She walked over to introduce herself, and after a brief chat, they invited her to join them in an excursion to nearby Livingston Waterfalls.

She discussed with Dr. Mendez and the boys about how they should not feel responsible for Yvonne's wellbeing, that she could take care of herself and they would all see each other again in a couple of days in the capital. If not, then they could start to worry. In any event, she could not leave Guatemala without her personal items left at their house.

Dr. Mendez wanted to leave the port town soon because, as he said in secret to Yvonne, in the afternoon the whores come out dressed for business, and he wanted to spare Manuel and Jaime the exposure.

The French girls helped retrieve Yvonne's backpack and things from the car and all cheek-kissed goodbye. The girls waved as the Mendez family car drove away. Then they walked Yvonne to their hotel room. They carried her things up a creaky wooden stairway covered by a balcony walkway that surrounded the building's second floor. Inside, the room felt cooler, with green curtains and two large twin beds, much nicer than the weathered exterior led one to expect.

Yvonne: How can we go to this waterfall you told me about?

Marie: Tomorrow at 4:30 in the morning, we take a boat across the mouth of the Rio Dulce to a village on the other side.

Annette: You're welcome to use my shampoo. This community called Livingston, maybe in honor of the African explorer. Ironic, because the people come from escaped slaves, and in Belize they speak something like English, like Creole or Carib, I forget.

Annette: We can speak with them, I think. My Spanish is not too good.

Yvonne: I love the view from this window!

Marie: Beyond Livingston, a few miles down the beach, a river comes out of the jungle in a fantastic beautiful waterfall.

Yvonne: Ah, listen there, to the calls of the fishmongers, like the sea birds. Where did you hear of this waterfall?

Marie: From a Frenchman in Guatemala City. He saw it earlier, on a different trip. He exports pottery from Guatemala.

Yvonne: This place will fill with tourists this time of year?

Marie: I love it here because I have no desire to put on makeup, with all this heat.

Annette: No, they say not many people come here. They stay in the highlands where it's cool. We may get the place all to ourselves.

Marie: Safety in numbers. Better the three of us than two.

Yvonne: I'm in. Only a foolish girl walks into the jungle alone.

Annette: Or with a boyfriend.

The girls laughed.

Livingston Waterfalls

Dressed in her village's topless fashion, a Mayan maiden's coal black, mango shaped eyes open wide as she scrambles through the sodden rainforest to find the path. She stops to listen, then runs again through the lower branches that rake her smooth thighs and catch in the woven fabric round her hips. She claws the branches full of wet leaves out of her way, and turns her head to glance left and right, behind, and overhead in a frantic search. She knows a Tzók bird impregnated the Great Mother of the Corn God, her tongue decorated by his thick white defecation. The bird's whistle can fill the ears and drown out the world. It might immobilize her, turn her into a female snake, a sinuous cavern, a conduit to connect this earthly life to both the Underworld of Dead Souls and to all the levels of the Star filled Heavens. Her mind's eye fills with carved stone images of the Gods' Ancestors, whose thick fangs and great eyes protect the pyramids of dead God-Kings, nestled in layers on the pyramids. She felt them reach out for her from the Underworld, touch her skin, hold her down, as the Heavens must look down upon them all and demand blood.

She runs through the undergrowth, falls to her knees. She crawls under a bush and lies flat, still. Her heartbeat thunders in her temples. She slows each breath, and hears the drip of water, the hum of insect wings, and the distant bird's shrill call.

She lays down and peers along the ground, through the plant stems, to search for sunlight, the sign of a path or open ground, escape...

The next morning, felt like the middle of the night to Yvonne, the three French girls shouldered their backpacks and set off down to the docks along the sea. Marie walked along with her arms folded around her tote bag until Annette gave Marie a sweater. They felt grateful the backpacks helped to insulate them from the cold night air, thick with sea salt and the fetid aromas of flotsam.

They huddled together against a low wall, and watched the eastern horizon lighten. Canoes came to take people to, and from, a large ocean vessel moored offshore. More and more people gathered on the wide dock to sit among their bundles and stacks of cargo.

The barge arrived an hour late. Everyone boarded, they revved the engines and turned around slow to chug straight out to sea. The low shoreline disappeared with distance in the dark humidity. The sunrise glow turned to a gold light on the horizon. Small puffy clouds appeared , and formed a quilt design that advanced and grew over their heads, an exhibition of an infinite fabric that progressed in rainbow hues as sunlight marched across the sky.

On the eastern horizon, a low belt of clear cream yellow sky lit the earth, burned away the purpled blue with red, orange, and then yellow as the sun rose. The low clouds brooded above as the boat lurched through the ocean swells, the bow crashed through each to send a misty salt spray over everyone. When the boat dropped over the edge of a crest to free fall into the trough of the next wave, people whooped as they felt lighter and floated out of their seats. Waves crashed upon waves, and if timed right, wave intersections melded together to make a super wave, a mountain of water that leapt up to tower over the boat for an instant.

As the sun came up, its light outlined the boat and silvered the edges of somnolent people, the grease black machinery, and boat's salted crusted window frames. It shimmered off the ocean surface and shattered off its myriad small mirrors to throw tiny pools of light across the flat vertical surfaces of the boat. The spider webs of ropes drooped into wet spirals of sunlight, as if God's palette knife cut through layers of bluish black paint to expose the white primal canvas of reality, a cold bloodless matrix without comfort or care.

They approached a shore where little lights shone through the haze, little stars that denoted human activity on the distant shadow of land.

The boat drew close and the details filled in. People on board pointed and smiled, made last minute adjustments to their loads, or lay down again for another fifteen winks. The jungle flowed down to meet the sea, broken in places by narrow dirty beaches lined with tall palm trees, like mop headed snakes, bent under the weight of coconuts.

The boat docked with the groan of wood and metal, cushioned by the sun charred bumpers of automobile tires that hung over both sides of the boat, and garlanded both sides of the dock like a row of salt sprinkled chocolate donuts.

Livingston appeared much cleaner than Puerto Barrios. Rows of houses aimed at the junction of the road and the dock. A large Victorian hotel stood rigid halfway up the town's sloped waterfront, its spacious porches decorated with pauper tourists and the empty cocoons of hammocks.

The men, gracious and false, offered a steady arm as they urged the girls to pass over the flimsy gangplank.

The girls walked along the beach and stopped at flotsam deposits, piles of shells in pearly pinks and purples that marked the limit of the highest tides, and the pits of whirlpools.

The majority of the shells looked like tall, rounded right triangles with a flattened bottom, some as big as a thumb. When the two halves remained connected, the two triangle shells looked like the angel wings of Christmas decorations.

The shells made drifts along the shore and collected in the hollow palm tree stumps. They scooped shells up in both hands, to let it run like treasure between their fingers.

A few miles up the shore, they came to a riverbed with a trickle of water in the middle of its sandy bottom. They followed it inland, walked on huge rocks that torrential floods and hurricanes once carried down from distant mountain cliffs.

As they walked upstream in the riverbed, the jungle became a dark green tunnel, and the pools of water grew larger. Soon they entered the eternal gloom of a tall forest, and a leaf filtered greenish light fell in tiny bright splashes through the still haze. Butterflies flit between the pillars of tree trunks that rose up through the lower canopy of leaves. Flowers lay strewn about, fallen from the treetops, out of sight. Far above, they heard a wind among the highest branches, and a few moments later, it rained red flowers. The air buzzed and whined with the sounds of a thousand insect wings. The loud metallic caws of unseen birds punctuated the hum.

A half a mile or so up the riverbed, they encountered a series of semicircular dams that looked like a giant stairway into a tall, vine woven jungle lit by a few slanted shafts of light, like a great Cathedral. They climbed up the scalloped edges of the first dry waterfall and walked its semi-circular edge around a pool of coral blue water to the next scalloped waterfall. As they climbed above each of the travertine edges of these first clear pools, they saw more dams beyond. They climbed up each of these travertine dams, skirted along the edge of their deep blue pools, and came to more of the same.

Higher yet, they found the pools got smaller, and then streambed curved flat and disappeared into the jungle.

"Wrong time of the year for waterfalls," Marie said as she watched the water trickle over the edge of the travertine dam. "Dry season." She scratched one of the circular dam's surface, and under her fingernail collected some of the calcium deposit that formed the dams, left behind as the water trickled and evaporated in the tropical heat.

Yvonne looked into the clear waters of a deep pool with huge boulders at the bottom. "It's not what I expected."

"Nor I."

Large dragonflies swooped and hovered above the water.

"Very quiet and peaceful, no tourists. That's a blessing." Annette threw some sticks into the pool and the girls watched as they went over the rock dam and down into the next pool.

"Well, we're here. Might as well enjoy it. I feel like sunbathing."

"Where? It's all rock, and very little sun."

"Find a dry edge near a pool, and lay down a towel. I don't care much for bright sun anyhow. I burn."

The girls headed back down to the larger pools below, then separated to each find a spot where the limestone deposits widened enough to stretch out a towel. The girls waved to each other across the shady distances of semi-circular limestone dams, stained black with algae where the waters cascade with gleeful chortles and silvery reflections. They disrobed like wood nymphs, white against the oily dark greens of the wall of jungle behind, and lay naked alongside the clear waters of intense blue pools.

"They should cut more trees down, let in more sun."

"Great idea. And with the wood they could build a diving board and a snack bar. And get some handsome lifeguards."

"Sometimes nature needs a little improvement. Isn't that right, girls?"

"No men to stare at us."

"I feel safer with the handsome lifeguards watching me."

Yvonne lay naked on her back and looked up into the branches far above her head. After a while, she closed her eyes. The sounds of the jungle, the buzz, the flap of wings, the cry of a distant nest of baby birds, soothed her. She felt the earth move in a warm spin.

Eyes, like fingers, ran along her nakedness, traced the outline where her tan body contrasted with the transparent greenish blue of the pool behind her, and touched her soft flesh where it deformed against the hot gray limestone she lay upon, as if atop an altar.

Fourth Section: Culture-shocked Together

CHAPTER 14: Dirección de Migración

After I returned to the guest house and rested from the hardship of the twenty four hour bus trip from Tikál, I noticed my Visa about to expire in a few weeks.

No money arrived at the Bank of America.

The Dirección de Migración offices lay near on my route to the Post Office, so I dropped my passport off one day and asked if they could stamp me with a visa for another three months.

I could leave my passport with them, but they would need proof of funds to stamp me a visa extension, so I should return to show them a quantity of money or traveler's checks.

Tourists, expatriates, and travelers made daily pilgrimages to Guatemala's main Post Office to receive their mail at General Delivery. The clerks' constant communication problems, a daily battle with the babble of foreign tongues, seemed infused with a black humor that rescued them from contagious stress. They mangled pronunciations on purpose, and almost smiled with each increase in a tourist's frustration. Mail Clerks refused to follow Spanish pronunciation rules, which every client expected, and instead attempted to repeat the exotic glottal sounds of foreign tongues with exaggeration, as if cosmopolitan themselves

To a man they seemed too stone faced. I thought they got a kick out of our shocked facial expressions, and probably hungered for one that registered the first dim recognition of their joke.

I decided to avoid their jokes and wrote my name on a sheet of paper to hand them, like a deaf-mute, after I suspected my mail retrieval depended on clerks who didn't know enough about the pronunciation of the English alphabet to file mail in the correct quarter of the alphabet.

Some of the letters arrived so late I wondered who else read them in transit, yet I received them with no sign that someone tampered with the envelope.

Shotgun and Ida led me to believe that the Guatemalan authorities might investigate anyone and everyone as a potential threat to some powerful interest's security.

Maybe all the mail to general delivery went through a process to screen out the dangerous correspondence.

Life in the Pensión grew comfortable, if not private.

The people that stayed here, which I first thought all belonged to the same family, often ate dinner together and breakfast on Sunday mornings, because most of Guatemala closed on Sundays and nobody went to work.

On most days, the older Spanish couples looked dressed for church. Because I knew their private lives, their home life, I started to appreciate that Guatemalans keep up appearances much more than Midwesterners did, not only because we dress in layers of old clothes to fight frigid, dangerous winters, but as a philosophy of life. Appearances mean everything when so many live in poverty. Respectable Latin Americans dressed up every time they went out in public.

Two young men about my age worked all day and on weekends dressed in T-shirts and jeans, yet they stayed out all night dressed up in pants and shoes, colorful polyester shirts with pointy lapels, sunglasses wore at night, and put on light jackets designed for Polo clubs.

Another bachelor in the house, tall, thin, once-upper-class middle-age Spanish descent Guatemalan who lounged around chain smoking in sleeveless T-shirts, liked to tell jokes at dinner. In a slow but gradual process of intuition, I gathered he resented my presence as a foreigner, as a Gringo, a Yankee American.

When I ate with them the first few times, nervous and unsure of every movement with knife and fork and every utilitarian Spanish phrase, he grilled me in Spanish to determine the extent of my comprehension. He decided I didn't understand a thing, in spite of the protests of others that I could speak and understand a little.

When he made his comments about me, I first thought people looked at me to see if I understood his jokes, then I realized they looked at me to see if I would react to them. He knew I would not understand his jokes, and so I became the convenient butt of many.

My inklings turned into his broad brushstrokes, when I began to recognize phrases of his anti-American comments, his hatred of Gringos, and thus his disdain of me by association. I didn't come to Guatemala to represent my country, my culture, my tribe, or my lifestyle. I represented the purity of youth, the untrammeled mind that struggles to bootstrap itself out of the mud of its origins, the curiosity of those who dare, for no good reason perhaps, but for no bad one either.

He let up after the matron of the house, who served the food and lurked about, came to my defense and scolded him, and probably told him to lay off.

Through shear will power, I almost purged myself of urges for late night ice cream. I recognized will power as one of the weakest forces of nature.

Masturbation helped cure me.

To bathe in the Pensión, each person arranged it with the housemother and servants who heated bathwater over the fire and dumped it into a giant iron caldron in the semi-public bathroom. Without a private bath, I tried to release my sexual tensions alone in the room I shared with my absentee roommate, but the thin walls made me paranoid that others could hear me breath in sexual excitement.

Most days the Salvadoran student roommate took classes and worked nights, but the maid and other members of the family could walk in at any moment. Several times I tried to close the door and read a book, and soon learned that if the door remained closed too long, they thought something wrong and investigated. I felt the others passed my door more than I heard them, imagined they stopped to listen. Guatemalans do not read much, and they rejected the possibility that a person could enjoy time alone in a closed room for hours.

I studied Spanish for a couple hours a day outside in the courtyard, and some times atop the Cerro del Carmen in the gardens. I occupied the rest of the time in explorations of the city. I watched the parade of tourists that filed through the Post Office, the Cathedrals, the Dairy Queen, and I mixed in with the pageant of life around the Central Plaza.

I could hear my internal dialogue make excuses to fool myself that I did not wander just to catch a glimpse of Yvonne.

I intended to stay home in the Pensión more than I managed to, but the thickheaded Italian Guatemalteco in the adjacent room, with whom I shared a small bathroom with a sink, loved to irritate me. Stout, no-neck, doe-eyed, beak-nose, fleshy lips, black greasy hair, he doused himself with colognes and liked to spit on the floor, my floor. I asked him not to. He spat, rubbed it in with his foot, and then glared at me with provocative insolence to dare me to react. He worked as a part-time fill-in temporary bartender or something, and he ribbed me nonstop while he dressed and shaved and greased his black hair into an oil sludge of bluish obedience. He would monopolize the bathroom if he realized I needed it, or plant himself in my doorway to adjust his tie and irritate me with obscene swine noises, sucks of nasal mucous, or a long fart.

He went out of his way to find opportunities to tease me about the two maids, young girls a little overstuffed, whose lack of athletic activities bulged their bodies' lower half. When one of the girls came near, he teased with increased frequency and intensity, and enjoyed it when anyone took offence. The unfortunate girls fought against their captivity within the dilemma of their role as professional servants and as human beings that deserve respect. They followed his orders and suffered his vulgarities with a wince and a cold shoulder.

He stirred up rumors of a love affair between I and one of the young girls, a stocky, good humored girl with Mayan's beautiful brown skin, Arabic features, and thick hairs on her arms and ankles, and a fine black fuzz on her upper lip. He told each of us, in private, different lies about how passionate we felt for each other, then made allusions to those lies in public. Because we felt privy to that information, although untrue, our uneasiness at the shared misinformation lent credence to his farce.

He looked like the fat child of a New Jersey Mafioso. He tortured both me and the younger servant girl, a stocky quiet twenty year old, with ashen brown skin and coal black eyelashes top and bottom, so thick they looked fake. Her big nose's nostrils flared permanent, and a mop of black curls that she wore tied up in a bun let curly tendrils escape and stick to her sweaty neck and temples. Whenever she served me, he made comments that made people laugh. She blushed, and I sat still as a rock.

After a while, I caught myself in fantasies about her, which made me feel as if he read my mind, or influenced it to think about things with her I never considered before. She didn't attract me, except the lovely exotic curves of her lips, the mysterious soft bulges under the front of her loose white blouse, the muscular calves that showed when she hiked up her skirt to climb the stairs.

Older than I by about five years, he tried to assume the role of guide to Guatemala's rituals of passage into manhood, a perverse father figure. I refused to let him show me the whorehouses, all fabulous, each full of beautiful friendly women, and cheap.

"Boy", he said in a combination sign language and the baby talk Spanish he used to insult me, "When I sixteen," he holds up fingers to count in English, one to sixteen. He points to his chest, and says "I work hard." He pantomimes work with a pick and shovel, "Earn money, everyday." He pretends to put money into an imaginary billfold. "Knock knock at house of girls." His hands outline the flanks of a curvaceous woman.

He wipes his sweaty brow and nose, spits on my floor, smears it with his foot, hikes up his baggy dress pants, looks from side to side, then tilts his head fast so his neck cracks.

"Give them money, and chingar, chingar," he pantomimes sex doggy style, his hands on imaginary hips. Then he shows me his fist up close, with his thumb inserted between his first two fingers. He wags two fingers up and down around his stubby thumb.

I smile and shake my head Yes, I understand.

"You come, I show you girls."

"No, gracias."

"Come, I buy you girl. You like, you buy one for me. Deal?"

"No."

He starts over. "Be like me. Work and earn dollars, knock knock. Go back to work, get money, go knock knock. Three, four times a day." holds up two fingers, pantomimes oral sex on a woman, another bout of doggy style, work, knock, etc. "All day, five, six days a week, when young like you."

What an excitable boy, I yawned at him.

I did give it some serious thought. Imagine, a visit to a bordello with him, a shameless and vulgar brute, too much of a jerk. He seemed incapable of decent concern for others that might translate to respect, let alone care or affection. I considered him a risk to my personal security. He might force me to shell out for both of us, or give me a practical joke in return. I figured he would try to spend any quantity of money I brought along, at best.

The House Mother warned me not to go anywhere with him. She hinted that he might rob me, or get his friends to.

I imagined him capable of a set up where a couple of his friends rob me, or a whore rolls me while my pants lay on the floor, or he 'rescues' me from some similar situation and expects a reward, or he abandons me to some fate which he pre-arranged.

In exchange for one sordid, base, and regrettable twenty minute act, I might make life a little easier for a single mother whore and her children or maybe her own single mother and siblings, but in return would receive the chance for a free dose of a venereal disease and long term fear of symptoms, or I become a vector of contagion to those I most cared about (Yvonne and the Ice Cream Queen), while my available funds suffer a drastic cut.

The cost of that twenty minutes might pay my expenses for a month somewhere else in Guatemala.

Another young man in the Pensión invited me across town to see the apartment he would move into.

We decided to walk the twelve blocks. On the way, we see this modern Ladina girl approach, dressed to show off her body in painted-on blue jeans and tight T-shirt. As she passes, he leans toward her and says something. She stops, turns around, and looks back at us. So we stop and walk back to her. I could not follow the exchange but read the body language. He leans over her, a little too close, and she shuffles her feet real coy while her shoulders oscillate like a street sign in a hurricane. At the end, she takes a pen and scrap of paper out of her purse and writes something, hands it to him, then walks away. She turns around and walks backwards with a little extra bounce which enhances her frontal jiggles, and waves, big toothy smile outlined in red lipstick, a wave with each bounce skip, then turns, her buttocks in a silent drumbeat of retreat.

"What was that all about?"

"I invite her to go out tomorrow night."

"Did you know her?"

"We just now meet, Brandon. You see everything."

"What did you say to her?"

"A piropo. You know piropos?"

"No."

"The things men say to girls on the street, you must say them in the States. Teach me English, what you say to meet a pretty girl on the street?"

"Nothing. I mean, construction workers and house painters in the city yell vulgar things, but I don't think girls don't like it. Girls get scared, or insulted."

"In Spanish the girls like it, at least they expect it. If you don't say something, they know you're not interested."

"You say Hey, mamacita?"

"Maybe, but better, classier sayings we call piropos. Come from Spain's culture. You want to learn one?"

"Like what you said to that girl?"

"That one's a bit complicated for you. Try this one. Tus ojos, morena, son de tal virtud, que a los mismos que les matan, les dan la salud."

He made me repeat the rhyme after him line by line until I got it right, sort of, then again as I wrote it down, and then again as we translated it word for word. We arrived at his cement apartment by then, a glass fronted room on the second floor over a main drag. Looked to me like office space.

I stood in the window and looked out over the bowl of Guatemala City as the streetlights struggled to get up to full voltage. In the distance, they twinkled yellow in the purple mists of twilight at the foot of the mountains.

I practiced my piropo in Spanish, and tried to understand it in English.

"Your eyes, brown skin girl, are of such virtue, that the same ones they kill, they make healthy."

I tried to find the best translation into English, while he swept the floor and explained his plan for the interior décor, and how he would find the furniture to match.

"Your eyes, my tanned child, pierce like knives, but those you kill, you have made wise." Ugh. Seemed way too corny in English. I added a stiff upper lip twisted into a wry intellectual smile, and tried again. "Your eyes, blonde vixen, cut me to the quick but I'd come back from the dead for one little kiss."

The rust belt girls I knew stateside would belt me aside the head, and Jap slap and cold cock any stranger that recited corny poetry to them on the street. They would think me a fool, homosexual, or someone who tries to make them look stupid. American girls expect nonverbal flirts, like the long stare and a slow smile from strong, silent types or, at most, 'oneliners,' hack cliché pickup lines. Women share and compare these often vulgar witticisms to ridicule men as simpletons, at least some female friends told me that in an attempt to train me in how to pick up women.

The poem translates into pure corn in English. I could not believe women love that stuff, until I saw it work. That day, I wrote in my journal the first "inkling" that I began to understand a tiny fundamental axiom about the reality that underlay my trip outside the borders of the good old USA.

I glimpsed the enormity of the task of language acquisition, the acceptance of phrases from a tangential historical trajectory that leads to distinct culture, politics, and traditions and creates macro-structures of institutional religion and educational systems nuanced by the micro-expectations of social grace that makes song lyrics sound correct and translations always difficult, if not impossible, once removed from the native context. I saw myself trapped within a WASP context, a White Anglo Saxon Protestant cultural framework, whose foundations diverged eons ago from the Hispanic Romance languages of institutionally Catholic nations.

As if a barrier to my comprehension broke, I began to see realities from two sides, as an inhabitant of a window between them. I saw the impossibility of any comprehension of Spanish and Latin America through word for word translations into English. Such a brute exchange of symbols cannot remain faithful to the original.

More than geographical regions separated by manmade borders, two realities struggled to maintain an uneasy co-existence, one with obvious technological and economic dominance, yet as if through a veil, I began to see the focus change. A halo of innocence, of sensual camaraderie in nature, surrounded these pedestrian Guatemalans, as perceivable as the metal and glass automotive alienation of American society.

In my journal, I wrote: "I feel like an alien, trapped in a parallel universe."

Back home in Michigan, the winter set in with six feet of snow and subzero temperatures. I felt nostalgic about skiing and the aesthetic purity of a snow covered landscape in hibernation, the effects of ice that sterilizes and freezes to kill off the insects and halt the decomposition of dead leaves and any other detritus. Guatemala City's constant nippy weather came with wood smoke and diesel fumes, flowers and birdsong. Each morning, a tropical sky clotted with ocean-driven clouds that billowed behind the silhouettes of palms and epiphytes, volcanoes and mountains. This Land of Eternal Springtime reminded me of spring in Michigan, when winter's white blood unclots and sends young men off across the muddy landscape in high rubber boots to search for adventure.

New flowers bloomed every month here. I wanted to pick them and give them to all these beautiful brown girls, but I didn't feel confident with my piropos.

A couple of pre-dawn mornings, I walked through the dew jeweled trees that lead up to the Ermita del Carmen, the church where I first heard the Nuns singing. The birds come alive as the light swells on the horizon. The morning's fog and haze flows between the tree trunks and coalesces into low clouds that break apart and shrink into puffs so low they leave water droplets on the top branches of the trees. This uneven cloud cover burns off by midmorning, when the city fills with the honks of traffic and birds, the squeals of brakes and children.

The bright colors of indigenous Guatemalan clothing echoed the flowers, insects, birds, and sunrises of the Land of Eternal Springtime.

Mayan Calendar:

The Mayan calendar cycles through two distinct year counts, plus five "nameless" days of bad luck called Uayeb, that together depict a 52 year Calendar Round. The Sacred Year, or "tzolkin", consists of 260 days the Mayans count as 13 months with 20 day-names. That year intermeshes with a "vague" or a solar year called "haab" which demarked 365 days with 18 month-names of 20 days, numbered from 0 to 19, plus those five "bad" days.

They also counted time through a series of cycles of days, called "kins": the uinal (20 kins), tun (360 kins), katun (7,200 kins), baktun (144,000 kins), and the alautun of 23,040,000,000 kins, which counts sixty three million, eighty thousand and eighty two years of 365.25 days each.

The first two year-counts allowed all of the Meso-American civilizations to determine, with great accuracy, dates within each period of fifty two years, because the least common multiple of 260 and 365 works out to 18,980 days, or 52 years, perhaps also useful as an average lifespan, or two generations.

$$260 \times 73 = 18,980 \ (52 \ years)$$
$$365 \times 52 = 18,980 \ (52 \ years)$$
18,980 divided by 20 = 949 months of twenty days, (52 years)

In Mayan cultures of the Guatemalan highlands outside of Guatemala City, they still use the 260 day calendar, secret sacred caves, and ancient prayers and processions to Mayan deities incorporated into the iconography of thin veneer of Spanish Catholicism.

After a late sidewalk brunch of corn tortillas and refried beans with white salty cheese, I visited the general delivery window of the Post Office.

I walked out from under clouds that threatened rain and into the unusual brightness of the interior of the Post Office, and saw Yvonne in a floor length light blue cotton dress, accordion pleated and full up to the waist, then tight and sleeveless.

She waited for her mail at one of the window's old walnut counters.

I stood behind her in the small crowd, unnoticed. I watched the men watch her. The Westerners tried not to appear too obvious in their interest, but the Guatemalans and other Hispanics engaged in a genial competition for her attention. They made comments and jokes to each other with each casual movement of her lithe body.

When she turned around to leave, she ignored them and her eyes bumped into me.

"Oh! Hello Brandon." she smiled and held out her hand.

"Yvonne, I recognize your hat."

"Did you?" She teased the hair that poked out from under her Jamaican beret as I looked at my feet.

"Where you headed?" I asked.

"Nowhere. And you?"

"To get my mail. Wait for me? We'll head for nowhere together. Will you wait?"

"I'll wait for you outside. Don't be too long," She turned to walk down the white stone stairs.

I turned around to find one of the clerks waited for me with a face of feigned politeness. I wrote my full name on a piece of paper and gave it to him.

He went off to search for my mail. He came back with nothing.

I could feel Yvonne watch me, but when I turned around, I did not see her.

I walked down the stone stairs two at a time, calm, deliberate. I scanned the little gardens with shade trees, but did not see her.

She got up from a bench, tucked a book into her handbag, and walked over. Her dress hem flipped forward with each step.

She glanced at her watch and said "Any mail, Brandon?"

"Not a thing, Yvonne." I opened my empty hands, and smiled to think she remembered my name.

She smiled back. "Expect something?"

"Yeah. Word from a friend."

"A friend?" She said as we stepped through a flock of pigeons big as a carpet, their iridescence a drab gray in the gloomy afternoon. "A girlfriend?"

"I wish."

She shielded her eyes from the sun and studied my face.

I winked at her and continued. "Haven't seen anyone lately. Left the country. Abroad."

"I know how it feels, so far from friends." She linked her arm with mine and we walked down the uneven sidewalk, alert to the potholes and shattered cement that sometimes opened to reveal a shallow drainage ditch below.

It felt good to walk with someone again, in the hot sunshine on a cool day, to talk to someone attractive, someone who acts interested.

My doubts about Dennis' story resurfaced. If Dennis told me the truth, did that mean Yvonne must manipulate men, or that the French in general trivialize relationships more than Canadians do?

"You miss your friends and family, Brandon?"

"I try to miss them about as much as I think they miss me. Everyone's busy with their own problems."

"I bet you left behind a lot of broken hearts. Be careful, women can feel each other's pain, even long distance."

That reminded me of women who told me they believe in the dark powers of witchcraft, but they call it a white magic. They warn men to treat women right because it angers their collective femininity, their Goddess powers, as if in revenge for all this talk of God as a man or his son, and the way males dominate women in marriages, the workplace, in society, and in general.

Modern women attack in the name of all the women who went before, all the "slaves of a paternalistic society," the ubiquitous niggers of the known universe.

It did not make sense to me, the way Dennis said they broke up. People should invent some correct way to break up with others, some quiet unemotional method to walk away, a pleasant card covered with flowers, birds, and bees that says "It didn't work out," as a guarantee of distance and civility, to keep everyone out of danger from emotional vendettas.

"Do you believe in Astrolgoy?"

Dennis' story helped me distrust Yvonne, but then everyone knows the moon rules women, right down to their twenty eight day periods. Women who live together often menstruate together, and a significant percentage of pregnant women give birth on the full moon.

Lunatics.

"Did you hear me? I asked if you believe in Astrology."

"No. I might believe, if one more person comes up to me and says something like, I moved here on the advice of my Astrologer, bought the raffle ticket as instructed, won a car, and found you here, as my horoscope said I would. Wanna go for a ride?"

"I asked an Astrologer about us."

"You and me? You don't even know my birthday."

"You don't remember? You told me because you don't believe in astrology."

"What's my horoscope?"

I didn't really listen. I bet Yvonne faked everything, all that dream mumbo-jumbo, to make it easier to break up with Dennis. If she did, she showed a lot of creative intelligence, or feminine wiles. O.K., so our sun signs seem compatible and our moons both rest in the seventh house of bedlam. Auspicious and rare, she says, and probably doomed.

"Where do you want to go?" She asked. "Have you seen the Merced?"

I winced, remembered Dennis and I puking our hearts out on its steps. I wondered if she talked to him since then. "A couple of times." I said absently.

"Have you seen the inside?"

"No. Have you?"

"No, and I want to." She slipped her arm into mine and pulled me along.

Short people with black hair filled the main square. Crowds gathered at bus stops, street vendors with their wares spread out on blankets stretched between pillars that held up the arched stone roof over the sidewalk. People hurried across the sunny, traffic clogged streets to enter the shade. Pigeons flocked in the square where mothers helped children throw snacks on the worn stones.

The Bank of America building reminded me of the lost transfer of funds my mom sent three weeks ago. Every time I complained at this Guatemalan branch of B of A, they tried to trace my money.

Yvonne and I walk in. I feel out of place because of our típica pursed, clothing made by Mayan Indians, me with blue jeans and sandals, she in her embroidered skirt. We looked somewhat like an indigenous couple with white skin.

No one gave me the impression they disdained us for it.

The teller recognized me, because of my regular fruitless visits over the last weeks, and my insistence that they try to trace the transmission. Mom said the Michigan bank traced it into the stateside branch of the Bank of America.

He smiled and said "Good news," and walked to another window to pick up some documents for me to sign. He asked if I would like cash or traveler's cheques.

"Did you ever figure out what happened to my money? Why it took so long?" I wondered if the system did this kind of thing to sequester small amounts of money from thousands of people, to make quick investment turnarounds on sure things, like daily rate of exchange fluctuations.

He said "The money got lost between the New York branch of the Bank of America and their California branch."

I wondered. His explanation didn't let Guatemala off the hook in my mind. It sounded fishy to me, that the most advanced international United States bank would lose money, but not the bank in a country without dependable electricity or a functional telephone system.

Yvonne and I both resented the mysterious and unfriendly presence of tall Gringos in suits. They waded among the short black haired Indians, giants in a squat, peaceable kingdom, top predators through a lower level in the food chain. A six foot tall blonde haired 'guero' Gringo sticks out like a snowman in a coal field.

Many indigenous older women look upon us Gringos with superstitious glances; they cross themselves and kiss their thumbs to ward off the Evil Eye. Maybe these Indians harbor doubts about their own state of grace in the face of such large and affluent humans from the Colossus of the North. I wondered what Mayans from rural areas think, the first time they come to the city and see these huge specimens of Northern European bloodlines raised on milk, corn, and beef.

When I began to travel, I felt excited at the thought that I might meet powerful people who lived complex and colorful lives, members of foreign governments, or even the CIA, who might take an interest in me to show me the ropes and influence the direction of my life.

Some of these giants probably worked as CIA agents, young, well dressed, huge and tall men with military haircuts and dark sunglasses who walked head and shoulders above the sidewalk crowd, farmers through a field of wheat.

I told Yvonne about Ida and Shotgun's experiences, and how they thought these American agents kept an eye on things we really shouldn't know about.

Yvonne felt repugnance when confronted with their superior attitude and self assurance, the elegant veneer that spoke volumes about their ability to hob-knob with the rich and powerful, to receive preferential treatment and protection.

The ones I heard speak Spanish didn't do well.

They didn't respect the language and customs. They looked down their noses at the rest of us, as if they thought of themselves as genetic superiors, the cream of a super race from a super power. Whether from families with generations in the military elite, or the sons of old money and military education, I sensed them as cruel mercenary muscle-heads who train at West Point or other military academies, schools that attract the young cream of the corrupt ruling classes from around the world. Like the television images of the legendary few good men the U.S. Marines seek every year, they seemed like football players in suits, extraterrestrial gorillas. They lacked humility, elegance and style, and their casual grins and proud aloofness robbed others of dignity, which they seemed to enjoy as they muscled their way through the crowd without a downward glance.

Their behavior betrays a psychological need to make others feel they live inconsequential lives. They communicate a disdain for their surroundings, and treat entire nations of diverse people as nothing more than another pawn to manipulate in their geopolitical game. They pushed through the crowd without eye contact, devoid of the altruism that marks real heroes. People who belong, whose beauty shines from within, whose labors of love continue without cease day after day without pay, deserve recognition for their heroism and their influential place in history. We should stop the memorials to people who owe their heroism to a special moment in some extreme situation of brutish conquest.

My heart went out to the prematurely aged women with five kids camped out on downtown sidewalks to sell things, dayglo candies made of sugar and coconut, fudge-like substances of granulated brown sugar and burnt milk, home implements, baked goods, or huge bundles of woven products.

What would it take for these CIA bastards to recognize their own mother's or grandmother's hardship sprawled across the sidewalk at their feet, and help her get back up?

They represent the fruits of boot camp, where in the national interest, they take young, patriotic citizens and break them down, erase their instincts for moral behavior, to build them back up into military personnel trained to murder on orders, without reasons, happy to receive 'intelligence' on a need to know basis.

You can't put the killer into a soldier until you erase their instincts to belong.

CHAPTER 15: Rites of Courtship
Iglesia del la Merced

Many Meso-American cultures, in both southern North America and northern Central America, believed that around the year 1519 the universe would pass through its fourth destruction and leave them near the end of eternity (whatever that means) to enter the Fifth Sun (which the Spaniards later learned about from the Aztecs, and called the Quinta Sol). As the end approached, the Aztec empire, centered in Mexico City, needed people to sacrifice, victims captured from the tribes they dominated over their vast holdings in Meso-America. This made conditions ripe for a civil war.

We talked on the sidewalk, admired the beautiful amber stone of the Iglesia del la Merced in the full afternoon sun, then walked across the rust red tiles of the courtyard to enter, through the vacant yawn of the dark vaulted doorway, the netherworld of Guatemalan Catholicism.

Our eyes opened wide to watch the fade-in of the immense arched purple darkness of ceiling ,where the four walls surged upward in an illusion of an endless curved perspective that held the heavens in a giant embrace. The few shafts of light from tiny windows painted amber highlights and hollow echoes, as they bounced off the shimmers of gold trim, the semi-mirrors of glass display cases, the mirror-polish of marble pillars, and the wine dark varnish on the hand worn wood of pews, altars, and banisters. Confessionals lined both the walls, a testament to the necessity of redemption. Chambers that flanked the main Cathedral area contained paintings and garish wooden saints, two thirds human size, that suffered Christ's wounds with red paint and big spikes. Some lay clothed in white satin and gold trim, inside clear glass caskets that look like tiny greenhouses, or giant cut glass jewels.

The paintings also depicted scenes of Christ's suffering and death. All around me I saw torture, mutilation, death, and what might deserve the label of necrophilia.

"Yvonne, do you think we're safe in here?"

"Of course, Brandon. Don't be afraid. It's just Catholicism."

I directed her gaze to the altar and the cross behind it. "They don't kidnap unbelievers to sacrifice on the cross each Sunday?"

"We could come back and find out. I'm Catholic, remember."

"I don't think I know enough Spanish."

"It's in Latin anyway. It's not important that you understand the words."

"So that's why Catholic countries remain illiterate. They rely on graphics, pomp and circumstance. Priests show Indians all these paintings of punishment or death, and then link it to this glorious gold leafed cross behind the altar. The Indians see it as another one of their cracks between levels of the universe. They should put one of those big red Exit signs over the cross, alongside a neon blue arrow that flashes and points up."

"Brandon, just shut up, will you? Have a little respect."

"I'm very respectful, when earned."

"Atheist."

We walked towards the altar and examined each of the little statues of Saints that bled and mourned, eyes open, tucked away into niches in the walls, or as macabre decorations high on the pillars. Behind the altar, a wall of sculpted foliage and birds, a gold leaf waterfall, fell from the ceiling to entangled Saints, pillars and the Angel cherubs, called Putto, or cupid.

Worthy of any One True God, or a couple of embezzled National Treasures. And all this splendid ornate ostentation remains in Guatemala like the faint echo of a Big Bang, a whisper of the thousands of tons of gold the Spanish tore from the fingers, ears, and necklaces of the beaten, diseased and dying Indigenous American people, while their victims hallucinated that either their Gods abandoned them, or these vulgar, metal-clad whitish bearded people represented the return of the God Coatzecualco to herald the Fifth Sun, the Quinta Sol, the end of their eternity, or maybe the start of their ninth hell.

Something in the human psyche makes people believe that prophecy fulfilled always works out for the better, so better to rely on imperfect memory to create a past full of destiny.

Gold leaf covered the entire baroque wall around the cross. Perhaps they electroplated some of the metal filigree plants and leaves, or painted with a gold powder mixed with brass flake, but most of it they applied as tissues of gold leaf, some say a mere a molecule thick, made with a sheet of gold hammered thin, folded, hammered again, folded, etc. Hard stuff to work with, I thought. Gold leaf that thin must smear like pencil lead.

The Saint, with mouth slightly open, lay within his glass casket and stared up through the fingerprint-smudged facets. The casket looked like a big diamond. The Saint suffered, in a wordless though openmouthed silence, the wounds of Christ's agony that wept bright red paint from his hands.

The images of the Virgin Mary inter-mixed with that of Mexico's Virgin of Guadalupe, like Spain's Lady of Fatima. They place her image, or little statues of her, into niches to surprise those who entered. She accosts with head bowed and hands open, as if to part the fog of confusion, welcome children, or perhaps to say "What are you telling me for?" Her red heart radiates gold skewers, a shared shish kabob of multiple heartbreaks, all the fantasies of sexual frustration cowed under her prudish cowl. Her body, shapeless and covered head to foot in thick folds of cloth, repulsive in its virginity or its shame of unmarried sin, reminds the most vulgar parts of the male psyche of the ubiquity of mischief and naughtiness. The original sin expresses itself in the omnipresent lust of the lying braggadocio of men, and in the short-term improvisational availability of women who keep secrets to the grave, both of which seem like a divine plan to diversify the gene pool against the harmful effects of either large harems for the few kings, or the ancestral inbred incestuous tribal marriages between cousins, Aunts and nephews, fathers and daughters.

Yvonne said, "Do you feel the sexual repression here?" Her words echoed and reverberated off the hard stone, her feminine voice came out too loud for the dark and ominous silence.

"I was just imagining the Virgin without clothes."

Three old women with black headscarves knelt between the pews. One of them pulled her shawl down farther over her face and crossed herself. They interrupted their prayers to give us a brief glare that made me wonder if they understood a bit of our English.

Yvonne continued. "That's what I mean. There's no nudity in Guatemala. In Europe, people enjoy nudity."

"Guatemalans don't touch each other, barely touch when they shake hands. Mexicans kiss each other on the cheek and give hugs like we shake hands."

"And Mexican men try to father as many illegitimate children as they can."

"Maybe the Guatemalans do too. I mean, think about it, Yvonne. What else do poor people have to do? In the tropics, they can't do much in the heat of the day except sleep. They stay up all night, and when they see someone attractive down at the fountain, in line at the corn grinder's place, on the bus, they try to score. Where else you gonna meet people?"

"In church?"

"Or on a dock in Santa Catarina. And with the Pope's stand against Birth Control, we're in for a massive population growth of Catholics on all Continents. If you can't lick 'em, join 'em. You're a practicing Catholic, aren't you?"

"I used to practice, until I mastered the material. It's dark in here." She said.

"You ever think that these vaulted church doors look like a vagina?"

"A vagina?" Yvonne laughed. I don't think so."

"You know what I mean, between a woman's legs, pussy. See the lines along the side, inverted V in the middle?"

She shrugged. "I know what a pussy is. Don't know. Symbol of rebirth? It's God's house. God knows that Man is nothing without woman. Most people enter the world through a pussy, eh?"

"Ever wonder what motivates young men to enter the priesthood? What is that, homosexuality, altruism, need for authority and divine power, instant respect, or is it a fear of women?"

"God is a woman." Yvonne walked away distracted, straight up to the altar where hundreds of votive candles burned on a slanted table, a great plain of little fires, little souls stretched up with steady feeble flames shaped like leaves, the translucent wax slumped, white grubs lined up like soldiers.

She found an unlit candle, a squat little red one, and picked it up, slow, and deliberate, to tip the wick into another candle's yellow tongue of flame.

I walked up on the right side of the altar and watched the profile of her face in the candle light. She set it amongst the other lit candles, crossed herself, and touched her lower lip with the thumbnail of her right hand.

"What does that mean? Did you wish for something?"

"I can't tell you."

"We need to go camping."

"Camping? Why?"

"My church is much bigger than yours, and the points of light always shine, even beyond the clouds. If you wait long enough, a star will fall to wish upon."

Yvonne smiled, and said, "Better hope it's not a big one."

"The bigger they come, the harder they fall."

Catholic Confessional

Quetzalcoatl: The story of the Toltec Empire revolves around a legendary yet real person, the son of a king named Mixcoatl, ruler of the most successful tribe of a group collectively called the Chichimecas, known by their symbols as the People of the Dog. The son's name, Topiltzin Ce Acatl Quetzalcoatl, means Our Prince One Reed Bird Serpent, which reminds us how the Aztec choose a new home on Lake Texcoco, where they saw an eagle eat a serpent atop a prickly pear. An assassin murdered his father and became king even before his mother died in childbirth, so his mother's family raised him in the city of Tepotzotlán, where he became a priest of the God Quetzalcoatl. As a man, he returned to the Toltecs and avenged his father's murder in a battle to the death with the usurper, and took the throne. Then he founded a new city, Tula, fifty miles north of Mexico City, and dedicated it to the peaceful pursuit of the arts. Ancient chronicles suggest he meditated and became convinced of man's duty to the Supreme Creator, the god both near and far, male and female, the force that called into existence the sky, sun, earth, and moon, and decreed that humans should create, not destroy. He preached for the acquisition of wisdom as the ultimate good, earned through abstinence, personal sacrifice, mediation, and creativity. The culture of the Toltec people blossomed with artistic creativity, and a renaissance spread across Mexico that brought artistic motifs, metals, metallurgy, and a new scratch-resistant glazed pottery known as plumbate. Pottery vessels took the shapes of animals like birds, turkeys, quail, lizards, tapirs, armadillos, dear, squirrels, toads, and snakes, with and without feathers.

I left Yvonne at her ritual of self anointment and examined one of the confessionals. First, I snuck a quick peak inside, and then looked around and saw no one, so I checked it out thoroughly, inside and out. Then I opened a small door and got into the Priest's section. It looked like a good place for a couple of stereo speakers and a small light to read by, a great place for sensory deprivation or meditation. You could give orders to the house cleaner through the cloth partition meant to separate the priest from some crouched sinner who kneeled to confess and beg forgiveness. I bet the Priest yawned ninety percent of the time, as he heard the endless repetition of mundane and unoriginal sins.

Do the best sinners, those that put much creative thought and effort to commit original sins, share the same pedantic faith of those who find solace and constant amusement in the rote Latinate mumbles of Priests? Do the lackluster drones of automatic choral responses give the faithful an inflated sense of togetherness and dilute their crimes against God? Do those who partake in the Mass's splendor like royalty with the gowns, robes, scepters, humble themselves when they wait in lines for wafers, pews, soot smudged foreheads, and a splash of water? As if to convince themselves that God takes a personal interest in their activities in return for the decorations within His house.

All in service of medieval notions of sin and redemption.

I felt sure that the more people educated themselves, the more transparent the relationship of church and state, where both seek to control people's thoughts and actions, hypnotize them into the rituals of tithe and tax.

I wanted to buy a confessional for my future home. A confessional that folds down into a bed, with a little refrigerator for ice cream, a color TV with headphones. With a little modification, the expanded confessional might retain its dark, woody coziness for two people two enjoy together. Easier to adjust the microclimate and cool things down when things overheat.

A psychologist could use them to specialize in Catholic psychosis. I could rent out my enhanced musical confessionals as a dark space to absorb the evil sinfulness of their confessions, a Pandora's Box for any Catholic soul's litany of agonies and self flagellations, those who seek guilt first, redemption later, through self punishment to purify one for a final absolution, and ensure the certainty of an afterlife of clouds, winged babies with harps, and utter boredom for eternity ,except for the memories of their sins.

Catholicism institutionalizes the dissolute. Reminds me of the joke about someone who beats a hammer against himself because it feels good when he stops, or the definition of neurotic obsessive behavior, when someone does the same thing over and over and expects a different result. Catholics perfect the process. Men serve their families with elaborate parties of fun and games for the slightest excuse, birthday parties for one year olds, so the adults can drink and meet each other and share the silent, culturally appropriate expectation of the males' persistent carousal for extra-marital liaisons to beget more illegitimate children. Maybe those married women who accept another man's proposition, do it to exact revenge against their own husband's dalliances. Then all the Catholics confess to start the cycle over again.

They should meditate, not confess.

Meditation trains people to see that logical, verbal left brain hemisphere from another viewpoint, and increases our quality of life from mere lip service to tradition into a macro-perception of our own internal dialogue, so our inner nonverbal language and thoughts can break through the repetitious tape-loop circular logic of words.

We WASPs get pushed out of the nest too young, uneducated and too infected with rugged individualism to recognize our interconnected lives. Most of us land on our feet, and then the school of hard knocks makes us swallow the unhappiness, to let society's rules and regulations create frustrations that wear away at our young adult's ideals, until we shed them like useless pin feathers. The few fly high for a while, and the luckiest see themselves below, while still young, as dupes about to dedicate their life to a comfortable prison from where they service a debt on car, house, insurance, and medical bills that comprise a system designed to make someone else, some other class of human, rich.

A faith in the basic goodness of human beings works against the media brainwash, the madness and fear caused by relentless newscasts of victimization, rape, dangers to children, robbery, spontaneous and senseless violence, corporate crime, war and terrorism, etc. Fear keeps us imprisoned within our cars and homes or apartments that serve as both prisons and receptacles for an endless procession of 'necessary' consumer goods and services.

Fearful people end up in church, but hell cannot motivate altruistic creativity. No wonder religious fanatics added so little to the shared wealth of human accomplishment.

The Jewish faith produces the physicists and doctors, the scientists and artists that push the frontiers of human accomplishment. And they learn a dead language to practice their faith.

Maybe bilingualism opens the doors of perception.

The Market

At Tula, Meso-Americans built temples, at least four dedicated to the god Quetzalcoatl. One portrait, carved on rocks above the city, depicts the man Ce Acatl Quetzalcoatl in the costume of a king with a scepter. In his legend, like Theseus in Greek mythology, he offers himself as a human sacrificial victim, as food for a dragon and he cuts his way out of its stomach with a copper knife, which perhaps speaks to Coatzecoatl's opposition to human sacrifice.

The legend also describes battles with the sorcerer-priest Tezcatlipoca (Smoking Mirror) depicted with a mirror for his right foot. This sorcerer sent devils, disguised as old men, to get Quetzalcoatl drunk and seduced by a woman to break his vows of abstinence and continence. Other spells, perhaps aided by the influence of peyote or psychedelic mushrooms, made the king Quetzalcoatl feel shame and disgust about himself. He destroyed his palaces, burned his cacao plantations down to cactus and charred rock, banished all birds from his kingdom, hid his treasures and artwork in the mountains, and left with a retinue of dwarfs and cripples.

When this priest-king Ce Acatl Quetzalcoatl crossed the high volcanoes with his retinue of dwarfs and cripples, most of his followers froze to death. He continued on, and suffered many hardships before he rested in Cholula. He then set out for the coast of Veracruz, where he built a raft woven of serpents and sailed south.

Yvonne made her way around the far edges of the Cathedral, and I followed. As we walked through the Church, she opened doors, and laughed when she noticed how I kept watch to see that no one in authority rose up to stop us. We went where we wanted to, and in a cul-de-sacs anteroom in front of an encased wooden Saint who stared in blind agony at the murals on the ceiling, she gave me a little kiss.

I took it as a reward for my lapdog behavior, unconditional support and two steps behind in slack tongue adoration.

Painted blood ran from the encased Saint's hands and temples, as usual.

At any one time, we saw no more than three or four groups of Guatemalans knelt in prayer, the majority old women, wrapped in layers of shawls and blankets. The echoes of their soft mutters padded like mouse feet between the pews. Did they entreat God to cure sick members of the family or otherwise improve their lot? For the benefit of their friends and neighbors? Maybe they grumbled and demanded damnation for those they perceived responsible for life's discomforts and disappointments.

I followed Yvonne to the glare of the front door. The intense sunlight filtered around a couple of wooden screens to stab our eye as we neared. With a final look back that lingered on the wall of gold far off in the candle-lit interior, we squinted and stepped out onto the red flagstone apron that shimmered transparent in the sunlight.

As if a new day dawned while we loitered for that half hour inside, the dark and damp clouds thinned to bright, windy and dusty.

I felt hunger. "Let's go to the market and Eat."

"OK." She pulled me along. "I need to buy some things to send to France."

"You don't plan to stay longer in Guatemala?"

"I don't know. I don't know anymore. I bought some beautiful fabrics and sent them home already. My sister wants me to send more so she can sell them. I bought the first ones because I want them, not to sell. One of a kind. At least I thought so at the time."

We walked the diesel scented streets through the smoke of the outdoor grills.

Nearer the market, a long line of street vendors set up to take advantage of the hundreds of people who pass these corners every hour. In any country with few refrigerators per capita, housewives or sent servants make daily trips to buy the day's supplies of food and drink, the fruit, vegetables, meat, and all the multi-colored sweet breads and candies made from Guatemalan sugar. They squatted next to open fires on the street to prepare oil drenched fast food. The aromas wafted from their wok-like vats of oil where pouches of dough sizzled and boiled. These corn dough pockets contained bananas, or cheese, or strips of meat, chicken wings and legs, squash flowers, or chunks of fleshy plant stems and leaves. Draped on the dry edges of the woks and grills, tortillas browned with char.

Inside the market, another line of stalls served Guatemala's version of take-out foods, the aromatic, partially rotten meats cooked in smoking vats of used oils, then wrapped with a stack of tortillas handed over in a paper bag with a few paper picnic napkins and a couple of teaspoons of hot sauce in a small plastic baggie sealed with a wire and paper twist top.

People crowded the market's aisles. Yvonne pushed me down the narrow aisles to careen against the high walls that threatened to overflow with merchandise. She felt my attraction to the guitars and let me examine one, but then steered me away to keep me focused on fabrics.

The tourists came to the market like metal filings to a magnet, sharks to a carcass. They gaped and pointed cameras, dressed outlandish in Hawaiian shirts, white shorts, and plastic thong sandals. Tourist families gaggled together, chicken squawked at each little discovery, and rubber-necked while they asked each other who would like what for Christmas or Birthday, Mother's day or Father's day. They shared vague paranoia in long reiterations to no one in particular, worried about hygiene, hotel security, prices, itineraries and bus schedules.

They chatted with strangers, compatriots or not. They compared notes on prices to make sure they didn't commit the consumer's error to get gypped, or pay too much, which helps many Americans and those from consumer cultures of the Developed World feel competent as Democratic Consumers, those who shape reality by the virtue of their votes with ethe pocketbook. If you pay too much, you lose in the grand game of International Capitalism, where winners must always receive more value than they pay, more bang for the buck.

The Traveler adheres to the motto "take nothing but pictures, leave nothing but footprints." A great excuse for the miserliness of those on a budget, though it frustrates merchants and the beggars, who learn to resent cameras in their face and the zoo-animal treatment from people who do not buy. The casual tourists do not appreciate that Guatemalans must live from each sale's meager profit. Tourists regard their presence in the workplace as fashion models of local color, paid for by the government, like Mickey and Goofy at Disneyland.

Tourists resent it when a colorful native tries to charge per photo. The tourist may walk away and feel anger, but the Indian's family feels hunger.

Yvonne made a beeline for the section of stalls that sold fabrics and clothing.

I followed.

"Fashion changes often in France, for every season. Look at this." She pulled out of a rack a green dress with complicated embroidery. "Peasant look for Spring in the French countryside, no?"

"Yeah. Or Winter in Alabama, hippie Earth mammas could hide their rubber boots under it to run out to the end of the driveway to check the mail."

"What?"

"Never mind."

We walked on and showed each other things that caught our eye. She enjoyed the hand woven intricate details on the fabrics, the interwoven colors that blend into stripes of patterns through centuries-old techniques of tie-dyed threads to make the skeletons and geometric animal designs.

I looked at boxes with hidden compartments and enameled paintings of Guatemalan scenery on top. On some paintings, you could tell the painter worked fast on hundreds of boxes. Most scenes depicted the same old volcano and palm tree, a man with a machete, but some offered a rarer vision. The artist experimented with another interpretation of Guatemala in scenes of a hut in the moonlight at the water's edge, or a Ceiba tree with cattle huddled in the shade, or a scene of hammocks strung from the pillars of a house made of sticks. Once I found a box that showed a jungle path in moonlight where fireflies flit around a curvaceous female figure with one arm upraised to steady a huge basket on her head.

Yvonne and I separated, lost in the huge market, as we followed our respective interests.

I watched her work the stalls hung with hand woven embroidered peasant dresses. Then I stepped into a couple of stalls that sold complete business suits made out of colorful Guatemalan Indian textiles. I tried to imagine myself in the suits, to parade in their woven textures, the fluorescent colors and Mayan designs, and could not think of one social function in Michigan where I dared to go dressed like an emerald extra-terrestrial.

Yvonne snuck up behind me and grabbed me around the waist. "You're so easy to find. The Gringo in a white Sololá Bat jacket."

"You notice how much some Indians resent that I wear the Bat instead of the abstract embroidery, like your jacket?"

"I wondered how you got that jacket."

"Long story. Not pretty. Someone died," I kidded.

"Maybe its better I don't know."

"Yes. Hungry?" I pointed to the fresh meat vendor who cut little chunks of meat off of a misshapen oblong lump of something once alive.

Yvonne leaned close to decipher a large goat head on a staff. It stared back with lidless bugged eyes, face white and pink and stripped of skin, empty gray veins that dove through bone tunnels like worms. The countertop held a pyramid pile of smaller, meatier goat heads, babies, that stared as if frightened, wild, skinless and bloodless.

"Oh yes." She laughed. "Mmmm. Makes me sooo hungry." She bent down and met the stare of one, close enough to kiss, and turned to look at me. "Let's eat this one. This one will do. It's the most beautiful, don't you think?"

So French, or European, as if some primal human logic still prevailed in her culture. In the search for quality in life, to acquire beautiful thngs tht endow our environment with grace, elegance, excellence, and intrinsic worth, to bless us through association.

When beauty touches our life, it attracts us, and as if by instinct we stop to appreciate, enjoy, use, buy, take possession of, or eat it.

I felt a connection between the attraction of Art, and the way people couple. Sexual selection for beauty directs evolution, the life force, God if you will, which drives us toward increased order in a universe destined to die in a bland, homogenous low hum of thermodynamic chaos.

Disowned by Phone

The legend of the priest-king Ce Acatl Quetzalcoatl picks up again in the Mayan regions, in the Yucatán peninsula's cities of Chichén Itzá and Mayapán, where archeologists interpret artifacts and architecture as evidence of the history of a new priest who brought the Mayans aspects of Tula's culture. The Mayans call him Kukulcán, and when he leaves by boat to sail off to the south, they chose a site on the coast of Quintana Roo, in front of a break in the reef, to construct a temple complex called Tulum, where priests can wait for his return.

In the market, I bought a ten inch by seven inch wooden box because the artist painted, in glossy enamels, a Guatemalan beach hut at night, rendered with more care than the majority. To open it, one first opened hidden panels to extract the key.

I also bought some semi-precious stone and silver jewelry, some woven table cloths, a couple of serapes, and a large blanket. I packed them into a sturdy, flexible, waste basket woven from palm fronds twisted into thick rope cord, sewn together to make a cylinder.

Yvonne and I carried it between us a couple of blocks to the post office, and learned that the cheapest postage meant it would go by boat all the way to Michigan, from the Atlantic, up the St. Lawrence Seaway, and into the Great Lakes, to arrive in a couple of months.

Outside the post office, I pulled Yvonne over to one of the deep blue science-fiction cowlings that protected Guatel's street phones. "I need to call my grandmother. I wrote her a letter from Guatemala. Should have arrived by now. She just remarried, some rich industrialist, and she might help me get to South America."

"Why would she do that?"

"I don't know, because my father, her son, died so young when I was six, and I thought she might enjoy my exploits. Vicarious adventure, maybe."

I dialed the number and waited. Yvonne reached out and squeezed my hand. "Good luck." she said, which I took as a "Fat Chance."

The receiver crackled with static, and I knew it would never connect. I heard it ring in a strange tone, like an old man's gargle with salt water.

Then grandma's weak voice, "Hello?"

"Hello, Grandma? Brandon."

"Hello. You call from Guatemala?"

"Yes. Then you got my letter."

"Yes. I did not vant to read your letter to my husband," I hear my Austrian Grandma, Antoinette, say over the phone. Her voice's octogenarian quiver reminded me of how her head shakes form side to side, as if in negation of everything around her. "You understand, he vouldn't like it either. You remember I remarried?"

"Yeah, what a surprise to hear from you after fifteen years. I got your wedding announcement. After you married. Why didn't you like my letter?"

"Vat have you got against the United States? I'm from Austria, my husband, from Germany. This is a Vunderful country."

"Wonderful. They don't think so in Guatemala."

"Then why do all those Mexicans come here illegally?"

"To look for work. Don't you think immigration problems stem from United States' Foreign policy since the fifties?"

"Vat's dat supposed to mean?"

"We use over a third of the world's resources, and practically control two thirds. That doesn't leave much for anyone else ,who must follow the money, chase their nation's resources out of the country. . Where do you think they should go to find a decent life?"

"They can stay vere dey are, verk hard, scrimp and save, just like we did."

"There's not much left where they came from. You didn't stay in Austria, you came to the United States. Why shouldn't they?"

"I came legally, a long time ago."

"You notice in my letter, the part about what those teachers said about the U.S. Government overthrowing the President of Guatemala?"

"Yes. He vas communist. Vat's that, the fault of the United States?"

"No, no. Maybe. Why should the dollar equal one Quetzal, for decades? Since the fifties, when the United States overthrew their democratically elected president."

"Now hold on, dat's vat we cannot agree with you, ever. They ver Communists! So vee decide to disown you."

"What?"

"Vee decided to disown you. Disown you, you understand?"

"Disown? Like I'm not your grandson?"

"Yes. Exactly. Goodbye."

Click.

Dial tone.

I hung up the phone.

Yvonne looked at me and seemed concerned. "You turned white. Didn't go well, did it?"

"She disowned me."

"Brilliant. Best way to avoid grandchildren who might ask for money."

"Do you think she knew?"

"Doesn't matter. She could say no a million ways. Everybody's on their own in this world."

"Jesus, I can't believe it. Disowned. I never thought it would happen to me. I didn't have much family to begin with."

"Well now you have even less to worry about. Don't be sad. Let's forget all about it, and go on a picnic."

Bread and Guatemalan Cheese

In the year fifteen eighteen, Hernan Cortez arrived in Mexico with a couple hundred Spaniards and some horses. The arrival date and physical appearance, his white skin and beard, offered parallels to the expected return of the beloved God of art and culture, named Quetzalcoatl, Coatzacualcos, or Kulkulcán. With a small band of men, canons, and horses, he made contact with the tribes along the shores of Tabasco and Veracruz. The Spaniards, with horses and canons, won battles against the frightened and confused Meso-Americans, and earned an uneasy peace. The Tabasqueños gave nineteen maidens to the Spaniards, which included a young slave girl, a noble by birth, who could speak two languages, the Aztec's language of Nahuatl, and Mayan. One Spaniard, long shipwrecked on Cozumel island, could speak Mayan, and thus they forged communication between the three cultures. Hernan Cortéz took the girl Malinche (also called Marina, or Malintzín) as his lover. She fell in love, and learned Spanish, to become his loyal translator and trusted diplomat. With her intelligence and skill, the two hundred Spaniards and a few horses enlisted the aide of many tribes resentful of Aztec domination. Together, they engineered a siege of the Aztec's island city Tenochtitlán, both by boat and over the long causeways. The combination of European diseases, steel and gunpowder, mounted equestrians, similarities between the white skinned, bearded Spaniard Cortéz and the God Quetzalcoatl, and perhaps most important (and unsung), the diplomatic skills of the noble woman Malinche, together enabled the coalition to topple the Aztecs and win this civil war, first called "The Conquest of New Spain."

As Yvonne counted her centavos, I thought about where to picnic. "Do you know the Cerrito del Carmen?"

"I don't think so. Near here?"

"Yes and no. Truth is, I feel too hungry to walk all that way without a snack first. We could buy food, eat a snack, and take a bus to have a picnic on the hill. There's a great view of the city."

On the way back to the market, Yvonne spied a long loaf of French bread in a bakery window, and bought some.

In the Central Market, we also bought some small rolls and a smooth white Guatemalan cheese, and bought some sturdy fruits to put in our daypacks for later.

We headed out of the dark market, and as we neared the corner door to the streets, a noise came from outside. A roar grew in volume around us, from the roof. Water, tracked in off the street on shoes, made the floor slippery with greasy mud. The rain hammered down hard on the corrugated metal ceilings of the enormous Mercado. A knot of people formed in the doorway, pressed together huddled into the dry areas almost out of reach of furious sprays of water and wind.

People rushed in off the street, some with newspapers tented over their heads. Some retained their dignity and ignored the rain, carried their bundles as if nothing mattered until a sheet of wind driven water knocked them off balance. Some people walked unaware around the corner towards our little group, and we all watched the funneled wind slam against them.

They gasped and tucked their arms in to hold their jacket shut, or hold onto their hats and umbrellas. Those that did not lean forward, staggered back a step or two.

We waited for the weather to let up as thunder boomed above our heads. Lightning, much brighter than the dim yellow electric lights of the market interior, strobe the scene like a camera flash and reflected shiny highlights of pure white light on metal surfaces or puddles of water. Each flash burnt a single, short lived negative photo to linger on the retina.

"I'm hungry, but I don't want to eat the food we bought here." Her eyes searched the little restaurant stalls within the market.

I ate in the market all the time; cheap and hot, the pageant of humanity as entertainment, but I did not feel hungry. "Maybe we should eat later. Want to see a movie?"

"Sure, let's get a taxi. He might know what movies the cinemas play this afternoon. Here comes one."

A Guatemalan man rushed out and got to the Taxi first. Other people crowded onto the sidewalk to hail another taxi, but then fled back for cover.

"Let's walk around the corner to the next street and catch a taxi before they pull up in front of the market."

We both ran out into the thick gray rain and ran down the sidewalk. Our feet stamped and created little explosions of water. We stayed close to the walls of buildings to get out of the worst of it, and ducked under canvas awnings where possible. We stopped under the doorway an inch out of the rain, in front of a store that sold flowers that fluoresced in the artificial light. Their perfume permeated the atmosphere around us.

"We didn't get too wet, did we?" I lied.

"You must be joking. Look at us; we caught all the rain with the whole front of our clothing. Better to walk, I think. Just the head and shoulders get wet."

We took the first bus that stopped. It took us south instead of north toward the Cerrito del Carmen.

I looked ahead just in time to point out the Red Tile Church to Yvonne. "Have you seen this before?"

"I never noticed it. Looks like a castle instead of a church. Too red, all that shiny tile, like a holy whorehouse, don't you think? Red's too passionate a color for a church."

A few minutes later, we got off the bus to head back into the city's center. We splashed through more rain on streets where people huddled under canvas canopies and in doorways to wait out the storm.

We flagged a taxi.

The taxi driver tells us that only one movie house plays matinees, and today shows a well advertised movie about love in deepest, darkest Africa.

That piqued Yvonne's curiosity. "This movie I think is a, how do you say, documentaire?"

"Documentary."

"Documentary about how they cut children with knives when they get old enough for sex, do you know what I mean?"

"Circumcision?"

"Yes, and on girls too!" Her eyes widened and a little alarmed.

"Are you sure?"

"Sure. Positive."

"Sounds too horrible not to be true. Who ever thought of that first, was one sick puppy."

"A man, for sure. Men try to control their wife, rob her of any sexual pleasure."

"What about women who think it's OK to cut off a baby boy's foreskin?"

"That's for health reasons. Everyone knows that."

"Yeah, well I've still got mine, and I can't imagine being without it. The thought of the rub of dry cotton underpants... like nails on a chalkboard, or getting an eyelash in your eye. I can't stand that when it happens. You think uncircumcised men less sensitive down there?"

"How should I know?"

"Better you than me."

"So why aren't you circumcised?"

"Don't know. Made me feel pretty strange, as a boy."

"Why?"

"I think the other kids, when we took showers for gym class, said I was deformed, had no willy."

"You had someone, a big brother maybe, to tell you it was OK?"

"I'm the oldest. One older boy lived next door to my brother and I, about four years older than us. Two sisters, one a beauty queen, big hooters."

"Hooters?"

I put my cupped hands before my chest, palms in, fingers splayed to approximate their dimensions.

"Oh, those. You never had sex education?"

"Oh yeah. From him. Before we reached puberty, we used to ride bicycles to town and buy things. One day, he tells us about a gas station, way out in the country, that sells Playboy. So we make a plan to ride our bikes the five miles to steal a copy. My brother and I distracted the clerk as we bought candy, so he could walk to the door and throw the magazine outside as he spits real noisy, you know, to cover the sound of the magazine's flutter when he tossed into the weeds. We took the magazine way back into the fields with us, and hid it in plastic bags under slabs of bark at the Old Tipped Over Tree. Then we would hike together to the Tipped Over Tree to flip through the pages, and check out all the nude women, and the centerfold. My brother and I, boys about twelve and thirteen, didn't know what to think, but our sixteen year old neighbor did. I imagine he snuck back there without us often enough. We invented names to describe breasts; bananas, or cupcakes, snow cones with a cherry, bags of milk, but our favorite was giant doorbells. We would fall down laughing if anyone mentioned doorbells in public."

Yvonne laughed. "You still a virgin?"

"Maybe. Does it matter to you?"

"It would be interesting if you were, in some ways."

"In some ways, then, yes."

"How mysterious, I love it."

The taxi driver asked if we came from Usa."

Yvonne asked me if I remembered puberty.

"Puberty hit me in a state of complete innocence. On our farm, I must have ignored all the dogs, goats, horses, ducks and chickens that mounted each other right in front of me. Did not understand what cats wailed about, all the weird howls, like fights in the night. Until one night, I woke up terrified in the darkness, thought I might die, all out of breath, wet stuff all over my stomach, between my legs. Thought I might bleed to death. I turned on the light and saw what looked like chunks of tapioca. Thought I rolled over on a tarantula or something."

Yvonne laughed.

"I wiped myself off, and crept downstairs with my hand cupped around this traitorous thing between my legs. I knocked on the bedroom door where my mother and stepfather slept. He and I weren't close, you can imagine. They didn't open the door right away, but called out What's wrong? I don't know, I said. Something happened. Open the door, tell us what happened. I stayed in the doorway and said I don't know what, I woke up and felt funny. The sheets got all wet. How did the sheets get wet? Maybe something came out of my penis. I'm sick or something."

Yvonne laughed aloud, bent forward in the back seat of the taxi, and resisted the temptation to beat the driver's seat with her hand.

"After a few seconds of confusion, my Stepfather said Oh, oh oh. I get it. Then he laughed a smug little chuckle I cannot forget. He threw aside the sheets to get his nude ass out of bed, looked at my mom and said Don't bother to get up. I'll deal with this. He chuckled as he led me all the way back up the stairs to my bedroom, because for the first time, my mom shut up and let him deal with one of her two precious boys."

"Did he clear everything up for you?"

"He mostly asked me questions, about if I knew what the other kids said about pussies and penises. I heard about birds and bees, the usual stuff. Imagine how that feels to connect sex with your own pisser at such a late age. Not a clue. I couldn't get it out of my mind for months. For a couple of years, I rode the bus to school and looked down at all the people in their cars that drove by, and could not believe it. All the people on the street, old frail wrinkled women wrapped in winter clothing, old men that tottered on canes in the Rexall pharmacy to order a cherry phosphate like they'd done all their life, all these people screwed around with someone at some point in their life. Or still screwed with someone, or had sex all by themselves. I supposed they committed sex acts undreamt of by me. I thought of sex as some monstrous practical joke, an appetite that awakens at puberty. Couldn't happen at a worse time, I thought, right when I felt on top of everything, great grades in school, read a lot if books, exercised, and got enough control over my uncoordinated body to fail at the pole vault. Still, it improved my social status among my schoolmates at my new school. Then this one night, like a vampire or some undead monster, this thing rears its serpent head to spit venom and change my life forever. Later I learned these needs return, every few hours or days without reason, until I die. I felt this sexual awakening woke me up to a hell of insecurity and intellectual noise, fantasies, and appetites for things that refused to take form and become concrete. Imagine what that did for the way I looked at girls."

Yvonne laughed. "How did you see girls after that?"

"How did the girls see me? That's what drove me nuts. Girls know long before the boys. I don't know how, but I could feel it. Women look right through a boy. I felt them laugh, like when somebody sees a kid on a bike out of control. Sometimes I walked around like a zombie in school, on the bus, because I got erections and used my books as a shield to hide the bulge in my pants. Then what do I do with my hands? Use them as a shield, or a distraction?"

"Oh you boys do suffer."

As we rode on in silence through the rain, she punctuated the scenery with a couple of sporadic chuckles that repeated for several minutes.

I felt that even the windshield wipers and the sheets of rain we drove through made sarcastic sounds.

The taxi pulled up in front of a grandiose old building that for years served as the main theater for all of Guatemala City. The first movie theater in the country, he said. "Nowadays, investors build drive-in theaters and modern cinemas in the newer parts of town, in the tourist area south of the city, near the airport. Few people come to this old movie house."

We both helped pay the taxi fare and tip without much scrutiny to equity, and ran up the sidewalk stairs through a light rain to the open foyer that sheltered the ticket booth. We bought tickets, went inside, and found a thick red velvet rope, which matched the wine red carpet, blocked off the stairway that leads up into the balcony. We ducked under and snuck up into the balcony anyway, like a couple of kids, where we hoped to at least finish our food before they caught us.

Stinky Rites of Passage

Older Yucatecans, interviewed by Spaniards in the fifteen hundreds, claimed their ancestors did not worship idols until the arrival of a man named Captain Quetzalquat with people from central Mexico. The people of Chichen Itzá (Chichenyza) said a Captain Kukulcán (Ku Kalcan) taught them idolatry and rituals with offerings. Nevertheless, this foreigner convinced the nearby Mayan city-states to help him erect a new city as a wellspring of goodness. They founded Mayapan (flag of the Maya) and thrived with increased emphasis on the arts, good government, and commercial trade routes. Mayapan formed an alliance between Uxmal, Chichen Itzá, and other regional city-states and for two hundred years ruled over the rest of the Yucatán kingdoms. After Kukulcán left, at some point his successors increased the culture of ritual offerings and instituted human sacrifice, perhaps when the tyrannical ruler Cocom brought in mercenary Mexicas or Nahuatls from Tobasco and promised to give them Mayapan in return for their help in the subjugation of the other city-states. Cocom became the first Mayan to enslave other humans. By the late Post-classic period (1250 to around 1530 when the Spanish arrived) after the tyranny and oppression of Cocom's heirs, a tribe called the Xiues adopted the technology of bow and arrow from the Mexicas, conquered Mayapan, and ended the last ceremonial civilization in Central America.

The movie started with drums and montage footage of what would come: strange rites of passage for African boys in loincloths and pubescent bare breasted girls, their black skin beaded with sweat, scarification, wounds from crude tattoos, and lots of blood at times. The Negroid mammary glands took unfamiliar shapes, triangular and bouncy, hard black bumpers of gelatin.

The witchdoctors marked the initiates to scar them. They lifted little puckers of punctured flesh with sharp wooden tools or metal nails, or used knives to cut into the faces and bodies of both sexes. They pinched up the tortured skin to massage mineral pigments into the wound. Faces, dusty black, contrasted with the inside of the gums and lips, a vivid shiny redness that intensified the whiteness of their teeth when they grimaced in pain, and stood still for more.

The camera lingered on images of the circumcised young boys, uncontrollable shivers in reaction, seated in shallow streams that ran with streaks of blood from their groins. Other tribesmen fanned them gently with long bundles of soft, fresh, green herbs and grasses bundled together as a ritual wand. With smiles as if in play, elder tribesmen flayed their laps and shaded the scene with great umbrella-like palm fronds. Around them, long black bodies draped in beads, cloth woven into their thick hair, sang to the initiates as they entered a numbed state of shock. They sat with a slight rock, leaned over their groin, with each blow from the stalks of leaves, and moved their hands in weak gestures, as if they held an invisible basketball, to protect their mutilated genitals.

Another cloudburst fell upon the lofty roof of the theater, and added a muted boom and the roar of thousands of small impacts, a background static or white noise underneath the movie soundtrack.

Then the movie turned to the initiation of topless pubescent African girls, with their immense collars of beads in a half moon over their tight mammary glands. How could these gap toothed old women, these black African mothers, who once upon a time themselves submitted to female circumcision, witness their daughter's pain and let a man scrape off their daughter's clitoris with a sharpened seashell? Did their culture teach them to fear a woman's sexuality, and blame it on the devil, or some imaginary inevitable social chaos, that women who feel pleasure will bring forth?

We shrunk against each other in horror at the scenes, and opened the bag that contained the French bread and cheese.

The Guatemalan cheese stank. It smelled like unclean sex, like sweaty smegma cultured under foreskin or labial folds after a number of days without a good shower. It did not crumble like Mexican cheese.

I thought my imagination ran away with me, until Yvonne said "This cheese smells like sex."

It tasted better than it smelled, but with our hunger, we held our breath and ate it. Tasted like normal cheese with the nose held. We ate it up, and chased it with the French bread.

The cheese odor hung about us. What a first date.

A calm settled over the movie theater. The rain slowed to a stop. The static of rain on the theater roof, which our brains filtered out to become unnoticed, now became noticeable by its absence.

After the movie, we stepped outside under clear skies. Long streaks of light slanted through the street canyons and lit up the white haze of steam that billowed off the hot asphalt streets.

As we walked toward the city center, I asked her if she had plans for the evening.

"No, not really." She then added, "I want to call a friend, a Doctor, but it's not important."

"A Doctor friend? A rich boyfriend?"

"Doctor's aren't so rich here. He and his family took me in, as you say. I think they want me to be a good influence on his youngest son. We went to Lago de Izabél together. Did you go there?"

"No. I'd like to. Looks like you go through there to get to Tikál, but I didn't notice. Probably passed at night. Nice?"

"There's a Spanish Castle, on the river mouth, to protect the lake from Pirates that came in from the Caribbean."

We sat together on some benches in a park. Yvonne threw the last of our bread to the birds while she told me about her trip to the eastern shores of Guatemala. She paused often, her cool green eyes gazed up and to the right, into the sky, as she thought in French, English, and Spanish.

Her hair moved in the light breeze, it beckoned and made me feel dizzy. The air grew chill and damp. She felt warm as we snuggled together.

A large crowd of pigeons assembled and waited for her crumbs, and I identified with them, all together in a peaceable kingdom, a union of happy creatures.

We looked like a couple of good friends who might become lovers; same skin color, almost the same language, we got along well and felt comfortable with each other, the way we shared our warmth and quiet conversation. Her beauty shined into my heart and I resolved that she would see no dark corners, no failed compromises, no strings, no deep scars from in my past life of twenty two years, only four years since high school, only one as a legal adult. Even so, I felt those years contained plenty of things not to feel proud of. I considered my past dabbles into alcohol abuse, live-in girlfriends, hitchhiking, Buddhism, psychedelic drugs, gratuitous sex, and lots of rock 'n roll, comprised a rite of passage into industrial strength adulthood, which I ran away from.

Powerless, I let her sweep me along to fall under her intentional spell of irresistible womanhood, even as I recognized my vulnerability due to the lack of human contact these past months of travel, and the months before I left.

The sun set as Yvonne and I left the park. We watched the street lights come on with a noisy buzz and a dim ultraviolet and orange spark, a weak glow against the purpled twilight.

She pulled out a lipstick called Deseo. It reminded me of cherries, succulent sweetened cherries, more dangerous than the apple Snow White stole from Eve, as troublesome as the Golden Apples that Paris gave to Aphrodite so he would make Helen lick his fingers. Yvonne's cheeks glowed with youthful flush, rouge rubbed in by the cold, gentle as a rose petal falls into a white tiled Spanish Arabic fountain.

I could smell the flowers on bushes all around us, and her perfume made me feel sad, an instant maudlin nostalgia that life held not enough of such moments between people. She snuggled against me.

"I feel comfortable with you, like I've known you forever, and that's good. I like that." She held my hand.

"Should we fall in love?"

She laughed. "You think too much. Go with the flow."

"It feels kind of, French, you know, romantic, don't you think?"

"Maybe you won't like me after you get to know me."

"I think a man likes a woman who is not afraid to show him her bad side. We all fall victim to bad moods, don't we?"

"You are so naive. You know nothing about women. You want to believe they think like men. They don't."

"How do they think, then?"

"For starters, spend some time to imagine what it would be like to bleed every twenty eight days. You think a man could put up with that?"

"I think the military once used cramps and bloating as torture, didn't they?"

She looked at me, almost said something, and then gave it up. "Let's walk down to Guatel and call my Doctor friend."

As we walked, she took my arm, and glanced at me as if to judge my reaction every seven steps or so. Her green eyes became dark mirrors that flashed with all the colors of the sunset sky along the mountain horizon. She dropped her lashes and eclipsed them, as the earth's shadow pulled itself across the zenith.

Near the Post Office, Guatel, or the Guatemalan Telephone Company, occupied an old building with a flight of wide stone steps in front. The five bright blue fiberglass cowlings lined up on the sidewalk made the turn of the Century central Guatemala City streets resemble a Science Fiction film from the Fifties, about extraterrestrial fantasies projected onto our consciousness. Each housed a telephone that hung like a black dung beetle on a stainless steel box.

I waited a discreet distance away as she made her call.

She returned in a few minutes and said, "Ready?"

"For what?"

"Anything. Are you hungry?"

"Not yet. What did the Doctor say? Did the rabbit die?"

"He said I should go to bed and call him tomorrow."

"No aspirin?"

"Oh yes! That's it! Take two aspirin, go to bed, and call him tomorrow!" She laughed and pulled my arm. "Let's go get drunk."

She moved fast, hustled me down the city streets and across a little square park. We walked up a wide, short flight of stone steps and through a huge colonial doorway of chocolate wood and cut crystal glass windows, like church doors.

Inside, a short flight of wide stairs led to the open glass doors of an elegant restaurant with red velvet wallpaper on the upper two thirds of the wall above the booths, wrought iron fences around islands of ferns and palms, and cut glass mirrors on the walls. We sat at a table near the middle of one end of the room, along a partition of wrought iron and flower boxes that divided the dance floor from the dining areas.

Although a Tuesday night, the restaurant offered live music. Along one wall, six gentlemen in suits played on marimbas that looked like four long tables of dark wood slats, each near a pair of men who wielded, in each hand, two strikers, long sticks with a hard ball on the end. The strength of the blows controlled the dynamics, loud and soft. They could play an entire run, from low note to high note, even though each musician played a small section of the complete set of wooden slabs, like one section of piano keys. When a melody or a fast run crossed the boundary of one player's keys to the other's, the second player picked it up with identical speed and dynamics in a display of joyful virtuosity.

After a couple of drinks, I felt relaxed and sat back to pull out a cigarette. Then I noticed a waiter beside me, ready with a lit lighter. Waiters brought little trays to each table, botanas, or bar snacks, like chips and hot sauce, "Japanese" peanuts coated with a crunchy, dark red sugar and chili lumpy crust, or a tray with triangular sections that contained various little hot pickled snacks, like hot peppers, hot carrots, hot onions, and spiced chopped meats.

The music inspired an elegant, well-fed older Guatemalan couple to leave their seats for a waltz and whirl across the dance floor. Some minutes later, five or six couples filled the small dance floor. Sometimes they would follow other couples down the aisles between our tables, without a misstep or mishap.

We ate, enchanted by the old world elegance, the classical and tropical music on the exotic instrument, and the love of life of the well-dressed middle aged Guatemalans, and wondered aloud at our great luck to discover this place.

No place like home.

As the youngest ones there, the token tourists, we felt few foreigners stumbled upon this place, although located in the center of Guatemala City, because of the unmarked entrance.

"I first came here with Dr. Mendez's son. He explained to me about the marimbas. See the gourds that hang down under the wooden xylophone? They amplify the tones, and sometimes buzz with sound. They look like goat things, where milk comes from, don't they?"

"Udders. Goat udders, or something. How many people in the doctor's family?"

"The father and two sons. His wife divorced him and went back to the States, I think. The doctor doesn't talk to me about it. The whole family speaks English. They travel to the United States to visit family there. Will you excuse me? I've got to go to the lady's room."

I sat back and dug into my pocket for another cigarette. Our elegant waiter, black suit and white tuxedo shirt with frills, stepped out of the shadows with a lit lighter almost before I thought about a cigarette. He would lean forward in one brisk movement, eyebrows quizzical, one hand curled around the lighter to keep the flame alive, protected from the wind of his motion.

When Yvonne returned, we talked a little, but then our main course came, and I think we both felt relieved to not talk so much, but to eat, relax, and listen to the Marimba music. Yvonne recommended I try the squab, because I didn't know anything about it. It looked like a miniature Thanksgiving turkey. Took a long time to dissect and eat, so many little bones.

Yvonne said "Maybe you eat one of the pigeons I fed in the park."

Yvonne disappeared for a while, another trip to the bathroom. When she returned, she said, "I'm sorry. I've got a bladder the size of a pea. Classy place, you should see the bathroom, like Europe, the first place in Latin America where men act like gentlemen. I've gotten used to men who try to pick me up in the most vulgar way, I almost forgot how civilized men treat a lady."

After we finished our meal, the waiter asked to take our plates before we thought of it ourselves. He suggested another round of drinks, and when we said yes, he reminded us of what we ordered the first round.

Before he returned, Yvonne said, "Let's dance."

"You think we should? We're the only tourists. This place feels like a private club."

Yvonne leaned over to the next table, and through sign language, she pointed to herself and I, and moved her fingers in a walk toward the dance floor. The man started to pat and push her chair with the back of his hand, smiled and said "Si, si," to urge us to go dance.

Yvonne grabbed my hand, got up from the table and said, "Don't worry if you don't know how to dance. Relax and try to follow me."

I felt lost, unsure, my Sololá Bat jacket on, a cultural artifact from the Mayan Indian Highlands which might remind everyone of the conflict between the restaurant's culture, the dominant class of Ladinos' Old World Spain verses the mixed Spanish and Indigenous bloodlines of the lower class. I felt out of place, dressed in one of the forbidden Bat Jackets of Sololá, a tourist that flaunted the prohibition of its sale to outsiders, whatever that meant.

She led me to the almost empty dance floor. I held Yvonne in my arms and followed wherever she moved, and we danced to the percussive buzz of the five men who played the giant wooden xylophones. They smiled at us. The other dancers smiled at us. People at tables smiled at us.

When the song ended, enthusiastic applause filled the air, for our benefit, I think. We walked back to our seats as the Guatemalans smiled at us.

We drank a few more drinks, talked, danced a little more, and after several yawns at each other, noticed half the tables now empty. A man, who wore a suit so elegant it looked like a tuxedo, got up and pulled the chair out for his companion, a portly woman with hair an unnatural gray. He took her jacket off the back of her chair, and then helped her stout arms house themselves in the tight sleeves. They walked through the bar with smiles or a nod to whoever met their eyes.

We followed them out of the bar, down the steps and into the street.

After they got into a parked car and drove off, Yvonne yelled "That was incredible!" to the starry sky.

"It was, wasn't it? I feel sorry for all those back home in Michigan that can't experience such a thing. It almost makes me forget I've been disowned." I wanted to live forever like this, every night, and remember every moment forever.

"Maybe we can do something, to help you forget."

It didn't feel late, around eight thirty, but we walked past closed shops, their fronts covered by the corrugated metal that unrolls like a garage door with a horrendous thunder and screech It padlocks to loops of iron set into the cement. Most thieves probably leave them alone out of respect for the sonic nightmare. The streets, once lined with shops and glass windows, now looked more like lines of loading dock doors for truck trailers.

A few people roamed the streets.

I offered to walk Yvonne to her hotel, several blocks away.

"I can't believe you asked. A true gentleman always walks a lady home."

"Well, my pensión is in the other direction."

"I can get a cab, and you can go your way, if that's what you want."

"What do you want?"

"I want to believe that Americans can be gentlemen. You should to learn how to be a gentleman, like those men in the club, and walk me home. Then you can do whatever you want."

I felt tired and stupid, a rural Michigan hick who didn't know that old world courtesy required me to walk her home. No gentleman should let a decent, respectable female walk the streets alone after dark in Central America, or perhaps anywhere. I might get a goodnight kiss for my gallantry at the hotel door.

She took my hand, and we walked hugged together against the chill air.

She said "If I knew it was this cold, I would order another drink."

As we neared the front of the Spring Hotel, she pointed it out and said, "I like my room, very nice, I do. Expensive for one person. My own bath tub, and a huge bed with purple sheets, ceilings up to the sky!"

"You ought to share it with someone then."

"I plan to. With you."

I laughed. "I paid up for the month at my Pensión. Where were you two weeks ago?"

"Looking for you."

"All the way to Puerto Barrios and the Castle on Lake Izabél?"

"So I got... how you say, distracted? But for short while. Does this mean you won't stay with me tonight?"

"I would love to, really, but I fall in love very easily. And when I fall in love..."

"Yes? Then what happens?"

"I don't know, and that's what bothers me. Maybe I don't really fall in love. Each time it gets better and better, so I think the time before wasn't the real thing."

"You sound like one of those people who think too much, and really needs to fall in love. Let me warn you, when a French girl says I love you, watch out. The word means something most Americans never understand.

We French feel the romance of life, and we express what we feel. We live the difference, and long live the difference."

She stopped a little ways away from the hotel entrance. "One little problem. I need to hide you into my room."

"Hide me? I have to sneak in?"

"Yes, that's right. Sneak."

"Why?" I tried not to get as over excited as I felt, now that I knew she wanted me to spend the night with her.

"The management might catch us and kick us both out."

I jumped in the river. "It's your room, you paid the rent. I'll pay for the double occupancy rate, if you like."

"No I do not like. You forget ,this is Catholic Guatemala. The people that run the hotel, if they know you stay all night, they will think me a Puta, and they will kick me out. That is how their minds work, that way. Women don't have money unless men give it to them."

"Next time we can get a room as a married couple."

Yvonne turned aside and left me with the impression that she detoured, to not say something to regret, or say too much. Then she looked at me and smiled. "Sure."

That thought awakened my naughty, youthful, foreign, First World superego. Of course we could out-smart them tonight. She implied we, our relationship, might last into the next few days, at least. Yikes.

She looked up at me and put her hand on my chest. "Let me go in first, and you wait out in front of the hotel a few minutes. Don't go through the door. My room has another door onto the street, on the first floor, but it doesn't open. Stay out there, and listen to hear me knock on the door. Three knocks, one two three. Then you can go into the hotel and walk straight to my room."

"And the front desk?"

"Don't worry. It's not so near. The night watchman sleeps behind it, a boy. I'll ask him to get me some water or something. He won't notice, and if he does, you came to visit for a few minutes, and he falls asleep again. Or else you pay him to shut up for tonight, and we work something out tomorrow. Here." She kissed her finger and put it to my lips. "A few minutes..."

She walked down the sidewalk, shook the jacket off her shoulders and dropped it around her hips to exaggerate the sway, whirled around to blow me a kiss, and stepped into the gray stone building.

I walked casually past the entrance, noticed 'The Spring Hotel' carved into the polished granite arch over the doorway, and walked on.

Down at the next corner I turned around to look back. Noticed another sign, lighted and modern, that said The Spring Hotel, mounted up high on the corner of the this colonial building, about three stories high with a little wrought iron balcony for each window.

A little mist fell from the clouds that skimmed over the dark, quiet city. The dense moisture carried sounds from far off down the back streets, doors banged, excited shouts, a distant confusion of sounds and shrieks from children or brake shoes, a fight or a garbage truck. I heard a car door, then a starter motor's cough until the engine purr, then tires squeal, and then silence floods back like dull pressure on the ears.

All this day I thought about sex with her, connived and planned how to make it happen, how to trick her or control her, and manipulate the situation but she beat me to it. I felt nervous to realize she wanted me, at least it seemed that way. Maybe she wants to get to know me better, and we will talk all night.

The two of us, young, alone abroad, no one to answer to, somehow accelerated the land of Mañana, and my life streamed like water, a rapid rush toward the unknown. I left home five months ago to discover the unknown, and now here I stand, cold feet on the wet Guatemalan sidewalk, under a turn of the century streetlight that makes cloud mist look like fog.

I feel dizzy, on the edge of an abyss, an abyss of time.

What if the hotel boy calls the Guatemalan police to arrest us?

What if she's crazy, and starts to yell or throw things, break glass? Maybe she robs tourists. Maybe her boyfriend waits inside, to roll me.

I lit a cigarette and took a few drags. A little beggar child wrapped in filthy blankets came up to me, palm up, his dirty mouth moved as he squeaked out some noises I thought he hoped sounded like 'Quarter'. I spoke Spanish to him, and his face lit up, so I tried to talk him into a performance, to work for my money, do a little dance or a song to earn a quarter from me. He looked down, then up at me and smiled. I saw a perfect picture of pathetic dejection, but he refused to acknowledge that he understood me, and I felt sure he did, so I decided not to pay him anything. He made me dance to try and convince him to. The brat. He wouldn't go away. I gave him a Quetzal as an investment in his future loyalty to me, in case I needed a witness for an alibi.

Then I walked back and forth in front of the Spring Hotel, counted the sealed doors and stopped in front of the one I decided once gave street access to Yvonne's room.

The mist thickens into droplets that fall through the bright haze around the antique gas streetlight. Their combined motion makes me feel like I fly upward against the mist, into the sky, a phantom movement like a when you sit on a parked bus and the bus next to yours starts to back up, you feel it as a forward motion.

In a few minutes, I heard three deliberate knocks come from the inside of that sealed door. I returned three knocks and took a drag, then flicked the cigarette out of my fingers like a movie star, I hoped. It bounced against the curb and shattered into a miniature firework explosion, an orgy of sparks, and then over the curb into the wet street to disappear forever into a puddle that reflected the misty streetlight like galaxies.

I walked quiet, with smooth silent steps through the main entrance, and tried to muster a nonchalant invisibleness as I continued down the short hall until it opened up into a large courtyard beside the front desk, tucked under a wide stone stairway. A wrought iron banister leads to the second floor. As I passed the counter of the front desk, I leaned over to see the empty cot behind.

A couple who seemed European in earth tone sweaters, the man with a couple of weeks of beard, sat and nursed drinks at a wrought iron table top in the courtyard. Electric lights, hung under the second floor's walkway around the courtyard, cast elongated shadows, triangular slashes of light and dark, across the stucco walls.

Three foot wide earthenware planters held tall bushes, treelike succulent plants, and yuccas balanced off the ground on delicate wrought iron stands.

The couple watched me, bored, as I glanced around and acted confused.

Then I moved to the first door on the left and gave it a little rap with one knuckle.

She pulled the door open, stuck her head out and looked both ways, and said "Hi."

"Hi."

"Like to come in?"

She closed the door, grabbed my head with both hands and planted her mouth on mine. When we separated, I asked "Now, why won't they think I'm here?" and felt stupid.

"I don't care if they think you're here. Even if they see you, they might forget, or think you left when they weren't looking. Or maybe they listen at the door, and hear us in bed together. So what? If we make beautiful music, they should think twice, no? Anyway, if they knock to ask me who I have in here, I will tell them to go away and let me sleep, I don't want to be disturbed."

"That easy? They have a right to more money for double occupancy."

"I tell them it was a nightmare. Nervous? You can leave when you want, but promise to leave a tip with the night watch boy to keep his mouth shut. I told him you would."

She turned on the radio, at a volume that helped to cover our conversation, or other noises.

"Maybe I tell them you are my brother, arrived late last night. Then I pay for two people, and everybody stays happy. But you won't like being my brother."

"Why not?" I sat down on a simple chair at the antique desk beside the bed.

"I hate my brothers." She sat on the bed's purple sheets, leaned back propped up by her arms. "You wouldn't survive, believe it. Come here." She crossed her legs and teased with a smile.

I sat still and looked at her.

She stretched one long leg out slow, and began to massage my knee with her foot. "Why don't you take off that Sololá Bat jacket?"

"Protects me from evil." I took it off and crossed the room to the coat rack, stretched it out between two pegs to dry.

"Does that mean you're in the mood for a little evil?"

"Where did you learn English? In the States? At times, you sound like you're from Chicago."

"I've studied since elementary school, and my parents know a little from both of their families."

"Both families?"

"They do business in New York, and traveled. They learned all over. I love Hollywood movies, I learned English with them. I wish we could find a good movie. I saw a sign for the movie Jaws at a theater downtown. They call it Tiberón, shark, you know."

"Did you go to Hollywood?"

"I couldn't live there. Hated it. In Los Angeles, everybody drives, everybody needs their own auto. I hate to drive, I want to look out the window, or read. People there, they act like product to sell, sell themselves, do you know what I mean? Everybody with a business card and a lie."

"Did you like it?"

"Hated it. Unless you like crazy people."

"Crazy people everywhere, don't you think?"

"No, not crazy like normal, but crazy like bizarre. I asked this one man, a handsome homosexual black man who worked in a clothing store and knew how to dress, I asked him, What do I need to look like I belong in Los Angeles? He says, A Tan."

"You've got a nice one now. Feel glamorous? I felt tall and glamorous the minute I stepped foot in Guatemala."

She squinted and pointed at me. "I knew there was something about you, something tall and glamorous. The people here look so much the same, all Mayan. That's not true, but sometimes it feels like I can't tell them apart."

"The people are mass-produced in a factory out by Cobán. Owned by the Japanese. That's why they all have that gorgeous tan."

"Why is that?"

"Quality controlled ovens."

She laughed. "Little mass-produced Indians. Good, we'll go to Cobán and order a gross in all the colors of Santa Catarina."

"Red, white, and blue, the colors of Old Glory."

"Old Glory?"

"The United States Flag."

"Right." She got off the bed, ran her hand under my chin as she walked by. "You want a drink?" She reached for something on the dresser, then turned and waved a small bottle of whiskey in a limp hand. "Water, no ice?"

I felt too nervous to spend the night with her. How would I undress, lights out first? What if I needed to use the bathroom, or fart? How could I get out of here? I said "OK."

She prepared a little glass of whisky for each of us, and said, "We both feel exhausted. Let's get to bed." Then she lit a couple of candles and turned off the lights.

We set our drinks on the nightstands that flanked each side of the bed, and sat down.

"What do you like to do before you go to sleep?" she said, and took a book off the nightstand. "I like to turn the radio on low, and read."

She turned on the radio. An AM pop station played Creedence Clearwater Revival.

I felt tired, my mind raced. I thought this nervousness would counteract the happy dull lull of alcohol. She knew about my pensión, so she must want me here. The invitation came not as a favor, nor as a charity case.

Maybe she invites me to spend the night because she wants sex, or she wants to get to know me first, see if I'll attack her or something worse. What happened to the long series of talks, the dates, meet the parents, tentative kisses, furtive feels, first base, second base, third? She wants me to step up to the plate and hit a home run? "I didn't bring my book." I thought about us in bed together, and wondered at what moment the monster between my legs might rear its one-eyed little head to take a look around.

"Here, try this one. I've finished it."

We both lit a cigarette and read a while.

She prepared more drinks.

A friend of mine once confessed that he felt objective when he made love, as if he looked down from the ceiling. He said it bothered him, and did not add to the experience. I wondered how he did it. I mean, how do get objective viewpoint about pleasure? Or did he obsess about the moronic physicality of a man's repetitious insertions, like the black silhouette of an oil well against the sunset, or one of those blown glass lever birds on a fulcrum that sips water to demonstrate perpetual motion?

Footsteps passed the door, cheap dress shoes that sounded like wood blocks on stone.

She stood up. "Excuse me. To the bathroom again. Remember, my bladder's the size of a pea. Get out of those clothes, make yourself comfortable, and get into bed if you want," Yvonne said in a half whisper.

I sipped my third drink and felt a flush as her toilet flushed. The room and I swayed and listed like a ship at sea. I needed a jolt to my nervous system to sober up, so I stepped onto the throw rug, a thick cotton weave of Indian fabircs, and jumped up and down in place.

"What are you doing?" Yvonne called out over the rush of tap water.

I ran to the bathroom door and whispered "Ssssshhhh. I'm not here." I went back to the bed and started to undress. I took off my shirt, sat on the bed, and noticed nervous sweat run down from my armpit. I tried to untie my shoes. Head down, bent over, and couldn't get that double knot untied, leather laces hardened with dirt, shrunk by puddles of muddy water and dry heat.

I'll fix that, I said to myself, and lay back on the bed with my shoes up in the air. Dirt fell on me. I put my feet on the ground and bent down to work the knot out with my fingernails.

As I undressed, I felt more nervous with each layer of clothing stripped away, layers that cloak the human animal and distance our natural instincts from our daily impersonal existence. What a sham. I heard most honest men admit to thoughts of sex every hour of the day, and I bet women did too. Healthy men look and lust as if controlled by a genetic imperative to spread their seed, analogous to why most women exaggerate their beauty to show and tease, in acknowledgement of that fact. Women primp and fuss, exaggerate the lips and shadow the eyes, shave off the eyebrows and paint new ones, select the fashions to best flaunt their secondary sex characteristics to swell breasts and tighten butt over reduced waists, where open skirts instead of pants, all subliminal solicitations to copulate, to excite all men. What else can explain why women spend so much time and effort on body creams and face makeup, push-up bras, low-cut blouses, and skirts that reveal more hide than a discreet man should look at? Does the more attractive woman get to pick and choose the best mate, and also keep her mate grateful and faithful? Or does beauty provoke insane jealousy and possessiveness?

I kept my underpants on, although four months of busses put holes in them. Didn't want her to see them. I planned to slip out of them under the covers, and drop them over the side of the bed before she noticed. Tomorrow, in the full light of day, my strategy demanded I get up before she did, in case I needed to escape.

She took forever in the bathroom. I waited, under the purple covers, and resisted the impulse to down the rest of my whiskey and serve myself another.

She came out naked under a man's long sleeve white shirt, and stood before the bureau to use the mirror by candlelight. Her tan stretched all the way from her toes to her shirt tails, where a bit of the under curve of her white buns peeked out.

She moved the two candles and then walked back to the bed, her hand on her shirt's middle button. Without a word, she slipped in between the covers beside me.

We both reached for our drinks on our bedstands. I started to say something and she said, "SSsshhh. You're not in here, remember?"

"Uh huh."

As we settled down, the radio dominated.

She sat up straight beside me.

I slumped into the pillows with my book.

She said "Look at these walls and doors, made of adobe blocks I think. Look over at the door, see how thick the walls are." She whispered, leaned over me and pushed against the wall, then slapped it. "Thick."

She go ton her knees and stretched over me supported by her two hands on the wall. The shirt fell open, both nipples inches from my face. "With the watch-boy asleep, we can make all the noise we want. These walls are thick."

I looked up into her smile and said "Good. Wouldn't want anyone to crash through it."

She laughed and fell back onto the bed beside me.

"What are you laughing at?"

"What might make me lean against the wall so hard I might crash through?"

"What do you mean? I was thinking someone on the other side might fall through it. What were you thinking about?"

"Never mind." She fell back into her pillows and grabbed her book.

Every time I started to say something, she turned toward me and said, "Sh sh sh sh..." with a finger to her lips. "You talk too much."

"Let me give you something for that." I lifted her finger from her lips and moved toward her.

She smiled, and pulled up the sheet to glance toward my crotch. She seemed disappointed.

I kissed her.

She turned towards me, and our mouths stayed together to explore new worlds. I felt her soft warm lips, and tongue on tongue, we breathed the same air. She flushed hot under my touch. Her legs held me in a scissor hold as she stretched and flexed. She ran her tongue over my lips, her hands through my hair.

I felt smooth curves under my hands as we nuzzled.

She reached down to search for the bulge in my pants, and then pulled my hands out from under her shirt. "Like another drink?"

"Sure."

She stood up to walk across the candle-lit room to get the bottle, a leggy cat in a long sleeve shirt.

"Freshen your glass?" She held the bottle at her side and pulled at the front of her shirt. "Feels warm in here. I think I'll get comfortable." She walked toward the bathroom and when she passed the dresser, put the bottle on top ,and disappeared into the bathroom.

I thought she wanted to run a bath with the hope I might fall asleep.

I padded on bare feet to the door of the bathroom to listen, and heard her breathe so that I knew she also heard me at the door. "Do you think", I called out to her, "they forgot about me by now?"

"Get back in that purple bed, and be quiet."

I got back in bed.

She opened the door a crack and peeked out around the edge.

The bathroom's light streamed into the bedroom and hurt my eyes.

She clutched her incandescent nightshirt to her abdomen with one slim fist, but let it fall open a bit.

Then she opened the door and flowed into the bedroom with the shaft of lightt. She looked at me and let the white shirt open to fall a bit across the back of her shoulders. She held her arms out and forward to stop the shirt's fall, and turned her face to the side and down, while she stuck out one leg.

The radio played 'Heard it Through the Grapevine', by Creedance Clearwater Revival. How much longer would you be mine?

She stayed within that narrow shaft of light and began to dance. She used her shirt's loose cuffs as a veil, as a towel, as a belly dancer's scarf, as a rope of bondage. At the end of the song, she fastened the buttons on her cuffs, turned off the bathroom light, and walked to me through the candlelight.

She pulled me out of bed to my feet. The purple sheet fell sideways to the floor. She laughed at my underpants, and said, "What do you have those on for?"

I jumped out of them.

With our mouths upon each other's, she maneuvered us to the bed and then she fell backward onto it to pull me on top. I slipped the shirt down over her shoulders, and nuzzled each soft discovery unveiled, until my tongue tickled her belly button. She laughed and tried to get away or push me off, but her elbows remained fastened to the bed on either side of her hips.

Her buttoned shirt cuffs trapped her inside her own shirt, elbows tied behind her back. She lay there, nude in front but with her hands caught short, like an inmate half out of a straight jacket.

"You bastard!" She laughed softly, and grabbed my waist with her legs to give me a bear hug. "Help me get my hands out of this shirt, and I swear, you won't regret it."

Intimate Relations

In the Yucatán, an ancient Mayan site from the Classic Period (600 AD - 1000 AD) called Uxmal contains exquisite examples of the Puuc architectural style. One group of four structures forms a rectangle called the Nunnery Quadrangle. The architects adorned the rear façade of the north building and the front façade of the west building with phallic sculptures. The phallic motif continued on the façade of the apt-named Temple of the Phallus. To the east of a platform that supports a structure known as the Governor's Palace, the excavators found a collection of phallic sculptures. Archeologists' drawings of Stela Fourteen bring out the erect figure of ruler Lord Chac, who stands on a platform under which two naked males recline, knees apart to display their genitals.

Once free of the shirt, she jumps on me with a knee on each side of my chest. She pushes her groin against mine, both of her hands on my shoulders, and moves her hips like a dancer. I feel her coarse nest of black hair like the moustache on a wet mouth that searches for the hairless helmet of my little soldier.

A network of dark vines over her moist cave, the heat shone through the branches and leaves, I feel wetness, and look up to see her face through the tendrils of damp black hair, her face indistinct, a pale ghost with lips pursed in moans of pleasure.

I hold onto her strong thighs, her hips, and pray to stay erect for a complete launch, and not feel too nervous or drunk or worried and then fail to achieve lift-off.

Her pubic hair feels like sandpaper. This could disappoint both of us.

Then I felt the free fall of warm space, a universe of comfort and bliss, my skin and hers felt smooth and the night turned into chocolate we both swam through. She disappeared, the forest of coarse jungle fell apart, and between my legs I floated into orbit like a happy electron around a hot radioactive isotope.

Then I wondered if I could remain in the valance ring long enough to see her toss a couple of neutrons, and lost the mood.

She cries out, then a little whimper, and she lifts her broad hips to move in little surges, a bit at a time so I would not fall out. My softened pointer worms deeper and deeper, and I kiss her and begin to feel it thicken. She stretches up to kiss my forehead and drag her nipples over my chest hair and mouth, and when I curl forward to help, she brushes my face with the tips of her softies to tease my hungry mouth with each bounce.

I strain up into her, as she wags her butt up and down on my lap and works me deeper as my antennae unfurls. She moves like a dancer to the music, her ribs like fingers that want to open and engulf me.

As Gibraltar rises over the Mediterranean, my pulse throbs blood iron hard against the inside of her. She sits up and bends backward, bends it backward inside her. It hurts me, feels like it might break off. I pull her arms and bring her forward, down to me, and hold her soft shoulders as we kiss. Her upper arms become the strings of a kite, and I direct how we fly. She flutters like a flag, and digs her nails into my shoulders as if afraid she might fall.

The bed scootches in tiny jumps across the floor with each thrust, and I notice a rhythmic chirp rise above the soft late night music from the tiny radio speaker. We adjust, she bends forward, and with her lips on my forehead, she takes all of me inside and changes her bounce into an undulation, forward and back like a greyhound, as she chews my ear and makes noises that remind me of a rusty swing set.

I want to back off, to hold her still to stop the inevitable, but she bites my neck and growls like an alley cat, mutters something in French. I lose my breath, every muscle tenses and King Arthur's sword plunges again and again into the anvil of France.

She gasps and holds me in the vise of her ironwood arms, surrenders her hips to my rhythms, her legs spread wide, then her fingernails scratch down my chest.

She lists to one side, thrusts one hand to where we join together, and starts to move.

I surge up into her, we tense and I grab her hipbones and mash our groins together. I bury it as deep as it goes, and we grind together like one whiplash body. Then I come and it hurts, it squirts like a grease gun into a clogged bushing, the spurts feel like they rip something open, like my banana burst, as I spasm my milkshake into her.

I roll on top of her, push myself up to look at her tan body dappled with our sweat. She lays spread eagle below me, her eyes intense, her mouth open a little. I push into her with the last few contractions of my exhaust hero.

She says something in French, her eyes turn the color of the wine dark sea, and I know she does not want it to end just yet.

I try to keep up with her rhythm, but my soldier falls out of his foxhole, soft and shrunken, muddy from battle. Her hand between us vibrates and tries to put it back in, then moans her disappointment and continues to writhe against me and her own hand.

I kiss each moan, and suck her lips. I lick them like a dog licks a wound, and she licks back, bites my lip. Her legs caress my flanks, up and down my sides and thighs.

We straighten and intertwine our legs like serpents, constrictors, stretch, and mesh together at the groin, tangle and untangle, tense and release, tremble, collapse and pant. We stay glued together by the hot wetness of our groins, roll across the bed and surrender to the waves of purple night and glitters of stardust that waft through our field of vision. I lick her neck, a dry, unexplored desert with little rivulets of salty tastes, the aromas of earthy lust and sweat around the shy caverns of her ears. Her toes grab mine, a handful of painted fingernails rake my back and butt. Up and down the valleys of sensation and rhythm, we climb and fall with each slow exhausted pant.

We kick the blankets and sheets away to let our bodies cool. The rest of the covers slide off the bed in slow motion and land on the floor. They appear to quiver in the candle-lit darkness, as my fingertips do, as her lips and eyelashes.

The cold climbs up off the tile floor and spreads over our bodies that hum as if the distant thunder of tropical storms awaken deep in the mattress.

"Mmmm " She murmurs, her eyes like a cats. "You came fast."

"Too hard, it hurt, let me tell you. Been a long time, too long."

"How long?"

"Can't remember. Maybe since Santa Catarina, when I used to fantasize about you."

"How do I compare with your fantasies?"

"Blow them out of the water."

"Is that a hint?"

"About what?"

"Never mind." She kissed me.

My groin felt mangled, kicked in the ass, at the root of my testicles, deep in my abdomen. She still seethed a little, hissed and writhed beside me, an Anaconda that squeezes and sucks at my neck.

The candles ebbed and wavered. We breathed, relaxed, and stared at erratic hints of movement up on the ceiling. My eyes go out of focus, and our skin disappears against the purple sheets.

She reaches for my manhood and by instinct, I twitch away but she follows like a cat and grabs it, to massage a few slippery drips out.

I put my hand between her thighs, feel her soaked hair, both of us a mess, everything soaked with the soup of us, slippery and sweaty. My fingers roam over, around, and through her swampy thresholds, to the wide delta of her pubic mound, to the junction of her swollen lips again.

"Oh, it's so sensitive, careful, there. Yes. Oui oui oui oui oui."

She guides my hand to the right spot, forces my fingers to stay right there, then arches her back, twines her thighs through mine, her soft skin slides against me.

We kiss. Her open mouth rubs against my lips. My fingers move in random trails across the wet tangle of her hair, her lips down there. She gasps, her hands over my head to trap me in an underwater world of pure sensation. I could feel the heaviness return to my machinery, a little sore but a pulse remains, and soon I set sail under a full mast again, a tense log which, when she noticed it, she grabs to milk up and down.

She slides her hand over its wet head as if to polish a brass bedpost. She takes my root and pulls, moves my hand from her pussy, and puts me at the entrance to her hot spring.

I enter her, smooth, and feel her wrap hot around me. This time, my scraped up little post hole digger dives into her and feels every ragged, sensitive millimeter. With hands on her hips, I try to stretch her pelvic bone-frame box until it seems to creak and bang like the crude wooden bed frame under us.

She pushes me off and pulls my shoulders onto the bed to mount me, this time with her hand between her legs.

I buck and heave under her, send her up into the air, the candlelight and my hands play across the round softness of each bouncy breast.

A soprano moan builds from a low hum as it escapes her lips. She mashes my hand into her mammary glands and pinches her own nipples, then bends forward to increase the tempo on my staff.

She spreads her legs like a cheerleader and bucks on with violence. She slams her hands onto the bed next to my head, hard enough to scare me.

Then her hand dives between us to work her secret buttons. She sounds as if she feels some great pain, tenses up, and seems unable to move.

"Fuck me! Oh Jesus Christ, hard, harder, now! I'm so close. Give it to me hard, more!"

I tried, but at that moment, her French accent made me think how little in common we shared, not even a Catholic upbringing. I became objective, and wondered where and how she learned such language, with such a precise and situation-specific, appropriate American vocabulary. I tried to forget about it and remember to ask her later, and begin to thrust up harder, with a rhythm as fast as I can maintain, as if to crucify her on the staff of my life.

Her fingernails shine in the candle light, I see them flash and scrape spastic across my chest, belly, and dive down to the darkness where we meet. She leans against me, bites my shoulders.

She muffles her squeals with a mouthful of her own fingers, recovers her coordination, and humps me even faster and harder, takes all of me and wants more, rubs herself against my pubic bone. Then her face pants near mine, teeth bared, eyes squeezed shut. I watch her, and then she opens them wide.

"I'm coming don't stop, keep going I'm gonna come... Please, please, harder harder. Oh, Jesus, Jesus Christ!" Her face contorts as if with pain ,as she burns with pleasure, the ultimate altruism and reward of life, self abandonment in the union with another's pleasure. She shakes and bucks and bull rides me like a half drunk cowboy.

I roll her over onto her side, and manage to stay inside as we turn. Then onto her back, with the thought that her submission might excite me enough to give her what she needs. Her erratic gasps reminds me of a heart attack, but I don't care, I push her legs open farther, and try grind into her. My thrusts inch us up the bed, and push her against the headboard.

She places her feet flat on the bed to push her groin up in the air and meet my thrusts. The bed squeaks and groans a rhythmic accompaniment again, but we don't care, we don't listen to the radio's insipid polka music this time. My balls hang lose and hot, I feel them swing cool and wet to slap against the juncture of her inner thighs. She holds me around the neck, hugs me to her breast, and tells me to come, but I came once already, and this time I'm in control. Colors flash behind my eyelids, electric tingles start to shoot down my spine and behind my balls. Sweat drips off my face as I allow myself to slide past the point of no return.

I feel the brightest sunlight shoot up behind my eyeballs, and I gasp with the strength of sensation, the sunlit entrance of a dark movie theater, the end of a root beer when the straw collapses, a gasp of air, the rush of dogs and children who push their face out the window of a fast car. I push up, extend my arms and rise over her to squint, thrust, and spasm rainbow-hued hurricanes of my ancient seas into her, and then fall on top as we mash our groins together like two beached boulders rocked together by immense waves.

My excitement rekindled hers, and I feel her push and buck under me, desperate. "Take me, hard, now! More, f___ me!"

I almost laugh, and want to roll off her and fall asleep.

Her hand rubs herself as her hips push up into the air, a bronco that bucks in slow motion. I stay with her, but it begins to soften.

She calms down, lies still, and says "You. You don't know what you do to me."

"What?"

"You awakened the tiger I keep hidden, and now you must feed it."

"You sound like a gasoline commercial."

"Out of gas?" I try to stay stiff and in there, and tensed my buttocks to squeeze the blood into my eyedropper to stiffen it. It softens, sags, shrinks, and falls out anyway.

Yvonne overheats. She rubs herself, ready to take on a Brazilian soccer team. I saw something in her sexuality that frightens me about women. Some women, maybe.

Some scientific studies show an overwhelmed majority of men need at least a half hour or so to recuperate after they pop to get another woody and reach another orgasm, yet many women enjoy multiples of cyclic spasms of their pleasure centers, and may need continued stimulation to satiate their sexual urges, to reach homeostasis, the comfortable bored and sleepy equilibrium where they no longer feel like wrapping their legs around the nearest erect object. If ancestral women evolved with such an endurance and desire, so far beyond one normal man's capabilities, it suggests evolution selected for women who get too hot for one man. Orgy queens.

For this to happen, for evolutionary processes to influence such 'over sexed' women in modern populations of humans, some female ancestors with this ultra-passionate potential birthed more children, especially similar daughters, who tended to reproduce more than less excitable females. Or men enjoyed more reproductive success with such women, and worked harder to ensure their children, especially the excitable daughters, survived. I tried to imagine why multiple orgasms and redundant sexual pleasure sequences increase the "fitness", the percentage of the population which demonstrated such capacities for sexual pleasure, over a simpler female sexuality.

Perhaps those ancestral anthropoid men gathered around those excitable women, perhaps as their queen, for group sexual favors. Maybe the female's "fitness" describes the woman who more than survives (enjoys?) the gang rapes that the modern human male member's shape suggests to some scientist. The functional shape of the penis's head acts as a plunger, designed to rake out any previous deposits of ejaculate. Perhaps the tribes that survived best enjoyed another utility of a few multi-orgasmic women, with a few females who go along on the long hunts as concubine, to care for men's sexual needs, while the other women back in the village care for the children, which includes the concubine's. So maybe it stands to reason, at least for conjectural reasons, that at least some, probably many if not all, modern women inherited capabilities to enjoy experiences with multiple men, or women, or a mixture that includes machines.

When she calms down, she runs her fingers through my sweaty hair.

I feel that she wants to make me feel OK about my inability to please her when she asked for it, begged for it, demanded it. She coughs and the emptied sausage falls out of its nest.

She rolls over and clasps my thigh up tight between her legs and grinds her groin against my hip bone.

I lay exhausted, sweaty and out of breath.

She massages my bruised manhood with one hand, buries her face in my neck, sucks on my ear, insinuates her sweaty thigh between mine, then pushes me away and says "Too hot!"

"We're covered with sweat." I blow on her to make her feel cooler. My voice echoes in my ears, maybe a drop of sweat on my eardrum adds a dreamy quality.

She stretches out and twists her torso so that she lies on her side, a voluptuous horizon that undulates alongside me.

Her fingers pull at her sweaty hair, matted inky on the whiteness of her throat and upper chest. She glistens in the candle light. Her golden tan, jeweled and deepened with sweat, contrasts with her white breasts and their pink pools that change shape in slow, tectonic processes. Her nipples pucker in a volcanic uplift, the plains folds and small galaxies of spiral mountains build and disappear soft again into the rounded expanses. Then they relaxe, and the rosebud cone subsides.

I watch a red flush fade across her neck, chest, and abdomen. She lifts one leg and the whiteness of her inner thigh glows against the purple sheets. She looks at me with those long black lashes. A river system of wet hair runs in strands across her forehead and cheeks. Her perfect teeth reflect the candlelight. I kiss her, tell her she's the most beautiful woman in the world.

"Even like this?" She pulls a strand of hair that wicks sweat onto her cheek.

"Like this."

"You too, are very easy on the eyes. Texans say that." She smiles and speaks out of the side of her mouth.

"I like to watch you when we make love." She rolls over on her stomach, supports herself on her elbows so her breasts hang against the sheet. "I mean, what do you think, a good fuck or not?" She brushes the hair from my forehead, smiles, stares into my eyes.

"Aren't the French supposed to know better than anyone?"

"Experts we are, and it takes a lot of practice. Like anything else, practice makes perfect." She pushes her knee into my side. "You don't think mankind suffers from the shortage of casual sex? Don't you think everybody deserves enough casual sex to satisfy them. Imagine all the people who can't get enough. All that frustration, not healthy. Or do you think it better that Americans reject sex and sensuality, and instead follow all those fake religious leaders with plastic hair on television?"

"You didn't have a good time with American men?"

"Most American want to brag, I fucked a French girl, you know what I mean? In America, I became too popular when I made everyone think I came from a wealthy family."

"Americans love money."

"We French think Americans love violence. Your culture, your movies, so full of violence and action, and see heroes only as soldiers or policemen. American men want virginal women, even children, who do not know what they're doing, or they want women who don't say what they want. Those men prey on little girls. They can't stand it when a woman thinks, and is not impressed by muscles, a gun, or deadly friends."

"With virgins, competition doesn't get into the bedroom."

"Maybe that's why American men don't care about aesthetics and culture. They want to compete, join a winning team, become leader, achieve, get rich, and be the big boss over others. They join the military, or a big corporation, so they can move up and dominate others, earn a certifiable success."

"We're taught to become winners, that's all. What's wrong with that?"

"Your education teaches you nothing about what it means to be human. Americans cannot appreciate natural beauty, don't know how to treat a woman, and don't respect each other. They cannot love. America creates men like its movies, teenage fantasies of stupid nude women, car chases, explosions for a climax, and too much violent death."

"Tool and die."

"What's that?"

"A type of business, metal fabrication."

"Seems like hours since we smoked a cigarette," she said.

We both startled at a funny sizzle sound. The play of light changed, so we sit up in bed and find a conical pile of soft wax near the bed. Unbeknownst to us, at some point a candle overheated, and the liquefied wax buried its own little metal cup of a candleholder, flowed across the surface to the edge, and fell straight down in a translucent cascade, to create a stalagmite topped by a flame.

"We almost set fire to the bed."

She blows out the flame, gets out of bed, and walks nude to the bathroom to get a wet washcloth. "What a mess we made. You still feel like a virgin? No? Did I deflower another virgin? It's a habit of mine, sorry."

"I think I made love to a woman before, but can't remember, because of the drugs and alcohol. Maybe she was just a girl. It feels different with someone who knows what they're doing."

She hit me with the washcloth, then threw it towards the bathroom and blew out the other candle.

We sat together on the bed.

She lit two cigarettes.

That night, with her in my arms, I couldn't sleep. Tried to sleep, but with this woman beside me, the smell of her, her warm skin pressed against the entire length of my body, I wanted to live forever like this, every night, and remember every moment forever.

She woke up and reached out to me. "Something of yours pushes into my hip. Does it mean anything special, or do you need to pee?"

"I believe in jumping on opportunities. Who knows what tomorrow will bring?"

"I know." She kisses my ear and whispers "War."

"War? What do you mean, war?"

"Didn't you hear the radio in the taxi? For the last couple of months, Presidente General Kjell Laugerud wants war, to reclaim Belice as a part of Guatemala, just another state, like the Petén. He says England never made a road they promised in some contract to cut down trees in Belice, so Belice never was the British Honduras, it was always a part of Guatemala. Today he says Great Britain must call him by midnight tonight to say that they agree that Belice belongs to Guatemala, otherwise, Guatemala will go to war with Belice."

"Reminds me of something I learned on this trip, about choices, about going from bad to worse, you know, from mala to peor."

"What's that?"

"It's a saying that goes De Guatemala, a Guatepeor."

Fifth Section: Guatepeor

CHAPTER 16: Terremoto

Humans anthropomorphize objects, a mountain becomes a regal human the way it stands upon the Earth, clothed from head to foot in pine trees and crowned with snow or cloud. Water passes through it as if through an animal; it drinks the rain and gives birth to springs that leak from its sides and base. Clouds exist as mountains of the sky, kingdoms of the Heavens, and contain the voice of thunder, the fire of lightning, the water of Life, and the fierce breath of deadly wind. Water courses through the earth like blood, and so we can imagine how blood, water, and spirit pass through stages, or levels. Through channels and portals, underground rivers pass through the mouths and veins of mountains. The mountain births clouds, springs, and caves. The same way blood flows through our veins, water flows through a mountain, and spirits flow through all. The portals remain shut most of the time, but the Mayans, some modern Mexicans, and mystics in general, believe that ritual opens the portals that link levels of creation and allow an exchange of influences. People go on pilgrimages, venture to mountain tops, drink from sacred springs, enter the dark unknown of caves, or meditate and go within, to open their own metaphysical portals, to find that great spirit that inhabits everything. Through traditional rituals of blood and lives, and sometimes human flesh, humans around the world offer, or bribe, or even pay the Gods to influence reality. Through bloodletting and human sacrifice, the Meso-Americans implored the Gods to open the portals between the layers of Heavens, Earth, and Underworlds, and let them intermix.

The cars screeched and careened through the snow covered guardrail and plunged into the ravine, smashed through the thick black pipes draped with icicles and then crumpled, with the roar of slow motion, into the river. Ice explodes towards the charcoal overcast sky in tall geysers of diamonds.

As a rain of giant icicles falls around the tiny one room log cabin where a wisp of white smoke spirals from a black stovepipe chimney against the soft sky fall of white flake.

The hot breath surged like steam of war horses from under the parka hoods of a hundred black clad Boy Scouts. With red bandanas across their mouths, they jump up from foxholes beneath the snow. They bellow with voices of lakes locked under four feet of ice, they wade through waist high snow and advance, fill their mittens with wet snow to pack into ice balls and hurl against the cabin.

They throw in unison, a volley from all sides. Hundreds of wet snowballs fall upon the cabin at once, explosions of shattered snow on the sheets of tin that cover the windows, sheets that thunder and reverberate without end, a roar whose echoes return muffled by the thick snow piled along the sides of the river's ravine.

The train loomed out of the pines with horn blasts that shook snow from the unseen heights of the pines. The smokestack belched coals and molten iron of night over the diffused light of dawn's snowfall, a dream of heaven's virginal white sterility lies in deep prayer at the feet of a juggernaut of blackness, a brimstone hell of soot. The railroad tracks bent up from the ground to break through the snow as blackened mastodon teeth in front of the bloodied bars of the cowcatcher. This cyclone of snow and steel banked against the side of the ravine, west through the wet-black trunks of trees along the cabin's side, west North West across the cattail swamps, then northward as the train's wheels spun and threw showers of blue welder's sparks. The train made a complete circle to enclose the cabin in a cyclone wall of steel and soot colored boxcars that tightened with each revolution.

The cabin flickered out of sight as the train roared over us, full speedahead. The boxcars circled behind the locomotive and came closer to the cabin, a tornado of soot, fire, and snow.

Again the boy scouts hurled their thousands of wet snowballs to bury the one room cabin in a vortex of snow. It crushed the roof in a torrent of tarpaper, creosote shingles, alligator logs of wood splintered with teeth on the ends, glass shards, a hail of nails, as the walls folded in upon themselves.

I woke up.

The bed lurched and bounced in the blind darkness, as we boys woke up to do battle with the invaders from the adjacent camp, but the roar filled the room with dry dust. I tried to get out of bed and my feet hit the warm cement and confused me. The bed creaked and lurched across the floor. I heard chunks of the wall and ceiling crack and pop. The darkness fell and smashed into little pieces that skittered across the floor.

I reached for Yvonne and felt her shoulder, muscular and tense, almost awake. She woke up angry and yelled at me, "What are you doing? Stop it!"

By a little moonlight that streamed through small cracks in the shutters over the sealed street side door, I began to differentiate shapes between the black and less black.

Yvonne struck out at me once with her arm, but the mattress bounced. She lurched sideways and missed. She jumped out of bed and then bent over at the waist, unsteady, to touch the ground, then to get down on all fours.

I sat on the edge of the bed as the ground heaved. The bed lurched and trembled, as if a team of unruly sled dogs dragged the entire room down a gravel road. I hear more plaster fall off the walls and ceiling, from the corner, then near the bathroom. From overhead, a fine chalk dust rains upon me.

The building groaned and roared, the walls pulled apart at the corners where ceilings cracked and stucco exploded into the room.

I remembered the three floors above us.

"What's happening?" she said, her voice terrified.

We heard noises through the door, from out in the courtyard, muffled cries of people in other rooms cut through the ominous din of the earth's roar punctuated with glass breakage, the crash of heavy pottery shards, the deep crackles as masonry pulls apart.

We heard sounds from the street through the sealed door; the sounds of doors pushed opened, bricks and stone kicked around on the pavement, the muffled cries of people as they rushed into the street.

Yvonne screamed "The flashlight! Where's the flashlight?" and scrambled across the room towards the dresser. She lost balance and fell backward, pulled the entire drawer out onto the floor. She grabbed the flashlight and turned it on. Dust swirled in the wide beam that splayed about the room.

The roar diminished, and the bed settled into a tremble of stillness. A hum remained, a vibration from deep under the floor, walls, and street, indigestion deep in the earth's bowels. We felt it through the floor under our bare feet.

I found my pants and put them on, got out the lighter, and lit a candle. "Get your clothes on."

We started to pack our backpacks with the meager light of Yvonne's one flashlight, but neither of us could get enough light where we needed it. We remembered the clothes hung in the bathroom to dry, and found other clothing strewn about around the room as if it walked by itself. My shoes lay separated by four feet. Maybe kicked in our confusion, or maybe they walked. Yvonne found another candle, lit it, and we both dressed and packed.

Another vibration amplified into a quake that made the earth lurch. We stuffed our clothing into the packs, put them on, and hurried out the door to join others who rushed into the courtyard.

People streamed into the hotel's courtyard in various states of undress. Bewildered faces questioned each shocked other, neither yet awake. Shadows from flashlights and a gas lantern animated the walls and gave sleepy numb faces the appearance of mummies in subterranean catacombs.

The Guatemalans talked in hushed tones and used the word Terremoto over and over. The hotel staff lit a kerosene lantern, took down the parrot's cage, and hung the lantern in its place in the middle of the courtyard. They set the terrified bird in a corner.

"Anyone hurt?" Someone called out in English.

We watched a group of rescuers walk around the balconies and down the stairways by flashlight. They helped a dazed woman in her nightshirt.

As they eased her into a chair, they answered our questions. "We got up to the third floor, how the Guatemalans built the Bridal Suite as a separate room, a wood shack on four cement block pillars. At least two of the pillars fell apart in the quake, and the whole room fell off on one side and slid about six feet. When we got inside, everything bunched up against one wall, the desk, the chests of drawers, the bed, the shattered mirror, the table and chairs tangled together. She lay unconscious next to it all. Thought she got hit on the head. Looked like the higher floors amplified the earthquake. As we examined her, she woke up. She thinks it's all a joke."

The young woman gazed without comprehension at the fallen potted palms and other plants that lay on the ground to sprout horizontal from broken ceramic planters. The heavy ceramic pots fell when the thin legs of the soldered wire stands bent and collapsed. She talked, but could not accept the reality of the earthquake. She believed, or found it easier to believe, that we all conspired in a complex joke, or that she still slept and dreamt all of us.

We felt the earthquake hum underground, as the earth settled into new positions. Flashlight beams cut through the dusty haze in the air and revealed the damaged architecture. Bricks and plaster flaked out of the cracked walls of the courtyard and hinted at structural weakness beneath. Below each damaged area, piles of white plaster, powder, and rubble grew as more sandy mortar and plaster trickled down onto the conical piles, hourglasses of doom, that formed along the walls.

The quake's soft hum continued. When it grew strong enough to threaten, people dashed towards the blackness of the exit doorway to escape into the relative safety of the middle of the street.

"Best to stand in a doorway, that's what I've read." said a male voice in the darkness.

"You stay here in the doorway then, I'll be in the street," countered a female voice.

"Nobody better block that doorway when I'm getting out of here!" A garrulous man's voice, pirate tones, a motorcycle gang member's humorous threat of violence for the pleasure of it.

When the vibrations died down, people wandered nearer the narrow dark passageways back into the buildings. The quake faded, and we walked back into the interior courtyards.

"Do you think it's safe in this building?"

"How can we know without lights?"

People seemed to dash around with their shadows. Erratic flashlight beams stabbed through the dusty air like frantic air-raid searchlights. People hauled backpacks and clothing into the courtyard to pack up their things in the light of the lantern, hung to sway with the quake's residual vibrations. The shadows it threw danced in fits and starts across the courtyard walls.

The balconies groaned under the weight of people headed downstairs with their backpacks and suitcases. People scurried through the bat-black shadows of other people who eclipsed the light as they walked near the lantern.

The vibrations ebbed and grew, then waned, and each time they strengthened, people stopped to listen. If the vibration reached an amplitude that alarmed someone, they called out and rushed toward the street, which made the others panic. The vibrations sent all of us through the entrance to stand out in the open street, under the dark starlit city sky, with the most panicky neighbors.

The centuries old colonial buildings, yesterday an unbroken wall of houses strung together by electrical lines, looked old and fragile. The buildings' highest parts consisted of unsupported facades to add curves and arches, to individualize the houses. These architectural decorations, which added height to the tops of the street's walls, now lay in piles on the sidewalk. Most of these additions probably fell before the first people rushed into the street to escape the building's collapse. Many people emerged, in an effort to escape the disintegration of their home, to face torrents of brick and mortar.

The red tiles of Spanish roof lay in shattered heaps on the sidewalk. Up close, they impressed me with their size, a truly lethal bulk of almost inch thick ceramic. Roof tile production comes from a tradition where women bend soft damp clay slabs over their thigh into a half-pipe curve. When dry, they painted them with a clay slurry, a slip, that would turn into the familiar bright red glassy coating when baked in kilns, the ovens that melt clay minerals into ceramic. Roofers then laid the half-pipes in close rows, face up, then capped the seams with rows laid face down. These heavy double rows of half-pipe tiles slid off during the earthquake, heavy missiles, cluster bombs, which smashed onto the sidewalks to create a ruby necklace of destruction around each building. The piles of tile spoke to the intensity of the murderous bombardment that greeted residents as they ran from their buildings.

The electrical cables and telephone wires lay broken in the street or swooped low, due to the lean of broken telephone poles. As quake vibrations fluctuated in intensity, the electric and telephone lines trembled and swayed, their motion amplified by the height of the poles. They oscillated in the stillness of a windless night.

The earth calmed, yet continued to tremble, a vibration hard to separate from our own nervousness.

We walked back into our room. Yvonne packed her things while I shined the light on the bed, and on the walls.

One wall in our room suffered a diagonal crack, an inch wide chevron where thick flakes of plaster chipped away to expose the broken mortar beneath. The other wall cracked like a tic tac toe game, two horizontal cracks and two vertical. We scanned the floor for the splashes of white powder and chunks of plaster that indicated damaged parts of ceiling and walls.

"We can't staey here." I said. The ground still vibrated and threatened to quake again. "This place could fall down on top of us."

"Do you know a place we can go?"

"The Cerrito del Carmen. The church on a hill, with a park around it, all trees and bushes. We could pass by my Pensión, see how it fared, and pick up my things."

Yvonne finished with her things and we went into the courtyard.

A young man decided to stay in his room in the hotel. "I don't think it's so serious. The ground shook a little. So what? I don't see anything a couple of two by fours and a bag of cement couldn't fix."

One young woman in pants and a night shirt cried, while she held another in her pajamas to comfort her. They stared around with wide zombie eyes as people described the quake.

The rescued woman from the top floor sat on the floor in her night gown and repeated the same things over and over. "I rented the little bridal suite on the top floor, a little room on little block pillars, and you people say that it fell over, dumped me off the bed onto the floor, and I didn't wake up. I cannot believe this happened to me. It's a joke, this isn't happening. I'm still sleeping." She refused to function. As she sobbed, another girl sat on the ground beside her and hugged her about the shoulders.

The woman from the Bridal Suite repeated "This isn't happening" so many times people wondered aloud if she suffered a head injury, then someone said hit her again and make her shut up. They examined her scalp as she whimpered.

Everyone wanted to hit her on the head for her stubborn incredulity in the face of the tipped over potted plants, fallen mortar, the chaos of everyone awake at three in the morning, the mood of fear and anxiety, and the constant vibration underfoot. In sum, all the subtle and brute irrefutable manifestations of what occurred couldn't put this Humpty Dumpty together again.

She stood up by the lantern with her mouth open, and repeated, "I can't believe it. I don't understand."

Easier for her to believe she still slept, or that an entire hotel full of people got together to play an elaborate hoax on her, than admit she slept through an earthquake of magnitude 7.5 on the Richter scale with waves that moved 22,000 Kilometers per hour and released an energy equivalent to 3,000 atomic bombs like the one dropped on Hiroshima, a total energy of over 20,000 tons of TNT. The quake affected sixty thousand square kilometers, almost half of the entire region, an area which includes their neighbor Belize, which they considered illegally occupied by Great Britain.

Yvonne and I set out down the city streets, all dark without electricity. The cold night air made the breath fog out of our mouths and noses.

No cars, very few people. Dogs howled all over the city. We could hear sirens, and sometimes we saw, far up a long city street, a police car cross the road, its red and blue lights flashed upon the buildings and announced its route.

We passed holes in the once walled streets of colonial blocks where an entire house collapsed. People walked over and through the ruins in search of survivors. In the dim light, I could make out three men atop the rubble. They who carried a person, or a body, on a blanket wound around two poles to make a stretcher. They walked slow, each step deliberate and tested across the treacherous loose brinks and chunks of wall, ceiling, roof, or floor.

The dark city seemed abandoned, a mere hour after the quake. The ground trembled, and electric wires, those that still hung loose between broken and inclined poles, still whiplashed with the strongest tremors, and danced on a night with no wind.

We found out where many of the people went.

At the base of the Cerro del Carmen, we looked up the forested hillsides to see a tent city. Every available plot of ground covered by people and makeshift shelters of cloth, erected in this first hour after the quake. Behind us, we could see other people trickle in to seek safety from the city's damaged buildings, which threatened to crumble in a cascade of rubble and entomb the residents.

Within one hour after the first quake, people erected cloth shelters and cooked and watched their alert, traumatized children. Mothers breast fed their babies, and fathers busied themselves about their tent homes in silence, as if part of their normal life, as if these emergencies happened often, countless times before.

We walked up the road that curved to the church on top, and overlooked the entire Valley of the Cows. All around us, the tents of blankets and plastic sheets stretched on ropes between the trees. People searched the underbrush for wood to light cook fires. The Indian men in their típica pajama outfits, and the Indian women, with their long hair in two braids, sat with children in a pile of blankets they wrapped around their bodies. It gave the scene a timeless innocence.

Men carried fire in metal coffee cans from one campsite to another. A mysterious aromatic white smoke curled about and swirled in the lantern lights. It wrapped around tree trunks and filtered through the leafy branches. The Indians burn Copal, their incense, or green wood.

From the walkway around the back of the church, high over the city, we saw no fires, nor plumes of smoke, across the wide expanse of the valley.

When that quake hit that Wednesday, February 4th at 3:03 in the morning, emergency switches cut off the electricity. Without street lights, the city looked like a dark jumble of blocky rectangular crystals. From up high on the Cerrito, we saw the city stretched dark and ominous below, and melt into the distant mountains around the Valley of Cows. Police cars and ambulances made mobile pools of red blue light changes, as they traversed the network of streets. We could follow their route by flashes that illuminated the tops of buildings along the invisible arteries. The greater their distance from us, the more the siren's sound lagged, and our ears located its source a few blocks too far behind. These emergency vehicles traveled the city in spasmodic jumps from section to section. We could tell when they slowed to a crawl to avoid piles of rubble and the huddled groups of dumbstruck people, then sped up on clear streets, in a hurry to get to the next emergency.

We walked around the front of the church. Our feet still felt the vibrations of the broken earth as it settled into new positions, a sleepy giant awakened to emit low growls that bubbled up from the realms of the underworld, where it turned over and drummed against the earth with subterranean fists.

Through the clear mountain air, cold splinters of starlight illuminated the damage to the ancient Ermita del Carmen church. A portion of one thick corner collapsed to form a talus slope on the grass. The earthquake also bisected the round tower in the center of the circular drive in front of the church, a diagonal crack displaced the top section a couple of inches. Another good shake and it might slide off and leave the base to resemble a giant open lipstick applicator of gray cement.

A busy hour after the first quake, a couple of hours until a cold and cloudy daybreak, the entire nation huddled terrified around radios. More and more radios blasted out at full volume from perches hung in the tree branches, the fast frantic Spanish distorted by tiny overdriven speakers into a mechanical crackle, the squawks of rusty parrots of a land that turned itself into a junkyard in thirty seconds.

Smoke from around a hundred campsites wafted horizontal through the lower branches of trees, ephemeral white rivers, illuminated like ghosts in the light of lanterns, flashlights, and campfires. Men broke off the lower branches of trees to feed cook fires between the lean-tos and tents of cheap plastic and cotton blankets.

Under the trees that lined the north side of the circular drive, we found an empty stone bench to use as a bed. We spread our bags out to make a mattress, and hoped to sleep until daylight. The two of us barely fit together, wedged sideways like two spoons with Yvonne behind me. My legs hung over the edge of the cement bench, a discomfort which kept me awake. I hoped Yvonne felt warm enough to sleep, with her back against the cold stone backrest.

I lay tight alongside Yvonne, and we shared our warmth. I wonder if she felt as I did, on that narrow stone slab, that God punished us. Did we all share the same guilt, a beaten look in our eyes, as if we all deserved it? Everybody must feel that God kicked us in the teeth for about thirty seconds, each of us shaken awake at 3:03 AM, each reminded that we live in a lethal world where death waits with the easy grin of instant inevitability.

The earth's constant but quiet rumbles grow strong enough to alarm us every hour or so, then die out again. I felt the vibration, heard it through the cement of the park bench, and I became convinced I made a fool of myself, a victim of my own wild imagination. Then the vibration grew fast, into another unmistakable tremor, strong enough to make children cry, strong enough to change my mind.

The vibrations continued, and our shocked nervous systems kept us awake to listen. Whenever tremors increased in intensity, we repeated this conversation.

"Do you feel that?"

"Yes."

"Getting stronger, no?"

"Yes. Do you think we should get away from these trees?"

"I'm too tired. Trees don't fall easy. Most of them, anyway."

One strong quake felt as strong as the first, startled us all out of a half-slumber. From all around us on the slopes came the sounds of panic. We hear the calm voices of mature Indians as they hush and quiet children who cry in terror.

I wrote in my journal that "Neither of us slept. The ground continues to vibrate. If you concentrate, you feel it, but you don't want to."

Babies cried low in a strange moan, all cried out, too tired to put much energy into it. Once in a while we heard laughter, and it sounded out of place.

I lifted my head off the stone bench and turned to Yvonne pulled on her arm to get her attention. "You know what really makes me feel like shit in the middle of all this?"

"What?"

"I've been disowned."

"Everybody's been disowned."

As dawn broke and the sky grew light enough to see, neither of us felt as if we slept more than a few minutes at a time. Yvonne decided to get up and cook porridge on her camp stove. "Never used it before this trip. Carried it all this way for something. Destiny. Fate."

We could hear people around us talk in Spanish or Mayan. Radio's blared from various directions, and announcers counted the after-shocks and reports of damage, estimated death toll, estimated 'damnificados,' lists of villages damaged, inaccessible except by helicopter, communities buried under landslides to disappear, communities reported missing, without contact, without a clue.

The radio's relentless litany convinced Yvonne and I that these problems would not go away with a couple of two by fours and a bag of cement.

The earthquake invalidated everybody's normal daily ritual, all plans thrown to the winds, everything now the wreckage of a former life, most possessions now meaningless, most real estate a liability. Without safe buildings, nothing would open, and no stores could sell the necessities of life, no trudge back into a town for food, water, or shelter.

Each sunset would mean another night at the mercy of the elements for thousands of extended families, for one fifth of the population lost their homes, over a million dwellings destroyed.

We mixed dry milk powder with canteen water and boiled oatmeal, sweetened with cinnamon sticks. We ate on our stone bench, and watched the pigeons and parrots fly by along with the smoke from a hundred small breakfast fires below us in the park. The breeze wafted up the hill and brought us the aromas of tortillas and oregano, eggs, and boiled rice.

As the morning progressed, the low fog and white smoke lifted higher and pulled apart to let the blue sky background shine through with unbroken promise. Low clouds scudded along, not cumulus, but airborne puddles of fog with indistinct edges and colors.

After breakfast, we packed up and walked back towards the center of the city. The people on the streets stood around and talked, assessed the damage, or helped families pick through collapsed buildings to pull out the injured, or the bodies of the deceased.

Some women lit candles and set up little altars on the sidewalk amid piles of stone and brick.

Our route took us past the huge Cathedral of La Merced. All around the immense Cathedral, tremendous blocks of stone lay on the apron and sidewalks, toppled from the tops of the massive walls.

Guatemala's world changed overnight.

Today people cleaned and tried to make the city function. They swept up the streets, shoveled rock and glass into misshapen mountains of rubble on the sidewalks that overflowed into the streets, or piled it into towers on the street corners for pickup.

These piles represented pieces of buildings, proof the earthquake damaged the structure, and the building's internal structure might also sustain enough damage that the rest of it could fall at any moment.

When we reach the square in front of the National Palace, Yvonne notices the clock tower, the Big Ben of Guatemala City, stopped at 3:02. I wondered how long the first violent quakes lasted, and how quickly we both awoke.

I asked Yvonne how long she thought they lasted.

She said "Brandon, tell me the truth. You did not shake the bed?"

"No."

"You didn't shake the bed at all?"

"That's right."

"I thought you acted like a child." She laughed, her eyes darted about in thought, and she breathed in short quiet gasps, almost a pant. "I awoke so angry at you. How long do you think it lasted?"

"I don't know. I thought a train full of Boy Scouts threw snowballs at our windows. They surrounded us."

"What?"

"I incorporated an old childhood memory into a dream, like when your alarm clock gets into your dreams and turns into a fire engine, because you don't want to get up. It goes back to a winter campout I went on as a Boy Scout. We stayed in a small cabin near a railroad track, and one night the Scouts from another cabin attacked us. They threw snowballs at the sections of tin nailed over the windows. As a boy, I woke up slow, like last night, and thought the noise came from a train that passed right through the center of our cabin. So all us boys got up and threw on our jackets and snow pants to run out and do battle in the snow, in the middle of the night. Never thought about that campout in all these years, until last night."

"The highpoints of your life flashed before your eyes. All eleven years of it."

"I'm still a Boy Scout at heart. That was the closest thing to an earthquake I ever experienced before last night."

The frozen clock face stared down at us. Yvonne looked around the streets at the dazed inhabitants of the dead city, and bit her lip. "We could call my doctor friend. I should call today anyway."

"I bet he's busy today, Joanna."

"Joanna? Who's Joanna?"

"Sorry. Someone I traveled with a short time."

Yvonne stayed silent.

I said, "Forget it. A slip of the tongue, means nothing. Met her at the border. A friend."

"Now you really insult me."

"Do you think the phones work? Want to call that doctor friend of yours? I bet he's busy."

"Who knows. He works as a cosmetic surgeon. I hope someone's home. I don't think the schools will open today." We walked towards Guatel, to try the long distance phone booths in front of the company's building.

A large crowd milled about, full of tourists and extra-nationals, that stretched far down the street. As we approached, people's attitudes gave us the impression the phones did not work. People's eyebrows seemed bent at crazy angles, foreheads corrugated, a bunch of sleep-deprived traumatized people, seemed half of them chain smoked. People on the street told us a Guatel employee came out once, to announce that they hoped to establish a few emergency lines in a little while.

"I imagine everyone with a relative in Guatemala wants to call today, to find out about their family, and all that."

Yvonne looked worried. "I wonder how many people got hurt, how bad it looks..."

"We don't even know where the center of the quake is yet. Imagine if Guatemala City is on the fringe of it, away from the epicenter."

"Do you think any volcanoes will erupt?"

I shrugged and said, "I wish we had a radio."

The range of uncertainty made me dizzy, as I thought about my status as a foreigner, and worse an ugly American, in a country full of people that felt the United States of America corrupted their democracy, absconded with their natural resources, and dominated their economy through the influence of a very few privileged families.

Some French tourists caught Yvonne's attention, so she ran across the road to talk to them as they walked away. She jogged back with her eyebrows pointed skyward, and crossed the road with her backpack and breasts in full bounce.

She panted too much for the short run, more than out of breath. "It's bad. Real bad." She came close and talked low, "They just bussed into town from the countryside, saw many dead people, saw people die, whole villages disappeared. Bodies piled alongside the road. They heard reports on the radio about collapsed bridges and landslides that block the main highways. The radio talks about scenes shot from airplanes and the President's helicopter, things shown on television. Looks bad. They say foreigners should all leave the country."

"Who said that?"

"The radio. Those Frenchmen over there. The President. Everybody. How the hell should I know? Where should we go?"

"If you're not part of the solution you're part of the problem, as hippies say. We must wait to see if the road to Mexico is open. Where did they just bus in from? Maybe we cold go back the way they came in, make a tour of the death and destruction."

"Oh yeah. Great idea."

"OK, a sick joke."

"What a time to joke. What if there's no food or water?"

"It's always raining in the highlands. I've got enough oatmeal for a couple of days."

"Don't say that loud, we'll get robbed. And what about all these bodies, and buried villages. You have any idea what that could do to things?"

"Epidemics?"

"Epidemics."

"OK, we should leave. At least go somewhere not so damaged. Belice."

"Belice? I bet they cancelled the war."

"Of course they cancelled the war. God probably punished the Guatemalan people for going along with that stupid idea of war. Good for God, if you ask me. Good for her."

We walked through the city toward the south, without any idea of where to go ,and we came upon a city block where people lay lined up along a wrought iron fence, behind which lay a luxuriant landscaped yard around a modern hospital, bushes in full flower, tall aromatic eucalyptus trees. People lay scattered about on the grass inside, and outside with their backs against the fence and their legs outstretched across the sidewalk. As we stepped careful and measured each footfall between their outstretched legs, we noticed their soiled and dirty bedclothes, IV stands and plastic tubes, the older people's vacant gaze, and the bandages stained by overnight blood flow, now caked with dried blood. The hospital probably sent these people outside to make more beds available for the influx of people with more serious injuries.

Inside the fence, people, many with bandaged wounds on their arms and heads, lay spread out on the green grass. Some lined up along the fence to beg for food or money with arms stretched out between the wrought iron bars.

Inside the compound at the hospital entrance, people helped each other get out of taxis and move toward the entrance. People who came out of the hospital wore fresh bandages, white as the nurses' uniforms or the orderlies' shirts who walked with them to and from the metal gate, guarded by two armed men who held back a desperate crowd. Some people in that crowd stood on tiptoe to call out with a piece of paper in an upraised hand, perhaps prescriptions for drugs, but each with the hope of special consideration for treatment.

As we walked along the sidewalk, we saw more and more injured victims on the grounds around the hospital, most still in their bedclothes from the night before. They stretched out on blankets in the warm sunlight, and most slept. Some sat dazed, and stared through the portions of chain link fence that separated the hospital grounds from the street.

At my feet on the sidewalk, a gaunt ancient man sat, his face filled with deep wrinkles. He peeked out from under a thick woolen sleeping cap, his legs spread eagled over the sidewalk. He looked up and gave me a weak smile. He raised his arm, bandaged from the shoulder down his forearm and over his hand in a thick mummy wrap, as if to greet us, or to say "Look at this... these sunken eyes saw so many years pass, and now this misery just makes me want to smile at young people, who know not what they're in for. Life is a constant defiance of mortality."

I smiled back and responded in English, "Hey, how's it going?" an automatic answer to this telepathic greeting. A stupid thing to say, I thought, and didn't know why I said it.

He smiled at me again while he closed his eyes, as if reassured about something.

We walked toward the downtown area. People walked haphazard, into streets without traffic, to peer up at the buildings. We all felt alien this morning, from another city, or another planet.

I turned to Yvonne and held her arm to slow her down. "As long as we're near downtown, I've got somewhere to go, a few blocks from here."

"Where?"

"The Dirección General de Migración, they've still got my passport. How could I leave without it?"

We walked fast. Soon we stood on the sidewalk outside that office, and stared down the wide, rubble-strewn stone steps that lead down from the sidewalk level to the steel trap door of the Migración offices.

The expressionless gray metal door relayed a clear, mute message. Closed.

We decided to head away from the city's center, towards the suburbs, and with a luck, away from the confusion of all the people who would spend the day in frantic attempts to fathom the damage to their shattered lives and property. Everyone in Guatemala wanted to get in touch with loved ones, reassure each other they still lived, and hear who else survived, or if they did.

I suggested the three dimensional relief map at the north edge of town. We hopped on an almost empty bus north, and it cruised nonstop because so few people traveled anywhere today. The earthquake closed everything, no electricity, no water, no food, no business.

Through the bus windows, we saw pile of blanketed corpses lined up on a couple of side streets. We noticed people, and that included all of us on the bus, dazed and numbed, as if in denial of the realization that last night's intense terror brought a dawn of horror without end, well into the predictable future.

Yvonne wondered if the earthquake damaged many of the taller, modern commercial buildings, built fast and cheap, perhaps more fragile than the older stone or cement traditional architecture. We passed many new vacant lots filled with the chaos of rubble where buildings once stood, reduced to piles of loose brick and bent reinforcement bars. People climbed over and through the wreckage, on the lookout for the dead and those still alive.

We saw a long, rectangular three story hotel with one third of its length collapsed where the lower rooms' walls failed. Two floors above dropped one floor down, to smash flat the first floor rooms. The middle third of the long building sloped on a diagonal to connect the fallen section to the intact section.

To me, it symbolized life in an earthquake; the fallen, the injured, the still upright but vulnerable.

Women walked the streets with all kinds of containers of water on their heads, large clay pots, metal cans, but most balanced plastic buckets in bright blues, oranges, and brick red. A line of women with containers balanced on their heads meant a source of water, clean or not. Often people opened the spigots on the sides of tall buildings to draw water from the storage tanks on the rooftops.

From the bus, I saw women line up to dip water from a hole in the sidewalk where workers once removed a square of the cement to make repairs. The earthquake broke a water pipe, and now the water flowed under the sidewalk, alongside other pipes that probably carried other effluents. People cannot live without water. They could boil it to kill bacteria and viruses, but that won't remove chemical toxins like heavy metals, or some of the poisons from bacteria.

Residences, spread out along the road, became luxurious mansions amid groomed lawns and offered a glimpse of the extravagant comfort of the privileged few.

A line of large trees in the median shaded the boulevard. We flew through their shadows with almost an audible sound, a vulture's wing beat. The bus sped past the entrances of other peninsular enclaves of residences, with no passengers to hail us.

At the far northern edge of the city, this road stops because of soft, volcanic ash cliffs along a large river valley. The bus left us at the last stop, at the top of a circular turn around drive.

We walked over to the fence that encloses an area that looks full of pointy termite mounds, the 3 Dimensional map of the entire country of Guatemala.

We did not know yet where the experts determined the quake's epicenter, although we heard several names of villages that we couldn't find on our maps of the country.

Yvonne laughed at the three dimensional map, with its stiff plastic flagpoles akimbo and crooked to label place names on the gray, lifeless comic caricature of the topography. With the vertical scale exaggerated hundreds of times, the map resembled a cave floor full of stalagmites made out of goopy cement.

The map did emphasize one fact. This country, the size of the state of Tennessee, rides on a spine of twenty seven volcanoes, all with the potential to erupt. These volcanoes belong to the great arch along the Pacific mountain chain, a continuation of the volcanic regions of Mexico, Baja California, California, Oregon, Washington, British Columbia, and Alaska which forms the eastern edge of the Pacific Ocean's famous Ring of Fire, a volcanic shoreline that continues through Russia, Mongolia, China, Japan, Philippines, and southern Asia.

Guatemala's tight group of volcanoes form one of the most active parts of this "Ring of Fire." Its string of volcanoes leads through Central America, then down through the Andean region of South America.

I wondered if earthquakes trigger volcanic eruptions.

Indigenous American folklore and cosmology visualized the land mass of the world as the back of a huge tortoise that swims in the sea. Today we call a similar vision plate tectonics.

With Central America and the entire Caribbean caught in the middle of the major pressures from mid-ocean volcanic ridges that spit out new seafloor, this relatively small isthmus between the Americas cracks into hundreds of small plates. The myriad chunks of the earth's crust grip against each other, but over eons of time, they slip and release some tiny portion of the huge potential of geologic energy. We perceive the earth's miniscule corrections and accommodations to volcanic seafloor expansion as cataclysmic events, earthquakes and volcanoes. After a few years, things settle into place again, and may remain quiet for years, decades, centuries or even millennium, but the pressures build up again. To a human's seventy year life span, it looks like a slow process. On a geologic timeframe, we live a heartbeat from the next gigantic disaster, a rapid flutter of an eyelash to the next cataclysm.

The first quake lasted only thirty five seconds.

The ground still trembles, and so do we.

"Have you been to Antigua?"

"Yes."

"Imagine what could happen if some of those volcanoes start to erupt."

The park lawns spread northward, to a line of tall trees that mask an abrupt and bushy drop off. We walked along the lip of the valley's edge, and skirted thirty foot square sections of sod, bushes, and trees that dropped several feet in last night's quake. Sections as big as a house's footprint cracked off and split, slipped down the cliff edge in angles that stair-stepped eight inches at a time to drop ten feet or more. We looked down into the cracks from the unstable edges, and saw powdery dirt walls that dove down deep into a stygian darkness. A volcanic eruption probably produced this soil, a powdery dirt, as water flow and ancient rivers deposited ashes and pulverized rock from the mountains that encircled this high valley. Wide, flat valleys, where not created by glaciers, reflect the action of rivers and erosion that filled in what once looked like a deep V-shaped valley between steep mountain slopes.

We climbed out on one of the huge broken chunks of ground, tested each footfall, and peered over the edge. Seemed solid enough to support our weight, but still loose at the broken edges.

The valley stretched northward between an the escarpment to the west and a low line of eastern mountains. Both faded to blue in the milky distance of the horizon, where a thin line of more distant mountains seemed to appear and disappear.

We noticed banks of yellow dust meandered through the valley floor.

"Rivers. Those yellow clouds must mark river valleys, canyons through some yellow ash deposit. The sides fell off in the earthquake."

The valley's streams joined together into a main river down the center of the valley. All the canyons belched a dusty haze, like white smoke, into the lower atmosphere. It looked like fires raged below as if rivers of embers smoldered through the dry grass riverbeds across the distant valley floor.

This haze lay thick over each long canyon and billowed out of each of the gashes in the valley. As the billows wafted and changed shape, we glimpsed the fresh face of exposed chalk dirt on canyon walls, last night's contributions to erosion. Right below us, we looked long and hard to sort out the crumbled mass of earth and twisted trees that fell last night.

The billows of dust moved as if alive, a slow serpentine movement as if diaphanous lemon sea monsters swam through solid earth. The vista changed as we watched, optical illusions, the haze moved and disappeared and reappeared, tendrils and tentacles of a sensuous octopus that devoured the land as far as we could see. Maybe chunks still broke off and sent up those yellowish clouds.

Our little broken piece of cliff seemed stable. We sat down and used it as our little lawn. It overlooked a beautiful vista draped in pain, a land shaken and torn, its breath writhed as low clouds of dust.

Yvonne reached into her bag and got out her small wooden flute, a recorder, to put it together. She sat cross legged and played to the valley, as I lay back with a long strand of grass to chew.

I closed my eyes and daydreamed. All through the day, when I closed my eyelids, I saw a nightmare recur, over and over, all last night and so far, all day today. People clambered over ruins, they stepped through debris and poked around with flashlights, they bent down and called out with care and waited, to listen for an answer, so that others who searched the rubble and called out for survivors could hear the faintest of replies from within. Ruins lit by candle light, once homes, poked and examined by families that searched and kept searching, energized by hope, while some contextual realization took place, a psychological adjustment to prepare them for the sight of corpses of loved ones, and the eternal absence thereafter.

Yesterday in the Land of Eternal Springtime, young men muttered piropos at the exotic beauties that passed. School children played and fought, ate and took classes together and went home to their families, traditional old-world Guatemalan or Latin American multi-generational families, extended families with grandparents and their sister's kids who all lived together under the same roof. They did laundry together in the same courtyard, where plants flowered and roosters crowed. Dogs barked and wagged tails to tease a couple of cats (who learned to ignore the chickens that laid eggs) who lay about with regal dignity to keep the mice out of sight. A couple of parrots squawked at the cats who got up undignified to get out of the way of the peacocks that yelled "halp!" and scared foreign visitors like me.

The beauty and peace of Yvonne's flute music helped bandage the wounds that an impersonal natural cataclysm left upon all creation. I respected and admired the fact that in the face of such senseless destruction and emotional upheaval, she needed to play music, and I benefited to hear it, and it seemed that all creation improved. Music brought peace and hope into a world in shock, God-betrayed, disowned, on the verge of a nervous breakdown as a prelude to the end.

It made me think about the role of art and music in human society. In fact, the day, so unlike other urban days, without traffic, no throngs of people on the streets, soothed me, and maybe the other sleepless people on the streets. People looked at each other all day, direct and open, as if to appreciate those who survived, to acknowledge our coexistence and shared calamity, to give each other a small smile, a nonverbal greeting that might say "Wow, wasn't that something! Glad to see you're still here too."

On the way back into the city, we asked the bus driver to drop us off at any store he could find open in spite of the earthquake. He said he knew of one, and dropped us off on the edge of a suburban area.

We stepped inside the modern grocery store, and saw most of the stock lay right where it first landed, shaken off the shelves to smash and scatter. The broken glass containers oozed puddles that that merged and cemented things into sticky masses. People picked through this carnage to retrieve anything undamaged to purchase. We found oatmeal, crackers, tins of tuna, some dried beans and a couple of bags of rice to carry as emergency food for the uncertain days ahead.

Late that afternoon, we stopped by Guatel and after a half hour wait, Yvonne got a telephone and called her friends, the doctor's family, and they invited us over. We took the bus out to Dr. Mendez's house, and through the radio on the bus, we started to hear the whole story, at least as much as we could understand from the way the overexcited announcers machine-gun it out in Espanól.

We heard most often one phrase, total destruction, as Newscasters repeated the damage reports for town after town. Unknown, ignored villages now claimed sudden fame for their complete disappearance. Whole villages of adobe flattened under rockslides, the occupants of the houses crushed or perhaps alive in spite of their injuries, trapped under the weight of their house. Entire buildings fell to crush the dust filled breath out of them, or leave them trapped in the earth's pitch black tremble to hope for rescue that may not come for days.

I tried to imagine how adobe houses might crumble in an earthquake, turn into an adobe dust that kills by asphyxiation. If people could survive the weight of the walls and tile roof that fell over them, they might breathe the dust and cough throughout the night and for innumerable days to come, as long as they could, as long as they had energy to hold on to that spark of life fueled by oxygen. So they lay and waited for rescue, buried alive, each breath forced by the bellows of rib and diaphragm, breathed with bloody lung froth and foam around the mouth, as their sense of place and existence passes in and out of consciousness until their deepest exhausted sleep brings eternal relief.

Entire villages of adobe brick crumbled to dust in that first intense thirty five seconds of vibration, that violent back and forth of perhaps a foot, perhaps less, up and down, side by side, the circular motions of compression waves as the tremors shot through the soil and rock to reverberate across the width of the entire country.

The tallest points of structures amplified the motion to move perhaps a yard or two, who knows how many times in those thirty seconds before the break and collapse of heavy row upon row of red clay roof tiles that skidded off into piles of broken rubble like shatters of sewer pipe. Then the unrestrained adobe bricks of the upper walls crumbled into loose dirt clods with vertical tons of weight to slip, fall, and flow over the bewildered families snug in their shelters.

Thirty five seconds doesn't sound like a long time, but try it yourself. Start to rock a little back and forth, like a tall building or an adobe wall with a load of clay roof tiles, while you count One dit dah dah, Two dit dah dah, Three dit dah dah, Four dit dah dah, Five dit dah dah, Six dit dah dah, Seven dah dah, Eight dit dah dah, Nine dit dah dah, Ten dit dah dah, Eleven dah, Twelve dit dah dah, Thirteen dah dah, Fourteen dah dah, Fifteen dah dah, Sixteen dah dah, Seventeen dah, Eighteen dah dah, Nineteen dah dah, Twenty dah dah, Twenty one dah, Twenty two dah, Twenty three dah, Twenty four dah, Twenty five dah, Twenty six dah, Twenty seven, Twenty eight dah, Twenty nine dah, Thirty dah dah, Thirty one dah, Thirty two dah, Thirty three dah, Thirty four dah, Thirty five dah.

With the Mendez family

The Mendez family, delighted to see Yvonne again, regarded me with an elegant friendliness both wary and proper. It took a while for me to get them to laugh, but I found a way through the maid. I jumped up to help her whenever she came in the room, and resisted their instructions to sit down.

"I'm just a Gringo. We're supposed to help women with the chores."

"But you're in Guatemala know. Women do the chores, and men sit back and enjoy. Besides, she's the maid. We pay her to do everything for us."

And work she did, in continuous service for several years now. She smiled in gratitude for the compliments, attended to our drinks, cooked the meals, changed the sheets in the bedrooms we would sleep in, and attended to her own two children, one arrived three months ago. Sometimes she wore her baby in a light blanket, like a sling under one shoulder and tied at the back of her neck, so the baby could nurse while she worked.

Yvonne knew Dr. Mendez could not allow us to sleep together. Out of respect for his family, and Yvonne's belief that Dr. Mendez found her useful to educate or control both his sons, she decided we should hide our relationship.

Although they didn't ask about our relationship, they soon clarified things. They saw it in our eyes, or felt it in how we evaded each other's touch with a deliberateness that spoke to our desire to touch, or how we glanced at each other reluctant to look away.

By bedtime, Dr. Mendez announced what everyone deduced anyway. He told us that our visit as tourists, in a Catholic and conservative country such as Guatemala, meant that he, Dr. Mendez, could not in good conscience allow two young lovers to share a bedroom in his house, no matter what his personal feelings on the matter. "Word gets out, and I want no stain on our reputation, on this respectable house, not even in times of national emergency." Later in private, he talked to both of us, together, and asked we respect our influence on his sons, and behave according to Guatemalan standards, not the United States. "I personally do not judge you two. I met my wife in the United States. But this is not the United States, and I must teach them how to behave as Guatemalans."

Just before sun set, Yvonne and I hung out with the boys in Jaime's room and discussed some radio DJ's opinion that Led Zeppelin ranks as the greatest Rock and Roll band in the history of the known universe.

"Without Jimi Hendrix or the Doors, I might agree with it."

"What about Pink Floyd, Dark side of the Moon?"

Yvonne came in with some candles, and broke into our masculine face-off, to say "I'm nervous, you know. Real nervous."

"On edge?" said Jaime, as he gave Yvonne his complete attention. "Earthquakes. The whole world chingada, everybody no got nothing now. We wait for the Terremoto to happen again."

As the light from the window faded and the candle light illuminated our faces, Yvonne and I sat on the floor while Jaime talked to us from the top bunk of the bed. I noticed Yvonne put her hands on the floor, as if to determine if the floor her body trembled.

Jaime watched her and said "I like it up here, it exaggerates the motion of quakes."

With a sixteen year old's naughty grin, Manuel said "Reminds me of a drunk I saw on the street. He walk around and hit walls, like he can't stand, and he walks bent over to watch the ground. He put his hand out, on the wall, the ground. Then he throw up, you know, vomit. That's what the world like now. A sick drunk who throw up and might do it again."

"That is so gross," Yvonne said. "But it does feel ugly like that."

"Dr. Mendez will not go to sleep soon." Jaime said. "He likes to drink late and when I stay home, he stays up to watch me, to stop me from a drink, a little of his whisky. Just a little."

Jaime took one of the candles to light the way for Yvonne to shoulder her pack and head to the guest room down the hall, a room she liked to stay in because it gave her a separate bathroom. He gave her a flashlight.

"To read with?"

"Do you have batteries? We need the flashlight. No electricity."

I sat around with Manuel in the boys' room and waited, while nervous sweat dripped from my armpits, for Jaime to return from Yvonne's room. I feared she might take the opportunity to give Jaime a heart to heart about me, about our relationship. I knew Yvonne traveled with them at least once, and I could see how much Dr. Mendez respected her influence over his two sons, and how much they liked her.

Dr. Mendez liked to go to bed early. He organized his life through rituals of punctuality. Every week he planned with detail, so that even his days off became ordeals of accomplishments which his sons learned to endure. Tonight he broke from his schedule to stay up and talk with us.

"Since this 'terremoto', the earthquake, trucks and cars bring more and more people into Guatemala City. As soon as officials report another road open, the buses and cars come from the smashed villages. New patients arrive, with increasingly complicated conditions because of bad treatment, or no treatment at all."

"Lots more infections?"

"Of course. I've been incredibly busy the past few days," Dr. Mendez tells us. He says the hospital staff, exhausted and overworked, fall asleep while they attend to all the cuts, breaks, bumps, respiratory failures and heart conditions. "Now we deal with huge numbers of dislocated spines and fractured pelvises, which need the most care, and we have no more beds to put them in. I hate to see people suffer. The ambulance drivers and relief workers tell us about hundreds of towns destroyed, thousands of people dead. The body count climbed every hour for the city, and now the countryside. More planes return to report villages flattened, or that they'd flown over the locations of villages and can not find them anymore. Landslides cover the roads, cover villages, change landmarks."

The country faced food and water shortages, epidemics, and transportation problems, and the road to Puerto Barrios remained impassible where the earthquake destroyed the impressive Aguas Caliente Bridge. The entire middle section dropped out when the center two of four pilings failed, which left both ends to stand free in midair, like two giant diving boards high over the rocky riverbed.

Manuel said "Kids play hide and seek in the fissures, and risk a fall into the earth. They play on earth bridges, where sections of dirt and plants clogs a fissure from one side to the other. Sometimes it gives way, they fall, and get stuck, or fall into caverns underneath, deep caves."

"Things changed overnight," Dr. Mendez said, "last week you could buy sheet plastic for pennies, now you can't find it. People needed all there was to shelter themselves from the sun and rain. The entire population of Guatemala wants to live in a plastic tent right now. So the government helps workers set up impromptu Rescue Centers. They give emergency first aid, and administer other types of relief. International aid arrived at the Guatemala City airport from all over the world."

Manuel said "The Nicaraguans arrived first, because when a hurricane hit Nicaragua, Guatemalans arrived first to help them.

Dr. Mendez continues, "Everyone says more deaths will come, but the radio's warnings about inevitable epidemics and famine will make people panic. I don't like panic, people go crazy and fight. The first big problem is water, drinking water. The radio announcers tell everyone to boil water, to help cleanup the dead bodies, to burn trash. In three months the rains will come, so everything must happen fast.

"For example, now, with so many dead bodies, the government puts them in mass graves. They have to. The government and international health authorities believe that is the only short-term solution to protect people, food, and water. Refrigeration doesn't exist in Guatemala. Not even for beef cattle. We kill a cow or a goat and eat it within days, so it doesn't spoil. Local officials in smaller villages can't wait. They must burn the bodies with alcohol."

Doctor Mendez, perhaps due to his Catholicism, seemed most horrified by the news that in some places the quake's pressure waves and fissures cast up coffins out of their graves in the cemeteries, and concerned relatives headed to the cemeteries, to re-bury their dead ancestors and family members, to scrape out a new grave with machetes.

On the Machete's Edge

Dr. Mendez planned to show us around today, but crisis struck first thing in the morning.

The maid woke us all up with her screams. We threw on a robe or pants or something decent to run around in, and filed out of our rooms and into the hallway. I followed the boys down corridors I didn't know existed, to the maid's room.

Dr. Mendez beat us there. He held onto the baby's hand, as the maid hugged it and shook with sobs. The boys and their father talked rapidly in Spanish, and then they all pushed each other out the door to leave the maid alone.

As we walked back to our room, Manuel told me "The baby's dead. It died last night. My father doesn't know why. These things happen. The baby's already cold, nothing he can do. Not much to do today, the stores stay closed again, I think. We can take the bus to the 3-Dimensional map."

He seemed hurt to hear I visited it yesterday.

I wanted to go down to the Dirección General de Migración first thing, and, if open, find out what policy they would adopted for foreigners whose passport they lost.

Yvonne stayed with the boys at home.

I took my shoulder bag and hurried out towards the driveway gate into a cool, bright, cloudless day. The guard stopped me briefly to make a cursory search of my daypack, and pointed me to where I should stand to catch the bus.

I got downtown around noon, and noticed the tall clock tower still frozen at 3:02.

A small crowd of people in front of a couple of vans piqued my interest, so I went over and tried to figure it out. One of the Guatemalan gentlemen in the crowd spoke English, and he explained. "The Mortgage Credit Bank, el Crédito Hipotecario, now does business in these vans, outside, because they don't dare enter the building."

In the entrance of the open cavernous Immigration office, a large crowd waited, almost immobile. Then a man came out and tried to separate them into groups, the white-shirt missionaries along the west wall, the suit and tie foreign business consultants and engineers up one side of the stairs, tourists at the window to the left, and what I thought represented the elite of Guatemala, a small group of well dressed people that chatted as they waited at the center window for their turn with a clerk.

The officials repeated the phrase "tres semanas" with three upraised fingers, because the employees of the Dirección de Migración thought it would take at least three weeks to sort their files out.

In the land of mañana, delays that long sound eternal.

As I moved closer to the tourist's counter, I heard the clerks say to each client, with a practiced smile, "Come back in two weeks." Behind them, I saw a cavernous room, lit by fluorescent tubes, full of tall, military green, filing cabinets. They lay strewn about and even tipped over, drawers open like undershot jaws, their contents disgorged, the files fanned across the floor in broad, curved cascades of manila folders and paper, like fanned decks of playing cards in a magician's hands. The clerks estimated that in two weeks they could restore order to their system and begin to process non-emergency paperwork.

We foreigners that waited around shared our experiences of Wednesday night in a fellowship of an earth-shaking thirty five seconds that thousands did not survive.

Someone said a few restaurants, south towards the airport and the modern hotel district, served meals again.

With a sharp collective intake of breath, a pause mid-sentence from all, we felt the earthquake's return. We staggered as one shocked beast on our multiple unsteady legs. The ground shook and lurched under us. People walked fast without panic in a quiet rush for the stairway up to the street. By the time the first people got halfway up the steps to the sidewalk, the quake stopped.

I got lost on the bus routes back to Doctor Mendez's house, and found myself on the far west edge of town, past the corporate installations of Lilly, Parker, Dupont, etc., big international corporations from the U.S. and Europe.

The cookie-cutter, tiny identical workers' houses in vast residential areas near these centers of industrialization, did not escape damage. Again, I saw women dip plastic buckets into a break in the sidewalk to get water pooled there from a ruptured pipe, possibly contaminated with sewage.

I took a taxi back to the Mendez's house, and as I arrived, another car pulled up in front. Two men dressed in elegant black suits got out and walked, a little too brisk for their suits and the hot afternoon weather, to the door. Dr. Mendez came to the door in answer to their knocks as I paid the taxi. I noticed he did not invite them in.

They pulled papers out of a briefcase to hand to him.

After the taxi left, I stayed on the sidewalk and examined a thick riot of flowers and vines atop the neighbor's fence to let them talk a while.

As they left, the doctor walked out onto the sidewalk to light a cigarette. He saw me and waved, took a puff. "You know how to cook? The maid will be gone for several days."

"Spaghetti or oatmeal. Who were those guys?"

"Those were vultures. Imagine how it is in Guatemala. The maid's baby dies this morning, and already they know about it. They come here to make money. They sell funeral services, burial, caskets, things like that. Real sensitive, no?"

"How could they find out so fast? Did someone call them?"

"Maybe. The maid talks to the neighbor's maid, and faster than telephone, the whole neighborhood knows. Maybe someone's son-in-law works for that funeral home."

Dr. Mendez likes to drive us around, to show off his country. He ushered us all out to the car. "We're going on a tour of the city, earthquake or no."

The police or residents barred access to some streets with barricades of sawhorses and planks, or a row of large stones too big to drive over, to keep vehicles away from damaged buildings. Behind them, we could see the rubble strewn across the streets, and sometimes the ordered array of bodies under sheets.

Dr. Mendez drove to the southern edge of town, to the airport. We drove slow and saw the throngs of tourists and extra-nationals unload huge suitcases from the back of small taxis. The crowd milled around, most dressed like Americans, blue jeans and a rainbow of Hawaiian style shirts and embroidered Mayan blouses, some with Sololá jackets with stylized bats. On many people's wrists dangled the colorful pulsera cloth bracelets woven by young Mayan girls from the stricken central highlands.

I said "This gives a whole new meaning to the phrase tourist flight."

Dr. Mendez said "I hear on the radio that Nicaragua sent us the first plane to arrive with help." Then he pointed out planes decorated with flags of nations from all over the world.

Throughout the disaster, over one hundred nations sent planes with various kinds of aid, news crews, and an exit strategy for their citizens.

South, beyond the airport, beyond the planned expansion of new suburbs and the unplanned informal neighborhoods of squatters, lay a vast barren slope strewn with garbage, the municipal dump.

Three or four families picked their way across the refuse. The man in a cowboy hat and thick jacket would prod garbage with a strong staff, turn over a pile, and the woman and their children would pick through whatever surfaced.

"What do they come here for? What are they looking for?"

Dr. Mendez pointed to a couple of lean-to shelters on the edge of the dump. "They live here, in those piles of scraps. They pick through the fresh stuff everyday to find things of value to sell, and find something to eat."

I thought of friends of mine in Michigan, who lived communally, tried to live on the barter system, and raided dumpsters behind huge grocery stores to bring home unspoiled food.

When I moved into the city for college, I applied for acceptance into a collective and received a room within a giant house with people who ranged in age from over fifty years to preschool children, but most of them around college age. They tried to live cheap, and ate the outdated, but still sterile, packaged trash scoured from the dumpsters of giant grocery stores. They belonged to an almost invisible, polite counter-culture that reacted against the ambient industrial-strength alienation of our paternalistic rust-belt society, built on factories that contaminated indiscriminately to serve Detriot's auto industries. Our local communities made the plastic window knobs, and chromed bumpers.

In our collective house, we tried to create an instant family of unlike individuals, female mountain climbers, underemployed businessmen, college students, single mothers, bisexuals, lesbians. Most notable, the incessant interpersonal dramas between an upper class black woman that felt bad she didn't dance very well and wanted to cuddle all the time, and a manic-depressive, attention-starved Arab with luxuriant nose hair. He once came home from the bars so depressed that he lay on the kitchen floor and answered "I'm OK" to anyone who asked, until about nine thirty the next morning, when he went to bed.

We lived as if in a commune, but did not share ownership of the house, only the expenses, an arrangement called a Collective instead of Commune which implies joint ownership. We held house meetings every week to pool our dues, budget the money, discuss the week's issues, assign people to duties to cook and clean, and then eat a varied and healthy meal all together as an ad-hoc family.

So it felt natural to me when I asked Dr. Mendez, "Do they get food the grocery stores throw out because it's past its date?"

"Stores in Guatemala don't throw much out. Very little refrigeration in Guatemala. People figure out a way to cook it into something they can eat, store, or sell."

"What food do they find in the garbage then?"

"They eat what other households throw out."

I could see the hands of the children reach into the garbage and then bring something to their mouth. "Don't they get sick all the time?"

"They live sick. Their bodies are full of bacteria and infections, sores on their skin, in their mouths, gastro-intestinal problems, diarrhea, pneumonia or tuberculosis, parasites, everything. When they get a disease, their immune system has nothing left to fight it, and they live with chronic illness, diarrhea, fevers, brain damaged and breathing. Sometimes it's lucky they die first. We practice evolution in Guatemala, only the strong survive. Only the unkillable babies of the very poor survive. You've heard of them, the unkillable children of poor people?"

"Yeah, never seen them before. Why don't they go somewhere else, anywhere else?"

"They don't know any better, and they think it's easy here, close to something they know. They grew up with a hunter-gatherer way of life, maybe first in some village where people go out and look for food in the forest at the base of mangos trees, or papaya, wait for the bananas to ripen, climb a palm tree for coconuts. Why work when food falls off trees? Here, they consider Guatemala City's garbage dump a real treasure, and trucks bring new stuff to them every day."

"Yeah" said Jaime. "Like you say in English, they don't know any better. Ignorant."

"They're used to it, it's normal for them. They don't know better."

We drove back across town on residential roads. The suburbs fared well, few buildings of adobe, and few over one story high.

We noticed many of the most humble men, the Mayans who work as construction workers, bricklayers, and gardeners, now walked the streets with machetes in leather scabbards on their belts, like the campesino farm workers in the countryside often did, their multi-function machete ready to serve as axe, clippers, shovel, hoe, or as a sword. They wore machetes like pirates, Prussian Generals, or the Three Musketeers wore swords, like Old West cowboys wore two six-shooters. Some of the machetes dangled in tooled-leather scabbards decorated with tassels, a lethal piece of audacious jewelry that both feminized male vanity as it announced their virility.

The well off people, those with valuables or belongings to defend, began to fear these Mayan cowboy-pirate look-alikes as potential looters, invaders, usurpers, kidnappers, rapists, or murderers. The tiny, prosperous upper class, often called the "middle" or ruling class, distrusts the majority of the desperate and dirt poor population, and hides, behind a patron's mask of paternal concern, their deep disdain that mutates into fear. The ruling classes must refuse to recognize their common humanity with the lower classes, to prohibit social contact and lessen the chances of intermarriage. If worse came to civil war, the lines might divide by dress, Western verses indigenous típica.

The distrust that resides in socio-economic divisions exists as anxiety, and in a disaster becomes a blind panic the upper classes share amongst themselves. The rich and powerful overlook the immediate and widespread heroism among the poor. They devalue the generations of quiet and stoic altruism, the almost religious voluntary belt-tightening the poor do when the rich devalue their currency. The good faith of the marginalized sustains each generation of disadvantaged people, they reproduce and grow more numerous, which serves the purposes of the privileged few even while the overlords fear their increased numbers.

Many landed gentry and "middle class" Latin Americans feel that poor people need only the slightest excuse to take the opportunity to revolt against their bosses and rulers. In Guatemala's case in particular, the educated with some knowledge of world history, feared that all the Mayan Indians, eighty percent of the population in some areas, would turn into bloodthirsty revolutionary criminals bent on revenge.

That fear wells up like endless black, angry vomit inside any educated Guatemalan whose lips chap as they breath in short little gasps to acknowledge how the springs of hated might rise up out of a subterranean sea of social injustice and discrimination. That sea bubbles just under the surface in a modern continuity with four hundred and fifty hundreds years of domination, violence, rape, institutionalized theft, and murder which all Mayan families suffered from the Spanish and others, generation after generation.

Any person with obvious Mayan genes who remains alive today does so as an involuntary symbol of the survivors of broken bloodlines and promises, and their keepers, bosses, and rulers feel no compunction if they never get an education in how it happened.

Last night Dr. Mendez took his first turn to guard the neighborhood, the fenced-in enclave for the houses of the middle class.

I walked outside to smoke a cigarette with him.

Dr. Mendez told me his replacement sent word he couldn't stand guard, so the doctor agreed to stand guard for a double turn that night.

He confessed his incompetence about how to guard the community. "Should I stay in the light of the street lamps where someone might take a shot at me, or hide in the shadows and walked the perimeter? I do both, and when I'm in the light, I allow myself a Benson and Hedges. I don't have many cigarettes left, so I walk the perimeter too much."

The upper "middle" class, those that could get permission or afford to keep guns, wore guns now, to protect themselves and their neighbors. Property owners waved them around on purpose and fired them into the air without reason, other than to let everybody know they possess a gun. They began to fear the hired help who would return home to their slums after a day's or a week's work. They put on great shows of histrionic bluster to motivate the help to tell all their dirt-poor neighbors, all the potential looters, robbers, rapists, killers, all those communist insurgent guerrilla rebels, that these homeowners and their rich neighbors lay in wait, well armed, ready to fight back.

Dr. Mendez told us about his most recent dreams, nightmares. He dreamt of revolution.

"Look at all those little lights of houses on the mountain side, all those little cook fires, candles, and battery lanterns. Those are the most Catholic, superstitious, ignorant, and oppressed people in Guatemala. All over this country, the families in one room shacks of adobe and sticks suffered the most. The upper class live in modern houses, iron-reinforced cement walls and some in American style architecture made of wood with a peaked roof of tarpaper and shingle, which resists earthquake damage. My unfortunate brother constructed his house like that, but in a suburb built around some deep canyons, very dramatic, with a wonderful view. I heard from my brother's family yesterday. Half of Lorenzo's house fell into his backyard canyon. He got out in time, but they lost the master bedroom and the dog, who they think stayed behind and barked at the walls while that room fell off the house. He is afraid now, and thinks gangs of Indians will get inside and steal everything."

To me the fear seemed exaggerated. "Why do you think the Indians would revolt, when they live so peaceful in their tiny villages?"

Dr. Mendez looked down at me over the top of his glasses, which impressed me with the view of his bald planet of shiny skin ringed by a Saturnine wisp of grayish hair and two moonlike earlobes at opposite poles. "How old are you?" He said.

"Twenty two."

"Born in nineteen fifty four?"

"Fifty three."

"You know about Che Guevara?"

"He's that army guy on T-shirts with the beard and moustache, long wavy hair, wears a beret, smokes a cigar or something. Cuban guy, I think. That's about it."

"Argentina guy. In the year of your birth, Che Guevara graduated as a medical doctor in Buenos Aires. You know where that is?"

"Argentina. Land of the presumidos (self important, vainglorious, ostentatious)."

"And no one more presumido than Che Guevara. Even though he came from an upper middle class family that could afford to put him through medical school, this young Argentine thinks of himself as a Leftist, what you Americans call a Communist, and thinks that Guatemala's government under President Arbenz seems like a good place because they give land to the poor people. Many called it a Social Revolution. Che was charming and handsome, and all the women fall in love with him. Then the United States decides to stop all that. They throw out our President, and put in someone who will protect the American businesses. Did you know that?"

"A couple of people tried to tell me about it. Everyone likes to blame the United States for their problems."

"Maybe yes, maybe not. Yes, the problems belong to Guatemala, to Latin America, and we must take responsibility. But do not forget that the Americans don't care about the poor people in Guatemala, except when they work for free, for very low wages. That is very important to the American businesses in Guatemala. Che Guevara came to Guatemala as a doctor. He came filled with an idealism that believed in the greatest common good, an old notion from the Chinese philosopher, Confucius. That idea also inspires Communists, who want people t ounderstand Capitalism favors a small number of investors who own the businesses that employ the majority of the people who don't make much money but do all the work."

"Don't you think that investors, who risk their money to create factories and businesses, deserve more than a worker who does a job that anyone could do?"

Dr. Mendez looked at me and said "Hungry people will do almost anything for food."

"But food is so cheap in Guatemala."

"Only because few people have any money. If everybody had money, prices rise. Look, imagine the government took all the land away from the big plantations of coffee and banana, and cut up all the big ranches to give a little piece of land to every family in Guatemala. In a short time, maybe a decade, a few people own most of the land again."

"Why is that?"

"Not everybody wants to farm. Crops fail, bad weather wipes out a region's produce. Families suffer from ignorance and alcoholism, they get sick, develop chronic health problems. Eventually most sell their land. It's too much work, they don't like the farm, crops fail, a continuous battle against animals and insects and plant diseases, they can't afford fertilizers or pesticides. They don't know how to farm, so many will go into debt. Then they get a little educated and want a better education for their children, and move to the cities. Some families cheat and steal from others. Some sell their land to run to the United States and make more money than they ever could in Guatemala. So again, you end up in the same situation, a few people control most of the land, most of the natural resources. People who control resources either work with American businesses, or learn to fear them."

"So you shouldn't give land to the poor?"

"To everything, there is a season. We reap what we sow."

"So the United States should have left Arbenz in power?"

"I don't know if that mattered, except to prove Che Guevara correct about one thing."

"What was that?"

"He feared the influence of the United States. You better go in the house and get some sleep."

That night in the darkness of a house without electricity, Manuel and I listened to Led Zeppelin and argued again the relative merits of various popular rock bands on Guatemalan radio. We shared the comfortable communion of young people across nationalities, with English language pop music, American, British, and the Australian Bee Gees and Olivia Newton John, as a common culture. We both spoke its language, a mantra of catch phrases and opinions voiced in song lyric. Music's counter-culture pretended to criticize what young people perceived as the Establishment, a traitorous world of hypocrites who inhabit a corporate world aligned with a nebulous, and perhaps subconscious, international conspiracy known as The System.

In the Sixties, many fans lived for music, and watched their favorite musicians and groups as if in worship of idols and avatars, scouts of alternate realities, and messengers with new ideas and ideals. Musicians competed for the recognition and sales, and many lived to play, and played nonstop in tiny alternative clubs, stadium shows, and rock festivals, where multiple groups would play over a two day weekend. Most of these so-called alternative rock musicians, even those with an anti-establishment posture, competed to one day become the respected and successful artist who fans criticize because they "sell out" their artistic freedom and meaningful significance as the price for superstardom. Then their producers, The Corporation or faceless Company, in order to fulfill their mandate to maximize profits, requires them to pander to the lowest common denominator and record vacuous and infectious pap about love. They betray the youthful ideals and radical rebelliousness that made them popular among the young cognoscenti in the first place. The fans notice when the artists change their vision of art for social change, or self help, into aural decoration for the mating ritual. Those artists lose their most 'hardcore' fan's trust, which

366

erodes the artist's power to affect social change, but with the income generated by increased audience, the artists don't mind. So far, none apologize.

With more economic success, the most visionary among them, who can see the future, stop their incessant tours, get married, and recreate their life to a new equation that considers their wife's happiness and the future economic security of their children.

We tried to go to sleep. One can't make an effort to sleep, you must surrender, or succumb to it. Our sleep deprived nerves felt every vibration, intrinsic or extrinsic, and refused to yield. Sometimes the world did shake, and Manuel let out a little giggle that spoke volumes about how we all felt, how we waited for it, and dreaded that it might happen again.

I suspected that our youthful immortality unified us, like the poorest of the poor, like all overconfident young people too distracted by hormonal urges to notice we tend to fall into a dull repetition of our parents' worst mistakes. We didn't know any better. Our nervous systems didn't need sleep, they needed to listen for the next amplification of vibration, and mull over the day's new information.

All animals learn in their sleep. Sleeping dog's run, children dream nightmares. A person attempts to learn something, a musical instrument or dance gymnastics, or new concepts that must incorporate, although they seem incongruous, such as mathematics or politics, and the brain sorts it all out in sleep. The next day, the person can play that tune, do that dance step, and see the previous day's error. To the alert mind, everyday brings a flood of information for sleep to sort through.

Dr. Mendez stood outside to guard the other households in the walled community.

I went outside to smoke, saw him under the streetlight, and walked over to chat. "From the bus window, I saw huge factories, big drug companies. Enormous buildings."

"Guatemala is the manufacture and distribution center for the entire Central American market. The big companies ship the chemicals to subsidiary companies here in Guatemala for distribution. Often you don't know which American company produces the drugs, because they change the factory's name and create new drug names to advertise and export throughout Central America and the Caribbean."

"Is it good medicine?"

"Who knows? They don't test it like you do in the States. Nor do they protect workers. In Puerto Rico, after they started production of birth control pills for women, men started to grow breasts."

"Men grew breasts?"

"The factory workers. They worked with the hormones used in the birth control pills and too much exposure caused breast tissue to grow in men. Imagine what could happen with other kinds of medicines, other chemical contaminants and poisons. Doctors down here can never be sure about anything, not even the medicines. We can't afford to do research on the medicines, the pills, the dosage. We assume the factories base everything on the literature from parent companies in the United States, who test everything and present results to the American Food and Drug Administration before market. But when medicines get withdrawn because of health concerns in the United States, we keep selling it."

"Why don't they take it off all the markets?"

"To make money. The corporations need the new markets. As workers make more money in other countries, other businesses earn money because of the new affluence. That creates jobs, and jobs give people more money to spend on medicine. Those jobs, the factories, the urban congestion and lifestyles, can also make people sick. So if a big company sells something they withdrew from the market in other countries, small governments look the other way, because as long as the United States makes money, we can too."

"I don't see how you can blame the United States for bad decisions other countries make. Everybody wants to believe in conspiracies."

Dr. Mendez said, "To you, it seems improbable, because you don't understand international politics. Even war is politics. War is, in a way, a conspiracy to sell arms."

"What war? Who's talking about a war?"

"You never heard Guatemala almost went to war against Belize?"

"What's that got to do with the United States?"

"Maybe nothing, maybe everything. To make war, people need guns. Who makes guns? The US, Britain, Israel, China, and the Soviet Union manufacture and sell weapons. So they like war, they need the threat of war. They sell to both sides, and make money no matter who fights. They pray for war, like farmers pray for rain. War means profits, especially from areas with constant conflict. When Presidente 'General' Kjell Laugerud wants Guatemala to go to war with Belice, arms merchants know both sides will buy guns."

"How can two poor countries afford to go to war?"

"The United States Government guarantees loans to governments so they can buy arms. Then both countries remain indebted to American interests. To America, that's a win-win situation. The corporations, the arms suppliers and distributors, the factories, the investors, and the American people, all earn profits from war."

"You sure about that?"

"Sure." Dr. Mendez said. "Then the United States can influence the rulers of indebted governments to gain access to natural resources and a favorable political climate for businesses."

I didn't know what to say, so I said nothing. I thought about the slight hostility I felt from many people in Mexico when they learned my nationality. I figured the Viet Nam war bothered them. Friends of mine, kids I went to school with, went to war in Viet Nam, some died in Viet Nam, others came back so damaged you risked your own life if you touched them when asleep. They explained to us that because the military trained them to kill when threatened, the trauma of war left them in a semi-permanent state of lethal readiness.

In the United States, we debated the war for years, yet few came up with a reason why the United States warred against Viet Nam, except for the lame excuse to stop the fall of another Communist Domino.

To the Vietnamese, they saw it as a continuation of their three thousand years of armed resistance against domination by foreign powers. If you didn't believe the hype about a 'Domino Theory,' where communist countries, like amoebas, engulf and swallow all adjacent countries, you could imagine the war driven by capitalists, politicians, and military leaders motivated by their testy middle-age male libido waned, so they became vampiric harpies on a mission to ensure penetration and insertion of consumer societies in virgin areas of the world.

The popular rumors churned out conspiracy theories of mysterious international forces like the Trilateral Commission, but few studied more subtle information like how war affects the net gross product of national and corporate economies thus the health of local suburban supermarket chains and the stock portfolios of a global network of investors. For nations that produce arms, war serves their ideology of deadly profit.

Dr. Mendez said "Look, I like the United States. I liked living there, but my family history belongs in Guatemala. The future remains to be seen. Corporations exist only to make money for their investors, people who know nothing about Guatemala. They do not care, or want to, or need to, know the details about where profits come from, or how they come, or how it affects people, cultures, and environments. Everybody in the world, Americans and everybody, wants to make lots of money. Money is energy, the power to do work, the source of the freedom to choose and take control of your reality. With money, you change your life and the scenery whenever you want. Business makes money, and business controls governments, and some business people can influence the CIA to overthrow democracies and install puppet dictators."

"How can you know for sure? Why would they?"

"I told you. Money. Why does anybody do anything?"

"Why don't we hear about it on TV, radio, or in newspapers?"

"You do, in many countries around the world. I've seen books and magazines from Europe, the United States, and Mexico that talk about these things."

"What about here in Guatemala?"

"Or Central America, or South America, or places like Southeast Asia, Africa? The United States, through the CIA's secret operations, use radio and newspapers to control people's opinions. When they cannot directly control the broadcasts, they use Public Relations campaigns to rearrange the facts. They do not have to control the media, because the media can only repeat the official facts, even if not exactly true. They control hearts and minds all over the world when they control information. They change the way things look. When they can't, they control the media itself."

"How is that possible? I mean the media is made up of people, of employees. How can they control a whole industry? "

"Control the owner ,who would lose the most. Let's say I'm with the CIA and I want control over you. I invite you to a party, and convince you to pose for a picture with your arm around a friend of mine, a man you don't know, but I know as an important local Communist. Now you look like a Commie too. If certain people see that photo, you would soon be a dead Commie. After I develop those photos, I show them to you, and explain things so you understand that when I tell you to do something, you do it. Period."

"Why would the CIA or the United States make such an effort? Why spend time and energy on little countries?"

"Because it costs so little. Imagine I pay some people to start a Communist demonstration, then arrest some of those people, and I convince some of them to swear you are a leader of their group. Now newspapers in the Free World call you a dangerous Commie, and no one will care what happens to you."

"You believe the United States controls all the other countries?"

"Not all. But the countries with valuable resources must listen to America very carefully. A hundred years ago, the United States conquered Mexico, a big country, but decided not to make another State out of it. They didn't want the headache of governing a Catholic country that spoke Spanish. Imagine a protestant Anglo saxon culture that tries to annex a country like Mexico. Just look at England and Ireland to see what could happen. Mexico and the United States base their entire legal systems on separate histories. Instead, the United States decided to influence Mexico's economy, to make sure that Mexican oil, cheap labor, bananas, chocolate and vanilla, and probably even illegal drugs come in through the proper channels. It is not by accident that only one political party rules Mexico for the past half century."

"So you're saying that the United States lets people run their own governments as long as resources and products flow north across the border. Why don't people get wise and talk about this stuff?"

"They don't want trouble."

"Why trouble? These are democracies, right?"

"Unions and Labor movements start democratic organizations for better wages and improvement in conditions at work, but that would lower profits. The stockholders, owners, managers, and governments of those countries don't want to lose profits. They're Capitalists, they own the means of production and the right to profits. So they say that Unions, even though democratic, lean towards the left, towards socialism and communism, but the people only want to share profits and live better. Capitalists try to convince people that with Unions, the price of everything will go up, the businesses go bankrupt, and that will lead to Communism. In smaller countries, when Union organizers organize strikes to demand higher wages, those organizers might 'disappear', and the members lose their jobs. After that, no one hires them again. So, no unions."

"So factories are not democracies. No surprise."

"Does it not make sense that a truly Democratic society would vote for socialism? Would not most people vote against anything that makes a small group rich, and keeps the majority poor?"

"Isn't that the tyranny of the majority? That the largest group always gets its way? Then society falls victim to any popular fad or stupidity of the moment."

"Representative democracy means people elect representatives, not vote on policy. Quality of a one person's decisions, not the quantity of ignorant votes. But political campaigns don't educate people about a candidate's character, they push a platform based on issues that people care about. You would think people would vote for someone they trust to do the right thing, but instead they vote for people who know what to say in public, while in secret they plan other things with powerful people who finance their campaigns. Only ignorant people think everyone has a right to vote on each issue. Representative democracy tries to free people of social responsibility, so every voter doesn't have to learn about every issue and vote on it."

"What about competition, and Capitalism? The right for anyone to create businesses and jobs?"

"In Latin America, no one saves money in the bank. Hand to mouth, as you say in English, all the family income spent to buy food. Most people cannot start a business, only a class of people already friendly with banks and government can afford to get educated or start a business. Indians don't get educated or own their land. They use other people's land and pay debts that last generations. That's the same way big business arranges big loans to the governments of small countries, to build roads or dams or ports, which helps the upper class, the educated people with resources, make more money. When things don't go as corporations planned, the United States can often change things by threat or force."

"Why should the United States care who becomes president of Guatemala, if they control everything?"

"In the year nineteen fifty three, they made our Presidente Arbenz look like a dangerous Communist for a reason."

"Maybe he was a communist."

"No crime in that. The people elected him, and he remained popular. But dangerous, I don't think so. President Arbenz helped reorganize the Guatemalan labor movement, the PGT, and gave members important positions in his social security and agrarian reform systems. Then the Guatemalan government took unused land from big landholders and gave it to peasants. They took land from Arbenz's own family. But when they took land from the United Fruit Company, an American company, that created a problem with one of Guatemala's largest landowners. So the CIA got rid of Arbenz."

"You really believe that one little fruit company can influence what the CIA does?"

"You ever hear of the Dulles brothers? One worked as a head of United Fruit, and his brother worked as the Secretary of State for President Eisenhower. Interesting coincidence, no? By 1954, the United States' CIA trained men in Honduras to help a Guatemalan Colonel, Carlos Castillo Armas, organize a revolt. Anastasio Somoza, Nicaragua's dictator, helped out also. "

"Why would a Nicaraguan dictator help the United States?"

"In 1909, the United States supported a revolution in Nicaragua. Then in 1912, they sent in American soldiers. The U.S. Marines remained on Nicaragua soil until 1925, then left, then came back in 1926 to stop 'another revolution', as they called it. But the second time, the U.S. forces trained and created a special 'National' Guard for Nicaragua, which replaced the Nicaraguan military and oversaw two presidential elections. Then General Augusto Cesar rebelled and led a guerrilla war against this fake 'National'

Guard until 1933, when the U.S. Marines finally left Nicaragua. They convinced the rebel army's leader, General Sandino, to sign a cease fire, then the 'National' Guard killed him within a year. After that, the 'National' Guard's commander, Gen. Anastasio Somoza Garcia, took power. Then General Somoza rules Nicaragua like a Mafia Godfather. When somebody kills him in 1956, his sons, Luis and Anastasio, rule Nicaragua with obvious support from the United States."

"I still don't see why the United States cares who rules Nicaragua."

"Commerce. The Somozas run the government, own the businesses, and they sell cars. They're car salesmen. Who buys cars, I don't know. Maybe just their friends, the government officials, businessmen, farm owners, who knows? Maybe Nicaragua's drug dealers and prostitutes can afford to buy American cars. In the United States, the investors want to help little countries develop into consumer economies. Then people buy televisions, and see everything else they should buy, all the new products, the clothing, soap, fast food, refrigerators, dishwashers, automobiles, alcohol, cigarettes, medicines, everything for the consumer lifestyle."

"So you believe the US controls the governments of small countries to sell televisions, and that will make Americans rich?"

"It will make stockholders rich, or richer. Stockholders and investors from all around the world. In the marketplace, people vote with each dollar they spend, and corporations compete to get that vote. But in a dictatorship, only one person matters, the boss. So the United States finds it easy to overthrow troublesome democracies, which may get voted out of office next election anyway, and install friendly dictators or fake democracies that last for decades. One dollar, one Quetzal."

"Why doesn't it get in the papers, or on radio and TV? You think someone controls American news media?"

"American media gets its international news from our local media. Radio and TV makes money the same way newspapers make money. They sell ads. Who buys the ads that pay for radio and newspapers? It costs a lot of money, a lot of electrical energy, to broadcast radio and TV. Big corporations buy the ads. The company can take away ad money, if they broadcast the wrong thing. The angry businessman might call the owner of the radio or TV station, or the owners of any newspapers that run a bad story, or maybe he calls other businessmen to do the same. They call up and say, why you say that on the radio? We're not gonna pay you for advertisements, we go to another radio station. So the United States steals elections, forces governments to change leaders, and no one cares, because they make sure people hear about it as an anti-communist action, never as anti-democratic. Most people believe newspapers and TV, and even if they don't, they do nothing. They hope someone else will do something about it, but nobody does, until it falls on their own head."

"So you think the CIA overthrows President Arbenz to stop communists from stealing unused banana land from an American Corporation?"

"No. The Guatemalan government paid for lands taken from United Fruit, at the tax-assessed value. Think Consumerism and rich people, not communism and poor people. The rich invest in the future. It scares them to think Latin American countries change governments leaders so often, by revolution or elections. Dictators supported by the United States stay in power. Mombassa in Africa, Stroesner in Paraguay, now Pinochet in Chile. If American corporations see any president as a threat to business profits, anywhere in the world, that president lives in fear the United States can replace him with a dictator that knows how to carry on business as usual for decades."

"What about Fidel Castro? Cuba's communist, and only ninety miles offshore. Why doesn't the United States overthrow him?"

Dr. Mendez smiled. "I think the United States attacks Fidel in many ways: the embargo, biological weapons, attempts to discredit him and his communist government, the threat of the Miami Cubans, secret militias, assassination attempts. But they also take advantage of Cuba's independence. The United States can get rid of him at any moment. But they don't. Not because Cuba doesn't have enough bananas, oil, or minerals, but because every time people run away from Cuba to Florida or the Yucatán, when they float on inner-tubes to escape Communism, it makes Cuba look bad, and proves the superiority of the American dream. Cuban refugees believe in the American dream, that people can go from inner tubes to the life the see in Hollywood movies. Where do you think they end up?"

"Some crime-infested, big-city slum, and if lucky, they get a job where they work harder than they ever imagined, and can't afford to quit."

"Right. And many don't find work. So some Cuban women become prostitutes, like they did with tourists in Havana to get money. The Cuban revolution creates the very thing Castro hated the most about Old Havana under Bautista, when the rich went there to gamble."

I needed my jacket, so I went back inside. I could see his whole point of view framed by jealousy, or a hysterical paranoid neurosis rampant in Guatemala about U.S. domination. If Guatemala ruled the United States, we would complain. Everybody complains about their boss. The CIA probably did a lot of people a big favor, if they really did take out President Arbenz.

The boys helped prepare the evening meal without the maid's help, and once prepared, we brought food out where to Dr. Mendez stood.

Inside the house by candlelight, we set the dining room table with the Mendez's most elegant china, then ate and cleaned up all by ourselves. The Mendez boys acted as hosts, like responsible young adults, to prove they could do housework as well as children in American families who don't hire servants.

After the meal, we boys took our candles and retired to the room with the bunk beds.

Manuel said "How you like my father?"

"He's great. He knows lot about the United States, Cuba, Guatemala, everything. He must read a lot."

"He's an asshole. He wants to control everything. You really want to know anything, ask Jaime."

"OK. So Jaime, what do you know about Che Guevara?"

"He came to Guatemala once."

"Your dad thinks what happened in Guatemala made Che join Fidel in Cuba."

"Look, Che Guevara and others saw the CIA throw out Presidente Jacobo Arbenz Guzmán. The connection between the United Fruit Company and U.S. Government through the Dulles brothers makes it obvious. One brother as Eisenhower's Secretary of State, the other as the head of United Fruit Company. Because of what happened here, Che believes the United States creates social injustice all over the world. He believes people should expect the United States and the CIA to support dictators and tyrants to serve American interests. So Che goes to Cuba, to fight alongside Castro."

"What's the connection between Castro and Che Guevara?"

"Castro and Che saw Bautista in Cuba as a puppet of the United States."

"Why do you think the United States cares anything about a little island country like Cuba?"

"To get tons of cheap sugar for Coca-cola, and Havana for gambling and whores, as an American Mafia playground for rich gamblers from around the world. Castro hated to see prostitution, the poor Cuban women, sometimes very young girls and their mothers, who sold their bodies for American dollars. The revolution promised to change all that, and they did."

"So you like Castro's Cuba?"

"Today, most Cubans know how to read, no one's hungry, and everyone gets free medical care. Cuba educates many people to become doctors and nurses, and then sends them all over the world to help. But the United States will not sell Cuba medicines or technology. No one goes hungry because everyone shares, but that means the government must control everyone. Castro controls all books, radio, and television, just like he controls the food and clothing each person receives."

"How do you know all that's true?"

Manuel spoke up. "Jaime went to Cuba. You can too, from Mexico. But you cannot go there from the United States, your free country, right? Big superpower that can't even kill Castro." Manuel laughs and jabs his boney finger into my ribs.

"Very funny, Manuel." I wondered why they enjoyed this evidence of United States impotence. "Maybe the United States allows Cuba to exist, allows Fidel to stay in power, because Castro proves the United States doesn't interfere. If things are really so bad in Cuba, they probably expect the people to revolt, a civil war. But what happened to Che?"

"People with egos like Castro's and Che's can't sit in the same room together. So Che goes to Bolivia to start a revolution. Che fears the United States, but he thinks he moves too fast. When he goes to Bolivia, the CIA already there. He planned to make a revolutionary army to defeat a weak and corrupt Bolivian regime, but his little band of farmers confronted an army equipped and trained by the United States. So they kill Che within a year."

"So why is he such a big hero?"

"He's like a rich man, the son of bourgeois Argentinians, a teenage rebel. People forget he abandoned his wife and children to be a revolutionary hero, bigger than life. I think he went to look for his own country to dominate, like Castro dominates Cuba. He thought he could liberate all of South America. He hoped everyone in Latin America would fall in love with him, with his idea of a democratic Communism of equality and justice. He, from a rich family, pretends to know how it feels to suffer injustice and racism. I think that like Fidel, he would reject democracy as too dangerous, and become dictator, to control everybody."

"So why do people put his face on everything?"

"'Because he's handsome. They know him as a revolutionary. Most people don't hear about the wife and kids he left behind, or the women he slept with, about how his men learned the wrong language for Bolivia. They tried to learn Quechua, spoken by highland Incas, instead of the Amazon languages of his revolutionary Bolivian farmers. They don't see Che as someone who made mistakes, as a weak man. He suffered from asthma so much his band of revolutionary farmers raided pharmacies to get medicine for Che."

"Did he die like a hero?"

"The United States and the Bolivian Army hunted him down and wounded him in the leg. They say a bullet hit Che's rifle, so he surrenders and screams 'Don't shoot! I am Che Guevara, worth more to you alive than dead!' They kill him anyway. They tie his hands to a board inside a schoolhouse before they shoot him, and his last words were 'I know you will kill me, but you are only going to kill a man.' He dies for his beliefs and for that, he dies a hero in many people's eyes. The army hid his body in the jungle, so no one could make a martyr out of it."

"How do you know it's true? Maybe he's still alive, with Communists in Colombia or Peru. How do they know he needed asthma medicine?"

"They published his Bolivian diary. They cut off his fingers, and sent them around the world for positive identification. He's dead."

"Why so popular?"

"If the United States let Arbenz be president in Guatemala, maybe Che starts a Guatemalan family, with beautiful Mayan wife and lots of mestizo children. Then he is famous as an Argentine doctor who helps the poor. Probably he would abandoned that wife too, and run away with a pretty communist soldier girl to some other revolution."

"How do you feel when you see Che's face on a T-shirt?"

Jaime shrugged. "Che Guevara reminds us of how the United States sabotages everyone's future when it destroys democracies, supports big business, and installs puppet dictators. Che's life shows us how the United States can destroy democracies, unions, and revolutionaries, and the poor people's opportunity for social justice. Even the United States' embargo against Cuba helps keeps Fidel in power. It doesn't make sense."

The next morning as Manuel prepared breakfast for the three of us, Yvonne and I noticed the empty shelves. Since the maid left, no one shopped as usual. Every other day a maid goes to market for fresh produce. The household's food stocks dwindled to near nothing.

Alone with Yvonne for a moment in the kitchen, she says "I want make love to you."

"No chance in this house."

"Let's leave. Why stay in the city, with the threat of violence, looting, epidemics. How can we repay this hospitality? Pay rent to Dr. Mendez? Become his servants?"

"Yeah, stand outside all night with a gun, and they will still run out of food."

"Let's leave, go where we can be alone."

"I think Dr. Mendez hopes you might marry one of the boys."

"You know he married an American woman?"

"Where is she?"

"In the States, I think. She left him."

"The doctor fantasizes about you too, you know."

"No, I don't know, how should I?"

"No? Healthy man, no wife, beautiful female."

Yvonne and I kissed and our eyes agreed to leave together. That should allow the Mendez family to adjust to life after the earthquake without us as a distraction or liability. In this conservative, Catholic, repressed, indigenous, uneducated, and God terrorized country the Mendez family did not need the added burden of two unmarried foreigners all steamed up and ready to fornicate at any moment.

The servants might blame us for the earthquake. I did.

Back in Manuel's room, we listened to the radio and scanned the map of Guatemala by candlelight to find somewhere else, somewhere solid, to hang out for a while. With the boys' help, we listened to the radio, and decided on a small undamaged town called Huehuetenango, pronounced Waywaytenango, in the central highlands of Guatemala near its eastern border with Mexico.

The radio said the roads, although damaged, allowed light traffic and buses with few delays, but rockslides narrowed the road to a single lane in places.

It looked far from the areas of destruction, yet close to an easy exit into Estados Unidos Mexicanos should things fall apart with epidemics, riots, or revolution. The high altitude of Huehuetenango also promised a healthy climate with pure water.

That night while on watch, Dr. Mendez chatted with a companion and guard. He came into the house to take breaks, and pass on the gossip he heard. "Everybody scared. Radio talks about uprisings, murders, riots, gangs with guns, looters shot by policemen. Everybody afraid Mayans will invade the suburbs to take back their ancestral land and reinstall Mayan kingdoms."

"Could they?"

"Rumors come from ignorant people, too lazy to read. The radio tries to make everything exciting, so people hear advertisements. Everybody get nervous, they gossip and invent things when they don't understand. We don't need silly rumors in a time of National emergency."

That night, while Yvonne and I slept in our own respective beds, the earthquake struck again, a voracious animal that trembled with rage and wanted to swallow the rest of us. Maybe a turtle that carried the earth on its back.

I awoke, flailed about in the pitch dark, and recognize Manuel's voice. He cried out and tried to wake up. Jaime whispered "shut up and listen" without a hint of terror in his deeper young man's voice.

I listened for the sound of a wall in collapse, or the shatter of glass. The China cabinet in the dining room rattled, full of the clinks of wine glasses.

The house groaned and banged as if two hippopotamuses mated in one of the rooms, then silence.

For now, the ominous rumble from some subterranean God diminished into a dog's nightmare growl that slinked back into the bowels of the earth to curl up and fall into a twitchy sleep.

Every once in a while, I glimpsed another answer to the question of how the other half live. The other half fragmented into dozens of realities, and provoked the realization that I assumed I knew how my half lived. I couldn't describe the economics of my own family, let alone my neighbors or the inhabitants of other cities or states, other agricultural or economic regions, or anyone with another lifestyle.

Like a mountain climber on the summit of the first mountain, I glimpsed, from this Latin American vantage point, more mountains, valleys, jungles and deserts that blocked a more general overview to fundamental, important questions that needed some framework.

We boys lay in the bunk beds in Jaime and Manuel's room, and listened to Led Zeppelin, whom they supported some radio disk jockey's opinion as the World's Greatest Rock and Roll band. I defended Jimi Hendrix as the best rocker, and the Beatles as the best composers of music that passed as rock although they split up and mostly produce vinyl artifacts, not live music.

In secret, I would rather listen to Guatemalan Marimbas in that restaurant near the Central Plaza, with a mouthful of golden-brown roasted squab and another forkful on the way, pried from that naked pigeon stretched out like a miniature Thanksgiving Turkey. I would rather watch the fat grandparents dance that slow circle around the dance floor, like bright-colored plastic ducks in a tub at the fair. The rotund dancers, in their own way, reminded me of gleeful children at the fair. These retired people become again as little children, who treasure each new day and decorate it with their own graceful existence, and so enter the kingdom of heaven on earth.

Jaime wanted to live in the USA.

I couldn't understand why. Their family lived in paradise, with servants, at the top of Guatemala's food chain.

What more could they want?

To "Xela" Quetzaltenango

Some Anthropologists suggest Meso-American cultures mythologized a separate creation myth for each class. Aztec conquests became official with an exchange of women from the two Noble Classes of the winners and losers. Members of the ruling classes became family, from the lineages of Noble bloodlines, from the women who birthed the successors to the thrones of conquered City-states, until all these far flung nobles belong to a single kin group.

Archeologists noticed that skeletons of Maya upper class tombs measure, on average, much taller than the agricultural classes, which points to a complete separation of culture and nutrition, and perhaps genetics, between the nobles of the ruling classes of City-states, and their subjects ,slaves, and workers.

Mayans believe in duty and predestination by birth into a social rank, and a fatalistic submission to the inevitability of events instead of reliance on free will. The similarities to the Catholic Church's culture enabled the Spanish Catholics to preach understandable messages about disobedience and sin. These cosmologies teach citizens to submit to the will of the universe, to the Mayan and Catholic forces of nature, seen as the wishes of the Gods, which come direct through the human conduits of the Fathers and priests, like the Mayan's shamans and King-gods of their ceremonial centers who removed live human hearts. Today, the Mayans submit to rule by the Catholic Church and the Catholic governments and presidents of Mexico or Guatemala and other Catholic Central American countries, who all listen to the Pope, who talks to God.

The next day, the Mendez boys reminded us to fill our canteens while the water lasted, and then Manuel walked us out to the bus stop.

A lot of people wore machetes on the streets, but Yvonne and I felt confident, or at least hopeful, that nothing bad would happen to us. The Guatemalan people's polite and meek character made it hard for us to imagine a little earthquake could transform their complacent servile personalities into wanton thieves, kidnappers, torturers, rapists and murderers.

We walked past many men who wore machetes on our way to the bus stop, and no one looked at us too long, or sized us up as potential suppliers of useful items. We talked about the value of our stoves, supplies of dry foods, and water purification tablets in our backpacks.

The terminal appeared as busy as normal. Travelers with suitcases and duffle bags, Mayan people who wheel barrowed around huge quantities of fruits, grains, and vegetables in nets, burlap bags, crates, and cardboard boxes, groups of tall and stout Ladino women who towed an inclined train of children. We found a bus destined for Huehuetenango and spent hours seated while the drivers tried to round up more riders.

We took off late in the afternoon, the bus almost empty. I figured most people busied themselves at home with repairs to guard, and reinforce, damaged buildings. The normal daily activities take a lower priority when you suspect your building might fall down in the next temblor.

The Red Tile Church still stood, flawless and shiny, solid and upright, like a launch pad to blast away from earth's human misery, a cross on top of a tower as red as a dog penis, attentive and happy as a Golden Retriever. Although its doors and windows remained shut and lifeless, I thought I saw people camped under the trees on the narrow alleys of ground around the sides of the building.

Once out of the city, the highway skirted the slopes of the massive volcanic uplift on the Pacific Ocean side, and sometimes the haze of the humid lowlands cleared enough for us to imagine we glimpsed the sea.

We passed through the rubble of a number of small villages, where groups of people sorted bundles amid the ruins. Several times when the bus stopped, I noticed people came over to stand outside the bus windows and plead with up-stretched arms, listless and without energy, their words soundless, lip movements on blotchy faces, dirty cheeks tracked with dried tear streaks, uncombed matted black hair now reddish from dust. Their eyes stared at us with a numbed vacancy, like trapped animals, trapped on the wrong side of a bus window.

At sunset we reached Quetzaltenango, the ancient capital city now modernized into a big city that retains much colonial quaintness in its narrow cobblestone streets and steep grades. Here, powerful indigenous Mayan families run the town, a rare situation in all of Latin America.

Guatemalans take pride in beautiful Quetzaltenango, and refer to the city by the Mayan name of Xela, pronounced Shay la.

We decided to get off the bus and spend the night.

Most of the people on the streets of Quetzaltenango, an Indian name that means ethe Quetzal's City, bear the unmistakable Mayan features of straight black hair, almond shaped eyes, beautiful tan skin (men without much facial hair), and fine sculpted large noses, and full cheekbones. We saw these Mayan faces on well dressed affluent citizens, in marked contrast to other places in Mexico or Guatemala.

Quetzaltenango's champions claim that here, the social structure of ancient Guatemala remains intact, the royal bloodlines of a few Indian families trace the histories of the upper class citizens both merchants and governors.

The city reminded Yvonne of parts of Europe, a medieval narrowness to the streets, and the centuries old three story colonial architecture.

On the sidewalk at one side of the tree lined Central Plaza of Quetzaltenango, on the open cement area under a row of trees, men busily put together a wooden platform and strung wire for the speakers and microphones of a public address system. As we walked around the square, we spotted a balcony on the second floor across the street from where men constructed the soundstage. We found a nondescript doorway below the balcony, and entered to discover an elegant and old world restaurant, twelve foot ceilings, luxurious curtains draped over the windows.

No customers.

To convince the mesero (waiter) to move a table and two chairs upstairs so we could eat out on the balcony, we promised to order two big dinners and leave a big tip.

Repeated Sins

From a people now called the Zapotecs, from 300 BCE to 200 years CE, elite Artisans of the earliest period at Monte Albán, near Oaxaca, built their ceremonial city high on a mountain that once supported a population of up to twenty thousand people. The Zapotecs created the earliest writing in the Americas, and used it to record names and events. They carved heads, upside down, labeled with dates and names of nearby towns, which may commemorate conquests. In low reliefs carved into sandstone, about one hundred fifty nude male figures, known as 'danzantes' or dancers, cavort in odd, rubbery positions. With eyes closed, mouths agape, they might represent corpses, yet from their loins a liquid, maybe blood, spews out like smoke. Might memorialize enemies captured and sacrificed, or signify sexual ecstasy.

The waiter spoke English pretty well. He relayed to us the most recent earthquake news, both from radio reports and from the people who came into town from the chaos of the countryside.

From Panajachél on Lake Atitlán, he first heard that people drowned by the busloads, that busses rolled into the lake. Then he heard that only two people, the bus drivers asleep inside, drowned when their bus slid into the lake.

"We already received aid from Nicaragua, the first to arrive."

"Why from Nicaragua?"

"When the big earthquake struck Monagua years ago, the aid from Guatemala arrived first. We are very friendly with Nicaragua."

The waiter took our order, and then said "You know the nickname for Guatemala?"

"Land of eternal Springtime?"

"That is true, but even more true, it is the Land of Eternal Tremors. We name tremors the way Eskimos talk about ice, or the Hawaiins name lava, you know what I mean?"

"Many names for tremors?"

"Vocabularies. First, we say sismos for the smallest tremors you cannot feel. Only the instruments sense them, on the news we hear about ones so small they call them microsismos. If we can feel them, if people feel them, then sismos become tremors. We have several kinds of tremors; suave, regular, fuerte, and muy fuerte. Then you run and put yourself in the doorway in case the house falls. Unfortunately, that only works with certain types of construction."

"So we had a muy fuerte tremor?"

"Today?"

"The earthquake."

"Oh no, not a tremor. That was a Terremoto, the worst. I thought you ask me about the tremor today, muy fuerte. It caused a landslide on the road to Antigua. Road closed, buried a camioneta from Costa Rica."

"Camioneta?"

"You know, a little truck, open on the back to load things."

"A pickup truck?"

"Yes, a little pickup. That's how you call them."

Yvonne said "We didn't feel any tremor."

"You came today by bus? Maybe only the driver feels it then."

"Maybe that's why we saw all those people knelt in prayer as the bus through that village."

This Friday, the sixth of February, nineteen minutes after noon, a major tremor struck and caused landslides and widespread panic among the traumatized population. In the Miguel Angel Asturias Press Club, with its wooden courtyard walls painted in a style reminiscent of Pompeii, members of the legislature, in the midst of a meeting spoke about the need for calm in this emergency.

When they felt the tremor, they panicked and ran for the exits.

Two Mexican photojournalists, Mario Gallindo and Victor Payés, take statements from various neighbors in Antigua after the tremor subsides. They note the exaggerated fear in those who survived the Terremoto two days ago.

In Antigua, crowded with terrified citizens who fled into the streets in fear of their own damaged buildings, a man climbs up atop a pile of rubble and makes a long speech about the need for sanity.

In Chimaltenango, the quake brought down the walls of the large jail facility and allowed many jailed survivors to escape. Officials decide to free the rest of the survivors.

At the very end of a forty kilometer dead end mountain road headed northeast out of Guatemala City, the quake survivors in the Mayan Indian town of San Pedro Ayampac discover the road closed by landslides that isolate them from supplies of food and water. The tremor inspires the townspeople to kneel and pray. The town sits atop the dry highlands at the head of an arroyo which leads down past Rincon Grande, Great Corner, to the valley of the Rio Montagua, the fracture of the earthquake. They pray to all their gods, both Christian and Mayan, and as if in answer, this terrible tremor opens up a spring of pure, fresh, cool water nearby.

A radio blares in the square below. The announcer pleads for news or a report of conditions about various remote villages now cut off by landslides, if not buried under them. Our waiter tells us many remote towns communicate through one person who operates a radio transmitter, but now, no one answers. The reporters say that in a few cases, people walked across landslides to reach the roads on the other side and relay information that helps estimate the total of destroyed homes to almost one million.

We sat on the balcony and waited for our food to arrive.

A man came to the microphone to read announcements as part of a live radio broadcast. That attracted more people to come near and stand around, cold hands in warm pockets, colorful thick scarves wrapped around their necks.

A small crowd below grows larger, as this announcer and public address system become part of the national radio broadcast.

The waiter brought out three forks for each of us, and a linen tablecloth, with the first round of drinks. We held our drinks and stirred them with the straws, swirled the ice to jingle against the side of the cut crystal glasses, while we read the menu and listened.

The night fell like cold feathers into our collars and across our necks and hands. I felt it creep up my ankles and across my socks to whisper up into my pants.

"This city is built upon the ruins of an even greater Mayan city, a complex of temples and markets. The Spanish took it apart stone by stone to build these colonial buildings." The waiter explained that the man said the government would provide more plastic tarps so that people could roof their house, or protect belongings if they lived in the streets.

Then the cold of night rode in fierce. White knots of small moonlit clouds streamed overhead, one after the other, flocks of gentle spirits, the souls of the recent dead.

The announcer's amplified staccato delivery echoed and boomed across the square, hit the buildings to slap back in echo and ring down narrow cobblestone pipes of streets and alleys. People arrived with blankets and household goods, which relief workers added to a pile accumulated earlier, for distribution tomorrow to those in need.

"The government has a plan, a one hundred day plan." Our waiter told us. "We have to get everything working before winter comes." e

"What do you mean, one hundred days until winter?"

"In Guatemala, winter, el invierno, refers to the rainy season. Right now we're at the beginning of February, the crazy month. Next come two months of dry heat, too much heat. After April starts our winter, with rain, rain, and rain. The roads, the water system, the landslides, the how you say, system of black water, all must be fixed before the rains come."

We ate in silence to listen, secure on our balcony high above the distraught citizens of Quetzaltenango, to the speaker's voice, a sporadic reminder of a nation ruptured, a country still too shocked to grieve.

"Winter in April." Yvonne said.

"It's another world down here. You'd think people could agree on the seasons."

We ordered another round of drinks to fight the chill.

Like someone lost inside their own television, or an explorer transported to another planet full of unfamiliar elements, I felt separated and alien. This cold darkness, the unfamiliar shapes of wind blown trees across the Central Plaza, the time blackened slabs of flagstone, the colonial architecture streaked and stained from four hundreds of years of rain or perhaps a thousand years as part of Mayan temples, created the sense of a four dimensional image congealed in a moment in time, with roots far in the distant past. It existed as an alternate reality, one we could turn around and walk out of, and probably should.

After dinner, we found a cheap hotel room to stash our backpacks, then decided to explore the city. The hotel management told us Quetzaltenango offered nothing of nightlife until Saturday, so we walked to the bus station nearby, checked the schedules, and then returned to our room to go to bed.

We lay together, exhausted, for the first time since the earthquake, free to hold each other with neither worries nor undue considerations for others. Neither of us felt energetic enough to more than kiss before we fell asleep.

Without the hum of the earth's tremors, we slept for ten hours straight, the first unbroken sleep in the past four days.

We woke up at about the same time, looked at each other and started to kiss.

Yvonne looked at me and said, "I want to make love but I don't know if we should."

"Why not?"

"Look what happened the first time! Do you think we sinned against God or something?"

"Well if that's the price of sin, we survived it."

"So far."

Instead, we went out to explore, but the cold wind and the old dark, rain stained stones of the city hurried us back to the comfort of the hotel. As soon as we got back to the room, we made love, and then took a hot shower together.

Why should people feel guilt, anguish, and torture themselves because of sin? If there is a God, he deals us a lethal hand as birthright, no escape from mortality, and then adds injury to that insult with little tricks like earthquakes, bad parents, and other personal disasters. Religious people suffer from a need to believe that God destroys so much, kills our loved ones, thwarts our plans, and expects us all to take it all in stride, as a punishment or a test of our faith, our character under stress.

CHAPTER 17: A way to Huehue

Itzamná, the supreme Maya deity who created all, serves as the lord of fire, hearth, and authority. Carved into stela from the Classic period, he often appears in his serpent form on ceremonial bars held in the arms of Maya rulers.

Mayan folklore talks about four Gods, the Bacabs, assigned to the four directions of the universe to hold up the sky. Each one an Itzamná (depicted as Celestial Monsters or Two headed Iguanas) or Supreme Creator God, and each associates with a color and a sacred symbol such as a bird, a ceiba tree or silk cotton tree, the Earth as the Green Center, Red to signify the East, Black for the West, Yellow to the South, and White meant North.

We put on our heavy backpacks and hoisted our tote bags full of Guatemalan memorabilia to walk to the bus station, until a taxi hailed us. We got in and let him drive us to the nearby terminal. We thought of these trinkets as export examples, in the fantasy that we might make a business of it and return to Guatemala every year, or every six months if possible, to purchase more.

The bus departure time gave us a couple of hours, so we each downed a beer in front of a store, and asked around for a restaurant.

The bus left for "Huehue" around noon. We sat high and comfortable in a spacious, un-crowded modern bus, the earthquake and all the uncertainties forgotten for the moment in a climate controlled coach.

We held hands, felt no hunger, and enjoyed a gorgeous mountain landscape on a clear, crisp afternoon all the way to Huehue.

Huehuetenango

Through the bus window, Huehuetenango appeared on the horizon in late afternoon, and looked like fifteen or twenty streets of one story adobe structures, most painted yellow ochre and unadorned. We didn't see any earthquake damage at all on the drive into town.

The main market's emptiness told us the street vendors all headed for home hours ago.

Many of the people who stepped off the bus looked like earthquake refugees, like us, who wanted to sleep secure, in safety, far from the zone of the quake. We asked around for hotels, but even the taxi drivers said we would not find a hotel room, so long after the arrival of the first earthquake refugees.

We looked for a restaurant, and people pointed us towards tourist class establishments. "Algo más barato?" Cheaper, we asked in Spanish. They mentioned a small place near the center of the village, hard to find, no sign, but everybody ate there, they assured us.

We found it with the help of a Guatemalan who led us there in person. We walked through the thick adobe doorway and entered a small room with about five tables, walls bare except for a Virgin of Guadalupe calendar behind a cash register on a small glass case that enclosed the bright fluorescent dye colors of shredded coconut candies. A worker's restaurant with one soup on the menu, and lots of beer. A few Guatemalans played pool in the back section of the room.

Dust covered Cowboys filled the place, hats on, sheepskin jackets with hide side out, thick colorless scarves around their throats. The sun baked their skin into a reddish bruise color, the stiff clay of their corrugated faces and hands fired in the kiln of intense sunlight. They each sat in front of a bowl of soup that steamed when stirred with the rolled tortillas they used as spoons.

No one talked as they ate, but custom dictates that one finishes a meal and stands up, with a final mouth wipe with a tiny paper napkin, and says, "Provecho," a contraction of 'buen provecho' which means To Your Advantage, or Good Fortune.

Everbody answers "Gracias" with a mouthful of food.

We talked about where to sleep.

The dry bushy scrublands of the countryside we saw from the bus window on the way here, a few minutes walk down the road, might harbor a place where we could camp alone in the wilderness.

The late afternoon's cold mountain air made us walk fast as a few planets appeared in the sky. Two kilometers or so beyond the outskirts of Huehuetenango, tiny houses spread out over areas of grassy hillsides.

One large house atop a hill squatted amid a scrub wilderness. They might let us camp and even permit us to make a small campfire, we thought. We walked up the long gravel drive to the house to ask permission, but the aloof matron that came to the door turned us away with obvious suspicion. As if she faked her response, she acted irritated first, then refused to understand our Spanish as we explained our flight from the earthquake in Guatemala City. We pantomimed our need to sleep outside on her property, and repeated "hotel full."

She shut the door in our faces.

We walked back, but when out of sight of the house, due to the curve of low hills that intervened, we stepped off the driveway and onto a gravel jeep trail that took us to a footpath through the scrub along a slope.

No one saw us, we felt sure.

Surrounded by bushes about four feet high, we found a gravel area between the shrubs, free of sticks and cactus, and spread out our sleeping bags and unpacked our packs. The breeze died down as we made camp under the stars. I gathered some sticks and made a tiny fire to boil some 'instant' dehydrated beans and rice. We ate, surrounded by desert shrubs and thick bushes that danced to every flicker of our campfire's tiny flames.

The thin air at this altitude made the sky crystalline, filled with the myriad discrete dots of stars, galaxies, and our own galaxy the Milky Way. We could see Huehuetenango in the distance. It twinkled and gave the illusion of a much bigger city, much farther away, with its straggle of 60 Watt street lights to give the illusion of a much more distant view of an urban superhighway.

By the faint starlight, we scurried up and down the footpaths in the darkness, to collect soft grasses and leaves to cushion the stony ground under our sleeping bags.

We both got ready for bed. I watched her undress beside the tiny campfire's light. She looked at me with a smile that expressed her confidence in herself as a desirable woman.

I undressed.

We looked at each other nude. The firelight's soft yellow light gave a false warmth to our skin, covered in goose bumps from the cold air. We decided to use our two bags as one, mine on bottom and hers on top. The zippers wouldn't zip together. We lay down on my down bag and felt our soft cushion of grasses become as hard as rock, then threw her bag over us.

She wrapped her legs around mine and whispered "Why did you take your shoes off laying on your back?"

"I don't. Is that a joke?"

"You did our first night together."

Then I remembered. I did take my shoes off that first night on her bed in the Spring Hotel. Drunk, and flat on my back. How could she see me? She undressed in the bathroom. "Well, I didn't tonight, did I? Or any other night?"

"No. But you did in the Spring Hotel."

"I don't know, don't remember. Drank a lot, so did you. You saw me?"

"Yes."

"I don't believe you, and why should I tell you anyway?"

"Am I the first woman you sleep with?"

"I don't remember. The first real woman, yeah I guess so."

"Tell me about the others."

"What kind of a question is that? You're not supposed to talk about things like that. Only in locker rooms."

"You seem so, how can I say, inexperienced?"

I laughed. "Maybe I needed a good teacher. Do I have much to learn?"

"Plenty, though I don't want to scare you." She lay still, and I felt her start to fall asleep.

"Horny?"

"Yes," she murmured, "but too tired. Tomorrow, OK?"

Yvonne's Stew

Amaranto or Amaranth, a weed that once formed a large part of the staple diet of Meso-Americans, grows in a variety of soils, temperatures, and elevations to produce a miniscule seed the size of a pinhead. The seed contains the majority of the twenty essential amino acids needed to fabricate the proteins and enzymes to sustain human life. By weight, it offers up to thirty percent more protein than corn or rice, and more than sixty five percent more than wheat and other grassy grains common in Europe, which at best offer incomplete amino acid compliments. When boiled, the little seeds form a mush with a taste similar to boiled beets, which may explain the Meso-American reliance on spices, hot peppers, tomatoes, and the discovery of delicious flavors like vanilla and chocolate to create flavorful mixtures like 'mole' sauce, made of chocolate and seeds. When toasted, the Amaranto seeds blow up in the same manner as popcorn, to form a weightless powdery mass of snow white grains like small Styrofoam beads. The Meso-Americans mixed the popped Amaranto seed with pastes made from honey and nuts, and molded the mass into sweet confections in the form of serpents and skulls, and other representations of their Gods. To "crush the indigenous culture" as some people describe it, to ensure the superiority of the Catholic God and Iberian cultures, the Spanish outlawed the use of the ubiquitous food plant from the southwestern United States through Mexico and Central America, down the Andes Mountains of the Incan civilizations to Chile. Under Spanish rule, Under Spanish rule, Meso-America's use of Amaranto almost disappeared from human memory..

We lay close together in our separate sleeping bags, and watched our sun's other planets peek out, one by one, the first star-like objects to pepper the deep violet between muskmelon horizons. After so many nights without electricity, I felt the strict solar rhythm of day and night liberate me from some silly intellectual work ethic of reading myself to sleep only to awaken in the night with the light on, guilty about the wasted energy, the book in my lap.

We tried to read by flashlight, but the light attracted bugs.

In the darkness, Yvonne threw back the sleeping bag and sat up to say "Hungry?"

"I feel something, but it's not hungry."

"Can't men think of anything but sex?"

"Not usually, but right now, I mean I feel sick."

"What kind of sick?"

"Headache. My stomach. All day long, I waited to feel hungry, I wanted to feel hungry, and never did. Even when I ate, I didn't enjoy it. Now I feel full of wax, like I need to sleep or throw up. I don't feel sleepy or hungry."

"I'll make a fire, maybe we could read by the light, and the smoke will keep the bugs away. Want some oatmeal?"

"No. You go ahead. I feel like crap."

She stood up and walked toward the bushes for firewood. Her eyes scanned the ground for sticks and branches with dry twigs. Then she circled where I lay in our bed, and searched for a long time without a move into the vacant spaces between the bushes. Then she moved between the bushes quiet as a deer. Maybe her eyes grew accustomed to the starlight. Soon she returned with a small armload of sticks and long branches.

She labored to break green branches the right size to pile into a beautiful teepee, a yard from where I lay.

I asked her "You want to start a fire so close to all our stuff?"

"Not such a good idea, is it? OK, I'll move it. I thought we might use the light. You could jump up and help anytime, you know."

I still wanted to sleep or throw up. She could take care of things on her own. Or did she always manage to travel with men that take care of her?

She squatted over her teepee of sticks and stared at me a little while. "You like?"

"What? Oh yeah, great way to start a fire, but you need some tinder inside."

"Tinder." She stood up and pushed all the sticks further away with her boot. She rebuilt the teepee, but without any tinder at the center.

"Yvonne, you ever built a fire before?"

"Sure, lots of times. Sleep. Don't worry about me."

She sounded irritated, more so than her normal adorable, haughty, French attitude. She lit a match and held it against some sticks too thick to ignite, then flicked the match to the ground when the flame burnt her finger. She did this several times, and then threw the matchbox down in disgust.

"This wood must be wet or something."

The dry yellow fields bore testament to months without rain. Even though this high altiplano might get a little dew in the mornings, all the tall whitish straw color grasses spoke volumes about dry days in intense sunlight.

"Yvonne, start with a pile of grasses mixed with tiny twigs, and when that starts to burn, add the bigger stuff."

I felt bad, sick to my stomach, and her angry frustration did not help. Perhaps the altitude here affected me.

She reached out and gathered a ball of grasses. I asked her if any of it looked the slightest bit green, and she said yes. I explained that green grass and wood makes more smoke than flame, and she should start with wood long dead and dry. She scuffed around and gathered a ball of dry grasses, but then noticed the some of the twigs and branches showed green under the gray bark.

"How can these be green inside? I picked them up off the ground."

"Let me see it." She showed me some almost leafless branches that a woodcutter trimmed off a live bush. "Our woodcutters left you a present. Put this in the fire after it gets going enough to bake the water out of the wood."

Hunched over, she trudged off again, farther away, and found some very dead and dry sticks to bring back. She gathered up another ball of dry grass, mixed it with tiny sticks, and laid it near her teepee of sticks, lit a match and pressed it to the top of the ball of grasses.

It lit up with a brief flame, and went out. She moved the match and the same thing happened. She lit another match.

"Yvonne, you should hold the match under the stuff you want to burn."

She picked up the ball of grasses and held the match under it until it caught fire, then she dropped it near the teepee, which she tipped over on top of the grasses, and put out the fire.

Without a word, she rebuilt her little teepee, gathered another ball of grass, lifted it up off the ground and relit it. She set it down aflame, near the teepee, and tried to push small sticks into the grasses. That put out the nearby flames, and left a mass that smoldered and died, with a few red glows on the ends of dry grasses. Ash squirmed and fell like thin worms.

She snorted exasperated, and looked at me. "Could you help me with this?"

"You're doing fine. Next time you light a ball of grasses, push it into the teepee, so the thinnest dry sticks get the flames. Then blow lightly on the grasses to keep the fire going, and feed more small dry sticks in. They'll catch fire."

She kneeled down to try again. She lit the tinder, and bent forward to blow hard on the lit grasses which fanned up in a spray of flame and ash. Sparks flew into the grasses around us. She blew harder, then sucked in as much air as she could to blow again. Time after time, she blew with so much violence her lips made that sound horses do. Her efforts scattered sparks that flew far into the tinder dry landscape. She sat back each time she raised the tiniest brief and useless flame.

She panted, blew and blew, got smoke in her eyes and throat and started to cough. She stood up in anger, stuck out her lower lip and blew upward to blow the bangs off her forehead.

"It's no use," she yelled. "It won't stay lit! Look, it goes out again. Could you please get up and help?" and stomped her feet in place.

"Listen to me. It's easy. Get down close to it, lay down on the ground if you have to, and blow gentle and slow, little more than a whisper. You blow too hard, it scatters the heat. Talk it back to life. You'll learn how to blow, nice and gentle."

She looked at me as if she suspected something, crouched down on her folded legs and elbows, her big butt highest.

I reached out as far as I could, managed to pull her pant leg, and said, "Now that's what I like to see."

"Leave me alone!" She shrieked. "You don't act so sick."

"Trust me. I feel terrible. What if I get diarrhea out here? Won't that be fun?"

Yvonne lit a match and poked it under the ball of grasses, and as flames shot up, she blew a long, gentle current that pushed the tiny hot red embers deeper into the tinder. The glow lit her face as she blew, and then a mass of flames shot up. Her other hand pushed sticks into the fire.

She said nothing, tried to keep her back to me.

The flames died down again, and she repeated the long breath and coaxed another ball of flame to ignite her sticks. Then she built another little teepee over the fire, cautious to not burn her fingers, until the fire stayed lit without her help.

"Hey, congratulations, Yvonne. You're now a Boy Scout."

She turned to me and I saw angry tears run down her face. "You bastard."

"What?" I looked at her in shock. "What did I do?"

"Nothing."

"I helped a little, but you did most everything."

"You sat there and told me what to do. You know what I'm talking about. I'm not even hungry anymore." She turned away from both me and her little cheery campfire and stared out over the valley. Outlined by the firelight, she hugged her knees to her chest as the wind blew her hair off her face.

"Yvonne, you look beautiful."

She did not move.

She sat there and I drifted off to sleep.

When she got into her sleeping bag beside me I awoke to notice that, for the first time in our entire life of less than a week together, she did not reach out to touch me, nor give me a kiss goodnight.

Honeymoon over.

I drifted off to sleep with the impression that Yvonne revealed an inner self that she hated, something she kept hidden. I felt she loathed herself in some secret way, beyond low self esteem. In a flash of non-verbal thinking, I imagined her inner self as an angry child, the dark side of the mature sophisticated French woman she tried to present to the world, a slick self constructed veneer. Inside a sultry, seductive radiant moon of passionate madness lived, an angry manipulative tramp. What began as an exploration of the world turned into an exercise in domination of men as a method of cheap travel. Maybe her lack of independence her feel infantile, self conscious, and reluctant to return to France, her home, and her family. How would she explain it?

Because we could not get the sleeping bags to zip together, all night we played tug of war with the top bag, to reheat an exposed back, side, or backside.

The earth moved that Sunday, February eight at thirteen minutes after midnight. As we slept light with our ears on the ground, we felt the distant thunderous tremors of a quake that measured 5.5 on the Richter scale, centered under Puerto Barrios, where the motion of the waves in the earth liquefied the saturated sandy soils and caused the buildings and port installations to sink further into the muck.

In the past four days, the count of aftershocks reached six hundred twenty five.

I woke up in the darkness, a knife of pain in my left kidney, a cold sweat on my forehead. I became one with the tortured Earth, and we trembled together into the night. When the pain subsided, I rolled onto my back and listened to the quiet sounds of night birds and desert toads. My eyes felt as wide as the full moon, that blind man's pupil so white with cataracts, as it swims amid a black iris decorated with the stars of the Milky Way galaxy, and other galaxies that looked like stars.

Maybe I should see a doctor.

Weaver's Valley

Mayan art depicts a peaceful afterlife, of rest and peace, in the shade of Yaxche, the Sacred Tree, the World Tree, the ceiba tree.

We used up most of our water the next morning, as we washed all the utensils and the mess kit, and ourselves. We left our packs hidden in the brush and walked down toward the road into the valley to ask for more water from one of the houses.

We did not see any livestock to speak of, but the distant grassy hillsides looked grazed so short it left rocky fields to shine in the sun. Green areas surrounded larger, older buildings with an apron of pants, lawn, and trees, evidence of a water from a well or seep.

All morning, since before daybreak, we puzzled at the strange woodblock percussive sounds that echoed across the wide valley. It sounded like hundreds of woodcutters chopped with their axes, each in a nonstop, mechanical, even rhythm. The rhythmic sounds of wood blocks went in and out of phase with each other, sometimes the nearest synced, then would disintegrate into a chaotic sprinkle. The sounds came from all corners of the valley, clumped together in a vast dull echo towards distant Huehuetenango, a one story mirage that shimmered over a mile away across the undulations of the scrub plains.

We walked down the hillside to approach the first square adobe house. The individual sound of its part in the magical woodblock cacophony stood out more and more, an unmistakable thok! of wood on wood, over and over, without stop, from the house.

Inside a lean-to built like a carport onto the side of the house, a man sat high on a stool in front of a wood contraption that resembled the ribs of a giant baby carriage, a full scale loom. His feet moved up and down, as if on a bicycle. With one upraised arm he tugged at the black rubber of a bicycle inner tube, an action which somehow propelled a wooden shuttle through the woof of the fabric. His loom held a wide bolt of bright green cloth patterned with long lengthwise stripes. With each change in the position of his feet, half of the lengthwise strings of the fabric's warp raised up. Then he tugged the bike tube and the shuttle shot through the middle to bang to a stop on the wooden side of the loom. He switched feet to exchange the two layers of threads, and banged the shuttle across the warp again.

Those chock sounds came from across the wide valleys around Huehuetenango, from every one of the hundreds of one room shacks, each a small home for a weaver's family and the loom.

The loom design came from Europe, I felt sure, and this Latino man, so absorbed in his work that he didn't noticed us for a while, wore store bought clothes, a short sleeve solid color shirt and a pair of baggy khaki pants with black dress shoes.

All these hundred or so houses across these hills probably harbored looms where people wove long bolts of cloth. Every morning, all day long, they continued with their cottage industry, a foot in the Mayan past and a bicycle tube to the present, amidst this picturesque simplicity. Their existence based on an ageless economic reality, a continual need for new fabric, and their earnings came in exchange for a virtual imprisonment to the labor done in each of these tiny rectangular homes.

From our timid perch in the doorway, we called out "Buenos Días" until we broke through his machine trance mantra of wood, string, metal and the snap of the bicycle tube tension. He looked at us as if part of his own daydream for a while, then startled awake.

He stopped and got off his stool. Filled with a strange apologetic politeness, he walked over to us stooped, and straightened up to smile when he realized we wanted water. He took us outside to a small barrel, and grabbed a large tin soup ladle that floated on top. He would not listen to another word until each of us drank from it. When we asked to fill our canteens, he gave us all we wanted.

From the looks of his house and the lack of toys or women's clothes, he lived alone. We saw no well in the vicinity, and asked him where the water came from. He pulled out a yoke, from which two huge buckets hung, and slung it across his shoulders to show us how everyday, he retrieves water from a nearby well.

I asked him if we should take the yoke and go for water to refill his barrel.

He shook his head no, and I wondered if he understood. He motioned again to take all the water we wanted. We filled our two canteens and another plastic bottle, and he offered us more plastic bottles, but we refused them.

The patterns he wove reminded me of the Mayans of the Atitlán area's striped designs, but instead of tiny stripes with miniscule designs inside each, he wove broad stripes of solid colors.

We walked back to our camp and spent the day in pastoral peace. We read books, wrote in our journals, talked, and ate our meals together to the accompaniment of the atonal wood block marimba. We heard the echoes mesh and then march out of step, in and out of phase to each other, throughout the day until midafternoon.

Yvonne wondered whether these ranchers from Huehuetenango knew how to buy nutritious foods with their hard earned Quetzals. The men we saw yesterday at the restaurant all looked so skinny, and acted stiff, cold, and lethargic.

Yvonne wanted to go into Huehue and find the public schools, to see how Guatemalan teachers educate their children about the world. Did teachers expose school kids to the great ideas, the highest and varied expressions of the human mind? Did Guatemalans learn to appreciate and value the pinnacles of human achievement as the true treasures of our collective heritage as human beings? Even more important, did they know about the French Impressionists?

She suspected that values and lifestyles from the developed world would constitute dangerous prohibited information that they might provoke rebellion away from traditional values.

One thing I felt certain of, the experience of this pastoral valley, the idyllic sounds of nature and unarranged marimba music, this endless work of creation between weaver and loom, individual and society, lent itself as an analogy to a God of Time who paints this reality upon a canvas of matter with electromagnetic radiation. The image of this valley exists in my mind as both perfection and prison.

Maybe someday the people of the whole world would value their modern luxury of lifestyle choice, and choose with a healthy future as the goal. That won't happen as long as education teaches children only the reality within their parent's fences.

Guatemalan citizens, probably like most Latin Americans, live a ritualized life of toil and religion, punctuated by holidays, fiestas, dances, birthdays, and the Day of Your Saint celebrated by those who share a Saint's name. They conform to a strict Catholic interpretation of reality, even if the indigenous Mayans decorate and infuse their Catholicism with the pantheon of Indian icons and beliefs. The Mayan Indian's culture, so domestic they weave and eat small animals (instead of big animals that would take the men away from home to hunt), enables them to exist in isolation, distant from their overseers, the landowners and businessmen who market their weavings. Both the Ladinos and ruling classes, and the Indians, define their lives in servitude to the status quo.

This social structure serves Guatemalans as a map for their life's trajectory. From birth, to full flower, and old age if lucky, most people accept the narrow limits of what others expect from the phases of their life. Tradition defines what society will permit them to be, where they can go, and what they should think about it.

The Christian heaven remains the one redemption for each person's lifelong conformity in this Catholic universe. A lifetime of incomprehensible Sunday Masses in Latin (until Vatican II in the late Sixties) accustoms each citizen to give the ten percent of their income as tithes to the Church, in spite of hungry children, in spite of the grandeur, pomp, and gilt covered ostentation of the Cathedrals. How convenient that the ancient Meso-American religions, like Catholicism, taught that this life suffered leads to a better life in the great beyond.

Imagine yourself a priest with duty inside a confessional. You hear believer after believer confess many a damned good reason to, and then you forgive them in God's name to renew their entrance pass to Heaven. Catholic confessionals become the telephone booths for super-gossip with God. That might help explain the Catholic nation's cultural sluggishness. Many Catholics feel comfortable in their passive fatalism. They shut their eyes and ears, ignore reason and history, and fail to educate themselves enough to see beyond their bleak world of magic realism stuck in Medieval notions of guilt, sin, and redemption that blinds them to the intricacies of the modern world's rainbow of alternatives. They live in a paternalistic society modeled after God's, with the Father on the throne, Jesus seated on his right, and no significant female in sight. The local priests, up to the papal father, relay God's communiqués like lackeys on a baseball field who run messages to the pitchers who think they control the game, or the umpires, who make the decisions, and tell others what to think.

I could see how the Catholic religion overlooked, or maintained, maybe enforced, illiteracy among the Indians. The Mass in Latin must rate as the church's worst long term practice in its two thousand years, which lasted into the nineteen sixties until Vatican Two. I bet all that Latin didn't help any Mayan students learn Spanish as a second language. The mass in Latin made it easy for Catholics to undervalue books and education, and rely instead on the authority of the church, on holy hearsay, little better than gossip. Without functional literacy, their lifestyle gave them plenty of free time to dedicate to gossip, to philander as a God inspired pastime, and to magic thinking, which makes everything that happens in a person's life seem preordained, as fate and destiny, inevitable.

After a life led by the nose by what amounts to Astrology from Rome, the believer expects death to come on little cat feet, to shut the doors and windows, pour wax into the ears, fill the mouth with sand, bury the feet in mud, wrap the body in a cement overcoat, and pulled the plug so the body returns to the subterranean realms of water and clay, while the spirit drifts free, either upward to Heaven if one got that last confession in on time, or downward to burn for eternity in Hell, with all your friends who missed Mass on Sundays.

I do not know what Mayan cosmology offers the Guatemalan Indian as an afterlife, but judging from their willingness to exist as downtrodden underdogs, it must resonate, it must ring to the depths of their souls with joy and happiness, in a sympathetic and harmonious vibrations to some simplistic version of a Catholic Heaven. Instead of harps and clouds to lounge about on, maybe Mayans dream of a heaven with rainforest landscapes of flowers, walkways lined with little candle shrines, and lots of bare patches where they could sit on the ground and weave to the birdsong while Quetzals and parrots fly above, iridescent unchained jewels to decorate the sky. They could gossip as a group of happy weavers seated around a hot spring that bubbles up little cooked crabs to eat.

Yvonne asked me "Did you ever wonder why people in Latin America appear so relaxed?"

"What do you mean? Lazy?"

"Too relaxed. Yeah, maybe. I think winters would kill off any lazy Europeans. That would leave more people with a predisposition for work to interbreed."

I defended the tropical lifestyle. "It's too hot to work down here. They've got the right idea. Get up early, work, eat after midday, go to sleep in the heat of the afternoon, and go back to work late so you can stay up all night and party with the neighbors. I bet the European's work ethic demands that people watch each other, to criticize and judge, with an interpersonal style that forces people to conform. It makes everyone pull their own weight, or people disrespect you. The work ethic demands that people volunteer to help out when needed. How else could a French family with a dairy farm ever expect to build a barn? Wait till the kids get old enough?"

The contrast of idyllic cottage industry here in Huehuetenango played against my industrial rust belt background, and clarified one distinction. The modern industrial society exists in a dysfunctional and suicidal relationship with nature. One could make cloth cheaper with a factory in this valley, with a coal generator and big wells to suck out water to wash fabric and machinery, but the people wouldn't share in the greater profits, and the valley would suffer from pollution and contamination from metals, lubricants, chemicals, dyes, and other wastes. Even in the best case, with a clean operation, workers would soon want to buy a car and drive to work, which would again worsen the situation. Car culture brings all the support industries of tire repair, oil changes, antifreeze spills, broken glass, auto parts stores, the ooze and canker of junk yards, and the subterranean leakage from gas stations, not to mention increased mortality from auto accidents.

Most examples of successful industrialization allows the owners and stockholders to streamline production at the expense of human culture. Industrialization divorces humanity from sustainable local cultures and economies that for centuries or longer, coexisted with nature, depended on nature, and became part of the ecosystem. When people eat only industrially grown foods trucked in from far away, human survival depends on fertilization, pesticide, irrigation, and transportation technologies that dirty the air, contaminate water, and ruin soils to produced lower quality foods. The appeal of packaged foods inspires new dietary habits that convince people to depend on factory products of lesser nutritional value while they gain security in the cleanliness and standardization of their food. Industrialization does not compute the costs of compensation for contamination of the environment, loss of productive land, nor the term repercussions on human health. Industrial farms count only the lower cost of food, which translates to an decrease in the percentage of a worker's income devoted to groceries as their unique gift to society. The eventual biosphere loss becomes a cost to the locale, not to the industrialists, who diversify and move on to other croplands, and use the waste lands as feedlots for animal crops.

When the un-industrialized people adopt lifestyles of the industrialized 'Western' societies. They learn to live to work, to service the debt for a car, house, children, and buy toys and gifts for the whole extended family on their traditional Catholic festive days that honor Easter, fifteen year old girls, elaborate two year old's birthday parties, the day of your namesake Saint, and several other days around Christmas into February. They feel like members of the developed world when they can drive to a fast-food restaurant for hamburger, and never see the thousands of acres of forests that get cut down each year to turn into open range for cows. Then greasy hamburgers, the deep-fried chicken, the mint-jellied pork chops, the cloven ham hocks, and the sprinkles of bacon bits on the empty nutrition of water-leaf salads and pastas (with more neurotoxin monosodium glutamate than salt) replace the old sustainable cultures of vegetables and fruits, the complete protein combinations of a legume and grains, beans and corn, or all twenty essential amino acids found in amaranth and soy-based tofu.

Unfortunately for the future of humans on this tiny planet of limited resources (which some suspect already overheats from the influence of human activities) the Great Creator inspires people to invent seductive advertisements to excite a basic genetic need within all humans, the desire for a wristwatch, a Television set, a personal auto, a charge card, and a house with a garage to store all that stuff we buy in huge quantities at wholesale prices from superstores.

Stuff we can't find time to use, but make us feel we keep up with the neighbors. It makes work-ethic Americans feel good to live to work.

Americans feel too guilty to slow down to smell the roses or clean air. They can't change their lifestyle to work to live, and can't imagine how to leave a sustainable, cleaner future for our children.

Of course we would give up a lot of things, and lower our standard of living, and that feels wrong, just plain wrong.

'Third World' people and governments do it all the time. They devalue their national currency, and ask citizens to tighten their belts, again.

Over the past centuries, they possessed very little to begin with. Now they must tighten their belts to the bone.

Confronted by Woodcutters

The Mayans belief in the World Tree, the sacred ceiba tree, included ritual consultations with "talking crosses" as wooden oracles, another fortuitous coincidence which gave the Mayans a smooth transition into the Spaniards' Christianity.

On the dark morning of Monday, February 9 at 5:44 AM, we awoke to a slight tremble in the earth. Its epicenter, Lago de Izabél, lay near the epicenter of the original quake. This one measured 5.5 on the Richter scale.

We stayed inside our sleeping bags until the sun lit the ground around us. Dewdrops decorated all the stalks of grass with crystalline globes that sparkled with rainbows.

We squirmed out of our separate bags, slung them across bushes to dry, and made a fire to cook hotcakes and coffee. The dew moistened soil caked on our shoes.

I looked up and my eyes met the stares of three men in cowboy hats who stood chest deep in the brush around our camp. They came out of the bushes and walked with caution into our campsite, machetes in hand.

They snuck up on us without a sound, and now acted polite and respectful, with their machetes held relaxed but obvious, out of their scabbards, at the ready.

"Buenos Días."

"Buenos Días."

The three said things to us in a strange Spanish we did not understand, but that happens to everyone in Guatemala, where most Indians speak an illiterate Spanish as a second language.

They looked like woodcutters, the one profession older than prostitution. All over Guatemala, men and women roam the morning hours for dry cellulose, the most abundant sugar on earth. Woodcutters operate like miniature one-man oil companies, the source of the archetypical concept of windfall profits.

They shuffled closer, machetes in relaxed hands, serious droll expressions. They wanted to know where we came from, our names and who sent us, why we camped there, where we headed, what we planned to do.

We understood very little of what they say. We said "Si" a lot and smiled like idiots.

They didn't smile. They didn't understand our Spanish either. "Turista" meant little or nothing to them. Gringo, Estados Unidos, USA, America, California, even Ooosah (USA), all elicited blank stares tinged with more suspicion, as if they thought us evasive. They asked us earnest questions we did not understand as they invaded our camp a little deeper, step by step.

They began to poke through our packs with machetes.

One of them spotted the hardback book beside Yvonne's bedroll, and said something brusque with his long machete pointed at it. They all started to talk at once, very interested, so we handed it to them.

They looked at it with awe, and one said, "La Biblia."

They handed it back and forth among them, and talked.

"Si, si, eso es. Aquí esta."

"Pues, son evangelicos."

"Si pues."

It all made sense to them, our camp, our lack of purpose, our mystery. They identified us as evangelists on the road, those who roam in poverty, with little more than the bible to rely on. They smiled as if consecrated, enlightened, faces effused by sudden joy, big yellow teeth came out like a sunrise between thick chapped lips. They holstered the machetes, crossed themselves, and with undue reverence, backed away into the shrubbery and disappeared.

Yvonne and I sat and looked at each other. The coffee water boiled, birds sang, the marimba of a hundred looms echoed around the valley.

"What happened?" She asked.

"If we had bicycles, they might think we're Mormons."

With simple logic, when they saw a book, they saw "The Book," the Bible, and they remembered that Evangelists read Bibles. Therefore we, as Evangelists for God, earned their respect and reverence, and an instant logical reason and excuse for our peripatetic ways, and our camp in the middle of God's country.

Lucky for us, at this moment she did not read a romance paperback with a lurid cover of a bare-chested muscular man who manhandles the ripped bodice on a buxom maiden who swoons from a kiss she fought against and yearned for. That might inspire the woodcutters to capture us and march us into Huehuetenango on a morals charge.

After we ate, we both remarked about how that wake-up call by three men with machetes convinced us to look for another campsite.

They helped me refine a theory about how illiterate people do not use words, but entire phrases. Many people refuse to reword sentences, but instead, repeat with insistence the same thing, over and over. Some do not slow down, separate words, or try other words and phrases to help another's comprehension. In Spanish, people talk with machine-gun staccato, and worse, link words that end in a vowel sound that the next word begins with, to run them together. So two words share one vowel sound if the end of one word sounds like the beginning of the next. To the uninitiated, it throws word recognition into the bushes.

People who don't know how to read and write don't depend on language to think the way literate people do. Instead of words, illiterates think in actions, pictures, fantasies, and magic. Phrases become sound sequences, instead of discreet words strung together into concepts linked by rules. Like children, they string phrases together with oral language's impromptu grammar. Children borrow constructions from similar phrases and whenever they come up with some phrase that sounds incorrect or awkward to an adult, we correct them or laugh at them. For illiterate older children, this probably creates a reluctance to express themselves with the freedom necessary to learn from their mistakes, to learn social conventions from literate society, to expand their tools for efficient communication and further education.

So their minds never value vocabularies of expansive possibilities, nor thrill with alternative and elegant grammatical constructions that invent new ways to communicate. You ask them to repeat themselves, and they do, word for word, over and over, exact copies of the first time.

Even though word-linkage receives the seal of approval from the Royal Academy of the Spanish Language, the committee in Spain that oversees international Spanish grammar and dictates whether particular words merit inclusion in Dictionaries, I hate it.

Imagine the strong accents of Hillbillies or Southerners as the 'official' way to speak English. American school children would learn how to sound ignorant and illiterate, or overly polite and class conscious, and pat each other on the back about it. Oh yes, ideals of tolerance of others in our multicultural societies demand that we accept our individual differences, and de-emphasize that everything sorts out on a scale from bad to good, feeble to efficacious, contemptible to attractive and excellent, when evaluated towards goals of mutual understanding and respect.

The U.S. Southerners fake culture and 'good breeding' with respectful, mannered conversations full of 'Sir' and 'Mam,' a model taken from the class-conscious mentality of Old World societies that the first immigrants sought to escape. Southern U.S. society relied on slaves, on captive humans, and today, relies on a failure to understand the United States Constitution's prohibition against the use of titles of nobility, and the modern interpretation of their efforts as a beautiful dream of a classless society that respects equality and civil rights for all. People who say 'sir' to each other belong in some hierarchical sub-humanist society, like the military, and should feel shame for their inability to find language that expresses their respect without a word steeped in domination, subjugation, unchallenged authority (not really respect by any means), and slavery.

In accordance with my Yankee upbringing, or perhaps to all humanists and anyone who respects human rights and social justice and the ideal of a classless society, when someone addresses another as Sir (sometimes spelled sir), without the addressee in possession of an honorary title from the Queen of England, it amounts to an insult of fake respect. As a term of respect, it also fails as sexist ('Mam' does not connote equivalent respect) and so merits elimination. In whatever part of the United States, 'sir' deserves its unconstitutional status, and deserves elimination from the national vocabulary.

Provincial attitudes often survive simply because they survived, a circular proof often offered to prove merit. Whatever the grandparents did should work well enough for generations to come, so let the kids marry at thirteen years old. Improvement fights against traditions, because to evolve (increased complexity) and progress, demands a recognition of the old way's insufficiencies, a criticism of the previous generation's unassailable and traditional veneration. Respect elders, whether they ever deserved it or not, to lower them into the grave with a smile on their face.

Not that I dislike tradition all the time. I want to believe that merchants do not cheat or overcharge customers, whether on ethical instincts, a developed moral code, or because of a simplistic Christian ideal. It does matter to me which, because if people don't make their own moral decisions based upon reason, then they tend to let leaders do it for them. Catholicism permits one to do whatever, and confess later. The military only permits one to do as commanded, on a need to know basis.

Around nineteen fifty nine, my atheist mother told six year old me and my five year old brother about the Scopes Monkey Trial thirty four years earlier, and how it foretold troubled times ahead for the truth seekers, skeptics, secular scientists, and non-Christians such as Buddhists, Freethinkers, Muslims, Hindus, Jews, Animists, meditators, philosophers, and everyone else who seeks their own knowledge of fundamental realities, paths to morality and personal happiness, and deserves respect and permission to continue.

As far as the woodcutter's motivation, what if the book didn't lay about where the woodcutters could see it? What if the dominant personality among them decided to blame the earthquake on the presence of foreigners?

What if the woodcutters sit in Huehue right this second and talk to someone who tells them the police look for a young couple of foreigners wanted for murder, or worse?

May my atheist mother forgive me. I prayed.

I thanked evolution that God exists.

We walked down to the road after breakfast, and spent the midday hours in silly explorations of Huehuetenango's municipal palace and other public buildings, to keep out of the intense sun.

Some bilingual, middle class, cowboy-type Guatemalans who wanted to talk English tracked us down to talk, eager to confess they lived for a time in the United States of North America. They told us how easily the typical Guatemalan travels around this beautiful country, and how they appreciate God's splendor out the bus window or through their car's windshield. Some of their own family, though not close family, women with children, often traveled far from home to do seasonal agricultural work. In the Pacific lowlands for example, workers might stay in communal huts with their babies and young children in tow. Most of what they earn, less than a dollar a day, they spend for their immediate needs. When faced with unexpected need, they must beg for help.

They told us of mountains nearby in the Sierra Los Chuchumatanes, covered with forests of perfect little Christmas trees.

That day, as we walked around Huehuetenango, we felt relieved, out of the earthquake zone, and now invigorated by the earthquake, as if it gave us a new lease on our young lives. We escaped death, and now talked with hope and optimism, determined to use what remained of our youth to help people. We felt aged and wizened by the last week's catastrophe.

I thought people in Guatemala needed earthquake proof adobe houses. Maybe with a framed layer of chicken wire inside, to force the walls to fall outward. Tile roofs represent the worst possible solution to shelter in a region of earthquakes. Go back to palm fronds, or forward to asphalt shingles.

We both wanted to return to our traveler's life of perpetual motion and irresponsible action, but with a new goal: To acquire more life experiences and knowledge of the world so that we could decide what we want to do with our lives before circumstances forced us to look for whatever job available just to make money to survive.

We both made our original decision to travel based on a conviction that better sooner than later, before we succumbed to the necessity of career choices, college, or a long apprenticeship with an illusory opportunity, like an unfair climb up some corporate ladder to nowhere. We both jumped out of the nest young to fly into the face of the unknown, and in a blink, we almost died. We wanted to see things now, while young, instead of after that long wait for retirement, if we remained healthy and energetic, if we still felt curious and brave, if we survived. We wanted to see the world not as tourists but as travelers, ready to settle down if we fell in love with someplace, or somebody, that might make the compromises worthwhile. Even as international paupers, our back pockets filled with a guidebook instruction manual to survive on five dollars a day, we believed in the quality of our existence, and felt we reaped more valuable rewards than our friends and schoolmates back home, stuck in situations they hated and couldn't escape. Our friends 'found themselves' in dead end jobs, or wallowed in junior colleges that promised to train them for a vocation like shop (car repair), truck driving, or nurse's aide. The luckiest and most affluent tried to maintain excitement about a university career in institutions that existed to grind out carbon copy humans that could write academic tomes in wordy passive-tense riddled English, and share them with peers who deigned to explain anything to those not as educated, for fear of ridicule. Many dropped out to wrestle with bad marriages, unions between two immature people who gained expertise in how to anger each other as advances in intimate knowledge. The worst off made plans to deal with unplanned, unwed, uncoupled, single parenthood without parental support.

Even if we couldn't put into words why we felt so rewarded, we both felt our escape from the social normalcy of our country's cultures forced our eyes to recognize home's limitations, a prison of traditional choices that that gives our compatriots comfort and continuity, generation after generation. Viewed from outside, that homespun normalcy seemed arbitrary, foolish, and flawed with both nearsightedness and a lack of self examination. Traditions help people avoid social frictions and discord, and guide the lost into a sensation of belonging, but also condemn groups of people to exist outside the realm of ideas which would force the examinations and changes that make progress possible.

We felt changed, forced by unfamiliar circumstances to metamorphose into something better than the person who started our travels. We learned how to change plans and adapt, and our world widened. The school of hard knocks lay around the corner, and the earthquake, a wake-up call.

As we walked down a gravel road in search of a campsite, Yvonne and I talked about how, in the wee small hours of that Wednesday morning at three minutes after three, we both stared into the sooty eye sockets of the grim reaper, and felt grateful he looked away. We noticed the Guatemalans around us suffered an anguish that increased with the desperation of each new day. As more news came from the re-connected villages, it also came with new revelations of more family members gone forever, perished in those thirty seconds of chaos. Each hour, any phone call could bring news of tragedy, another friend, family member, or entire family gone. Many survivors died as a result of injuries, and those who lay in hospital lay amidst too many others with serious wounds in a country of low medical standards, overworked staff, and depleted medical resources.

"I worked as a nurse, and I know what can happen in hospitals. Germs everywhere, people go there healthy and catch all kinds of disease. I mean, I would like to help, but the real problem comes from a lack of food and water and what to do with dead bodies, not from the survivor's bumps and scratches. We're two more people that need food and water, and a place to sleep. We don't belong here."

We tried to put our finger on who bears responsibility for the state of modern Guatemala, its poverty, substandard houses, the hierarchy of class, the military presence in the city and countryside, the rumors of death squads and the disappeared, the few families who own most of the land, and the resistant culture of the Mayans who worked it.

Yvonne said "Society always looks like a pyramid, those on top don't hear the voices of those below. The ones on top stay there on the backs of others. Here, a few rich families own the land, then the middle class of store owners and merchants, then the young ladinos compete for jobs or for work as servants to get out of agriculture. On the bottom, the Mayans live in their own culture, and don't know how much better life could be for them and their children."

"Maybe the Mayans reject progress, like Mennonites, with religious reasons to want simplicity in nature."

The lushness and variety of Guatemala's landscapes spoke of a natural abundance that contrasted with the poverty that complicates of low birth survival rates and short life expectancy. The chiaroscuro of colorful Mayan fabrics reflect the bright tropical birds so conspicuous against the jungle backdrop. In the jungles and cloud forests, I could feel the silent green walls as a presence, it broods and sees all, as if to harbor and hide the shadowy influences of class repression, and allow the worms and corruption of the lowest levels of dirt rise to the heavens. The mountainous forests and steamy jungle ravines of Guatemala guard the graves of the disappeared.

I felt stupid and worse, wanted to return to ignorance. I did not understand Guatemalan society, the gentle kindness of the Mayans, and I wanted to ignore the paranoia and callousness exhibited by the middle class people I met, among individuals I considered decent and moral.

One afternoon in Santa Catarina Palopó, when I attempted to thrill a Guatemalan Indian lad with pictures in a magazine from the United States, pictures of airplanes and modern conveniences like dishwashers, toaster ovens, and blenders, which they know as a class of consumer goods called electro-domestics.

He showed no interest. As I thought about it over the weeks, I doubted he could even see the items, because he couldn't understand the images in the reproductions. His culture didn't know about or use such items, maybe because electricity arrived in Santa Catarina Palopó within the past couple of years.

One day it dawned on my that he didn't need to. I thought he would thrill to imagine himself inside an airplane. But if he saw his place in the universe as a mirror of his father and grandfather, it didn't fit.

Perhaps we should first seek a balance of nature within ourselves, a balance that the Guatemalans inherit by grace through the tight bond woven between each mother and the quiet child she carries all day in a blanket slung across her shoulders, before we dare to think they lack, or live deprived of, the advantages of the high-wire act of modern urban life.

Too much freedom and movement for each individual makes balance difficult. How do couples balance their needs? Where does a family find balance between two working parents and their individual personal needs, between the parents and the familial needs of their children? The modern economics of cement and asphalt urban centers depend on people with automobiles, who don't value the need to walk through nature for health and happiness.

Does a bridge exist between the secure neighborliness of snoopy citizens in the fishbowl of a small rural town snuggled in nature, and the big city's crime-friendly personal freedoms of anonymity and alienation within a cement and steel jungle where various cultures coexist in uneasy truces?

We must find a new 'natural' balance, an education for both right and left brains, to bridge the divide between the logic of linear verbal thought and the nonverbal qualities of instinctual aesthetics to create a new order, a consciousness of our place in history and nature. Then we might decorate reality with arts and music, instead of billboards and advertisements, and imagine a future of both quality and quantity, to reconnect us to our lost graces of simple existence, shaped by millions of years of evolution, and help everyone benefit from science and mathematics.

Each small step for humanity keeps our feet on the ground as a caress, not as a footprint of death and annihilation, as if we belong to it, and relearn to respect and nurture the thin layer of green that supports us, as it supported our parents and grandparents and all our ancestors.

As we lay together for warmth under her sleeping bag, I asked Yvonne how France's standard of life compared to the United States.

"People in the United States want to buy buy buy, more more more, and everything must look new, clean and sterile, so that one can show off, prove themselves more than all the others. France has centuries of culture and history. America's lack of history forces it to invent itself in lies. We honor the history of our culture. America defines itself by war, endless movies about military leaders and the victories in both World Wars, and never mention the contributions of other nations. America invents its history to sell as pop culture, for sons to become soldiers, so parents feel honored when their soldier boy comes home dead."

"You don't think people owe a debt to their country?"

"Oh yes, it's called taxes. But not the rich, they don't pay their taxes, and they don't send their children into the army. Their children go to college and their families stay rich, so they can buy art from other rich kids who pretend to be artists in New York or Paris. They buy art without value, which anyone would throw away, useless except for that artificial history that ties it to its own small circle of friends."

"You don't like modern art?"

"I like decorative arts and conceptual arts that mean something beyond the art world. If it's ugly and says nothing, where does it belong, but in the garbage? In France, we love things intellectual. We make television shows and movies too, but we do not blow things up, chase each other with cars, or shoot it out with machine guns."

"I've seen some France movies, about photographers, or sensitive kidnappers, love affairs between teachers and students. I thought maybe French filmmakers don't have money for explosions and hundreds of used police cars to destroy every year."

"You Americans like to say France is backwards, that our telephone system does not work, a national joke. We still talk to our family, and pass each other as friends in the streets. We live in villages full of people who stop and talk to each other. We don't need so much a telephone system, because we don't live inside our automobiles. I suppose France, like everywhere else, will one day look like the United States, full of MacDonalds and Dairy Queens, because everybody wants a car, you know."

"You think the French live a happier than Americans do?"

"I can't tell you that. I can say, I feel happier here, right now in Guatemala, even with this disaster. People get lazy and stupid everywhere, and elect the government they deserve. American elections look like a joke to me."

"How so?"

"With two parties, only two parties, you call it democracy. How can it represent society? Each party tells lies to get elected, and everyone knows they will never do what they promise. Americans think when everyone votes, that's democracy. Who makes the decisions, when people from corporate offices get appointed to Government jobs, or work for the CIA, or work for your stock exchange in the Security Exchange Commission. Your presidents put people into agencies that regulate the same industry they used to work for. Imagine, you want to control the forests, you appoint a man from the lumber industry. You want to regulate oil, you appoint a man who works for oil companies. That's OK for Americans. Good experience for the job, they say." So corporations run your two-party system through money. They support only the candidates who they trust to do what's best for business, and everybody around the world, except the Americans, knows who the president works for. Your free and democratic election puts one of two identical candidates into office of president."

"At least there's continuity. We don't vote for socialists, or Christian Democrats or change things too much every four years. The president doesn't have more power than the senate and house."

"The all works for the same bosses. It's a holy trinity in America, you got Democrats," Yvonne holds up one finger. "Republicans," she extends another finger, "and corporations," she shows three fingers. "Both candidates serve corporations. Take away your precious Democrats" down goes the index finger. "And take away Republicans," down goes the ring finger, "and you get this." She held up the middle finger.

"Who told you all that?"

"This guy I traveled with for a while. Said he used to work in the State department. You know it's funny to watch the TV news in the States. Dennis calls it hypnosis, a suggestion of reality. Not the same as news in Canada nor in France."

"He told me that too."

"Oh, and when did you talk to him?"

"We ran across each other one night in a bar in Guatemala City. We got drunk together, sat on the steps in front of the Merced. He told me about hypnosis, suggested reality." I shut up fast, looked up at the stars, and prayed for a meteor flash to change the subject.

Yvonne didn't say anything, but I felt her stiffen and lay immobile in my arms, like she forgot to breath. Then she said "So you talked to him before you and I met again."

"Yes. A couple of weeks ago, I guess."

Her shoulders shrugged a little.

I thought they communicated annoyance.

"Did you two talk about me?"

"Sure. I wanted to know where things stood between you two, because I loved you from the very first moment I saw you."

"Liar." She tipped her head to blow into my face, and asked "What did he say about me?"

"Nothing that didn't make you even more attractive." I did not want to mention her sleep-talk, which I believed she faked. And I did not want to hear some defensive confession about how she awoke to play with Dennis' emotions, and make a fool of him. Whatever she might say happened between she and Dennis, I felt no good would come of it, and at worse, might leave me to think of her for the rest of my life as the complex and beautiful French girl that got away.

I decided to take the Hallmark card approach. "He said he missed you a lot, wished you lots of happiness."

She rummaged through her pack and pulled out her flashlight to read her book.

I closed my eyes and waited.

She didn't turn the page. Nobody takes that long to read two pages.

She turned toward me, so I opened my eyes to see her stare at me.

She said "You must be almost out of money." She turned back to her book. "Aren't you?"

Yvonne's Oldest Profession

The Mayan's book called the Popol Vuh reveals influences from many cultures of central Mexico. It tells us how the Sun, God of song and the hunt, once married the Moon, Goddess of cloth and pregnancy, when they both lived upon the earth. When the Sun God learned of his wife's infidelities, he poked out one of her eyes to punish her, and they both became banished to the Heavens. The myth makes a case for the Moon's lesser brilliance, with an unmistakable warning to women.

In the morning, I awoke again to that sharp pain in the small of my back. As if an interrupted dream, another memory of Michigan came to me. A local farmer, very religious, could not understand why I wanted to travel to Guatemala. He said, "I hope you find what you're looking for."

The clatter from the looms filled the beautiful valley with their incessant music, the pop of buds in spring, an force of creation made tangible to the ears in this pastoral valley. Over the past two days, we often lost ourselves in thought as we stared out over the valley, the waves of heat and sound felt as if they meshed and radiated in spherical ripples throughout the firmament.

I stared right through space and distance, out of the tropics, to a reality more than two worlds away, through Mexico and across the States, or across the Atlantic's Gulf of Mexico and up the coast. I could see the special isolated circumstances of the subset culture represented in the Midwestern WASP communities. Blind chance selected it for me, out of all cultures of all the cultures on this planet. I tried to construct a personal culture that used few resources, respected nature, valued civil rights, and supported a secular humanism as the only ideology that offers protection for all the rest of man's philosophies, cultures, religions, and lifestyles.

The Golden Rule of secular humanism: If what you do doesn't hurt you, me, or anyone else, and you can live with it, then no one else has the right to stop you.

Yvonne and I talked about elementary particle physics, before we crawled out of our sleeping bags. We concurred in a belief in a pop culture version of the Heisenberg Uncertainty Principle. In elementary particle physics scientists study what goes on when you smash atoms into smithereens and let the smithereens make bubbles in chambers full of liquid hydrogen. They find subatomic parts of protons and neutrons, named quarks, gluons, muons, anti-protons, etc. and they expect to find other exotic particles predicted by theory and mathematics. The mathematics describes matter as both particle and wave, and measures interactions as clouds of probabilities. The Uncertainty Principle exposes the impossibility of a discreet measure of the speed of an object at the same time as a measurement of its exact position at any point in time. You measure for speed, and you don't know where a thing is. Measure it's position, and you lose its speed. Measure one or the other, but not both at the same time with any precision, because the observation of one interferes with measurement of the other.

For humans in a Space-Time continuum, in constant relative motion to each other and in reference to our own lives, a Pop version of the Uncertainty Principle might suggest that when we know where we stand, we can't know how fast we move. Travelers know how fast they move, but can't stick around long enough to stand for anything.

This principle of uncertainty helps me define my connection to the river of life which ebbs and flows, stops and goes, within and without me. It gives me a framework to see and understand the frustrations of an analysis of my life as a work in progress, and allows me to feel satisfaction if I can maintain the motion even when I don't know my position on the map of life.

A beautiful uncertainty.

The appearance of the illiterate woodcutters morning helped us decide to leave this pleasant valley of weavers early, now that people knew where we camped, and people talked. One night they might bring a sick child for us to heal, or some rowdy village boys might want to provoke an international incident. We packed our bags and went without breakfast, to walk on animal paths across the bushy hillsides towards the long road back to Huehuetenango.

"Yvonne, what makes you happy?"

"When I feel alive, very alive, fully alive. The first night with a handsome man. When I'm naked on a windy beach, or when I dress up for an elegant party. Once I took a skinny dip off the side of a yacht because someone dared me to do it."

"You can't do those things all the time. How will you stay happy?"

She thought about that, as we walked down a gravel road toward the main highway. The flanking trees drew shadows of ragged stripes across the gravel. "I don't know. My mother is very religious. It comforts her. She never did anything with her life. She became so boring as she got older. She repeated the same stories, the same memories, judged everything against bible scriptures. She makes me crazy, really crazy, but I love her, she's mom. Couldn't be like her. Religion should help a person feel good, or why bother, you know?"

"You need a job?"

"Oh yeah, with plenty of travel."

"And lots of money to spend."

"Oui, but of course. I don't know what to do next. Something always comes to me. I work as a waitress, secretary, typist, telefonista, anything until I find a good position as a nurse, somewhere they give me what I want. People think I should wait in bars, for the tips. There's work everywhere you go. Maybe I could work on a cruise ship, then I could travel, and stay employed, no?"

"The attractive barmaid travels the world without any scruples."

"Screw pulls? What are they?"

"Scruples keep people like you and me from selling our bodies."

"Prostitution?"

"It's all prostitution, about selling yourself, eight hours at a time, your work as a nurse, my work as a mindless cog in a machine. Most work doesn't pay as well as sex."

"I worked as a prostitute." She waited for my reaction, then took on a pugnacious stance as she spoke slowly and carefully, "Mindless, almost like a machine, like you." She laughed.

She fell silent as we walked, so I said. "You worked as a prostitute? What's that about?"

"Oh, once. My boyfriend made me do it, actually. He didn't pimp me. We bet, he thought I would find it disgusting."

"Did you?"

"Find it disgusting?"

"Prostitute yourself."

"Yes. But not with him. I liked him too much, and did not want to win his stupid bet and lose him. Later I did it, alone, to prove to myself I could do it.

"How did that happen?"

"A man robbed me one night in Paris, when I first dared to go across town to bars where I didn't know anyone. At least he didn't rape me. I felt so angry, I didn't have any money to get home, and I could not call anyone or my parents would know where I went that night. So I tried to figure out what to do, and in a flash, I propositioned this middle aged man, because he looked nice. We went to a motel and he paid me."

"Lose respect for yourself afterwards?

"I think I gained self respect, and I learned a lot about men." Yvonne looked at me as we walked.

I looked at her and smiled.

She said "Don't you want to hear about what I learned?"

"Well yeah, I guess. Don't tell me if it'll make me feel like a bad lover."

Yvonne laughed. "Men are little boys, insecure liars who need a woman to mother them and be there whenever they need to jack off."

"You had to prostitute yourself to learn that?"

She laughed again, "No, I knew that. He wanted to talk, about his 'fat-ugly' wife, how they no longer had fun together. She refused to do things he waned, or hated to do them. With me, when I did what he asked, he rolled his eyes up like this, and moaned 'I've died and gone to heaven, I've died and gone to heaven. Praise the Lord.' He complained that even if he convinced his fat-ugly wife to play sex games with him, she acted like it was dirty, and not fun for her. She tried to look miserable on purpose, he thinks, to make him feel bad, like he forced her to do them, like a rapist or worse, so she would think they sinned. But then he also says she never excited him, even in their youth, when everyone said she was young and pretty. It was like an arranged marriage within their church. She keeps her church clothes on in bed."

"Think you might end up an fat-ugly wife?"

"Never. I can survive without marriage, thank you. At least for a while longer, no?"

"Maybe that's the start of your research on men married to women who hate sex. You could write a book, Marriage to the Frigid."

"Who would publish it or read it? Unmarried men? Can you imagine what happens when the wife finds that book under his pillow?"

"Yvonne, ever think that sex keeps people in shape?"

"Hey, you don't burn that many calories, ask me, I know."

"I mean if someone uses their body for pleasure, I mean if they enjoy their body, wouldn't they be less likely to let it go out of shape?"

"They get married, no sex, and eat too much."

A light rain began to fall, tiny droplets from the bottom of a misty sky. We ignored it.

Yvonne acted older, more experienced, and mature. She never told me her age in a way I could believe. I knew we shared approximately the

406

same amount of time since our birth, if not the same experiences. She attended some college to become a nurse, she wanted no children, and did not respect marriage. A new breed of woman, self sufficient, worldly, brusque and impetuous, one of those who hunger to demonstrate their strength, eye to eye and opinion by opinion, with any man in a man's world, to prove their equality.

I thought Yvonne, due to the influence of sixties feminism, took advantage of the fact that the modern man must recognize a woman's personhood, and grant her independence. He respects her right to travel alone, even while he takes responsibility for her safety. The men who helped her travel this far underplayed the importance of a young woman in their life. I knew, as Yvonne probably felt, that those men never admitted how much they valued Yvonne's sex appeal as a decoration to their life, more than any altruistic need or educational project to keep their interest. Her Paris and New York escapades on other men's credit cards filled her mind with dreams of a future with her own international credit card, a ticket to equality and mobility, freed from the drudgery of children and sexual slavery to a man.

I wondered how I would fit in to her long line of stabled ponies. One look at me, and any woman would sum me up as a limited resource.

She said, "Did Dennis tell you stories about me?"

That pulled me out of my reverie like a hooked fish. I floundered about and stammered "No. Are you afraid he might say something?"

She shrugged. "Don't believe what people tell you. You Americans are still uncivilized. You don't care about the thousands of years of culture in other countries." She made me laugh with her pouting, as she continued. "American men make love like an Olympic event. They have to be the best lover ever or they feel like a failure. No romance. They don't have time to seduce a woman, make her really hot. Without grace, no sensitivity, no tact, no sense of diplomacy or proportion, because they have no culture, and they're too ignorant to care about people who expect that." She said something in French to irritate me.

"Whoa, that's not fair. Americans try to be straightforward and honest, no nonsense. Practical and inventive."

"Inventive? So invent something. You Americans, Canadians too, you bore me to death. A fucking bore, that's what you all are."

I reached for her hand and pulled her to look into her eyes. "Do I bore you now?"

"Yes, completely."

I dropped away from her and stopped to put a little distance between us. We continued down the road and each nursed their private thoughts.

Up the road a ways, she sat down and waited for me. When I approached, she said, "Don't walk behind me angry."

"I'm not angry. I like to think, look around."

"What do you think? Did I hurt you?"

"You're French. You can't help it, anymore than I can rescue you from boredom with me. These trips we're on, they're like an escape from ourselves. We fled our homes, jobs, friends, and our own lives, and ran into an earthquake."

"Calm down. Yes. Walk with me." She stood up and walked in front of me without a glance backward. She held her hand held out and wiggled her fingers until I caught up and grabbed it. We held hands as we walked, but she said nothing. I felt her sink deep into her own head again.

We came to a fork in the road. One pavement led northwest towards town and the Mexican border, and one went southeast into the heartland of Guatemala. We crossed the road to a little window store, and the woman who lived there told us the bus to Quetzaltenango stopped right in front of her store, so we might as well relax and eat something. First she said the bus passed by every day in about three hours, but since no bus arrived on schedule since the earthquake, she thought road conditions made them arrive later. She suggested we stick around, relax, and buy food at her store for the bus ride, and spare us the trip to Huehuetenango.

We decided to walk into town anyway, and wave the bus down en route if it passed.

On this walk, I felt the knife-sharp pains in the small of my back. I sat down suddenly on the side of the road, out of breath.

"What's wrong?"

"My back." I tried to breath slow, deep. "I feel pains like this in the middle of the night, since I took two twenty four hour bus rides to Tikal and back without sleep in between. Bumpy roads, too."

"Maybe you bruised your kidneys. Or you have a kidney stone."

"What can I do about that?"

"Go to a doctor, and hope it isn't true. Luckily, most of us carry a spare kidney. You feel the pain on one side, right?"

"I'm not sure. It's a big, wide pain."

As the misty rain about us stopped and the air cleared, we saw a great thunderstorm swirl above the mountains. We watched the lightening strobe inside the cloud mass and cause the mountain peaks and cloud shadows to change shape and merge, as if gods locked in a dangerous battle threw silhouettes on a curtain.

Yvonne said "Nurses know men can't handle pain like women. Men think women exist to give birth, as if they hope for nothing more than house full of kids in the suburbs. They think all women become happy when they have children. Men want to believe that any woman will forget about her dreams, abandon her career, when they get pregnant, or find any opportunity to raise children, either their own or others. But the men also want to run away from a pregnant girlfriend. Even when a wife gets pregnant and becomes a mother, the distance between husband and wife grows. Sometimes they try to fill that gap with more children, and their children's friends."

"You like children?"

"Men are children. Even before they open their mouth to talk, you can see it in their faces, they think they know everything. They demand, cry and cry, or they get older and ask and ask and ask. You cannot make them understand, they learn by being stupid. Children cannot see danger, not even as teenagers. They pester their mothers, they want mom to be a child too, they want daddy to play with them, make them feel good, or they make their parents miserable. They never think they do wrong, never want to apologize.

If they do apologize, you see the birth of a real hypocrite. They're like salesmen who won't take no for an answer, but parents can't shut the door to escape them."

"Doesn't sound like you want children."

"Too needy, so crybaby. Too much like men. Especially men without money."

A little after sunset, we got off the bus in Quetzaltenango, hungry enough to eat a menu. We found a hotel, cheaper and better than our previous one in Xela.

I convinced Yvonne to take a shower later, with the argument that we should go eat first, then get back to the hotel room to clean up and go directly to bed.

"You know, we could probably get a phone call through from here."

We found one of Guatel's egg-shaped blue cowlings for a public phone near the Central Plaza. After a short wait for two Guatemalans to place their calls, I dialed the international operator and made a collect call back home.

The connection crackled, but we could hear each other.

"Where are you?" My mom asked.

"In Guatemala. Xela. It's called Quetzaltenango on the map."

"Why aren't you out of Guatemala? The news said they asked everyone to leave Guatemala. Aren't you worried about the epidemic?"

"So far, there isn't an epidemic. I can't leave yet, they have my passport in immigration."

"Why do they..."

"Before the earthquake, I asked for an extension of my visa. I need to get it back, because I don't want to get caught in Mexico without a passport. They could throw me in jail and make you guys try to prove my innocence."

"We worried about you for a few days. Didn't you try to call us?"

"The lines for the phones stretched around the block. We," I pinched myself and bit my lip, oops, almost let my French cat out of the bag. "A lot of people left Guatemala City for places less affected by the quake. You only worried a few days?"

"We got someone to call your guest house, that pension or whatever they call it. They said you passed by after the earthquake, so we figured you were OK. What's all this about a radio and a guitar?"

"What radio and guitar?"

"They talked about a radio and a guitar."

"Oh. I left my guitar behind, because my roommate's radio fell off the dresser and landed right on it. The radio crashed through the strings, broke some, smashed the wood and buried itself in the sound hole. Radio killed my guitar, basically."

"I bet you woke up in a hurry, all that noise."

"Oh it made a racket all right." I didn't want to let on that the earthquake caught me in someone else's room.

After we hung up, Yvonne too asked me "What's that about a radio and a guitar?"

We went to the same restaurant and ordered another unpronounceable Old World Spanish meal. We allowed our waiter, so happy to see us again, to suggest what we should order. He described the elaborate culinary process, which neither of us understood. We enjoyed his enthusiasm and excited gestures, at times so spastic that in his tuxedo uniform, he looked like a maimed bat.

After he left, Yvonne said "I think he likes you."

Up above on the balcony, we again dined all alone, in romantic tranquility, and with a proud pomposity inspired by our perch above the Central Plaza, as if Eva and Juan Perón, who dined on the balcony while they waited for the crowds to assemble in front of the National Palace. Below us, the scene repeated from a few days ago. A young well dressed Guatemalan man used the public address system to do a live broadcast on the radio, while he oversaw the Quetzaltenango citizen's donations of blankets, food, clothing and relief supplies for victims throughout the country.

The night fell down the slopes of the highland mountains that surrounded Xela. I wondered if this cold climate influenced the city's development into something of obvious superiority when compared to other Guatemalan towns. Xela exists in a temperate climate within the tropics, in the highland regions where cooler weather inspires activity, and allows industrious people to undertake productive projects. People could trust other's intentions, instead of a learned doubt due to tropical humidity and heat that sabotaged plans and buttressed fatalism.

The Spanish tore down the Mayan architecture; the temples, palaces, pyramids, walkways, ballcourts, and used the stone to construct public squares like this Central Plaza and park, and the colonial buildings that surrounded us. Mayan cities and temple complexes, built up over a thousand years, tumbled to the ground after the Spaniards' conquest in the year fifteen hundred and twenty two. Then as now, construction unearths artifacts and ancient sarcophaguses, and permits people to loot the archeological record even from the tombs of ancient royal lineages.

The piles of humanitarian aide for earthquake relief, clothing and blankets and stocks of canned foods, appeared smaller than before but big enough to remind us that this national tragedy continued.

Tomorrow morning, we head back into its black, quivering heart.

After we ate, we walked arm in arm as a defense against the cold winds that blew across the Quetzaltenango's Central Plaza. The announcer stood before the microphone and waited for his cue to go live on the national radio show.

The black sky shredded under moonlight, and we could see the ragged edges of clouds speed over the city toward the mountain peaks. The electric wires, strung from pole to pole down the streets, hummed and vibrated in the wind. Bits of airborne paper flew over tin cans that rolled in half-circles across the black cobblestones.

The entrance of the hotel felt hot inside as we walked the long hallway to our room. Yvonne started to undress. She wore her jacket open, and unbuttoned the front of her shirt so that her bra peeked out. She undid her belt and let it dangle in front of her loosened pants "more room for the food," she said.

Once inside the room, I threw my jacket across a chair and watch her leave a trail of clothing to the bathroom. Then I hear the shower turn on full blast. The water runs a while, then she screams. "This goddamn water's freezing! Doesn't anyone in this country shower before they go to bed? I hate to shower in the morning. I get sweaty in the day, not overnight!" She took a very quick cold shower.

I climbed into bed with some of my clothes on under the piles of blankets to warm myself up.

Yvonne came out with a towel wrapped under her armpits, and another as a turban on her head. She said "I want to apologize for how I acted up on the mountain."

"Which time?"

She stared at me for a few seconds. "I got upset, and I acted badly, because I felt you didn't help me. You might help me next time, you know."

"Oh, you mean about the campfire."

"Yes, the campfire. I feel bad about it, because you felt sick. I should respect that. You complained of a headache all day. I think the altitude got to you."

"Forget about it. Maybe the altitude got to you too."

"I never get altitude sickness. Never."

Her feminist attitude irritates me. "Wrong day of the month?"

"Bastard." She rubbed the towel deep into her ear. "You men always say that. I try to apologize for my actions, and you try to blame it on my womanhood."

"Don't you think certain days of the month make you moody?"

"Men think so, whenever a woman gets upset. They feel superior."

"What about it? Don't you feel that you lose control easier on certain days?"

"When you get cramps, then you talk to me about it, OK? People think women lose control, get hysterical, faint or something, so women who believe that shit, do faint and get hysterical. It's expected. Useless. I try to apologize for my behavior because I lost my temper, but you blame me. You knew how to help me, but you get some sick pleasure out of my problem, or what?"

"I felt sick. Didn't enjoy anything. I analyzed your technique lighting campfires to find out how to correct it. After you light so many fires, it comes natural, like instinct. I don't think about it step by step anymore, you know."

"Well, thank you for the education. I want to apologize, not for you, but for me. I get a little crazy sometimes, and it scares me."

"Happens all the time. Don't worry about it."

"But I worry. You don't know how angry I felt. It happened other times, you see."

"Forget it. Apology accepted, though not needed. What's the worst thing you've ever done?"

"Promise you won't tell?"

"I promise. Don't worry. Who'm I gonna tell?"

"When I lived with my boyfriend, I drop him off at his job, so we leave for work together every morning, and argue the whole way. We walk to the garage and it starts, every day the same. We open the car doors and argue from one side to the other, until we agree to stop and get in the car. One day, I got so mad, I didn't wait for our agreement and sat down inside the car. He stood there and yelled Will you answer me? Answer me! I didn't. I started the car, and put it into reverse, and just pushed on the gas, and it took off backwards." Yvonne said, and looked at me with a scared innocence.

"So? You run over him?"

"I don't know if I should tell you this. Promise not to tell anyone about this?"

"Who am I going to tell? We have friends in common? I promise. OK, I promise."

"I backed out of the garage with both doors open." She looked as if she expected a response from me.

"So?"

"I almost hurt him. I didn't think about him or anything, I was so mad."

"What happened?"

"I knocked both the car's doors off. They hit the garage door, so narrow, both doors caught and snapped back, bent and fell off."

"Could you bend them back?"

"You're not listening. They both fell onto the garage floor. He got really angry, but scared, too. I sat there with the engine running, looking at the garage with these two car doors on the cement inside, and him standing there next to them."

"Did he hit you or something?"

"No, he was so scared and mad he stood like a statue, looked at me with his mouth open. Then he put his hand into his hair, like this, you know?"

"What did you do then?"

"Me? I laughed. You should see his face. I laughed at him so hard, and that's what scared me."

"Scared of what?"

"When I stopped laughing, we both realized I could really hurt him. He turned around and went back in the house. It was my car, not his, thank God. We broke up soon after that."

"Better late than never."

"Better sooner. Always better sooner. We wanted to, a long time before."

"Most people say that, after it happens. Self-defense. Makes them feel like they fought a noble fight against the inevitable."

"You promise not to tell anybody?"

"Yes, yes. No, I won't. I promised already."

"I learned a lot. I know how to break up with men, like this." She snapped her fingers. "Easy. Now I move so fast, I knock their doors off."

"Blow their doors off. You pass them by so fast it blows their doors off."

"Exactly. There's more than one way to blow a man off. I can think of five or six now. And you're next."

I wondered what she meant by that, but decided to smile and take it in the best way possible.

Because of a reputation for unfriendliness, France didn't interest me. I would rather go to the Amazon than Europe, too civilized and uppity, from what I heard. And the French don't bathe enough. Prissy, pissy, and pissed off. Yvonne's attitude pushes others down to raise herself up, and at times she expects the rest of us to confess our inferiority. She jokes about people as pigeons in the park, docile and harmless, so silly all they do is eat and shit, too numerous to count or kill. I thought she wanted to train me to share her hypocritical laugh and fake my ride on her wavelength, as someone to support her every pose and charade, as she slummed her way through a Universe that didn't deserve her.

Months ago, at first sight on that dock over the bottomless waters of Lake Atitlán, Yvonne attract me with her lithe form stretched out to bronze on the gray wood. Seemed like a miracle when we met again. Now, I realized that most travelers meet each other several times over the months in a small country where all roads run to the post office. We guidebook-driven travelers swept along together in the mighty currents of the main tourist flow, which revolved around the post office as the central vortex. Yvonne and I spoke the same instinctual language of youth. We felt immortal not immoral, clean of all sin or blame, and the desperate instinct to couple and procreate took us by surprise.

Our physical attraction for each other imploded us together with the push of an external reality more foreign than either of us to each other.

Both Yvonne and I neglected to bring a camera along on our journey.

She liked my drawings, and said God blessed me with a bit of talent, which insulted the amount of hard work I invested to accomplish the little I could. I knew my lack of natural talent all too well from contact with people with talent, yet she claimed that with my artist's eye, by duty I should take advantage of all technologies and take advice from accomplished people, like the German at the Christmas party on Lake Atitlán, who took photos to cart back home and create artwork from later in his studio, in homey comfort, with all his necessary tools at hand.

I showed Yvonne the sketches of fallen palm fronds on a mountain trail in Santa Clara, the hole in the tree alongside the Ermita del Carmen, the dragon I drew on the morning of the Sea Snake, the sketches of small groups of Guatemalans, the Chihuahua desert Ocotillos like frozen grenade explosions, quick ballpoint pen portraits of Mayan faces in Indian Village típica costumes, and other sketches of the feminine side of Meso-American beauty.

After dozens of searches through my small backpack, extractions of the metal blades of its internal support, turning every article inside out to find some forgotten stash of traveler's checks or a big wad of almost worthless Mexican Pesos at twelve and a half cents each, I still refused believe I could run through that much money so fast. Though a meager sum in most American's eyes, a little went a long way down here.

I imagined myself stranded in a few weeks, poised to shatter my American ideal of rugged individualism in front of a telephone, ready to ruin my adventurer's reputation back home. My estimate put me in some tiny Mexican town in the desert mountains, where I would enter a small notary public office to use one of their three rough lumber telephone stalls to talk into a nineteen fifties black desktop telephone and beg for financial aid to get me out of this mess, and then beg a ride to the nearest major city with a Bank of America.

Travelers with funds take courage from the fact that they can retreat, return home, and look for work, even though it feels like a failure, an aborted mission, a scuttled attempt to continue the dream to its unknown conclusion. To arrive at that point of surrender makes it reasonable to ask someone for just enough money to finance a luxurious six hour flight back to whatever we spent these long months of meanders to get away from, which inspires a hundred fantasies of how to find a job, or how to make money, to repay that kindness.

In our simple tiny hotel of wood and diagonal striped wall patterns painted with a carved rubber roller, Yvonne and I felt confident to sign in as husband and wife. Yvonne told me about the embarrassment of one male companion who asked for the honeymoon suite in a luxury hotel, and the desk clerk asked for a copy of the marriage license.

We made love, or shared sex, as proud, strong, and healthy young people in a companionate relationship, not as newlyweds on a lovey-dovey romantic honeymoon. As a goal, we tried to stay excited about our surroundings and vibrate in harmony with the basic frequencies of life, the rhythms of morning, noon, and night, and we didn't care much about how our vibrations looked to others. In this manner, we also insulated ourselves against the prospective matchmakers and sexual predators, even thought we confirmed the Guatemalans' opinion that Americans and Europeans enjoyed too much sexual license, and therefore the females deserved their reputation as 'easy' sluts, prostitutes who don't charge. Latin American men probably saw white men as too attractive competitors for, and predators of, the local virgins.

I asked her if she used any birth control, even though I felt foolish and ashamed that we never mentioned it earlier. that day I felt an itch down there, sensations that made me wonder if we shared a venereal disease. I began to appreciate the value of condoms.

"No, I'm a good Catholic girl. I use the rhythm method."

"You menstruate exactly every twenty eight days?" I could feel my body break into a sweat.

"Yes. Clocks' work. To the hour. Like a clock's work, how do you say it?"

"Clockwork."

"That's me. Regular like clockwork."

Some nights we lay in bed together and tried to read, but felt obligated to talk, or mumble, to each other for hours until no response, until our own lids shut and our faces sagged. We jerked ourselves awake again, for neither wished to insult the other and fall asleep first.

One night, far into the wee small hours of the morning, an instinct awakened me with the insane urge to impregnate her, no matter the odds against it. She rejected my advances, at first, but then surrendered and seemed to enjoy it.

Said she did not remember in the morning. "You know, I like to travel with older, experienced men. Men who could be my father. At least they let you get a good night's sleep. Young men act like sex junkies."

"You don't like sex?"

"There's a big difference between quantity and quality. You represent quite a break from my normal standards," she said.

I looked puzzled, I'm sure.

Yvonne laughed at me and said "The rich older gentlemen offer a lifetime of wisdom and culture, and love to instruct young girls in the romantic arts, as tour guides for the finer things in life. They try so hard to please a woman in bed."

"I don't please you in bed?"

"You have no idea how."

"Like what? You have orgasms, don't you?"

"Not with you. It's not your fault you've got plenty to learn. The journey's often better than the destination."

"So why do we have sex at all?"

"You need it for us to stay together."

"What's that mean? You need me to be older, or richer?"

"When a rich old man and a young woman like me become intimate enough to know how to fight with each other, then all my youth and supposed beauty becomes superficial, useless. When I can't understand them, their superiority pisses me off. I try not to believe it's my inexperience, but when I never figure it out their way, I refuse to change my opinions just to make them happy. Then the silences grow longer and longer, and the man looks like Dracula, a vampire who needs fresh blood to maintain his illusion of youth."

"Any man would feel lucky to be with you, at any age."

"Thank you. Men say my presence compliments the room. I take it as a compliment, but feel like a decoration. I learned to promote myself as a classy woman. Classy men want to be with me, because I talk about music and art, and not embarrass them at dinner. That earned me invitations to wonderful parties and intimate gatherings. A man once paid me to fly to a New York party. I told you? Men helped put me through school in Paris. After I graduated, I planned to travel with men around the world."

"Why did you stop in Guatemala?"

"A rich old man selects the game, and controls the prizes. He calls the shots, takes his turns, and pays the bills. See how well I learned the American language of games? Bridge, poker, badminton, ping pong, skeet shoots, polo, I've seen it all. One day in Baja California, I couldn't stand it, the heat of the desert, the deep sea fishing, and I hated myself. Any girl can abandon a man in an instant, but I learned how to convince most of them to give me a little money to get back home."

"Don't you miss the luxuries?"

"Luxuries are a prison. All the luxury hotels look the same. You forget the name of the country you travel in. When you meet other travelers in first class, they have endless discussions about hotels, food, and restaurants and who they know where. They name celebrities as close friends, invite each other to visit when its clearly impossible because they're never home, they're always on the road. I got so bored I was ready to light my hair on fire if I heard another discussion about someone's personal friendships with the famous chefs of five star hotels."

We fell asleep between the crisp sheets, wrapped around each other's warmth against the chill of night.

I woke up to a low rumble, the ground shook, windows rattled, and the walls groaned. We did not move. I thought OK, go ahead and kill us. I'm tired of days and nights full of false alarms. I'm here, off to sleep. Shake, rattle, and roll all you like.

We heard a big truck outside. No one stirred,
felt like everyone listened. Everybody awake. No sirens.

Silence.

Yvonne said, "Do you feel like the ground trembles every moment, ever since the first quake?"

"I thought it was just my imagination, but it comes back by itself." I listened for the rumble of the truck to return.

"I feel really scared when I feel a truck pass."

"Me too."

About seventeen minutes into a new Tuesday, February tenth, we felt a brief and weaker reminder of the first deadly 7.5 quake that tore apart roads, collapsed bridges, imploded churches, and sloughed of mountainsides to bury entire villages under mudslides or their own adobe walls. It destroyed families in flight with a rain of heavy ceramic roof tiles, and ripped northern and southern Guatemala apart with a crack from east to west, sometimes opened up nine feet across, a deep vertical chasm that displaced the two halves of Guatemala by a yard and a half.

Seismologists measured the Tuesday, February tenth quake at five on the Richter scale, centered under the town of El Progreso, though not many people there cared one way or the other. The first quake flattened it six days ago, and killed twelve percent of the population, which included the governor, the mayor, and the justice of the peace.

In El Progresso that first day of the earthquake, forty six year old President Kjell Laugerud arrived at six PM to find the village's buildings destroyed and seven hundred cadavers lined up in the street. The earthquake left only one big building undamaged, the modern Catholic Church.

When he returned a month later, people worked at unburying their houses, and threw the rubble into the street for heavy machinery to cart away. The Emergency committee used the church as a storehouse, with medical supplies and piles of corn dumped on the floor.

The President ordered all that stuff moved out of the church.

"But where do you expect us to ride out the rest of winter, under a tree? February weather is crazy, but March and April are the hottest months, then the rains come. Where will we store everything?"

"I will provide you with a provisional shelter."

Nearby, a full-figured ladina Guatemalan woman with pox on her face, complains to no one in particular. "What's the use of talking to the President, when those who hand out aid only give things to the pretty young girls. Isn't it true you're my girlfriend, they say, all smiles and flirtatious, then they give out clothing and supplies. For you, my love, because you are my love. Que falta de educación. Malcriados." Bad manners, bad upbringing, lowlifes.

A bystander says "If it's true they give only to beautiful young girls, you must have a houseful."

"Hey, listen to me," she says. "I deserve respect. I'm a señora, a married woman. I'm forty five years old."

"That's one year younger than the President. He likes younger women, too."

When I returned from my shower, I found Yvonne still tucked in bed with one of those tiny but thick Mexican comic books. I looked at Yvonne and said, "That feels so much better."

She grunted in response.

My clothes, washed in the shower, I draped across my backpack and hung around the room to dry. "Got plans for today?"

"I should say goodbye to you."

I stopped and looked at her. She still read, or pretended to.

"What made you say that?"

She put the book down. "I don't want to go back to the city."

"Neither do I. I need to go back and get my passport." I felt stunned, sluggish. "Is this goodbye?"

"Might as well. Must happen sooner or later."

"Alright." Lately, I couldn't understand her until she filled me in with a detail of one of the fine points of European history. Neither of us belonged here, nor to each other, nor to the same continent. Not much to base a relationship on. I didn't speak French, and at times I doubted that she meant what I understood, what it sounded like it meant in normal English, or the way she translated it to imperfect English. Other times, I decided she did mean to say what it sounded like, and I did not much like that either. She's French. Big difference in how French people think and act, and it took a long time for me to acknowledge that I didn't understand Yvonne. So I felt neutral about this separation, looked forward to the opportunity to continue alone, and felt certain I would feel worse without her. For a while, anyway. I'd get used to it.

In sum, I failed. I failed to see things from her point of view.

She laughed. "You're not angry with me then?" She lay back on the bed with that smug crooked French smile.

"I'm throwing in the towel." I threw my towel at her, followed it and jumped onto the bed beside her to give her a little kiss. "I don't want to lose you."

"I think you'll survive." She turned away, cold again. Then she smiled at me, reached out, put her hand on my thigh, caressed it absent minded, without affection. "We must make the best of it, every moment of our lives. We are young. Alive. Survived an earthquake together."

"And now it's lose the girl and gain your soul."

"I like the way you speak English. At least I can learn grammar from you, even when I don't like what you think. I learn from you, when I really listen. But you never tell me the truth, do you?"

"Truth about what?"

"About anything."

"Maybe that's because I don't know myself. I'm always guessing."

"Tell me, why did you come to Guatemala? Tell me the truth. Una vez al año no hace daño."

We both sat and looked at each other a while, then she said, "I want to know. You come here alone, to Guatemala, instead of College, or the family business in Michigan. Why."

"How far back should I go?"

"The beginning, perhaps?"

"You want to hear about my preschool memories of a babysitter who put some little girl in the bed with me, and I remember she smelled like corn? After that, whether it happened or not, as I boy I practiced giving her all the space on the bed. I scrunched to my side of the bed, to give her all the room, if she ever came back."

"You expect me to believe that? A little girl who smells like corn brought you to Guatemala?"

"My eighth grade teacher deserves the blame, then. Young guy, Mr. Kimble. He taught eighth grade social studies and geography. One day, he lost control of the class. Almost all the class showed no interest in South America. They wouldn't quiet down, and ignored him. But I watched. He leaned over his desk, and said to no one in particular, over everyone's head, that "if you get the chance to go to South America, go. Go" he said. "South of the border." He told the whole class and nobody but I heard him. At least I saw his lips utter those words, or something similar, and I thought I heard his voice through the noise of rowdy kids. "Learn a little Spanish, and go when you get the opportunity, just go."

I saw a tear start in one eye, I swear, a little trickle he wiped away as if an itch. Not sure, but I thought so, and remembered it with more clarity than the observation deserved, unless by instinct or some nonverbal recognition, I got it right. I remember that moment more vividly than any other moment in all my years in school."

"Is this going to be a horror story, somebody gets killed, or what? Why Guatemala?"

"I discovered Guatemala in my mom's Encyclopedia Brittanica. I took two semesters of Spanish in college, and afterwards, my mom dropped me off on the freeway so I could hitchhike to the Texas-Mexican Border."

"Your mom dropped you off to go to Mexico?"

"Saved me at least a three mile hike to the nearest big road."

"No friends, or girlfriend?"

"No."

"No one else you wanted to go along?"

"I asked everybody."

"Even Joanna?"

"Joanna? How do you know about her?"

"You mentioned her. Called me Joanna a couple of times."

"She means nothing to me."

"Maybe I mean nothing to you."

I didn't know what to say for a while. "I guess you think that we must say goodbye sooner or later, because... of what?"

"Because it cannot work out between us. I have no plans, you have plans. Or you don't, and I do, vice versa, whatever. Anyway, you are too American. No culture, it would take too long to educate you."

"To give you orgasms?"

"Ah! He knows! I can't believe you. That too, but I was thinking about how you embarrass me."

"So this is the end."

"I think it's for the best. Don't you?"

"You are right, as usual. Any last requests?"

"A little thing, really. I want to get to know who you really are. I'm tired of your strong, silent, farm boy act. I want you to tell me the truth."

"I told you the story of my life."

"Oh yes. The brief version. You left out your trip through Mexico, before you met me."

"Not much to tell. I passed through Mexico to get to Guatemala."

She laughed. "You mention trains, Guadalajara, San Blas, and some Communists who kidnapped 'us, oops! I mean me.' Then you confuse me with her, this Joanna, right? Sometimes something reminds you of something you did with her, and you ask me about it like you expect me to remember it too. You can't jog my memory about something we didn't share, so stop trying. Tell me about her, and all your trip."

"Was it good for you too?"

"No. You're a young one, you are. You need to learn how to please a woman. I don't know where you hid for so long. We probably won't see each other again, from the sound of your pocketbook. And since you have no urge to visit France, and I saw too much of the United States already, it doesn't sound hopeful, does it? So tell me everything. That is my last request."

"Last request? What's this, you want me to assassinate my own character, right here, now? Am I the executioner here? Am I supposed to take the hood off of myself, or take it off you?"

"Off of me. Let me see you as you really are."

I saw no way to escape. I took her new curiosity about me as a compliment. "Do I get a last request?"

She laughed. "I already know what you need. Money, and a mother. You're still a little boy when it comes to women."

"You say that about all the boys. Let's make a deal. I'll tell you everything, if you'll teach me how to love."

"Deal."

CHAPTER 18: Life On Another Peninsula

Yvonne wanted to know everything, and peppered me with her questions until I stumbled upon things she thought formative. Then she grilled me about the details. Sometimes she led me to an insight, or a probable cause, or a psychoanalytical anti-Freudian feminist insult, which made me think she aimed me there from the beginning. At any rate, she plucked these incidents out of my personal oral history, though not in this refined literary form, of course.

Here goes the gist of it.

In High School, most of the kids I hung with didn't merit the label of friend, though I called them that at the time. My fault, in retrospect, that I didn't know better.

Some people think families should avoid arguments. My mother's parents came from England. I heard a joke once about a twelve step program for the children of the Brittish. Imagine, a whole nation proud of their stiff upper lip. How could you tell when someone's excited, or whose the wit? If nobody laughs, everything's monotone. The English need to believe that their newly independent colonies will wake up every morning and thank God for the extreme good fortune that the English colonized them, instead of any other country.

I remember breakfasts at Grandma's house in Detroit, my egg nestled down in a little wooden chalice with a painted smile. All our breakfast eggs wore little woolen caps to keep their heads hot. Then we crack their heads open and eat their soft boiled brains with a spoon. My brother and I fought over the Charley McCarthy spoon.

The English love animals. Some Brits count bird species they see over time. One famous group of bird lovers identify each individual wild geese in every winter's returned flock. In this viewing room, they made a wall chart that depicts the feather markings of each bird. All the English love dogs, high class, low class, and over the centuries they selected and bred utility dogs to create specific breeds. They hunt ducks with retrievers, rats with terriers, and foxes with "hounds on horseback" as the English grammar book put it. Imagine all those English animal lovers as spectators who enjoy the bizarre cruelty of foxhunts. Those older aristocrats with monocles do look like hounds on horseback.

My family's brand of English reserve means we forego all normal niceties, the small talk of the human primate in full groom. Our six to fourteen housedogs served as conduits of familiar affection, each petted and cooed to, then passed along to the next person, as if we loaded them with affection cooties.

Get togethers offered the more well read family members plump opportunities for rapturous excursions into the forbidden territories of sex, religion, and politics, but never personal income. Everyone partook of a little Devil's Advocacy to provoke Granny, and we all tried to hide the earnest desire on the part of all present to bump Granny into new heights of outrageous exasperation until she reached that state of stammering speechlessness, when her teacup clatters against its saucer and she falls back in her seat, one hand over her heart, and starts to pray. Sweet victory.

We all felt proud of our rigorous intellectual tradition, cold, humorless Grandfather Arthur, a "walking encyclopedia." This patriarch scheduled trains. When he retired from the railroad, it took six men to replace him. Mom inherited the gene for repeated stories, like one about the shocked look on the faces of members of her Dog Club when she shared the results of her IQ test. Our family tradition of vigorous debate also allows us to attack ad homonym and go to the quick of each other's well known vulnerabilities. We relish those comic facial expressions at that delicious moment when old wounds reopen. Confirms our intimate knowledge of what makes each other tick.

In junior high and high school, I started to become an autodidact, and studied arts and letters, but before I could let either side of my brain dominate, the sixties happened.

Junior year, and I did not lose my virginity. Loser.

A senior girl, short black hair and eyelashes like tangles of dead spiders around a drainpipe, came on to me. She easily seduced me with her two big eyes as echoes of the round frontal offer of weekend intimacies, which gave me five days of anxiety.

I met Debby in a Volkswagen. These two senior girls offered me a ride home from school one Spring day, because they heard I played guitar. They even talked to me, a mere junior, and they asked me if I listened to Jimi Hendrix. No, who is Jimi Hendrix? They played some Jimi Hendrix for me, and asked me if I smoked dope, No, what is dope? and they laughed at me. The big eyed girl admitted she tried LSD, only because her doctor prescribed some kind of medication derived from chemicals similar to LSD. She had this glaucoma eye condition, or something. This dope smoking, girl, who's wearing a black and white op art checkered polyester pantsuit, told me she felt attracted to me, wanted me, and would I help her break up with her boyfriend, her famous and long time steady relationship with her popular and sought after and respected boyfriend, Chuck Tardeman, who always wore a Salvation Army military jacket.

With all the brutish aplomb of immaturity and the most fearless hippie philosophy of free love and recreational drugs, a recent import to Michigan from California's Summer of Love two years before, she asked me "Are you still a virgin?" Her big eyes shined behind those lashes that looked like spiders stuck in asphalt, her pink frosted lips in a half smile. Freckles started to work their way to the surface layer of base, cream, color, and powder. "I mean, have you ever been drunk?"

When I said no, she said, "That won't last long."

Both girls laughed together at me, a lot.

When her best girlfriend Barbara leaned over the steering wheel, and her long straight black hair fell in a curtain around her face. Her laugh coughed each lung full of air through bright red lipstick, lips that looked crowded on her face, and changed shape often, two sausages of swollen cherries.

Debby says "This weekend, I promise, I swear to God, this next weekend, I'm not joking, I'll change your life forever."

Four six days, I obsessed about it, every moment. Sweat blossomed in my armpits. In one lucky minute of one otherwise unimportant day, I realized, at a sluggish pace due to my inexperience in the detection of duplicity, hypocrisy, cowardice, and the instinctual lure of naughtiness, that she wanted me to be the bad guy. She wanted me to take the blame for the destruction of one of the most popular and visible couples in our High School. In my Junior year. What I do this year, I have to live with next year.

She offers me a weekend like it's the beginning of something, and I suspect she wants to dump him and me, and go on to bigger and better things.

I talked to her on the phone a couple of times that week. When that big night came around, she did not answer the phone. I called a couple of times, but gave up and knew she played a cruel joke on me.

That next Monday, at school, I found out that she drowned in a bathtub, home alone, that Friday night. A victim of her Doctor, some said. He prescribed her a medicine derived from LSD.

At least, that's what her best girlfriend Barbara told me, as she hugged me and cried, chewed cinnamon gum, and taught me to French kiss in earth shaking sadness. She and I made it very clear to each other to keep our conspiracy quiet and never reveal my secret date with the late Teenybopper.

Of that Fall, I remember the funeral most of all. Barbara and I went together, as the secretive, demonic Anti-couple. Afterwards, she drove that Volkswagen through drifts of fallen leaves in Fallsburg park, where she gave me French kiss lessons with proof of her expertise in how to block men's hands before they reach their targets.

Most of the senior and junior classes went to the funeral in the Episcopal Church. Many marveled at how well her boyfriend appeared as he walked in, in that baggy green droopy military jacket, how he kept himself together, eyes so sad, cheeks still wet from a waterfall of tears. We watched his slow stride, and saw that one wane, brave smile on his way into the church, and we watched him drag himself out afterwards, crumpled, another lost soldier of the vanquished, who limps home in disgrace.

He'd feel worse if she ditched him and ran off with another guy. Dead, she wouldn't pop into view all the time and torture him with her desirability and aloofness, the way an ex-lover might.

Now I wonder if age and experience, or an incomplete recollection of events, allows me to accept the possibility that maybe he killed her in a jealous rage. If Barb or I ever opened our mouths, the police would investigate us.

Maybe Barb did it, furious about some trashy free love incident I knew nothing about.

Anyway, when the Sixties happened, the new interconnected world of Egghead youth collectively thought they lost their innocence, and then freely proved they could inhabit states of pure innocence for years. Through new musical forms and instruments, drugs, government repression, cultural ideas from the world's universities, Eastern religions and exotic cultures, widespread use of The Pill which liberated women, the Viet Nam war, the antiwar movement, and then a couple of deadly skirmishes with police against college students who exercised their human right to civil disobedience, many young Americans lost faith in the conservatism of the fifties, and the blind loyalty that makes military might right. Young Eggheads around the world examined other nations as Eggcrates for the development of equally valid cultures with different philosophies, lifestyles, and religions and drugs, or meditation that defined alternative realities. So through the popular consumer culture of superstars that traveled to other countries (and California), people began to recognize other realities as valid cultures, with their own languages, psychologies, religions, and sciences that ensure survival of society for thousands of years, and made us innocents feel secure in our common humanity.

This led some Eggheads to the idea of the Universal Yolk.

After a varied number of failed relationships, us eggcrate siblings eventually awoke to the inappropriateness of our interpersonal style within our common culture. Not a pretty process. After the third or forth time one hears "Didn't your mother breast feed you?" it cracks your eggshell a bit. The whole family compared notes about our eggcrate, incubated the results, and sat a long time, blank and unmoved, shoulder to shoulder.

Somebody in our family came up with the idea we should get religion, become Born Again, to get in touch with our hot and runny Universal Yolks, the part inside that cries out to merge into the company of other human beings. The idea of membership in any religion repulsed us committed rugged individualists, but in the end, after we considered the alternative as a long Hard Boiled Alone, some agreed to give God a chance. We got a religion for a time, at the same time, to experience the Universal Yoke.

When we compared notes, we recognized a common point about religions. Most religions complain about the other religions. Each splinter group uses their individual interpretation of sacred texts to prove only their cosmology, their method of worship, and above all, their forecast for the end of the world. Imagine a restaurant full of hungry people with the same menu, but each sees only what they want to eat. By the principles of evolution, any religious menus full of bad food won't last long, so any religion that survives probably offers the same essential ingredients for the benefit of its followers. The side dishes get us into trouble.

Within each religion, exist two kinds of disgruntled members. The Eggheads who never examined their own Universal Yolk, and those with a personal relationship with their Universal Yolk, who recognize those who have not, and probably feel sorry for them. Those without contact with their Universal Yolk play power games, and react defensively to contradiction and sometimes feel so frustrated they act aggressive toward their own supporters. Both the most fanatical of those, and those who almost maintain contact with the Yolk but then lose their way, try to crack other eggs to kill the messengers, and forever lose their own message. They cannot see the fertile power of a thermodynamic counterbalance called life, the anti-chaos, the germ of an idea of increased order, the thing that wills itself into self existence in the Universal Yolk. This power causes life to evolve in fits and tweaks, till it develops self consciousness, so that the aware feel indebted and responsible to try and ensure the continuation and perpetuation of life for the good of the Universal Yolk.

Satan does not exist, unless one considers the Second Law of Thermodynamics, the increase in chaos, the tendency for things to break down. The universe does not exist as a battleground between God and Satan. Two kinds of moralities cause conflicts in the world. Those who recognize the moral right of every individual to chose their own path as long as it doesn't hurt anyone else and respects that right in others, and those people who try to control others. Both of these moralities, the controller and the exerciser of unconditional love, may exist in the same individual at different times, in different situations, or in regards to distinct moral issues.

As a family, we youngish ones compared notes about our explorations of other eggcrates, incubated the results, and sat a long time, blank and unmoved, shoulder to shoulder, until one Egghead jostled us to mutter "It's like God uses atheists to practice juggling, because we always make him laugh."

When the neighborhood decided to close the "one room school" (in the basement of the church and inside an adjacent one room building), they forced us kids into separate school districts by age. Some members of the same family, like my brother and I, split up and took long bus rides to either of the two local villages about seven miles distant.

Our family lived on the edges of two public school bus lines, which means we , got off last at the end of the day, and at six thirty AM waited for the empty bus to arrive in the subzero predawn winter. We wore scarves across the face, mittens over gloves on our hands thrust into deep into pockets, and peered against the papercut cold of wind gusts. A distant yellow blur of the bus's lights through the snowfall preceded its struggle up the icy hill to the corner of our street, a quarter mile distant.

At the end of the day, we rode the bus all alone for the last mile to the last stop, our house, and got off at four o'clock on frigid January afternoons that slipped into darkness at five like a cold gray marble dropped into a bucket of old engine oil.

Things improved after the sixth grade, when my brother and I both excelled at Junior High School. The village daughters of the best families warmed up to us, and once invited us to a birthday party. A couple of male teachers hinted at good things to come, "remember to come back and visit after graduation."

I thought they respected and cared about me. Perhaps they did, in their misguided way. Maybe they received compensation for each seventeen year old child they helped conscript into military service.

After my first year in high school, our mother, in a fit of maternal responsibility, fell victim to the hubris that This Village School District's Not Good Enough For My Kids and decided to redraw the local school district borderlines. With our new stepfather of four years, they canvassed the neighborhood to convince everyone of the certain benefits, in both education and property values, that would follow upon inclusion into the rapid growth of the nearby upscale suburban school district.

Our future lay assured, and waited for us to discover it.

The Neighbors Brauwnought

My stepfather related his experience with a very poor and humble family, the Brauwnoughts, of less than adequate intellectual resources. Their children bounced from Special Education classes to normal classes with kids several years younger than themselves. My stepfather hung out with them to get their vote for the other school district, and told us about one dinner he shared with this extended clan of four generations. They all lived in one rectangular cement block structure, which us kids laughed at. When they got a stove with a stovepipe, they broke one windowpane out of a window and forced the stovepipe through. It leaked fumes which blackened the other three glass panes with soot. Then they tried to clean it with varnish.

Mr. Brauwnought tried to seal the space between the round stovepipe and the empty wood window frame with old woolens, which even the preteen kids looked sideways at, so obvious a fire hazard. The fire trucks came out to their place several times a year, for grease fires on the stove, or when their untended garbage fire jumped out of the rusty oil drum and licked across their meadow towards my mom's forests. One time, their kids played with matches out back and made a fence of fire that danced across the fields. The fire trapped them atop one of the piles of boulders and field stones left a hundred years ago by farmers, who every spring before they plowed, plucked this winter's crop of frost heaved boulders out of the sandy glacial deposits that roll like dunes of gravel under the pine forests of those days, which they wiped out back then to construct Chicago.

Our tall oak forests came in as secondary growth.

After each time my step dad eats dinner at the Brauwnoughts, he returns so brim full he overflow with guffaws and giggles. He tells the tales at dinner with us, many phrases meant for my mom's ears only, with double meanings and mature innuendos. He describes how, even before they finish dinner, the fat tattooed husband of their slack jawed, wet lipped, blonde and always pregnant daughter, gets up and wipes the chicken grease off his mouth with the back of his meaty hand and, without a word to anyone else, grunts at his wife. He pulls on her arm to drag her off her seat and into the bedroom.

My stepfather could recreate the husband's grunts with great skill around our own dinner table. I know this for a fact, because he did it often for six months to get a laugh. With that aural joke up his sleeve, he would wait, as our family ate in complete innocence, for the right moment to make that noise and crack everybody up, which wiggled his pesky figurative fingers under the uptight British ribs of mom. At the precise inter-gulp moment of the youngest child's drink of milk, he would grunt like that Brauwnought girl's husband, and in fear of milk spray, we laughed out of control, compounded by mom's exasperated and dishwater tenderized little fists clenched to make ineffectual bangs that made the silverware clatter.

The neighborhood's property value did increase, along with school tax rates, and some neighbors felt the pinch and moved out. Mother's property increased in value. She thought she always did the best for her kids, and felt relieved as she watched the bus from the village school district pass us by while we stood out in the cold and waited for the suburban district's bus. The village bus went on its way to pick up the unlucky families that lived on the other side of the road.

Our bus came along a little later, and took us to a brand new school in a brand new suburb full of the Nuevo Rich. Their children amplified their parent's socio pathologies; the cliques of status, greed, rampant one-upmanship, consumerism, and neurotic corporate group-think in a constant search for more status, which in a child's simplistic thought process, meant put others down or underfoot to raise oneself to a position of superiority.

Early in my career at the new school, I remember one exam in biology where only I knew the answer to all the questions, one hundred percent correct. The other kids looked at me like I'd done something wrong. I learned what it meant to forget your place. It means go back to the end of the line, the back of the bus, through the servant's entrance.

In other words, you don't belong, and that need to belong comes in at number five in my version of Maslow's Hierarchy of Needs towards self actualization, right after food, clothing, shelter, and sex.

The School of Cliques

The new school district encircled a wide rural area where two rivers came together and included a wooden covered bridge near the rumored ancient site of a Native American "Indian" village. The old township became a "bedroom community" for workers who commuted into the nearby city, fifteen miles away. The community benefited from a local-turned-national pyramid scheme business that exploded into a global enterprise, and with the new tax resources and economic power, a modern suburbia arrived with construction projects that built roads to wind through woodlands punctuated by driveways to elegant homes, almost out of sight of each other due to the intentional construction around all the trees.

The first of these mansions, a little larger than normal for that decade, nestled in the woods along the rivers. Those blessed with the money for this brand of rural upward mobility moved into what once resembled countryside, dairy and hay farms separated by leafy acres of elm and oak forests delineated by a rusty wire or a low rock wall.

Their kids imitated the parent's snobbery, and soon we all knew who came from the richest families, the same ones teachers pandered to, considered the most intelligent by administration for the "advanced placement" classes, and by the subliminal virtues of status, voted in as candidates for the Kings and Queens of homecoming by their sub-peers.

As if to prove the rich kids superiority on all levels, the coaches took it upon themselves to promote the children of favored families as the most talented adolescent athletes. Coaches trained them with special consideration, as opportunities for invitations to their parent's house to receive pledges of economic support. Coaches help promote the gifted and privileged into the limelight as sports heroes and in this manner, become personal family friends to the community's power elite.

As ex military men, these High School sports coaches stood at such a severe salute they looked ready to slap their own backs. They basked in the blind, tribal loyalties that exclude moral thought and came alive in efforts to invoke the killer spirit in their young athletes.

The kids clumped into cliques based upon each trendy forest-enclosed neighborhood. Their conversations often passed over my head, or underfoot, face offs that contained keywords to competitions in areas I found invisible and unintelligible, the brand names of fashion, cars, alcohol, the names of the developers or architects, the size of incomes and houses, the names dropped to earn status by who their parents knew, and vaporous concepts like their family's "net worth" and extent of political influence.

My interest in this school and its segmented society plummeted over the next three years. Senior year, everything crashed and burned, along with my grades, in a quiet Midwestern way, through a responsible and cautious debauchery, a library researched and open eyed exploration into alcohol abuse, and a search for alternatives to marijuana and tobacco to roll up into cigarettes. For a few months, my brother and I tried various house plants when mom stepped out for the three mile drive to the local grocery store.

I couldn't keep up nor understand the changes in my body, mystified by the disappearance of smooth hairless skin, and attempted to find satiation of my nescient sexual urges through pornography or callous treatment of short term girlfriends, and with one longer term love achieved a level of sexual openness from which I fled, terrified. This beautiful girl, a high school junior and not a great student, loved me and wanted to get pregnant and I could see her magnificent hips as a spring-loaded, thigh-muscled bear trap that could imprison me in a life of underpaid work for her father and lots of kids who played around piles of dirty laundry.

Seemed horrible at the time, but decades later, I sought it out as real life.

I worked to make a reputation for myself as someone in the cool group, though I never felt membership. As social collateral, I used the family's summer cottage on a rural lake as a Senior Class party palace. We students slipped off on cold nights and drove twenty miles through the blown snow highways to livened up that semicircular lakeshore ghost town for two winters. My new friends, the fat Football jocks, started a lifelong career of alcoholic hobnobbery. They told jokes and insulted each other with young voices just shy of mastery over the boom of a mature male's. One cold dry winter night, a jock fell out of an open jeep driven too drunk and fast down the gravel access road to the cottage. He hit the ground with his face first, and knocked out a front tooth. We all left the cottage to go look for it, we combed the gravel road in between the headlights of two cars, but couldn't find it. Someone drove the wounded one to the hospital, and the rest went back to the cottage to party on.

In the morning, each woke up where they fell the night before, each large, elephantine boy groaned and brushed aside the aluminum cans and spilt ashtrays. One blinked in dull awareness to find himself semi-upright, propped up seated but slumped inside one end of a long, narrow closet, a drool of pretzel puke to decorate his letter sweater.

I found out they didn't count me as their friend, didn't invite me into their social world, and for good reason. They felt uncomfortable with me, they couldn't talk about music, art, and literature, and I felt no interest in sports, except the pole vault, gymnastics, and lady's synchronized swimming.

In my old village school, I got good grades, and felt admired and respected by my peers. I kept to myself, and wandered the woodlands. They invited me to social functions, I could dance with everybody, and all the girls wore welcome smiles.

In the new school, I never received invitations, the uppity girls flew glances down flared nostrils, and I considered it ugly makeup. I let my grades fall, and I discovered that neither good looks, intelligence, nor physical prowess really mattered. Your car and clothes and your ride to school mattered a little, your neighborhood mattered among a general society, and your reputation mattered with those close to you, or with complete accuracy, you share your family's reputation and responsibility to maintain the social order. The police handle the horizontal social order, while snobs enforce the vertical.

Students got messages from both to teach us our place in the classless society.

In the country schools, I believed in America as a meritocracy. They filled me with a utopian faith in justice and equality of opportunity, where those who put out the most effort, with the most talent and luck and hard work, surely rise to the top.

Maybe it looks that way from the top, but from below, you only see assholes.

Discovery of Guatemala

Mayan scientists invented the concept of zero before most of the civilizations of Europe and Arabia, if not India. The descendants of those advanced Mayan societies still exist and populate sections of the Yucatán peninsula and Central America in a network of tiny villages, yet entire regions remain separated by distance and language dialects. From its earliest origins in the Petén and the Guatemalan highlands, the most ancient Mayan influences left evidence unearthed in archeological discoveries and legends, spread across six modern geopolitical regions, north into the Chiapas region of southernmost Mexico and north across the Yucatán, and southward into Belice, Honduras, and El Salvador in Central America. Archeologists explain the spread of cultures through two mechanisms, conquest and trade, which sometimes blur together and promote the intermarriage of the elite classes.

At home, I ran across Guatemala in mom's nineteen sixty eight Encyclopedia Britannica. It said Guatemalans earn an average per capita income of three hundred sixty five dollars a year, a suspicious number, the number of days in a year. I reasoned that since the richest citizens must earn considerably much more than an dollar a day, the poorest citizens made less than a dollar a day. I researched more in the city's library, and found color photos that showed coffee plantations, bananas, Mayan ruins, Indians in ropa típica, volcanoes reflected in Lake Atitlán, and the proximity to the United States.

Guatemala resembled some far off place in Asia, and yet so close. By the map's mileage, I estimated a bus could take me there in sixty hours, nonstop.

I earned a dollar twenty five each hour, when I washed dishes at Uncle Johnny's Pancake House on Twenty Eighth Street, the major beltway on the new South Side of the city. For each day I worked, I earned a week's worth in Guatemala. As I washed dishes in that industrial kitchen, the thought of Guatemala bubbled up shiny, pristine, primitive, and multifaceted, like mountains of soapsuds that floated in the wash bin of my stainless steal environment. I dreamt of volcanic mountains blanketed in the sweet green of forest surrounded by clouds of sunset flower petals, mint horizons, and vanilla rainbows. This balanced my disgust with dirty dishes from a pancake restaurant, tubs full of dishes covered in artificial butter grease and synthetic fruit flavored syrups. Each time someone opened the foot thick, stainless steel door of the walk-in cooler, out wafted a stink from the racks of quartered cold-rot chicken. Whenever I smelled it, I saw in my mind's eye the candy apple red pools of congealed gelatinized beef plasma on the floor in the corners.

I worked with the constant fantasy I might save up the money to live in Guatemala for a while.

I slaved, sweated, and tried to avoid the aggressive frustration of the head cook, an intelligent high strung, athletic young man who dropped out of high school and hated me at the first sign of knowledge. He cooked furious everyday, tortured about the most recent turmoil with his girlfriend, a gorgeous buxom and cultured young woman from a fine family, from my school district, but who never talked to me as an underclassman until after we both graduated.

She wore real leather boots up to her knees, and owned various several pair in various shades of shiny white, chocolate browns, or textured blacks, each with a dangerous needle of a high heel. Winters, she belted herself into real furs that exaggerated her ample bosom. Whenever her boyfriend made himself scarce, a too rare and brief an occurrence, she treated me with a cautious friendship and respect, perhaps to enlist me later as a spy. She respected me for my courteous behavior and respect for her, neither of which he displayed.

Unfortunately, he noticed. Maybe he saw her laugh with me, or she suggested he model his behavior on mine, but in any event, something made him hate me even more.

Adolescent standards of the age meant one took a man's punch in the shoulder as a humorous "love tap," or you earned title as a sissy. I learned to avoid the blows, or roll with them to decrease their intensity, and with luck, I benefited from an unwritten rule of bad form for him to insist on a punch. He nailed me good a number of times, and some weeks I sported a bluish yellow bruised area on both my shoulders.

Our boss managed a number of restaurants, and did so in absentia, which left the head cook in charge. I learned to fear his anger and insecurity most on days when he or argued with her and made too many phone calls from the pay phone on the back wall. I knew he either looked for her, and could not locate her, and it drove him mad.

He like to set up practical jokes to distract himself, sadistic plots to provoke workmates against each other, to get them to take sides and trap people in a kitchen food fight, which always put the busboys, in their white shirts, ties, and black pants, at a disadvantage against the filthy kitchen staff.

When he needed to get a strong reaction out of us to forget his own problems, he took one of the empty plastic buckets that came packed with quartered chickens in water, filled it with cold water, and snuck up behind someone to empty five gallons of cold water over their head. Then he might run into the cooler, and come out with a naked headless and footless chicken to clown with, to dance with and kiss, or use as a voodoo doll and insult our girlfriends. He might walk by casual and flip a half cooked pancake at us, to stick the dough side on the back of a shirt, or on the ceiling over our head, to watch it slowly detach and fall.

When all else failed, he called us to dare him to hawk a nose full of winter mucus to spit into some poor old lady's hamburger.

Special Sauce he called it, a code word that he used to gross us out, to threaten us, as he trained us well to respect and fear him, and his psychosexual adolescent dominance, which I recognized years later as a common personality disorder that mixed narcissism with manic depression, and causes a megalomania of low self esteem and performance anxiety that makes men buy sports cars and join self destructive sports like American football or the military, or hit their girlfriends in jealous anger.

His relationship illustrated the gene-inspired illogic of adolescent love, where a boy believes he can beat a woman into an amorous mood, and believe her pledge of lifelong love sincere under threat. Sometimes the girl stays with such an adolescent mentality, even after several children and trips to the hospital for stitches.

We knew she should blow him away, rather than blow him off.

Lifelong love comes true too soon when it ends in a lethal tragedy.

Like many able and conscientious young people, I did not last long at a series of jobs over the next five years. I did feel proud as a factory worker, in my white cook's apron, a card-carrying member of the Teamster's Union, founded by truck drivers. This membership allowed me to work inside a quarter mile long brick building to operate the shiny machines that hummed and rumbled all night long to kick out thousands loaves of bread, and hundreds of cellophane wrapped packages of various kinds of donuts and cinnamon rolls.

The innocent white dough rose in huge wheeled metal troughs, fifteen foot long and four feet around, to flow over the sides and fall in slow-motion cascades, a thick butter colored curtain, until someone walked by and flipped it back in like a limp octopus. Some drips escaped, and if not swept up, grew and then dried out to form dry hollow spheres, some as big as a fist, kicked into dark corners.

Up the assembly line one department, a big black man took a trough of dough and pulled out a tentacle of it to slash it onto trays, each one beat flat with his flour covered fists. Then he stacked the trays into seven foot tall racks to sit and swell for a couple of hours. Then he took each tray and pummeled it flat, knead it, made a slug out of it, centered it on the tray, and put the tray back to rise again. When the dough matured, each looked like a swollen white grub, twenty inches long. Then he pushes the rack into my department.

In my department, I take each slug and beat it flat onto the rubber mat of the conveyer belt's entrance, then take the next one and pounded the ends together into one seamless yellow ribbon of dough. As a conveyer pulls it along, a shaker machine sprinkles sugar and cinnamon, and then a diagonal metal roller lifts the dough up and curls it over itself into a tube. Then a sharp metal blade cuts the tube into spiral slices just before they drop into a metal grid that floats under the surface of a vat of hot oil. They fall onto this metal net to sizzle and boil. Halfway across, where another mesh revolves to flip them over to fry on the other side, then they get pushed by other floated donuts to the other side of the oil. Another steel conveyor belt lifts them out of the oil and moves them along under fans to cool the top a little. Then they summersault over the edge of a precipice to fall face down onto another mesh that drags them through a molten pool of sugar or chocolate. Another metal flipper pushes each cooked round of dough out of the sweet stuff and onto another conveyer belt, where some receive toppings, nuts or colored candy sprinkles, before another stretch of fans to cool them down. Then a machine partitions the correct number of cinnamon rolls or doughnuts, and with a burst of compressed air, shunts them into shiny waxed white cardboard trays. These cardboard trays pass through a machine that wraps everything in cellophane, then pushes the box over a heater to seal the plastic. At the end of the conveyer belt, a young girl dressed in white smock and shoes, white pants, and white paper mushroom hat to contain her hair, grabs three packages with her transparent rubber gloves to stack on pallets until they form a cube about four feet tall. A full pallet get wrapped in a clear, wide, plastic wrap and sealed with transparent shipper's tape. Every half hour or so, a forklift takes the palettes out to the truck docks.

She, like many factory workers, suffered an addiction to donuts and cinnamon rolls, coca-cola, and vending machine snacks imbided on each and every one of her fifteen minute breaks mandated by law for every two hours of work. She loved conversations so insubstantial that I could not make light of it. She told me "A person smart as you shouldn't work here" and communicated in no uncertain terms, through glances and endless smiles that bared her gray, soft-drink eroded teeth, her readiness to accept me as a donor to her family's genetic diversity.

The good old days.

When I first started work at the factory, they put me at the ovens' mouth. I wore a t-shirt and thick gloves made out of multiple layers of a crude woven cotton that stretched to my elbows. I cowered before the roar of the gas flame in its gut, but did not flinch when I needed to swap those oven-hot trays of bread loaves for trays full of cold dough. I passed that initiation. The oven shuddered and howled, a constant roar and ping of stressed metal deep in its bowels. Each time the conveyer belt tongue opened its maw to eject another load of bread pans in a fast slide through the long black teeth, I grabbed one at a time to swivel and place it into the racks to cool. Then we placed a full load of raw dough bread trays on the apron before the bowling alley rake arm pulled everything into the oven again.

I worked with a partner, a skinny old man named "Ody" Odenthal. We waited together, side by side, for each load of baked bread to emerge.

They did not bother to introduce me to him. They brought me to the mouth of the oven, and told me his name. "Ody. He always works the oven. Don't bother to try and talk to him."

In the break room, they tell me the rumors. Ody survived World War II, but not right in the head.

On top of the normal atheistic existentialism and disillusionment with God that survivors of World War II suffered, the rations at home and abroad, and all the female factory labor to give birth to women in the work force as part of the war effort, many believed that this holocaust signified a new low in humanity's record of achievement. The entire generation felt proud they confronted the evil of man's inhumanity to man, personified by the racist (and vegetarian) Adolf Hitler, but never confront their own history and an even greater inhumanity, and a true genocide, in the eradication of Native Americans north of the Rio Grande.

Every time I looked at this shell-shocked Yugoslavian I saw a mummy, with pockmarked skin like a peeled and forgotten potato. He walked about so bloodless he looked covered with flour and dried dough scum even when I saw him in the supermarket, dressed in street clothes.

I could imagine him at the input mouth of some concentration camp oven. Instead of incineration and annihilation of whatever he threw in, he now took the staff of life out of ovens.

When the oven belched, we (protected by thick gloves that covered the forearm) removed the seven hot bread pans, each with five browned loaves. We took one quick step away from the heat to pivot ninety degrees on our dough-splattered black work shoes, and set the bread pan on seven foot tall wheeled racks to cool. Then we turned one hundred eighty degrees to similar racks on the other side, and grabbed cool bread pans filled with yeast-raised raw dough that bulged over the top like fat white slugs. We lined up the seven bread pans beyond the metal tongue of the oven's metal apron, fast enough to avoid the dangerous bar of hot black metal. A vampire bat's black rectangular tongue came out, with a long rusty scrape and a hoarse roar, to drop over the top of the bread trays with a clang, and drag them into its fiery gullet.

After one week of 4:00 AM night shifts alongside the non-communicative Ody, I knew every move he made, and the subsequent months confirmed it. As each load of bread pans cooked inside the oven, we waited about five minutes for the next batch to come out. Ody sat down in the same spot on the oven's bench (a metal ledge meant for a quick step up to reach into the ovens) with his back to the radiant heat of the oven, which he did not appear to feel. He slid his hands along his thin, pasty white arms and talked to himself.

Ody never talked to me. He might smile and react, change his mouth so that I glimpsed a few craggy stumps in place of teeth, but he refused to say anything intelligible, and did not wait for replies. Seated all alone on the oven's foot-ledge, I saw him carry on long, serious conversations in the time it took for another load of pans to eject. His eyebrows animated, his arm moves in back-of-the-hand brush-offs, shoulders shrug, hands open and implore, and then he looks exasperated and gives his face a rub with one of his bony white dog-carcass hands before he slips them into the huge gloves again.

To Ody, his internal dialogues deserved more attention than any reality with people around him. He often put his face between his hands and stared across the factory. He gave me the impression of someone trapped in painful memories, a daydream nightmare in the wee small hours, provoked by this factory, a noisy purgatory of cold, stainless steel with this black monster oven at its heart. The heat, and years of buttery fumes from the oven's mouth, colored the apron with a caramel patina of baked grease. The black rubber slats of the heat-barrier curtain swung as violent gusts of heated air, perfumed by baked bread, wafted out.

Nearby, troughs of dough burped with yellowed flesh colored mounds, swelled up to sometimes drool over the sides like tentacles bent on escape.

One day, the floor supervisor brought a young man over to replace me, and took me to where two other supervisors gave me a couple of donuts to try. I wondered if the six foot tall, blue-egg bug-eyed Norseman hit on new employees this way. He wanted me to be the judge of which tasted better, a factory version of an intelligence test, or verification that I spoke intelligible English. After that, they moved me to the donut department under supervisor Mr. Snieder, a diminutive hunched cynic with a twinkling eye and a conspiratorial smile.

At the factories, I saw grown young men, once someone's children, remain boys at heart, and try to earn their place in a society of factory rats through automobile culture. They dumped their money into "cherried-out" cars, lavished attention on their "rides" with transparent candy colored metal flake paint jobs, expensive chrome rim steering wheels and fancy hubcaps, hood ornaments in the form of jets, rockets, cobras, lions and tigers. From the rear view mirror, a four inch piece of cardboard cutout dangled, a picture of some cheesecake seated nudes from Playboy magazine perfumed with air freshener. The outside of their car sported pin stripes similar to what tole painters in Austria would paint on dinner plates. To make the car sound worthy of all that decoration, they put in high octane overpowered motors and glass pack muffler systems so it would roar in acceleration, backfire in explosions on a downshift, and sound like indigestion and equestrian flatulence at idle.

This completed the fantasy art of the motorhead, except for the girl.

Motor heads took advantage of the exodus at shift change to compete. They 'squealed out' through the factory parking lot in a blue cloud of acrid smoke from the layers of melted rubber burnt off their obese tires, some so large they looked swollen, reminiscent of the rear end of a female chimp in estrus. The burnt rubber stripes on the surface of the parking lot recorded the competitions in a rich tapestry of tire tread braids in hundred foot long rubber burns.

Taxonomical logic forces biologists and other scientists to admit that birds represent feathered reptiles. We eat reptile for Thanksgiving and Christmas dinner. Deep in the human brain, a bird still exists, and when humans succumb to environments that dehumanize them, this birdbrain takes over and forces people into courtship behaviors patterned by the epochs before human evolution.

In response to these thunderbirds' gasoline fueled high octane fantasy courtship displays, a certain class of women took notice. She wanted to belong and feel noticed, to become one of the "most sought after" girls, the blessed few tall and svelte blondes, thin protuberant women who smoke and drink and avoid marriage, or at least monogamy, to play the field of men in a desperate race to believe they lived life to the full, while they still "had their youth." This urge probably existed in direct relation to the unhappiness of their home life in infancy, or their mother's string of failed relationships, whichever came first.

Motorhead factory rat men worked hard to earn a little fame in the local rock and roll bars where they hung out. Nothing like a little notoriety to help a man take advantage of that breed of aggressive factory class women psychologically traumatized by factory rat frustrated fathers long suffered by factory rat wives that also worked, themselves factory rat daughters of factory rat mothers who worked. The rapid decay of older sisters shocked young women to recognize their own temporal and tenuous hold on youth, and that desperation exaggerated a young girl's instinctual urgency to couple. Factory class girls in a factory town sat in bars with girlfriends after work, and drank toasts to the future, committed to the pursuit of every advantage afforded them by the short term blessings of youth for however long they retained their beauty or sex appeal, and mercenary intelligence. Every girl could count on, and believe in, her sex appeal, for nature blessed all men, every single one of them, with the God-given ability to go to bed with any female, if both drink enough.

Unfortunately, the factory girl's low self esteem lowered their horizon of possibilities and blinded them to life's wider vistas, so few ventured farther than to flirt with whichever factory rat motorhead the girls regarded as the most sensitive, handsome, virile, and safely ineligible male that week. Although those who did more than flirt the men called sluts, easy, not bright enough to whore, for behavior that twenty years later would characterize a respectable, professional, and common urban lifestyle known as serial monogamy. In secret, those girls became the most popular, and discreet.

A motorhead believes the fantasy that the car will bring them a 'most sought after' girl, a skinny sex maniac, who judges the worth of a man by his automobile. He sits low in the driver's seat, jostled by the vibration of the super-charged motor at idle, while his glass pack muffler blows smoke rings out the tumescent twinned exhaust pipe extensions, fat chrome fingers that poke out from under, two per side.

Out of nowhere, she responds by instinct, and surrenders to the impulse to strut toward him, toward those twin billows of smoke, while the people in the parking lot stop in their tracks, transfixed by her beauty and the throb of her halo of sexual urgency that surrounds her like fog lights at the airport. The double flow of crowd movement, in and out of the factory when the shift changes, slows down to a molasses thick motion as this primeval drama begins.

Her eyes fix on his sunglasses under cloudy skies. She advances, arrow-straight to where he sits with one arm draped out the car door window and the other, with the cigarette, hung over the steering wheel made of chromed, welded chain with enormous links. His chariot trembles and sputters like a racehorse on speed forced to sleep.

He can see the future. After hits of hash on a bong pipe with hoses that lead into the eye sockets of a silver skull, he conjures up a vision of her in a hat and thick boa, both made of black crow feathers. The boa wraps around her neck and falls to her wasp thin waist. She wears a bra with a long fringe of black South American Night Monkey fur that contrasts with the white smoothness of her perfect spherical orbs, so rare in nature, so common in low class male fantasy, which creates a market for cosmetic breast implant surgery as another consumer item, promoted on television by Los Angeles' failed fashion models that work as helpers on game shows and televised wrestling matches.

Below her boa-hidden hips, her long panty hosed legs dangle and almost reach the ground to scissor-cross as she puts one foot down in front of, and a little overstepped across, the other. Her footprints stay within whichever straight line of charred rubber leads to the passenger side door.

She stands before the passenger door. When she sees his cigarette wiggle, her straight legs open and shut, a silhouette of scissors, as she opens the car door and stoops to step into his car with a flash of milky cleavage between crow feathers. She nestles into the bucket seat and stares at him motionless as a chicken.

When she looks at him, his false smile of bravado freezes.

She knows it, licks her thin lips, and gives him a wordless smile that leaves blood red lipstick chevrons on her tobacco yellowed teeth. Her wide eyed glazed gaze shoots out under her mascara to skewer him between her baling-wire eyelashes, crosshairs, bear traps, giant black clams.

As if in an alien spaceship's tractor beam, he feels the tug but must ignore it. His hand out the window opens to caress his car door. At last they confront their destiny. She answered the mating call, that smoky banshee shriek of burnt rubber. She saw her future mirrored in the provocative fishtail of his taillights through the billows of blue smoke, burnt rubber, and cigarette ash. She feels his power, this sound, this car, and knows this man could tame the flame lights up her life from the place where she feels the cushion of heat from the sun drenched, black patent leather of the bucket seat.

Soon they would both realize their auto-centric culture's biggest mistake, to pour all that money into a car with an uncomfortable back seat.

I know all this, because I know a couple of these guys. I went to their houses and examined their bedroom walls, and the garages where artisans work on their cars, the walls hung with the calendars that depict these mythic women, calendars sponsored by companies like Snap-on Tools, Hard-On Tools, Inc. or Tool And Die Corporation.

Through a short-term friendship, for drug purchase purposes, with the talented, longhaired, dope smokin' drunkard who lives down the street and went to school with these guys which entitles him to design their car hood murals, I perused the original artwork that depicts these mythic women. He will airbrush the hood, trunk, and sides of any vehicle with his automotive enamels, until the ride becomes a decorated pinstriped puddle of candy apple aluminum flake quarter inch thick transparent goo with murals of semi-naked girls with cars, hubcaps, snakes, dragons, and the American flag.

The artists needs to scrape the money together to finish several projects, which depends on some inaccessible person who took the little money he had and promised to come up with the right assortment of drugs to unload at a profit, through his brother in law the dentist, or through his young cousin Nicky, who at thirteen needed to repeat his loss of virginity because he couldn't remember the first time.

All this bird brained motorhead sexuality, in all its frigid reptilian glory, expresses the fundamental truth of the human male, driven by a genetic mandate, to sire children with as many women as possible, and get away fast before someone forces them to become responsible.

This demonstration of their virility, their readiness to express the anger of contest and challenge between males, functions almost as a homoerotic sex act in itself. The motorhead culture distances them from normal, worthy females that would seek a kind, disciplined, protective, strong, and committed man who could devote his life to her and their kids.

What kind of a woman lets a road warrior father her children?

Motorheads tend to attract those women who, by virtue of their own father's culture or lack of it, or through substance abuses and addictions to self medications, grow accustomed to hard language, tobacco and alcohol, drugs and violence. They put up with the promiscuity of un-bathed, unshaven, unfaithful men who beg forgiveness only after their public infidelities. They blame alcohol, their man's uncontrollable masculinity, and the other wom(a/e)n. If that doesn't work, they expect a "real" man to become violent as an undeniable demonstration of brutal, instinctual, and therefore a real jealousy of undeniable love. These women do not see jealousy and other violent demonstrations of possession as denigrations of themselves to the level of object, or as a male personality disorder. A motorhead woman recognizes these symptoms of mental chaos as signs of true love, the kind of love their own father demonstrated. She cries with her man, forgives him, gets drunk, forgets about it, and uses sex to kiss and make up.

At three in the morning when he, partially undressed, clambers over her, she recognizes him, perfumed by drugs, alcohol, and cigarettes, the unshaven stubble of his beard decorated by the pink lipstick paisleys of other women's kisses. Yet she doesn't recognize the insensitive lout as a complete waste of protoplasm. The slob's anaesthetized failed attempt at the athleticism necessary for some minor spurt or flutter, something that might pass for sexual release, instead of this emotional and physical impotence, requires them both to fall asleep before either recognizes or complains about their inability to stay awake.

After a good night of drugs and alcohol, she feels the multiple attacks, submissions, and mutual paroxysms of pleasure, pain, panic, and ecstasy flee from memory as if it never happened, or in retrospect, become so impersonal and devoid of significance that she might equate his performance as a drunken night piss with an unknown assailant(s), or an impersonal wet dream, a masturbation in one's sleep with a machine one doesn't know how to turn off.

Their spiritual human lies bound and gagged in the corners of these people's lives, and that amuses them. With a post-act cigarette, both puff out a sigh of relief to recall how they seethed with only each other's names on their lips, and not another lover's moniker.

I asked long-time supervisor Snieder how many years Ody worked in the factory, and he said, "I asked around once upon a time, and no one knows. We all remember Ody here when we started. He's the original old timer."

One day Mr. Snieder's wife called with a family emergency, so he trained me on the spot, in five minutes, how to change the donut line from white frosting to chocolate, then untied his white apron and took a brisk walk through the factory to punch out.

I grew more nervous as the end of the vanilla run approached.

When I tried to couple the four inch pipes from the chocolate vats to the icer vat, the pumps started. I held onto the spasmodic pipes as if a great Anaconda that ejaculated surge after surge of thick chocolate venom. It poured over my hands and hairy forearms as I yelled for help. A tall bespectacled supervisor, with straw hair that sticks out from under his white paper-boat hat, runs over from the next department to solve the problem with a few deft turns of the pipe fasteners. I hung in there, with my arms heavy with chocolate, hands wrapped around the neck of that great snake to steady it. I estimated over seventeen gallons of chocolate glaze puddle on the floor in a huge shiny lake whose edges crept across the floor.

Other foremen arrived.

I expected they would escort me out, but body cared.

"Don't worry about it, kid." One foreman said to me. "Sugar's cheap."

The factory stayed open twenty four hours a day, three shifts of eight hours each. Some volunteered to work two shifts, "back to back" as they say. The double-backed beast, a euphemism for fornication. Not easy to see who really got screwed in this nest of industrial activity, this infestation of localized production and poisonous waste. Like a legion of white uniforms, ants in the bowels of a nest built around ovens, ants as part of the machine of production, ants anonymous and identical except for the name tags, ants unanimous in the belief that money buys freedom.

In our secular humanist society proud of the recent civil rights movement victories that again reinforced the moral superiority of the Yankee's role in the Civil War, many of us tolerated the various skin colors of our rainbow workforce, and even strived to become people without discrimination, to recognize everyone as autonomous free agents and masters of our own destiny, even if we all felt trapped to do our daily stint as part of the machine.

We came out dirty, exhausted, but richer, and so dehumanized that many double-shifters claimed they got off work only to go home and eat, drink a few beers, and sleep to get up early and do another sixteen hours or so the next day.

They lived to work.

The Raccoon

We three, high school freshmen me and two of my three years senior Senior class neighbor boys, enjoyed hikes through the woods on gray spring days when the last of the snow lay in the permanent shadows on the south slopes of the ravines in these deep leafless woods of tall oak, beech, maple, and ash.

We found a tall hollow tree stump, smooth and naked without bark, about a yard across and eight feet tall. We beat on it with our hatchets, for no reason at all but to hear what it sounds like. The face of a raccoon peeks out of a hole about six feet up, then disappears. We beat the tree with our hatchets until the coon dashes out the hole to leap through the air over our heads.

Instead of a prolonged terrified flight, it stops about ten yards away and comes back, slung low, full of snarls with teeth bared.

We turned and high-tailed it through the trees, slippery slides on the thin snow and wet leaves. The sounds of that animal's scuffled footfalls and angry growls sounded like the muffled chirps of a piece of cardboard stuck into bicycle spokes. We scampered up the wooded slope on fear and adrenaline. I got the farthest away quickest, which surprised me, because I never beat those two in a foot race.

The other two boys stopped to face the coon's attack.

The coon stops and stands with its arms out, a devilish snarl of pointed white fangs that lead back to the shiny eyes squinted through a black furry mask.

The boys maneuver the raccoon between them, one distracts while the other takes a swing with the hatchet.

The coon swirls between them, fast as lightning, all snarls and darts and feints. It lashes out at their knee-high rubber boots and slashes one with a front paw to rip out a big chunk of rubber, which flaps like a hunk of black rawhide and wakes us up to the danger of the situation.

The lean, muscular, smaller lad gets low and lets his hatchet drag through the leaves to distract the raccoon. That gives the biggest boy an opportunity. He holds his hatchet about shoulder high and moves in like a knife fighter. He winds up like a baseball pitcher and swings a terror-driven overhand hatchet blow aimed at the coon's head. The coon hears him and whirls around to face him as the hefty rusted-iron hatchet comes down full force atop the crest of the coon's skull.

The coon stops in mid snarl, shakes it off like a mosquito bite, and lunges at the boy. We all back up in retreat, and breath relief when the coon backs up also.

They all retreat from each other, as if in recognition of discretion as the better part of valor. When the coon estimates the distance as sufficient, he makes a run for it. It scampers faster than a dog across the snow and leaves, down the gentle slope of the wooded ravine, splashes through the ice crusted water in the creek and corners around the smooth eroded boulders to jet straight up the embankment, a cliff of soft sand eroded into a scalloped horseshoe twenty feet tall, to disappear over the top.

The boys let it go.

When we hoisted each other up to look into the hole, we discover three baby raccoons inside. We decide to enlarge the entrance hole, but first run the half mile back to the house and get the thickest work gloves to reach in and extract the cute little bundles of needle-toothed fury.

Each of us boys took home a baby raccoon in a cardboard box.

Mom scolded us for hours about cruelty to animals. The other boys tuned her out, accustomed to her culturally inappropriate ideas since she moved here, to the boondocks, and proclaimed herself an anti-hunting, animal-lover, the Dog Lady, a city girl from Detroit and Chicago. She first peppered our property line, every thirty feet, with fluorescent red No Hunting signs, and earned instant infamy with the neighbors, until she told them personally that since she knew and trusted them to act responsibly, they could trespass to hunt in season.

Our raccoon grew up in a couple of months, and acted more dangerous every day. Each of us experienced situations that made us less and less disposed to play with it. The thing angered, and often wanted its own way.

Dogs and cats don't do that. They stay immature and needy their whole lives.

We learned to respect it, kept it caged behind the house. We didn't like to open the door to feed it, so we gave it too much food to minimize the number of times we opened the door and would need to fend it off with one hand covered by a thick glove, kept nearby for that purpose.

Not only did it try to escape, when out, it considered itself a member of the family. It demanded increased rights to explore anywhere it wanted, and eat anything it found. It became harder and harder to maintain the necessary diplomacy to get it back in the cage and avoid damage from those razor sharp teeth that slash out from under the tip of his upturned snout.

It knew we feared it, but we fed it. He considered us family, whatever that means to raccoons. Not much.

Flies infested the area around the cage, due to the quantities of dog food it smeared around with its wet little knurly hands. In its instinctual habit of raccoon-ness, it washed handfuls of dog food, to produce a mush it refused to eat. Flies loved it, and maggots mysteriously multiplied.

Like any creature out of its natural environment, the raccoon looked miserable, trapped in that small cage. Flies covered its face, sometimes it looked like a welded sculpture of drippings with a metallic green patina, until it gave its head a quick, violent shake to dislodge them. The flies buzzed around in a cloud, as the raccoon snapped at them to pluck them out of the air. When the raccoon settled down, the flies returned to the coon's snout and cheeks, to start the cycle all over again, until sleep granted the raccoon unconsciousness and temporary relief.

Flies became more of a problem that summer. Near its cage behind the cottage, we kept a fly sprayer, which looked like a bicycle pump with a testicular canister on one end full of insecticide. A few quick pumps of the sprayer produced a fine mist, directional, but as an aerosol, it floated about and smelled similar to kerosene.

My thirteen year old brain wanted to alleviate the raccoon's misery and free it from the torture of more fly bites. I sprayed the chicken wire of the cage where the flies sat like miniature vultures. I sprayed the coon's water bowl, where the flies congregated on little coon handfuls of food mush the coon forgot to stuff into his fang-lined mouth.

Later that night, my stepfather came in and said, "The raccoon is dead. Anybody know anything about it?"

No one spoke. He said, "Come on, something must have happened. Baby raccoons don't just up and die."

A terrible realization grew inside of me, and forced me to confess. "The raccoon looked miserable, always covered with flies. I tried to help it. I thought fly spray would only hurt flies."

After all the blame, short lived and emotional, they forgave me, and then the relief grew. No more would we need to undertake the dangerous maintenance of a wild beast without manners, a mature animal that did not know better than to bite the hand that feeds it.

It died because I did not know better. I resented that I did not know better. I thought fly spray killed flies, not raccoons. If not, why would humans spray poisons on foods and in houses, if the poisons could kill anything?

With the death of that baby raccoon, a sense of the destructive power of chemicals and poisons grew within me, a vision of certain defeat for man and all life in the suicidal war of Man against Nature.

In Michigan, as I stood in line at the bank to withdraw money for the trip, I noticed an arrogant schoolmate in line, behind me. I said hi. Out of school, without the social context to snub me, he greeted me and we talked. Although we both graduated in the same class from the same upscale suburban High School, I doubted we ever talked before. He came from one of the townie families, the novo rich that made local kids uncomfortable, unless they came from families of Amway distributors with newfound wealth. Some families came from abroad, to avoided taxes in Canada and probably many other countries unfamiliar with the profit potential of person to person pyramid hierarchies of catalogue distribution.

I asked him what he planned to do. He proudly stated that Arizona State University accepted him, and he would leave in a week to start classes this fall.

"I should be in Guatemala by then." I said.

"Guatemala," he says, eyebrows registered confusion, non-comprehension. "Where is Guatemala?"

"below Mexico. Closer than Asia, and people there live on less than a dollar a day." I felt embarrassed to tell him that.

He huffed, a surprised exhalation, and says "More reason to stay away."

I shrugged, didn't know what to say.

He stood there with a thought that gave him a smirk. I felt sure he wrote me off as a loser, to allow him to feel ahead of me in this race called life. Maybe he heard his father's deep authoritarian voice reinforce his silent observation that I must be a crazy, a dirty hippie, an enemy of the State.

My own father died when halfway through my first grade of public school. That spared me the influence of a macho womanizer that spent few nights home, and, to judge from his actions the first six years of my young life, cared little for his own children. Even Christmas and birthdays became a toss up as to whether he would bless us with his presence.

The insurance company tried to rule my father's death a suicide, instead of accidental death in a fire, to avoid payment of life insurance to my mother. She found a good lawyer, and when they settled out of court, she received a sum which enabled her to buy a play farm in the country, seventeen miles outside the big city, over a hundred acres of land whose value would skyrocket over the next forty years.

And so it happened that she gave her elementary school sons the strange and fortuitous opportunity to walk, every morning, through the snow covered fields and woods to one of America's last one room schools, and then attend high school in one of America's wealthiest and most pretentious new enclaves of a right wing conservative anti-nature, pro-war, American Capitalist consumer culture.

Before Gerald Ford's rise to the presidency, our area's most famous citizen lived a half mile, or ten houses, down the street and wrote the Top Forty radio hit called "An Open Letter to My Teenage Son." Victor Lundberg, a spokesman for the Libertarian Party, threatens to disown his son if he burns his draft card. "And I will remind you that your mother will love you no matter what you do, because she is a woman."

Might makes right, and Right wants nothing left.

In nineteen seventy five, after two semesters of College Spanish, four jobs, and the end of the Viet Nam War, I made good on my pledge to not cut my waist length hair until after the war ended. I visited a trendy, upscale hair salon in Aspen, Colorado where I worked as a maid ,maintenance man, and on-call night clerk in a Chateaux, a pretentious motel for skiers. My glorious three feet of sun bleached blonde wavy hair seemed to terrify the two who attended me, both intelligent, handsome, homosexual hair stylists, as opposed to barbers.

They did a beautiful job, of course. I became James Bond, sophisticated and sarcastic yet quizzical, my ears rang with the 007 riff with the complex timbre of an electric guitar's new-strung bronze E-string plucked close to the bridge.

I felt unstoppable, immortal, immoral, lethal, shaken not stirred (a little scared but not emotionally involved), and ready to take on the world and see for myself, first hand, how the other half lives.

Sixth Section: Life goes South

CHAPTER 19: Two to Mexico

Twenty two years old, I got to the Texas-Mexican border from Michigan in late September, nineteen seventy five. I remember that frosty dawn, a silvery sunrise in a cloudless sky. I stood alone in the barren heart of Texas, outside of a place called Van Horn, a place where two skinny State Highways crossed. My last ride dropped me off long after midnight, when I realized I missed the turnoff.

I planned to take a train ride from the remote Mexican border town named Ojinaga to Los Mochis on the shores of the Sea of Cortez. Instead, I stand alone in these sparse grasslands, the eroded limestone mountains filled with shells from a quarter of a billion years ago.

As if in a trance, the driver let the car roll at seventy five miles per hour for hours until he dropped me off. I thought about the night's experience of almost invisible exotic flat scrublands, trapped in a purgatory, a TV show without commercials, hour after hour of this endless flat asphalt ribbon of road with one feature, a single line of white dashes illuminated by our flat pool of yellowish light from the two headlights, the end product of sunlight stored in forests and plankton from over sixty five million years ago. We scattered it along the darkness of West Texas, a brief spray of photons and heat. These two State highways meet in a vortex in the Space-time continuum, I could feel it.

No cars now. Not even distant headlights. The wind blew a few strands of hair across my forehead and felt chilly on my skin. With hands thrust deep in pockets, I wear my backpack for added warmth and stomped my feet in the gravel alongside the clumps of tall white grasses, tough dew-drop decorated stalks with a pinprick on the end.

I watched the birth of this cold September morning in gray charcoal and graphite. The wind gusts sometimes blow sustained, a tremendous yawn of air rushes through mountains. As the sky lightened, I could an see a mountain top catch the sunlight and tint it with a rusty glow. A shadow falls from a cloud as a misty drizzle wafts across the plains.

I walked a little and noticed grasshoppers, almost as big as sparrows, tucked into the grass along the shoulder of the road. Over three inches long, shiny black with silver trim and decorations, I estimated several hundred might lie across this dry-stubble acre of my immediate vicinity. Black and silver lined like fine jeweled sculptures that shined in the cold. I picked one up, and drew it close to eyeball its details. It moved slow and stiff, an alien from another dimension of time, then the entire segmented abdomen, two thirds of the armored critter, contracted and let out a big hiss that scares the nerves in my elbow so fast, I drop the thing.

It fell like trash and broke the spell. One cold wing cover propped up at an angle and multiple transparent wings fluttered out. I picked it up again and watched it hiss. Air rushed through decorated holes near the tummy side of the plates, holes in its exoskeletal segment that wraps over the back of the abdomen, where contractions caused air to stream out and hiss. Later I learned they called them Caballeros, Gentlemen in Spanish, or literally 'horsemen.'

Hours later, a truck and trailer came down the road. I wondered if I should stand in the middle of the road to flag it down, try to force it to stop. I could see it slow down to make the curve. The driver waved as he past, no surprise there, but then he pulled off the road and stopped to let me catch up.

A young man stuck his head out the driver's side of the cab. He looked down at me, out of breath from my jog, and smiled as he waited for my pant to slow, then asked "Going to Presidio?"

"How did you know?"

"There ain't a whole hell of a lot of anything else down this road for a couple hundred miles either way." His wavy light brown hair turned dirty orange where the sun bleached the longest strands. "Hop in. Name's Andy."

We drove through some mountains for a while, and he said "Don't suppose you ever been to Presidio before?"

"Nope."

"Not a whole lot there. What do you expect?"

"Sleep. That's all I care about, sleep and a shower."

"Why Presidio? The name means prison, so that should give you some idea of what it's like. You could get a better room in Van Horn."

"I want to take the train down to Los Mochis."

He never heard of the train, so I filled him in.

He drove us through mountains, and on some of the high speed curves, I watched the big rear view mirror mounted on my door to see the trailer tilt with its load of green peppers which sprinkled out from under the gray canvas cover. The roadway came alive with these round green things that bounced and fell apart, swept up in the turbulence behind the truck.

Then we arrived, sudden as a nosebleed, senseless as the discovery of a tick on your ankle. The mountain's beauty and the truck's high speed exhilaration disappeared when we pulled into this town made out of used plywood and un-maintained adobes with crumbled corners, rain splash erosion, and missing chunks of the outer covering of whitewashed stucco. One street parallel to the border, a couple of Laundromats. a few school bus stop signs, a wrecked auto in the tall grass next to the windowless walls of a plank shack. Everything appeared grey, flat, dusty, junky, and shoddy. The municipality whitewashes the bigger trunks of bushes and trees up to about four feet, even the big cottonwoods along the streets that offered a little dappled shade to horses tied to it.

Truck driver Andy said "What do you say we split the cost of a room, and save money?"

"You know a motel around here?"

"Several. None worth a shit."

We drove through town and passed a young woman who stood alone on the side of the road, backpack at her feet. She wore a necklace of beads, with a couple of oversize beads and feathers. At the end of town, a couple of blocks away, we turned around and go back to pull up alongside her.

I ask "Where you from?"

"New Jersey"

"I come from Michigan. You taking the train to Los Mochis?"

"How did you know?"

Andy said "There ain't a whole hell of a lot of anything else down this road for a couple hundred miles either way."

"Since we both plan to take that train ride tomorrow, what do you think about cutting costs and sharing a room with us?"

She appeared cautious and looked up with suspicion, so I said "You don't have to decide anything. Just an idea. Hop in, we'll give you a ride down the street to those hotels. You can see the rooms the same time we do, you have to look at them anyway."

She climbed up on the step to get in the cab beside me, but we realized at the same instant the door will never shut with all of us plus her backpack. Looks like the thing weighs a ton, so I get out and offer to carry it.

We talk while Andy drove the truck to the motel. She looks Italian, but says her name, Joanna Mujialski, comes from the Polish side of her grandparent's family, and that a great uncle of hers wrote the famous book Quo Vadis that inspired a bunch of movies in several languages about the situation of the early Christians in Rome.

We stash our bags in the motel room, and the three of us explore Presidio. A couple of trinket shops sell articles from Mexico to tourists who fear the drive, or the walk, to Mexico over the bridge, a one lane culvert with speed bump ditches on both ends, which passes over a dry section of a boulder-filled Rio Grande.

As we walk around and look at prices, I notice a man eyes us from over the top of the merchandise. He follows Joanna and I where ever we go.

Big guy. Texan, mid forties and the beginnings of gray hair, no cowboy hat, but a limestone color western shirt with a big cowpie colored brown yoke. Everybody in Texas wears blue jeans, so ditto the pants and boots. I don't give a hoot about cowboy boots since I bought a pair in Mexico and learned they slip on anything, cripple your walk, and give you bunions the size of apples. Maybe they work for someone who rides a horse all day, but as footwear, the cowboy boot deserves fame for the image of two people who help take off another man's cowboy boot. As footwear, a complete stinky failure.

I separate from her.

He follows me.

I get Joanna and we leave.

He follows us to the next store.

Main Street Presidio, with only three blocks of potholes and gravel covered broken asphalt, small enough that his presence does not surprise us. Anyone out and about in downtown Presidio at the same time will see everybody else downtown every couple of minutes. Probably less than two hundred people live here.

About thirty seconds after we leave the store, so does he.

Next time he came near, I moved closer to talk to him. He introduces himself, says he lives and works in Presidio, for the School District. Says Presidio exists as a place where Mexicans can do their laundry in the Laundromats and buy leather boots cheaper than those offered in Mexico. He seemed gay, too curious about me, too heavy with eye contact and overly earnest smiles. It made sense. A gay in this tiny town would cruise the male tourists either to protect his reputation or cheat on his partner in relative safety.

We say nice to meet you and I go off to find Joanna. When I explain, she breathes a sigh of relief, her shoulders sagged a bit, and she says, "I thought he was after me. A rapist or something worse."

I found a five dollar Chinese transistor radio and decide to buy it, to help me learn Spanish, and to offer it as a gift if the occasion arises. We bought fruit cups from a street vender, a waxed paper cup full of cut strips of mango, banana, melon, watermelon, and a crisp white vegetable called Jicama, first time I'd seen that. The Mexican man, who pushes this little glass case on four wheels to this same street corner everyday, convinced us to let him prepare each cup Mexican style, with red hot chili pepper powder and a bath of fresh squeezed lime juice. Tasted like the inside of a cucumber, watery.

We bought some tacos from a street vendor at sunset, and headed back to the motel room where the three of us must arrange ourselves between two double beds.

I assumed she thinks that us two boys might share a bed, but Andy hit the roof, said he'd rather sleep on the floor than sleep with another man in the same bed. Tomorrow he would drive more than ten hours, and he needed sleep tonight to stay awake all the next day.

I volunteered to sleep on the floor, "the filthy, damp, rock-hard, scorpion highway floor. Hope they don't have black widow spiders around here."

Joanna said she trusted me to sleep beside her, no funny stuff.

"I didn't bring any pajamas. Packed light."

"I didn't either," Joanna said. "Sleep in your underclothes. Clean ones."

Andy got undressed down to his underpants. He slid his tall, awkward frame between the sheets, said goodnight, and buried his face in the pillow to avoid the light that flashed into the room from the motel sign.

After we each showered, Joanna and I did the same. I surrendered her the only pillow. She looked attractive in the half-light; beautiful skin, though up close her face showed the pits of a few acne scars. Her nose reminded me of the statues of Greece or Rome, or Romanians, a beauty hewn from the marble sculptures of art history. He body's curvy strength suggested to me that in her later years, she might become one of those rotund Italian matrons in foreign films that beat up men with big wooden dowel dough rollers.

That motel sign blinked red and blue all night long, each change with a click-buzz noise. Every once in a while a car roared into our aural horizon, then passed us with at spray of gravel to fade off down the bumpy road.

Joanna rolls around a bit, and I try to give her more room for her comfort, but she insinuates a leg between mine and her breathing doesn't sound sleepy. Sounds like she dreams a nightmare, where she gets angry or something. She breathes like a horse after a run, a shallow pant like idled machinery, the pistons of hydraulics, a freight train at rest.

The cold of that high desert night crept into that motel room and clawed through the sheets, which pushed Joanna and I closer together. We spooned against each other and shared body heat. I put my arm around her, careful not to brush against her breasts. She snuggles a bit. I think maybe she's asleep. Then she pulls my arm tighter around her to place my hand over one of her breast, and wiggles her bum into my groin. I felt her nipple grow hard as a pencil eraser.

So I hold her close, to make her feel more comfortable and protected, and in the red blue lights of the motel sign that flashes its light through the thin curtains, I see she keeps her eyes closed as she reaches up for my face with one hand and turns her head to kiss me.

The two of is, so far from home in the exotic barrenness of the Chihuahuan desert, fell under the spell, the desperation to love in Wartime. Both of us wandered alone to reach the far edge of our own country, and both felt committed to tomorrow morning's big step, off the U.S. map, and into Mexico. Young, alone, curious, adventurous, and scared.

We kiss a while, and she grabs my hand and pulls it down between her legs. Wet. My hand slipped all over her thighs and stomach, we kissed, and she grabbed me and we fornicated slow and cautions for a while, to not awaken Andy, to relax ourselves and get some sleep.

Joanna might pass me a venereal disease. I remembered how fast her caution melted away. She agreed to share a motel with two men she never saw before in her life. I wonder if I should rummage through my pack for a condom, so I ask, "Are you on the pill?"

She says, "Don't worry about it." in a voice that reminded me of the quiet voices of dogs at a communal feed, good natured guttural half-growls of both complacency and urgency, but with authority.

We make love, in secret, in the throb of red blue neon light through the threadbare white curtains. We pant with faces buried in the sheets, afraid we might wake up Andy. The sky grows lighter and lighter, and I can see her better.

Joanna tasted like garlic. Under my hands, she felt thick and warm, pudgy, and not used to it, not used to her, not used to the situation, and the presence of a man in the next bed, all conspired to distract me, and I failed to get excited enough.

"You going to come?" She whispers, and of course, I say yes, but I don't know how or when. I mean, when you make love, the place should remove all worry and distraction that people might hear, or wake up. A place without another man asleep in the next bed.

"Get on your knees."

She looks at me with eyebrows in a V, as if to accuse me of something. "No funny stuff."

"Don't worry, regular." I said, and thought Ooops! Like a gas station. I should say Premium next time.

She rolls over and gets on her knees in the middle of the bed, pushing all the covers down with her feet. The position exaggerates her hips and the smooth curves of her buns. I get excited, think I could come in a minute or two, and then Andy wakes up.

He raises his head, bleary eyed, and looks over at us, so I stop my movements and say Good Morning. He raises up his head a little more and peers down his nose as if he wore glasses, as if to assure himself that in reality he sees Joanna and I, in the next bed, doggy style.

He mumbles Good Morning, nosedives into the pillow, and pulls up the covers.

We go back to our business. Joanna gets a little more vocal, reaches back to pull my thigh, to excite me and get it over with, I think.

Andy pulls out one arm, looks at his watch, and starts to get out of bed. Joanna dives down to grab the sheets and pull herself under.

Andy says, "Don't let me stop you. I need to take a shower anyhow. Carry on."

While we hear Andy's hot shower, we loosen up and finish our business.

Afterwards, we stretch out side by side half-covered by the sheet to smoke a cigarette.

Andy comes out with a towel wrapped around him, dresses, and leaves "to get my truck back on the road as soon as possible. I get paid by the job, not by the hour."

Joanna and I fall asleep in each other's arms. We wake up a little before the eleven o'clock checkout deadline, so we shower together to save time and vacate the room.

Outside, a beautiful sunny day in the seventies, gusty wind kicks up miniature dust devils between white, dry mud puddles on bulldozed white roads where pickup trucks raise a balloon of dust when they clatter and bounce through town.

Joanna and I walk arm and arm a little, tickle each other, feel light on our feet, full of energy as if gravity disappeared. We soar through the gritty goat-herder town of pickups and stock trailers, Indians in cowboy boots and hats, older Mexican-Americans with reddish brown faces grilled by years of sunlight into eroded badlands of furrows and micro-wrinkles, their expression now a permanent echo of the sum of their joys and sorrows, and the daily squints to avoid the sun.

It all appears so exotic to the Midwestern farm boy and the urban urbane East Coast girl. We beam at each other and flirt, enjoy the superficial rewards of glandular love, the drug of choice for all youth since time immemorial.

The Universe Publicist

The Aztecs believed dead people go underneath the Northern Deserts to Mictlan, where the Death God Mictlantecuhtli dwells. For four years, they follow this skull-faced God through eight levels of hell, until they arrived at the ninth, and disappear forever.

Mexico's world-famous Copper Canyon train does not leave from the Mexican border town of Ojinaga, as I thought.

We wandered around all day, then camped out on benches in the bus station to save money and sleep a little before we got on a predawn bus toward Chihuahua, Chihuahua.

In the day's first light, this strange desert resembled a curved bone decorated with the silhouettes of Yucca plants, Mesquite trees, and

Huisatche trees that drip with giant flat pea pods. The Ocotillo plant looks like comic book grenade explosions, shaky lines that radiate out of the ground. I make sketches of the landscape.

In the seat beside me, Italian Joanna from New Jersey slept slumped, her garlic-blonde hair stuck on the humid bus window. We met thirty six hours ago, and again I feet alone. I thought of my home state, Michigan now in the second of its two seasons of mud, when leaves turn colors and whimper to the ground to blow together and make drifts of shattered rainbows of black, red, yellow, and oranges, a fluorescence that announces winter's sterility, a party of multicolored death before the funeral.

I felt the familiar hollowness grow inside and empty hope and joy out of life. Suicide in Latin America on two College semesters of Spanish. Dead Boy. I didn't care what happened to me.

Later that afternoon, the bus pulled into Chihuahua, where I saw my first examples of Mexico's colonial architecture.

The sunshine and air temperature felt hot, in the eighties or nineties at least, so we got a hotel room and put on some shorts to go explore.

We walked the hilltop streets within Chihuahua, and saw its urban sprawl hug the skirts of statuesque desert mountains framed by buildings on each side of sunny, narrow cobblestone streets, canyons that divide the whitewashed walls of long colonial buildings.

People stared at us, and we don't know why.

We met a Gringo man who lives in Chihuahua, and he invited us to dinner after we walked with him to meet up with his wife, a Mexican woman. We eat in a restaurant with tables outside on the sidewalk. They smiled and waved at so many people while we ate, it seemed like the whole town knew them. What a difference from my tiny village, where it felt like people avoided each other, if they ever got out of their cars. And no one ate outside in public.

They own a disco. They tell us that people stare at us because we wear shorts. They don't often see shorts on either men or women, because the conservative people of Chihuahua don't wear shorts.

Next morning, dawn lights our way as we march through clouds of our own breath to get on an ancient train filled with wood church pews as seats.

The train rumbles slow across the desert for a half hour or so, then stops alongside a dust colored, tin roofed plank shack with a decrepit porch, alone a desert that shimmers like a hammered silver plate. Mexicans board with their burlap bundles, chickens dangled head down, bird cages with yellowish and bluish canaries, steel enameled buckets with a dishrag cloth to cover hot tamales for sale, a couple of hog tied goats, a calf, and a crate of young pigs. They shoved the animals into the corners of our car to bleat pathetic once in a while.

Three men board and shook the dust out of their sombreros to sit down in the pew in front of us. They stink like cow manure. After the train gets underway again, the middle one turns and drapes a dusty arm over into our booth and says something. His two compadres laugh like parrots with tongues made of parched red earth. He pokes his stubby callous fingers at Joanna's chest, then at me, makes a gesture and again his comrades put their hands over their mouths and snicker. Spittle bubbles out between dirty chapped lips over yellowed teeth.

"Want learn Ingleesh," says he, and for the next hundred miles he smiled, drooled, spoke slurred wet Spanish with his thick stuck between his teeth, and tried to touch Joanna's thigh or chest with a fingertip of tenderness, to punctuate another droop eye leer.

He burped, stood up, and swayed down the aisle, pew by pew, to find the bathroom. The wind roared through the open windows as the train clatters across Chihuahua.

Across the aisle from us, three stoic matrons sit silent and proud. Mexican women, outlined in silver by morning's horizontal sunlight. Each wears a knit black shawl, a "rebozo," across her head, which she clasps with one tight fist at the collarbone to hold it in place.

The nearest one leans across the aisle to tap me on the thigh. "Bad Man" she says, in English, and shakes her finger back and forth, "No."

Big help.

The cowboy swims back up the aisle, falls into his seat, and again turns back towards us to charm Joanna with a wide, kerosene perfumed gold tooth smile.

The woman looks stern and speaks to the cowboy.

He glares at her, his chin jutted toward her in challenge, then staccatos words that make her cross herself and turn away. He turns to us again, arm dangled, his finger idles up and down Joanna's thigh.

I sit up in my seat and take a deep breath to puff myself up and stare him in the eye. I pull his sleeve up and push his arm back into his booth, and poker-faced, slow and careful, I say in English "I am a Universe publicist, and I am of no wealth paid."

Joanna looks at me with a shocked expression, round eyes, mouth open.

I look at her without expression.

The man looks at Joanna and then at me, and then he and his two compadres look at each other. His friends pull him around to face forward.

He did not turn around anymore.

Joanna tugged on my sleeve and whispered, "What did you say to him?"

I pulled out my wallet and extract a business card to give her. "My stepfather laughed when he gave me this as a going-away present. A street person gave it to him. He passed it on to me."

The little business card read: 'Myron F. Thorstein. I Am A Universe Publicist, and I Am Of No Wealth Paid.'

Whenever the train comes to one of its abrupt stops, young Indian children and Indian women with babies board for a short time until the train departs. They walk through the cars and sell food or soft drinks. If you buy a soda pop, they pour it out of the glass bottle or aluminum can into a small plastic baggie, stick in a straw, seal it with a rubber band or twist-tie, and hand it to you. Little Indian girls, looked about four years old, haul iron cook pots covered with linen hand towels. Under the towel, individual portions of enchiladas or tamales lay wrapped in aluminum foil to stay hot and ready to sell.

When the train climbed into the mountains, scrub desert metamorphized into dry stream channels cut through the rock, and sparse forests of short, dry pines. A couple of times the train stopped, for no apparent reason, alongside small meadows nestled in amongst the pines. Joanna noticed cows alongside the track.

The train took us to Creel, a town about eight thousand feet elevation, where we got out to stretch our legs. I walked the length of the train, and saw the village dogs chew at the severed leg of a cow tangled in the undercarriage.

From Creel, the tracks crossed the continental divide about seven times with thirty five miles of bridges and tunnels, to give travelers world-class spectacular views of "Copper Canyon," the Barranca del Cobre, the Grand Canyon of Mexico. Not as arid as the Grand, tall pine forests of the continental divide crown this canyon, and the train's descent took us in long curves from the pine to deciduous forests, through long black tunnels where we breathed in the sooty smoke from the engines, across rickety wooden bridges that spanned the extreme depths of many a waterfall's canyons, past enclaves of primitive houses perched on inaccessible cliffs, through regions of extreme vertical barrenness which contrasted with the next bend's lush microclimate with explosions of green tropical vegetation full of banana plants and Papaya trees that clung to tiny flat areas on the sides of the canyons.

They say the Tarahumara Indians, who live in these remote canyons, still practice ritual worship and use peyote, the tiny cactus that produces the hallucinogenic drug Mescaline. Tarahumara Indians earn their fame by the way they hunt. They run after deer until the animal drops from exhaustion.

In the 1968 Olympics held in Mexico City, the Mexicans entered a Tarahumara Indian in an Olympic marathon. He ran well but did not win, and when he crossed the finish line, Mexicans said he complained "Too short! Too short!"

To see the Pacific Ocean, we passed Los Mochis at the end of the train ride and took a bus to a dirty little port called Topolobampa. From there, we decided to hitchhike south.

It took a while. We stood beside the road in the sun, got thirsty, and walked down in front of a tiny store-restaurant, built like a cement tent a couple of steps above road level, to buy drinks, then tried to hitchhike again, got hungry, decided to eat, hitched, got thirsty for another apple flavored soda pop, hitched, felt sun burnt, hung out in the shade of the store.

Then a truck stopped to pick us up. A funny, aggressive fat guy, "El Gordo," and his passive skinny "Flaco" sidekick became our tour guides.

The truck stopped along the roadside every hour or so, at one of the thousands of little house windows dressed up with signs and glass jars of candies to serve as a front room convenience store counter. They bought cold beer, the antidote for the heat and humidity. With the bartender's help, they taught us about the area, the industrialized agriculture's huge sprinkler systems, and loved each other's embellishments and reenactments of the bloodier episodes of local history full of revolutionaries, drug runners, and the gunslinger lawlessness of the big ranch families. Sometimes they asked the other soused patrons or the fat beer maids to jog their memories, or help them act out some phrase or word we didn't understand.

When we got back in the truck, the fat man El Gordo laughs as Flaco quibbles about the seating arrangements. El Gordo hoists himself up with a big groan and a fart to get in on his side. He leans across the seat and grunts and opens the door from the inside to call out for Joanna "Subete, Joe-Aahhnnna, Subete" to climb up into that colorless stale yawn. They think Joanna should sit between them, with me against the door. I try to tell them that the chivalry of Caballeros, gentlemen, forces us to give her the window seat. With gentle pushes and pulls, they try to push me along and up into the truck to sit next to the fat driver. I put my arm around Joanna, which confuses Flaco with hope for a moment and gives me a chance to give him a rough push upward into the truck to sit next to his boss. Then I climb in fast beside him, and Joanna gets the window.

On the road with the windows open, everyone with a beer, we see the road ahead dissolve and bubble into the sky. Cars appeared as blips on a bluish-green horizon that would not sit still. To enhance the extraterrestrial effect, sweat dripped into our eyes. Then El Gordo the Potgut began to off-gas, to subject us to each flatulence which he blames on his skinny sidekick with a cruel laugh and his elbow jammed into the man's tuning-fork ribs.

As the sunset painted the cloud layer with streaks of red so it looked like the hot ceramic of an electric stove element, we drove through the flat plains decorated with cultivations, swamps, forests, and open range. Far off, city lights bloomed on the horizon and spread their stardust under the earth's shadow.

El Gordo rasped his ham of hand across the forest of stubble on his porcine jowls and announced "Vamos a comer," time to eat. We stopped at a restaurant, another half-size circus tent set up beside the road in the middle of nowhere with a fancy beer company billboard.

El Gordo bought us more beer. Joanna whispered to me, with a flirty smile in case they watched her, but with a voice nervous and intense. "I don't like this at all. El Gordo stops to drink and get us drunk, then he tries to touch me."

"What?"

"Haven't you noticed him touch my leg?"

"No." As if through a portal, I enter Joanna's world, which changes everything. I feel her fear, and feel responsible to protect her. I also feel powerless in a land where we don't belong, don't speak the language, and don't know the culture or laws.

When young, most of us feel unsure of ourselves, and that helps us learn. People who know it all suffer from a learning disability, they must destroy their own ideas to make way for new and better ones. After we appreciate the differences between groups of people, our notions of good taste and a sense of humor change. We can't feel so sure about where appropriate behavior stops, and crude jokes or vulgar threats begin. Good manners depend on each group's tacit approval, each relies on tribal instinct for the creation of unique and arbitrary non-verbal clues to acceptable behavior.

Joanna might feel an exaggerated repulsion, due to the way her parents brought her up. I thought maybe El Gordo the Amoeba, and other Mexican men, might touch women casually and think nothing of it when among members of their culture, and the women might expect a hand on their knee, or else feel rejected and less attractive.

Even though they don't understand English, they understand too much. Joanna and I excuse ourselves to go find bathrooms, so we can express ourselves a bit more freely as we walk together.

When we get back to our table, learn they ordered for us, to speed up the process.

The food soon comes. We eat, nervous, and watch as they order more drinks all around in spite of our protest, which they wave off as an insult to their hospitality.

After all the beer consumed throughout this long day, at last, El Gordo the Fatman acts drunk. Night engulfs this circus tent in the middle of nowhere. The jukebox revs up to push high decibel tropical rhythms through blown speakers that buzz and cough the offbeat Omp-pah-paaaaah bass line of Cumbia music.

El Gordo the Doughboy wants to dance.

His skinny Ralph sidekick convinces the toady barmaid to come over and keep me company. Short, with broad thick shoulders and no neck, her hair once black but now dyed an improbable color, short arms with tiny hands that she can't quite let hang to her sides, but angle out a little. Her mouth manipulates a tiny piece of chewing gum. She wears a loose white shirt and khaki shorts covered in front by a blue denim barmaid's apron. I imagined her birth, ladled out on a huge greasy spoon, her makeup already applied with a hand accustomed to a spatula and a hot grill, her plucked eyebrows and overall image under constant refinement with pudgy fingertip adjustments as she watches her amplified image through the smeared concave surface of a little round pocket compact mirror. She sits down heavily in the chair, crosses her short bare legs, puts her hand on my thigh, and tries to teach me Mexican Spanish.

When a new song starts, she stands up and pulls on me, puts her arm around my neck to cajole me to dance with her. El Gordo and Flaco help push us out onto the empty dance floor.

I look over her shoulder and see our fat truck driver hustle Joanna. The four of us dance around the center tent pole, a large four foot think tree trunk that, at one time, sprouted here in what's now the middle of the dance floor. It makes a convenient obstruction which El Gordo uses, along with the expansive folds of his own curved back, to block my vision while he attempts to kiss Joanna. She tells me this later, at the table.

Joanna breaks free and runs back to the table. As we finish our plates of Mexican food, we hold secret conversations, disguised by smiles and pointing at the hot sauce, about how we can get away from these two. Beg sanctuary from this circus tent full of alcoholics? Run into the road and flag down one of the few cars that pass, and hope it stops? Run into the bush until morning?

When they decide to take off again, Joanna and I talk quickly in English, but they hate that, and get testy about it. We laugh, but talk terrified about how we can get away from them, away from this bar restaurant circus tent in the middle of a Mexican darkness, a void full of bird song that sounds like broken dishwashers, punctuated by mysterious loud noises that a deer might make eviscerated live.

They could murder us here, and no one would complain about the Yankee fertilizer.

As we walk back toward the truck, Joanna and I smile and chatter in English to disguise our conversation's subject, that we recognize our plight, stuck in a foreign country with a couple of drunken rapists, surrounded by miles and miles of darkness. We want to run, hide, and hitch another ride.

How do we get our bags out of the truck? Leave them behind, with all our traveler's checks? Perhaps these two clowns want our money, and the entertainment of anything else that happens before they get rid of us.

When we make moves to get our bags out of the truck, the men laugh and say, "No, it's not safe here. We can't leave you here alone."

We look back to the employees of the circus tent, and call the toady barmaid over, but even she helps push us back into the cab with the two Mexican men.

The employees think we are paranoid. When we say we want to stay there, at the restaurant, in the middle of the night, they all shrug and gently negate that possibility. They encourage us, with smiles and "please" in English, to get back into the truck's cab.

Later, I wondered if, on balance, they picked the lesser of two dangers. Maybe they thought it best that we not find out what might happen to a couple of lost Gringos at an all-night circus tent bar with easy barmaids in the middle of a region notorious for narco-traffickers.

Back on the road for the next couple of hours, the two men told us all about Culiacán, the regional center of drug traffickers and ranch violence, over the last decade. They pantomime battles with machine guns and marijuana cigarettes, show us how addicts tied off their arms to inject heroin, how people snort cocaine powder with a rolled five dollar American bill, which they urged me to lend them for the purposes of verisimilitude.

I thought they wanted to know where, and how much, money I had on me.

After midnight, we saw the lights on the horizon grow into the sprawl of a city. El Gordo pulled into some junkyard outskirts of Culiacán, and drove alongside a long corrugated metal fence decorated with stencil-like paintings of Ché Guevara, raised fists, and words like "Vencerémos!" and other communist slogans in bold letters that dripped blood red paint.

Then the fat man drives up to a gate, stops and honks. An armed guard comes to his window, they talk, the guard asks something about us, stares at us, then takes a step back, runs his hands through his thin, greasy hair, stares at us some more, and then he waves us through.

El Gordo drives on, and leers at us as he pans our surroundings with upraised palm. "Communists. You have a problem with communists? No? Well they have problem with YOU. You Americans, Americans hate Communists, so Communists watch, careful. Ten cuidado. We Mexicans, we like Russians. You understand? We like Russians." He leans over and stares into my face, pulls down one lower eyelid to reveal the bloodred raw meat within.

Flaco and he laugh.

We stop at another guarded gate, and after more intense discussions and some harsh words, we drive through and down a small dirt road along a cement wall punctuated with lit doorways. In the yellow electric lit rooms behind doorways draped with diaphanous fabric, I see domestic scenes of adults and children, televisions on dressers, walls of vibrant pure colors that clash with each other, and simple plastic furniture labeled with Coca-cola, or a brand of Mexican beer like Superior or Pacifico.

They park the truck along a dark section of that wall, and two fat women and some children come out. The fat man introduces us to his wife and sister, and a few of the older kids. Then he, his wife, and Flaco show us to a doorway a couple of hundred feet down the wall.

This they offer as our room for the night. No window, and a simple metal door, like a garage. Looks like a jail cell to us. One bare bed with a filthy bare mattress, one bare lightbulb dangles from the ceiling over a bare cement floor. The walls and everything look covered with cobwebs and coagulated dust balls. They promise to bring blankets or sheets. The fat man enlists some teenagers to bring us our bags, and as they leave, they lock the door "for our protection" from the outside, and promise to return "pronto".

We don't feel comfortable, try to decide what to do, but do not see many choices.

I wonder if the problem stems from our perceptions. "Maybe we overreacted. Maybe everything will turn out fine."

Joanna says "Easy for you to say. Slim chance you'll get raped in the next couple of hours."

"Slim, but not impossible."

"Have we been kidnapped?"

"Maybe we don't understand the culture. They might think they do us a big favor, save money, not sleep at a hotel. That's how they would treat a friend or family member that comes to visit."

"I don't feel like family, do you?"

We both admit that now, it feels like they treated us like prisoners from the start. We talk about an attempt to knock El Gordo out, but like Siamese twins, the two appear inseparable. Joanna wonders what might happen if we call out, because we know nothing about the loyalties of others nearby. Wouldn't do us Americans any good to hurt a member of a big, extended Communist family community that lived on hateful fantasies of how to roast Capitalist pigs.

We decide, for our own protection in the short term, to stay on their good side.

When they return, a couple of fat women boss El Gordo and Flaco around. I get the impression the skinny man's wife wants to kill him. The women try to apologize, and act ashamed of the men. They carry our backpacks for us and walk us to the truck to load everything back into the cab. Then they force the two men to take us into downtown Culiacán and drop us off at a hotel.

The women smile and wave as the truck pulls out of the wall enclosed compound.

We feel the heat of the asphalt as we drive down the black empty road. A fine mist peppers the windshield, and the wipers turn it into a smear of mud until a heavier rain washes it clean.

Within a half hour, we pull up in front of a three story hotel. They know the hotel manager, and get us a real low, special rate, they say. We look at each other in desperation and acknowledge it as a bit expensive for us, but the alternative seems worse.

They carry our bags up into a second floor street side hotel room at one thirty in the morning, then say goodbye and stomp down the stairs. We hear the rumble of the truck's motor as it starts.

We sit silent on the bed, sobered by fear and nervous exhaustion, then hear voices call out our names from the street. We open the window and lean out over a tiny balcony about a foot wide, decorated with a wrought iron fence.

Below on the black rain wet streets, they both lean out their window to smile and wave up at us. "Tomorrow," El Gordo whispers hoarse, hand cupped around his mouth, analogous to the exhaust pipe that issues drum rolls from the truck's pistons. "We pick you up at eight, tomorrow morning."

"Ok." we wave and smile. "Bye. Adios. Hasta mañana."

Next morning, we walked into the bus station at seven AM, worried that The Fatman and Skinny might head us off to strong-arm us out of the bus station with lots of laughs to wave off their compatriots. Then we boarded a bus and, paranoid, keep watch out the window to see if The Fatman and Skinny might show up to encourage the bus-line personnel to point us out.

Only when we felt movement as the bus backed out of its slot, did Joanna say "Finally, I can relax and not worry about those two Bozos."

I didn't relax until several miles after the bus left town, and even then, I looked with untoward attention through the bus window and into the cab of any big rig truck that passed us for the first hour or so.

No wonder the United States hates communists.

I thought about what communism means, and wondered, did they plan to share us with everyone?

San Blas Hurricane

The Mayans believed in thirteen levels of heaven, with the Earth as the first level, each ruled by gods called Oxlahuntiku, The branches of the Ceiba tree (the World Tree) reach up into these heavens of peace and leisure reserved for Priests, warriors killed in battle, women who died in childbirth, and the sacrificed. They visualized the Earth as the back of a huge tortoise or crocodile creature that swims through an ocean of stars and time. Below that, nine levels of subterranean underworlds, each ruled by one of the gods called the Bolontiku, with the lowest level called Mitnal by the Yucatán Maya, and called Xibalba by the Quiché Maya. The God of Death, Ah Puch, rules this ninth hell, and sometimes he stirs all the levels above, all the way up to the heavens, in a deadly maelstrom that whirls with water, earth, plants, and the breath of the Gods.

Many archaeologists think the ancient Mayans also believe in a paradise after death, as did the Aztecs in central Mexico. Today's tribes of Lacandón Indians, who live remote and isolated in the southern forests of Mexico, believe the dead's spirit flies to a land of plenty above the earth, and live without work, worry, or strife.

San Blas owes its popularity to surfers.

As the highway neared the Pacific, it took us through green canyons where walls of jungle vegetation parted in temporary openness. The bus thundered through pools of red or yellow flower petals under trees that looked as if God iced the topmost surface of their canopies with that color flowers. In some places, where the dense leaves opened up a little, I could see into the shadowy forest. Small explosions of pineapple-like bromeliads and vines made of thick spatula-shaped succulent leaves flattened like chains of foot long hotdogs, covered the thick silvery tree limbs. Networks of large, long vines looped from tree to tree, from nests of lacey tendrils wrapped around the limbs and elbows of the forest giants, creatures trapped in great spider webs.

The bushes along the road looked impenetrable, and divided our asphalt ribbon world from the primordial, and kept us out of this Eden so pregnant with threat and danger. With its exuberant fecundity that depends upon death, the temporal present eats the past and toasts it with the wine of forgetfulness. Those who enter here and get lost, not only never return, but cease to exist with a suddenness that makes all doubt if they ever existed.

The Californian surfers' influence displayed itself in joyous psychedelic colors in much of the business signage. These establishments learned how to attract all classes and groups of tourists to their establishments with hucksters on the sidewalks in Hawaiian shirts, or with signs made out of old surfboards. Restaurants and clothing stores accessorized their name with English keywords. Panadería bakeries advertised "Banana Bread", the hotels advertised 'showers,' the price of rooms in dollars USD, specials for the "Bridal Suite." Clothing stores hung out starburst signs that declared "Swimsuits" as fluorescent flowers to attract the busy-bee tourists.

Joanna picked out a San Blas restaurant for our next meal, because the sign outside mentioned a live alligator.

As our eyes got used to the dim light, we noticed the rustic drift wood incorporated into the bar and stools. The vertical bamboo walls, and plastic palm leaves stuck on the top of support pillars, added to its tropical charm. In the center of the building, a little circle of wooden fence marked the periphery of an excavated pit about five feet deep and five yards across. Inside the pit, potted plants arranged around a small pool of black water became a tiny zoo exhibit, a home for a large, motionless alligator over ten feet long. It took Joanna a while to see it, because she looked for something small, not a massive breakwater half beached and half submerged.

It looked like peninsula of dirt and rock.

Talk among tourists and travelers centered on the overcast skies and a powerful hurricane offshore in the Pacific, which weather forecasters said would hit this area for the next four days.

The Pacific ocean and San Blas' beach lay about a mile away, maybe more, a walk out of town down a long, jungle lined, grassy road little used by automobiles. It takes us to a clear area of sand and rock next to an abandoned hotel within view of the ocean. We heard that hippies hang out in the abandoned hotel, to spend the night for free, soothed by the complex long crashes of ocean waves on a long rock peninsula and the sandy beach.

Joanna and I walked it in midday, under overcast skies. We walked fast to keep ahead of the mosquitoes. I think Joanna feared the dark forest. When we glimpsed the ocean's vast openness ahead, she ran as if to rid herself of her claustrophobia. I walked out into the soft, windblown sand of a area of sand dunes, and felt heartened to see trails of footprints that led up to, and from, the abandoned hotel's entrance. A couple of tattered shirts hung on the low cement fence around the porch area.

The hotel leaned in mute testimony to the power of the a past hurricane that all but destroyed it and San Blas.

Even though intact, the entire two story colonial style hotel listed on the sand at an angle, as if the ocean floated it here from somewhere else, or the waves of a storm surge excavated underneath the structure.

Under a dishrag sky, long rock peninsula, black as motor oil on the gray sludge of ocean, jutted off the beach and floated across the horizon of water. A low palm thatch restaurant perched on the point. Huge waves broke against the boulders, fifty foot high explosions of whitewater from the collision with hurricane-generated waves smashed into the peninsula and scraped their way down from the far point to the beach. Each one lit up that rocky peninsula like a struck match head, all along its quarter mile length, with giant geysers of spray that sputtered like white flame.

The air hissed and shook past us full of the vibration of the sea and the sizzle of bubbles, the sounds of windblown sand and the cymbal shimmers of whitewater crests that double over upon themselves. The air filled with static white noise. Cloud troughs of the hurricane's edge arched in spiral arms overhead, evidence of the power of the distant hurricane's center of deadly turmoil a couple hundred miles out to sea.

A few people waded in the shallows, but the waves created sudden changes in the water level, from knee deep to shoulder deep. Only the bravest, or most foolish, of adults entered the deeper water.

Neither the shouts of Johanna, nor the relentless roar of static could dissuade me from a dip in the ocean. I let the ambient whoosh drown out Joanna's objections, and I shouted into her ear that I wanted to swim, but she clutched my arm with bony fingers and begged me not to.

"I won't sit here and watch you drown." She looked like she might cry. She feared the ocean, and to avoid a miserable time with her eyes glued on me for the next forty five minutes with the morbid fantasy that I would drown any second, I urged her to head back into town to get some sleep in our hotel room.

As she walks alone across the sand dunes towards the break in the green wall, I notice another swimmer, far out and even with the peninsula's point, who tries to body surf down the face of a huge wave. Then I see another swimmer. They hold one arm extended like superman as they cut like a knife and fall at the same speed that the water pushes upward to carry them forward toward shore. I wanted to try it, wanted to swim way out there, past the three or four people that waded in waist deep water to wait nervous for the next big wave to lift them off their feet and force them to dogpaddle for a few minutes until the water ran back out to sea and let them down.

I took off my shirts, shorts, and sandals and put a big scoop of sand on them as an anchor, and ran into the sea. The peninsula and its little restaurant offered a haven, should I get tired or water logged. I battled the waves, but didn't feel like I made much headway against the onshore push of the breakers. After a while, I got far enough out so that my feet didn't touch the bottom at all, and only the biggest waves piled up into whitewater crowns that curved over to fall upon their own chest. The cumulative effect of waves and surges of water changed the depth by three feet every half minute or so.

I swam out far enough to get even with the end of the peninsula, and noticed the body surfers all wore fins, mask and snorkel. I didn't. I never tried to body surf before, but when I managed to catch one big wave for a short ride toward shore, I wanted to do it again. I tried to swim out to sea and catch another, and when another big breaker came in, I tried to ride it. This one curled over and scrubbed me along the bottom like a washing machine as it dragged me back toward shore.

I tread water and looked around, deafened by a static sound that came from the bubbles that boiled up underneath me. Little bubbles wiggled up my legs, into my swimsuit, into my armpits, and popped at the surface all around me, an after-effect of the frothy breaker that passed a few moments before. I tried to swim out again, and felt pretty good about myself, until a man who swam near me called my attention to the fact that the rip tide carried us farther and farther from the beach. Without notice, sound, nor sense of motion, the sum of water the bigger waves heaped up near shore must sweep back out to sea again, corralled along this peninsula. While we both attempted to swim farther out to sea, this offshore current carried us farther and farther away from the long peninsula of rocks.

The dilapidated restaurant on the rocky point shrank into a distant symbol of safety and rescue.

We both swam like mad towards shore, and didn't make much headway. I decided to swim parallel to the shore and towards the peninsula, and he followed me. We both touched bottom much sooner than we expected. We fought the urge to swim into the rocks of the nearby peninsula because waves crashed there with explosive violence. We struggled to parallel the peninsula back to the shore, so far away that people looked like pencil marks.

Swim strokes, splash splash splash, impotent flails against an inexorable force. The powerful mixture of waves and wave bounce off the peninsula mixed with the rip currents, and I felt like a frantic mouse in a flushed toilet. I tried to walk underwater a little, dove down and bent over till my hands touched the bottom to dig in with fingers and toes with every step, but came up exhausted every time I managed to hold my place. I hugged the bottom to escape the waves and current, curled my toes deeper into the muck sand bottom, but couldn't dig in enough to walk.

In fear and exhaustion, we looked at each other.

He raised one hand flat, and said "Calma, calma."

We waited for the seas to calm between sets of waves, then swam like madmen until a wave lifted us and we could try to slide or surf down its front. When the water deepened and flowed backwards, we went underwater and dug our toes in to try and walk forward, bent double. By this strategy, we swam both toward shore and away from the peninsula, which soon liberated us from the rip currents. After that, we swam relaxed, grateful, and scared, to shore.

As I walked back towards town, I examined the decrepit hurricane-smashed hotel. With its foundations undermined by the waves of a hurricane, the walls leaned south, as if a head nod toward the jungle path that exited the undergrowth behind it. Through the open double doors, I saw a small group of people inside, seated in a semi-circle just within the dark interior. I walked across the sand to check it out.

About five people sat in the dark interior near the door and passed a joint around with furtive movements. They wore Mexican tourist sarapes, with leather hats copied from Dickens' England, blue jean shorts, and sandals.

One of them appeared much older. He wore his hair long and uncombed, thin hair that sprouted from a scalp almost bald. So skinny, his blue eyes sunk into deep sockets in his cheekbones, and his emaciated hands seemed made of bones, veins, and fingernails. His white skin flaked off in the edges of his white scraggly beard, and framed his face up into his dishwater blond temples.

They stopped their conversation as I approached the hotel veranda. Moments later, they confessed they worried I might work as a spy for the cops, and felt relieved when I shared their joint and "didn't seem like that type of person." Each of us took a hit, and then as if by secret signal, when one of them refused to accept the joint, the four decided to leave. They thanked the older man for the smoke, and left us two alone to finish it.

We watched them walked off, wrapped in wind-tugged sarapes, each sandaled footstep surrounded by a puff of blown sand.

I took a hit and asked him his name.

"No one has any names down here. What are you doing down here? You should be in school."

"I'm older than I look. I'm twenty two.'

"I'm younger than I look. You should be in college, then."

"I tried college. Took a class in Spanish. Now I'm headed for Guatemala."

"Guatemala, Guatemala. Why Guatemala?"

"People live on three hundred sixty five dollars a year. Dollar a day."

"People die on three hundred sixty five dollars a year."

We smoked the joint, and in the muffled static roar of the ocean that reverberated within the dark silence of the old hotel's deepest interior, I felt the spirits of life, of the visitors that once stayed here, their breaths like the sounds of the distant surf that crashed and sizzled across the sands.

Tall palm trees swayed in an erotic flirtatiousness above the low forest, a forest, I realized, lowered by hurricanes. Winds driven to landfall by hurricanes as strong as the big one that approached the Mexican coast today, contained eyewalls that spun over a hundred miles an hour, to trim and top any tall trees that dared to grow so near the ocean.

This skinny death-mask of a young man lay back and closed his eyes while he held in his hit of marijuana. He exhaled and seemed exhausted.

I asked "Where are you headed?"

"Nowhere."

"Where do you live?"

"Here."

"In San Blas?"

He made a movement with the hand that held the tiny end of the spent joint, the brown roach, which no longer glowed with fire.

I asked again, "You live in San Blas?"

"Whatever. Here, man. Here. Here." He pushed the dead roach at me.

I took it from him, and wondered if I could get it lit without cooked fingers. "What do you do here?" I thought maybe he camped out in this hotel, sold drugs or hippie artifacts to tourists.

"I live here."

I tried another tactic, another tangent, a circuitous route. "What are you doing down here in Mexico?"

He opened his eyes and looked at me with what I thought at the time seemed like suspicion or fear.

Quick as a wink, I added, "You have a job or something?"

"No. I live here."

"Don't you do anything?"

"I told you, I live here. Live. That's all. Live." He glared at me, then lay back against the doorjamb, and closed his eyes again. "You should be in school."

"Maybe you're right. Well, I'm taking off now. See you around."

He did not react.

I think of him often, wonder if he suffered from a heroine addiction, or some terminal disease. Maybe he lived out some fanatical religious philosophy, or dug himself into this trench to minimize the world's impact on his life, or his impact on the world.

Maybe he came back from Viet Nam so damaged that he considered himself a high risk, a mortal danger, to family and friends, to anyone that might wake him in the middle of a nightmare flashback, and open the portal from the real world into his inner vortex of violence and chaos, the trauma of wartime service in young adulthood, now an indelible part of his character.

Before fully awake, he might react, as trained, by killer instinct, and even those closest to him could cease to exist before a wakeful thought crossed his mind to temper a lethal reflex of self preservation.

He looked like a heroin addict that eats only beer and peanuts. Maybe he dropped out of college in reaction to a string of bad luck and cruel girlfriends, and did something that caused his family to disown him.

He might consider his escapade a heroic act to protect his family. Maybe he chose this way to die, of cancer or worse, a missing person till the end, to spare them the worst of it and earn them life insurance money.

Something about him convinced me we thought in common, when I felt like Dead Boy, that he too enjoyed the thought he could disappear in Latin America, and indulge in cheap amusement as a slow suicide.

Round House in Santa Clara

We got off the bus in a tiny beach community called Santa Clara because some fellow travelers told us about a situation near the beach, a Mexican family in a round cement house managed like a Youth Hostel, where guests may work to defray the cost of a room. We found the place, thanks to the usual hospitality. When you ask about the location of hotels or other landmarks, many Mexicans want to take your hand and lead you there.

A young Mexican student, Antonio, lived there and managed the guests when his mom couldn't. He rented us a wedge shaped room, and then explained he must leave for the afternoon. When home from college for vacation, he picked peanuts, the local product.

I disliked him right off, because his three day beard looked more beatnik hip than mine.

Later we got to know his mother, a sexy compact woman, a Mexican hippie with a thick wild frizz of black hair, a college educated polyglot who wore the loose white clothes one might see on a rich woman at an urban Whole Earth store. This curly haired dynamo moved so fast, on so many projects, she became both invisible and omnipresent.

"You can come and go as you like, but at night, about ten o'clock or so, we lock the doors until next morning. You won't find any discos in Santa Clara, and no bar that would let a girl go in, so better do any drinking during the day and stay in at night."

Our first night in the round house, we fell asleep fast, exhausted from a tour of San Blas with backpacks, then a long ride on a bus that stops in every village and crossroad along the way.

I needed to pee sometime after midnight. I crept out of our room and across the main room to the bathroom, a pie section with a steel sink and fancy modern porcelain toilet that flushed with a bucket filled from a nearby tap.

No light. I forgot to bring a flashlight.

I went to get one and returned to regret it. The flashlight illuminated bathroom walls that resembled an Egyptian tomb covered with hieroglyphics. Serpentine geckoes, huge winged bugs with wings akimbo, the fat exclamation marks of cockroaches, scarab beetles in iridescent blues and greens, punctuated by the asterisks and pound signs of black spiders with rhomboid abdomens and legs splayed out to about three or four inches across. Most of the bugs and geckoes remained motionless, but every once in a while one moved and set others into a short motion. I darted the flashlight over all the wall space and counted twenty or thirty of the big black spiders as they maneuvered for position. The spiders moved most often, to avoid the geckos, transparent runes of soft lightning that leaped into brief sine-wave action then stopped to emit mechanical chirps.

I hate and fear spiders, with reason. Daddy Longlegs bite me, though no one believes it. Maybe to them, I smell like a bug. I backed out through the bathroom doorway and decided to pee outside in the jungle.

I crept through the silent house, and tried to keep my bearings. Every direction looked the same, a doorway to one of the peripheral wedge shaped rooms. I tried to keep my sense of North aligned with the couches in the center room. Any one of those three dark masses of couches might hide a sleeper. I tiptoed to the main door, gently tried the medieval iron latch, and then remembered why they impressed upon us the need to get home early each night. They lock these doors at ten.

I went back to the bathroom and peeked in with the flashlight. It looked more horrible than I remembered from five minutes before. To avoid a ruptured bladder, I looked down to ignore the spiders, and felt relieved to see none on the floor. I rationalized that they must fear me more than I fear them, and both our instincts should reinforce the reality of our relationship. If any one of those spiders touched me, I would use the flashlight as a club to make sure it died as a tinted smear on the cement, with a trail of peepee to mark my panicked exit into the darkness. I stood before the toilet and tried to aim my stream of piss to make the least noise. The bugs, beetles, and geckoes minded their own business, to prey or avoid predation, so I ignored their presence.

In my mind's eye, I could see and feel the spiders, big black rhomboid six inchers, that lowered themselves in silence on thin threads, legs akimbo, toward the back of my neck.

First morning, I awoke before Joanna, so I took a hike alone, out of the little patch of forest that hugged the house, and down into the nearby slopes of a treeless settlement of adobe shacks and sapling fences on reddish sandy dirt. On the edge of town at the base of the jungle mountainside, I found a trail that went up the mountainside, into the forest.

In a few places, the trail skirted cliffs that overlooked the ocean.

A palm frond fallen onto the trail forced me to appreciate their size and ruggedness. While on the tree, they look delicate and flexible, and when they move in a strong wind, they look like pompoms of feathers. When I walked the trail alongside some fallen ones and counted my steps, I measured them between twenty to thirty feet long.

I sat on some tree roots to do an ink pen sketch. I included the path, a frond, some tree trunks, and jungle plants to capture some of the complex interwoven tapestry of thin bushes and muscular vines amid these big fleshy leaves.

Then I walked back down the steep path and turned towards the ocean with the idea of a little swim, if I could find a beach.

I decided not to pass by the house to see if Joanna might come along, to spare her forty minutes of speculative fantasy of my death by drowning, and the profound guilt should it happen. She should feel guilty, because she never learned to swim enough to rescue anyone.

From my point of view, without Joanna, I would spare myself the ridiculous last image of her frantic screams as I disappeared under the waves to reappear to sink again, over and over, till drowned.

The windy beach confronted me with a big problem, bigger than the medium sized waves that came in fast to smash and send up geysers of seawater. The beach consisted of rounded black boulders, about one and a half to five feet across. Up close, they looked like charred rye bread, a black volcanic glass filled with tiny bubbles, sized from a pinprick to the size of a pea, each with sharp broken edges. They formed a black band of beach which contrasted with the geysers of spray from powerful waves that outlined the shore around this two mile wide bay.

They arrange themselves into two banks, one at wave level, and another one higher, from hurricane-strength storm surge waves, a beach with two tiers of gigantic bowling balls.

On the exposed face of the mountain, where wind and waves cut away and left a cliff-face of dirt and sand, I could see the black bands of boulders, ancient deposits from where these boulders fell, black lines of boulders twenty or thirty feet high on the mountainsides around the bay. They fell out already rounded by ancient wave action from seas perhaps ten thousand or even millions of years ago, from higher ocean levels, or before an uplift of the land. I reasoned they formed when a volcanic lava flow of foamy black glass pumice broke apart, and waves bounced the almost floatable rocks against each other to round them. Then floods buried them in sand and gravel. Geologic uplift elevated the deposits, or ocean levels fell, and now they fell out of the sandy matrix from high on the cliffs to again form a beach. When the powerful waves of the Pacific Ocean crashed against the beach, they unsettled the underwater boulders, whose porous consistency made them much lighter than normal rocks. They bang against each other underwater, and make a tremendous dull groan that runs up and down the coast, the gnash of gigantic teeth, a gigantic sub-aquatic bowling alley that stretched for miles around the bay.

It didn't look possible to get in or out of the water. But after a few moments of study under the impetus of my determination to swim in the ocean again, I thought I could do it.

No one else about, so I took off my clothes and piled them under my sandals.

I studied how the waves came in, and thought I could time my leap to avoid the smash of wave upon boulders, to propel myself over the top of the danger and into deeper, wave swelled water.

A large wave smashed into the boulders and covered me with a mist of saltwater, and as it fell back into the Pacific, I leapt into the surge and rode it away from shore. I swam like crazy with images of my legs between big black boulders, smashed and abraded into pink gummy appendages, remnants of their former length.

After a few minutes I calmed down. I felt so refreshed and clean, but grew fearful of the waves, their power and unpredictability, and of the fin-filled darkness beneath my legs. I submerged and swam down with outstretched arm to feel the bottom or whatever, but the jade green milky waters darkened with depth before I could see or touch the bottom.

I swam out a ways and tried to lurch up higher out of the water to find a better place to exit, but couldn't see a soft sandy beach anywhere along this coast. I propelled myself under the waves with dangled toes, but no touch within nine or ten feet, so I swam closer to the shore.

From sea level, the waves looked much stronger, they crashed and roared like beasts against the gristmill of the boulders. Around the bay, I saw waves rear up like stallions, or white-mane lions, that attacked and pawed the black boulders, they exploded in long geysers of spray that danced in the breeze, a harem of veiled maidens. I felt the Sirens' invitation to the soft caress of treachery, the veiled enticement of a wet kiss upon the sands, and I remembered those waves would deliver me to the blind blows from immense black boulders that lurked beneath the surface.

I tread water as close as I dared to the boulders, where waves lifted them up and slammed them together like waterlogged sections of tree trunk. I watched, and recognized that I could take advantage of the energy and height of the largest waves to throw me up over the majority of the boulders.

When I felt sure of the necessary magnitude of a large wave's strength, I needed to swim as fast as I could.

With each minute, my sense of loneliness grew in direct proportion to the certainty of a large hungry shark below me in the jade green waters. I felt tired, and tread water with my face low in the haphazard jostle of waves and wave reflections off the shore. I swam upright to look out to sea, and the next time a larger swell approached, I swam furiously and incorporated myself into wave as it slammed into the boulders. I became one with the gush of water that threw itself on the boulders.

The wave swept me up in its death throes, and I landed full force onto the boulders with my chest, where my fingers clung to the sharp glassy sandpaper of a large boulder. As the waters retreated, the ocean pulled at my bare legs. I scrambled up the crushed black glass surfaces to get away before the next wave carried me back out to sea.

Naked, I searched along the shore until I found my clothes, then put on everything but my shirt, to give my bloodied chest a chance to dry and scab. The abrasive boiled lava surface of the boulder sanded completely through some of my chest hairs and left weepy, bloody abrasions that streaked down into my abdomen.

To escape the humid, sunny heat of the afternoon, Joanna and I lunched on Mexican sweet bread, bananas, oranges, toasted tortillas, and peanuts inside the cool shadows of the round cement house. Since we entered Mexico, it seemed we lived on Mexican sweetbreads. We could find them in most stores, in bus stations, at every panadería (bakery). To me they resembled an oversize hamburger bun baked with a decorative cover of a flattened spiral of bright pastel colored sugar and white flour. This topping crumbled off with each bite to decorate the lips and fall into your lap, so I invented various methods to eat them. In the most recent method under development, I plucked the topping off with my teeth and lips first, until it looked like a skinned hamburger bun.

We talked about the ashen-tanned owner's son Antonio, how he didn't look Mexican, but like a mulatto with nappy black hair and full lips, who said he went to college and yet worked in the peanut fields. When he came by for lunch, he promised to hang around and help us learn Spanish, if we could help him improve his English. He pulled out a joint and shared it with us, told us this joint represented the last of his stash. When he heard that I play guitar, he brought out an acoustic guitar for me, so that he could play blues harmonica. We tuned the guitar to the harmonica, then he asked me to play in a key other than the harmonica's scale, to play blues. That impressed me. We started a jam session so he could show off on the harmonica.

I started to play some intellectual Art rock, something off The Rise and Fall of Ziggy Stardust most likely, but he wanted blues, just blues, and I got bored after each fifteen minutes of another of the same simple chord progression {one-four-one, four-one, five-four one, one-four-one-five repeat} and the twelve beat rhythm. Then I thought to interjected some other chords in the scale, and other improvisations I learned in jazz class at college.

It sounded cool.

His eyes shot at me with alarm, then disapproval, over the top of his cupped hands. The harmonica bleated, and when that didn't stop me, he put down the harmonica to give me a lecture in broken English about the blues.

Antonio said "You move your fingers good, but play too much. The less you play, the better. More tasty you know. Feel it here, not here." He pointed to his head. "Play less. You play not too much, and makes it tasty."

He wanted me to play pure backup and give him plenty of space and time to lead. Even though I knew that, his words rang true enough to hurt. I decided that he lacked creativity, and the willingness to go with the flow, to change with the currents of others. I shouldn't let myself feel bothered by a fledgling Mexican intellectual, a recent arrival to blues music. He would benefit from a primer in a sensitive appreciation of Blues and Jazz as a unique American art form, and learn to expect improvisation.

After a few minutes more of this Mexican blues, he excused himself and left to head back to work in the peanut fields.

Joanna and I decided to go out in search of marijuana to replenish Antonio's supply, and ensure his future generosity. We both felt very nervous about carrying drugs on ourselves in a foreign country. Better Antonio, as a member of the modernized hippie generation of college bound youth of Mexico, face charges of possession of marijuana than us. As Antonio said, if the authorities catch young Americans with drugs, they throw them in jail and wait to see how much money their parents will spend to get them out.

We walked around the village. It sprawled along the valley floor, a conglomerate of wooden shacks made of saplings and mud, each surrounded by a bare yellow ocher plot with pigs or goats and chickens and/or turkeys, with a few plots of vegetable gardens. The owners often surrounded each household with a wire fence constructed with living saplings as fence posts planted a couple of feet apart. The whole community seemed built on a three quarters scale, with doorways to stoop through.

We debated how to make connections and find the drug users. Joanna thought the local alcoholic men who hung out in the shade by the window stores might know, but I thought they might rob us or hang onto us as fountains of money for more liquor. So instead, we kept our eyes peeled for adolescent young boys, and zeroed in on a few of the wilder adolescents in T-shirts emblazoned with icons from the world of Rock and Roll. We would start a light conversation, talk about their shirt, and then ask if they smoked pot, or did they know anybody who did, or anybody who could get some for a friend of ours?

At last, one boy led us down the village paths between the tiny one room stick and mud houses' sapling fences. Everyone seemed to notice us as we marched through the village to the edge of town, where the commercial fields begin upstream.

The boy knocked at the open door, and a hammock strung across one corner unraveled like a spider's nest to release a young adult man dressed in long pants. He came to the door sleepy, his stiff black hair pushed up on one side, and after some fast conversation with the boy, he motioned us inside and at the same time, shooed away the boy.

Inside, one tall, tiny rickety wooden table and two chairs stood by the door for light, while against the back wall a military-style wooden cot lacked a cushion, not even straw, nothing as a mattress. We communicated easily, he smiled a lot and said he could get some dope. He asked us for the money up front, which scared us at first, but with the price so cheap, we could afford it if he ran out on us. We knew where he lived, and everyone in the village saw us arrive. He told us to wait inside his house till he got back, then he took off on a barefoot dogtrot run through the village's powdery ochre trails.

We expected his quick return, but time dragged its dusty feet. The village quieted down in the intense heat of mid afternoon. We watched little dust devils move across the village, panic turkeys, and disappear. Even in the shade of his house, the heat made us sweat. We felt dull and listless as we repeated our conversation about whether we should admit he robbed us, and go back to the round house, or wait a while longer. After all, he let us enter his house, stay inside with all his personal belongings which could fit in one paper grocery sack. He expected us here when he returned, and we didn't want to cause any problems in the village. Everything moves slower, takes longer, in Mexico, the land of mañana.

We stared out the doorway at the tiny mud houses and the flowers on bushes along their fences. In some yards that served as tiny pastures, goats with their kids and pigs with piglets ate most of the vegetation down to the powdery, rusty dust. The air stifled us into silence. Sweat streamed down our temples. We wished for a breeze, said so, but nothing moved.

Both of us, at the same moment, noticed an orange on the table start to move. It rolled almost imperceptible, on its own, then picked up a tiny bit of speed. It wandered in a slow zigzag up to the edge of the table, then in numb suicide, fell off to thud without bounce, exact and precise, in the heel of the young man's tennis shoe.

"Did you see that?"

"Yeah."

"Well?"

"Can't explain it."

When the young man returned, he wanted to smoke with us, but we couldn't find a paper to roll a joint, nor did we have a cigarette to empty the tobacco out of. Joanna knew how to carve an apple to make a pipe, but without an aluminum foil liner, that would waste most of the marijuana stuck against the wet sides of the bowl. The young man looked around and spied a newspaper in the corner. He carefully ripped off a small square, then manhandled it, wrinkled and folded it into tubes, scrubbed it against itself, until it became soft as suede. He rolled a joint, licked the edge with copious amounts of saliva to make it stick, dried it with a lit match, then lit it. We inhaled and ignored the harsh flavor of burnt newspaper.

Back at the round house, we offered our marijuana to the other visitors to help use it up and avoid the paranoia with it in our possession.

When the sun sets and the lushness of jungle darkness invades the round cement house, guests retreat from the wide central lounge to their separate pie section rooms.

A little after we get into bed together each night, Joanna asks me if I want to, in a way that makes me suspect that she doesn't, but thought I would. Of course I do, so we did most of the time, as quiet as possible, with the presence of other guests in nearby rooms to dampen our expressiveness. Joanna and I felt nervous each time we wanted to make love in the almost silent house, and some nights we kissed and fooled around for hours in the darkness to wait until we felt sure everyone slept.

We didn't go around kissy-faced by day, we didn't hold hands, we acted like brother and sister, in true Anglo saxon aversion to corniness, soft fuzzies, and public displays of affection. We felt it easier to say we were family, than deal with all the Catholic unease whenever we checked in to a hotel and the conservative hotel manager asked each of us in turn, indiscreet questions, such as how long ago we got married, to trip us up.

One day, with his three day growth of peach fuzz shaved off to reveal mestizo features that made him look more beatnik than ever, Antonio took me aside to talk in private. He said "I know you two not brother and sister, or not married. So I ask you, about you and Joanna, have relations sometimes, after night. Because I hear things, no trouble. Everybody do things together, natural. It's small, this house, we get lots of strangers stay here, all here together, and everybody can hear things, but if its none of my business and everything OK, no trouble, right? Why should anyone care, natural, right? I want to know only, because, I mean, are you two cool? Do you two only see each other as friends like, who hang out together, like it seems? Or something else?"

"Sure, we're friends."

"Well friends like what kind? Friends don't mean same thing in Mexico. In Mexico, when a man like a girl, they hold hands so ever-body know she belong to him. Mexico friends do not make love to friends, like Spaniards, tourists from Europe, you know. But in America, hippies, ever-body makes love to ever-body, right, OK. I don't mind. Ok by me. No problem. So what about it?"

"What do you want to know?"

"Because, because, I think Joanna beautiful. She beautiful, to me. But I don't cause problems. If I want to date her, I think to ask you first, to avoid problem."

"She and I make love. But don't tell anyone, because I never talked to her about how she feels, you know, to tell other people about our private life. I don't know what Joanna thinks. You must ask her, not me."

Antonio said, "How do you feel about her?"

"We met on the border. I don't know her well, yet."

"I don't see any great love between you two."

I felt hurt to realize the truth in this. Young and in love differs from young and in need. We both met at the moment we felt most terrified to step across that border and travel alone in Mexico, so we clung to each other like two strangler figs.

Antonio said, "You don't get upset if I talk to her? Ask her out on date, maybe?"

My first thoughts ridiculed him as a young impoverished Mexican mulatto man who worked in peanut fields for a little more than a dollar a day. I said "What happens between you and her depends on her, not me."

To consider things from Joanna's point of view, I didn't offer her much, either. An impoverished American traveler with a backpack. At least with Antonio, she could learn Spanish and get to know a lot about Mexico. He looked so scholarly, Antonio did. Maybe he knew more than how to pick the correct key for blues harmonica. I could imagine Joanna and he as urban beatniks in Mexico City. Might work out great for her, and him, to learn each other's language.

With Joanna, I began to realize how we both traveled in a bubble of English which impeded our exposure to Mexico. I would not learn Spanish as fast as I could without her, and I felt certain that a Mexican girlfriend would teach me the most.

Joanna and I kept each other from Mexican friendships that might offer things otherwise unavailable.

I never learned what happened between Antonio and Joanna, if anything. Two days later, Joanna decided we should leave. She said the place made the hair on the back of her neck stand up.

I wondered if she felt the presence of that spider, that black hieroglyphic that hangs by a thread over each of us.

We took another long bus ride to Guadalajara, where Joanna wanted to see a famous Catholic Cathedral and its superlative ornate gold trim.

Once inside, it overwhelmed the viewer with its intricacy. I felt insignificant in front of all that Holy art, all that human effort to design the two story area in back of the pulpit, all the stonework pillars and niches and then sculpt all the woodwork into filigrees of floral designs, then cover the immense back wall with gold leaf. The volume of decoration spoke of exorbitant incomes, the paintings and statuary in the alcoves and niches, the paintings at the Holy Stations that depict significant events from the Bible or the lives of Saints, the altar with thousands of candles, the pews with special bars along the floor to kneel on. Funded by what, I wondered. The great land owners and pre-industrial families of politicos that controlled the taxation on thousands of peons and workers didn't seem like enough to pay for the incredible size and ostentation of this house of God. Maybe they forced the tithe out of everyone, or took a percentage of all the gold shipped out of Mexico to Spain.

We watched as people came inside to pray; the cowboys with gold teeth and silver spurs, young couples with children, the Old World gentlemen in formal attire with canes, lonely old ladies shrunk into a curve under black shawls. They sat separated and spread out in the pews. The old women pushed back their black shawls and muttered things which echoed like water in a cave, punctuated by the sound of thumb kisses and the rustle of clothing when they crossed their hearts. A middle age man dressed in dirty clothes shuffled around, perhaps a repentant criminal, a mental patient, an alcoholic, or the janitor.

The loudest sounds came from outside the small windows placed high above, when pigeons landed with a rustle of feathers against the textured glass. Their coos echoed and sounded like spirits asking "Who, who?"

I couldn't leave fast enough.

Near the center of the big city, restaurants placed tables and chairs outside on the sidewalk. We ate at one because a lot of other extra-nationals ate there. A couple of Mexican men at a table near us struck up a conversation to practice their English. Did we like Guadalajara, what did we see, and where we should go, all that rot.

Then they started to tease me about how I liked the muchachas in Guadalajara, as if they could read my mind and knew I felt stunned by the feminine beauty in Guadalajara. As Joanna and I walked down the streets today, the women fascinated me, mixtures of Amerindian black straight hair, black eyes, and high cheekbones that mixed with the sculpted features of Spanish Arabic Ladinos, their full Arabic lips and pronounced eyebrows, eyelids that covered the roundness of the eyeball instead of the native Chinese-like eyelid that hides under a fleshy eyebrow. Their skin color shaded from a delicious brown sugar tone into white. Some eyelashes grew so long they looked plastic. In the city the urban women and girls' features revealed European bloodlines of various intensities. Sometimes they lost some of the better qualities of the Amerindians; less bronze and too white, their hair thinned, or long black hair grew on whiter forearms. That attracted my attention, the contrast between white skin and black arm hair.

The men explained that Mexicans use regional names to identify where people come from, and they call people from Guadalajara region Tapatíos, and the women Tapatías.

"Watch out for the Tapatías, hombre." one said and laughed.

"Why?"

"For you, they too dangerous. They see a güero like you, a blonde man, and they..." he made motions as if to grab me.

"What should I do if that happens? What's the right thing to say?"

"You look up to the sky like this, and say Thank you, Lord." The men laughed. "You wait, you see. These girls not like American girls, no offence. It's something one cannot explain, and certainly not in the presence of a lady."

Joanna didn't take kindly to the direction of our conversation so we all turned to eat our meals. I watched the people walk down the sidewalk as I chewed, and found myself again fascinated with the beauty of these Tapatías.

We left the restaurant to walk around, and Joanna grabbed my hand. We talked about her adventures in New Jersey, but I couldn't understand a lot of it. so foreign to my rural upbringing.

Joanna bored me with her urban stories in New Jersey about ethnic groups and cars and fights and weird dates and especially the stories of one-upmanship related to brands of merchandise that meant class, of which I knew nothing. That robbed her stories of their intended snobby purpose and expected reaction from me. Each time her story depended on the brand names of quality clothing, food, wine, or cars I made her explain it to me, but I forgot all of that tripe. She didn't like to hike, hated bugs, didn't like solitude or quiet. Swimming did not interest her, neither did camping or wildlife, nor could she partake in my favorite pastime, girl watching. No surprise there.

We both aspired to write, but our perspectives differed so much that we criticized, analyzed, poked holes in each other's observations, till we learned to undervalue each other's commentary.

Our worst moment came when she confessed to he ruse of seduction as a research technique. She wanted to know her own capacities and live with faith in her attractiveness, so once she seduced a man for money to prove she could do it in a pinch, as she said.

I re-examined the whole idea of self knowledge after that. I couldn't understand any benefit for a person to plumb the depths of their capacities with a freefall to whore, seduce, drink, fight, steal, manipulate, coerce, and even kill when the other direction takes so much hard work and self control, the higher capacities of love, tenderness, beauty, song, art, and become motivated by altruism to solve problems with creativity so that everyone wins.

She represented a dilemma of whether people should gain confidence through an extreme range of experience, from sublime to vulgar, or should people seek the middle ground, in accordance with some preconceived value system, some arbitrary conjecture in the grand macro-cultural scheme of things.

She called me an innocent, and said she did not invent the world as it is, but came to it on its own terms. She said human history gets written by the strong, the warriors, the conquerors, the people who dare to do what others do not.

I thought the importance of history lies in the technological and philosophical advances that better the human condition, in techniques that produce plenty, in the warm hands of mothers that produce brave and empathetic members of their civilian community. I felt neither allegiance nor respect for military personnel, who seemed like fearful bastards that want others to decide everything in their life for a constant paycheck and unearned benefits. Macho men tend to see enemies everywhere, start fights and wars they believe they can win, aspire to become leaders but become dictators, and demand the love and respectful glorification they believe, by tradition, due them as heroes. Then they pontificate from the bully pulpits of reigns of terror.

Seemed to me that Joanna looked at everything and everyone with a superiority complex, so stuck on herself that she saw others in relation to her own nose. I could relate to it, since that day a long haired Colorado house framer that played bass guitar said I should come down out of my ivory tower. Joanna and I both shared the view.

Her disdain I thought urbane and East Coast, even though I know little about the Eastern seaboard's metropolitan areas. Because of the New York area's reputation for brash aggression, and their constant feigned anger which looks like unfriendliness to people from other places, her 'center of the world' no longer interested me.

Nevertheless, as liberal college-age ex-hippie Yankees, we did share a rejection of our Industrial Age culture's protection of everyone's Constitutional right to the pursuit of personal happiness through material acquisition, an automobile, and loud noises.

From the early stages of my adolescent life in the ivory tower, my addictions to literature, drawing and painting, and the guitar left me inexperienced with baser aspects of reality. So far on this trip, these mysterious and picturesque, exotic and risqué lands south of the border promised to reveal important ancient truths which the First World forgot. My imagination ran away the first time I laid eyes on Joanna, and I could imagine us together, basked in the brilliant rainbow hues of drippy rainforests and noisy sun drenched seascapes. Even though we met on the harshest, driest, most remote port of entry between Mexico and the United States, the sun-drum rhythms of those noontime deserts, or the sunsets seen through the silhouettes of songbirds atop phallic cacti, inspired a romantic fantasy of us. I could almost smell the starlight on the wind-churned faint greenery of a wheat field path made by two pair of bare feet, and the pungent perfumes that rise invisible from double-backed procreation in the sweat-silver moonlight.

Colorless green ideas sleep furiously.

To think of our separation, both of us faced the last step of a plunge out of our reality and into the great unknown of Latin America. When our eyes met on that dusty West Texas street, we fell in love in an instant. Our subconscious minds considered it a good idea to hook up, and for safety's sake, probably decided correctly.

Both young and healthy, how could we not feel a physical attraction for each other, and the implosive force of our new foreign reality made us reach out to each other with the desperation of non-swimmers for a life raft.

Two magnets pulled us toward instant intimacy, in spite of our rust-belt origins in separate worlds, urban and rural, due to the glandular magic of youth and the instant liberation of travel.

The lone young traveler abroad exists in a terrible isolation, inexperienced, ignored, and unskilled. Natural to deduce that many of those with the energy to jump so easily at risky chances to feel, experience, and explore probably suffer from an exaggerated lust for life.

Back in our home communities, our cultural taboos, code of ethics, and the potential of social shame and a ruined reputation often dampens what we do anyway under shallow subterfuges. As a traveler, you realize that no one around knows your name, your friends, or your spouse or family, and you decide to enjoy the moment and reinvent yourself. Many travelers wallow in the prohibited, because they feel liberated and anonymous.

Travelers follow a tradition known to criminals, knights and paupers, merchants, peddlers, and the politically uprooted. We live like tramps and hoboes, with the lifestyle of Gypsies, thieves, outcasts, musicians, homosexuals, exiles, pilgrims, and other internationally peripatetic itinerants. We mix in, but do not join the society that surrounds us. Like another social class, pennywise travelers on budgets exist on a separate marginalized plane within other countries. We count our pennies and allow ourselves to spend only so much everyday, and sustain ourselves on dreamy estimates of the amount of time our money will allow us to stay on this road without a job or income. Whenever we need income, we consider work in the local economy, but most jobs pay so little it would take many perfect months with no unexpected problems to save a pittance.

Meanwhile, I distracted myself easily. Mexico teemed with the unsung beauty of Aztec princesses, often dressed in Western clothes. Or I would a glimpse a girl in colorful ropa típica, her black hair danced in two braids alongside her face as she peeled potatoes into a large plastic pot of dirty water in some rustic counter of planks that served as a restaurant, and feel love-struck. On occasion, the exotic beauty of these Mexican women took my breath away, but if I held my breath, or returned my gaze for an instant, Joanna picked it up as if she could hear my pulse.

I made some excuse, a plea to stop so I could draw a quick sketch, so I would feign interest in some nondescript article or other commonplace distraction to convince her to move on ahead without me.

The urge to look at women grew stronger in Joanna's presence, because my fear of her jealousy forced me to hide my novice connoisseurship in the appreciation of the neglected Amerindian beauty. It became a game for me, to play our brother-sister charade to the hilt.

For example, in the market Joanna and I might pass a beautiful Aztec girl seated cross legged on a blanket full of cut flowers for sale, her skin a flawless bronze, her long hair blue black as crow feathers, the exotic slant of her eyes exaggerated by the upswing of long luxurious eyelashes, and sometimes ruined by plucked brows and penciled eyebrows. Her baggy fluorescent blouse bulges with hints of buxom adornments, and maybe one mahogany work-hardened thigh outlined by the blue denim skirt stretched so tight it restricts her seated movements.

Joanna could sense my interest like radar, even before I saw the girl.

I might stop to ask the price of flowers, and see her blush in response to my own nervousness, an instinctual awareness of my adoration. She might reciprocate with a blatant mutual admiration, with me as the exotic in her land although my young blood ran too hot to realize it. I might hang around at another vendor near one of these rough-hewn beauties, and pretended to examine some trash from China or another horrid black silver-embroidered Catholic matron's dress made on a kitchen table sewing machine, to take a few surreptitious glances to verify my first vague impression of an unfamiliar beauty.

If, or maybe when, Joanna caught me, she turned away with a stern look that communicated her expectation that I should follow like a dog. If I didn't, she gave me a homicidal smile that made me giggle in secret. So I would move on, slow, with a surreptitious glance backwards, for the opportunity to give a little wave. Then the flower girl surprises me with a furtive wave and a "Gracias," with such a gush of exaggerated elation I imagine at that moment she felt the world open up, a sudden realization that her exotic beauty might buy her a ticket out of her poverty to the Golden Land of Oz. This Gringo male's unabashed attraction to her lent credibility to any light hearted Hollywood fantasy life she dared dream of.

This First World traveler's brief infatuation with her exotic beauty seemed to warm the cockles of her heart, and I took it as a good deed.

I once belonged to the Boy Scouts. It became my mission to seek out these opportunities to do these good deeds.

One day, Joanna changed tactics, and began to point out women for me, as if I needed her urbane haute culture to refine my sense of Amerindian beauty. She pointed out both pretty girls and ugly girls, which made me suspicious.

I asked her, "Why do you think I should look at that girl?"

"Oh, she's your type. Skinny, long stiff course black hair, almost no breasts, one bigger than the other. She's so thick-lipped she can't close her mouth. Mottled skin, dry patches on her arms that look like cigarette ash, hairy legs that match her moustache. She's your type."

In Guadalajara, when I caught her in a similar act of coy adoration, I said "Hey, if I can't look at women, you shouldn't look at men."

"So we both look at people, so what? But I don't look at them for the same reason you do." Her curved nose flew like a sail up in the air.

"I look because they look nothing like people back home."

"Liar. You look because they're female. The thing that really bothers me is that you have no taste. That last girl looked like a wolf, a mix of Spanish, Arabic, and some peyote-addicted Tarahumara Indian, I bet. She could run you into the ground."

"Why should it bother you if I look at women?"

"It's not that you look at women, men always look. Deep down, they all make fools of themselves with this dog-faced Sultan fantasy. Their eyes comb the kingdom to assemble a harem."

"It's in our genes."

"Along with stupidity. You want to know what hurts me the most?"

"Sure."

"The women who attract you look nothing like me."

Our conversations became testier, something we both seemed to enjoy, due to our respective families' culture of intense confrontation.

Both our families owned dogs, and participated in a culture where the voice to yell commands at dogs crosses over into the realm of humans.

One day I would hear that you speak English to talk to dogs, and Spanish to talk to God.

We found it more difficult each day to see eye to eye. We compared notes, and found little in common between my rural to suburbanite high school experiences and her Gritty City East Coast urban public school.

As we got to know each other, we assumed the erroneous too often, and thought we knew how the other would react to things and said so with lines like "I know what you're going to say. I know what you think, so don't even bother."

The worst assumption of all. "You don't understand... you couldn't possibly understand."

At one point, I said, "I'm glad I didn't go to your school."

She grabbed me by the arm and wheeled me around to shout, "What did you mean by that?"

I told her that I didn't think her urban point of view merited more respect than my rural hickdom, and some of the things she did supposedly to enlarge her life experience made me feel sorry for her.

That gave her cue and permission to dump all over me. All that she thought about me and bottled up inside came bubbling out, like a fermented champagne of ruined sweetness turned acidic and flat. "I'm sick of your silence, your criticisms. I can almost hear you thinking how you want to get away from me. I see you look at other women right in front of me. You disrespect all women and me. Look at me when I talk to you! I'm tired of your distance. You act like you don't like me, until we get into bed. What do you think of me anyway?"

"If I tell you what I think of you, you get defensive and tell me I'm too critical, even if I mean it as a compliment."

"That's what I can't stand about you. I can't tell when you're sarcastic or making a fool of me."

So she considers me as so critical by nature that she must distrust even my compliments to her. That didn't leave me any choice except to fall on my knees and beg her to marry me, to blubber with the primordial seas of tears and snot to prove my lost soul authenticity.

Not likely. Instead I said, "I thought writers practice critical thinking. Isn't that the most important part of a writer's duty to truth, and art?"

"I don't criticize you half as much as you do me."

"I'm sorry you feel that way. I don't see it that way, but I respect your feelings."

"What do you know about feelings? When have you ever said anything nice about me?"

She got me there. Since she told me she wanted to write, we competed, and analyzed each other.

We walked on in silence through the hot, sunlit colonial streets of noonday Guadalajara. I looked at all the beautiful Tapatías without reservation, whenever they attracted me, not to hurt Joanna, but because I never saw so many exotic and beautiful women before in all my life. Every glimpse a short-lived phenomenon, a few moments of grace, like the sky opened up and heaven shone down upon me. To not look would constitute a sin against beauty and the Grand Creator.

Ok, I admit I felt a little tickled it bugged Joanna so much. My declaration of independence made me taller, older, more confident, as if the terrible two year old that lived inside me became the center of the known universe. Nobody controls me as center of the universe. I became magnificent, glorious, sanctified.

The central streets of this colonial city felt like canyons between three floors of stonework, cement, and stucco. Balconies cradled some buildings' second floor windows. Balconies where, sometimes, two or three beautiful young girls sat and sucked on thumb-sized candies on little white sticks, and stared down at the streets as if they waited for a rescuer to ride up.

I wondered if I could ever inspire one to let her hair down.

Joanna and I spent a frosty night far apart in our colonial hotel room, the door's wood trim and jambs decorated with floral shapes carved by craftsmen trained in Old Europe. The room vibrated with the ghosts of three hundred years of lodgers; the love, the fights, the families, criminals, the salesmen and tourists, the old and infirm that died a sudden death here, perhaps a birth or two in this room, right where we slept.

Even though we snuggled against each other, it felt good to think about travel alone tomorrow, when we would both leave the bubble of America we wrapped ourselves in, and enter Mexico, as young individuals, vulnerable and impressionable, with few expectations, open to everything .

The next morning, without any verbal agreement, we dumped the contents of our backpacks onto the bed to separate the things intermixed along the way in a nonverbal symbolism of our union and commitment to travel together.

She said "I want to take a nice hot shower without anyone to interrupt it, run the water as long as I want to, so why don't you shower first?"

I took a long shower, and afterwards, thought about a shave, but considered it bad form to tidy up to leave a woman who never before saw your shaved face. I wanted to know what I looked like with more of a beard anyway. I put on my little-used long pants and shoes, hoisted my backpack, walked to the door, opened it, turned around, shuffled my feet, and searched for something to say. Joanna lay in bed with her glasses on, a book on a pillow on her lap.

She waved without a glance, so I said "Bye," stepped into the immense hall, and shut the door.

It felt bad, as I descended the old hotel's steps, to imagine how Joanna threw the book aside to spare it from the flow of tears that formed rivulets down her cheeks, her neck, across her two conical volcanoes, tremulous gelatin cups, creamy as the flan offered as dessert throughout Mexico. I imagined her shaken by sobs of anguish. I saw myself retrace my steps and return, to knock on the door, a few quiet, cautious knocks. She wouldn't answer, instead she would wrap herself in her tear-soaked robe and nestle deeper into the bedcovers. Even if she comes to the door, she might only lean her temple against it, steady her voice, to intone through the thick varnished dark oak wood, "Who is it? Did you forget something?"

I couldn't go back, no matter how much I thought she might expect it, or resent it if I did. Even if she opened the door naked and threw her arms around me to smother me with kisses, the next day on the street full of Tapatías, I'd regret it, and I knew she would even more.

The early morning sun turned Guadalajara's streets silver, and the chill quickened my pace. The workers and business people strode by on their urgent missions.

My eyes connected with an elegant Mexican business woman, short black hair, her eyes deep black, her delicate cherry red lips drawn, filled, and softened by God within exquisite dove-wing lines. She almost stopped before me as the crowd jostled us into a collision course. I felt small as I looked upon this natural tan Cleopatra in a double-breasted business suit, swelled and rounded in front. She looked interested for a millisecond, and then averted her eyes in a way that made me think she feared me.

What would we have in common, except a glandular attraction due to opposite genders?

I wondered what keeps couples together when most women and men do not share much common ground. Does love truly conquer all? Do women want to feel conquered?

My eyes saw a different Mexico this morning. Over the past month in Mexico with Joanna, I grew accustomed to Mexicans as Amerindians; their black hair, loud happy extroversion, the flawless tan skin, their exaggerated attention to appearances, their ubiquitous symbols and decoration of a flowery European Catholicism, their natural flirtatiousness. A great contrast to Joanna and I, with our secular humanist background and our Spartan wardrobe rooted in frumpy no-nonsense utilitarianism. We didn't hold hands when we walked.

By noon, I walked all the way through the downtown to its heart, to stand beside the central gazebo in Guadalajara's main Central Plaza. Something hit me on the head. I looked up and saw three teenage girls in school uniforms, plaid skirts, white knee socks, white blouse, their long, straight, raven black hair that framed brown faces, their eyes pure black and almond shaped, thick dark lashes, their lips graceful and cherry red. Each one held a pale green section of something like bamboo. Sugarcane, a foot and a half of sugar cane, and they bit into it and stripped off the outside to break off a chunk of the pithy sweet core, which they sucked the juices out of. Then they spit out the sponge of cellulose that remained.

I looked down at the cement at my feet and noticed the little wads of chewed sugarcane pith. I looked up at them and they laughed. They looked pure Indian to me, and pure beautiful. They smiled, pulled at each other and waved to me with furtive restrained flips of their hands, which fluttered to cover their mouth in laughter. They pulled each other by the arms, tangled in each other's hair, and hugged together in a mass of skinny arms and soft protuberances of puberty.

They looked about thirteen, yet flirted with me without shame, in fact, as a playful game, a natural and wholesome exercise of their new status as female. I could not imagine any of the uptight Christian Reformed girls back home comfortable with such blatant flirtatiousness, at any age.

Without Joanna beside me, my eyes wandered free, and I recognized another area of fault for our failed relationship. No matter how we held hands, or how tight our hug as we walked together in the cold, something insinuated itself between this Eastcoast dishwater blonde Joanna and me, which impelled me to let go, drop her hand like a hot rock.

I felt the exotic beauty of a Mexicana as a palpable presence, which engendered in me a fascination that grew day by day. I felt my appreciation and expertise in the identification and categorization of their beauty deepen with each hour this twenty two year old male human animal walked among the Tapatías of Guadalajara. For among the women of this, the second great city of Mexico, I began to see groups of differences in their features, differences that I associated with great regional tribes of ancient Meso-America.

After the split from Joanna, this incomprehensible and exotic land came alive to me as I tried to understand the everyday activities of a population without personal autos, where everyone walked to bus stops, or waved down little vans and other vehicles that served as public transportation. Signs displayed long, unpronounceable Aztec names I couldn't read long enough to figure out how to write down. With so many people on foot, stores decorated most street corners. The variety of shops, street venders, fruit carts, markets, hardware stores, restaurants, etc. seemed to cycle a good walk from each other.

All the contact between these urban people, on the streets, buses, or crammed together inside the sweaty little vans, repulsed me at first as primitive and backwards. After I grew a little more accustomed, I didn't mind the lucky snuggles against some delightful bouncy girl, even though I blushed and stood still as a rock, which seemed to make them bump against me in time to the Creedence Clearwater Revival music the driver played.

Girls don't act that way back home. The more deeply I entered Mexico, I discovered things that contrasted with my own culture, and at first I distrusted my observations. Then I wondered why the same things occurred over and over. I started to appreciate this new mystery of Mexican girls, of Latin American women, the way they dressed and looked at me, as social and sensual, natural in recognition of the base vulgarity of sexual attraction, instead of rejection of it as a personal flaw, embarrassed and forced to hide the inevitable and natural. Even though overdressed and conservative in little schoolgirl uniforms, Mexican girls acted more flirtatious and sensual in the street than any American women in the bars.

None of my old girlfriends could compete with the flirtatiousness of Tapatías. They wouldn't want to, and American boys don't know what they miss.

Mexico enveloped me, and I felt my English as less a barrier, because without Joanna, nothing softened the need to understand in Spanish.

I felt the shock of unfamiliarity and my own incompetence, until I learned to use the excuse of my foreignness, my Gringo-ness, as an advantage. I used it as often as I could, to insinuate myself into people's confidences, to fake innocence and gain access to prohibited areas, to ask the stupidest or rudest questions which I often repeated to various people to compare results and build my own conceptual constructs with their vocabulary.

That's how I began to decipher this land, and all these various peoples. I began to recognize Mexico as not just a country south of the United States border, analogous to Canada with a different language, but a much more distinct reality, separate and distant in both time and history, in roots and in directions, from anything in my background, from any other place on earth.

Mexico, a small Hispanic and Meso-American part of a region known as Latin America, itself a portion of an almost global language, Spanish, spoken in South, Central, and North America, the Caribbean, Spain and parts of Europe, some other Mediterranean countries, the Philippines, parts of Asia, and in Africa's Equatorial Guinea, Spain's port for nineteenth century slavers.

I stumbled into another reality, planet Mexico, and I wasn't ready for it.

CHAPTER 20: Alone In Mexico
Every traveler should get lost on occasion, if only to verify the appropriateness of the planned route.

I can't figure out why I bought a bus ride to Manzanillo, especially after I took a bus out to the tourist zone, a new development with fancy hotels like miniature skyscrapers. I fantasized I might sleep on the beach, but the line of huge hotels intimidated me. I walked and walked through the sand fields behind them, and debated if I should spend the money on a hotel room or not.

So I planned to make a discrete camp, dress in my best pants and shirt, hide my backpack, make it invisible under sand and leaves, go to a couple of discos, and spend the money a room might cost. But would I find my backpack later, even if only half-drunk? In addition, if I got lucky with a tourist girl, could I remember how to find it tomorrow in the daylight, hung over, when everything would look different? If stolen, it might take me a day or two to admit someone stole it. If I did not find my backpack, or if stolen, I ruined this trip on the slim chance of meaningless sex.

I could see children nearby, young people's eyes watched me, and I imagined their curious conversations and thought how easy the thief among them would know about my presence.

After sunset, in the near dark, I walked into a large sand field behind two five-story beachside hotels. I resigned myself to a good night's sleep, and started to take off my shoes and socks. Sand burrs in my socks drove me crazy, stuck to my clothes as I tried to pluck them off, one by one, and crawl into my sleeping bag.

The wind blew sand in my face all night long. Way past the normal two o'clock hour the bars closed back home, the bass notes of music from two discos, one from each hotel, pounded into my brain as they fought and phased with cyclic discord into each other's rhythm.

Early the next morning I dressed and discovered the sand burrs missed the night before. They found their way to my most sensitive spots, in armpit, torso, inner thigh and higher.

I walked out of those dewy sand fields with fingers and thumbs punctured and painful, to reach the asphalt road and sit on the curb for fifteen minutes and pluck the hundreds of new ones out of my socks and pant legs.

Didn't much like Manzanillo, and the resentments and insults of that night gave me a hatred of hotel discos, sandy beaches, and sand burrs, in that order of intensity, which served me well over the years.

Lago de Patzcuaro
In Mexico's central highlands, a fresh climate with cold nights in the Fall, lies the reed lined shores of Lago de Patzcuaro, where Indian men in wide cowboy hats fish from dugout canoes with large, stiff nets shaped like rounded butterfly wings.

In the middle of an inhabited island in the lake, the government erected a giant cubist geometric bust of a man with one arm upraised, like the upper torso of a male Statue of Liberty. The guidebooks claim that one should not miss the festivities of November first and second, the Night of the Dead on the island, when the indigenous people offer food and all-night candlelight vigils to honor their dead.

I got on the ferryboat with a bunch of Mexican tourists and a few colorfully dressed indigenous people. As we pulled out, a young man with a guitar started to sing. Another young man in the boat sang along, and then a good natured competition ensued as they traded verses and sang to each other.

My guidebook advised tourists to respect the dignity of the occasion, as outsiders, as we walk among the festivities in the cemeteries where Indians camp out to offer food atop the graves of their ancestors.

Tourists should not drink, nor talk loud, nor snap photos without the consent of the subjects, and respect the serious gravity of their traditions.

In a variety of ways, Mexicans express a morbid fascination with death, through a mixture of Catholic fatalism with Indian animism, which cross-links the Pope to sugar skulls and woodcuts of skeletons in sombreros that dance with cigars in their mouths. Altars with candles, food offerings, and flowers fill little shrines along the highway to mark the locations of fatal car crashes where loved ones perished. On these two special November days, the graveyards become campgrounds, and Mexican families worship their departed in all-night vigils. Perhaps over half the dead honored on the second night represent children, who died in childbirth, in their infancy, or as pre-adolescents.

That afternoon, the urban Mexican nationals arrived en masse, in an overdressed imitation of the ugly American tourists. The cemetery changed over the afternoon, as vendors constructed booths and Indians spread blankets to sell their wares of candies, flowers, candles, trinkets, and clothing that appeared hand made, with lots of embroidery. Musicians wandered the streets dressed in wooden masks, and sometimes stopped to put on a little show.

Vendors sold beer to everyone, tourists, Mexican tourists, and Indians, as they watched loud parades of festive people pass through the plaza on the way to the cemetery. Actors in large wood masks with beards of real human hair represented the Spanish conquistadors. One masked actor played a rusty-string strung guitar, and sang with a whiskey voice along the edge of a crowd of parents and children. He bent over his guitar, danced up to the children to make them shrink against their parent's legs, then he stomped with menace to scare them even more. Rock'n roll.

Various balladeers with guitars strolled the walkways. On this trip so far, I noticed that when Mexicans group into crowds, some men emerge to sing along on popular or traditional songs. A good natured competition ensues, with contestants that knew how to croak, wheeze, and shriek the famous grito, the Mexican shout, which sounds like a stuck pig, or a broken police siren, or what might ensue from a male opera star at the moment he discovers his own castration.

People bought fireworks and threw them at each other, from family to family, up into the air, over the heads of the crowd, over the beer tents as advertisements.

The riotous and colorful festivities lasted throughout the night, but I tired and left the island of Janitzio. I took a dugout boat ride back to my hotel room on the shore.

So much for the sanctity of indigenous tradition.

Morelia Burro Cart

Near the town of Tepexpan, northeast of Mexico City, archeologists excavated the skeletons of two mammoths, butchered thousands of years ago at the site where they now lay. They found evidence that primitive humans killed these mammoths with spears fitted with stone points.

This geologic layer, dated to 8000 BC, also produced one human skeleton, a female, with bones comparable to a modern Amerindian woman.

I got up before dawn to leave Morelia and head to Mexico City. From the street, Morelia seemed like an ancient maze built of a single story colonial wall that ran almost unbroken. Windows, protected by iron bars, and massive double doors of wood punctuated the faded and peeling wall colors that mark one residence from another.

No cars or taxis on the dark streets. Cocks crowed and answered each other.

I heard a distant clatter of wood on cobblestones. From far down the dark street, I saw a small open cart pulled by a tiny donkey, as if a dream that reoccurred and disappeared. It became visible as it passed through pools of yellow light under the old cast-iron street lamps.

I walked in a direction I thought might lead to the center of Morelia and the bus station.

Within a half an hour, the donkey cart overtook me. An old man, wrapped in a sheepskin coat with the collar pulled up around his neck, drove the cart alongside me for a ways. He pulled the donkey to a stop and asked "Donde va?"

I said, "Centro de Camiones" Bus station.

"Lejos", far, and then he motioned me to get on the back of the open cart. I took off my orange backpack and let it slip onto the gray weathered boards, and then pushed it into the corner with the wind-blown remains of green hay, which the streetlamps' yellowish light mutated into psychedelic paint swirls.

We tried to talk. He couldn't understand me well, and I could not understand his answers to my labored questions, so it ended up I nodded "Si, si" in assent and smiled, as he chattered and lightly whipped the reins onto the donkey's back to keep it awake. The wooden wheels clattered down the cobblestone streets of the somnolent one story city.

I watched the horizon lightened into the muskmelon tones of a new day, over the fishbone TV antennas atop three hundred year old, flat colonial rooftops decorated with sagged electric and telephone wires strung between haphazard poles and struts of wood made of scraps.

Mexico City and the Chicano's Aztlán

In 1967, archaeologists at the site of Tlapacoya, southeast of Mexico City, found an obsidian "knife blade" in a matrix of soils which scientists dated (by radioactive carbon isotopes) to around 21,000 BC.

The Cuicuilco-Ticomán culture, credited with the site, fades away by the Middle Formative years (900–300 BC) in villages of the Valley of Mexico, but later cultures retained many aspects of their culture, for example their solid figurines.

On the southwestern edge of the valley, lava from a nearby volcano covers the site of Cuicuilco and the lower part of a roundish temple pyramid. With ramps to the summit on two sides, it rises up in four tiers of worked lava blocks over a core of rubble solidified with clay. Archeologists analyzed ceramics and carbon from the site, and found evidence that suggests the lava engulfed the region around the time of Christ.

Early Meso-Americans probably dedicated their live heart extraction sacrifices atop such circular temples to Quetzalcóatl, the Feathered Serpent, who some think served as the main deity of Cuicuilco. The description of this peripatetic God as a bearded white man enabled Hernan Cortés to win the confidence and aid of many city-states subjugated by the bloody Aztec empire. With the invaluable help of an intelligent and beautiful Indian woman named Malinche (also called Marina, or Malinalli or Malintzín) as translator between the Mayan language, the Aztec's Nahuatl, and Spanish which she learned from Cortez when they became lovers, the Spaniards instigated a revolution against the oppressive Aztec regime. The people from City-state tribes across central Mexico won their civil war to end Aztec domination, and enabled the Spanish to put an end to the practice of live heart extraction and other human sacrifices, which some archeologists think characterized Time worship in Meso-American cultures for over twenty thousand years.

The Valley of Mexico, with a perfect climate place for a city, cradled a system of high altitude lakes and a central island. The mountains that encircle the lake help stabilize average daily temperatures about seventy degrees Fahrenheit, twenty Celsius, year round. The Aztec name of the lake, Texcoco, signifies the Lake of the Moon. With mountains on the south rim near eighteen thousand feet tall, they provoke rainstorms and fogs which replenish the lake's waters through over eighty freshwater springs. The Aztecs made artificial islands of mud and vegetation which the Spanish called chinampas.

To the east, on the clearest mornings the snowy peak of a volcanic cone, Volcán Popocatépetl, appears as it has through the centuries, filtered by the contaminated haze of burnt atmosphere, once the product of the volcano, now the product of automobile and burnt hydrocarbons of the city's millions of inhabitants.

My first destination, the world-famous Sanborn's restaurant in central Mexico City. I find it housed in a beautiful building covered in blue tiles.

This began my indoctrination and enthusiasm for mass transit systems. I moved with the crowds through an immense city on little van-buses, big urban buses, and underground on the modern and clean subway system. I ate meals from street vendors and co-existed amid a dense population, on average, a head shorter than I.

From my taller vantage point, Mexico City looked like a sea of black hair. I wandered around and began to feel confident, though not completely safe, within their public transportation system, once I felt comfortable with the folded subway map in my back pocket.

The detailed map of Mexico City in my shoulder bag made me itch to explore all its museums and points of interest. The sprawl of the anthropological museum alone overwhelmed me with cavernous rooms dedicated to permanent displays of just one culture's artifacts. The archeological record of Mexico reveals a rich mosaic of cultures that influenced contemporary cultures. Beautiful books in the gift shop would help decipher the names, cultures, regions, artifacts, architectures, and perhaps even facial features of these exotic denizens around me, but I didn't want the extra weight.

I learned a lot in the magnificent Museum of Anthropology, and even more as I talked to students my age who attended UNAM, the National Autonomous University of Mexico, who wanted to practice their English with me.

Aztec Legend claims their migrant ancestors left Aztlán and searched for a homeland through a Vision Quest. The Shaman dreamt they would next settle where an eagle eats a snake while perched atop a prickly pear cactus, and that image adorns the Mexican flag today.

So the Aztecs' migration brought them to this volcanic bowl that forms the Valley of Mexico. They settled to create one of the world's most beautiful cities, because, as goes the legend, some Aztec with incredible eyesight saw a hungry eagle lunch on a snake atop a nopal prickly pear cactus on an island in the middle of a lake.

To build their island city, they connected it to the shore with mile long causeways that also served as dikes to separate the valley's lakes into impoundments, each with a varied level of salinity, flora, and fauna. The Aztecs thrived, prospered, and multiplied in this productive valley center, and over the centuries expanded their rule across Mexico and into Guatemala.

The Aztecs own legends reveal they put their origins in the East, near the Pacific Ocean. Modern anthropology thinks they hail from the shores of Nayarit, where a much smaller version of the Aztec's island city, Tenochtitlán, exists today.

The island town of Mexcaltitlán, just off the Pacific Ocean shore, shares with Tenochtitlán a street plan of circular main streets cut by radial streets. Mexcaltitlán's economy depends upon shrimp, caught in hand thrown nets and sorted by size, with the smallest "Popcorn" shrimp the most expensive, dried whole and sold in little bags like spice, or shaped into various sized balls.

Not so far inland, a village exists that appeared on maps from fifteen seventy nine with the name "Aztlán," but for Chicanos to recognize that would erase their mythic right to re-inherit all of North America.

The Aztecs inhabited a paradise, a region between mountains of tropical lakes without winter, where the two American hemisphere's plants and animals mixed. The flora and fauna from the temperate climates spread along the central spine of the high Sierras, a mountainous continental divide that spans two continents, mostly continuous except for a confused sections in Central America, especially in the northernmost part of Colombia, part of Panama's Darien Gap.

Many scientists believe Mexico's variety of climates support the greatest bio-diversity in the world.

Many Mexican students wanted to know my opinions about why so much racism exists in the United States. They knew about the civil rights movement, and considered Mexico free of such racism.

But whenever I watched television in the hotel lobbies, it looked like another world, a part of Europe, filled with blonde, blue-eyed people, or dark-eyed Spanish with Moorish Arabic blood, a legacy of a couple of hundred years of domination by the Turkish Ottoman Empire.

I noticed only one person on Mexican television that looked like ninety percent of the Mexicans I rode the busses and Metro with. She called herself La India Maria, "Indian Mary" a comedian who made movies about how an energetic, illiterate, good hearted Indian woman gets the best of hardened criminals and inept politicos.

And Mexicans see the United States as bigoted, racist, and rife with social injustice.

I stayed almost a week in the Gran Ciudad of Mexico City.

Whether from food from street venders, or the non-potable tap water I brushed my teeth in, diarrhea almost kept me in my hotel room, but I often got outside to walk around weak and subject to recurrent headaches. Diarrhea can make gastro-intestinal hot air substantial, the worst of all social nightmares, when a person must live with a Fear of Farts. I continued to explore, and made sure I carried a quarter of a flattened toilet paper roll and a liter of water. In the cavernous museums, I would sit down often to rest and knew the location of clean, modern bathrooms. Everywhere else, I became hyperaware of the whereabouts of the nearest theoretical bathrooms in restaurants, museums, bus stations, or businesses, and in a couple of emergencies, prided myself on how well I could communicate in Spanish.

People suggested I ask a pharmacist to help me. The first one suggested some pills sold only by prescription in the United states. I asked if any over the counter drugs worked well, and he sold me something that ended my misery. Now, I recognize a particular flavor in a burp that terrorizes me into a trip to the pharmacy.

On the streets in urban Mexico, impetuous schoolgirls, most dressed alike in uniforms, enticed me with insolent Flamenco stares from the safety of groups. They strutted toward me like angry hens with flirty hip twitches, and then ran away, arm in arm to giggle in the safety of their group.

Polyester-dressed urban businesswomen dazzled me with their perfect brown skin and attention to their appearance. With eyes over-outlined with unneeded mascara, they rarely met my needy gaze head on, and when they did, they most often avoided me as if afraid of a ghost, a peripatetic vagabond, a thief, a rapist.

My sexual innocence and low self esteem, coupled with what I recognized as a false perception of cultural superiority, banished me again into a bubble, a self imposed exile into an ivory tower I constructed as a psychological refuge deep in this enemy territory, where I suffered battles between my plans of writing, my lack of money, and my incompetence with Spanish, to divert me from the instinctual hunt for nookie.

The urban Mexican women's constant, instant rejection of me probably saved my life.

And theirs.

After a few days in Mexico City's combination of contamination and overpopulation, I could appreciate what the world lost when the Spanish tore down the island city's pyramids to build the first colonial structures. The valley once enjoyed the world's perfect climate, and now those same temperature inversions trapped the airborne contaminants, from the activities of overpopulation and primitive cooking, automobile fumes, industrial plumes, and petrochemical processes, too close to the ground.

Other travelers and I watched the news in the hotel lobby. People translated some of the important stories for the others, like me, not quite up to speed in Spanish. It became apparent, over the days in the Penny Hotel, that each year, the increased influx of rural Mexicans, many who spoke Spanish as an imperfect second language, created a marginalized subclass of people that lived on the streets, perused the garbage dumps for food, suffered untreated medical problems, slept on and under portions of cardboard boxes, and birthed children between parked cars.

Oaxaca

The upper class of Monte Albán, the ancient Meso-American mountiantop ruins near Oaxaca, developed the rudiments of a written language first among Meso-Americans, when they invented a written form of a calendar. They wrote dates in bar-and-dot numerals, a system that characterizes the Classic Maya, and still survives within today's Mayan communities.

After more than a month of travel towards Guatemala, where I hoped to live on a dollar a day, my expenses in this exploration of Central Mexico and the Gran Ciudad revealed how tourist destinations suck money from wallets. I noticed an even sharper daily decline in my funds while in Mexico City. Seemed like I cashed a couple of twenty dollar traveler's checks every day.

I decided to make a beeline for Guatemala, but under estimated the amount of Mexican pesos needed to get there.

The bus left late at night, and I hoped the bus route from Mexico City southwest to Oaxaca would show me some real hot steamy jungle all the way to the Pacific.

I dressed light in shorts and sandals, and hoped the next day's dawn might reveal huts and banana trees, Howler monkeys, and vine-tangled trees under which barefoot brown skinned women with huge mats of frizzed black hair walked topless. I dozed off with visions of those big breasted women in simple shift dresses that fly open with each step to reveal the smooth expanse of mahogany thighs flexed under their burden, buckets of water balanced on the head with one upraised arm, the other around a child or two that straddled their broad hips.

Instead, I woke up to see high, dry desert of barren mountains, where goats outnumbered Indians. I saw a fat man in a dirty T-shirt blow cigarette smoke through broken teeth while he scratched his distended beer belly and emitted a stream of steamy pee into bright clear morning air. He waved at us, as the bus passed.

My assumption that tropical rain forests extended throughout southern Mexico to Guatemala proved my ignorance of winds and ocean humidity related to mountain slopes and the rain shadows produced by them. The west side of the steep Pacific Range of Mexican mountains causes the air to rise and release its load of evaporated Pacific ocean water on those western slopes. Because the moist winds rise and cool, the clouds drop their moisture on the first upraised flanks of mountains. These more eastern ranges of mountains looked like the scaly back of gigantic bone dry iguanas, and from the highest passes, the jagged horizons marched off into the distance in faded shades of blue. The bare rock hosted sparse grasses, isolated bushes with tiny leaves, large yucca plants, gigantic agaves and Magueys, ocotillo, and sometimes a low cover of tiny plants in flower that hugged the ground, and when viewed from the side, the sparse ground cover of weeds in flower gave the illusion of a lush blanket of fluorescent violets or yellows.

I must look real hungry and skinny, I thought, because in the bus stops something motivated people to offer me things to eat. Much of the stuff, miniature French bread tortas, or tortilla-wrapped deep fried meat tacos from street vendors, I felt reluctant to eat since recurrent intestinal distress in Mexico City. To avoid hurt feelings, I would confess to a bit of "bad stomach" as they say down here, and then listen to lots of advice, most of which I heard before. Drink liquids, down a couple of rapid shots of Herradura Tequila, drink pepto bismol and kaopectate, kill all the parasites in your system with pills from a pharmacy or make a drink of those black pissy stink papaya seeds chopped up in a blender

I needed some Imodium AD, and plenty of rest.

I didn't want plenty of rest. I wanted to arrive first and get to bed last.

In Oaxaca, I got off the bus and felt an unexpected late afternoon chill. I didn't want to stay even one night in these high mountains. I needed to put on long pants and a jacket. I walked around the downtown streets and found a place behind some bushes to change clothes. The next bus toward Guatemala would leave tomorrow morning.

When I asked around for a cheap room near the bus station for the night, I fell in with these three Mexican travelers, young college boys with long hair, sun glasses, sandals and serapes, something most modern and affluent Mexicans avoid as 'tipica,' an insult to their self image. They explained to me, with a laborious and creative use of their broken English, that they knew a way to spend the night cheap. They led me to a hotel where we each paid very little money for permission to sleep outside, on the second floor balcony. Thus protected from the street, we enjoyed a great view of high dry Oaxaca, and I learned a fierce and cold lesson about tropical night wind gusts.

I slept fitful, paranoid about thievery from my balcony mates, curious about every exotic odor and sound. The wind blew in fierce gusts till three AM, a north wind, propelled by a dip in the jet stream that pulled upper Arctic atmosphere southward, deep into the southern United States, which chilled

Mexico's winds to dart southward and whistle through the iron guardrails of our balcony with a selection of the city's perfumes.

All night long, in the light of the motel sign and two streetlights, I watched the stiff smooth blades of banana leaves clatter and whip against each other as they shred into long fringes of green curlicues.

Huixtla

As our bus neared the Guatemalan border, whenever we stopped in a new city I took the opportunity to talk with other travelers headed North out of Guatemala. I learned to recognize them by the intricate colorful designs of the Guatemalan fabrics they carried as handbags, or wore as shirts, jackets, or bracelets of little strips of cloth called pulseras.

They impressed upon me the necessity to show substantial amounts of money to get into Guatemala. "You must change your traveler's checks into cash money before Tapachula, or any other border town, because the money changers on the borders will jack up the service charge and the rate of exchange so much you can't believe it. They know you won't want to go back to a city just to avoid it."

From the map, only one important city remained on my route before we reached the border town, Tapachula. A town called Huixtla became my unscheduled stop to visit a bank and cash travelers checks.

Without a schedule, I lost track of the days. Everyday seemed the same. I learned about the need to cash checks on a Saturday morning. The banks would close before I arrived in Huixtla on Saturday afternoon, and don't open on Sundays.

I struck up a conversation with a very proper young Mexican lad seated across the aisle.

He calls himself Xavier, and I call myself Brandon. He goes to college in Mexico City, speaks English, and heads back home now for a long weekend.

When he says his parents live in Huixtla, I asked him to suggest a cheap place I could stay until the banks opened, a place that might front me the credit for a couple of nights.

Xavier told me, in good English, "Huixtla has no hotels that I could recommend you to stay in. They are dirty, for cattle people, ranchers. They won't lend you money, anyway. And Monday, all the banks stay closed all day, because of elections."

Great. A pessimist. "I need a place to stay, anyplace, low cost. I feel a little distress in the stomach, since Mexico City, and I need to get a good rest. I haven't eaten well for days with these stomach problems. Let me stay at your house. I can pay you on Tuesday, after the banks open, for all the food I eat, and the room."

He decided to ask his mom to take me in until Monday.

We got off the bus at a tiny bus station located across from the city's main plaza, and walked kitty corner across it to his house.

Xavier's family lived above their business, a counter under a wide arched storefront behind two pillars, where they sold ice cream and frozen fruit Popsicles made from real fruit and milk. Felt like I sampled everything over the next three days. When they close the store on these relentless hot humid evenings, they reach up and pull down wide metal doors, like heavy-duty garage doors built of interlocked slats, and padlocked them to loops set in the sidewalk's cement.

Xavier eshowed me to an upstairs bedroom with a window and balcony that overlooked the main square, the Huixtla Central Plaza, a small city block of cement with a central gazebo and tiled courtyards surrounded with symmetrical gardens. The large shrubs and small trees grew out with branches and leaves so dense with foliage that artistic professional gardeners, employed by the city, sculpted them into exotic animal, bird, and chessmen shapes that marched around the square.

I took a shower and fell asleep, grateful that I landed in a upper middle class Mexican home.

Next morning, the sunrise painted the Central Plaza's file of bushy green animal Chessmen with golden brushstrokes of burnished sunlight. The light streamed through the morning mists of humidity that rose up like awakened clouds. The Chessmen cast long blue shadows through the haze that looked like suspended transparent tubes one could reach out and touch.

From safe inside those green chessmen, birdcalls filled the air with sounds like bells, pings, swoops and whistles, and one that sounded like the obnoxious metallic screeches of a cartoon factory in Toyland. This species of bird remained invisible to me, but called out for over an hour everyday, around sunup and sundown.

I got up and dressed in my cleanest clothes, and slipped cautious on bare feet down the cement stairway of the cement house. Someone set the table earlier for two people; two bowls, two small plates of something, two glasses, and a large central plate of something, each covered by an open paper napkin that flies buzzed around and landed for a quick stop.

Xavier came in from another doorway.

"I've been waiting for you. Ready to eat?"

"How long ago did you get up?"

"We get up early to enjoy the day, because our business gets busy in the afternoon and night."

Xavier's friend, Raul, stopped by at breakfast, and announced he could take us on a journey into the countryside to visit another friend.

We three crouched into this friend's Volkswagen bug, and before we took off, they asked me if I liked the beach.

"Yes, I like the beach." I thought about the Manzanillo sand burs. "Not as much as the water."

When they understood I loved to swim, they sent me upstairs for my swim suit.

We drove on a skinny asphalt road full of potholes which followed a tropical river valley between jungle covered hills. The car zipped around curves and under stretches of forest that arched over the road, then alongside reed-filled drainage ditches next to fields of Brahma cattle that rested in the shade of tall palm trees. After the road turned into reddish dust for about an hour, we arrived at a tiny collection of houses.

We greeted the people outside, and a young boy ran off to get the boys' friends. We walked along the open grazed grass along the river to a wide bend. Upstream, beyond the rapids that emptied into the sluggish wide area of the river, I could see women wash cloths. They used bushes as clotheslines. Shirts, pants, and dresses covered the bushes and lawn along the riverbanks. Where the bushes in the sun in front of a deep shadow, visible water vapor rose from the sunlit clothing.

The river water looked milky. We walked to the edge of the clearing behind bushes to change into swimsuits, hastened by mosquitoes.

"Any villages upstream from here?"

"No. Clean water, from the mountains. Go ahead, jump in."

I worried and jumped in anyhow. Of the others, only Raul wanted to swim, or try to, not very well. I didn't feel comfortable enough to open my eyes underwater, and since I couldn't see to my elbow, it didn't matter.

Some young boys, small fellows around ten or eleven, followed us into the water and wanted to show us how to get out on the other shore, walk upstream, and ride the rapids down. They screamed as the white water bounced them around, shot rapids over stationary waves caused by submerged rocks. Neither Raul nor I wanted to risk our shins.

Raul and I got out after about fifteen minutes, and stood around to dry off and bat at big horseflies to avoid bites.

We changed into street clothes in the bushes, and threw the wet suites onto the car's hood to dry.

The others stood at the edge of the clear area and talked to a slim cowboy who rode bareback atop a white horse.

As we approached, Raul said "You want to see a horse race?"

"My friend wants to race his horse against another, to prove who owns the fastest horse."

"Where's the other horse?"

"Soon, soon."

The young man leaned forward and kicked the slim white mare into a nose-arrowed frantic gallop along the river in several short bursts of speed, to warm it up and impress us.

He rode bareback, almost as out of breath as his horse, full of that hubris that the smiles of counted eggs provide, a brief revel in an easy pipe dream of youth, full of illusions of youth's invincibility and immortality, ready for a fall as a wake-up call.

The other horse arrived, a wild eyed, large chest, silver gray stallion with straw yellow mane. Both this horse and its rider looked much more thick bodied and healthy, and their attire more finely wrought and expensive, the man with a big silver watch and a huge silver belt buckle, and the horse with silver medallions on the bridle and saddle, tied with long thongs of leather.

"Who do you think will win?"

The riders busied themselves with jackknives to find a slender, flexible branch to strip the leaves from and use as a switch to goad their horse to greater speed.

"The grey." I hated to admit it. I pointed with a tilt of my head and my eyes, and then without a thought, pointed with pursed mouth, like a blown kiss, a gesture learned from many similar pointed gestures I saw performed here in Southern Mexico.

We walked into the forest on a little used two track worn into the forest floor by autos. We walked until the two horsemen agreed on an appropriate distance to race. Then they lined up, faced back towards the river.

The horses chomped at the bit and tried to bite each other. The excited gray reared up a bit as the riders wrestled with the reins and got them side by side.

Then Xavier called out the Spanish equivalent to Ready, set GO!

They thundered away down the lane and out of sight in a cloud of yellow dust.

We waited for their return.

Insects, stirred from the foliage, swam zigzags in the golden dust illuminated by shafts of sunlight.

We could hear a distant staccato of hooves change cadence, but then they seemed to take too long, and the forest fell quiet, a faint buzz, a snapped twig, and a low birdcall. Then we heard the sound of hoofs grow louder.

The big gray stallion rounded the curve, its rider hunched low over the neck. The rider glanced back with each energetic slap with a small switch.

The gray horse and rider thundered past us.

The stocky rider leaned back with force to haul the reins up to his jutted chin. The horse hunched down and dragged its back hoofs to stop. The rider turned its head with a violent tug of the reins to turn around and trot back towards us.

Then the white mare streaked into view, diaphanous in the film of dust that lingered from the other horse's passage. The bareback rider hugged the white mare's mane and switched her rump, and she ran like an arrow, nose down and forward.

The money changed hands. The winner said little. He touched the brim of his cowboy hat, and turned to ride off. Both the horse's and the rider's buttocks bounced esassy from side to side.

The dispute now settled, the skinny man took off his hat and batted at his jeans to shake off the dust kicked up by the grey. "But you have to admit, my horses is fast, right?"

We admitted his horse looked fast, like an arrow.

If spirit counted for anything, the slim white bareback mare and her skeletal loving owner both deserved to win, for they possessed something more important that the privileges of money and health enjoyed by the dominant class.

People often overlook the most important things.

Turtle Eggs

That Sunday afternoon when we returned, another of Xavier's friends, Marcos, waited for him at his house's ice cream store. When he learned I love to swim, he talked Xavier and Raul into a trip to the Pacific Ocean.

We took a nice highway without traffic straight to a small community of shacks and beached boats on the sea, which seemed 'pacifico' calm under a bright gray sky that hurt my eyes.

The beach sprawled empty for miles along this little two track access road, and then the road disappeared in sand. The Volkswagen got stuck, the front wheels buried up to the axle, until the three of us passenger all got out to lift and push it back onto firmer ground.

Back at the fisherman's encampment, we drank a few beers, then decided to eat a fish dinner in a thatch roof restaurant without walls. A table served as a counter for a gas stove, with ice coolers for the beer and soft drinks underneath. They recommended I try a huge reddish pan-shaped fish with large scales.

While we ate, a man came up to us with a bag of turtle eggs. He seemed sad that he must sell the eggs, even though he knew it illegal. He told us how he chanced upon the turtle nest this morning, after someone raided the nest and took the majority of eggs. These few eggs he found by light of day would die either way, left in the nest or harvested, whether we ate them or not.

Then Raul made a comment I couldn't catch, and Xavier and Marcos laughed. The man made an obscene gesture with his fingers, thumb rubbed between index and second finger, and the young men slapped each other on the back as they machine-gunned a staccato Spanish. I felt some of the comments involved me.

I asked "¿Que pasa?"

"Estos huevos te hacen duro, mano." They say it makes you hard, like the bony fists they held at the end of an upright forearm with little up and down motions and a suggestive leer.

"Afrodisíaco." They smirked and laughed, slapped each other on the back some more.

An aphrodisiac for males. It never occurred to me before that any healthy young man would need, or care so much about, aphrodisiacs. It struck me that their interest might reflect cultural myths, their inexperience with the opposite sex, or perhaps a plethora of access and opportunities that I could only dream about.

The salesman convinced us in the time-honored tradition of sales. He ignored our refusal, bragged about the quality and freshness of the eggs, talked about their healthy virtues, laughed too much, and hammered the point home that the eggs would either rot or get eaten, so why not by us, for a Gringo that never tasted a turtle egg before, and probably never would again.

"No hay nadie por aca pa' decir nada." No one else around to say anything.

We bought one for each of us, about three bucks.

They taught me the proper way to eat it. Open the shell on top with a pen knife and fold it back to form a little cup, sprinkle in the salt, and then squeeze a lime over the top. The citric acid cooks it, they said. Down it in one mouthful.

Tasted like egg-flavored chalk, with acidic limejuice and sweaty salt.

Don't mothers prepare a similar tonic to induce a child to vomit?

Alley Cats

Archeologists see evidence that Post-Classic Mayan societies engaged in intense warfare with sophisticated campaigns of domination and subjugation, perhaps motivated by the need for sacrificial victims, that demonstrate advanced military organization. The stone records on stelae hint that the kings and royal families concerned themselves with empire and conquest of cities. The stone record further suggests a metamorphosis in those empires, that an increase in militaristic influences at the expense of the secular, humanistic, and religious, a consequential artistic decline evident in the artifacts left behind.

Yvonne extracted much of that history out of me with the skill of an orthodontic surgeon, and once said that she knew why I journeyed to Guatemala. Still, she asked for more.

By now, I tired of it, felt ready to receive her side of the bargain. I told her "You know the rest. I went to Santa Catarina and rented that house from the Mayans."

We strolled around the streets of Xela hand in hand, as if to fulfill all our romantic fantasies as foreplay to a final goodbye.

We ate in a tiny hole-in-the-wall restaurant, the front room of someone's home decorated with old movie posters and calendar scenes of Guatemala. We stopped at a few bars to drink a few beers, serial drinks, one in each bar. Sometimes they would smile and suggest that Yvonne wait outside, but she knew enough Spanish to tell them that as a French woman, she knew more about beer and wine than they did. Her macho attitude they understood, and they let her enter without another word.

As we walked around the steep center of Quetzaltenango, high on alcohol and energized by the crisp mountain air, we kissed and flirted with each other. I felt attracted to her physicality, and felt angry about the fact we would split up tomorrow morning.

She looked adorable in a loose knee length skirt of deep blue Guatemalan denim. We walked alone down the cobblestone streets etched in gold under the last rays of the sun. I surrendered to her beauty, my horniness, and dared to pull her hand to the urgency in my crotch.

"Stop it."

She looked so beautiful in the sunset, her face glowed in warm hues reflected from the sky. Her cheeks flushed pink from the cool air and our exercise.

We passed an alley, narrow and dark, and I pulled her into it to give her a kiss, long and passionate.

She pushed me away and stared into my eyes. She said, "What do you want with me, really?"

"I want to kiss you where nobody else can see us, to not upset any Guatemalans. They're too conservative, they all look depressed."

"Might give them a needed rise in blood pressure, help them, God help them. Nobody can see us here. It's a dark alley. Who looks up dark alleys?"

"I feel better not to worry about it."

"So why do you want to kiss?"

"I don't. Not exactly. I want to make love to you. I'm crazy for you. Feel me."

"All right, I can feel it. Back in the room?"

"Now, right here, right now, and do it again back in the room."

"You're crazy."

"You're right."

We kissed and our mouths ate each other. She got hot fast, and let me lift up her skirt and touched her there. She pushed my hand away. I kissed her, squeezed her butt, lifted up her skirt again, and rubbed against her.

She moaned.

I took it as an OK. She didn't stop me. Her tongue probed inside my mouth like a frantic, warm slug that looked for a place to hide.

I massaged her mound with my fingers and she threw her head back, so I kissed her neck. She backed up and leaned against a brick wall, next to a drain pipe from the roof. In a few minutes, my fingers worked under the thin veil of her panties and slipped through her wetness. I bent down and massaged her chest with my face against her sweater and bra as I unzipped my pants. She rubbed her knee against the outside of my thigh, so I grabbed that long, tan leg just behind the knee and lifted it up.

She helped me pull her panties to the side.

We moved together and kissed, and somehow maintained our balance, as we breathed together, slow at first with the paranoia that someone might see us. We began to throb together, in a pantomime of a desperate mouth to mouth resuscitation. I hoped we looked like lovers who slipped into an alley to kiss, but in a few moments, I didn't care.

Yvonne tried to dig her nails through my jacket and into my back, then up to my bare neck. She pulled her head back and rested it against the wall, her eyes closed, as if to connect herself to the earth or remove herself from the situation, I couldn't tell which. I put my hand around the back of her head to protect it from the brick wall, gave it to her quick and hard. She steamed up and panted hard as I finished too fast.

She put her leg down and I zipped up.

We kissed, let our heart rate return to normal.

She said "What was that all about?"

"I thought you liked it."

"This is crazy. You're crazy. Did you ever stop to think about how I might clean up out here?"

That little problem never occurred to me. "The hotel's a couple of blocks from here."

"You expect me to walk all the way back there and let your stuff fall down my legs? What did you do that for?"

"I don't know. Uncontrollable urge. Didn't you like it?"

"Disgusting. You asshole, I hate you."

Back in the hotel room, I started to read as she showered and complained about no hot water.

She came out wet, a towel around her head, walked over and kissed me, but a book captured my interest more at that moment. She turned away from me in a huff. I recognized my mistake as she stormed into the bathroom.

She came out dressed in her street clothes again, and sat in a chair to read a book. She stared at the book and appeared angry.

"Something wrong?" I said.

"Oh no, not at all. I see two beds in this room, don't you?"

"What's that supposed to mean?"

"You don't care about me. You care about sex. I feel dirty, ashamed of myself, after what you did to me in that filthy alley. I do not know how you could think that if I let you kiss me, that gives you permission to use me like a whore, that I must let you fuck me in public, on the city streets in the afternoon, in daylight, in an alley. In that dirty, stinking, garbage-filled alley, rats and puke and black water. Worse than a whore! A real man pays for a hotel room with a whore. You disgust me."

"I'm sorry. I made a mistake, I thought you were in to it."

"I think I was in shock, because I couldn't believe what was happening." She sat down at the desk and looked into the mirror.

"You don't sound like the same person who made a deal to show me how to make love to a woman. I trusted you."

She reached into her makeup purse and took out some lipstick or chapstick, looked into the mirror, and painted the open O of her soft lips. "Trust. So sorry. I can't give you what you need. I don't have enough money, and I'm nobody's mother. You can't make a woman climax if you disgust her. No way. Sorry."

If I could believe what I read in the letters section of pornographic magazines, all sorts of people did kinky things; unspeakable things with amputees and their stumps, two or three or more people in bondage, couples in costume or nude but disguised, and some do it in semi-public places because the fear of discovery excites them. Maybe I should enlighten her, and add that 'everybody knows that,' but it didn't seem worth it. She'd take it as a criticism, get mad, and use it as another example of my American vulgarity.

I wondered if Yvonne discovered something about herself in that alley, that she felt something that reminded her of something she didn't like about herself, something half remembered or not understood, something she didn't want to face.

That knife-sharp pain in my back returned. I wanted to hide it from Yvonne, so I writhed and bent to the left as I lay down to ride it out. Maybe I did have a kidney stone. Maybe I should see a doctor. Worst case, I might die before I learn how to satisfy a woman.

Death would also eliminate my financial problems.

Before dawn the next morning, I awoke to go pee, and saw my breath in the mirror. I took a quick hot shower, and dressed while I scanned the bedroom for anything else of mine to squeeze into my backpack.

Yvonne pretended to sleep, naked under the sheets.

As I hoisted the backpack to my shoulders, Yvonne raised her head once to blow me a kiss goodbye, then buried her face in the pillows with a mumble about how tired she felt. She rolled over onto her stomach and raised her face to look at the wall and say "I hate mushy goodbyes. Thank you for everything, it's been great, lovely. I can't wait to take a hot shower for as long as I want."

"Can I have your address in France, so I can write to you?"

"Write down your address and leave it on the dresser."

There it ended, Yvonne and I, with the one-way exchange of addresses and a wish for each other's wonderful life.

I thought I would never hear from her again. She would prove me wrong.

She blew me a wet kiss that evaporated in the humid tropical air.

Once outside, I turned to look up at the black stone face of the hotel that eclipsed the dark sky and stars. Hundreds of years of dew, dust, diesel and daydreams ran in black stains down the hotel's stones, now Colonial architecture, a previous part of a Mayan temple complex, and before that, part of a volcanic mountain thrust through sediments that recorded hundreds of millions of years of evolution that brought us to now.

A couple of pigeons rustled themselves awake, then snuggled into the corner again and bent their heads to sleep.

I felt relieved and tragic. Maybe people who go to conferences and meet other business people of the opposite sex feel like this after a short term affair. They mutter things like "You're beautiful, you're wonderful, I had so much fun." Then, as they stand in line at the airport, they smile as they remember all the "Was it good for you too?" questions, asked while fascinated by the twin cobras of pale cigarette smoke that curled against the darker recesses of a motel room. I bet most of the time, each follows American cultural programming learned through television and their friend's parent's gossip, etc. They want to run home, get drunk, wax nostalgic and reminisce with tears and anger, then hope to erase the entire memory with more alcohol. Others probably take a long shower, first to disinfect themselves, then to cleanse themselves of their self loathing, and then, as they dry their hair, they swear on everything they hold sacred to never do it again, yet can't stop the nervous smile in recognition of how much they enjoyed the naughtiness.

I got out early enough to see Xela, the colonial city built atop the ancient Mayan city, in the indirect silvered light of a dawn hidden on the other side of the mountains. Street sweepers dragged and pivot-rolled fifty gallon oil drum garbage cans in a thunderous route across the cobblestones of street, sidewalk, and square. The garbage men settled their oil drums upright and took out their brooms to sweep the streets. Old women, at least they looked old wrapped in shawls against the cold, ventured out of their houses, locked doors and gates behind them, and hurried off to another house to continue their work as servants, or catch the first public transport buses to the markets.

An ambulant line of women in shawls led me to the bus stop, where I caught a public transport and asked how I could connect to the line that goes to the Terminal de Autobuses.

By the time I arrived, all Xela seemed awake, and the crowded bus station invigorate me with the freedom to look at women without the fear of a poke in the ribs. The world filled with possibilities and discomfort, full of an infinity of choices that might lead to a hope for a better future, instead of the prison of pricey comforts and moral contradiction that threatened to turn me into a zombie of compromise.

I enjoyed the bus ride back to Guatemala City, alone.

Guatemala City reminded me of the seriousness of the post-earthquake situation in Guatemala. While Xela and Huehue allowed one to forget about the recent cataclysmic catastrophe, I needed to go back into the belly of the beast on the chance that the Dirección General de Migración might process my passport. I didn't like the idea of a trip through Mexico without passport, because I needed it to get money and to present at the periodic military checkpoints, where army boys, ignorant and uneducated young men in battle fatigues and a duckbill cap atop shaved heads, came onto the bus to stare without comprehension at our papers, while their youthful, delicate fingers worried the trigger of a gun they cradled like a baby, a gun with the safety off, a gun with the power of death over life, a power too big for their comprehension.

Maybe I could make a couple of phone calls and ask for money, enough to hang out in San Jose or Hawaii, where the quake probably didn't do a thing, to buy time to wait to see if in another week or two they find my passport in the scrambled files.

I thought Yvonne a much sadder person than the girl that embarked alone from France over a year ago. Her innocence still bubbled, buoyed up by not much more than her own conscious efforts at effervescence, though I felt that deep down, little remained to evaporate. My influence in her life added to her litany of the cruel feminist clichés of why men befriend women, how men use women, how men don't deserve women. In addition, all her picture postcard idyllic views of the world wore thin to show a fundamental reality beneath, a dangerous world that popped her most beautiful buoyant thought bubbles to make her sink further. I imagined her as a deer caught in the headlights of a moral compromise, between social responsibility and personal freedom, the immature wish for independence and unrestrained hedonistic pleasure at someone else's expense.

Sometimes her speech patterns, when she talked about herself, created an image of Yvonne as her own daughter.

I don't think she resented our affair. I didn't. We communicated and trusted each other, and over those few days together, twenty four hours a day, we fought very little, and grew to know and understand each other a bit, both the physical and intellectual, if not the spiritual. We grew in self knowledge, and discovered that what physical attraction brings together, bad timing and incompatibility separates with ease, in peace or war, disaster or fortune. It depends upon something bigger than us. A couple's longevity depended upon the antidote for war, and a parent's problems with teenagers, the concepts of peace, unconditional love, and understanding remain empty words, too complicated for the immature, who seek to control others.

Scratch those conservative, right wing, warmonger Republicans and you find an Average Random Mean just below the surface, a tribal instinct to blame and hate. Everything makes mistakes, even computers, and the brain is a computer on hormones.

We shared a shallow physical love that first night, and then the earthquake gave us a mountain of guilt to chew on throughout the days, as we awoke to the magnitude of this national disaster. We both felt chastised by God for our impertinence, and the importation of the developed world's personal freedom, the impertinence of a belief in a classless society, and our secular liberal morality to the ultra conservative Guatemalan culture of traditions, Catholic and Mayan, and the rigid social stratification by class.

My plans changed in a heartbeat, every time that knife-blade of pain in my lower back returned.

I could go to the relief workers to ask for work, or maybe a quick flight back to the states on an empty relief supply airplane, or on a donated military transport, back to the United States. Or I could go to Doctor Mendez to ask about these stabs of pain in the small of my back, which now occurred almost every night.

Dr. Mendez will ask about Yvonne, and I didn't want to risk some instantaneous emotional reaction on my part, because I didn't yet know how I felt about it, our relationship, the way we ended it, how I felt about Yvonne, what she meant or means to me, and our failure as a couple, or as individuals.

We lived beyond the edges of Guatemala's social frameworks of birthright, blind nationalistic loyalty, clerical authority, fatalism, and superstition. We clung to each other frightened, our eyebrows arched like South American Night Monkeys that stare out from among the coal-tar roots of a tree whose leafy branches form a crown, an atomic blast's mushroom cloud.

Without the earthquake, that first night might bring a morning of nothing more than a kiss and a shared breakfast, a hug and a thank you, and a goodbye.

The traveler's anonymity becomes a social asset that offers a quick, easy intimacy. Travelers can bear their soul and share their innermost secrets, or perhaps try out their new persona, because every day, every acquaintance, every situation becomes a transient phenomenon. People can reinvent themselves, or even try a dash of total honesty, to see how they feel about it without social repercussions. Whatever happens, they can move on and forget about it.

Maybe we should all live that way, with the goal to create a world where gossip doesn't rule the tribe, where everyone in consortium gives permission to each person to make their own mistakes, like everyone does anyway, and the rest try not hold it against them for as long as human memory serves.

Reputations, created over the long haul, people love to destroy in a heartbeat. We all make mistakes, and people should appreciate honest mistakes, their own and others', as long as one learns from them.

Maybe we fail whenever we do not consider all hypocrisy and dishonesty a crime, an individual's acquiescence to their family or tribe, to protect reputations and seek personal benefit, when contrasted with service to the truth, for the bigger all-inclusive tribe that everyone should belong to, a tribe dedicated to a better future for humanity.

That won't stop the instinct to wag the ol' judgmental tongue, the prejudicial tongue. Nothing wrong with judgments, but prejudice relies on ignorance of a deeper knowledge. Nothing like an enforced ignorance coupled with good intentions as the two cornerstones for chaotic evil. The tribe that hates together, stays together.

Religion, and most religious people, err when they simplify things as a battle between good and evil, God and Satan. Two kinds of people inhabit the world. The humanists who try not to judge, and allow others to take their own steps and make mistakes as long as no one gets hurt. The most common, traditional, and primitive people need to, want to, and feel a sadistic enjoyment to control others.

Humans evolved as tribal monkeys, and I left my tribe at home.

The bus headed for the earthquake-shattered Guatemala City on nightmare roads cracked and crumbled with car-size potholes and curves without guard rails that marked landslides of dirt, boulders, and trees. Road crews let the cars trickle through on narrow one-lane passages cleared by small bulldozers. We skirted slow around new cliffs that dropped off into deep canyons, where the bus inched forward along the edge of broken asphalt.

Across the countryside, curtains of yellow dust swirled up on wind eddies from deep inside the contorted canyons. As the bus neared the city, the yellow dust squirmed and mixed with gray smoke from hundreds of campfires scattered across the forested hillsides.

Once inside the city, from the bus window it seemed like bigger piles of rubble blocked more streets than I remembered. Mayan men walked around with their machete scabbards, and I thought I detected more suspicion and avoidance in the way people looked at each other. Children and dogs played atop the piles of rubble in front of damaged buildings. Bleary-eyed people walked with painful determination, one hand elevated to ease the pain under crusty, bloody bandages on hands, arms, or head.

I got off the bus with one hope, that I could get my passport and leave.

A group of Caucasians walked down the street in work clothes, some carried duffel bags and one walked with a sturdy professional camera tripod across his back. Each wore an identical armband. I hailed them in English.

"Are any of you American?"

"Yeah." One replied like an American.

"Were you guys here for the earthquake?"

"No, we're part of international aid. Through the Red Cross."

"Any jobs available?"

They laughed.

"I need to get a little money, that's all."

The leader spoke. "Not much chance of that. Most of us volunteer. You need a sponsor, mate." He motioned for the others to follow him and walk on.

Canadian, or Australian, New Zealander. I said "Thanks, sport. What is it you guys do?"

"We make photographic and video documentaries of disasters and relief programs."

I joined a small crowd of people that walked slow in front of the Dirección General de Migración. Then I turned off the sidewalk and took the wide stairs down to the subterranean entrance and mixed in with the groups that waited at the windows.

Open for business.

Over the tops of the heads of the people in front of the counter. I could see that most of the file cabinets stood upright in neat rows, although some disordered piles of manila folders remained scattered along the aisles.

When my turn came at the window, the man who took my name and numbers asked me to step back and wait, to give others access, while he looked for my file. I waited fifteen minutes, almost gave up hope, but he came back with my passport. The official asked me how much additional time I wanted, or needed, to leave the country. I asked for a couple of weeks, he stamped it with permission to stay one week more. We both knew it didn't matter to anybody. No one would keep tabs on a few misguided tourists in this demolished country with so many problems.

I felt my heartbeat calm down, with my breast pocket stretched by my passport stamped with a week's worth of time, time I could spend anywhere in Guatemala.

In order to decide where I should go next, I talked to travelers and tourists who ate in the central market's restaurants. They told me that the main bridge over the Montagua river to get into the Petén fell apart, and many major roads remained covered by rockslides or closed because of earthquake damage or potential for new landslides. The needs of relief efforts to make runways for small planes often closed other highways, and other access roads remained closed to provide safe tent cities near mountain communities.

I walked out of the market and across the Central Plaza to the National Palace. I wanted to see the murals. The Guatemalan artists adopted the Mexican mural movement and filled the wall surfaces with painted imagery of Mayans, Spanish conquistadors on horseback, and men in suits to symbolize the compression of five hundred years into a colorful eye candy.

I could not decipher it. Guatemala remained an enigma, a mystery with no explanation. I did not want to rush away from so much intrigue, where colonial Eternal Springtime cities sat like spiders in the center of a web that led out of small Mayan villages Guatemala City. Mayan ruins in the rain forests, sulfuric desert mountains, an Atlantic coast with coral reefs, lakes surrounded by volcanoes draped in coffee plantations, a Pacific coast of long black volcanic sand beaches, and a lost state full of black African descendants that spoke English. I could not decide which way to go. I could stay in the city another week, even if it meant another stare into death's eye sockets. I wanted to stay, and risk that kidnap into a limitless night of unanswered questions about the future.

More rumors of epidemics, malaria, typhoid, dengue, encephalitis, toxic contamination of water and food supplies from industrial spills and rotten corpses, kidnappings by gangs of policemen, riots over food, wars between gangs of looters, class warfare, even wars of international intervention, all these rumors aggregated to seem intentional, meant to push me, the affluent, the travelers, the tourists, and all other extra-nationals out of the country.

It also made me want to stick around, if only I could find a way to hide somewhere in safety, and watch this theoretical expansive butterfly of disaster unfold its wings and cover the land in shadow, or not.

Better not.

With my passport in my backpack again, on this third cloudy day with intermittent rain and drizzle, I hoisted my backpack and walked toward the Guatemala City bus terminal, paranoid about the diminutive Mayan men who passed with machetes in scabbards.

The sky darkened, and it began to rain. I found the right bus, the one where a burly man hung out the doorway to yell "Tapachula! Tapachula!" We waited for over an hour for more passengers.

The bus driver fired up the engine to idle and attract those anxious to leave right away, and after fifteen minutes or so, he revved the engines and double clutched to make the bus lurch through the mud puddle potholes, some almost a foot deep, in the dirt of the parking lot and driveway.

Under the black skies of the downpour, the lights of a few buses lit the scene and created shadows that moved and took on a life of their own. They painted the walls with silhouettes of people who scurried for cover, or lugged suitcases and cardboard boxes tied with thick jute rope. Some tried to keep their heads covered with torn plastic garbage bags.

I took a good, long, last look at the details of scattered garbage; pieces of broken wood, plastic candle wraps, old auto parts, skins and peels of banana and mango, amid the piles of fallen squashed vegetables that drained into the black rivulets of sewage and fresh raw bones gnawed by stray dogs. This fetid soup and salad of human activity perfumed our drive out of this gravel and pothole football field parking lot.

CHAPTER 22: The Red Tile Church

The bus lumbered its hulk through the city on streets black as char. The dark streetlights stood lined up like dead sentinel vultures, a blind white eye under a bald head that crowned a vertebral curve of steel. On straightaways, I could hear the bus wheels sizzle as they spit a spray that spread like two angel wings on either side, gossamer in the headlights of other vehicles.

The bus headed south, towards the suburbs near Guatemala's International Airport, an area that suffered little damage and housed the affluent international community of retirees, professionals, upper level factory management, and the well off expatriates or immigrants.

Sleep snuck up behind me and put its cool fingers over my sandy eyelids. Vignettes of possible futures floated through my mind and refused to coalesce. I needed money, and might do anything to get it. I might stumble into a situation where a beautiful woman would take me in, buy me a ticket back home, or travel with me so I could introduce her to my mother. In my fantasy, she never appeared Guatemalan, but older, cosmopolitan, and more like that red haired Irishwoman that married the ruler of Paraguay and started the War of the Triple Alliance, which wiped out eighty percent of Paraguay's men and left a Shangri-la of females for the survivors.

With a girl like that, who cares what mom thinks.

I might get off the bus and look for a little work, find some reprehensible amoral arch-villain as a boss, someone with a workable plot to take over the world. Of course, I would thwart his plans and free his over-affectionate supermodel sex kitten, who loves me as any real woman must love a fresh idealistic young boy-toy with too much energy. She buys my love with false promises to stay by me no matter what, and will, as long as I control the creep's wealth and keep her in expensive clothes and earlobe-deep in the latest fruit-based schnapps.

Friends joked with me that I could "Go anywhere in the world, if you get your hair cut and learn some manners. You could escort rich old ladies to social functions, and on the way home in the taxi, work out payment for special in-house services." They waxed envious, and looked at it as a reasonable short term career choice, which I considered impossible. As I said in not so many words, my ovation rarely stands for the first performance, not even with a beautiful young girl who jumps between the sheets and pants in my ear like a lioness latched onto the dusty backside of a wildebeest.

"There's an art to every profession," they told me.

I looked out my window at the wounded city's blackness, and tried to make out the rectangular shapes of the near horizon, vague buildings a little darker than the charcoal drizzle that fell out of the dense air.

The Red Tile Church came into view. Almost invisible, save for the glitters of reflected light off the red tiles. A sparse light scattered from the cars' headlights and bounced off the slick pavement and puddles, and mixed with gigantic rivers of lightning that spread horizontal across the sky and tickled the bellies of fat, black clouds.

A light shone from a lower window, from inside the church.

I grabbed my backpack from the seat beside me and started to run towards the front of the bus, but the pack caught on the back of the seat. Jerked backwards, I almost fell, but managed to hoist the pack to my shoulders and yell "Baja! Baja" to mean down, down, let me off the bus!

The pneumatic brakes hissed through the sizzle of spray, and when the bus stopped, I heard the thousands of finger pats of rain against the roof. The driver grabbed the baton handle to open the door with a squeak as I stepped out into the soaked blackness and ran back toward the church.

Would someone come to the huge door of the Red Tile Church when I rapped the brass knocker against the metal plate? Would anyone hear the wooden booms from the kicks of my waterlogged boots against the heavy door, so wide and tall it would act like a tympani drum, and send waves of sound, reverberation of my desperation, to echo down the empty halls and swirl in the cavernous, candle-lit cathedral of the interior?

Any church should feel obligated to give shelter in such a storm. I imagined Guatemala's refugees filled all the intact churches, and those inside might demand this strange extra-national leave, out of a suspicion of the truth, that I possessed resources enough to buy my way out of danger and take the next flight out. The gold leaf ostentatious wealth of all the Catholic Cathedrals in Guatemala could offer little more than faith to millions of earthquake victims.

I knocked and knocked, but the wind and rain beat too, branches of trees moved like stiff hula arms, and rubbed their green fingers against the church with the sounds of slaps and scrapes and thuds. A loose window above me clattered as if something tried to get out. The heavy wood door muffled the blows of my knuckles, and then I opened my hand to slap the wood, to get a sharper sound. It sounded like a finger snap in the howl of the wind. I kicked at the bottom of the door, but it felt as solid as stone, and refused to ring.

Big raindrops hammered on shoulders to form rivulets that streamed into the space between my shirt and backpack.

I stepped away from the door, turned around, and looked down the black tunnel of the lightning strobed street with the hope I might see a bus. Without streetlights, every vehicle looked the same, two cones of light that ricocheted off the wet pavement.

The door opened, and I turned to see a brown, elder Guatemalan gentleman, taller than most, black almond shaped eyes and hairless chin with one black spot. His arms wrapped a green woolen blanket over his shoulders. We stared at each other for an interminable ten seconds as each waited for the other one to speak.

He looked me up and down, and then said in perfect English, "Can I help you?"

"You could ask me inside, out of the rain."

He stepped back from the door and waved me in with an elegant gesture.

When the door shut, the storm almost disappeared. The tempest whispered, and we walked past a shelf where a candelabra burned with flames as motionless as glass.

"Take your boots and socks off, I'll get you some slippers. Put your wet things in this room to dry. I do not usually open that door, but then, no tourist in a backpack ever knocked at night, in the middle of a thunderstorm. Lucky a car passed as I looked out, or I would've never seen you."

He looked about sixty years old, perhaps a Spanish nobleman, but spoke perfect American English, with an accent like mine. I could believe he came from Michigan. I took the slippers from him, and asked, "Are you an American?"

"More American than you. I come from both Central America and North America."

"Where did you learn English?"

"I spent the summers of my youth in Canada. When my parents divorced, they shuffled me back and forth from Regina to Antigua. It's not often I get a chance to talk in English. That's why I decided to open the door. My name is Diego Garcia."

"I call myself Brandon, as they say in Spanish. Nice to meet you."

We entered a small room with a book case that covered one end. It looked like a living room, but without a fireplace or rug. We sat down in plush upright chairs with wooden lions feet.

"Are you the Father of this church?"

"I take care of it sometimes. I know the family that built this church."

"This church belongs to one family?"

"I don't know all the details of ownership. The man who built this church made a lot of money in Guatemala, back in the fifties. I know that, because I helped him earn that money, before his wife got sick. He loved his wife very much, she meant the world to him. As she grew weaker and weaker, he went crazy. He couldn't sleep, and stopped eating. He prayed all the time, in the Cathedral of La Merced, downtown. He prayed all night, all day, whenever he couldn't stay beside her in the hospital. Here, a family member stays with hospital patients because there aren't enough qualified nurses. He begged the doctors to do something, but she stopped responding, and eventually, the doctors gave up and sent her home on a stretcher to die. Even then, he stayed beside her and prayed. He prayed to God to protect his wife, to give life back to her. He prayed to God to give him a few more years with his wife. As he prayed, he promised if God would spare her life, he would build the most beautiful church in the world. And then, miraculously, his wife recovered. So he built this church, even though it bankrupted him, and probably sent the both of them to the grave before their time."

"So where is he now? Buried under the church?"

"I couldn't say. Or shouldn't say. I don't know who you are. Why do you come here in the middle of the night?"

"It's not the middle of the night, it's just dark out. I've been curious about the church since I first saw it, and when I saw your light, I got off the bus to see if anyone would answer."

"There are no lights you could see from the street. We don't have electricity yet. I'm afraid you came here because of a reflection of light from elsewhere, a car or something. Anyway, you're here now. Can I offer you a glass of wine, if you're old enough to drink? About eighteen, I should guess?"

"Twenty two."

"Old enough. What brings you to Guatemala? ¿Hablas Español?"

Before I could answer, he raised his hand to silence me as he strode out of the room. He stayed away for a few minutes, and came back with a bottle. After he rummaged through a drawer and pulled out corkscrew, he uncorked the bottle with a practiced expertise, extracted the cork as fast as one could dig a red pimiento out of a green olive with a toothpick. He soon lined up two tall wine glasses filled to their tipsy elegance, and asked "So tell me about your trip so far."

I gave him the short version of my trip to Guatemala, the desire to see how people lived on a dollar a day, Lake Atitlán, Hawaii, my pensión, and how in the earthquake I struck out for El Cerrito del Carmen.

I asked him about his family. Most left Guatemala over twenty years ago to live in the United States. He said that made it easier for him to decide to "enter a dangerous and lucrative line of work."

"You mean what by 'dangerous and lucrative' work?"

"When a person, perhaps not unlike yourself, has only one person to think of, one can afford to take risks that a family man would not dare to, if he loved his family."

"You mean something criminal, like drugs or arms merchants, stolen cars? Some subversive organization, like communists?"

"Subversive, yes. In my case, I mean the military, and the police."

"What's so subversive about the military?"

"You don't think of the military as a subversive organization, because you do not have an education in history. Militaries tend to overthrow their own government. Or the military-industrial complex. Eisenhower's warning became famous as a convenient shorthand to describe reality, as do most prophecies that become reality."

"Prophecy? How's that?"

"The Military Industrial Complex. Only he knows exactly what he meant, but to my mind, it resembles Fascism, the wolf in sheep's clothing that cries wolf and sees enemies everywhere, an elite class of industrialists that control the power of a military that struts bellicose over the face of the earth. The entire earth should tremble when governments make money from rich industrialists, and militaries protect their capacity for production and profit among all other nations. They manipulate the rest of the world, to exploit cheap labor and extract resources."

"So what's wrong with that? Anybody that tries to live on a dollar a day needs a better job."

He lifted his head like an eagle, and split his narrow jaws in a wide grin and then opened up to laugh carcajadas. "As sure as my name is Diego García, you speak the truth. And people do offer them a better job, one that pays a dollar and ten cents a day, and if they don't like it, plenty people line up to take the job. Many never notice the job becomes a prison, one they can't afford to break out of. They accumulate more debt and babies than income or equity. Their own ambition for the house and car damns their children to quit school and go to work to service their debt."

"Everybody's in debt, everybody owes their lives to the State that protects them. Why shouldn't they get a factory job? I worked in a factory, beats digging out peanuts in the hot sun."

"You chose to move on, didn't you? Many of them cannot. The factories offer houses and cars with endless maintenance costs, and the luckiest qualify for long-term debt. In Latin America, you see families in a nice car with clean new clothes on malnourished children."

"Don't they see their children get sick?"

"Children always get sick. They go to the neighborhood curandero, the bruja or witchdoctor, and he rolls up a cone of newspaper, inserts it into the sick child's ear, lights the wide end, and everybody feels so relieved the child doesn't dare complain that he no longer hears in that ear."

"Why don't they want better, to improve themselves?"

"They do. They copy what they see in magazines and on TV."

"Why don't they get educated?"

"Our government says it can't afford it. And it can't. People would get wise to who robs them."

"Somebody must see through it every once in a while."

"The Asians say the nail that sticks up gets hammered down. That's how society enforces loyalty among the ignorant fools that choose tradition and a simplistic view of life to avoid the hard work to understand the complexities of reality. The dream of money controls their hearts and minds. Everybody wants to be rich.e"

"What's wrong with that? Sounds to me like the dream that fuels the American miracle, doesn't it?"

"This isn't your America. This is my Guatemala, and I declare myself, Diego García, its ruler. Now I'm responsible to protect my country, and promote industrial expansion. So what can I do against the threat of instability and social chaos? I must control people. Think of it as discipline among the undisciplined, of the superior man over the animals. To protect the country from political chaos, in a heartbeat I would disband government, the parliaments, the congresses, and declare a state of emergency. I would enforce curfews, and see to it that no one held meetings or spoke out in the streets. When people must be reminded about how to act in dangerous times, nothing reminds them as well as the pointed toe of a well polished boot."

"Sounds like Cuba, with Fidel in army fatigues all the time."

"No, not really. There's no industry to protect in Cuba, except sugar. Fidel saw to it that citizens valued education, and now they say everybody can read, although the bookstores control which books they can find. Cubans do get free health care, and their colleges put out so many doctors and nurses each year, thousands of them get sent around the world for free, as ambassadors for Castro's brand of communism. That's more grassroots aid than the United States sends to other countries. Unfortunately, since they have no access to American-made drugs and medical technology, I bet those doctors know less than most nurses in the United States."

"So you, too, think the United States military forced Guatemala to change presidents, something about protecting bananas or some such rot?"

"There were no bananas."

"What do you mean? Then why do people think America overthrew President what's-his-name?"

"Arbenz. He tried to give lands to poor Guatemalans, lands that United Fruit owned but weren't planted yet, because the Guatemalan government paid United Fruit the full tax-assessed value. So the CIA paints Guatemala's President as a Communist in the press, while they secretly train a rebel army in Honduras with a Guatemalan Army Colonel. They planned the whole invasion with air support to look like a military coup. It was funny, actually. Everybody panicked. This little CIA-backed army from Honduras came into Guatemala, a few planes flew over the harbor and strafed some ships, and Guatemala City panicked. Advisors told Arbenz to run for it, to save Guatemala City the horrors of war, and so almost without a gunshot, the government changed overnight. I know, because I was there. That's when I started to earn money."

He sat back in his chair with wineglass in hand, and rubbed his brow with his other. His skin took on a reddish hue in the candlelight, and glistened as if he sweated. The way his shoulders moved as he breathed made me wonder if he might cry.

"Diego? Mr. García?"

He put his hand up in the air, palm toward me, halt. After about a minute of brow rubbing, he said "Migraines. I get these terrible headaches sometimes. Please forgive me for worrying you. When you want to go sleep, let me know. You can stay in one of the rooms in the nunnery, though the bathroom is down the hall. You can shower there when you like."

"Thank you. What time do you usually go to bed?"

"Mornings. I try to work all night. That way I won't be bothered. You go on to bed whenever you feel tired."

He took me on a candlelit tour of the church while we nursed our drinks and listened to the hiss of the rain from inside the airy cathedral.

Then he asked "Do you believe that poor people demonstrate their laziness through their poverty?" His voice echoed in the vaulted space.

"What do you mean?"

"If you see a poor person, do you judge that person as less deserving, as lazy, like a drug addict, a no-account?"

"No, most people in Guatemala don't have money, but they work hard."

"So you think they should be rewarded with money. Have you heard of Spinoza's Social Darwinism?"

"What's that?"

"I have money, therefore I am, and you aren't."

"Reminds me of Ayn Rand. The Virtue of Selfishness, Atlas Shrugged and the slackers fall off."

Diego sighed. "So American. The glorification of industrialists and entrepreneurs, as if people get rich only by merit. Ayn Rand accepted competition as the only model, even when flawed with uneven starts and nonstandard rules."

"You've read her, then?"

"Not much. What do you believe, Brandon? You believe in altruism or selfishness?"

"Some think all behavior comes from selfishness. Even if you give money to someone, you do it because it makes you feel good, or more moral, to redeem yourself or feel superior."

"Do you believe in Capitalism or Communism?"

"I believe in Democracy."

"That's a political system. But let's say you run for office and must decide on an economic model, would lean toward Capitalism, or Communism?"

"I'm not sure I understand the difference."

"Think of it as jungle or zoo. Should government allow free competition between the wolves and the sheep, or satisfy everyone's needs as if in a zoo, where all receive equal benefit from taxation?"

"A zoo might be nice and peaceful, but unnatural. Why would anyone get up in the morning? Nobody would work hard unless rewarded for their ambition and hard work. No opportunity for individual freedoms."

"Maybe, maybe not. The jungle favors the predators, the top of the food chain, those who feed on the hard work of others. Some people think an impoverished childhood fuels ambition, and creates people that don't care about others. Sociopaths and criminals would find illegal and immoral ways to make money that people with conscience couldn't dream of. Do you feel a responsibility to your fellow humans?"

"Do onto others as they would do to you. Or maybe, before they do to you. Or when in Rome, do as they expect you to do."

"Is that the extent of your responsibility?"

"You think I am my brother's keeper?"

"What if your brother was in this earthquake, you think you would be doing something else right now?"

"Sure I would. I'm here because I don't know what I should do. I don't speak enough Spanish to be useful. Everybody tells me to leave, that epidemics, looting, and riots will start soon. My passport lay in a jumble of papers downtown, on the immigration office floor, until a few days ago. What do you think I should do?"

"That depends entirely on you. You could stay here a few days to go downtown everyday and watch it all unfold, and everything either settles down or gets worse, in which case you head out of the country as fast as possible."

He sat back in his plush chair and looked at me with eyes of an eagle. "Would you like to see the future of the United States of America?"

"I don't know. That's the problem with fortune tellers. Maybe I would live happier if I didn't know where my life headed."

"I'm not a bloody oracle, you know. Follow the trends, it takes a lot to change trends once things get set in motion."

"What's in store for the United States?"

"More oil shortages, longer work hours, more contamination until they move production overseas, and eventually the standard of living must fall to allow other nations to rise. If things keep on the same track, more and more Hispanics will immigrate to the U.S. which makes it easier for others in their family to come, legally or illegally. Because the Pope says that God will not allow people on birth control to go to heaven, Hispanics will reproduce like rabbits, while the Anglo saxons continue to see two children as the perfect and socially responsible size for a family in an overpopulated world. The Anglos will decline in number, while Hispanics become the dominant group in the United States, become the majority, and take power through the democracy."

"When do you see that happening?"

"It could happen early in the next millennium."

"Next Millennium. So what?"

"So what? That's the trouble with young people. Their frame of reference is like a keyhole into their own room, and ignorance makes them tedious. You think twenty five or fifty years from now, a distant future? With the best of luck, you'll survive and see it happen as a fifty year old man."

"So I should become Hispanic?"

"Couldn't hurt to learn Spanish. Your Spanish right now is atrocious."

Throughout this trip, I heard that criticism every couple of weeks and learned to take the insult as a sign of intimacy and confidence, that the source considered me a friend. "You think everyone in North America should learn Spanish, or should Latin America learn English? The United States makes most of the money in the world."

"Either way, it's time for a change. No one noticed The Constitution of the United States became outdated. The men who wrote the Constitution wanted to guarantee each citizen's right to equality, forty acres and a mule, and keep them free from unreasonable taxes, but they owned slaves. Your Founding Fathers missed the boat on Human Rights. They let Americans traffic in human beings, on purpose, for profit."

"On purpose? How do you know that? How can you know if that is true or not? That was hundreds of years ago. Different standards. Everybody had slaves, throughout history. How do you know their motives?"

"That makes it alright then, tradition. We should all go out and buy a couple of wives too. Actually, this year on July 4th the United States will celebrate two hundred years. You ask me how I know they wrote the Constitution with the intention of protecting slavers? I know because I know history. Would you like to know how to decide the truth about most things in history?"

"That would be worth a million dollars. Tell me."

"That's my point."

"What point?"

"Allow me to let you in on an underappreciated secret of the Universe. Did you do good in history classes?"

"No, not really. I couldn't get into it. Seemed like history contradicts itself all the time."

"You're right, any national history as taught emphasizes national pride and blind loyalty at the expense of the truth."

When he led me to my room to deposit my backpack, we walked the corridors with our hands up in front of our candle's flame, to protect it from the wind of our passage. We padded soft, our slippers as soundless as spirits that drift up and down the small flights of stone stairs in this House of God, all the way back to his study.

"So how do you know the truth?" I asked.

"It's very simple. Look for the motive, ask yourself why people would do things, why one group wins and another loses, why one nation declares war on another."

"Like Guatemala's war on Belize? Treaties must be enforced or what good are they?"

"Partly true. Guatemala wants Belize as an English language tourist destination."

"What's that got to do with how you decide the Founding Fathers supported slavery?"

"Like Belize and tourism. They do what makes money. Slavery permitted powerful people to amass fortunes. The more moral among them might hope that one day, some core of goodness in all people would recognize the immorality, the criminal intent to treat humans as property. They never imagined that some people would extend that protection to animals, and create government institutions to protect domestic animals from cruel or irresponsible owners. The Founding Fathers lived in times of great open spaces, and couldn't imagine a world like ours, where scientists say the last place with clean air in the United States, in Arizona, disappeared around nineteen seventy one, due to the growth of Los Angeles. Almost everybody in the United States breathes contaminated air and drinks tainted water."

A flurry of shadows fluttered high over our heads in the gloom, and I heard a hiss and screech, like tiny fingernails on a chalkboard.

"So what do you do about it? Talk everybody into a return to the family farm? Convince everybody the United States is evil?"

"No. That's not it. I agree the Constitution of the United States tries to ensure life, liberty, and the pursuit of happiness. From the agrarian viewpoint of those early days, it meant the protection of each family's right to earn profit from their forty acres and a mule."

"What do you see wrong with the way things are now?"

"The corporations of the developed world, the First World, move production overseas to cheaper labor markets, like Guatemala, El Salvador, Honduras. There, corporations can re-institute the immoral and profitable practices that the United States outlawed. They start up sweatshops, use child labor, force people to shop in company stores, and show developers how to build factory housing projects financed by long term debt for workers to keep them on the job. Then they manipulate the economy or wages, and workers cannot support their household. This profitable exploitation by corporations tends to institutionalize social injustice, even though it leads to civil unrest and international tensions. So the underdeveloped world learns to distrust, dislike, and eventually to hate the developed world, and at the same time, they learn to see the United States as the leader of that free world, the refuge of the capitalist class and their own deposed leaders."

"So write your own constitution. If you have faith in people, if you believe people recognize the good and will always reject the bad, why don't you try to change things?"

"People do recognize the good and reject the bad, but only what the powerful people let them see as good and bad. What's good for powerful people tends to be bad for the rest. Since powerful people control what others read, see, and hear, they control democracies and education systems, the news services and book publishers. They control who becomes a candidate, and after elections, they educate the winners in how they must vote. As you've probably heard, in Guatemala, even democracy exists only as long as it serves the interests of the United States. Capitalists like to say the market works on democratic principles, one dollar, one vote. In Guatemala, one Quetzal, one dollar, no vote. They need that dollar to eat."

I didn't say a word, I needed sleep.

I felt tired of Guatemalans who blamed the United States for their failed government. The majority of people in Guatemala don't even speak Spanish, let alone read, so how can Guatemalans take their democracy seriously? A few centuries ageo, they ripped each other's hearts out to influence reality, and now they wanted to make a sacrificial victim of America through an extraction of its Capitalist heart.

The middle class people in Guatemala seemed like poor people in the United States. At least the poor people in the States don't need to live behind cement walls topped with shards of broken glass. Guatemala's poverty imprisoned even the middle class people.

I suspected the true cause of all this anti-American sentiment came from jealousy. They could see no future where they could advance with the same degree of freedom and mobility as the poorest of Americans. All the people from the United States enter Guatemala almost like Gods, with their silly shorts and Hawaiian shirts, cameras that cost more than several year's wages for the average Guatemalan. I bet the average American tourist serviced more debt every month than the average Guatemalan could earn in a decade.

Of course they hate the United States.

When normal people see someone who looks great, a handsome man or a gorgeous woman, they feel intimidated. If that beautiful person also wears expensive clothes and looks like a magazine cover, other people resent it. People who get to know a beautiful person, at first feel good and privileged to bask in their glow, but often the time comes when they resent the ease with which the beautiful live, with all the unearned favors, the opportunities, and the preference given to them for no true merit beyond their beauty. Worst of all, if a beautiful person appears intelligent, it insults others, it rubs their innate sense of justice and equality, and forces everyone to admit that a few people get born gifted, which means most of us exist with a lesser status.

The existence of talented, gifted, beautiful people allows the rest of us to fall into low self esteem, which makes us fearful and angry. Our insignificance inspires a quiet hatred of smart, beautiful people who smile at us and try to charm us with their unfair advantages.

Even though beautiful people decorate life and amuse us all, most of us must look for a way to tip the scales and achieve a balance in this game called life.

One can resort to subterfuge, corruption, even crime. Networks of corrupt normal people can compete with networks of beautiful, intelligent, noble people. The ignoble path will level the playing field, and let the devious find a way to rule the day against the injustices of God, who so unfairly doles out the attributes that make us valued by others.

They can hate the United States all they want. My citizenship gives me the right to escape their lazy complaints and go back to the land where hard work, discipline, and the innovation of a creative class of people makes life better, decade after decade.

After all, ever since Thomas Edison, the creative citizens of the United States of America wrote most of the entries in the big book of human progress.

So let me click my rosy red calloused heels together three times and say, "There's no place like home."

What do Guatemalan's expect when they choose to live in a country the size of Tennessee with twenty seven volcanoes? Does anyone with half a brain think that bodes well for, or paints a rosy portrait of, the future?

Losers.

Señor Diego Garcia, with two lit candles in hand, woke me up in my chair and led me down narrow hallways to one of the nunnery rooms. There, he used a long staff with a lighter on the end to light two candles high on tiny shelves mounted on the stone walls. Frozen waterfalls of old wax flowed from each candle, over the shelf, and piled up from the floor in a sheet of drippings against the wall, a translucent glaze of icing.

The ceiling disappeared into a darkness I could see stars in.

I surveyed my room and discovered clean sheets over a hard, thick mattress stuffed with something crackly like straw, on a wooden bed frame.

One window in the wall set so high up that only if I stood on the desk, could I look out into a black void.

I undressed, hung my wet clothes on the chair, desk, and headboard of the bed to dry, then climbed into bed and wrote in my journal as much as I could remember about our conversation. Before I got too sleepy, I knew I must blow out the candles to avoid a fire, with all that wax around.

Naked, I climbed that slippery translucent wall of wax, hugged it tight and dug in with my toenails and fingertips, until I got high enough to blow out the candles in self defense and relax to turn and slide down into a deep, dark sleep.

Light streamed into the window and painted the opposite wall with dusty a yellow that hurt my eyes. I got out of bed and stood up. The chill air convinced me to put on my long pants and shirt, and some socks.

I stood on the desk to look out the window.

The early morning scene seemed washed out and transparent, with small things that moved around without order, molecules that grouped and boiled apart. My eyes felt blinded by the whiteness of cement basketball courts within whitewashed walls that surrounded a playground of swing sets, geometric constructions of pipe, and the whitewashed lower tree trunks of Norfolk pines.

School children, about a hundred of them, dressed in uniforms. The girls wore long black hair in braids, plaid skirts and white blouses, white knee socks, black pilgrim shoes. The boys wore khaki shorts, white shirts with black tiese, white knee socks, black pilgrim shoes, and a beanie skull cap. The smaller kids pushed and chased each other around in games like tag and hide and seek. They ran through small groups of older children that talked amongst themselves, or jumped rope, played hop-scotch, shot baskets, or lined up for tetherball.

The ten biggest and probably oldest boys all wore orange and black "Letter Sweaters," part leather and part knitted jacket with their names across the back yoke. They hung out with hands in pockets, bellies out, and walked around in groups of threes to talk with other students, who stopped their activities and regarded them with respect.

I counted the students, around two hundred. The rainbow hues of their skin tones ran from the deepest black through the so-called yellows of Asia, the 'redskins' of indigenous America, to the bloodless fish belly white of Caucasians like myself. At first glance, they all played together, but the more emotional outbreaks divided them by color.

The kids also grouped by size, which probably meant age, and for most of them, the girls stuck to the small group activities like jump rope and hopscotch, while the boys dominated the large team sports of basketball and soccer.

The three trios of letter-sweater jocks dominated their turf, a third of the playground, and the smaller kids would gather around them for a few minutes and dig through their pockets. They handed over something to the older boys, who looked into their hands as if to count coins. When the older boys gave a little hand motion reminiscent of the Pope's when he blesses a crowd, the children ran off to continue their game.

Then the older boys gravitated to the center of the playground to lean on picnic tables in a half sit.

Six of the older girls hung around the big boys. They wore their plaid skirts high to expose a wide expanse of young thigh that funneled the eye down to the knee socks bunched around their ankles. They liked to throw their heads back and laugh, teeth all white or glittery with braces. Some flirted with earrings that gleamed when they brushed their long hair aside, or played with necklaces pulled out from beneath their blouses.

Three couples clung to each other's arms as they strolled. One couple held their faces close, talked, and punctuated their conversations with little kisses.

One couple stood out. A short stocky boy with a shaved head walked with a giraffe of a girl, an open jackknife with long, straight black hair that fell to her narrow hips. They talked and walked toward an open area near the playground's perimeter.

He stopped in mid stride, tensed up, and pinned her arm to his ribs to reach across her with his other arm and put his big hand on the back of her head and neck. Her free hand went to his shoulder to push away, but he ignored it. He overpowered her, bent his head to mouth something into her ear, then gave her a little kiss on the cheek and relaxed.

Her eyebrows gathered. She squinted up at him. Her arm lashed out and she knocked the chip off his shoulder with the back of her hand. looked like she spat out whispered words, then hit him in the solar plexus. She stamped her feet near his, extricated her arm from his and pushed his arm away. Then she stomped away to approach one of the other couples.

She grabbed the arm of a muscular blond girl who gently oscillated in the arms of her boyfriend, and tried to pull her out of his grasp. The blond looked at her and pushed the spidery girl away.

Two other older boys stopped and pointed at her with their mouth and chin, lips pursed the way Guatemalans do, to attract the attention of their buddies. Then the boys worked their way across the asphalt playground towards her, as the center of a circle of orange and black letter jackets. Her boyfriend stayed out in front, and held one hand as if to snap his fingers, or hold an imaginary cigarette.

She looked back, looked around, and then stopped. Without escape, she waited there for them to approach her. The boys came up and encircled her in a tight group, with her boyfriend in front of her.

She did not look at any of them, but looked down at her feet. Her hands pulled down at the hem of her dress, as if to make it conform to school regulations.

The boy held out both hands, low, palm up, and waited. The others folded their arms and put their weight on one foot as if ready to kick out.

I could see her wipe her hands on her dress and as she reached out to take his hands, her own seemed to tremble. She did not look up, but her hair shook and her shoulders hopped up and down and I knew she sobbed.

As they held hands, the other boys applauded soft, without a sound.

The other children on the playground quieted down and continued to play in a deliberate manner, without laughter and expressiveness, that seemed contrived to cover their observations of events near the wall of the Red Tile Church.

Behind me, the door opened.

I turned and peered into the dark interior, and my eyes grew accustomed to the light from the shafts of sunlight.

There in the doorway, in the same robe I left him in, stood Diego García.

"Good Morning," he said. "Are you still up, or did you just get up?"

"Just got up."

"I'm on my way to bed, myself."

"Who are all those children?"

"From the school next door. After they finished building the church, the neighbor started a school, and asked if they could use the grounds as a safe place for the children." He came over to where I stood on the chair and held his hand out to help me down. "If you want, you can go outside through the back door and talk to them. Be sure to lock the door again, when you return."

"You've had problems?"

"Are the big boys out there? With the jackets?"

"Yeah. What is it they collect from the other kids?"

"Money. Those ten boys, just five percent of all the children, terrorize the others into giving up a quarter of their lunch money."

"Doesn't anybody stop them? Can't the other kids get together and do something?"

"How? They're stronger than the rest. It's a tradition now, year after year the seniors do it. The teachers hope they'll grow out of it."

"Like domestic violence, I suppose."

"What do you mean?"

"You know, wife beaters, that attitude that if I can't have you, then nobody can, so they threaten to kill their girlfriend."

"Many adolescent boys go through a stage where they think they can bully and threaten somebody else to love them. The power of love."

One girl's terrified scream came from the playground, then faded, muffled. I jumped onto the desk to look out the window.

I saw all eyes centered on an orange and black huddle right below my window, the backs of the ten older boys in a clump. The girl's screams sounded exhausted, then changed to feeble moans of "No, no, help me, stop" as her shoes flew out of the huddle, then her socks. Her white blouse and plaid shirt shot up into the air and floated down with an oblique trajectory. Then her bra and panties.

The jump ropes fell slack, the tetherballs wound slow around the poles, Some of the other kids stood up in the sandbox. The swings slowed down, and no one slid down the slide. Children dropped off the monkey bars like leaves in October.

I tried to lean out the window so far that I bumped my head on the bus window, and woke up.

The bus lurched slow across some potholes and banged my forehead against the window. I looked through tinted glass at a candle-lit scene of food vender's stalls. Another nondescript Guatemala City crossroad, where the bus would sit and idle as the driver waited for passengers to get off, or show up.

As I sat up and looked over the heads of the passengers to the pool of rain filled light through the windshield, I remembered events in my past that influenced the dream.

In high school, at the last assembly of the year when the school honored the class of seniors who would graduate, we senior boys worked out a plot with three of the adventurous "Pom Pom Girls." After they did their dance number, dressed in uniforms similar to a cheer leader's tennis miniskirt and sweater top, a group of the biggest boys, all on the football team, rushed out of the bleachers and corralled the three co-conspirator Pom-pom girls in the center of a large huddle.

Deep inside the huddle, the girls quieted their laughter between their fake terrified screams, as three of the boys took hidden paper bags out from under their letter-jackets. From inside the paper bags, they extracted the three extra Pom-Pom Girl uniforms, and threw the articles of clothing one by one, out of the huddle and into the air in front of the astounded assembly of high school students and gape-mouthed teachers.

The bus continued to wind with care through a broken Guatemala City under black rainy skies, dark enough to turn on the streetlights, if the city could restore the electricity.

It took a long time to leave the city, a long slosh through the suburbs, with a few stops at major intersections to wait for passengers. Then we headed out of the valley of the cows, through the forested mountain passes, and swung around the volcanic piedmonts, invisible high overhead, somewhere above the dark clouds.

The rain let up sometimes, as bus skirted the sensuous inclines of the Pacific mountain slopes on roads that, in the headlights of other vehicles, appeared cracked and broken off in places. Chunks of roadway fell into deep canyons that yawned invisible below the visible treetops, on a level with the road. Other places, the lack of vegetation drew my attention to the fresh scars of landslides, and the yellowish rust colored stains on the black asphalt, where road crews cleaned off the muddy debris.

As we came through the last pass toward the Pacific, the sky cleared. I could see the flatlands that stretched westward to the ocean, and up ahead, on the flank of a volcano, a small volcanic cone sprouted with a new plume of smoke or steam that made a horizontal sulfuric S to fan out and disappear over the coastal lowlands. Maybe the earthquake brought it to the surface, a rude pimple of adolescent magma that spat out a signal, a horizontal aerial pathway that demarked the border of a land of doom.

Felt like only a couple of hours passed, with a couple of scary pauses to inch around damaged mountain highway, when the bus reached the border. My young Guatemalan seat-mate turned to bid me well and shake my hand with that limp Guatemalan handshake that feels feeble and insincere. We got off the bus single file, and I watched him walk among the quiet throng of loaded-down indigenous Guatemalans, colorful zombies, shell shocked by the earthquake.

I turned toward the Mexican border, towards my escape northward to my homeland over a thousand miles away, an escape I could not share with them.

The Mexican officials waved me through.

With my beautiful white Sololá bat jacket on for warmth, I took the first overnight bus north, and as the miles and kilometers rolled underneath the bus, Guatemala lost reality and faded away like a bad dream, a recurrent nightmare. I wanted the past to lose substance, to become transparent. I hoped life's more , recent images would superimpose over my Guatemalan memories, with so little in common, they would become the cover of a closed and forgotten book.

My experience in the Land of Eternal Springtime would exist in my memory sandwiched between other realities. Before I forgot, I took notes while memories existed fresh in my mind. All the alien impressions of Guatemala, its jungles and beaches, its arid wastelands and mangrove swamps, the ancient pyramids and prehistoric volcanoes, the rich variety of its people. The people mystified me the most. At their happy and peaceful best, they lacked ambition. When surly, their reserved and conservative culture created zombies of traditional ignorance.

Who would they become as a result of thirty seconds of tectonic movement, when Guatemala's entire population felt as I did, at best, betrayed by instinctual faith in solid ground.

Mayan Guatemalans continue on as before, within their reality, as if nothing happened, although insulted and injured by their own Gods and given a timely reminder of the nine levels of hell that plunge deep into the cavernous maw of the earth beneath their feet, where the dark dendritic channels writhe like worms, or clawed fingers, just below the surface, eager and hungry for blood and human sacrifice, to fulfill Mayan destiny, and their hope for a union with the souls of their ancestors, to become bats disgorged from the cave mouths at sunset, hummingbirds, mosquitoes.

Seventh Section: The Diminished Chord

CHAPTER 23: Return through Mexico

Carbon-14 dates associated with the deposits at La Venta, an archeological site in the Mexican state of Tabasco, suggest that the Olmec civilization flourished 1,000 years to 1500 years BCE (Before Current Era, before Christ). The artifacts unearthed there, and at Olmec sites in Mexico's Isthmus of Tejuantepec, look like the root of later cultures that spread across Meso-America, cultures like the Toltec, Zapotce, and the Mayan cultures in Guatemala, Belice, Honduras, El Salvador, and shaped the culture of Mexico's Aztec warlords until the arrival of the Spanish.

Late the next morning, the bus slowed down in another Mexican village. I looked out the bus window and saw two muscle-bound hippie-hitmen Narco-bikers. They looked like the two I met months ago in Casa de Pies in Panajachél. A girl rode on the back of the Harley-hog, behind the macho without a shirt, just a leather vest.

She looked like Yvonne. She splayed her legs wide over the saddlebags, and I imagined she wove her fingers into his chest hair, and rubbed her chin and breasts into his back.

I wondered if she would remember me fondly, the two of us in dark hotel rooms nestled in the diesel fumes of Guatemala City, or surrounded by the cloud forest drizzle of Xela.

Once I admitted to Joanna that in order to become a good writer, I wanted to live and examine life without the influences of academia, or any one else's literary tradition. I wanted to examine the world as I found it, without preconceived notions of propriety or correctness. I believed that my secular humanist background, from a family of uptight Anglo saxon atheists, might give me the objective viewpoint and opportunity to write something worth while, if I lived long enough to know what to say, and how to say it.

She said, "If you write about me, be kind."

At that time, stuck between the current in-vogue stupid movie phrase about "Love Means You Never Need to Say Sorry" as if Your Partner Does Not Expect You To Apologize And Won't Get Angry, or some such rot, and my family's expression of love through altercations meant to raise the hackles as proof of familiarity, I stood unformed and immature.

I thought uneducated meant an opportunity to create something pure, free of outside influence. My ambitions first led me into graphic arts, then into rock music with the electric guitar. And innocent with no idea of what I missed. Ignorant I thought meant a purposeful act to ignore, because of a distrust of knowledge and reliance on the old traditional ways, which doesn't sound like me. I ignored nothing, and tried to pay attention to everything, a Zen exercise in macro-consciousness. I could not consider myself ignorant, far from it, my curiosity also pulled me into trouble, ever since those toddler home movies of me in a curious march at the camera, to find out what made that noise.

So if I wrote about Yvonne, she would prefer lies. I wondered if she wanted to protect herself from the truth and destroy the meaning and utility of one's observations turned literature, or did she fear some mean streak in me?

Every youth feels normal, and the rest of the world crazy. The best form of maturity should force each one of us to accept everybody else's specific right to their own craziness, as long as it doesn't hurt others. Nobody can cause envy, or belittle another, or inflame one's low self esteem, if that person remains centered in confidence, graceful in their belongingness, and sure of one's self and their place in this universe.

The danger comes when a person gets fans, fame, and supportive people and lets it boost their ego into the superclasses, a stratosphere far removed from eathly concerns, where the powerful and corrupt put on angel wings to fly around and pat each other on the back.

My anti-establishmentarianism and intellectual openness to ideas from around the world, brought to the United States by poets and writers and scientists and the Beatles and Baba Ram Das and counter-culture celebrities, predisposed me to think in terms of improvements to the status quo. The more radical the road to social change, the more it excited me.

Few people respect anyone who tries to improve things from the bottom up. Most people chose to decorate what exists, rather than dig down, find the flaws in the foundation, and correct what went wrong from the beginning. Constant repair over the long term feels cheaper than demolition, and the fundamental flaws remain.

Destruction clears the way to build something new, as the Meso-American pyramids and temples gave colonial architects their first building blocks. Perhaps this next time we can all help build something so solid it might last forever.

In contrast to Guatemala, my first Mexican hotel reacquainted me with the crass bar noises and black-water belches of a Mexican city. I now understood enough Spanish to catch the suggestive jokes and macho aggression of Mexican men, a competition to determine who barked with the loudest laughter and the filthiest words per minute.

Nostalgia overcame me.

I longed to go back into polite Guatemala, and hear the pitter patter of ignorant Indians on their midnight candle-lit processions, and wonder every time I saw a blue pickup if it carries a death squad. The elder expatriates, former United States citizens, intrigued me and I wanted to hear how they felt about their life as a continuum of diminished expectations. The caste system offered comfort and security for the eternal springtime of deadly oppression, within the threat of torrential rain and mudslides, volcanic eruptions, hurricanes, or earthquakes that would ensure a future of shattered families and mass graves.

A fit antidote to youth's perception of immortality.

From Tapachula, the bus driver defied death on a bus ride over the mountains. He passed cars on blind curves, and played chicken with the other lane's traffic to get to Mexico City in a hurry. At least that's what other passengers told me when I woke up, "You missed all the fun."

From across the aisle, a Mexican fellow handed me my pen and journal, and explained, with hand motions and a polite smile, how he rescued it from the floor.

I looked at the bus-vibrated penmanship. The zig-zag scribbles ran all over the page, with some on top of previous literary jewels.

The return trip home to the Midwest occupied my mind, with possibilities of an itinerary of vaporous destinations, unknown villages with cheap hotels, or camp outs, and all night bus rides to avoid the cost of hotel rooms.

I needed a rest, and wanted to feel comfortable. I missed my childhood room on the second floor of the old farmhouse out in the Michigan countryside. I wanted to wrap myself in the big queen-size bedcovers, reach between the box spring and the mattress to pull out the three or four girlie magazines, switch on the light on the nightstand, and pleasure myself for a half hour to the moans of a wind that made the big black walnut tree's branches scratch against the glass panes of the tall window. I wanted to wake up and see the three long shelves on the wall loaded with my painted plastic monster models, the encyclopedia of nature, an almost complete paperback collection of twenty five Tarzan books alongside the microscope and chemistry set. I wanted to get up and pick my clothes off the electric guitar amplifier, and dress while I leant over to read a book set on the bed. The morning sunlight turned everything a vague green as it bounced off the life-size photo mural of a rare and little known, very shy African antelope called an Okapi, within a bamboo grove.

On the bus and in each of the bus stops, I talked to travelers about hotels in Mexico City, and got a number of good leads, the majority too expensive.

Near the Arch of the Revolution in Mexico City, I found the recommended and inexpensive Penny Hotel, near the Avenida Reforma and the Parque de Chapultepeque and its museums, with El Metro subway access nearby, and not too far from the Central Plaza, if I didn't mind a long walk.

In each bedroom, a bidet graced the side of the bed. Bid-ay, the dictionary calls it a porcelain bowl with a water supply to wash the crotch. It shocked me. I knew nothing of bidets, except that the word spells and sounds French. It provoked much thought about sex and personal cleanliness. Years later, I appreciated the utility and functionality, the commonsense hygiene of it, and how it corroborates esoteric Yogic practices. The bidet offered more than a prelude to sex, it made it easy to sanitized the groin, front and back, and inside the sphincter after each bowel movement. A clean butt hole eliminates skid marks in the undies, which should become a relic of the past as a sign of cultural immaturity, a chevron that marks one's distance from one's own body, and the end of nightmares of embarrassment for those who fear what paramedics think as they do their jobs. Without those skid marks, your underpants stay clean enough to wear even if you know, for sure, for certain, of your anticipated involvement in an auto accident.

Every morning, the lobby of the Penny Hotel attracted people who liked to watch the news. I sunk down in a plush white couch before a long, low coffee table to sip free coffee, write when commercials came on, and try to understand the international news items in Spanish.

Sometimes one silver haired older man in a suit came down the stairs and set his briefcase on the coffee table. He stood and watched for a while, then looked at me and smiled. He asked, in English with a European accent, if I understood the news.

"No, not much. Some words here and there."

"Keep trying. You will someday. You're doing the right thing."

"How much do you understand?"

"Almost everything."

"How did you learn?"

"Like you, but I know four languages already. I'm from Belgium you see. Hardest to learn the second language. After that, it becomes easier."

He watched the news for awhile, and when another advertisement came on, he said "Have you noticed any anti-American feelings from the Mexicans?"

"No. Why?"

"Because many people resent the United States, and you travel all alone."

"Why should they resent the United States?"

"You know the difference between a machete and a sword?"

I shook my head no, and waited.

"A sword has two edges, and cuts both ways. A machete only cuts one way. That's how many people view the border between the United States and Mexico. But it's changing, with so many Mexicans going to the United States."

"Why do they go north, if they hate the United States?"

"You remember what Deep Throat told the reporters, the phrase that helped reporters get information on Nixon that led to his impeachment?"

"No."

"Follow the money."

"So you know the United States overthrew President Arbenz in 1954?"

"Yes."

"Maybe you can explain why. Bananas cost pennies, even in a grocery store back in the States. So why should a United States company feel threatened if the government gives unused land to peasants? Why should I believe a handful of people from the United States could overthrow Guatemala for a banana company?"

"It's not about bananas, and not only about Guatemala. The CIA used agents in Honduras and El Salvador to train exiles from Guatemala, to make a small, 'counterrevolutionary' military force led by Colonel Carlos Castillo Armas. When they attacked, the Guatemalans thought an entire army invaded, and it threw the capital into a panic. The Guatemalan army refused to fight, and forced Arbenz to resign on June 27, 1954 to run away into exile. Colonel Armas became president, and his government reversed all the reforms of the previous decades, and made generous offers to businesses and foreign investors."

"Is that why everybody hates the United States?"

"I don't hate the United States. I'm a businessman."

I walked around the main square, the wheatfield sized, brick paved open space of the Central Plaza of Mexico City called the Zócalo, and threaded my way between rows of parked cars, and almost stepped on a baby.

His little head of black hair slowly turned up toward me from where he squatted at my feet. We looked at each other steadily for a few seconds. He seemed about two years old, street wise, dirty and skinny, nude from the waist down. I looked around for his mom, thought I might pick him up to get him out of danger, then thought about our language barrier and how he'd scream and cry, and people might think I kidnapped the child.

In that instant, I realized how people from the developed world, due to fears inspired by television and radio's nightly news, would first think I try to kidnap the child. That level of paranoia, of distrust and tendency to assume the worst, robs us of our basic humanity, and damages our instinctual ability to belong to a common human family.

He got up and took three steps away, then stopped and turned to look at me for about three seconds. I looked at him, then down at the smooth, butterscotch colored poop that steamed with its aromas. He saw me look at it, laughed, and ran in a clumsy trot around the chrome bumpers of the car. I stepped over his load and walked out of the rows of cars, but didn't see him anywhere.

He disappeared, vanished into Mexico City's thin polluted air, but left a trace.

Linares

The recurrent pain in my back made me want to make a run for the border. I bought a ticket for an overnight bus ride, to save the cost of a hotel room, and got off in Ciudad Victoria, which I don't remember much of, except bullfight posters.

I took another bus to Linares.

The town seemed like the old west, low, dry, and dusty. That afternoon, I found a café with a modern all glass front wall that advertised itself as a Café de Arte y Libros, a book and art coffeehouse.

As usual, no air conditioning. They propped the door open with a chair to improve circulation.

A very beautiful, tall, and slender Mexican girl waited on me, her one customer. She hovered like a black eyed flame that bent to my will with a smile. She captivated me, and flattered me with overlong stares that made me believe she too felt something. This rapport encourage me to ask where her family came from. I wanted to know the roots of her beauty, her almond shaped eyes, her white skin, her small nose with that slight hook, her aerodynamic nostrils that made me think of an exquisite racehorse from the stables of a Persian king.

Her grandparent's came from Syria and Spain.

Her name, Lourdes, gave my tongue a problem. After I wrote it down to sound it out, I repeated it until I pronounced it to her satisfaction.

The shop's ovens in the back room, and the solar gain from the big glass wall, created an oppressive heat inside. She wore her thick golden hair pulled tight behind her, but strands from the sides of her forehead pulled free to hang down and stick to her sweaty face in loops and arabesques. She didn't mind, did not pull at them much. She let them frame her face.

I ordered a fruit smoothie, a licuado, made with milk and bananas, and she convinced me to try it with Amaranto. She showed me a bag that looked full of pinhead size white Styrofoam beads which stuck to her hand with static electricity.

She said "Good protein. Made from a seed that pops into these tiny white puffs, like popcorn. Mom says the Aztecs grew Amaranto for food, but the Spanish made them stop, to destroy their culture."

She walked over with the full blender and a glass to serve me.

I noticed deep, long scars that ran from her slim wrists, up her forearm, and disappeared under the baggy short sleeves of her kitchen shirt.

She set the glass down, then poured a glassful of smoothie into it. She set the blender pitcher beside it. "This is all yours. Enjoy."

"¿Lourdes, me permites preguntarte algo?" May I ask you a question?"

"OK."

"How did you get those scars?"

"A couple of years ago, after we built this restaurant, a man came in with a knife to rob us, and I ran away. I was not yet accustomed to this new place. I didn't see the big glass door, and I ran into it. When I broke through it, I fell down and the glass fell over me. It cut me all over my face, my legs, but worse on my arms. I bled so much they though I would die. They called an ambulance, and sent me to Mexico City in a helicopter. For months they gave me physical therapy on my arms."

I hung around and read a book for an hour and a half, drank coffee, ordered another smoothie. She introduced me to a couple of affluent young men, friends of hers. I thought they looked too manicured, too clean and concerned about their appearance, maybe homosexual. They chattered with her in Spanish, and after a while turned to me and asked in English how long I planned to stay in Linares.

"I don't plan very far ahead," I told them. "I'm so close to the border now, I can make it home easily."

They invited me to go out with them that evening to see some of the sights of Linares. After they left, I asked her if she thought it a good idea to accept their offer.

She laughed and asked what I worried about.

"Would you come along with us too?" I asked her.

"No, my family wouldn't let me." She blushed, and busied herself with something behind the counter.

"Lourdes, don't you ever go out on dates?"

"You must ask my parents for their permission first, but they will not give it to you. I am sorry."

"How old are you?"

"Sixteen. How many years do you have?"

"Twenty two."

She came out from behind the curtain and stood by my table. "¿Brandon, estás acostumbrado de salir con muchachas?" Are you used to going out with girls?"

I shrugged. "Un poco. Yah hace mucho tiempo." A little. A while ago now.

"Are you a virgin, Brandon?"

"No, pero no soy experto tampoco." No, but I'm no expert either.

"Is it true American girls move fast to bed with boys?"

"Doesn't seem fast to boys. We don't ask parents for permission. Boys hide from the girl's parents. In high school, if the girl likes the boy, she sneaks out of the house at night."

"You want me to sneak out of my house tonight, to go on this tour tonight?"

"We could have fun. I like you, you're a very beautiful girl."

"Even with no strength in my left arm?"

"I didn't notice till I saw your scars. I doubt anyone notices. Don't worry about things like that. Most girls would give their left arm for your beauty."

An hour or so before sunset, I went back to the Café del Arte y Libros, and met up with the two boys. I didn't see Lourdes around, and asked about her. They acted amused that I thought she might show up.

Their new sports car's motor purred and putt-putted through the little glass pack muffler. We wove around town to see the sights, the Catholic churches and city parks, then up a long inclined road to a mountain top with a dramatic view of the city in the last rays of sunset.

Lourdes filled my thoughts with scenarios of what we might do or say if she ever found the courage to step out with me.

The next day, before eleven, I packed my bags and stopped by the Café for a licuado lunch, and to buy enough sweet bread to hold me over for the long bus ride to the border.

I told her I planned to leave Linares for the border that day.

Lourdes worked alone, and after all the other customers left, she sat down at my table and told me how she couldn't sleep last night. She thought she made a mistake.

Then she took a locket from around her neck and gave it to me.

I didn't want to take it, but she insisted. It looked expensive, and even though her family owned the café, I did not think it right to accept so expensive a gift after such a short talk with a girl so young.

She showed me the back of the heart shaped ornament, where it said, "True Love" and then asked me "Do you think you might ever come back to live in Mexico?"

"Do you think you could live in the United States?"

We stared at each other and smiled, and then she said, "I couldn't live in the united States, because my family lives here."

I said, "I plan to come back through Mexico next year. I promise to come through Linares and stop to see you."

I meant every word.

CHAPTER 24: Revelation

In my bare wood hotel room in Linares, I estimated future costs to get home, to reach the border and take a Greyhound bus to Michigan. If I ate light, I could buy some Mexican things to take back home.

Saltillo interested me because of one line in a song that said For sarapes, Saltillo. The bus pulled into the city after sunset in darkness, after the shops closed. My next bus out would leave in a couple of hours on an overnight to Piedras Negras, the border town with Eagle Pass, Texas. A couple of hours to find serapes.

I hailed a taxi and asked the driver if he knew where I might buy sarapes at this late hour, and if not, if he could take me to a cheap hotel. He drove up a steep hill and down some narrow cobblestone streets, then across bulldozed streets scraped into hilly white limestone mud, then down a steep slope towards the city center to take a sharp right and park next to a long blank wall with one door. He got out and knocked.

A short man cracked the door to talk for a few seconds, then ducked inside and shut the door. The driver came back to the taxi to tell me this 'gran amigo mio,' great personal friend of his, out of the kindness of his heart, agreed to show me sarapes and ponchos.

The man reappeared at the door, came out sideways under a tower of textiles, and bent sideways to walk down the three cement steps to the sidewalk. He set the fabrics on the car hood in several piles for me to examine in the streetlight. The night's cold, dry wind parched our fingers and chapped our lips, and found every seam in my light clothing. So many designs, all beautiful, but many in a course weave that might cause an itchy feeling around the neck. I didn't know the value of these things, and didn't know how to bargain with someone after hours.

I figured they expected me to buy a big quantity to repay the favor of this special attention. I asked about a design I remembered Manuel wore, a light smooth black cloth sarape with a yoke in red velvet. He went back through the doorway and brought one out. I bought it, and another of blue stripes and cream, and a thin rainbow blanket, then took the taxi back to the bus station in time to catch the overnight to Piedras Negras.

Sometime around three in the morning at the U. S. border, someone saw me sleepwalk across, but I don't remember a thing.

The next day's Greyhound journey through sunny Texas again put me to sleep. That night I couldn't sleep, and saw twelve hours of the dark route along the agricultural flatlands of the Mississippi valley, with distant flat galaxies of streetlights reflected between the bus's glass walls.

First time I used the onboard bathroom, I brought along my own toilet paper. Of course thy stocked the bathroom with toilet paper and an extra roll. When the toilet flushed with that spiral of blue water, that bright chemical blue unlike any natural blue in the known universe, the same chemical color as the mixed drink called Blue Motorcycle and some popsicles, I felt reassured instead of repulsed for the first time in my life.

The next day, intermittent wakefulness punctuated the bus's drone and rumble across the vast American landscape down the almost flawless interstate highway system. The open spaces, enormous fields of corporate farms, tracts of forests that fade into the distance, all met my open eyes like a living green skin, punctured by abandoned small farms and a succession of gas stations near strip malls.

Rows of suburban houses, each within a small plot of grass, impressed me as the negative space of Latin America's colonial layout.

Where colonial buildings surround a verdant courtyard, here the greenery surrounds the house.

The hundred year old, three story brick buildings in the center of small towns seemed new compared to Meso-America's two thousand year old stone architectures or the five hundred year old colonial houses made out of those same structure's blocks.

We passed a major cities with their monotonous skylines, the darkened signs of big chain department stores and the lighted signs of fast food, and convenience store Franchises, and sometimes I could see the signs for all night inner city grocery stores, which attract the innocent and those who don't fear the local substance abusers.

Not until the bus approached the outskirts of Chicago, did I feel a return to the land of my birth.

Patches of dirty snow lurked about, tucked into the shady recesses along the northern sides of buildings, under abandoned cars, and piled near the tractors and farm equipment used to plow snow. I recognized the spring ritual of optimism and inappropriate fashion, when I saw Midwesterners, on these first sunny spring days over forty five degrees (seven degrees Celsius), dressed in sneakers, shorts, and short sleeved shirts to flaunt the long winter's chill that lingers in the frozen ground. People carried pails of soapy water and sponges as big as a small dogs to wash their car, and then rinsed it off with forty degree water from a garden hose.

From Chicago's immense gothic bus and train terminal, I called home to tell them my scheduled arrive time.

Back Home

Back at my parent's house, the family gathered to welcome me.

The family wanted to tell me how the earthquake affected them. When they first heard the on news about the earthquake, they wondered if it killed me.

They enlisted a neighbor, a young man who learned a little Spanish on a short missionary trip to the Dominican Republic, to help. He called my last known telephone number at the Pensión. For the next few days, he came to my family's house and they all gathered around the black, wall mounted telephone to ask the neighbors to stay off our shared "party line" and let him call Guatemala. On the forth day, the call went through to the Pensión. He talked to someone, but he didn't understand very much.

They didn't understand him either, until he said Brandon over and over.

He got the gist of it from their tone of voice, and relayed to those in Michigan something about a radio and a guitar, and that he thought I passed by the Pensión after the quake with a woman, and moved on, safe and sound.

Then they asked me questions, what does an earthquake feel like, did the earth shake, did the house fall down, where did I go, who did I hang out with, what woman, and "Aren't you glad to be back home?"

The answers evaded me. I stalled to let an appropriate response bubble to the surface, and none did. I watched their interested expressions sag into impatience, and then into mystified annoyance as I babbled about things they could not understand.

I did not mention Yvonne, except to a few close friends, and their reaction talked me out of any further mention. I bored them, through over enthusiasm or a reluctance to divulge, or they asked inappropriate questions that made it clear they could not care less.

As for where I went and what I did in Mexican America or Guatemalan America, one might as well talk about the surface of the moon. I couldn't expect them to understand a place so foreign that my own gray matter still worked overtime to sort it out. Once in a while, I came up with a sudden realization, a eureka moment to recognize a concept that surfaced like a breached whale, full of portentous obviousness, long hidden beneath my cultural assumptions and misconceptions.

I began to evaluate my trip into Latin America as a drug trip, an alternate reality, a dream without consequence or significance to others. My experiences intrigued others about as much as an account of a dream where I flew through a pine forest behind a snowy owl, or drowned naked in honey, or that dogs chased me around the deck of a ship in flames, or sirens wailed over the bombed city, and I woke up to turn off the alarm clock beside the bed.

In my body and subconscious, the earthquake lived on. My subconscious awareness tuned into, and maintained a diligent and inappropriate attention to, subsonic vibrations that when perceived, caused a physiological reaction. Adrenaline rushed into my blood, and I sweated hot, got tense and felt anxious and irritable. The rumbles of boilers and big trucks, or planes that flew too low, or my own body's paranoid hysteria, could trigger these events.

The earthquake continued inside all who lived through it. Imagine life in Guatemala, with the relief work and rebuilding, the necessary vibrations of the earth as men worked to rebuild, echoes of the earthquake. My own trauma brought home a small sense of the magnitude of losses suffered by Guatemalans. The survivors of those thirty seconds would all help mourn the deaths of twenty two thousand people, losses that each survivor would feel for the rest of their life. My sympathies lay with all the family members that would suffer those gaps in their membership for the rest of their lives.

There, by undeserved grace, the luckiest live long enough to mourn the rest, because they survive into old age. Only the worst of luck spares us from the deaths of loved ones, we go before they do, or we all die together.

My American friends didn't care. Their empathy and curiosity extended only to me, and since I lost no more than a ten dollar guitar in the earthquake, they lost interest. I could not explain my experience to anyone's satisfaction.

I knew they wanted to hear the lies about how I escaped the rain of rocks from a building's collapse, how I dug myself out of the wreckage and saved a family of eight. They wanted the quick heroism of normal people forced into extraordinary circumstances, like soldiers in wartime, or paramedics in ambulances.

I clammed up. I didn't know what to say.

Family remarked on how skinny I looked.

Over the past five years, I maintained an almost constant weight of one hundred forty five pounds since my senior year of high school when baby fat began its redistribution into muscle as I worked in landscaping, factories, and as a day laborer, and then maid in an Aspen, Colorado ski chateaux, a fancy name for an upscale motel.

Those six months in Mexico and Guatemala wore thirty pounds off my slim frame.

For the first weeks in Michigan, I woke up in the middle of the night with that barbed pain, like a thin knife blade plunged into the small of my back. I awoke doubled backward, with the back of my hand along my spine, my mouth wrenched open in agony.

An examination by our family doctor revealed microscopic amounts of blood in my urine. He suspected something amiss in my kidneys. He instructed me to rest and drink plenty of liquids, and return in two weeks.

I drank a lot of ice tea, and enjoyed Michigan in the springtime at my parent's humble cottage on the shore of a shallow lake about twenty miles from home. Because the cottage lay on the eastern shore of the mile long lake, the westerly winds push any sand, dumped into the lake to make a small beach for children, along the shore to our beach. The sandy shallows in front of our cottage made our dock the longest on the lake. Every spring when the sun heated up those shallows, we put out thirty seven sections of dock on wooden saw horses to reach four feet deep waters.

In the gray mists of April mornings in Michigan, the scene out the cottage's front window resembled Chinese ink brush paintings. A Great Heron stood immobile on the dock, its crown of feathers detailed in contrast to the blurry fog of distance, all framed in the weeping willow tree's long whip branches, thickened with new buds, reminiscent of a waterfall of bamboo shoots.

My grandfather's small black mechanical typewriter served to copy journals and notes, and add the material still fresh in my memory. I tried to rest and recuperate, but slowed my recovery with hours devoted to the task that resulted in two worn reels of typewriter ribbon, punched through and tattered by the repeated impact of the metal levers with their embossed letters.

A friend named Dick, a young college piano player involved in the downtown art scene, became a closer friend of mine. We first met three years before, when his girlfriend dumped him for me. He traveled to Spain with her, so he understood my trip into Mexico better than most. He urged me to write, and he offered to help me. He brought food and beer when he visited, and one day, "to help you avoid distractions," he brought over a large cardboard box that once held a small refrigerator about three feet high.

"What's this?"

"Open it."

Inside the box I found a foot high pile of magazines, a collection of pornography collected from who knows where, most of the last few years published output of Playboy, Hustler, Hustler Letters, Oui, Savage, Screw, and other magazines that specialized in photos, also called photo spreads (sic) that show unclad young girls, most of European ancestry, in poses and positions meant to addict men to onanism.

He told me "To help you concentrate. Keep you from wasting your time in bars. If you want, I could bring you a girl from downtown, but we split the cost."

"What makes you think I need all this?"

"I thought you might appreciate it, that's all."

"What makes you think I masturbate?"

"There's two kinds of men in the world. Those who admit they masturbate, and those who lie. Keeps your body healthy and your mind young, if not absolutely infantile. Don't worry, someday you'll meet a girl attracted to blind men with hairy palms."

One Saturday night, he came to my cottage with friend, a pretty blond girl with too short hair and artsy pretensions. We drank and chatted while "Magic Man" and other longer than normal songs played on the FM Alternative Rock radio station.

He reached into his sock and pulled out a small plastic baggie, really just the corner of a baggie, tied into a knot. It contained a white substance. He said "Do you have a mirror, and a razor blade?"

"Next you'll ask me for a ten dollar bill to roll into a tube. Cocaine?"

"Not just cocaine, but ninety six percent pure cocaine. I know, because it's been tested."

"By who?"

"By the police. I work as a photographer for the police department, and they give me access to the evidence room. Once they test the cocaine, they label it and lay it on the shelves."

We snorted cocaine through a brand new twenty dollar bill rolled into a tube.

They disappeared together for fifteen minutes or so, and when they returned, they acted too giddy. She came out with her winter coat on, but barefoot.

She stood before me like a statue, as he took off her coat with a magician's flourish to reveal her naked body wrapped in cellophane.

With her soft skin striated elephantine by the wrap, she sat beside me on the couch, snuggled and sandwiched between Dick and I. She acted coy, put her hands on our thighs, but without anything sensual. Sensuality in our city's Christian Reformed culture didn't exist, unless you count the bored, lifeless, awkward strippers at the Parkway Tropics bar, a one room bar painted black with a central dance floor cornered by four dusty plastic palm trees, an anomaly deep in the factory worker's residential area east of the river.

I didn't know what they expected. Maybe they bet money on my reaction, or maybe he wanted revenge for my acquiescence to his ex-girlfriend's infatuation with me in that round Big Boy Burger Restaurant that used to be a Pizza Hut. On this cold night, nothing happened, except she got goose bumps under the cellophane from the thermocline layers of cold air in the poorly insulated cottage, and left us to put her clothes back on.

As she left the room, Dick stood up and looked at me, put one hand up to rub his eyebrows, and extended the other palm up and open, both to implore and threaten to Japslap me, as he whispered insults. "Idiot, seize the day, why didn't you take advantage of this opportunity?"

I recall that his/my old girlfriend once said that she suspected Dick wanted a love life that included simultaneous bisexual experiences.

A month later, the doctor still detected blood in my urine, and said "We need to schedule you for a hospital visit" and then described how he wanted to use one of modern medicine's newest toys, a small cable with a tiny camera and its own light, to give my kidney a thorough examination. When I asked how they get the camera and lights into my kidney, he explained they would push the tube up into the little mouth of my wood mouse and continue up through the prostate gland, do a U-turn around the vas deferens, and down again to the nephritic chambers of my kidneys. Then they push the light and camera through those tubes.

As I paid for that office visit of bad news, the nurse asked me if I followed their directions to drink plenty of liquids.

Oh yeah. I drink all day long.

What do you drink?

Tea, lots of it. Iced tea.

Oh no, don't drink that. Stay away from anything with caffeine.

So I did, for that next month, and the pains diminished.

A week before my scheduled exam, I felt cured.

The morning of my exam, I checked in to the hospital. They extracted blood and made me void a urine sample for analysis, then gave me a bland meal of mashed potatoes made from powder, and a slab of flavorless white meat with a salty gravy.

In the afternoon, I called down to the lab and asked if they saw any blood, any microscopic traces, in the latest urine sample.

No. Not a trace of blood.

I untied the flat cotton cords of the backwards hospital gown, got into my street clothes, and walked out of the hospital with a backhanded hasty goodbye to the staff, to deprive them of time to convince me to stay, or call someone to restrain me, or call my doctor, or otherwise corral and intimidate me into obedience.

The next day I called my doctor.

He seemed upset that I left, and berated me for my irresponsibility.

I intuited that he utilized my predicament as an opportunity to play with new technology, and perhaps even torture me a little. I always distrusted his bedside manner and suspected on an interpersonal level, he didn't like me. I offered a great opportunity to 'practice' on someone young, strong, healthy, someone for whom he wouldn't bat an eyelash to see in pain.

We never spoke again after that.

While holed up in that cottage with the first drafts of this book, I thought about my experience in Guatemala, and gave thanks to luck and caution for my own survival, a feat and fate often out of our hands.

I also considered one of my original motives, the slow suicide, a partial success.

One day, more than two months after my return, a misshapen package arrived by mail from Guatemala. I took off the brown paper and string and recognized the large palm frond waste basket I sent from

Guatemala when Yvonne and I first got together. Although I feared the worst in broken and missing objects, my treasures came out whole, one after the other. First I dug through the fabrics to pull out the wooden Guatemalan jewelry box decorated with the painted beach scene. At some point in the three month long journey by boat, even wrapped in so much fabric, the cover cracked, either under some great weight, or because the wood dried out too fast. I tried for five minutes to remember the sequence of secret panels that slide against each other and give access to the key, and when I did, I opened the box and found the two clay pipes with human faces, Mayan relics from Lake Atitlán, unbroken inside along with jewelry of semiprecious stone and silver. Fabric items comprised the rest of the shipment; two small table cloths, Mexican doilies for mom's end tables, intricate Guatemalan cloths suitable for wall hangings, Mayan shirts, embroidered blouses for women, all wrapped in a large blanket.

The first time I explained to mom how the Mayans wove, with threads tie-dyed before use and staggered to make the geometric designs, she acted impressed for a few seconds, then returned to her knitting.

The monotony of my forays into the city on a quest for employment broke with the appearance of spontaneous memorabilia, the sight of someone with a purse made of Guatemalan fabrics, a hippie wearing a Guatemalan shirt with the colors and weave similar to Santiago Atitlán.

The most painful souvenir or "momento," (Spanish for moment), came in the form of a letter from Yvonne.

Dear Brandon;

Hope your grandmother forgives you. My family also gave me problems too. People asked how I, a Nurse, helped people during the earthquake. What could I say? What can you say? I feel shame, and guilt, and much anger at you. You convinced me to run away with you, to run away from the opportunity to serve, to use my education to help those in need. I feel selfish, a coward, and I blame you for that. I don't want to hear from you ever again.

Goodbye forever.
Yvonne.

That hurt. I'm such a bad influence, corrupted the sweet innocent.

She wouldn't give me her address, and this letter came in some insurance company envelope. .

I don't remember her arm twisted at any point. Nothing forced her to do, or not to do something, or anything. I decided she regards me as little more than a reminder of her personal failure. She puts me on her shit list, relegated to the deepest dungeons of her memory, to exist locked away, chained and out of sight, like prisoners in the bowels of San Felipe castle, condemned to wither and die as soon as possible, to ensure I cause no further damage to her fantasy of self.

I bet she judged our time in Guatemala as a lost opportunity to reinvent herself as a hero, to impress those who know about the angry moment when she knocked her car doors off and almost killed her boyfriend in the garage.

Didn't she remember we went to the hospital and asked? Didn't we stay with a Guatemalan doctor and his family? Didn't we bus across the country and see all the roadblocks and controlled access to the worst hit rural regions, where international aide arrived in Red Cross trucks with international camera crews?

How do you best help the survivors of such a disaster, and give aid to members of families related to those among the twenty two thousand people who died in the rubble of their own mud brick houses, asphyxiated on dust, or entombed in the rockslides of mountainsides shaken down by thirty seconds of tectonic movement?

A trained nurse should trust her instincts about where to go and what to do in the midst of a disaster, when a doctor friend complains about the lack of hospital beds, medicines, and facilities and doesn't mention a lack of nurses, but instead urges her to flee the threat of epidemics, riots, and class warfare.

He communicated to us how he felt in this confrontation with an uncontrollable chaos that everyone thought would worsen. For our own good, he encouraged us to leave the country. He magnified the perception of danger to ourselves, and in those first days after the earthquake, we gauged the depth of Guatemala's loss as Dr. Mendez's family took stock of its members and discovered who among their relatives disappeared forever from the land of Eternal Springtime.

Yvonne and I measured our collective resources, and judged them barely enough to save our own skins.

The earthquake branded us with a psychological terror and subconscious anxiety that took years, perhaps decades, to erase. Until erased, it welled up at any moment, provoked by the vibrations from the distant passage of a heavy truck, a long thunder, a neighbor's door slammed shut by the wind or any deep slow vibrations felt through our feet, the same feet that propelled two lustful sinners from the sudden genocidal wrath of a prudish Catholic Mayan God that lurked about invisible, capricious.

Our youthful optimistic hopefulness became a bent cringe as we looked at the heavens and yelped like kicked puppies, without comprehension, the way animals awaken gnashing their teeth from dreams of abuse.

Yvonne and I survived the earthquake traumatized, and then hung around too long in the aftermath of confusion and terror. As we fled north, we heard about or felt each aftershock as if God's shiny black Nazi boots stamped the ground behind us to hurry us along. We, eyes wide in glances to the rear, scurried like bugs back to our homes, back to where we came from, back to safety, back to where we hoped we still belonged.

Bicentennial

On Independence Day, the Fourth of July each year, firework displays celebrate the date the Founding Fathers signed Declaration of Independence.

This year, nineteen hundred seventy six, the United States of America would celebrate the two hundredth anniversary, the Bicentennial, of independence from England in a national orgy of self congratulation. Our collective and explosive pugnacious nationalism excites itself with mass-turbations of the atmosphere in colorful displays of pyrotechnical prowess. This special year, the displays promised to paint the dark zodiac backdrop like a reef full of sea anemones and coral polyps in a fervent idolization of war, to help us express our loyalty to the bullet ridden Star Spangled Banner as we sing the National anthem with tear streaked cheeks.

Imagine, Uncle Sam two hundred years old, a baby of a nation compared to Mexico, Europe, almost anywhere else.

For months, the nightly news chronicled the plans of various cities and listed how much each would each spend on firework displays in a friendly competition to garner tourist dollars. Seemed like every major city on the entire East Coast Seaboard spent millions and millions of American Capitalist Greenback Dollars to design and deploy unmatched and never before seen spectacles to boggle the mind and inspire the nationalistic heart, pyrotechnic displays of a modern technology and competitive consumerism wedded to Communist China's newfound capitalistic self interest.

So much for the seriousness of our Cold War on Communism.

A study of our National Anthem led me to some insights, like the fact the melody comes from a song popular among drunks in English pubs.

Take the first verse of The Star Spangled Banner by Francis Scott Key, 1814:

Oh, say can you see, by the dawn's early light,
What so proudly we hailed at the twilight's last gleaming?
Whose broad stripes and bright stars, through the perilous fight,
O'er the ramparts we watched, were so gallantly streaming?
And the rockets' red glare, the bombs bursting in air,
Gave proof through the night that our flag was still there.
O say, does that star-spangled banner yet wave
O'er the land of the free and the home of the brave?

We Americans learn in childhood, in elementary schools, of the glamorous splendor of war. We learn that images of bullet riddled flags should inflame our most nationalistic and patriotic blind loyalty, and inspire us to throw our mortal coil from the ramparts into the lethal fray. As long as bomb light keeps our flag visible at night, we live in the land of the free, the home of the brave.

Now examine the little known Second verse of The Star Spangled Banner.

On the shore, dimly seen through the mists of the deep,
Where the foe's haughty host in dread silence reposes,
What is that which the breeze, o'er the towering steep,
As it fitfully blows, now conceals, now discloses?
Now it catches the gleam of the morning's first beam,
In full glory reflected now shines on the stream:
'Tis the star-spangled banner! O long may it wave
O'er the land of the free and the home of the brave.

If children ever learn that verse, they might appreciate how our sneaky flag shows itself reflected on "the stream," probably the inspiration for a new global Monroe Doctrine that entitles us to dominion of everything from shore to shore, but this time, going over both oceans to circumnavigate the globe.

The Third verse of The Star Spangled Banner:

And where is that band who so vauntingly swore
That the havoc of war and the battle's confusion
A home and a country should leave us no more?
Their blood has wiped out their foul footstep's pollution.
No refuge could save the hireling and slave
From the terror of flight, or the gloom of the grave:
And the star-spangled banner in triumph doth wave
O'er the land of the free and the home of the brave.

Some missing band swore that war and battle will restrain our homes and country from leaving, as if they could. Or maybe they swear that havoc and battle will never leave. That band's blood washes away their own foul footstep's pollution. OK., but where did that band go? And why do hirelings and slaves find no refuge from flights of terror and the grave's gloom? More questions for elementary school teachers to answer.

Let's try the Fourth verse of The Star Spangled Banner all together, with feeling:

Oh! thus be it ever, when freemen shall stand
Between their loved homes and the war's desolation!
Blest with victory and peace, may the heaven-rescued land
Praise the Power that hath made and preserved us a nation.
Then conquer we must, for our cause it is just,
And this be our motto: "In God is our trust."
And the star-spangled banner forever shall wave
O'er the land of the free and the home of the brave!

So we can look forward to a forever where men stand between their homes and the desolation of war, and feel blessed with victory and peace. The Heaven-rescued land praises the Power of technologies that preserve the nation but today, make war look like a video game. And by the way, the

United States MUST conquer in the name of our just cause, and our motto to trust in our Anglo saxon Protestant Chistian God, until the whole world stares up at this flag that waves over the land of the free and the home of the brave.

No matter what the conquered think about it. They should feel grateful we pushed them at gunpoint into freedom and democracy.

My nationalistic blind patriotic loyalty disappeared, so I rewrote the Pledge of Allegiance to not feel like a hypocrite nor stand out as un-American. My America enlarged to cover two and a half continents.

"I pledge all legions to the flag of the United States of a Miracle, and to the Republican witness stands, Juan's nation, oh my God, with libertine justice for all."

I believe in the core values of the United States, ideals such as equal opportunity, equal justice under the law, the right to participate in democracy if not in legislation, freedom from other idiots and freedom to express my own idiocy, and privacy to protect my dalliances and mistakes.

Over the last one hundred years, us ignorant US citizens allowed our government to become kidnapped by a superclass.

We got the government we deserved, and reap the world's distrust and hatred for it.

Death of Jaime

The Mayans thought their Gods required blood and live sacrifices as offerings. Deciphering depictions on murals and stonework, some archeologists believe the Mayans used the competitions in the ball courts as opportunities for the losers, or even the winners, to offer their lives to heaven, or offer their blood through self mutilation. Artwork shows how priests, in feathered attire, stood and prayed while others squatted in bloodletting ceremonies.

They used spines jabbed through an ear or the penis, or a thorn studded cord pulled through the tongue, to spatter their blood into bark paper bowls to quench the thirst of their gods. The Catholic communion shared enough similarity that the rituals blended. These practices continued long after the Spanish conquest and created new Pagan-Christian ceremonies which sometimes included human sacrifices with death by crucifixion and the removal of a human heart. The last recorded case occurred in 1868 among the Chamula of Chiapas, Mexico.

Manuel wrote me a couple of times the first year after the earthquake, short notes that revealed the conceptual chasms of maturation between the six year difference in our ages, twenty two and seventeen years old, an impassable gulf widened by our distinct nationalities and cultures. He wanted me to find out how he could join the United States military and become a jet pilot, which he saw as a necessary step towards a career in commercial aviation.

In the last letter I received from him, he wondered why I didn't answer him, and did I know that his brother moved to North Carolina, and died there?

I didn't know what to write back. I felt curious about how his brother died, but I didn't want to come right out and ask about that. The confusions of my own life, the search for employment, food clothing shelter sex belonging and usefulness, did not motivate me to attach a high level of priority to international correspondence with a sixteen year old who grieved.

The flux of my own situation turned his letter into an irritation, a reminder of how easily I lived, worked, and made money in relative safety. I didn't forget about the letter, but buried it under stacks of paper tasks and projects. I intended to work through the stack from top to bottom, but my idle hands filled with guitar. I thought about him often, thought about what I could write and say to him. The dilemma created between my culturally appropriate plans to get out of the house as soon as possible, and the obvious reciprocal invitation for him to come enjoy my family's hospitality, knit the two halves of my brain. When I thought about what to write, my eyebrows felt like two arm wrestlers tied in strength.

I never answered his letter, and felt worse about it as the years passed. When I ran across his letter, I brushed it off with the thought that people forget each other all the time and go on with their lives, as Yvonne did to me. Years turned into decades, and with hindsight saw my twenty two year old irresponsibility illuminated by maturity as clearly as a midnight forest fire illuminates the cigarette butt that started it.

As a result, I found it easy to cease to exist for a number of acquaintances of mine, people who once befriended me with all the effervescent trust and honesty of youth. I didn't know what to say to them. I feared that anything I said about what I experienced might drive them away, because the few times I said anything, my words came with the black ink of negativity, instead of the broad colorful canvas that I tried to convey. I tired of listeners who seemed bored, so I shut up and shut the door, reached for pen and paper, or typewriter, to write it all down though I dared not share it. Any conversation that turned toward Latin America got sucked into nothingness down the vacuum of other people's yawns.

I felt embarrassed that other nations interested me at all.

When I graduated from high school, that September I hitchhiked through Chicago and Minnesota, across Canada, down the Pacific Coast to Tijuana, and over to New Orleans for Mardi Gras before I headed home. On that trip, a young woman showed some concern for me, and taught me to repeat something that sounds like Nam Meoho Rengay Keyho, over and over, whenever I felt bad, or got into trouble. Two years later, I found a guru, learned to meditate, and misunderstand the Nuevo Buddhist doctrine of nonattachment, interpreted as a commandment to not value things like cars, personal appearances, drugs, pets, friends, attachments, lovers, family, etc. to avoid the pain of inevitable disappointment later.

Jaime died in North Carolina, and I imagine Manuel grew up, but to me, exists as a memory of a gangly, obnoxious, seventeen year old teenager.

My inactions caused me to die also, to Manuel, and to other young friends who wrote letters I never answered.

I didn't feel very good about all this death, real and indifferent.

Meditation and Buddhism helped me find stability. Buddha never talked about God, or presented himself as one. He taught happiness to people, and so lived into his eighties adored by millions. After he died, his appreciative followers called him God.

I gained access to my core through the diaphragm, a muscle under both conscious and autonomous control. In other words, I breathed. I relaxed and concentrated on the physiology of my breath, to let the verbal side of my brain rant until it calmed down and shut up. Then I saw things, glops of purple and faint yellow in rings of light, recognizable everyday objects appeared in what some call hypnogogic imagery. I felt things with senses of emotion and aesthetics, pleased or off balance, and came to understand things without words. Through this meditation I learned patience with myself, to calm myself with an awareness of my physiological states, and this reconnected me to a deeper self, a primitive being that enjoys life, and belongs to everything, to the universe.

I learned how to belong, and felt a duty to live life the best way, for the greatest common good, with right thought, acts, feelings, and spirit.

Through practice and discipline, in meditation I could control this heartbeat that measures time, but for too many years, I let others control my heart.

Throughout the next two decades, I moved every two years to another city in an attempt to make a career as a rock musician and songwriter. I often prowled through the social world of bars and found that it offered little more than an alcohol fueled interpersonal dysfunction amid a social hypocrisy that cannot hide young people's most base and instinctual goal, irresponsible fornication.

The dangerous and counterproductive American myth of a Lone Ranger rugged individual existence influenced my lifestyle too much. I did some art, and played various types of music, but my Hierarchy of Needs remained unsatisfied beyond the physiological necessities of food, clothing, and shelter.

In general, I felt confident about myself and safe, even when I stumbled drunk out of some after hours bar or party in the inner city at three in the morning. Thieves don't rob healthy young men who look both drunk and poverty stricken.

Twenty years later, I realized that the earthquake left me with a mild case of Post Traumatic Stress aftereffects which lasted years. At any moment, adrenaline would course into my veins and produce a fight or flight response to subconscious terror provoked by vibrations felt through the soles of my feet. I could close my eyes and see the city's rubble again, and hear the strange low moans of confused and dying people, the cries of children and babies from within impromptu tents of plastic sheets stretched across the streets and under the trees.

I don't often remember my dreams, but for two decades, nightmares reoccurred. One placed me alone in a great city, the skyscraper canyons dark, without electricity. I picked my way across bloody streets, through the carnage of mutilated body parts that lay strewn between piles of wrecked autos, piled three high on the sidewalks as they leaked gasoline and plumes of fumes and smoke.

Once awake, I remembered the earthquake.

On the positive side of things, the earthquake spared Guatemala and Belize the horror of war. The earthquake probably bludgeoned all those that Guatemalans that favored war into a state of meek shock and awe, from where they might regain membership in the human community, and thus in the future, reject war in favor of a friendly, peaceful world.

Stereotypes

In American English, the concept of "going south" meant a fall into the process of failure. When a part on your car fails, that part "went south." Relationships "go south" and become dysfunctional. Mexico as a gestalt, an archetype, as myth and legend in the minds of citizens of the United States, perhaps limited to the Anglo Saxon psyche, exists as a Land of Mañana, where nothing happens on time or without corruption. This relegates Mexico to a small branch of the tourism industry, famous for Scuba, beaches, and gallons of alcohol to underage drinkers along the border and in March, throughout the country when Spring Breakers, the High School and College students far away from home and 'supervisory authority' for the first time, to test their limits and discover the price of excess.

Latin America puzzled me more and more, as I watched TV and listened to Mexican music. I mulled over my vaporous memories, experiences, and acquisition of Mexican Spanish, and together they amalgamated into another perception of human existence. That alternative reality called to me in dreams, and titillated my daytime existence with the rare sight of a Hispanic woman, or the sounds of Mexican music from a car stereo.

The lack of ethno-cultural common ground between the Hispanic and Anglo Saxon thwarted my efforts to communicate my experiences in Guatemala to friends and family. I estimated the one dollar twenty five cents per hour minimum wage for U.S. citizens ten times higher than the dollar a day average income in Guatemala. The Teamsters and other unionized factory workers earned ten dollar an hour, a hundred times more than the wages factory workers receive in Mexico and Guatemala.

That Third World average of a dollar a day might not take into account the unemployed, nor the non wage earners in agrarian societies, nor the urban poor, nor the poorest of the poor, nomads who lived on the margins of economies of barter in agrarian or inner city environments, or off garbage.

So my American friends lacked empathy for Hispanic American people, not due to a mean spirit, but to a tendency to relegate or categorize other people and places into objects, reminiscent of the two dimensional images in books or on TV screens. thus the rest of the world appears as if another planet, or long ago in the distant past. Because of the cultural chauvinism of United States citizens, they see other cultures and civilizations as a predawn of true civilization where everyone has a yard and an automobile. They see other cultures without value or utility to the modern world, dinosaurs en route to extinction that deserve little attention and no sympathy, remorse, nor reparations for whatever happens to them.

One of the most liberal and philosophically advanced among my friends perceived one great advantage for such poor people in times of calamity or disaster. Few possessions minimizes potential losses, as if involuntary devotees to the Buddhist doctrine of non-attachment, or the monk's vow of poverty.

Out here in the United State's suburban countryside, each of us drove our own car for twenty miles or more every time we went to work or to shopped in supermarkets for the necessities of life.

Most Latin Americans walk, or take public transportation, to work or stores. A pedestrian culture with shops on each corner, at odds with our automobile culture and a few superstores.

In the United States, each 'normal or average' suburban home houses one nuclear family, an arrangement of two parents and their children. The most upscale of these homes lay scattered about the countryside. Among middle class northern Yankees, most rural families like ours resided in a three or four bedroom wooden house that used hundreds of dollars of oil to heat each winter.

South of the border, most rural people lived in one room shacks of rock, adobe, stick and mud wattle, often grouped into commune-like communities called ejidos, to work or ranch land that belongs to someone rich. The middle class factory workers lived in poorly designed tracts of cement buildings with tiny bedrooms and a sink in the public area. Houses of cement turn into ovens under the summer sun, or ice box refrigerators on cold winter days. As the cities grew and swallowed satellite communities, an established family might build more rooms onto their building, sideways and up one floor, to shelter a large extended family of aunts and uncles and cousins, grandparents and grandkids, and other adopted members such as children born out of wedlock to sisters or uncles, and other rescued people.

On other forays into Latin America, I experienced again the enviable qualities of life I first experienced in Mexico and Guatemala. People accepted sex and vulgarity in direct relationship to the lack of books in the home. The newspapers and television newscasts cater to a superstitious uncritical reality oblivious to the United State's exaggerated fear of germs and premium on sterility. With the sensual as an integral part of life, unashamed newspapers carried drawings of nude women, stores sold popsicles made with real fruit, happy children learn to dance before their adult teeth come in. As I became more comfortable south of the border, I felt another personality inside me create itself, as an antidote to the unemotional logician of Capitalist acquisition and free market competition that measures success through economics, and progress through industrial growth.

It felt like a lost instinctual awareness of life, an appreciation of vivid experience as its own reward, ideas that people used to ridicule the Sixties Hippie culture. Qualities called family oriented, touchy feely, hedonistic, fuzzy, sensual, curious, tolerant or (better) accepting, and emotional hallmarked Latin America as it once decorated the lifestyles of long haired 'Hippie' men and Earth Mother women. They represent a humanistic version of humanity in opposition to the business suits of married, professional, salaried nine to fivers that put in sixty hours of work a week and thus can't find enough time for their own children. Hippies, in their long tie-dyed dresses, bare feet, and unshaved underarms, danced with their Earth Mother women, and spun themselves into a shut eyed dance till they disappeared in the United States, except for a few groups like the Rainbow People and those in marijuana drug cultures that followed that untalented improvisational country-rock group the Grateful Dead from concert to concert to trade surreptitious recordings of their jams.

I resolved to change, to resist the anti-sensual work ethic of repressed, stoic, 'stiff upper lip' Anglo Saxons that dominates my Midwestern community, and instead cultivate that nonverbal hedonist inside me, the antidote to my skeptical, critical, and judgmental bastard dwarf that elicited from Chicano Americans the response of "Your mother never breast fed you, or what?"

Poverty emphasizes another set of noble human characteristics, a counterpoint to the upper class's rigorous education in the appreciation of the reputed 'finer things in life,' like operas in Italian, modern art, and the table manners required to handle multiples of forks and spoons and a finger bowl to eat meals with each of the seven courses served on its own little gilt edged plate from some famous old world ceramics factory.

The high and mighty love to devise ways to identify and scorn the down to earth.

Indigenous cultures of simple people enjoy an easy sensuality expressed in impromptu song and laughter, with their sexuality on display and snickered about as an integral part of life. I remembered the laughter of children of all ages in multigenerational families, the ease of communication with neighbors, the genial vulgarities, and the reciprocal aide that guarantees help to those in need.

A fellow hitchhiker explained this apparent altruism to me. He said "It's not the rich who stop to help a motorist on the highway, or pick up a hitchhiker, but the poorest of the poor, or the faithful with the most faith in others. They know how much we all depend on each other, because they live that way. They help others out of an instinct of reciprocity, and expect that someone will help them in return. Everyone's life interweaves with shared events that bind people together."

Many of the poorest people in the world serve as examples to us all, as masters of the art of being human, of functional social beings. They depend on the most basic and ancient humanistic skills; altruism (to the tribe, at least), friendliness, and trust to create climates of cooperation, an expression of millions of years of genetic and social evolution programmed within us and our social learning, without which we probably limit our enjoyment of life, as no other life form can.

Animals don't commit suicide, or do they? I sometimes wonder about our black haired, family dog's midnight stray into the road in old age.

We animals need each other for our own happiness and wellbeing, for the survival of nature, for the health of the biosphere that we all belong to.

The inhabitants of small traditional Latin American communities revolve around the Central Plaza, with children in promenades with grandparents, girlfriends and boyfriends hand in hand, adolescents in groups that flirt, and parents with children in tow. The way Latin America's citizens parade around their community's Central Plaza demonstrates their place in the community, aware of the tribal responsibility of each member to decorate their community. Clothing functions as an expression of tradition or individuality, and helps others identify those who follow local customs, which puts them at ease. People announce their social reputation, their class, respect, resources, or social 'capital,' in how they dress, and with whom they chat. An artistic or eccentric individuality may threaten at first, but most villages easily accept their own homosexuals. They learn to accept the fringe elements, and from among those risk takers come the innovators, the entrepreneurs, the creative class.

Alongside Latin America's central plaza, the developed world's automobile culture looks subhuman, a mechanical alienation, an outgrowth of consumerism based upon one product as an ugly appendage that people believe amplifies human capacities as does the bicycle, but instead becomes an anchor. The automobile functions as a half ton piece of jewelry, a personal ostentation we pay to push around with fossil fuels everywhere we go, in an isolated existence that revolves around parking lots and shopping centers.

The rest of the world desires to remake itself in that image, that false freedom of mobility. Some Hispanics dress up like a million bucks, with their children left hungry back home in a shack, so they can drive a car that they believe gives them a little status. Rich Gringos wander around in worn blue jeans and floppy fabric hats and worry about their stock portfolio.

One college professor, through questions posed to his multicultural students, counts the hands raised and discovers that recent immigrant Hispanic students tend to drive around in new or late model cars or pickup trucks where culturally appropriate, while their much more affluent Yankee counterparts from the humanist side of the dominant society drive older used cars.

Latin America produces soap operas, called telenovelas, or Televised Novels, because they tell novel length stories in about twelve hour long installments, and then end. In general, actors of European ancestry portray histrionic personality disorders in plots that revolve around some mystery of paternity. Catholics cannot divorce easily, yet Latin America's superstition and illiteracy makes people susceptible to the vagaries of sexual attraction, which creates a society paranoid of illegitimate children, yet accept that husbands remain in good social graces although they publicly parade their lover and bastard children.

I wondered if I should turn Catholic, and indulge in the pomp and circumstance of serial sins cleansed through confession. Then I too might seek significant others for the express service of my genetic imperative, to sow my wild oats outside marriage and run away to avoid the cost of harvest, alimony, and childrearing, with the State to pick up the tab for the multiple single mom families I create. In that way, I too could share the wine, fool those girls, infiltrate that family to mate poach and sow my seed for her husband to support for the next eighteen years, and otherwise joust with elevated spear at those open armed windmills several times a month.

Once in a while, I would beat a stumbled retreat into the confessional to beg "Oh father, father, purify me for I have sinned" and prepare myself for the next go round.

After all, as an Anglo Saxon, the strength of my family ties weakened to almost nothing beyond the nuclear family of a couple and their kids, so if I became a Catholic and never got married, nothing could ever tie me down, and I could still go to the Catholic's heaven, if one exists.

Stereotypes work both ways. The work ethic that motivates cultural assumptions in the United States forces us to evaluate Mexicans as lazy, while their culture disparages us as antisocial Workaholics.

In one popular joke, an American business man berates a Mexican man asleep on a hillside as he tends his flock of goats. "Hey, Lazy. Don't you a job?"

"Para qué?" For what?

"So you can earn money."

"Para qué?" Why?

To buy a car, (Para qué?), to get to a better job (Para qué?), to earn more money (Para qué?), to pay for an education (Para qué?), to start a business (Para qué?), to make a success of yourself and your business (Para qué?), to earn a lot of money when you sell it (Para qué?), to retire.

"Para qué?"

"So you can relax and enjoy life."

"Que diablos crees que estoy haciendo?" What do you think I'm doing now?!?

As U.S. citizens people grow older, many think about retirement and continued part time employment and augment their social security and pension, because they believe they will enjoy life a little more in the process. "I can't see myself sitting around doing nothing."

In Latin America, people smell roses that citizens north of the border can't even see.

Even though the citizens of many Latin American countries suffered governments that, at almost regular intervals, humbled them into more 'belt tightening' as a response to inflation and trade imbalances that undermined their currency, which to many comes across as the meddlesome influence of the World Bank and the International Monetary Fund, both stationed in the United States.

Through all that belt tightening and lowered expectations of their future, the populations remain passive, full of interpersonal humility.

They also don't enjoy the right to bear arms.

They do retain their joy of life, ready to accept the presence of us strangers from the developed "First World." They invite us to dinner, to enjoy their country, to date their daughters, to share their vacations, and live in their homes.

To reciprocate, when they come to the United States, the richest nation on earth rounds them up and pushes them back into their poverty.

I educated myself about the world through shortwave radio broadcasts in English and Spanish from Germany, Netherlands, Japan,

China, Ecuador, Miami's Cuban Exile Community (Radio Marti), Fidel's Radio Havana Cuba, all measured against the apex of independent quality and universal coverage, the British Broadcasting Company (the BBC for short).

The public library became my classroom, where I could roam the complex world of arbitrary ethno-cultural geopolitical divisions, and the sample the currents of the free exchange of ideas, through books and magazines.

On one productive day, I learned that on my twentieth birthday, the third of July 1973, representatives of the European community attended a Conference on Security and Cooperation (CSCE) in Helsinki, Finland to analyze the responsibilities of governments. The meetings continued for two years to produce the Helsinki Accords.

The Helsinki Accords start with a Declaration on Principles Guiding Relations between Participating States, which includes promises to respect, support, and uphold things like "human rights and fundamental freedoms, including the freedom of thought, conscience, religion or belief," plus support for equality among people and the need to protect all people's rights, with special concern to "their right to self determination."

One might suppose the world's greatest superpower signed the accords, but recent history suggests otherwise.

I began to sense the existence of a super class within the United States.

The family and history of the two Dulles brothers illustrates an all too common lineage of power within America's "classless society" and the revolving door between the Corporations, the Security Exchange Commission, and the CIA. Academics consider the notion that an elite class usurped the United States government a mere theory, instead of a model with concrete examples in reality. Most teachers refuse to see, and would not allow in any case, anecdotal evidence that might sway their opinion as to how lobbyists influence the government in the interests of corporate profits for an elite class of world citizens, investors and top management. They call it the "Elitist Theory" of government, as if it deserves little thought, and don't recognize it as a model as old as civilization, one that helps us understand the trajectory of history.

The story of how one Austrian boy named Arnold Schwarzenegger becomes a champion body builder, then Hollywood movie star, and later in life becomes Governor of California gives us an example of more than the power of fame. His marriage into the illustrious Kennedy clan through Maria Shriver suggests socioeconomic nepotism as a sabotage of a process we would rather believe a meritocracy. Of course, one anecdote proves nothing.

The world lacks enough paper to list the rest of the anecdotes.

Take the Dulles brothers as another piece of anecdotal evidence, even though it proves nothing. I believe it illustrates a terrible truth about the world's most primitive and basic social structure, the pyramid built of stone to endure forever.

John Foster Dulles, designer of the Cold War.

Their father Allen Macy Dulles, a Presbyterian minister, married Edith Foster, whose father, John Watson Foster, served as President Benjamin Harrison's Secretary of State and helped plan the invasion and annexation of Hawaii. Robert Lansing, Dulles' uncle by marriage, served in Woodrow Wilson's Cabinet as Secretary of State.

Born in 1888, from early on in John Foster Dulles' life, he wanted to become Secretary of State like both his grandfather and uncle. In nineteen hundred and seven, at nineteen years old, he started his diplomatic career when he accompanied his grandfather John Foster to the second international peace conference at the Hague.

Allen and Edith Dulles raised five children who went to the Watertown, N.Y. public schools. John Foster Dulles shined as a brilliant student and went on to Princeton, George Washington Universities, and the Sorbonne. Around 1911, with a specialization in international law, he joined the law firm of Sullivan and Cromwell where by 1927, he became head of the firm.

By the time he celebrated his thirtieth birthday at the end of World War I, President Woodrow Wilson named him as legal counsel to the U.S. delegation to the Versailles Peace Conference, and became a member of the war reparation commission. In World War II, Dulles worked on the United Nations charter and served as adviser. With President Harry Truman in office, his secretary of state Dean Acheson thought a peace treaty with Japan impossible with the participation of the Soviet Union, so they gave Dulles the secret assignment to travel to the nations involved and, with great discretion, negotiate until Japan and 48 other nations signed the treaty in 1951.

After these successes, President Eisenhower appointed Dulles as Secretary of State in January 1953. Dulles took it as permission to design U.S. foreign policy, usually a responsibility of the president. He learned to become the leader instead of the follower of public opinion, and helped invent the field of Public Relations. Dulles trusted his own ideas, made detailed plans, and once he gained President Eisenhower's confidence, his concerns steered foreign policy.

He feared Communism both as a threat to his deep religious faith, and to America's values of Freedom and Democracy. He carried Joseph Stalin's booklet "Problems of Leninism" and pressured his aides to study it as a primer in conquest, similar to Adolph Hitler's "Mien Kampf".

Dulles thought the North Atlantic Treaty Organization (NATO) could only defend Western Europe, which left the Middle East, the Far East, and the Pacific islands unprotected. In 1954, he helped institute the Southeast Asia Treaty Organization (SEATO) to unite eight nations in a neutral defense pact. In 1955 he helped design the Baghdad Pact, renamed the Central Treaty Organization (CENTO), which united a defense organization for the 'northern tier' countries of the Middle East; Turkey, Iraq, Iran, and Pakistan.

Again in 1953, Dulles pushed around even the allies of the United States, as when he demanded the establishment of the European Defense Community (EDC) though it threatened to polarize the free world. He threatened that if France failed to ratify the EDC, it would force the United States into an "agonizing reappraisal" of the relations with France. That phrase, and Dulles' assurance that the United States planned "massive nuclear retaliation" in the event of Soviet aggression, became part of Cold War vocabulary.

The Brother: Allen Welsh Dulles

Born in 1893 in Watertown, N.Y., John Foster's brother Allen Welsh Dulles went to Princeton and earned a Masters by 1916, after which he somehow ended up in diplomatic posts. By the time he celebrated his 29th birthday in nineteen twenty two, the State Department named him chief of the Near Eastern Division, and somehow he found time to study for a law degree in 1926. Allen Welsh Dulles also served for a short time as counselor with the U.S. delegation in Peking.

Next he joins the law firm of Sullivan and Cromwell, which should come as no surprise as his brother became head of the firm in 1927.

So in World War II, Colonel William J. Donovan for the Office of Strategic Services (OSS), an intelligence service, recruits Dulles to serve as chief of the OSS office in Bern from October 1942 to May 1945 to take part in events that help lead to German troops' surrender in northern Italy.

Remember his brother at this time worked on both the United Nations charter and President Truman's Secretary of State's plan for a peace treaty without the Soviet Union.

So by 1948, someone picks him as one of three people to analyze the U.S. intelligence system.

In 1951 they established the CIA, the Central Intelligence Agency, and selected Allen Welsh Dulles as deputy director under General Walter Bedell Smith. By that pivotal year of 1953, with his reputation as a U.S. diplomat and intelligence expert, President Dwight D. Eisenhower appointed Allen Welsh Dulles as the Director of the CIA, which allowed Dulles to determine the CIA's mandate and the direction of future growth.

First they overthrew the Iranian government of the democratically elected Mohammad Mosaddeq in 1953 with the subterfuge of paid street demonstrations to make the president look like a communist leader faced with a civil war inspired by 'Freedom Fighters.'

The plan worked so well and cost so little, the next year they reworked it a little to overthrow Jacobo Arbenz in Guatemala.

These encyclopedia based bios do lack a clear reference to either one of the Dulles boys as CEO of United Fruit.

The United States, a global superpower after two hundred years of democratic independence, invents itself as the country that designed the modern world through industrial innovation. Its people believe they won both World Wars through noble interventions to make the Western Hemisphere (and Japan) safe for Freedom and Democracy.

America's World War II warriors dare to call themselves the Greatest Generation. Hollywood war movies give the impression that America did it all alone, which never played too well in the theaters of our Allies, especially those that hosted that theater of war, that suffered the cataclysms of death and destruction on their soil.

And so by the year of my birth in nineteen fifty three, the U.S. government, under the influence of the Dulles brothers, used a probably baseless fear of communism and the Domino Theory (or Principle) as the official excuse for four decades of violations of the sovereignty of other nations. (After the 'Fall of Communism' and a collective amnesia towards China, the 'corporatocracy' sought another excuse for its adventurism, and chose Terrorism.)

School children learn about our Manifest Destiny, and how the United States annexed lands from sea to shining sea as the spoils of war, but most of the textbooks gloss over the United State's appropriation of other sovereign nations since the original forty eight states took shape.

In the early eighteen hundreds, protestant churches from the Eastern Seaboard of the United States sailed missionaries to the Sandwich Islands. After they settled in for a generation, some realized they could make a killing with refined sugar. They followed their instincts and became rich, until the United States passed a tariff that threatened their fortunes.

They decided to woo the United States, so their leader went to Washington and got a promise of support from President Harrison and his Secretary of State, John Watson Foster, the Dulles' brothers' grandfather (small world, for members of the superclass).

Back in the Sandwich Islands, or Hawaii (the name of the South Pacific Polynesian people's afterlife residence and ancestral homeland, or "Heaven"), this leader of sugar farmers formed a triumvirate with the American ambassador and the commander of a U.S. naval ship anchored in front of Honolulu, on orders from the State Department to aid this 'revolution.'

The Queen of Hawaii didn't know what to do when they declared her government overthrown, then brought ashore two hundred fifty marines to keep order. She would rather maintain order herself, but when she talked to the dozen or so ambassadors from other countries stationed in Hawaii, they told her that any resistance would come to naught and ruin any future opportunities to regain her throne.

In the 1898 Spanish American war, the United States took the Philippines, and the 'government' of Hawaii offered itself to the United States as a way station, halfway between the Philippines and California. After the war, the United States gained the Philippines, Guam, Puerto Rico, and paved the way for Hawaii's statehood in 1959.

Under the Dulles Brothers influence, the American CIA overthrew the government of Iran in 1953, a nation with a culture that existed for thousands of years as the Persian empire. The next year, they overthrew the government of Guatemala, a Hispanic country three hundred years older than the United States, with an existent Meso-American culture with roots that extend back three thousand years to a millennium before Christ.

The need to avoid any public scrutiny, and possible criticism of the infant CIA and its covert destruction of democracies to install dictators, created a need for control, or spin, of information and public opinion. That need birthed the field of Public Relations, and brought into the fold of the United States intelligence community the innovation and vision of a man named Seyferth, who would preside over an American association of Public Relations firms for decades.

In the mid nineteen eighties, his lovely big eyed daughter Ginny, owner of her own Public Relations firm in Grand Rapids Michigan, served developers who would build the tallest buildings in town, taller than the Amway Grand Plaza hotel, on the West Bank of the Grand River (in actuality, a tall shell over the old Pantlind Hotel).

Amway started in the sixties as a door to door pyramid sales recruitment for biodegradable soap, with corporate offices in a small Michigan town of a couple of thousand residents and an antique covered wooden bridge. Although it sounds like a noble enterprise, the business next door put up a giant flag that said "When the wind blows this way, the smell is from Amway." The corporation grew into a factory and distribution center kilometer long decorated with flagpoles reminiscent of the United Nations, with its own tourist attraction called the "Hall of American Enterprise."

Ginny Seyferth kept it secret that her clients refused to acquiesce to Amway Corporation's offer to buy the top three floors of the new buildings, to avoid the need to build them. Amway wanted to ensure that the Amway Grand Plaza Hotel would maintain its dominance as the tallest building in Grand Rapids.

It didn't happen that way.

The developers rejected Amway's plot for skyline dominance, the three floors got built, and the Amway Grand Hotel lost its symbolic stature as a one fingered salute to Amway's international policy of Free Enterprise. Two decades later, accused of tax evasion and outlawed as a pyramid scheme in many countries, Amway sold out and the new owners changed its name.

Not many knew about Amway's plot to maintain that one fingered salute to pyramid marketing, until now.

Most of what I heard from all those crazy third world intellectuals, those rabid hateful anti-Americans, those jealous little nitwits that I characterized as Latin American closet Commies, resembled a reputable version of historical truth.

I couldn't understand why so few in my America, the portion north of Mexico and south of Canada, ever bothered to look.

Worse, few of those who look, see, and understand, ever give a damn. They ignore anyone who fights for social justice. That ignorance often frightens and sucks all the optimism out of those who care about other people's lives and deaths, about the quality of human life, about human rights, about the human right of each family, tribe, and nation to self determination as long as they guaranteed those same rights for others.

Competition for money serves as the fertilizer for both the flowers of human progress, and for the roots of all evil.

America's consumerist Capitalist society believes itself a meritocracy of Lone Rangers in a system that rewards any rugged individual with talent and ambition. Citizens of the United States believe in self-made people, those who bootstrap their way from poverty to personal success, and they search out their stories as anecdotal evidence to support this myth of rugged individualism, in the vain belief that each and every one of them might make it to the top. Even religious leaders tell them Jesus wants them to get rich.

Economic competition favors networks of co-conspirators, personality types who enjoy themselves when others fail, the hardhearted ones who take advantage and dominate others, the ruthless who do not value win/win situations, nor respect any peaceful philosophies devoted to the common good. Economic Competition favors individuals who form powerful socioeconomic tribes that conspire against social justice and excuse environmental contamination with the adage that 'it might not be ethical, but it's certainly not illegal.'

This worship of economic competition becomes a Logic of Self which cannot see, or understand, the social problems caused by unfettered self interest, because it cannot comprehend nor value social interconnectedness nor the importance of an uncontaminated biosphere.

The American school systems, a conspiracy of special interest groups and textbook publishers who acquiesce to them, offer a watered down, myopic, sanitized, uninteresting, untruthful, without embarrassment and unselfconscious version of knowledge and history. The system seems deliberate in its ability to kill the student body's capacity to build a reasonable facsimile of reality and put themselves in it as active participants, with meaningful work and political activism that promotes human progress.

What creates wealth in any society comes from their culture and value systems; whether big rocks with holes in them, coconuts, artwork, chocolate, gold, or oil. At this point in history, an automobile culture means that vast and easy sums of wealth come out of the ground in the form of oil. Drive down any commercial street in almost any major city in the world, and count the businesses related to oil and automobiles, the gas stations, oil change shops, auto parts, garages for service and repair, car washes, tire stores, automobile factories, used car lots, convenience stores and Laundromats, the roads themselves, and the superstores and malls with their immense parking lots.

Depleted oil supplies become a minor problem compared to a global rise in energy needs while the planet overheats.

The United State's public education system's greatest success lies in how it instills a blind loyalty and patriotism based on the ideals of equality, democracy, justice, and competition through a value system based on the oil dollar, with the theory that American society functions as a meritocracy of Lone Rangers, and the cream must rise to the top.

The cream may rise to the top, but when it drags the rot and corruption up from the bottom, it spoils the entire pyramid.

Fifteen Years Later, Antoinette.

The Mayan's ritual use of human blood, extracted from hearts in mid beat, emphasized the Shaman priest or God-king's power over life and death as a conduit from the Gods of Time to the lower classes. This Meso-American cosmology features male feathered serpents as portals of transformation, opened by the blood of live hearts, and perhaps serves as a metaphor to understand a male dominated society's pyramidal social structures.

Social scientists theorize that humans invented villages when some proto human Eve discovered agriculture, which freed the tribe from a nomadic life. Villages became permanent, women foraged and farmed, while the men hunted.

Their culture changed, attuned itself to the seasons of agriculture. The measurement of time and seasons offered advantages and let to more useful knowledge about plants, agriculture, and even architecture. In early agrarian societies, those who possessed the best gardeners became rich. They invented new cultures. Male domination of family allowed men to collect young females for procreation, and permitted the possession of women as mothers and domestic laborers, with older women to work as indentured servants until they died. Like Hollywood's mythic sexual vampires, the male human's lust for possessions and girls as "fresh blood" manifests the male animal's genetic mandate, to fertilize and procreate with as many as possible. This acquisitiveness and the need for genetic variation would encourage intertribal conquests. Feminist and 'evolutionary psychologist' scientists suggest that this need for genetic variation gives humans a secret promiscuousness, and extrapolates into imperial tendencies. Societies dominated by the male gender, especially with patrilinear inheritance, manifest this masculine genetic directive toward acquisitiveness to gather resources for multiple mates and offspring. These subconscious instincts also direct the male's ubiquitous dream to become top dog in a pyramid hierarchy, with exclusive access and control of all resources from the top down, through the Y chromosome's genes for linear two-dimensional thought; ambition, exhibitionism, greed, and violence mixed with lust, the lust for competition, the romance of wars both declared and undeclared between men, genders, families, tribes, classes, nations, and cultures.

Fifteen years after the earthquake, I received this letter from Grandma, my long dead father's mother, in the glorious Spring of 1990:

Dear Brandon:

How are you? My husband passed away. His children have given him many grandchildren, and since he was very wealthy, they're all well taken care of. Why don't you call me?

Your Grandmother, Antoinette.

So I did. I called her several times during those final years of her life, because I wanted to hear about her life, my roots, in Europe. Instead, she wanted to make sure I understood that the law allowed her to give family members gifts of up to ten thousands dollars each year. She told me about her "vunderful" life and travels with her rich retired husband, how they traveled the world and met all kinds of rich "vunderful" people although she could remember few details, when pressed.

I tried to get her to talk about her early life, and she would change the subject, which made me suspicious and created lurid fantasies about something she tried to hide.

"Grandma, tell me about your past, in Europe."

"Oh, there's nothing to tell."

"You must have traveled around."

"No. Only once. To Italy. I vent with my Uncle, a famous Archbishop."

"Tell me about it."

"Oh no. Nothing to it, really."

Silence.

"So, do you remember your first kiss?"

That opened the floodgates. She talked for almost a half an hour, nonstop. I know more about that young man's clothing than I ever did about Grandma's life with her two husbands. Over the next couple of years, I failed again and again to coax more information out of her about her own life, about our family. She thought herself too poor to go into detail, and refused to "say anything negative". Didn't want to "soil the nest", as she put it.

This made us grandkids suspect the worst about those silences. Did she go to Italy for an abortion, and then immigrate to the US out of shame?

She would talk about how rich all her husband's friends are, and that they don't come around to visit her anymore, and she doesn't want to see any of them anyway. Especially not his children. She suspects they never accepted her.

She always felt ashamed of her accent, she said.

She took all her silent thoughts and memories, our family's oral history, and her useless shame, to her grave.

I felt she should only regret her lack of self esteem, but as a good Catholic, steeped in medieval notions of guilt, sin, and redemption, she locked herself into a little glass coffin and clutched the key to her breast. It reminded me of my suspicion that people taught to despise sex as something shameful, dirty, or even unholy, can deny themselves and others sexual pleasure, and permit their bodies to get fat or otherwise unhealthy.

I once, and I mean one time, went out with a girl who got nauseous as she got hot because her religious mother equated sex with evil. Her ex-husband raped her to get her pregnant and give birth to two children. In general, whenever a Mexican sees a child somewhat naked, they tend to shout "Cochino!" which translates as filthy pig, or swine. Not the best situation, and to couple that with the misogyny inherent in Mexican Spanish merits an entire novel to explore its ramifications.

I don't believe in secrets or censorship. In a perfect society of acceptance and trust in each person's right to live and make their own gaffes, blunder, bloopers, and faux pas. We learn and benefit from other's mistakes, and artists create stories, books, and movies about them. No one wants to read about a perfect family without problems, although many want to censor all discussion about the most common problems. Few people respect the rights of others to chose and make mistakes, to let each individual take responsibility for their own process of becoming, as long as no one (else) gets hurt. One must assume that when people agonize over some decision and then decide what to do, they need to take that route. An open, tolerant with acceptance, Post-Industrial multicultural society of curious humanists should keep an open mind and a watchful eye, to offer helpful advice instead of judgment, and distrust the use of threats of punishment, which doesn't work.

For too long we've overlooked the vengeful hatefulness behind the oxymoron of our "Criminal Justice" system.

When people refuse to listen, or want to shut others up, they betray themselves as weak.

Information doesn't make people vulnerable, not even children, because they absorb at their level of comprehension. People benefit from information, not ignorance. People either try to understand what happens to themselves and others, or they refuse to for reasons that stem from their upbringing and education, or inherent in their personality, or due to social pressures. Each individual develops their own vulnerabilities and strengths from their environment and their own aptitudes, and they change over a lifetime.

Research about how images of violence or hardcore pornography affect children often show no conclusive results, but society's tolerance of violence in foreign policy, sports, and entertainment coupled with an almost complete blackout on sexually explicit information bodes ill for that society. With luck, all of us will participate in sex and avoid violence, not the other way around. People need information, not abstinence, which cannot help married people plan their families.

Some people remain ignorant and ignore others to avoid damage to their own self esteem. As long as the Untied States stays in its Ivory Tower as protector of Democracy and Freedom, home of the heroes of both World Wars, it can enjoy the view and look down at the rest of the world.

Those on the ground see the terrain in a different light, and far too many live in the dark shadow of the tower.

Antoinette could never face facts that might criticize or cause her to distrust the ostensible policies of the United States government, because she worshiped this land as her savior. She didn't need to forgive our trespasses, because she walked through Europe's valley of the shadow of death, and once inside the United States, she could see no evil.

She died in 1995, 95 years old, alone in her luxury apartment in an upscale Florida retirement community.

I wrote a poem.

In bed, powdered Antoinette winches her self up
Her white hair bunched and caught
Another warm white Atlantic morning
Streams through the second story windows
A mosquito net mist of white hot gauze.
She pulls a white mirror from the white headboard,
Purses her thin aristocratic lips
Does her crooked smile, the Old World flirt
Fingers fluff her hair.
"How Vonderful they Vould tink it here" she sighs,
A million miles away.
"Our yacht crossed the oceans
"Many times those fifteen years
"Before he passed a Vay."
She lays back down
Crosses her heart and did she think of us?
How fair she doled and saved

The best bought, at the best price.
Proud of what she sold well,
Ready to join him, atop that hill,
Their twin tombs encircled by a low brick wall
Around the bare cement that caps their graves.

I tried to understand the ease with which Grandma and her new husband disowned me. That anyone could disown family members surprised me, as oldest of her grandkids, because I didn't understand what motivates some of the "well off."

The worst of the rich assume everyone else's motives are the same as theirs, a lack of confidence in themselves which causes a deprecation of other human beings. Push other people down to elevate yourself. They become motivated by greed, and respect voracious gluttony over altruism. These people need to amass wealth because it allows them to enforce an artificial social superiority, to avoid the self recognition of their mediocrity, their spiritual weakness, their moral failings, their fearful vulnerability that someone would take from them the same way they took from others, due to the same base personality disorders that inspire too many people to amass wealth through competition and one-upmanship, instead of through a creative addition to human progress.

They limit the parameters of life down to a game of acquisitiveness, with net worth an easily quantifiable measure of their personhood. Some people feel more equal than others.

While Grandma's husband lived, they probably reasoned that fewer grandchildren meant they could concentrate their support on those deemed worthy.

They exercised the power of all those stingy, miserly, parsimonious, mean, tight, cheap, miserable, hoarding, covetous, pathetic, wretched, pitiable people that believe enough in American values like rugged individualism and the Lone Ranger ethic to shatter their own family. They became those tightwad, close fisted citizens ready to fight to keep their gains from the mouths of the hungry, the needy, the disenfranchised, the marginalized. They know they can recognize right from wrong, and they will finance the fight for the right to kill off all the wrong. Scratch any right wing, Christian coalition, intolerant Republican warmonger and you get down to the Average Random Mean, a mathematical construct from the stone age that gives them the authority to commit a nation to racist intolerance and extra-national adventurism, and if you don't like it, they call you anti-American and shout "My country, right or wrong, so love it or leave it!"

As top dogs, they earned the right to kick the underdogs back into the stone age, while their own garage fills with more forgotten and unused items than most people in the world would see in their entire lifetime.

What she tried to do to me, a young idealistic youth who thought he learned something and wanted to share it with his grandmother, goes by the name of kill the messenger. They tried to erase my existence, rather than entertain "my ideas," which never belonged to me in the first place, but exist in the world and deserve deliberation. I should thank her for what they taught me about how people think and act, what people become capable of, and how even when they feel shame about something, they do it anyway.

After her husband died, she tried to redeem herself through acceptance of me. She never opened up about her personal history, but she did leave me a couple of thousand dollars, slush fund money which made it easier to to continue my self directed education and become an autodidact, to travel as a pauper, to work jobs and know I could afford to quit and survive for a month or two should things not work out.

Don't misunderstand me and think I believe greed motivates only the rich. My poor dead father's sister, portly Aunt Widow Rufina who followed her mother's footsteps into the arms of a drunk, used to bore me with her inability to talk about anything other than gossip. Family members predicted that she waddled up the stairs to claim possession of the apartment before the body cooled. Gluttony comes from a neurotic exaggeration of the same fear and desperation poor people feel, insecurity about the availability of basic needs. Money becomes a currency in our social game to survive all the shit that happens with a little status, to get a little elbow room, to forgive ourselves our trespasses, and create a blissful cocoon where we can forget our influence upon others. A poor mother might prostitute herself to feed her babies, an ignorant or disadvantaged family man may learn to take advantage whenever opportunity presents itself, and with whoever he can. Everybody inherits those instincts for survival, but greedy rich people don't know when to stop.

Where business goes, the flag often follows. The United States of America supported corporate interests abroad not only when they helped to bring down other government's leaders, even if elected through legitimate democratic processes, but also to install and support military dictators as puppets, many of whom stayed in power for decades. They often act like extra-national political appointees, manipulated by fear and favor, and help protect corporate interests, the status quo, and maintain social order with military campaigns against what they call Communists insurgents or Terrorists bent on creation of a civil war. These dictators order their military to prune the citizenry of people they suspect disseminate 'dangerous' leftist ideas, like socialism or Communism or Human Rights, and do it by all means necessary; curfews, martial law, arrests, torture, disappearances, peole thrown out of planes over the ocean, drive-by assassinations, arbitrary blood bathes, razed villages, and other blatant signs of what reasonable people would call reigns of terror.

Taxpayers in all countries should demand their government respect Human Rights, educate children about Human Rights and civic responsibilities, make cities livable, and raise the quality of life, and avoid banker-elicited invitations for corporations to come and extract resources with slave labor.

My nightmares of shattered cities choked by burnt automobiles gave way to a new vision of the world, and I personally lived that vision for over twenty years. I biked to work, ate semi-vegetarian, drove my old car only when necessary, and saved thousands of dollars each year for travel into Latin America, to become familiar with, and appreciate the benefits and challenges of, the alternate reality of Hispanic culture.

People belong to the human race, no matter what their ethnic culture and social traditions. We all share the history of our species, and the responsibility for every one of the genocides, even the annihilation of the American Indians and the Holocaust. Even if we cannot avoid pyramids of socio-economic classes, we can try to reduce social injustice with true meritocracies, and work to correct other departures from the path of progress toward a safer future of tolerance and acceptance. We must all, as humans, take responsibility and learn to recognize those parts of our traditions that separate us into tribes and encourage us to not accept each other, and so live in fear and hatred, the fuel of intolerance, racism, war and genocides.

Many of us still wonder how the other half lives, not because of a lack of contact, but because we acknowledge the obstacles the other half faces; high infant mortality, malaria, HIV infection and AIDS, ignorance, illiteracy and aliteracy, and in general the lack of respect or knowledge of basic Human Rights and social justice. Those obstacles belong to all of us. Each and every one of us shares the responsibility for the future of the biosphere of planet earth, because we belong to it, we do not own it.

We are the other half.

The End

Postscript:

In 2003, a Guatemalan named Jose Antonio Gutierrez became the first US Marine killed in Operation Iraqi Liberation (Oil) war against Iraq, close to the city of Umm al Qasr. In the mid nineteen eighties, authorities placed orphaned Jose into a New York City affiliate program in Guatemala City, where he studied architecture through middle school, and left the program with high grades in nineteen ninety two. In nineteen ninety seven, the U.S. Immigration and Naturalization Service detained him as he tried to entered the United States illegally. Given asylum, he lived with a foster family in southern California, then joined the Marine Corps on March 25th, 2002, to die less than a year later.

Journalist Julio Godoy, from Guatemala's short-lived newspaper La Epoca which US-funded security forces blew up in 1988, stated "One is tempted to believe that some people in the White House worship Aztec gods, with the offering of Central American blood." He also quotes a Western European diplomat and says "As long as the Americans don't change their attitude towards the region, there's no space here for the truth or for hope."

Also in 2003, Cardinal Oscar Rodriguez Maradiaga, of Tegucigalpa, Honduras, called poverty and social injustice the real Weapons of Mass Destruction, with hunger and hardship the motivators of the subversive elements in Latin America. He warned that the current political direction of globalization creates a world where "the greediness of a few is leaving the majority on the margin of history."

The United States, with a small population, uses the majority of the earth's resources. The U.S. must lower consumption to allow resource allocation for the progress in other nations. To do otherwise denies the developing world's citizens their birthright to their share of resources, their political autonomy, and their right to participate in governance with the expectation of a better future for their children.

Yet few suggest the United States of America should abandon its automobile centered lifestyle, that its citizens should live nearer their jobs, or telecommute, or bicycle, or develop mass transit. Instead, we hear America needs smaller cars, better gas mileage, and alternative fuels to maintain progress and keep the oil barons of the superclass rich.

Unfortunately, the costs of materials and energy to produce the modern hybrid automobile for urban use, with electrical energy recaptured from braking, almost wipes out the benefits of increased mileage. The complexities of a national distribution of alternative fuels, such as alcohols or explosive hydrogen fuels, for personal autos cannot match the savings of mass transit, because each personal automobile moves almost a ton of extra weight per driver. Basic physics, of energy used per passenger mile, shows the bicycle as the most efficient transportation, followed by vans, then buses, and worst of all, one of those elevated monster show trucks with tractor tires and chrome goat testicles that hang from the trailer hitch that cowboys with tiny penises like to drive.

Each year, more evidence amasses that the earth's climate overheats due to human activities related to consumption of resources like fossil fuels. Solar power might heat things up faster. No cheap or alternative energy solution can change the laws of thermodynamics, which states that all forms of energy used must degrade into unusable heat. Most of the sunlight Earth receives bounces back into space, and it probably should stay that way. Maybe humans could lower consumption and lower global temperatures, before we reach a 'tipping point' and set off another mass extinction.

Today, with the scientists fast approaching unanimity on global warming, and the rest of us aware of pollution and contamination of food, water, and air, we can see that all people must take responsibility to protect the future, to help ensure a better tomorrow for the future generations of children on this planet.

The earth can no longer afford rampant consumerism, with human progress measured by consumption of oil and continued industrial growth. Progress includes scientific advancement, well funded scientific research and space programs, free medical care and education, containment and control of pollutants and contaminants, and sustainable methods of industrial and agricultural production. Those things will give us a higher quality of life, and we could do it all and enjoy life more, on what we would save in money and health care costs, through bike paths and mass transit to get to work. It would make urban air breathable again.

We've applauded when other countries underwent severe "belt tightening" in response to economic necessity. We should take this opportunity to consider other visions of our own future, where progress and quality of life does not depend oil revenues or industrial contamination, measured by automobile sales and personal net worth.

Where ever we live, we too can wean ourselves from the gas pump. We will lower our medical costs through healthier lifestyles of personal mobility without the automobile, and lower transportation costs and taxes.

Citizens can share in a collective dream, and mandate their governments to take responsibility for the safety and quality of life for both residents and the environment, to protect the biosphere. We all deserve time to visit parks and lakes, to enjoy healthy natural environments, to travel on safe bike paths, to use cheap mass transportation, and to enjoy it when our dreams come true.

Check out Curitiba, Brazil if you need ideas and examples.

Americans on both sides of all the borders of our two hemispheres need to invent a new form of Yoga. We who live inside the United States should expend personal energy not only to make money, but also to find quality time for children, friends, and family. We need to meditate long and hard on the true meaning of Human Rights, on the meaning of bloated diabetic navels, and commit ourselves to lifestyles that better ourselves, as we work toward social justice for all, and to ensure an uncontaminated future for the biosphere of planet Earth.

Then we could erase all the arbitrary geopolitical borders, and bike out to the lake in the farthest park, with swimsuits and baskets of fruits and vegetables, to smell the roses, listen to other languages, and enjoy the world.

U xul in t'an lá. (Mayan for "This is my last word.")

Statistics

(From Terremoto 76 by G. Asturias Montenegro and R. Gatica Trejo, DR© Editorial Girblán y Cia Ltda. Ediciones Pop. 22,000 printed by fourth edicion, June 1976)

Faultline: Follows the Rio Motagua valley from south of Lake Izabél to lake Atitlán, southern section moved northeast, northern part slipped southwest.

Longitudinal Displacement: 1 meter, 40 centimeters, a yard and a half

Width: Many pieces about 10 centimeters (4 inches) apart, total width from 2 to 3 meters, about nine feet.

Length: More than 240 Km, 150 miles

Speed of four main waves: 6 Km / second, 22,000 Km / hour, 13,671 miles per hour

Magnitude: 7.5 Richter scale

Energy released: 30,000 atomic bombs like the one dropped on Hiroshima, 20,000 tons of TNT

Duration: First main quake, 35 seconds.

One fifth of the population lost their homes. As of 1976: Death toll: 22,778 Injured: 76,504

In 2003, New York Times estimates 27,000 people killed and more than a million rendered homeless by earthquake. Fatalities in villages throughout Guatemala ranged from Santa Apolonia (Northeast of Lake Atitlán) with 22% killed, to the Huehuetenango area with no fatalities. Over a billion dollars in damage.

Update on GUATEMALA as of 2005:

Population about twelve million, 56% in poverty.

One and a half million people remain beyond the reach of modern medicine

80% of children under five years old suffer from malnutricion.

The infant mortality remains the highest in Central and North America, while the country spends the least in health care, at one percent of Guatemala's Gross National Product.

Two million adults illiterate, with numbers higher due to the language barriers of a nation with over seven distinct Mayan languages whose own sub dialects often cannot communicate with one another.

1.5 % of the biggest land owners hold 63% of the agricultural land while 95% of small producers work only 18% of it.

6% of Guatemala's privileged families make 50% of the money, and the other 94% of the population must share the other half of national moneys.

The indigenous population of Maya, many of which do not speak Spanish, comprise 50% of the population of modern Guatemala, with the rest "ladinos," a label applied to the mostly poor descendants of Europeans and people of mixed Indian and European descent, and some westernized Mayan. Although most Guatemalans consider themselves Roman Catholics, many worship Mayan gods disguised within Catholic traditions. Protestant and Evangelical movements made significant inroads since the rule of two Protestant presidents.

On the beautiful Chiquimulilla Canal, Hawaii, Guatemala became part of the Biotopo Monterrico-Hawaii nature reserve which protect four species of mangrove, the four-eyed fish, and the Pacific Ridley and the Leatherback sea turtles through a hatchery program. The turtles come ashore to lay eggs from May to September. On Saturdays at sunset from September through January, tourists can race hatched turtles against each other and win a dinner. The protected 28 square kilometres also serves the local community as a dump and source of illegal turtle eggs.

Historical Timeline of Guatemala

600 BC Mayan ruins and remains at UAXACTUN, El Mirador, and nearby Nakbe may date from as early as 600 BC. A site called Cival contained remains dated as two thousand years old.

1523   The Spanish conquistador Pedro de Alvarado conquered Guatemala around 1523 24 and ruled as the first captain general of an area that included most of Central America. Guatemala, independent from Spain in 1821, aligned with Mexico.

1773   The Santa Marta earthquake causes the side of a volcano's crater to fail, and the lake of water inside falls down the mountain to destroy the country's first capital city, Antigua. The Spanish crown orders the city abandoned, and the capital moves to Guatemala City.

1823   The Central American republics create the United Provinces of Central America

1824   the Central American Federation.

1838   Revolt led by Rafael Carrera, an Indian general, who declares Guatemala an independent country. Breakup of the Central American Federation.

Since Carrera, military officers allied with wealthy landowners govern Guatemala and cause the most extreme inequalities of income and resource ownership in all of Latin America

1839   Guatemalan Independence

1844-71 Guatemala ruled by conservative dictator Rafael Carrera and his immediate successors, mostly Conservative Caudillos or military dictators, rule until 1871

1940 Evangelical Protestantism introduced into Guatemala, and will one day infuse the ideology of military death squads with a murderous anti-Catholicism that results in burnt Catholic churches and a hated of Mayans, whose Christianity they perceived as a veiled paganism.

1941   Guatemala declares war on the Axis powers in 1941.

1871   Liberal caudillo Justo Rufino Barrios in control from 1873-85, attempts to modernize, build up the army, and promote coffee plantations. Barrios enacted anticlerical legislation, and tried to establish a national education system.

1919   A covenant establishes the League of Nations (1919) fails to lay down a principle of racial nondiscrimination which Japan requested, due to the resistance of Great Britain and the United States. The covenant supported several types of rights: fair and humane treatment of laborers, the regulation of trafficking in women and children, the prevention and control of disease considered international in scope, and justice for indigenous peoples under colonialism.

1931   Jorge Ubico becomes president in 1931 with repressive rule that improves the country's finances.

1944   Jorge Ubico, the last of the caudillos, overthrown, which allows a provisional regime led Juan Jose Arevalo, a university professor returned from exile in Argentina. Guatemalans elect him president. Liberals remained in control until World War II. He introduces social democratic reforms, sets up a social security system, and begins to redistribute land to landless peasants. Under Arevalo, political democracy encouraged the organized labor movement to help write the country's first labor code and successfully encouraged industrialization. The Arevalo-Arbenz years, 1944-54, are still remembered in Guatemala as a golden age of peace, prosperity and freedom: the "Ten Years of Spring."

1951   In 1951, Col. Jacobo Arbenz Guzman succeeded Arevalo and continues Arevalo's reforms. He launched a massive agrarian reform program, which took land from a large number of Guatemalan landowners, even from the Jacobo Arbenz Guzman family, to give to landless peasants.

The Communist party, one of the political parties that appeared in this "Arevalo-Arbenz period," used the name Guatemalan Party of Labor (PGT). Although with little representation in Congress, their ideas influenced policy. Arbenz became friendlier toward the PGT, and gave members and sympathizers important positions in his administration, in the social security and agrarian reform systems. He suggested the party should become the leadership of the Guatemalan revolution.

They made enemies in Washington, DC, capital of the United States of America, when the Guatemalan Government expropriated substantial portions of United Fruit Company holdings, although they "bought" the land from United Fruit at the tax assessed value. President Arbenz came into direct conflict with both United Fruit, with John Foster Dulles at its head, and the U.S. administration of Dwight D. Eisenhower, with John's brother Allen Dulles serving as the director of the CIA.

1953   International Covenant on Civil and Political Rights, with 11 additional protocols, enters into effect on September 3 and represents the most successful instrument of human rights. The convention's mechanisms of enforcement instigated a considerable body of case law which the state parties usually honored and respected, to the point where some European states deem the provisions a part of domestic constitutional or statutory law.

With a tiny investment in men and money, the U.S. government secretly overthrew the President of Iran (chosen as Time magazine's Man of the Year) in August 1953, by falsely painting him as a Communist. This operation worked so well, they repeated the strategy in Guatemala. After the trauma of the World Wars, the success of these covert 'peaceful' operations seduced even sober statesmen like President Dwight D. Eisenhower, who went along with the Dulles brothers as they directed the CIA to engineer the overthrow of governments in Iran and Guatemala and set precedent for covert support of long term military dictators in Africa, Asia, and South America. The 1953 coup led many intellectuals to recognize the hypocrisy of Western leaders who practiced democracy at home and destroyed it abroad.

1954   As a consequence, in mid 1954, Guatemalan Colonel Carlos Castillo Armas led a United States supported, CIA directed "revolt" (with the aid of car dealership owner Anastasio SOMOZA, the dictator of neighboring Nicaragua) to overthrow President Arbenz.

U.S. Central Intelligence Agency organized a "counterrevolutionary" army of exiles led by Colonel Carlos Castillo Armas in Honduras and El Salvador. Exaggerations of the size of the invading force panicked the capital;

The Guatemalan army thought they faced a huge invasion when the citizens of Guatemala City became panicked, so the army refused to defend Arbenz. The President resigned on June 27, 1954 and went into exile. Colonel Carlos Castillo Armas became president and not only reversed the land reforms, offered generous concessions to foreign investors. This US backed coup stopped what they termed the "nationalization of United Fruit Company plantation land" because the Dulles brothers and other powerful and capital rich Americans feared the expropriation of company land would impact their personal finances around the world another ramification of the "Domino Theory."

1960   UN adopts the Declaration on the Granting of Independence to Colonial Countries and Peoples In Guatemala, a failed coup which arose from internal causes helps transform the left-right conflict between the Ladino elites into a deadly genocide against the indigenous Mayan people.

1960s   For the next 30 years, rule by military men removed the Arevalo-Arbenz reforms. From the 1960s on, a leftist guerrilla revolt fought against the regime, and right wing "death squads" operated in the cities. Tens of thousands of Guatemalan civilians died. In an attempt to undermine support for the guerrillas in the early 1980s, the government forces herded more than 1 million Indian peasants into army run "model villages" enforced by "civil defense" patrols.

1963   Colonel Enrique Peralta becomes president, after Castillo's assassination

1966   Guatemalan elect Cesar Mendez and demand a return to civilian rule. The UN General Assembly approves both the International Covenant on Economic, Social and Cultural Rights, and the International Covenant on Civil and Political Rights.

1968   Assassination of the US ambassador deteriorates US policy toward Guatemala for 20 years.

1970   Declaration on Principles of International Law concerning Friendly Relations and Cooperation among States in accordance with the Charter of the United Nations includes language that states it is "the duty of all states to refrain from organizing, instigating, assisting or participating in ... terrorist acts."

1970   The military backed Carlos Arena elected president. Attempts to eliminate the left wing influences through "disappearances" (murders) of at least 50,000 people.

1973   Conference held on Security and Cooperation in Europe (CSCE) in Helsinki, Finland on the third of July. Representatives of the European community met to discuss the rights and responsibilities of governing institutions. The meetings, although moved to Geneva, continued for two years to conclude on August first, nineteen seventy five. The Final Act of the conference becomes known as the Helsinki Accords, and begin with a Declaration on Principles Guiding Relations between Participating States, a promise to respect, support, and uphold, among other things, "human rights and fundamental freedoms, including the freedom of thought, conscience, religion or belief," and the equal rights of all peoples and their right to self determination."

1975   Efrain Rios Montt, a Pentecostal Protestant, ran as an opposition candidate for president and appears to win the popular vote, but loses the presidency to General Kjell Laugerud, who many say received the backing of the United States. Laugerud plans to invade Belize, the former British Honduras, because of the unfulfilled terms of a treaty with Great Britain.

1976   February 4th, 3:03 AM, 1976 perhaps twenty seven thousand people killed and more than a million homes destroyed by the earthquake.

1976   The International Covenant on Economic, Social and Cultural Rights, and the International Covenant on Civil and Political Rights (see 1966) came into effect.

1982   Efrain Rios Montt complains of being "counted out" of elections. He seizes power with a military coup. Historians credit his regime of alleviating government sponsored terrorism in the cities, but exacerbated it in rural areas. Death Squads and soldiers believed to have "disappeared" around 11,000 people to stop the growth of guerrilla activity.

1983   Brig. Gen. Oscar Humberto Mejia Victores overthrows Rios Montt in August, then declares amnesty for guerrillas. He presided over elections and wanted to write another constitution with a unicameral legislature and a president, both elected for 5 year terms by universal suffrage. Mejia Victores stressed respect for Human Rights and wanted to end military involvement in politics.

These military regimes from the early 1980s disrupted much of the indigenous Mayan's way of life when they "relocated" Mayans as part of an anti-guerrilla campaign. More than 100,000 fled to neighboring Mexico. President Mejia Victores' period in office remains forever stained by an average of 100 political assassinations and 40 political kidnappings a month.

1985   Christian Democrat Marco Vinicio Cerezo Arevalo, wins elections while his party wind a majority in Congress under a new Constitution. Cerezo hopes for an amnesty for guerrillas, but without Congressional support, ineffective. Negotiations with the guerrillas fail due to right wing and military pressures. Both Amnesty International and the United Nations Commission for Human Rights denounce right wing "death squads" and publish evidence of politically motivated murders. The violence and terrorism from both left and right, with each sometimes leaving their victims to look like the other side murdered them, continued throughout the period.

1986   Election of the first civilian government in 16 years. Cerezo finds himself unable to make any significant reforms.

1988   In November the OAS adopts an Additional Protocol to the American Convention on Human Rights in the Area of Economic, Social and Cultural Rights, and of 26 Western Hemispheric states that signed the convention, only the United States refused to ratify it.

1989   An attempt to overthrow Cerezo fails. Since 1980, researchers estimate the death toll in this civil war at around 100,000 dead and 40,000 "disappeared". Sometime in the 1980s the Somoza family, rulers of Nicaragua, began the construction of a multistory hotel on the Lake Atitlán beach in Panajachél, which will remain unfinished and abandoned (November 1989)

1990   The UN covenant's Second Optional Protocol adopted in 1989 to abolish the death penalty worldwide, comes into force in 1991. Honored in most of the countries of western Europe and many countries in the Americas, the United States rejects it. In 2006, the Austrian people decided to remove the name of California Governor Arnold Schwartzenegger, the famous body builder and Hollywood actor, from a sports arena because he failed to stop the state's execution of inmate "Tookie" Williams, a reformed founder of a Los Angeles street gang convicted of murder.

1991   The violence lessons after Cerezo loses the second sequential civilian democratic election. Jorge Serrano Elias elected president. He restores diplomatic relations with Belize, and begins negotiations on the long standing territorial claims. Jorge Serrano Elias, a Protestant evangelist of the Christian Democratic party and one time member of the Rios Montt government, enters in place of Rios Montt when electoral authorities declared General Montt ineligible. Right wing violence continues. The Guatemalan government reaches an accord with the major guerrilla group the URNG after the arrests of a number of police and military men for death squad activity. Citizens experienced renewed hope for a peace in the region as the civil war in El Salvador wound down and the United States becomes less supportive of military and right wing elements throughout Central America.

1994   President Serrano ignites waves of protests, after his attempt to impose an authoritarian regime, that eventually force him to resign. The legislature installs Ramiro de Leon Carpio as president. Right wing parties win a majority in legislative elections. Peace talks begin between the government and rebels of the Guatemalan Revolutionary National Unity.

1995   Rebels declare a ceasefire; both the UN and the US criticize Guatemala for widespread Human Rights abuses.

1996   Around 200,000 people "disappeared" over the three decades of conflict before democratically elected president Alvaro Arzu, the Guatemalan military, rebels and armed opposition signed the UN-brokered Peace Accords to end what some called a civil war. President Arzu conducts a purge of senior military officers.

1998   Human rights campaigner Bishop Juan Gerardi found murdered. The International Criminal Court, a permanent international criminal court with a jurisdiction that includes crimes against humanity, crimes of genocide, war crimes, and crimes of "aggression" once they agree on an acceptable definition of the term, becomes adopted by 160 countries in July. Authorized by the Rome Statute of the International Criminal Court, the actual creation of the court depends on ratification by at least 60 signatory states and faces resistance by some countries, notably the United States.

1999   UN backed commission gathers evidence that senior officials oversaw over six hundred twenty six massacres in Maya villages, and says Guatemalan Government security forces authored 93% of all Human Rights atrocities which claimed 200,000 lives, throughout the period called "the civil war."

1999   The OAS's Additional Protocol to the American Convention on Human Rights in the Area of Economic, Social and Cultural Rights enters into force in November, but the United States refuses to support the additional protocol.

2000   Alfonso Portillo wins the 1999 elections, sworn in as president in 2000.

2001   Portillo pays $1.8 million in compensation in December, 2001 to the families of 226 men, women and children killed by soldiers and paramilitaries in the northern village of Las Dos Erres in 1982.

2002   In September, the Organization of American States (OAS) brokers talks that help Guatemala and Belize draft a settlement to the border dispute. Both nations agree to hold referenda on the settlement.

2003   A former Guatemala City street orphan, Jose Antonio Gutierrez, becomes the first US Marine killed in the war against Iraq, close to the city of Umm al Qasr. Orphaned by the death of his parents in the mid nineteen eighties, authorities placed him into a program where he became a good student, studied architecture through middle school, and left the program with high grades in nineteen ninety two. In nineteen ninety seven the Immigration and Naturalization Service detained him as he tried to entered the United States illegally. Eventually given asylum, he lived with a foster family in southern California and then joined the Marine Corps on March 25th, 2002, to die less than a year later.

In March, international forces persuade the Guatemalan Government to allow UN and OAS investigations in order to present and gather evidence on the activities of armed groups reputed to commit criminal violence. A constitutional court overturns the ban on the candidacy of former military leader Efrain Rios Montt, who registers in July to participate in November's presidential election.

"The C.I.A. intervention began a ghastly cycle of violence, assassination and torture in Guatemala," said Stephen G. Rabe, a historian from the University of Texas at Dallas and author of Eisenhower and Latin America: The Foreign Policy of Anticommunism. "The Guatemalan intervention of 1954 is the most important event in the history of U.S. relations with Latin America," Mr. Rabe said. "It really set the precedent for later interventions in Cuba, British Guiana, Brazil and Chile. The tactics were the same, the mindset was the same, and in many cases the people who directed those covert interventions were the same."

2004 CAFTA (Central American Free Trade Agreement) on the table; contains dispute resolution mechanisms similar to NAFTA's CHAPTER 11, to give corporations opportunity to sue governments for regulations, like local environmental laws, that "infringe on their rights". It extends new patent rules which serve to drive up the cost of drugs and delay, or obstruct, competition from generic brands. CAFTA diminishes protections for workers that the current Caribbean Basin Trade Partnership Act gives them. Previous initiatives tried to uphold the international labor norms recognized today, but CAFTA lets governments enforce their own laws, weaker and amenable to change.

Bibliography:

Terremoto 76 by G. Asturias Montenegro and R. Gatica Trejo, DR © Editorial Girblán y Cia Ltda. Ediciones Pop. Fourth Edicion, June 1976 (22,000 printed in total with previous editions)

The Ancient Maya by Robert J. Sharer, Fifth Edition, Stanford University Press, © 1946 - 1994 Board of Trustees of the Junior University, ISBN 0-8047-2310-9

The Mysteries of Chichen Itzá by Adalberto Rivera A., © First Edition published in 1995 by Universal Image Enterprise Inc.

The Mayas (on the Rocks), by Javier Covo T., 1st Ed. Coleccioón "MONO-GRAMS": 1987 © Producción Editorial Dante, S.A. (Translation by Gustavo Fernández, Ph.D.) ISBN 968-7232-63-3

The New York Times

Various editions, paper and digital, of Encylopedia Brittanica, Grolier's Encyclopedia, and World Book Encyclopedia, and the Website encyclopedia "Wikipedia"

To contact the author, or for further information or comments, please search online for Mark Plimsoll

www.ingramcontent.com/pod-product-compliance
Lightning Source LLC
Chambersburg PA
CBHW020821030726
47496CB00001B/31